Also by Anne Holt

THE HANNE WILHELMSEN SERIES

Blind Goddess
Blessed Are Those Who Thirst
Death of the Demon
1222

The Lion's Mouth

A Hanne Wilhelmsen Novel

Anne Holt and Berit Reiss-Andersen

*Translated from the Norwegian
by Anne Bruce*

SCRIBNER

New York   London   Toronto   Sydney   New Delhi

Scribner
An Imprint of Simon & Schuster, Inc.
1230 Avenue of the Americas
New York, NY 10020

Copyright © 1997 by Anne Holt and Berit Reiss-Andersen
English language translation copyright © 2014 by Anne Bruce
Originally published in Norwegian in 1997 as *Løvens Gap*
Published by arrangement with Salomonsson Agency

First Scribner hardcover edition February 2016

SCRIBNER and design are registered trademarks of The Gale Group, Inc., used under license by Simon & Schuster, Inc., the publisher of this work.

For information about special discounts for bulk purchases, please contact Simon & Schuster Special Sales at 1-866-506-1949 or business@simonandschuster.com.

The Simon & Schuster Speakers Bureau can bring authors to your live event. For more information or to book an event, contact the Simon & Schuster Speakers Bureau at 1-866-248-3049 or visit our website at www.simonspeakers.com.

Manufactured in the United States of America

1   3   5   7   9   10   8   6   4   2

The Library of Congress Cataloging-in-Publication Data is available.

ISBN 978-1-5011-2323-8
ISBN 978-1-5011-2325-2 (ebook)

It's no use being a qualified zoologist once you're inside the lion's mouth.

—*Gunnar Reiss-Andersen*

The
Lion's
Mouth

FRIDAY, APRIL 4, 1997

6:47 P.M., PRIME MINISTER'S OFFICE (PMO)

She wore a blue suit, the woman who sat doing nothing outside the prime minister's office; she just sat there, with a mounting sense of disquiet, staring alternately at the double doors and her own telephone. Her neat little jacket was of classic cut, with a matching skirt, and was topped off by an overly gaudy scarf. Although it was close to the end of a long workday, not a single hair was out of place in her elegant, if somewhat dated, coiffure. The hairstyle made her appear older than she actually was, and that might have been the intention, as if the fact that it had gone out of fashion in the early 1980s—feather-cut at the sides, with a full crown—somehow endowed her with a gravitas that her forty-plus years did not.

She had more than enough to do, but uncharacteristically, she couldn't settle down to anything. For some considerable time, she just sat there. Only her fingers betrayed her steadily rising sense that something was terribly wrong. They were long and beautifully manicured, with crimson nails and two gold rings on each hand, and they touched her temple at regular intervals, as though to tidy some invisible disorderly strands, before tapping the blotting pad with a hollow sound, like a series of shots fired using a silencer. Suddenly the woman stood up and crossed to the west-facing window.

It was twilight outside. April promised to be just as capricious as Bjørnstjerne Bjørnson, author of the Norwegian national anthem, had once described it many years earlier. Fifteen floors below, she saw people shivering as they hurried along Akersgata—the street where both the country's government and Oslo's newspapers had their headquarters—some of them walking irritably in circles as they waited for a bus that might never come. There was still a light on in the culture minister's office across the road in the R5 building. Despite the distance, the woman in the blue suit could see the secretary walking from the anteroom to her boss with a sheaf of papers. Tossing her blond hair, the young cabinet minister laughed in response to the older woman. She was too young to be culture minister. Not tall enough, either. An evening gown did not sit becomingly on a woman of barely five foot three. To crown it all, the young woman lit a cigarette, and placed an ashtray on top of the pile of papers.

She shouldn't smoke in that office, thought the woman in blue. *The finest cultural treasures are hanging in there. It can't be doing the paintings any good. And it can't be very safe either.*

She embraced the feeling of irritation with gratitude. It momentarily distracted her from the sense of disquiet that was about to tip over into unfamiliar and distressing anxiety.

Two hours had passed since Prime Minister Birgitte Volter had said, very specifically, almost coldly, that she was not to be disturbed, no matter what. That was what she had said: "No matter what."

Gro Harlem Brundtland, the previous prime minister, had never said, "No matter what." She would have said, "Regardless of the reason," or perhaps simply left it at that: she was not to be disturbed. Even if all seventeen stories of the government building went up in flames, Gro Harlem Brundtland would have been left in peace if she had given that instruction. But Gro had stepped down on October 25 of the previous year, and these were new times, with new methods and new jargon, and Wenche Andersen kept her emotions to herself. She carried out her work as she always did: effectively and discreetly.

It was well over an hour since Supreme Court Judge Benjamin Grinde had left the office. Clad in a charcoal-gray Italian suit, he had nodded as he emerged through the double doors and closed them behind him. Smiling faintly, he had indulged in a flattering remark about her new outfit before he had disappeared downstairs to the elevator on the fourteenth floor, carrying his burgundy leather briefcase under his arm. Wenche Andersen had automatically risen to her feet to take a cup of coffee in to Birgitte Volter, when at the last minute she had fortunately remembered her boss's resolute instruction about peace and quiet.

However, it really was starting to get extremely late now.

The undersecretaries and political advisers had left, as had the rest of the office staff. Wenche Andersen was sitting alone on a Friday evening on the fifteenth floor of the tower block in the government complex and did not know what to do. There was total silence from the prime minister's office. Maybe that was not so strange after all, because of the double doors.

7:02 P.M., ODINS GATE 3

There was definitely something wrong with the contents of the plain, tulip-shaped crystal glass. He held it up to see how the light refracted in the red liquid. He tried to take his time listening to the wine, attempted to relax and enjoy it, as full-bodied Bordeaux normally deserved. The 1983 vintage was supposed to be friendly and inviting. This one was far too tight in its initial phase, and he pursed his lips in astonished disgust as it dawned on him that the flavor of its finish in no way matched the price he had paid for the bottle. Abruptly setting down his glass, he grabbed the TV remote control. The evening news had already started, but the broadcast was completely banal, and the images flickered past without him noticing anything other than that the reporter's togs were thoroughly tasteless. A yellow jacket was quite simply not suitable male attire.

He had been compelled to do it. There had been no other option. Now that it was all over, he felt nothing. He had expected some kind of relief, the opportunity to breathe easily after all these years.

He really wanted to feel relieved, but instead he was gripped by an unfamiliar sense of loneliness. The furniture surrounding him suddenly seemed alien. As a child, he had often climbed on the heavy old oak sideboard decorated with carved bunches of grapes; it now dominated his own living room in all its grandeur, and he kept his exclusive collection of Japanese netsuke miniatures behind its polished glass doors, but today it seemed only gloomy and threatening.

One object lay on the table between him and the remote control. He did not understand what it was doing there. Why he had brought it with him was a mystery.

Giving himself a shake, he switched off the *Dagsrevy* reporter with a tap of his finger. Tomorrow was his birthday, when he would turn fifty. He felt much older than that as he strained stiffly to rise from the chesterfield sofa and walk through to the kitchen. The pâté could, and *ought*, to be made tonight. It would be at its best after twenty-four hours in a refrigerator.

For a second or two he considered opening another bottle of the wretched Bordeaux. Then he pushed the thought aside and contented himself with a cognac poured generously into a fresh glass. Cooking cognac.

There was no relief to be found in the cognac either.

7:35 P.M., PMO

Her hair was no longer so perfect. A brittle, bleached lock fell across her eyes, and she felt beads of perspiration on her top lip. Nervously clutching her handbag, she opened it to find a freshly ironed handkerchief, which she held to her mouth before using it to mop her forehead.

Now she would go in. Something could be wrong. Birgitte Volter had disconnected the phone, so she would have to knock on the door. The prime minister might be ill; she had seemed stressed recently. Although Wenche Andersen had considerable reservations about Birgitte Volter's rather reckless, unfamiliar style, she had to acknowledge that the prime minister was usually very friendly. During the past week, however, Birgitte Volter had been verging on dismissive; she had been irritable and sometimes even exasperated. Was she unwell?

Now she would enter. Now.

Instead of disturbing the prime minister, she paid another visit to the restroom. But although she lingered in front of the mirror, she couldn't find anything that needed attending to. She spent a long time washing her hands, then fished out a little tube of hand cream from the closet underneath the sink. It was unnecessary and made her hands feel sticky, but putting it on used up some time. Massaging her fingers thoroughly, she felt the cream penetrate the surface of her skin. Involuntarily she looked at her watch once more, and breathed heavily. Only four and a half minutes had passed. The tiny golden hands almost seemed to be standing still. Anxious and resigned, she returned to her seat; even the sound of the restroom door slamming behind her seemed alarming.

Now she simply *must* go in. Wenche Andersen attempted to stand up but stopped halfway, hesitating, and sat down again. The instruction had been crystal clear. Birgitte Volter was not to be disturbed. "No matter what." But nor had the prime minister said that Wenche

Andersen could go home, and it would be unheard of to leave the office before she had been given permission to do so. Now she would go in. She must go in.

With her hand on the door handle, she placed her ear against the door panel. Not a sound. Tentatively, she tapped her index finger on the wood. Still not a sound. She opened the outer door and repeated the action. It did not help: no one said, "Come in!" or "Don't disturb me!" No one said anything at all, and now it wasn't just Wenche Andersen's upper lip that was perspiring. Cautiously and hesitantly, ready to close the door again as quick as a flash if the prime minister was sitting there deep in concentration on something or other of great importance, she opened the door a tiny crack. However, from where she stood, looking through a gap that was no more than a few inches wide, she could see only the far end of the sitting area and the circular table.

All of a sudden, Wenche Andersen was seized with a decisiveness that had eluded her for several hours, and she threw the door open wide.

"Excuse me," she said loudly. "Sorry for disturbing you, but . . ."

There was no point in saying anything further.

Prime Minister Birgitte Volter was sitting in her office chair, her upper body slumped across the desk. She looked like a student in a luxurious reading room, late one evening right before exams, just taking a little nap, forty winks. Wenche Andersen stood in the doorway a good six yards away, but she could see it all the same. The blood was clearly visible; it had formed a large, stagnant pool on a draft of the proposal concerning the Schengen agreement—so visible that Wenche Andersen did not even cross over to her dead boss to see if she could possibly help her, fetch a glass of water perhaps or provide her with a handkerchief to wipe away the mess.

Instead, she carefully—but this time very determinedly—closed the doors of the prime minister's office, skirted around her own desk, and grabbed the phone with the direct line to the central switchboard of Oslo Police Headquarters. It rang only once before a man's voice answered.

"You have to come right away," Wenche Andersen said, her voice trembling only ever so slightly. "The Prime Minister is dead. She's been shot. Birgitte Volter has been killed. You must come."

Then she put down the receiver, moved her hand to another telephone, and this time got the security switchboard on the line.

"This is the Prime Minister's office," she said, more calmly now. "Shut the building. No one in, no one out. Only the police. Remember the garage."

Without waiting for a response, she disconnected the call in order to dial another four-digit number.

"Fourteenth floor," answered the man on the floor below from within a cage of bulletproof glass, the chamber that allowed access up into the holy of holies, the offices of the head of government of the Kingdom of Norway.

"This is the Prime Minister's office," she said yet again. "The Prime Minister is dead. Activate the emergency plan."

And so Wenche Andersen continued her duties as she always did: systematically and faultlessly. The only clues that this was a quite extraordinary Friday evening were the two expanding lilac patches on her cheeks.

They soon spread across her whole face.

7:50 P.M., *KVELDSAVISEN* EDITORIAL OFFICE

When "Little" Lettvik's parents christened their blond-haired baby girl Lise Annette, they failed to anticipate that her sister, older by one year, would naturally nickname her "Little" or that fifty-four years later Little would weigh two hundred pounds and smoke twenty cigarillos a day. Nor could they have predicted that she would push her exhausted liver to the limits by drinking a daily dram of whiskey. Her entire body invited ridicule: she still adhered to the 1970s rule about going braless, and her stringy gray hair framed a face that bore signs of almost thirty years in Akersgata. But no one cracked a joke about Little Lettvik. At least not in her company.

"What the fuck's a Supreme Court judge doing at the Prime Minister's office late on a Friday afternoon?" she muttered to herself as she hoisted up her breasts, which were spilling out in the direction of her armpits, finally finding support on her well-upholstered pelvic bone.

"What did you say?"

The young man facing her was her lapdog. He was six foot four, emaciated, and still suffered from acne. Little Lettvik despised people like Knut Fagerborg: boys with six-month temporary contracts at *Kveldsavisen*. They were the most dangerous journalists in the world;

Little Lettvik knew that. She had once been in that position herself, and although it was a long time ago and circumstances in the Norwegian press had completely altered since then, she recognized him. But Knut was useful. Like all the others, he admired her without reservation. He thought she would make sure his contract was extended. In that, he was totally mistaken. However, for the moment, he had his uses.

"Strange," she murmured again, really more to herself than in reply to Knut Fagerborg. "I phoned Grinde at the Supreme Court this afternoon. It's so bloody difficult to find out anything about what that commission of his is up to. A young chick in his office chirped that he was with the Prime Minister. Why in hell was he there?"

Raising her arms above her head, she stretched, and Knut recognized the scent of Poison. Not so long ago, he had been forced to pay a visit to the emergency doctor for antihistamines after a one-night stand with a woman who had the same taste.

"What do you want?" she said suddenly, as though she had just noticed him.

"There's something going on. The police radio went berserk at first, and now it's totally silent. I've never known anything like it."

Truth to tell, twenty-year-old Knut Fagerborg had not experienced very much in his short life. However, Little was in agreement: it did seem odd.

"Heard anything on the street?" she asked.

"No, but . . ."

"Guys!"

A man in his forties, wearing a gray tweed jacket, came shuffling into the editorial office.

"Something's going on in the government tower block. A great commotion and lots of vehicles, and they're cordoning off the entire place. Is the Prime Minister expecting some hotshot from abroad?"

"At night? On a Friday night?"

Little Lettvik's left knee was aching.

She had experienced pain in her left knee two hours before the Kielland oil rig disaster in the North Sea. Her knee had also been excruciating the day before the murder of Swedish Prime Minister Olof Palme. Not to mention how she had limped to the emergency room the evening after the Gulf crisis erupted, surprised that it had come on her so late, until that night she had received news that King Olav had died.

"Pop out and investigate."

Knut popped out.

"By the way, does anybody know anybody who had a child in 1965?"

As Little Lettvik rubbed her tender knee, she panted and puffed, bringing her stomach into a clinch with the edge of the desk.

"I was born in '65," yelled a snazzy woman in a mauve dress who entered carrying two archive folders.

"That's no help at all," Little Lettvik said. "You're alive."

8:15 P.M., PMO

B illy T. felt something he could only interpret as longing. It hit him somewhere in his solar plexus, and he was forced to take several deep breaths in order to clear his head.

The Norwegian Prime Minister's office would have been quite tasteful if it had not been for her lying there stone-dead with her head on the papers in front of her, a literally bloody affront to the interior designer who had carefully chosen the massive desk with its bow-shaped outer edge. The same undulating contours were echoed in a number of places throughout the room, including on a bookcase that admittedly was quite decorative, but its lack of straight lines made it seem totally unfit for purpose. And sure enough, there were not many books in it. The room itself was rectangular. At one end the furniture was arranged for meetings, and at the other end was the desk plus two visitors' chairs. It contained nothing that could truly be called luxurious. The picture on the wall behind the desk was large, but not particularly attractive, and Billy T. could not immediately identify the artist. The first thought that struck him as he looked around was that he had seen far more exclusive offices in other places in the country. This space was social democracy through and through—a sober prime ministerial office that would make Norwegian visitors nod in appreciation but which foreign heads of state would probably find conspicuously lacking in flamboyance. There was a door at either end; Billy T. had just entered through one of them, and the other led into a restroom containing a shower and toilet.

The pale physician had bloodstains on his gray jacket. He was struggling to remove his latex gloves, and Billy T. detected a hint of solemnity in his strained voice.

"I believe the Prime Minister died between two and three hours ago. However, that's only a provisional estimate. Extremely provisional. I am assuming that the temperature in this room has remained constant, at least until our arrival."

Finally, as the gloves capitulated, saying farewell to his fingers with a sucking sound, they were stuffed into the pocket of his tweed jacket. The doctor straightened up.

"She was shot in the head."

"Can see that," Billy T. mumbled.

The Superintendent sent him a warning look.

Billy T. registered it. He turned to face the three men from the crime scene division who had already set to work doing what they had to do, what they had done many times before: they photographed, measured, and brushed their fingerprint powder, moving around the huge office with a grace that would have amazed anyone who had not seen it before. They behaved as though they were used to this sort of thing, as though this was simply routine practice. But there was something approaching the sacred in the room, an absence of the usual gallows humor, an uneasy atmosphere that was exacerbated by the rising temperature. A dead Prime Minister did not invite frivolity.

As always when he found himself in close proximity to a corpse, it struck Billy T. that nothing was as naked as death. Seeing this woman who had ruled the country until three hours ago, this woman whom he had never seen in the flesh but had encountered every single day on TV, in the newspapers, and on the radio; seeing Birgitte Volter, the human being behind the public persona, lying dead on her own desk, this was worse, more embarrassing, and made him feel more self-conscious than seeing her without any clothes. Billy T. turned away and walked across to the window.

The Ministry of Finance was situated to the left, far below. The building seemed to cower in leaden resentment at the newly and very expensively refurbished Supreme Court by its side. Farther to the southwest, Billy T. could just discern the roof of the Parliament Building, which appeared rather reticent from where he stood on the second-to-top floor of the government tower block, a wispy, impotent pennant flying from the flagpole atop its cupola. The executive, the judiciary, and the legislature, observed from a somewhat skewed angle.

And the national newspaper offices of Akersgata winding through it all, Billy T. thought, turning to face the room again.

"Weapon?" he inquired of a young police officer who had stepped toward the door for a moment.

The officer drank some water from a plastic mug, then conscientiously returned the beaker to a uniformed female officer in the outer office. He shook his head. "No."

"No?"

"Not yet. No weapon." He wiped his mouth with his jacket sleeve. "We'll find it soon enough," he continued. "We have to search further. Bathrooms, hallways, corridors. Damn it, this building's a mammoth. But it's probably not in here. The weapon, that is."

"And this mammoth is actually filled with loads of people, even on a Friday evening?" the Superintendent said with some surprise. "They're starting to gather in the canteen downstairs. At least sixty or seventy people so far."

Billy T. swore under his breath. "There must be at least four hundred fucking offices in this building. Do I dare to ask for reinforcements?" He said this with a tense smile, rubbing his hand over his smooth-shaven skull.

"Of course," said the Superintendent. "We need to find that weapon."

"So much for the obvious," Billy T. said, just quietly enough that no one could hear.

He wanted to leave. There was no need for him to be there. He knew that the days, the weeks, yes, perhaps even the months that followed would be hellish. There would be a lengthy state of emergency. No days off and definitely no vacations. No time for the boys. Four children who should be entitled to see him at least on weekends. However, there was no need for him to be here, not now, not in this rectangular office with its fantastic view over the lights of Oslo and a dead woman lying across her desk.

The sense of loneliness seized him again. That was what it was: loneliness and longing. For her, his partner and only confidante. She ought to have been there. Together, they were invincible; alone, he felt that neither his height—six foot seven in his stocking feet—nor the inverted cross he wore in his ear were of any use whatsoever. For the last time, he averted his eyes from the pool of blood underneath the woman's shattered head.

He turned around and touched his chest.

Hanne Wilhelmsen was in the United States and would not be back until Christmas.

"Shit, Billy T.," whispered the police officer who had drunk the water. "I'm feeling really sick. That's never happened to me before. At a crime scene, I mean. Not since I was a rookie."

Without replying, Billy T. simply glanced at the man and flashed a grimace that, with a certain degree of indulgence, might be taken for a smile.

He felt really awful himself.

8:30 P.M., *KVELDSAVISEN* EDITORIAL OFFICE

"This must be something colossal," Knut Fagerborg gasped, flinging off his fleece-lined denim jacket. "Crawling with people, crawling with cars, cordoned off everywhere, and everything so silent! Fuck, everybody's so damn serious!"

He collapsed into an office chair that was far too low, his legs flailing about all over the place, making him look like a spider.

Little Lettvik's left knee was smarting intensely. She stood up and warily set her foot down on the floor, increasing the pressure with extreme caution.

"I want to see for myself," she said, fishing out a box of small cigars.

Slowly and solicitously, with Knut Fagerborg jogging on the spot, impatient to sprint ahead of her the few yards across to the government tower block, she lit her cigar.

"I think you're right," she said, smiling. "This is definitely something colossal."

She limped her way out of the editorial office.

8:34 P.M., SKAUGUM ESTATE IN ASKER

The black government car drew gently to a halt at the entrance to the royal residence in Asker, half an hour's drive from central Oslo. A tall slim man in a dark suit opened the right-hand rear door before the vehicle was properly at a standstill and alighted. Shrugging his coat more snugly around himself, he strode toward the entrance. Halfway, he staggered slightly, but only momentarily, and moved a foot to one side to recover his balance.

A uniformed man opened the door and led the Foreign Minister straight into a room resembling a library. In a subdued voice, the man asked the minister to wait. He had raised his eyebrows in surprise when the minister had dismissively waved away his outstretched hand, ready to take his outer garment. Now the tall, dark, ungainly Foreign Minister was sitting in an uncomfortable baroque chair, feeling that there was not enough room for him on it. He pulled his coat even more tightly around his frame, even though he didn't feel cold.

The King was standing in the doorway, wearing everyday clothes: gray trousers and an open-necked shirt. He looked even more concerned than usual, and his eyes glinted restlessly behind the heavy eyelids that revealed only the lower part of the iris. He was unsmiling, and the Foreign Minister rose to his feet abruptly, holding out his hand.

"Unfortunately, I have extremely grave news, Your Majesty," he said softly, coughing with his left hand clenched in front of his mouth.

The Queen had followed her husband and stood a couple of yards inside the room, holding a glass containing something with ice cubes. There was a homely clinking sound as she entered, like an invitation to a pleasant evening. She was wearing denim jeans designed specially for older women and a colorful sweater adorned with black and red cows. The professional expression on her face did not succeed in concealing a certain curiosity about the visit.

The Foreign Minister felt unwell. The royal couple seemed to be enjoying a rare evening of peace and quiet at home. Of course, other people too were having their evening spoiled.

He nodded to the Queen before looking into the King's eyes again as he continued. "Prime Minister Volter is dead, Your Majesty. She was shot earlier tonight."

The royal couple exchanged glances, and the King rubbed his nose slowly. Both remained quiet for some time.

"I think the Foreign Minister should take a seat," the King said eventually, pointing toward the chair the minister had just vacated. "Sit down and let us hear more. Perhaps I can take your coat?"

The Foreign Minister looked down at himself with an air that suggested he was not even aware he was wearing a coat. Clumsily, he extricated himself from it, but felt it was too much to hand it over to the King, so instead he hung it over the back of his chair before sitting down again.

The Queen's hand touched his shoulder as she passed to sit in a chair several yards away, a comforting gesture from a woman who had discerned a hint of tears behind the Foreign Minister's extremely thick glasses.

"Would you like a drink?" she asked softly, but the minister shook his head, almost imperceptibly, and cleared his throat once more, this time at length and with obvious difficulty.

"No, I don't think so. This is going to be an exceptionally long night."

8:50 P.M., OLE BRUMMS VEI 212

"My sincere condolences," the Bishop of Oslo said as he attempted to make eye contact with the man facing him.

It was impossible. Roy Hansen had been Birgitte Volter's sweetheart for thirty-four years and married to her for thirty-three of them. They had both been a mere eighteen when the wedding took place, and despite turbulent patches, they had weathered all storms and stayed together even while everyone around them was trying to prove that lifelong marriage couldn't survive such an urbane, hectic environment. Birgitte was not only an important part of his life; in many ways she *was* his life, something he had regarded as a natural consequence of their joint decision to prioritize her career. Now he sat on the sofa, staring at some nonexistent place.

The Labor Party Secretary stood at the veranda door, appearing very uncomfortable in the Bishop's presence. She had protested at his being there. "*I'm* the one who knows them," she had said. "For God's sake, Birgitte wasn't even a member of the church!"

But protocol required it, and protocol had to be followed. Especially now. When everything was crazy and upside down and the way nobody ever thought it could be, the dust was brushed off the *Crisis Management Handbook*. Suddenly it became something new and different rather than simply a book lying in a drawer for when the thing that was never going to happen actually happened.

"I'd like you to leave," whispered the man on the sofa.

The Bishop looked disbelieving for a brief moment, but only for a second; he caught himself and recovered his ecclesiastical dignity.

"This is a very difficult time," he continued in his east Norwegian accent. "I have the greatest respect for your wish to be alone. Maybe there is someone else? Family, perhaps?"

Roy Hansen continued to stare at something the others could not see. He did not sob, his breathing was even and easy, but a silent stream of tears ran down from his pale blue eyes, a tiny rivulet he had long since given up wiping away.

"She can stay," he said, without looking at the Party Secretary.

"Then I'll withdraw," the Bishop said, though he remained seated. "I shall pray for you and your family. And by all means phone if there's anything anyone else or I can do for you."

He still did not get to his feet. The Party Secretary stood at the door, keen to open it and hasten the man's departure, but something about the situation made her stand absolutely still. The minutes passed, and all that could be heard was the ticking of the oak-cased mantel clock. Suddenly it struck nine: ponderous, strained, hesitant strokes, as though it did not wish the evening to progress.

"Ah, then," said the Bishop, with a heavy sigh. "I'll be off."

When at long last he had gone, the Party Secretary had locked the door behind him and returned to the living room. Roy Hansen looked at her for the first time, a bewildered look that turned into a grimace as he finally burst into tears in earnest. The Party Secretary sat down beside him, and he rested his head on her lap as he struggled to catch his breath.

"Someone will have to speak to Per," he wept. "I don't have the strength to tell Per."

9:03 P.M., ODINS GATE 3

The liver was top quality. He held it up underneath his nose, letting his tongue just touch the pale slice of meat. The slaughterhouse at Torshov was the only one he could truly rely on as far as calf's liver was concerned, and although it was situated out of his way, the detour was worth the trouble.

He had bought the truffles in France three days earlier. Normally he contented himself with canned ones, but when the opportunity presented itself—something that happened relatively often—there was nothing to compare with the fresh variety.

Ding-dong.

He had to do something about that doorbell. The sound was discordant and atonal, and it startled him every time it rang.

He glanced at his wristwatch, and it crossed his mind that he was not expecting anyone. This was Friday, and the party was not until tomorrow.

En route to the front door, he suddenly stopped, remaining still for a split second, before walking resolutely across to the heavy oak coffee table and taking hold of the object lying there. Without further thought, he opened one of the sideboard doors decorated with carved grapes and placed the item behind the table linen, underneath a tablecloth his great-great-grandmother had woven in the 1840s. He closed the door again and brushed his hands on his flannel trousers before striding out to see who was ringing the doorbell.

"Benjamin Grinde?"

It was a woman who asked. She was in her forties, had three stripes on her shoulders, and looked as though she enjoyed being in uniform; it fit well and suited the matronly bust he could discern underneath her buttoned jacket. However, it appeared that she was far from happy about the business in hand. Avoiding his gaze, she instead stared at a point four inches above his head. At her side stood a somewhat younger man with glasses and a bushy, well-kept beard.

"Yes," answered Benjamin Grinde, stepping aside as he held the door open in invitation to the two police officers.

They exchanged fleeting glances before deciding to follow the Supreme Court Judge as he headed toward the living room.

"I expect you'll tell me what this is about," he said, using his palms to indicate the sofa.

He himself sat down in a deep winged armchair. The police officers remained on their feet: the man stood behind the sofa and fiddled in embarrassment with a seam in the leather, without raising his eyes.

"We would like you to accompany us to the police station," the woman said, clearing her throat, obviously feeling increasingly ill at ease. "We, that is to say, the attorneys at headquarters, would really appreciate it if you could come down for a . . . a chat, you might say."

"A chat?"

"An interview."

The voice emanated from the beard; the man straightened up now as he continued. "We would like to interview you."

"Interview me? About what?"

"You'll find that out when we get there. To the police station, I mean."

Supreme Court Judge Benjamin Grinde gazed first at the woman and then at the man before bursting into laughter. Muted, pleasant laughter. The situation seemed to amuse him enormously.

"I expect you know that I'm familiar with the rules here," he chortled. "Strictly speaking, I don't need to come with you at all. Of course, I'm happy to be of service, but I do need to know what this is about."

Then he stood up and, as if to emphasize his nonchalance, left them and disappeared into the kitchen. He returned immediately, carrying his cognac glass, and raised his glass to them with an elegant movement, as though he had already embarked on his birthday celebrations.

"I expect you probably don't drink while on duty." He smiled and sat down slowly in his chair again after picking up a newspaper from the floor.

The female officer sneezed.

"*Prosit,*" mumbled Benjamin Grinde, fumbling with the financial newspaper, *Dagens Næringsliv*, in his hand. Oddly, its pink paper matched the room's furnishings.

"I think you ought to come with us," the woman said, clearing her throat again, this time with more assurance. "We have a warrant for your arrest, just in case."

"*An arrest warrant?* For what, if I may be so bold?"

The newspaper was now back on the floor, and Grinde leaned forward in his seat.

"Honestly," the female officer said, moving around to the front of the sofa in order to sit down, "wouldn't it be better if you just came with us? You said so yourself: you know how things work, and it will be such a shambles if we arrest you. The press, for example. Much better to come with us."

"Let me see that warrant."

His voice was cold, hard, and incontestable.

The younger man fiddled with his jacket zipper and eventually withdrew a blue sheet from his inside pocket. Hesitant, he remained where he was as he glanced at his older colleague to find out what he should do. She nodded faintly, and Benjamin Grinde was handed the form. He unfolded it, laid it on his knee, and stroked the paper several times.

To top it all, they had used his full title: "Doctor of Law, Bachelor of Medicine, Supreme Court Judge Benjamin Grinde. Charged with violation of penal code section 233, c.f. penal code section 232, for the . . ."

When he read the basis and essential elements of the offense, he grew pale; his complexion turned completely gray behind the slight suntan, and as if by magic, a sheen of moisture covered his face.

"Is she dead?" he whispered to no one in particular. "Is Birgitte dead?"

The two police officers exchanged swift glances, knowing that they were both thinking exactly the same thing: either this man had no idea about what had taken place, or he ought to add "Actor by Royal Appointment" to his already incredibly impressive title.

"Yes. She is dead."

It was the woman who replied, and for a moment she was afraid that Benjamin Grinde would faint. The color of his complexion was frightening, and if it had not been for his seemingly excellent health, she would have feared for his heart.

"How?"

Benjamin Grinde was on his feet now, but his body seemed slumped. His shoulders were stooped, as if he were drunk, and he had banged the cognac glass down on the table, the golden liquid sloshing around, twinkling in the light from the chandelier prisms above the dining table.

"We can't tell you that, as you well know," the woman responded, though her voice had softened, to the irritation of her colleague, who interrupted brusquely.

"Are you coming with us now, then?"

Without uttering a word in reply, Benjamin Grinde folded the blue sheet carefully and precisely before unhesitatingly placing it in his own pocket.

"Of course I'll come with you," he muttered. "There's no need for any kind of arrest."

Five patrol vehicles were parked outside the venerable old apartment block in Frogner. As he slipped into the rear seat of one of them, he spotted two police officers heading up to his flat.

They were probably going to guard his apartment, he thought. Perhaps they were awaiting a search warrant. Then he fastened his seat belt.

That was when he noticed that his hands were shaking quite violently.

9:30 P.M., KIRKEVEIEN 129

The phone had been ringing continually, and in the end she had pulled out the plug. It was Friday night, and she wanted some time off. Real time off. Honestly. She shuttled to and fro between her office and the Parliament Building every day and wasn't about to have a hard-earned Friday evening spoiled as well. Both her children were out, and though they were almost grown up, she hardly spoke to them at all. Right at this moment, that didn't matter. She was exhausted and felt a bit under the weather, and had deliberately left her pager tucked away inside a clothes closet, even though, strictly speaking, she was meant to be reachable at all times. Half an hour ago, she had heard something come in on the fax machine in her bedroom, but she didn't have the stamina to go and see what it was. Instead, she mixed herself a Campari with a little tonic and lots of ice cubes, propped her feet up on the coffee table, and was on the point of searching for some kind of detective program among the plethora of channels with which she had never managed to become entirely familiar.

NRK, the state broadcaster, was the safest bet.

The news review program's graphics appeared on the screen. At half past nine? It must be the evening news. As early as this? She stood up to fetch a newspaper.

Then she noticed the vertical text on the picture, down the right-hand side. "News Flash." It was a special broadcast. She stood quite still with the Campari glass in her hand. The man with the fine, blond hair and tired eyes looked almost choked with tears as he cleared his throat before starting to speak.

"Prime Minister Birgitte Volter is dead, at the age of only fifty-one. She was shot in her office in the tower block inside the government complex some time this afternoon or early evening."

The Campari glass fell to the floor. From the hollow sound, she could hear that it did not smash, but the pale shag-pile carpet would almost certainly never be the same again. She did not even look at it, but let herself sink down slowly onto the sofa once more.

"Dead," she whispered. "Birgitte? Dead? Shot?"

"We're moving across to the government complex."

A breathless young man, who seemed tiny in a far too big all-weather jacket, gazed into the restless camera with wide eyes. "Yes, I am standing here outside the tower block, and we have just had confirmation that Birgitte Volter has in fact . . ."

He was obviously struggling to find the right words for the occasion and, as he stuttered and spluttered, she noted that he had not even managed to change into a dark suit, as the man in the studio had.

". . . passed away. From what we now know, she was shot in the head, and we have been informed that she must have died instantly."

And then he could not think of anything further to say. He swallowed repeatedly, and the camera operator was clearly unsure about whether to keep him in focus. The image veered between the reporter—strongly illuminated by a floodlight—and the scene of subdued activity in the background, where the police had their hands full keeping rubberneckers and journalists outside the red-and-white crime scene tape.

Birgitte was dead. The voices on the news program became distant, and she realized she felt faint. Lowering her head between her knees, she reached out for an ice cube from the carpet. Though it was covered in carpet fluff, she placed it on her forehead all the same. It helped to clear her head.

The anchorman in the studio was making a heroic effort to save his younger, far less experienced colleague standing outside the government offices.

"Do you know if any arrests have been made?"

"No, there's nothing to suggest that."

"What about the weapon. Do you know any more about what kind of gun we're talking about?"

"No, all we've been told is that Birgitte Volter is dead and that she has been shot."

"What's happening around the tower block at the moment?"

And so they continued, for an eternity, thought the Minister of Health, Ruth-Dorthe Nordgarden, who did not succeed in absorbing much of it at all. Then the TV picture moved from the tower block to the Parliament Building, where a procession of solemn-faced parliamentary leaders was hurrying into the studio.

Telephone!

She restored the plug, and only a few seconds later, the phone rang.

As she replaced the receiver after the call, there was only one thought in her head: *Am I going to lose my job now?*

She headed for the clothes closet in her bedroom to fish out her pager and look for something suitable to wear. Black. It must be black. But her winter complexion was pale, and black was not the most becoming color. She was aware she was beautiful, she was well aware of that—enough not to choose a black dress in April. They would have to be satisfied with brown. Something dark.

The shock had subsided, and instead she felt a growing sense of irritation.

This was a particularly bad time for Birgitte to have departed this world, to have died. It was extremely inconsiderate of her.

The brown velour dress would have to do.

SATURDAY, APRIL 5

Sure enough, the editor was pissed off that she had left, but that was of no consequence. She would not say what her theories were. That was her concern. Her business. If there was any business.

Benjamin Grinde's apartment was in darkness. Of course that might mean he was fast asleep. On the other hand, hardly anyone in the Kingdom of Norway was asleep right now: it was a Friday and the homicide of Prime Minister Birgitte Volter had struck homes throughout the country like an atomic bomb. Both NRK and TV2 had news flashes every hour, although strictly speaking they had very little to convey. They mostly were fillers and meaningless commentary, as well as obituaries that had clearly been cobbled together at the last minute. It was obvious that since Birgitte Volter had taken office only six months previously, the material had not yet been sitting ready-prepared in the editorial offices. By the following day, the situation would probably have improved.

The darkened windows might also mean that the Supreme Court Judge was out. At a party, perhaps, or "in company," as they said in this part of the city. However, it might also indicate something else.

She looked around before crossing the street. Cars were parked close together along the sidewalk, and there was hardly space for her between a Volvo and BMW whose bumpers were almost kissing. She huffed and puffed and finally had to turn away to try to locate a larger gap elsewhere.

Something was wrong with the lock on the entrance door at Odins gate number 3. Actually, something was wrong with the door itself; it did not close properly, and looked as though the timber had become warped. Odd, but she was spared having to use the intercom. Warily, she opened the massive wooden door and stepped into the hallway.

A smell of plaster and detergent assailed her in the unexpectedly

21

large foyer, and she saw a bicycle secured to the railings of the staircase adjacent to the door leading to the basement. The stairway was attractive and well maintained, with yellow walls and green decorative moldings, and the original stained glass windows on each landing were in exceptionally good condition.

Halfway up the second flight of stairs, she came to a halt.

Voices. Quiet voices in conversation. A peal of laughter.

She pulled back against the wall surprisingly quickly and blessed fate for having equipped her with soundless Ecco shoes. She continued her ascent, keeping as close to the wall as possible.

Two men were sitting on the steps. Two uniformed police officers, sitting directly outside Benjamin Grinde's apartment.

She had been right.

Just as carefully as she had gone up, she padded down again. Once she was well outside the damaged front door, she produced a cell phone from her voluminous coat and keyed in the code for a number that was one of the most valuable in her collection, the number for Chief Inspector Konrad Storskog, a thoroughly unpleasant social climber, aged thirty-five. She was the only one who knew that at the age of twenty-two, he had crashed his parents' car while in a state of intoxication that was never measured but must have been at least .08 percent blood-alcohol concentration. She happened to have been driving the vehicle behind him; it was dark and there was no one else around. She had contacted his parents, who had, quite remarkably, extricated him from this awkward situation without the young, newly qualified police officer receiving so much as a scratch on his record. Little Lettvik had tucked away the information for future use and had never regretted that she had neglected to fulfill her duties as a citizen thirteen years earlier.

"Storskog," was the harsh response at the other end, also a cell phone.

"Hi there, Konrad, old pal." Little Lettvik smirked. "Plenty to do tonight?"

Silence fell.

"Hello? Can you hear me?"

There was no crackling sound, so she knew that he was still on the line.

"Konrad, Konrad," she said indulgently. "Don't be difficult now."

"What do you want?"

"Just an answer to one tiny question."

"What is it? I'm extremely busy."

"Is Supreme Court Judge Benjamin Grinde at the station? Right now, I mean?"

Total silence again.

"I've no idea," he said suddenly, after a lengthy pause.

"Nonsense. Obviously you know. Just say yes or no, Konrad. Just yes or no."

"Why would he be here?"

"If he isn't, then there's a question of gross dereliction of duty."

She smiled to herself as she continued. "Because he must be about the very last person to have seen the woman alive. Volter, I mean. He was at her office late yesterday afternoon. Of course you have to talk to the guy! Can't you just say either yes or no, Konrad, and then you can continue with all those important tasks you're doing?"

Yet again, complete silence.

"This conversation never took place," he said, his tone stony and impassive. Then he disconnected the call.

Little Lettvik had received the confirmation she needed.

"Na-na-na-na-na," she sang contentedly as she headed toward Frognerveien to flag down a taxi.

The situation was getting urgent.

12:57 A.M., OSLO POLICE STATION

Even Billy T., who rarely noticed such things, had to admit that Benjamin Grinde was an unusually handsome man. His physique was athletic but not bulky. He had broad shoulders and narrow hips, though not exaggeratedly so. His clothes were extremely tasteful, down to the socks that were visible when he crossed his legs, and the matching tie, ever so slightly loosened. The dark circlet of hair around his head was cut very short, making the almost bald pate into something deliberate, something chosen: it suggested potency and a large dose of testosterone. His eyes were dark brown and his mouth full, and he had surprisingly white, youthful teeth, given that he was fifty years old, very nearly.

"Birthday tomorrow," Billy T. commented as he leafed through the papers.

A young trainee had already taken the personal details while Billy T.

had been occupied with a private matter. An extremely private matter. He had sent a two-page handwritten fax to Hanne Wilhelmsen before taking a shower. Both of these had been beneficial.

"Yes," Benjamin Grinde said, looking at his wristwatch. "Or actually today. Strictly speaking."

He smiled wanly.

"Fifty years old and all that," Billy T. said. "We'll have this out of the way fast enough so that your celebrations aren't spoiled."

Benjamin Grinde looked startled for the first time; until now his facial expression had been almost blank, exhausted, and virtually apathetic.

"Out of the way? I'll have you know that I was actually presented with an arrest warrant a few hours ago. And now you're saying that this will be out of the way quickly?"

Billy T. turned from the typewriter to gaze at the Supreme Court Judge facing him. He placed the palms of his hands on the table and tilted his head to one side.

"Listen to me." He sighed. "I'm not stupid. And you are *definitely* not stupid. Both you and I know that the person who killed Birgitte Volter did not smile nicely to her secretary and go home in an orderly fashion to make—"

He rooted through the papers.

"Pâté. Was that what you were doing?"

"Yes."

Now Benjamin Grinde was genuinely taken aback. Surely none of the police officers had been inside his kitchen?

"You're such an obvious suspect that it can't possibly be you."

Billy T. chuckled and rubbed his earlobe, making the inverted cross dance.

"I read crime novels, you know. It's never the obvious person. Never. And they don't go home to their own place afterward. To be honest, Grinde, this arrest warrant was a damn piece of nonsense. You were quite right to confiscate it. Throw it away. Burn it. Typical panic response from the bloody attorneys. Pardon my language."

Turning back to the typewriter, he let his fingers hammer out three or four sentences before he inserted a fresh sheet of paper. Then he faced Benjamin Grinde again and seemed to hesitate before he raised his extremely long legs and size 14 boots onto the edge of the table.

"Why were you there?"

"At the office, at Birgitte's?"

"Birgitte? Did you know her? Personally, I mean?"

Billy T.'s feet slammed onto the floor as he leaned across the desk.

"Birgitte Volter and I have known each other since childhood," Benjamin Grinde said, staring at the chief inspector. "She's one year older than me, and during one's teens that creates a certain distance. But in Nesodden, the community wasn't very large. We knew each other at that time."

"At that time. What about now, are you still friends?"

Benjamin Grinde shifted in his seat, placing his left leg over his right.

"No, I wouldn't claim that at all. We've had only sporadic contact over the years. Inadvertent contact, you might say, since our parents continued to live next door to each other for many years after we had left home. No. We can't be said to be friends. Have been, would be more correct."

"But you're on first-name terms?"

Grinde smiled faintly.

"When you've been friends in your childhood and youth, it would seem pretty unnatural to use surnames. Even if you've lost contact. Isn't it the same for you?"

"Probably."

"Well, I expect you know why I was there. You can certainly check in her appointments diary. Or perhaps her secretary can confirm it. I wanted to discuss an increased allocation of resources for a commission I'm chairing. A commission appointed by the government."

"The Grinde Commission, of course," Billy T. commented, putting his feet up on the desk again.

Benjamin Grinde stared at the tips of the boots belonging to the enormous figure on the opposite side of the table. He wondered if his behavior was intended as a police officer's demonstration of power now that he finally had one of the country's most senior judges under his heel.

Billy T. smiled. His eyes were intense, as icy blue as a husky's, and the Supreme Court Judge dropped his gaze onto his lap.

"Don't take these feet as a sign of disrespect," Billy T. remarked, wiggling his steel-capped toes. "It's just so cumbersome having such long legs. Look! There's quite simply not enough room for them underneath the desk!"

He gave a comical demonstration before putting his feet back into position.

"But you. If you were talking about this kind of . . . increased allocation of resources . . ."

Grinde nodded imperceptibly.

". . . why didn't you speak to the minister of health? Wouldn't that have been more normal?"

The judge lifted his gaze again.

"To some extent. But I knew that Birgitte was particularly interested in the case. What's more, it was an opportunity to meet her. In fact, we hadn't spoken for many years. I wanted to congratulate her. On her new post, I mean."

"Why do you need more money?"

"Money?"

"Yes, why did you have to speak to Volter about obtaining more money for this committee of yours?"

"Commission."

"The same thing. Why?"

"The work is turning out to be far more comprehensive than we anticipated when the commission was appointed. We have found it necessary to conduct in-depth interviews with five hundred parents who lost their babies in 1965. It's quite a task. And we have to . . . some investigations have to be conducted abroad."

He looked around and let his eyes rest on the window, where the blue light from a squad car in the backyard was pulsating on the glass. Suddenly it stopped.

"How long were you there?"

The judge considered carefully; he remained seated and stared at his wristwatch, as though he could not recall the answer.

"Difficult to say. I would assume about half an hour. I arrived at quarter to five, in any case. Actually, I was there for almost exactly three-quarters of an hour. Half past five. That was when I left. I know that for certain because I wondered whether I would catch a certain tram or take a taxi. Three-quarters of an hour."

"Okay."

Billy T. stood up abruptly, towering over the far smaller judge.

"Coffee? Tea? Cola? Do you smoke?"

"I'd really like a cup of coffee, thanks. No, I don't smoke."

Billy T. crossed the room and opened the door. He spoke softly to someone standing outside, then closed the door and sat down again, this time on the windowsill.

The judge felt the stirrings of irritation.

It was acceptable that the man's head was shaved smooth and that he was wearing old denim jeans that had seen better days. Even his studded boots were acceptable at a pinch; his feet were so large that it must be difficult to find suitable footwear. The inverted cross, however, was a downright provocation, especially these days, when right-wing extremists and Satanists were committing serious, offensive crimes almost every day. And it must surely be possible to sit still during an interview.

"Apologies if you think I look like a Nazi bastard," Billy T. said.

Could the man read his thoughts?

"I spent years in the drug squad surveillance team," the Chief Inspector added. "Haven't quite managed to rid myself of the habit of looking like a lout. In fact it's often quite effective. The boys get a bit matey, you see. The criminals, I mean. Don't read anything into it."

There was a knock at the door, and a young woman wearing a threadbare red corduroy dress and sensible shoes entered without waiting for an answer, carrying two cups of coffee.

"You're an angel." Billy T. grinned. "Thanks a lot!"

The coffee, piping hot and strong as dynamite, was impossible to drink without slurping. The wax on the paper cups was melting, and as the cups softened, they became difficult to hold.

"Did anything special happen at the meeting?" Billy T. inquired.

The judge seemed to hesitate, spilling some coffee on his trousers and then wiping his thigh with firm, angry movements.

"No," he said, without making eye contact with the Chief Inspector. "I wouldn't say so."

"Her secretary says she'd seemed out of sorts recently. Did you notice anything of that kind?"

"I don't really know Birgitte Volter any longer. She seemed very competent to me. No, I can't say there was anything that struck me."

Benjamin Grinde lived both from and for the pursuit of justice and truth. He was used to telling the truth. He was particularly unused to lying. It made him tense, and he felt nauseous. He put down his coffee cup carefully, at the far edge of the desk, before looking the Chief Inspector straight in the eye.

"There was nothing about her behavior that made me wonder if anything was wrong," he said in a steady voice.

The worst thing was that it seemed as if the chief inspector saw right through him, focusing directly on the lie that had coiled up like a poisonous snake somewhere behind his breastbone.

"Nothing seemed abnormal," he repeated, again looking out the window.

The blue light had returned now, hammering repeatedly against the dull windowpane.

2:23 A.M., NORWEGIAN TIME, BERKELEY, CALIFORNIA

Dear Billy T.,

It's unbelievable. I was in the middle of making dinner when the fax arrived. It's just incredible! I phoned Cecilie right away, and she's never rushed home from university so quickly. The murder has had quite a lot of coverage here as well, and we're sitting glued to the television screen. But they don't seem to be saying anything, just the same stuff over and over again. I'm missing home more than ever!

Be careful not to lock yourselves into any theories. We have to learn something from the Swedes, who obviously got totally bogged down in one definite "obvious" lead after another. What theories are you working on in the meantime? Terrorism? Right-wing extremists? As far as I've understood it, there's a certain amount of activity noticeable in those circles at present. Remember for heaven's sake the most obvious suspects: lunatics, family, rejected lovers (which you know more about than most). How are you organizing yourselves? I have a thousand questions that you probably don't have time to answer. But PLEASE: send me a message, and I promise to write more later.

This is just an initial reaction, and I'm sending it in the hope that you manage to read it before you go to bed. Though you won't be getting much sleep in the days ahead. I'm going to send this to your home fax machine as maybe the guys will be annoyed at a

*Chief Inspector in exile getting mixed up in matters that she
doesn't strictly have anything to do with any longer.*

*Cecilie sends her very fondest regards. Typically, she's most con-
cerned about you! I'm thinking more about Norway, my Norway.
It's all completely crazy.*

Write soon!

Your Hanne

2:49 A.M., *KVELDSAVISEN* EDITORIAL OFFICE

"Out of the question, Little. We simply can't do that."

The editor was leaning over his desk looking at a draft front
page, radically altered since the first special edition that had hit the
streets before midnight. He was now faced with a front page emblazoned with an enormous photo of Benjamin Grinde, accompanied by
a colossal, dramatic headline, SUPREME COURT JUDGE ARRESTED, and
a subtitle: "Last person to see Volter alive."

"We just don't have any proof of this," the man said, pinching his
nose and adjusting his glasses. "It won't do. We'll be sued. For millions."

Little Lettvik had no problem playing the martyr. She stood with
her legs apart and flung out her arms over and over again, shaking her
head and rolling her eyes in a grotesque fashion.

"*Honestly!*"

Her roar was so loud that the constant buzz of the editorial offices
was momentarily silenced. When they realized where the outburst
originated, everybody continued what they were doing. Little Lettvik
was no stranger to amateur dramatics, not even when they were inappropriate.

"I have two sources," she snarled through clenched teeth. "TWO
SOURCES!"

"Come with me," the editor said, moving his hand up and down in
a motion that was probably intended to be reassuring, but that Little
Lettvik perceived as patronizing. Once well inside his impressive
office, they plopped down in their respective chairs.

"What sources do you have?" he asked, looking at her.

"I'm not saying."

"Okay. Then there won't be any headline."

He grabbed his phone and indicated with his eyes darting toward the door that she should leave. Little Lettvik hesitated briefly, but then stomped out and along the corridor until she burst into her own little shoebox. The tiny office was in blissful chaos, with books, newspapers, official documents, food wrappers, and old apple cores everywhere. Rummaging around on the overcrowded desk, she located a folder she knew exactly where to find, amazingly enough, hidden between a pizza carton containing two dead pepperoni slices and an edition of the *Arbeiderbladet* newspaper.

"Bloody hell, it's hard work trying to sell newspapers," she muttered as she pulled out a cigarillo.

The folder on Benjamin Grinde was relatively comprehensive, as she had worked on it for several weeks. It contained everything that had been printed about his commission, from the very first interview with Frode Fredriksen, the lawyer who had initiated the whole enterprise. She located the newspaper cutting from *Aftenposten*.

NOTHING ABOUT HUMANITY IS FOREIGN TO ME!

Advocate Fredriksen celebrates 25th anniversary with acquittal in Brevik case

By Tone Vrebø and Anders Kurén (photo)

Frode Fredriksen has certainly not stinted on his personal effects. His office contains many items that his far worse-off clients would kill for, literally speaking. A gigantic painting by the acclaimed contemporary artist Frans Widerberg covers one wall of his office, sending reddish-orange rays across a highly polished mahogany desk. On the desk, a family smiles from a silver frame: two adults and their fortunate offspring, one of each, and a wife who could easily be mistaken for a model. Which she is not: Frode Fredriksen is married to the well-known psychologist and social commentator Beate Frivoll. Yesterday, Fredriksen's client Karsten Brevik was acquitted of triple murder, a serious setback for the prosecuting authorities. Today Frode Fredriksen celebrates twenty-five years as an advocate.

"How does it feel to have made a successful career from dedicating your life to losers?"

"First and foremost, it's really exciting. What's more, I wouldn't call them losers. I don't like the word. No human being is a loser. Some are simply more unfortunate than others, and the prize they have won in the lottery of life is not as substantial as what has come the way of the rest of us. Second, it is rewarding. Extremely rewarding, I would say. There's not a day goes by that I don't learn something new. In twenty-five years I've had the pleasure of meeting a large number of people in the most dreadful situations. Nothing about humanity is foreign to me any longer."

"Does it not take a heavy toll, working with violent criminals and killers?"

"No, I wouldn't say that. There's a definite challenge with such clients: acquittal, or a reduced sentence. Where injustice has occurred, but no blame can be allocated, then it is much harder. For example, I am currently helping a couple who lost a baby thirty years ago. In fact it happened in 1965, the same year that my wife and I had our first child. The death seemed both meaningless and unnecessary, and it has tortured this family for all these years. Now I am seeking an ex gratia payment on behalf of the parents. Such matters are difficult. Extremely difficult!"

The interview went on much longer, but she could not find the second page of the clipping. It did not matter. The date added in slovenly handwriting in the top left-hand corner was September 21, 1996. The article had given rise to an avalanche of requests to the elegant lawyer behind the mahogany desk. An amazingly short time after the interview, he had applied to Parliament for ex gratia payments on behalf of 119 parents. All of them felt that the death of their child had been unexpected and totally unnecessary. What all the cases had in common was that there was nothing to indicate malpractice. Most of the death certificates cited "sudden cardiac arrest."

The hullabaloo went on and on. The opposition parties in Parliament—apparently paralyzed by their battle against Prime Minister Gro, whom no one yet knew had decided to resign her premiership—had forced the government to set up an investigative commission, and this was finally appointed on November 10, 1996. It had become unavoidable, since just a few strokes of the keyboard at Statistics Norway could establish that many more children under the age of one had died in 1965 than in any year before or since.

Benjamin Grinde was the perfect choice to chair the commission, given his position as a Supreme Court Judge, embellished with a bachelor's degree in medicine like the top tier of a most unusual career wedding cake. The opposition parties in Parliament were still savoring the taste of success after another Supreme Court Judge had presented an investigative report concerning the Secret Services barely six months earlier. Since Grinde's dissertation had been entitled "Silence and Suppression: The Patient's Legal Protection in Health Examinations," he was an obvious candidate, and the integrity associated with his office underlined this.

Little Lettvik was worn out.

If she really were to think about it, she wouldn't be able to explain why, only a few hours after the murder of the country's Prime Minister, she was sitting reading old newspaper cuttings about a health issue no one discussed any longer and whose outcome was uncertain. Perhaps it was because she had worked on it for too long. These past weeks she had not unearthed anything new, and only her position as undisputed senior journalist ensured that she got away with that. The case concerning the infant deaths interested her. Maybe it was blinding her. But there was no time for that now. She needed to concentrate on the homicide.

Benjamin Grinde. It was Benjamin Grinde who had grabbed her attention. The mere thought of the man caused jabs of pain in her knee. It was impossible not to be intrigued by the coincidence. For weeks she had been digging to find out what the Grinde Commission was up to, without discovering anything but the most mundane and fairly obvious facts. Then the chair of the commission pops up as perhaps the last person in the country to have seen the Prime Minister alive.

"Now you'd damn well better set to work, Little."

It was the editor. As usual he shot a look filled with loathing across the tiny room before turning on his heel and repeating, "Now you'd better get to it. There should be more than enough to be going on with."

7:00 A.M., GOVERNMENT CONFERENCE ROOM
IN THE TOWER BLOCK

They all had felt the same insistent revulsion as they had passed the entrance to the Prime Minister's office on the floor below. Although there was no longer a police presence in the vicinity—at least not a visible one—and although the only obvious abnormality was a closed door that was usually kept open, they were aware that behind the wall they all tried to avoid staring at, Birgitte Volter had been shot and killed twelve hours previously.

The government ministers were extraordinarily quiet; only the Minister of Trade's singsong voice was just about audible.

"It's just so awful. I simply can't find the words."

She was sitting at the massive oval table on which stood several slim, modern microphones. One of them was audaciously pointing directly at her; she held her hand over it as she leaned forward to gain the ear of the Minister of Defense. It was no use. They were both sitting near the top of the table, as their age and seniority in cabinet required, and the sound carried right across the room.

The Foreign Minister was last to enter. The others were already seated. He was unusually pale, and the Minister of Culture could swear that his hair had turned grayer overnight. She tried to send him an encouraging smile, but he did not make eye contact with any of them. Standing momentarily beside the Prime Minister's seat at the head of the oval table, he made up his mind quickly and drew out the large leather chair, left it vacant, and sat down on the chair to its left. The Foreign Minister's seat.

"Good that you could all manage to come," he said, peering round at his colleagues.

The Minister of Agriculture was the only one dressed in everyday clothes: denim jeans and a flannel shirt. He had been fishing at his summer cottage when the government car came to collect him, and there had not been time to go to his apartment for a more appropriate outfit. Now he was sitting fiddling with a tin of snuff but did not dare help himself to a pinch, even though the craving was overwhelming. It would appear disrespectful. He stuffed the tin into his breast pocket.

"This is a terrible day for us all," the Foreign Minister said, after clearing his throat. "As far as the case itself is concerned—the police case, I mean—I actually know very little. No weapon has been found. No one has been arrested. It goes without saying that the police are working flat out. With assistance from their Security Service. I hardly need to tell you why they are in the picture."

He fumbled for the glass of Farris mineral water in front of him and drank its entire contents. No one took the opportunity to ask questions, even though there were quite a few of these bouncing off the soundproof walls of the room. All that could be heard was the sound of the Oil and Energy Minister sniffing.

"My primary concern is to let you know what is going on. Factually and constitutionally. I have a formal meeting with the King at nine o'clock today, and there will be an extraordinary meeting of the cabinet later in the day. You will be told when."

He continued to hold the empty glass in his hand, staring at it as though he hoped it would refill all by itself. He then reluctantly put it down and turned to face the Senior Private Secretary, who was sitting on the other side of the vacant chair.

"Could you provide us with a short briefing?"

The Senior Private Secretary from the Prime Minister's office was an older woman who chafed strenuously against the fact that she would be turning seventy in two months' time. Several times during the previous night, she had caught herself having the objectionably egotistical thought that this incident might mean the postponement of her pensioner status for perhaps a year.

"Otto B. Halvorsen . . ." she began, slipping a pair of reading glasses onto her narrow, angular face. "He passed away on May 23, 1923. He and Peder Ludvig Kolstad are the only ones to have died while in post as prime minister. So we do in a sense have precedents to follow. I can't see any reason why we should handle this case differently."

"This case." Finance Minister Tryggve Storstein felt a strong surge of irritation, bordering on rage. This was no "case." This concerned the dreadful fact that Birgitte Volter was dead.

Tryggve Storstein was basically quite a good-looking man. He had regular features that made life difficult for the cartoonists, short dark hair that showed no sign of receding even though he was approaching fifty, and anxious, downcast eyes that sometimes made him look sad even when he was smiling. His northern European nose was straight, and his mouth sometimes had an undeniably sensual quiver to it when he spoke. However, Tryggve Storstein did not make a big deal out of his appearance. Perhaps this was due to his upbringing in Storsteinnes in Troms County, or maybe it was that he had practically been born into the party. In any case, he had the peculiar trait that ill-tempered right-wingers ascribed to every former member of the AUF, the youth wing of the Labor movement: he was ever so slightly tacky. Although his clothes hung well on his athletic frame, they never looked quite right. Were never really tasteful. The dark suits were too dark, and everything else came from the Dressmann chain store. Now he was wearing a brown "tweed" jacket of synthetic material, black trousers, and brown shoes. He was upset and tinkered with a pen he continually pressed in and out. *Click-click. Click-click.*

"Of course, Otto B. Halvorsen died after a short illness," the Senior Private Secretary continued, glancing with irritation in Storstein's direction over the rim of her glasses. "So people had time to prepare themselves to some extent. That probably came in handy when Peder Kolstad died suddenly following a thrombosis in March 1932. The same procedure was followed then. In any case, the foreign minister takes over the post of prime minister on a temporary basis until the government resigns. That can happen as soon as a new government is ready. Until then, the present government functions as a caretaker administration."

She pursed her lips momentarily, which made her look like a bespectacled mouse.

"That is to say, it deals only with current issues. I have prepared a memorandum . . ."

She gave a peremptory signal to a woman who had just entered the room. Standing beside the coffee table near the door, the woman seemed extremely uneasy. At the sign from her superior, she moved rapidly around the oval table, issuing each of the cabinet ministers three booklets.

The Senior Private Secretary continued: ". . . that explains what can be considered 'current issues.' Mainly they are issues that cannot be said to commit the next government in any way. The appointment of judges, for example . . ."

Looking up from the paper in front of her, she sought eye contact with the Justice Minister, but he was gazing at the ceiling, his eyes fixed on the tiny halogen lamps that for the moment resembled planets in an alien universe.

"... must be put on hold. Well. Everything is detailed in the papers. We are at your disposal to answer questions twenty-four hours a day."

The Senior Private Secretary tapped the papers in front of her and looked at the Foreign Minister with a forced smile.

"Thanks," he mumbled, coughing.

He was coming down with a cold: a chill, tight band of pain was pressing into his head. "I have spoken to the President of the Parliament. There will be an extraordinary sitting of Parliament today at twelve noon. I expect to have a new government in place within a week. But we'll wait until after the funeral."

There was silence. Total silence. The Minister of Agriculture instinctively clutched his breast pocket but still let the snuff tin be. The Minister of Trade ran his hands over his hair. For once, his hair was not perfect, and several loose strands were hanging over his left ear. Tryggve Storstein broke the stillness.

"We are holding an extraordinary meeting of the Labor Party National Executive tomorrow afternoon," he said softly. "Until further notice, I will take on the role of Party Leader. You will be immediately informed about what happens in the party in the days ahead."

Health Minister Ruth-Dorthe Nordgarden looked up. Winding her blond hair around her ear, she glanced at the Finance Minister. Together with Tryggve Storstein, she was joint Deputy Leader of the Party. They had been granted these positions as a consolation prize following the dramatic confrontation five years earlier, when Gro Harlem Brundtland, abruptly and for personal reasons, had stepped down as Party Leader and concentrated on being Prime Minister. Birgitte Volter had won. There had been little to separate the three candidates until an hour before the result was announced. The Norwegian Confederation of Trade Unions had decided the matter. Birgitte Volter had originally come from the trade union movement and had wisely nurtured relationships there.

So they became joint Deputy Leaders. The most important difference between them was that Tryggve Storstein had accepted the defeat five years earlier with composure. He enjoyed widespread, universal respect, though most people disagreed with him on one issue or another. By contrast, Ruth-Dorthe Nordgarden had both a coterie of devoted, uncritical friends and a number of thoroughly malicious enemies. As long as the former were very much in the majority, she would manage fine. Tryggve Storstein did not belong to that group, and the mistrust was mutual.

"And one thing we must make clear," Tryggve Storstein added, leafing through the papers in front of him, "is that there is no guarantee—as the situation in Parliament currently stands, and given the appetite for government shown by the centrist parties in the past six months—that the Labor Party will be running the country in a week's time. Now they have the opportunity, if they want to take it—our friends in the centrist parties."

No one had yet thought that far ahead. They all looked at one another.

"Hell, no," muttered the Minister for Children and Families. Despite her young age, she had spent a long time in Parliament. "I'll bet my boots they won't take the chance now. They'll wait until the autumn."

Then she suddenly raised her hand to her mouth, as though it wasn't quite polite to bet your boots on anything.

8:00 A.M., OSLO POLICE STATION

"There are far too many bloody cooks around here," muttered Billy T. "This is turning into a real mess."

The woman at his side nodded gently. There had to be at least fifty people in the parade room on the third floor of the police building. The men from the Police Security Service were easy to distinguish, as they sat on their own and looked as though they were keeping an extremely big secret. What's more, most of them were well rested, in contrast to other members of the police force, many of whom had been working for almost twenty-four hours. A whiff of old perspiration permeated the large space.

"Damn Security Service," Billy T. continued. "It's sure to be a shambles. Those guys are going to conjure up the worst-case scenarios. Terrorism and devilment and threats from the Middle East. And we're probably only dealing with a lunatic. Hell's teeth, Tone-Marit, we don't need a Norwegian Palme case. If we don't get to the bottom of this in a couple of weeks, then it'll be too late. That's for absolute certain."

"You're just tired, Billy T.," Tone-Marit replied. "Obviously the Security Service has to be involved in this. They're the ones who know all about the threat levels."

"Yes, I am damn tired. But they can't have a particularly good handle on threat levels, since the lady's already dead. And so—"

Grinning, he tried in vain to find room for his legs between the rows of chairs; in the end he had to ask the man in the seat in front to move.

"And so they're in a catch-22 dilemma. Either *they* are right that the homicide has a political or terrorist motive, and they haven't done their job. Or else *I'm* right about it being the work of some madman, and then the Security Service doesn't have any business being here. That's the kind of thing *we're* good at."

"You'll just have to calm down now," Tone-Marit said quietly. "You never got over the fact that they had doubts about your security clearance."

"Just because I'm fond of women," Billy T. spluttered.

"You sleep with any woman who makes herself available," Tone-Marit corrected him. "And a few more besides. But that had nothing to do with it, and you know that perfectly well. You were once in the Communist Party. What's more, you can't possibly have any grounds for stating that this is the work of a madman. We don't have grounds for drawing *any* conclusions. None. You should know that."

"I've *never* been a member of the Communist Party. Never! I was a radical! That's something entirely different. I *am* a radical, for fuck's sake. That doesn't mean that I can't be relied on!"

The Security Service Chief and the Chief of Police had taken their places at a table at the very front of the room, and were sitting facing the others like two teachers facing a class they weren't quite sure how to tackle. The Chief of Police, who had been appointed to the post only three months earlier, had streaks of grime on his face and was scratching his dark-blue stubble. His uniform shirt had a dirty ring around the collar, and his tie was crooked. The Security Service Chief was not in uniform; he was immaculately dressed in a beige summer suit over a brilliant white shirt with a tan-colored tie, and he was gazing at the ceiling.

"A staff base has been set up in the communications room at the central switchboard," the Police Chief began, without any further introductions or opening preamble. "We'll continue with that arrangement in the days ahead. Time will tell whether we move out from there."

Time will tell. They all knew what that meant.

"We're left bloody high and dry," Billy T. whispered.

"In the meantime, we have very little to go on," the Chief of Police confirmed loudly as he stood up.

Crossing to an overhead projector, he placed a piece of acetate on the glass plate.

"Up 'til now, we have interviewed twenty-eight people. We're talking about people who can be closely connected to the scene of the crime. Staff at the Prime Minister's office, politicians, government officials, and office workers. In addition to the security personnel on the fourteenth as well as the ground floor. And a couple of—visitors. People who visited the Prime Minister yesterday."

The Chief of Police pointed at a red box on the sheet, filled with names. His hands were trembling. The pen he was using, outlined like a giant pointer on the wall behind him, moved up and down on the acetate and pushed it askew. For a moment or two he fumbled to try to straighten it, but it seemed to have attached itself to the glass, and he abandoned the attempt.

"At this preliminary stage, we have no fixed theories. I repeat: we have no fixed theories. It's of the greatest importance that we go forward on an extremely broad front. The Security Service will play a very important part in this work. The method used in this homicide . . ."

He switched off the projector, using both hands to remove the obstinate acetate. Then, placing another on the glass plate, he switched the machine on again.

". . . indicates a high degree of professionalism."

The acetate showed a diagram of the fourteenth and fifteenth floors in the tower block.

"This is the Prime Minister's office. As you can see, it can be reached in two ways, either through the outer office and in through here . . ."

He let the pen smack against a door opening.

". . . or via a conference room, through the restroom and in here."

The pen drew a route on the sheet.

"What both entrances have in common is that in both instances, you have to pass through this door here . . ."

Again he dotted the pen on the glass.

". . . and that is in full view of the secretary's desk here."

The Chief of Police sighed so heavily that the sound reached all the way back to Billy T. and Police Sergeant Tone-Marit Steen. This was followed by a lengthy silence.

"Besides," the Police Chief said suddenly, his voice breaking in the middle of the word. He coughed hoarsely. "Besides, in order to access the three top floors, the Prime Minister's section, you have to pass this point."

His stubby forefinger now covered the entire entrance to the four-teenth floor.

"This is a security gate, where a security guard is always present. True enough, there is of course an emergency exit . . ."

His finger moved again.

". . . here, but there is absolutely nothing to indicate that it was used. The doors are sealed, and the seals have not been broken."

"Where's John Dickson Carr and his supersleuths when you need them?" Billy T. said under his breath, his mouth at Tone-Marit's ear.

The Chief of Police continued. "For some time now, the tower block has been undergoing extensive renovations, both inside and out. Because of that, scaffolding has been erected on the outside of the building. Naturally we have checked whether someone could have come in that way, but we haven't found any evidence of that either. None whatsoever. The windows are intact, the frames untouched. Of course, we are also investigating everything to do with air vents and that sort of thing, but for the moment that seems to be a red herring as well."

The Security Service Chief had folded his arms across his chest and was studying something on the desk facing him.

The Police Chief went on. "The weapon has still not been found. So far it looks as though it was a relatively small-caliber gun, probably a revolver. We'll have more specific answers later today, when a provisional postmortem report will also be available. As things appear now, the time of the murder seems to have been at some point between 6:00 and 6:45. And guys . . ."

He peered out across the assembly.

". . . it should be completely unnecessary to say this, but I'm saying it regardless: if there was ever a time when it was important to keep our cards close to our chests, then this is it. Every single leak to the press or anybody else will be subjected to a thorough investigation, and I mean thorough. I will not accept *any* leaks; I repeat: *not a single, solitary leak about this case.* Understood?"

A murmur of consent rippled through the room.

"The Security Service will make a short statement."

The man in the beige suit got to his feet and rounded the table where he had been sitting. With a graceful movement, he sat on the tabletop, and once again crossed his arms over his rib cage.

"We're keeping all possibilities open, as the Chief of Police has suggested. We know that right-wing extremist groups have engaged in a certain amount of activity recently, and we are aware that this includes drafting so-called death lists. In itself, this is nothing new. Such lists have been in existence for a long time, and Prime Minister Volter featured on them long before she took over the premiership."

He stood up again and walked back and forth across the floor as he spoke. His voice was deep and pleasant, and his words flowed without pause.

"Neither can we disregard the possibility that the murder has a connection with recent events in the Middle East. The Oslo Agreement is in imminent danger of petering out altogether, and it is well known that Norway is working tenaciously behind the scenes to prevent the whole peace process from collapsing."

"Now our guys in Security will get to cooperate with their old pals in Mossad again," Billy T. muttered, almost inaudibly.

Tone-Marit pretended not to hear and craned her neck to obtain a better view of the man at the front.

"We also have a couple of other possible theories that we are in the process of scrutinizing more closely. It's not necessary to go into that in any detail here."

The Security Service Chief stopped, nodding briefly to the Chief of Police as a signal that the meeting was over. The Chief tugged at his grimy collar and appeared to be longing earnestly to go home.

"Do you still believe all that guff about a lone madman?" Tone-Marit asked as they left the parade room immediately afterward. "Must be an ingenious guy, in that case!"

Billy T. did not respond, but after staring at her for several seconds, shook his head lamely.

"Now I really *must* get some sleep," he mumbled.

9:07 A.M., OSLO POLICE STATION

It was impossible to guess the age of the woman in the black dress with a little scarlet scarf around her neck who sat sipping from a glass of Farris mineral water. Police Sergeant Tone-Marit Steen was impressed: the woman looked refreshed and immaculately turned out, despite having been interviewed until four o'clock that same morning. It was true that her eyes were ever so slightly bloodshot, but her makeup was perfect, and the small movements she continually made released a faint, pleasant waft of perfume into the room. Tone-Marit tucked her arms into her sides and hoped that she did not smell too rank.

"Really sorry to have to bother you again," she said in a voice that sounded sincere. "But in the circumstances, I hope you appreciate that we regard you as a particularly important witness."

Wenche Andersen, secretary in the Prime Minister's office, nodded gently.

"It's all the same to me. It's impossible to sleep anyway. It's the least I can do. Ask away."

"In order to avoid going through what we covered last night all over again, we'll do a short review of what you said. Stop me if anything is incorrect."

Nodding, Wenche Andersen cradled her hands in her lap.

"Birgitte Volter had asked to be left in peace, is that right?"

The woman nodded.

"And you don't know why. She was to have an absolutely routine meeting with Supreme Court Judge Grinde, a meeting that had been arranged a week in advance. No one else came to the office after you last saw Volter alive. But you say here—"

Tone-Marit leafed through the papers, and finally found what she was looking for. "You say that she had seemed troubled recently. Stressed, you say. What do you make of that?"

The woman in black gazed at her, obviously searching for the right words.

"It's difficult to say, really. I hadn't gotten to know her very well yet, you see. She was—dismissive? irritable?—a bit of both. Slightly abrupt, in a sense. More so than she had been before. I can't say any more than that."

"Could you—could you give some examples? About the sort of thing that caused her to become irritable?"

Something resembling a smile crossed Wenche Andersen's face.

"The newspapers are usually delivered by messenger at quarter past eight. On Thursday there was a delay of some kind, so they did not arrive until almost half past nine. The Prime Minister was so annoyed that she—well, she swore, not to put too fine a point on it."

The woman's cheeks had now acquired two small patches of puce.

"Foul language, in fact. I ran out and bought copies of *Dagbladet* and *Kveldsavisen* for her."

She sighed.

"Things like that. Unnecessary things. The kind of thing prime ministers don't usually waste energy on."

Tone-Marit lifted a half-liter bottle of mineral water and looked inquiringly at the other woman.

"Yes, please," she answered, holding out her plastic cup.

The Police Sergeant stared at her for some time, just long enough for the silence to become uncomfortable.

"What was she like, actually?" she suddenly asked. "What kind of person was she?"

"Birgitte Volter? What was she like?" The puce patches grew. "Well . . . what was she like? She was extremely conscientious. Very hard working. Almost like former Prime Minister Gro in that respect."

Now she smiled broadly, revealing a row of attractive, well-cared-for teeth, with flashes of gold in the molars.

"She worked from early morning 'til late at night. Really easy to relate to and always gave clear instructions. Very clear instructions. When something went adrift—with the kind of schedule a Prime Minister has, unexpected things happen all the time, but she always took it in her stride. And then she was quite . . ."

She was searching for words again, letting her eyes flit around the room, as though the words were hidden somewhere and refused to come into view.

". . . warm," she eventually exclaimed. "I would in fact call her warm. She even remembered my birthday and gave me a bouquet of roses. She almost always found time to have a natter about this and that."

"But if you were to say something negative," the Police Sergeant interrupted. "What would you say then?"

"Well, negative . . ."

Looking down, the woman fiddled with the edge of her jacket.

"Well, she could be slightly . . . slightly too . . . genial? I wasn't allowed to address her as 'Prime Minister'; she insisted on being called 'Birgitte.' That was unusual. And not quite proper, if you ask me. And she could get muddled—when it came to specific things, I mean. Kept forgetting her pass and suchlike. And in the midst of all this geniality, there was something . . . what should I call it? A kind of reserve? No, now I must be rambling terribly."

She was speaking softly, almost whispering, and shook her head dejectedly.

"Anything else?"

"No, not really. Nothing important."

Someone knocked at the door.

"Busy!" Tone-Marit called out, and faint footsteps disappeared along the corridor as she continued. "Let me judge whether it's of importance."

The woman looked her straight in the eye as she quickly ran her hand across her hair in a superfluous gesture.

"No, honestly. There's no more to be said. Apart from one thing that struck me last night. Or, this morning, in actual fact. A while ago. But it doesn't really have anything to do with this, not really."

Tone-Marit leaned forward, clutching a pen that she rocked between the forefinger and middle finger of her right hand.

"Last night I was asked to go through the Prime Minister's office," Wenche Andersen continued. "To see if there was anything missing, as the police officer put it. That was after Birgitte had been remo . . . been carried out, I mean. But I had already seen her, of course. Both when I found her and afterward, when she was lying there, or sitting there, I suppose. Across the desk. I had seen her twice. And . . ."

She stared expressionlessly at the pen tapping on the desktop with that nerve-racking, staccato sound.

Tone-Marit stopped abruptly. "Sorry," she said, leaning back. "Do continue."

"So I had seen her twice. And not to boast . . . in no way, but I am considered to be quite . . . observant."

Now the little puce patches were ringed with dark red.

"I notice things. It is extremely necessary in my work. And I noticed that the Prime Minister wasn't wearing her shawl."

"Her shawl?"

"Yes, a large, fringed woolen shawl, black with a red pattern. She was wearing it across one shoulder, like this."

Wenche Andersen untied her own small scarf, folded it into a triangle, and placed it over her shoulder.

"Not exactly like that, because it was a shawl of course, and much larger than this little scarf, but you get the idea I'm sure. I'm not entirely certain, but I think it was fastened with a hidden safety pin, because it never fell off. She liked that shawl and often wore it."

"And what about this shawl?"

"It wasn't there."

"Wasn't there?"

"No, she wasn't wearing it, and it wasn't in the room when I inspected it. It had vanished."

The Police Sergeant leaned toward her again; something had kindled a spark in her eyes, and the woman opposite her instinctively drew back in her seat.

"Are you certain she was wearing it that day? Quite certain?"

"I'm 100 percent sure. I noticed that it was hanging slightly crooked, as though she had put it on without looking in a mirror. One hundred percent. Does it mean anything?"

"Maybe," Tone-Marit said in a quiet voice. "Maybe not. Can you give a more detailed description?"

"Well, as I said, it was black, with a red pattern. Provençal pattern, I would call it. It was big, approximately . . ."

Wenche Andersen held out her hands a bit more than a yard apart.

". . . and it was probably made of wool. I'm fairly sure it was pure wool. But now it's vanished."

Tone-Marit turned toward her computer beside the window. Without uttering a word, she sat writing for ten minutes.

Wenche Andersen drank some more Farris and glanced discreetly at her watch. She felt fatigue seep through her, and the monotonous, rattling sound of the police officer's fingers on the keyboard made her struggle to keep her eyes open.

"And you never heard a shot?"

Wenche Andersen was startled; she must have dozed off momentarily.

"No. Never."

"Then we'll draw a line under this for today. You can take a taxi home and charge it to us. Thanks for taking the trouble to come back again. Unfortunately, I can't promise it'll be the last time."

After shaking hands in farewell, Wenche Andersen hesitated at the door. "Do you think you'll catch him? The killer, I mean?" Her eyes, until now only very slightly red, seemed full of tears.

"I don't know. It's impossible to say. But we're going to do our very, very best."

"If that's any consolation," Tone-Marit added after a few moments.

However, by that time the Prime Minister's secretary had already left, closing the door carefully behind her.

NOON, PLENARY CHAMBER, PARLIAMENT BUILDING

The half-moon-shaped plenary chamber in the Parliament Building, which resembled an amphitheater, had never been more crowded. Every one of the 165 seats was occupied and had been for more than a quarter of an hour. Unusually, no one spoke. The cabinet members were sitting in the first semicircle of chairs, at the front; only the Prime Minister's seat was vacant, except for a bouquet of a dozen red roses that had been placed there haphazardly and looked as if they might fall to the floor at any moment. No one felt inclined to straighten them. The spaces reserved for diplomats were chock-full of bureaucrats and foreign representatives, all in dark clothes and with pale faces, apart from the South African ambassador, who was black and dressed in colorful traditional costume. The only noise, other than the occasional splutter and cough, came from the whirring of camera motors in the press box. The gallery above the rotunda was packed, and two security guards had their hands full holding latecomers outside the doors.

The President of the Parliament entered from the left. She strode across the floor, actually strode, her back erect and eyes swollen. She had been one of Birgitte Volter's few genuine friends, and it was only long training in official decorum that kept her upright. Her curls trembled sadly on her head, as though they too were mourning the loss of a close friend.

She hammered three times on the table with a gavel before clearing her throat, then stood for so long without uttering a word that the atmosphere in the chamber became even tenser. In the end, she swallowed so loudly and so close to the microphone that the sound could be heard in every corner of the chamber.

"Parliament is lawfully convened," she said finally, before reading out the list of deputies, for once rather short, which was good, since formalities seemed misplaced on a day such as this.

"Prime Minister Birgitte Volter has passed away," she said at last. "And in the most brutal fashion imaginable."

Lost in his own thoughts, Finance Minister Tryggve Storstein missed out on the memorial speech. Everything around him seemed to blur. The golden decorations on the ceiling, the burgundy carpet at his feet, the sound of the Parliamentary President's voice; a glass bell jar formed around his chair and he felt totally alone. He was going to become Party Leader. Ruth-Dorthe did not have a chance. She was far too controversial for that. But would he also become prime minister? He did not even know if he wanted to. Of course, the thought had been there. Earlier. Before the final confrontation in 1992, when Gro Harlem Brundtland had resigned as leader of the Labor Party, thus launching the cat-and-dog fight that Birgitte Volter had won. But now? Did he want to be prime minister?

He shook his head peremptorily. People did not ask such questions. One did what the situation demanded. What the party required. Frowning at the old cliché, he closed his eyes. For one fleeting, liberating moment, he considered the possibility of the opposition taking over, but that blasphemous notion was swiftly displaced. They had to retain power. Anything else would mean chaos. Defeat. He was tired of defeat.

"In conclusion, I propose that the costs of Prime Minister Birgitte Volter's funeral be borne by the state," the President said.

Tryggve Storstein straightened up.

"Carried unanimously," the woman at the front declared, hammering the gavel, and stroking her cheek rapidly, in a gesture of vulnerability. "The Foreign Minister has asked to speak."

The ungainly man appeared even skinnier and more exhausted than he had that morning. Once installed at the Speaker's chair, he seemed to forget himself entirely, before pulling himself together sufficiently to face right.

"Madam President," he said with a brief nod, glancing down at a small scrap of paper he had set in front of him. "I have taken the liberty of asking to speak in order to say that, as a matter of course, all members of the government place their positions at your disposal now, since the Prime Minister herself is deceased."

That was all. Hesitating slightly, he adjusted his glasses, as if he was considering continuing, then stepped from the Speaker's chair and back to his place without taking the slip of paper with him.

"Then I would like to ask for one minute's silence," the President of the Parliament said.

The intense, empty silence lasted two and a half minutes. Now and again a sniff was audible, but even the press photographers did not disrupt the solemn pause.

"The meeting is closed."

The Parliamentary President banged the gavel again.

Finance Minister Tryggve Storstein stood up. Thirty-six hours without sleep was now beginning to make him feel intoxicated; he was out of sorts and remained on his feet, staring at his hands, as though they belonged to someone else entirely.

"When's the cabinet meeting, Tryggve?"

It was the Minister of Culture, in a charcoal-gray suit and makeup that looked as though it had been a long time since she'd glanced in a mirror.

"Two o'clock," he said abruptly.

They all immediately left the chamber in a quiet and orderly fashion, eyes downcast, like a procession of mourners rehearsing for the funeral. The press photographers noticed that the only person who actually looked as though she might be hiding a smile was Health Minister Ruth-Dorthe Nordgarden.

However, it might just as well have been a scowl.

3:32 P.M., GAMLE CHRISTIANIA RESTAURANT

"The Christer Pettersson sort. Quite sure. Dead certain."

The man wore a suit that looked as though it had been bought in a Texaco service station, its shiny material reminiscent of Beaver nylon from the 1970s. He raised his almost empty glass and continued speaking, with a foam mustache of beer above his lip. "The police are going to make fools of themselves. Just like in Sweden. They're going to get completely bogged down in all kinds of stupid, highly political leads. And then it'll be some peculiar guy or other who turns out to have done it. Somebody like Christer Pettersson, the Olof Palme guy."

"Or a jealous lover."

The woman with the not entirely original idea was relatively young, around thirty years old, her voice almost falsetto.

"Does anyone know anything about Birgitte Volter's love life?"

Four of the five others around the table, all men, started to laugh.

"Love life? She was having an affair with Tryggve Storstein, that's for sure. Hell, he's also the one who'll probably take over the whole shooting match, isn't he! A slightly delicate situation for the police, don't you think, since he must be on the list of suspects! I know that—"

The Texaco man sounded confident but was interrupted by a booming voice that came from the enormous beard of a man in his forties. His head was completely shaven, but the jet-black beard reached down to his chest.

"That rumor about Volter and Storstein is nothing but nonsense. Storstein's in a relationship with Helene Burvik now, not Volter. That ended long ago. Long before the big showdown in '92."

"I thought Tryggve Storstein was happily married," muttered the youngest of the journalists around the table, a young woman from *Aftenposten* who had still not managed to establish a regular seat in the Gamle restaurant. "How on earth does somebody like that have the *time* for a mistress?"

The silence was total, as they all froze; even the beer was left sitting for a short while. Though she blushed deeply and unflatteringly, the young woman was brash enough to continue. "I mean, how do you know it's *true*, what you're saying? If I believed half the rumors I've heard in the last six months, most members of the cabinet have a sleazy past and a sex life we all might envy. That is, the ones who aren't gay. Or them as well, for that matter. How do they find the *time*? That's what I'm asking. For all the sordid goings-on they're supposed to get up to, I mean. And how do you *know* all this? And is it actually so very *interesting* anyway?"

She raised her wineglass. She was the only one not drinking beer.

As though someone had waved an invisible magic wand, she was immediately pushed out of the group. She was sitting at the edge of the table, on a stool, and the two men on either side of her turned away, their shoulders expanding, forming a wall that separated her from the others.

"So sweet," the beard muttered. "Sweet and virtuous, I must say."

As Little Lettvik entered, she caught sight of them and lifted her hand in greeting; three swinging glasses of beer waved in response. She approached the bar, then headed toward her colleagues, carrying a glass.

"Cola, Little? Incredible!" The man in Beaver nylon shook his head. "This should be immortalized. Call the photographer."

"Unlike you . . ." Little Lettvik said softly, perching on a stool that supported only the small inner circle of her backside (the remainder overflowed so that it seemed as if four chair legs were growing out of her posterior) ". . . I'm now working twenty-four hours a day, and am staying sober. You can tell from your newspapers, of course . . ."

She raised her glass to the *Dagbladet* journalists at her side.

". . . that you have a different agenda from us. What's got into you today? The whole newspaper looks like one long tribute to Birgitte Volter. God's gift to the country, the greatest prime minister of our time! What's happened to your critical faculties, Ola? Your incisive journalism? The harsh spotlight? *Dagbladet* always to the fore! Today, to be honest, it's bringing up the rear."

"At least we understand that we shouldn't speculate in a wild, unrestrained fashion if we don't know a bloody thing."

The beard was insulted. A very experienced journalist, he was a prize winner several times over. He had been offered the editor's post on repeated occasions, but had always responded with a roared refusal, despite his satisfaction at the offer, since it basically confirmed how clever he was. He wanted to be an investigative journalist. He knew everything and was good company for those who recognized his sovereignty. But not for anyone else.

"When a Norwegian prime minister is shot in her office, it *really is* the time for speculation," Little Lettvik countered. "What do you think the police are doing? Of course they're speculating too. They don't know anything. They're inventing theories and thinking and acting accordingly. Exactly like us."

"This is not the day for speculation," Ola Henriksen said crossly. "Tomorrow will be time enough for that. When people have finished grieving."

"We won't have managed that by tomorrow," the ostracized woman piped up in a reedy voice.

"What are you up to, then?" Ola Henriksen said, staring at Little as he rotated his beer glass over and over again. "What do you know that nobody else does?"

Little Lettvik gave a husky, heartfelt laugh.

"As if I would tell you."

Suddenly she looked at her watch, a plastic Swatch with a wide pattern of eczema around its strap.

"Need to make a call," she said abruptly. "Keep my place."

The others remained seated, watching as she left. They were all struck by the same uncomfortable feeling—that they should really be somewhere else entirely, doing entirely different things, not just sitting in the Gamla drinking beer—and they were all struck dumb.

"When does that other bar, the Tostrup Kjelleren, actually open?" one of the eldest men muttered eventually; his words had already begun to slur.

No one replied. They sat watching Little Lettvik, who had not been content with simply leaving the dark premises; to be on the safe side, she had also crossed the street, where she took up position outside the GlasMagasinet department store, away from its café entrance.

It was chilly outside. The drizzle made her draw close to the wall, and she stood with her back to the street as she tapped in the secret number.

"Storskog," the voice snapped as usual.

"Konrad, Konrad, my very best friend," Little Lettvik purred and was met by the usual resounding silence. "Just one little question today. The same one as yesterday, in fact. After all, you weren't very cooperative."

The pause did not last as long as she had expected.

"This is the last time I ever give you anything, Lettvik. Do you hear? The last thing you're ever getting."

The voice stopped, obviously waiting to hear a promise that did not come.

"Do you hear me, Lettvik? I want an end to all this now. Agreed?"

"That depends. What is it you've got?"

Another long pause for thought.

"Benjamin Grande."

"Grinde."

"Okay. Grinde. He was in fact arrested yesterday."

"Arrested?"

Little Lettvik almost dropped her cell phone, and it chirped merrily when she inadvertently pressed a number of keys in her confusion.

"Hello? Are you there?"

"Yes."

"Arrested, you say? Have you *arrested* a Supreme Court judge?"

"Take it easy now. It was rescinded ages ago. It was all a damn mistake, the lawyers going over the top as usual."

"But it happened all the same? In print? A written arrest warrant?"

"Yes. The Head of CID who filled it out got a real dressing-down today. By the Chief of Police himself. *He'll* never get to be Chief of Police, that's for sure."

Little Lettvik turned to face the street, where a blind man was struggling through the stream of pedestrians on the sidewalk. He was waving his white stick in front of him and whacked Little on the shin.

"Can you get me a copy, Konrad?"

"No."

"If you get me a copy, then we have an agreement. No more phone calls from me."

"I can't do that. You've got enough now."

"Tempting agreement, Konrad. No more phone calls from me ever if you cough up a copy of that arrest warrant. Word of honor."

Chief Inspector Konrad Storskog did not answer. He simply disconnected the call. Little Lettvik stood for a moment staring at her cell phone, before snapping it shut and stuffing it into her coat pocket.

Then, smiling broadly, she crossed the street, waved to the six journalists sitting there expectantly, and disappeared in the direction of the Parliament Building. Her glass of cola was left behind, untouched.

"Thank God Konrad hates lawyers," she muttered, chuckling to herself. "Thanks, dear God!" She was fairly certain that Konrad Storskog would grab any opportunity to be rid of her with both hands. That was just before she started whistling.

7:04 P.M., NORWEGIAN TIME, BERKELEY, CALIFORNIA

Dear Billy T.,
Thanks for your fax. I'm impressed that you took the time to write.
Hope this fax doesn't wake you (does your machine make a
peeping sound?), because if you're asleep, it's certainly well earned.
You must get yourself a computer, and then we can use e-mail!
That's cheaper and better.

The assassination of Birgitte Volter is still receiving a certain
amount of attention over here. But thank goodness for the Internet,
I must say. I've been surfing the Norwegian news outlets for hours,
though it doesn't look as if they have much information either.
Apart from Kveldsavisen, *which is suggesting one scenario after*
another. Oh well, I suppose they need something to fill up all these
extra editions.

I was quite interested in what you wrote about the security
guards. When you can connect only four people to the crime scene
with any certainty—the secretary, the Supreme Court Judge (is
that the one in charge of the commission, by the way?), and the
two guards—then I would spend some time looking for a simple
method of entering the Prime Minister's area. It doesn't seem very
easy to construct a motive for any of the four who were actually
present. Therefore it must have been somebody else, *and this*
person or these persons must have found a way in.

Typical of the head of CID to investigate air vents and windows
on the fifteenth floor! I appreciate that this has to be done, Billy T.,
but both you and I know that the answer almost always lies in the
simplest solution. *Did the security guard take a break? It was a*
Friday evening, and as far as I understand it, there was very little
coming and going in the office. Someone might have entered by
the simplest route! *Does the guard smoke? Did he have an upset*
stomach? I expect that the guards have been security-checked, but
was there anything out of the ordinary there? Temporary staff?

And one more thing: if I'd been working on the case, I would
have left the access problem on hold to start with. I would have
searched for motives. I expect the guys on the top floor are going
berserk just now, with fancy theories about terrorism and that sort

of thing, but what about good old-fashioned police work? Did she
have enemies? Most certainly. The lady's been climbing all her life.
And not least: Was she about to disclose something or other? Was
the government about to pass something that major, powerful inter-
ests were afraid of? Okay, I don't mean that somebody would have
committed homicide in order to prevent a gas-fired power station in
western Norway, but all the same . . .

Simple, Billy T. The simplest solution is the best! First find the
motive; then the access issue will become clear. No one murders
without a motive. Not deliberately, at least, and it must have been
deliberate.

Don't let the guys in the Security Service push you around. But
try not to be so bad-tempered toward them. You've got enough
enemies up there from before.

I must say that every cloud has a silver lining. Cecilie and I had
been arguing for three days when we heard about the murder. She
wanted to extend our stay here. I said not on your life. It's true that
I love the good ole U.S. of A., but one year out of work is enough.
Now we're the best of friends.

On the other hand, probably nothing will now come of your
long-awaited visit. Am I right?

I'm crossing my fingers that the case is cleared up quickly, and
am quivering with excitement as I wait for your next fax. Give
Håkon my best regards if you see him, and tell him there's a letter
on the way.

Love and kisses,
Hanne

9:13 P.M., ODINS GATE 3

"I just couldn't let you sit on your own with your mother on an evening like this," she whispered as she placed her arm nonchalantly,
in an almost sisterly fashion, around his shoulders. "That wouldn't
have done you any good at all!"

Benjamin Grinde smiled without any emotion registering in his
eyes as he tied the apron strings behind his back.

"I'm sorry for phoning you last night, Nina. Hope it didn't prevent
Geirr and the children from getting a good night's sleep."

"Don't be silly," Nina Rambøl reassured him. "Of course you had to phone! You must have been beside yourself!"

She crunched on a raw carrot as she stood with her back to the kitchen counter.

"Sore back."

"What?"

"You have a sore back." She smiled broadly, now sitting on the kitchen counter, dangling her legs. Her flat shoes bumped repeatedly on the door to the casserole cabinet, and she pretended not to notice his disapproving frown.

"That's what I said. To the guests. That you had such terrible sciatic pain that the party had to be called off. I am to give you everyone's fondest regards and best wishes for a full recovery."

"Thanks very much," he mumbled, staring suspiciously at the ready-cooked roast beef he had grabbed for himself from the Smør-Petersen gourmet store, having popped in there only ten minutes before closing time. "I should have got salmon parcels. Salmon in puff pastry."

"Never mind," Nina said, aiming at the trash can that happened to be standing in the middle of the floor. The remainder of the carrot missed, and for a second it looked as if she was considering jumping down from the counter. However, she changed her mind and instead picked up the generous glass of wine at her side.

"You slurp terribly when you're drinking," he muttered.

Staring at him over the glass of red wine, she cocked her head.

"Benjamin. You're really not yourself."

Benjamin Grinde did not have a woman. A man who took an admiring touch on his suit jacket as an invitation to discuss the merits of alpaca did not attract women. He attracted female friends. Nina Rambøl was the best of them. She was five years younger than him, and they had met when he was a trainee doctor and she was a medical secretary. When she got married, her husband-to-be had been forced to accept the strange fact that his wife had chosen a male bridesmaid. But that was a generation ago now.

"Shall I send Jon and Olav home as well?" she asked in a childishly comforting voice, as she stroked his back with her hand. "Would you prefer that? Was I wrong to let them come? They insisted."

"No, no. It's all right."

"Boys and girls! Now you really *muuust* come and join the rest of us!"

The shrill outburst came from a woman in the doorway. She was clutching a glass of sherry and swaying slightly. Her face was tanned and wrinkled like a raisin, and as she raised her glass in a toast, the loose skin on her upper arms smacked gracefully against her sleeveless top decorated with enormous flowers. Her orange tights had gone out of fashion several years earlier, and even at that time they had not really looked very elegant on seventy-two-year-old legs.

"Here I am, having flown like a tiny bird from Spain just to celebrate my golden boy's birthday, and you're looking so down in the mouth! Come on, Ben, come in and join us. Come to Mother. You, too, Nina. By the way, that dress suits you. Beautiful! But then you've always had such a good eye for color!"

Tottering across the floor in four-inch heels, she grasped Benjamin's arm. He pulled away and refused to meet her gaze.

"Soon, Mother. I'll be through shortly. Just need to see to this first. You can tell the others to sit at the table."

He turned toward her with a salad bowl in his hands, but changed his mind and gave it to Nina instead. His mother did not reveal her feelings about his obvious lack of trust, but embarked on a fresh foray across the challenging kitchen floor, her glass held high.

"It's just so dreadfully, unbelievably awful," she began once the candles were lit and the food had been passed around the table. "Sweet little Birgitte. *Beautiful* little Birgitte! Yes, you know of course that Ben and Birgitte Volter were *best friends* when they were younger! She was always in and out of our house, Birgitte. A sweet, well-brought-up little girl. That's what makes all this so very much worse for Ben. Ben's so sensitive, you know. He gets that from his father. Can I come with you to the funeral, Ben? It's natural for me to go, I really mean that, she was in and out of my house for *years*! When is the funeral, actually? The cathedral? It has to be in Oslo Cathedral, of course."

She had seized the bowl of potato salad, and it was bouncing up and down in time to the torrent of words. Benjamin Grinde's mother did not talk—she chirped. Her voice was reedy and its pitch unusually high. And she insisted on being called "Birdie."

"We weren't *friends*, Mother. She was *not* forever in and out of our house; she might have come back with me three times. Maximum. I sometimes helped her with her homework. Now and again."

Affronted, Birdie Grinde opened her heavy eyelids, made even heavier with the weight of too much eye shadow.

"Now you're being really silly, Ben. Don't you think *I* should know who was coming in and out of my own house? What? Birgitte was a . . . a friend of the family, I would almost call it. You were so *taken* with her. A little bit in love, absolutely, that's what you were, Ben."

She blinked at Jon, who had given up waiting for the potato salad and was toying with his meat instead.

"You could have been a couple; I said that to my husband many a time. Just a shame that—what's his name again, Ben? Birgitte's husband? What was he called?"

"Roy Hansen," Benjamin mumbled, attempting to relieve her of the bowl of potato salad.

She moved it out of her son's reach as she continued. "Roy. That's right—Roy. What a horrible name, don't you think? Who on earth *gives* their children such names? Well. He wasn't much of a catch, if you ask me, and I don't mean to be indiscreet, far from it, and I don't have any prejudices either, and I've never been prudish, but . . ."

She leaned confidentially across the table, her chin almost touching the potato salad as her eyes darted conspiratorially from one to the other.

"They *had to* get married."

Delighted, she leaned back as she passed the salad to Nina.

"Mother!"

"Oops! I said too much there!"

Her hand flew to her mouth as she opened her eyes wide.

"Ben's so disapproving of gossip. Sorry, Ben! You must forgive your old mother for being a bit loose-tongued on a day such as this! Happy birthday, my treasure! Happy birthday!"

She raised her glass so abruptly that red wine splashed on the tablecloth.

"Cheers." The others smiled, looking sympathetically at the object of her toast.

The phone rang.

As Benjamin Grinde rose from the table, he had an attack of dizziness, like a sudden squall. He had to use the chair back to support himself, and he pinched the bridge of his nose between his thumb and forefinger as he squeezed his eyes shut.

"Is everything all right, Benjamin?" Nina asked anxiously, placing her hand over his. "Are you feeling unwell?"

"Fine, fine," he said softly, withdrawing his hand to answer the phone in the hallway.

The dizziness would not subside.

"Grinde. Go ahead," he said quietly, as he closed the living room door.

"Hi there! It's Little Lettvik, the *Kveldsavisen* journalist, speaking. Sorry for phoning so late on a Saturday night, but it's something of an emergency—"

"I can be reached at my office on Monday."

The receiver was on its way down.

"Wait!"

Resigned, he lifted the receiver to his ear again. "What's it about?"

"It's about the Volter case."

"What?"

"The Volter case."

Momentarily the world stood still, then resumed whirling around at accelerating speed. The series of five small lithographs on the wall immediately facing him raced along like an express train; he had to look down at the floor.

"I certainly don't want to talk about that," he said, gulping.

Stomach acid was making his tongue contract.

"But just listen, Grinde—"

"I've got company," he interrupted, with suppressed rage. "I'm celebrating my fiftieth birthday. This conversation is inappropriate and impertinent. I'm putting the phone down now."

"But, Grinde—"

Bang. He slammed the receiver down so hard that it cracked.

He could hear the faint sound of his mother's squeaky voice from the living room.

"And he was actually *flirting*! *Think* of it! A dashing, genuinely distinguished señor! Not that anything serious came of it, you understand, but since I'm down there eight months in every year, it's lovely to get just a little scrap of attention, you know!"

Birdie Grinde laughed ecstatically. It was more obvious to Nina Rambøl than at any time previously just why Benjamin Grinde had devoted his childhood to studying so diligently in his boyish bedroom.

His mother was still sitting with her glass raised when he entered.

"Cheers again, darling! Who was it? More congratulations, Ben?"

Her arm, the wrist jangling with masses of gold, swept across the table as she gazed at all the bouquets of flowers that had arrived during the day.

"Ben?"

Her face took on an unfamiliar, earnest expression.

"Ben, is something wrong?"

Jon and Nina, sitting with their backs turned, wheeled around abruptly.

Benjamin Grinde was swaying in the middle of the floor, his face ashen and his eyes sunk so far into his head that they looked like two bullet holes in the room's dim light.

"*Mother!* My name isn't Ben. I've never been called Ben. *I'm Benjamin!*" Then, closing his eyes gently, he fainted.

SUNDAY, APRIL 6

7:30 A.M., DEEP INSIDE THE FORESTS OF NORDMARKA, NEAR OSLO

The water clutched at him. It gripped him and would not let go, forcing him to breathe from the top of his lungs: sudden shallow gasps that made his skin contract. His heart was hammering rapidly inside his broad rib cage. He became aware of the passage of blood through his body; he felt the rhythmic pulsing beat spreading out from his heart through narrowing veins, in his legs and arms and toes, before the blood fought its way back to feed the struggling lungs and secure new strength, new life. He dove again, this time concentrating on extending his strokes, stiff, long strokes. He was an albatross in the water, a tiger shark; quick as a flash, he kicked with his feet in a fishlike movement and gained enough speed to push high, high up over the glassy gray surface.

He had never felt more alive. With a stealthy, continuous motion, he reached the shore and stepped onto a small silvery rock worn smooth millions of years ago in this amazing, beautiful landscape that was his home. He was naked, and his eyes scanned his body with pride, from the large, masculine feet with their fine, pale-blond hairs, to the shoulders that bore signs of hard work and even harder exercise. When he caught sight of his semi-erect member, he laughed. Cold water was the best thing he knew, and he always swam without bathing shorts, enjoying the discomfort of other men. But now he was alone.

Without drying himself—he had not even brought a towel with him from the cabin—he turned to face the lake. It had closed over behind him, and only here and there could he spot a tiny fish feeding, breaking the surface with minute, perfectly expanding circles.

The morning mist had settled between the trees, which were still naked, just like him. They peeped shyly at their own reflections in the water. Here and there, dirty clumps of snow clung obstinately to tussocks of heather and grass. The temperature couldn't be more than 40 degrees or so Fahrenheit, and the air was damp and fresh, with the unmistakable scent of the approaching spring. Smiling, he inhaled deeply through his nose.

He had never, ever been happier.

He had really not had confidence in the man, even though he had been recommended by several people, in fact: two group members had thought the man worth contacting. As their leader, it was he who had decided against it. There was something weak about the man. Even though he had never spoken to him, not then, but had simply judged him from a distance; one day he had tailed the unsuspecting security guard from the government complex. That was usually useful. A day spent following someone could tell him more than all the references in the world.

He was not sure what had decided the matter. There was something unacceptably feminine about the way the young man moved. What's more, he did not dress appropriately. Something weak about that as well. Perhaps it was his eyes. He had brown eyes, though that did not mean anything in itself. It was more significant that they wandered. Indecisive. Hesitant.

"Out of the question," he had decided. "That man presents a risk."

Precautionary measures. Double-checking. Triple guarantees. Such things had never been more important than now, when the security police guarding the traitors in Parliament were forced to direct their attention away from the real threat, the Reds, and toward them.

He had managed to build something resembling an effective organization. It was true they were not many, and there were only ten he actually trusted 100 percent. However, it was more important to be strong than to be numerous. They had to do their recruitment with extreme caution. A potential member was investigated for several months before the group even started to approach the person in question.

The security guard was a supporter of the Progress Party—not a member or anything like that, but quite openly sympathetic. That was not usually a promising starting point. Of course, they were often true patriots like himself, but most of them were totally stupid. If not, they normally suffered from what he called "a democratic surplus." He liked the expression: he had invented it himself. Adherents of the Progress Party had no real appreciation of the compelling need to use other means than those allowed by Norway's Jewish-dominated power elite.

So he had said no. The two referees had sulked, but he got the impression that they had accepted his decision. They had to.

"He must prove himself first," he had resolved, just over a year ago.

Immediately afterward, the two referees had told him that the guard was a friend of a guy in the underground organization Loke. That gang of romantic fools: debauched Boy Scouts who drank too much and damaged cars belonging to Pakistanis. Boyish pranks. They lacked ideological foundation, knew nothing, and had barely read anything other than the Wild West exploits of Morgan Kane. The security guard had an interesting job, however.

They had never before had the opportunity to recruit someone so close to the upper echelons of government. The security guard was as close as it was possible to get.

So he had continued the surveillance. Entirely on his own initiative, though not frequently. He knew everything about that guard. He knew what newspapers he read, what magazines he subscribed to, what weapons he possessed. The guard did own some guns and was a member of a handgun club. As leader, he had an entire folder at home containing information about the security guard; he even knew that he was screwing his supervisor's fifteen-year-old daughter and used Boss aftershave.

Slowly, ever so slowly, he had approached the man. By chance at first; he had asked to sit beside him in a café where the security guard was sitting on his own at a table for four. He had pulled out an American gun magazine. The guard had taken the bait, and after that they had met up perhaps five or six times.

The man was not yet a member. He did not even know about the group; nothing specific. But somehow or other, he must have realized there was an opportunity there. As leader, he had said as much as he could without admitting to anything concrete, without causing any rumors to circulate. And the security guard had understood. He had realized that there might be something there for him too.

The most important thing was to keep one's distance. Considerable distance. In no way connect the guard to the group. That was of paramount importance.

"At last we're up and running," Brage Håkonsen shouted to two crows that were skittishly taking off from an uprooted tree.

And so, taking enormous strides, the well-built young man headed toward the log cabin at the edge of the forest.

"At last we're up and running!"

In the cabin he had stacks of papers, organized neatly and tidily in folders and plastic wallets. He sat down, still without putting on his clothes; his skin was covered in red blotches from the cold.

"We're up and running," he murmured to himself yet again, as he remained sitting there, staring at a list of sixteen names.

8:14 A.M., HOLMENVEIEN 12

Karen Borg stared at Billy T. in fascination while trying, as discreetly as possible, to transfer a fresh loaf from the freezer to the microwave.

"Do you have any more?"

The man had eaten eight slices of bread and was still hungry.

"Coming up, coming up," Karen said, selecting the defrost program on the display. "Five minutes!"

Assistant Chief of Police Håkon Sand padded into the bright, spacious kitchen and plopped down on a rush chair. He was barefoot under his black trousers and his hair was wet; the small dark stains visible on his newly ironed pale blue shirt indicated that he hadn't bothered to dry himself properly. He rumpled the platinum-blond hair of the two-year-old in the high chair, but withdrew his hand abruptly, glaring at the child in disgust.

"Karen! He has jam in his *hair*!"

Hans Wilhelm laughed loudly and waved a slice of bread topped with strawberry jam in the air before leaning forward and slapping the whole mess on his father's shirtfront. Billy T. grinned as he got to his feet. The boy looked at him in delight and stretched out his arms.

"I think we'll pay a visit to the bathroom? Do you want to come with Billy T. to the bathroom, Hans Wilhelm?"

"Bath, bath," the little boy squealed. "Co' wi' Billitee to bath!"

"And then Daddy can change his shirt at the same time."

"Do I have any more clean uniform shirts?" Håkon asked sullenly, as he tugged at the front of his shirt, staring in consternation at the scarlet stain.

"Yes, of course." Karen smiled.

"Good heavens, Håkon! Don't you take care of your uniform shirts yourself?"

Billy T. was holding the toddler aloft like an airplane; the child laughed and waved his arms up at the ceiling.

"Is it a bird? Is it a plane? No, it's *Superman!*"

Describing an enormous curve through the air, Superman rushed through the doorway, moving up and down from floor to ceiling, giggling so heartily that he started to hiccup.

"There," Billy T. said when he returned; the boy now had wet hair and was wearing a fresh tracksuit. "Now I think we'll have some salami."

He grabbed one of the slices of bread that had just been set down on the table and made a substantial sandwich for Hans Wilhelm; for safety's sake he cut the slice in two and made a double-decker.

"Don't make a mess," he instructed gruffly, and the boy scarfed the food down at an amazing speed without dropping so much as a crumb.

"You've a lot to learn from Billy T., Håkon," Karen Borg declared, trying to maneuver her huge stomach between chair and table.

"When's it due?" Billy T. asked, pointing at her with his sandwich covered in Italian salad.

"It's a girl, Billy T. In a fortnight. The due date, at least."

"No way. A boy. I can see that."

"Let's go down to the basement," Håkon Sand interrupted. "Is it okay for us to borrow the office for a while?"

Nodding, Karen Borg rescued a glass of milk from where it teetered dangerously in front of the little boy.

"Come on."

The two men clattered down the narrow basement stairs and stepped into a remarkably pleasant room. It seemed bright despite actually being a cellar with only one small window opening onto the dim Sunday morning outside. Billy T. tried to make room for himself on a little daybed along one wall, while Håkon sat on the office chair, planking his feet on the desk.

"*Bloody* great setup you've got for yourself, Håkon," Billy T. said, scratching his ear. "Fantastic house, lovely lady, and super kid. Life's a breeze, eh?"

Håkon Sand did not reply. The house did not belong to him. It was Karen's. She was the one with money, even though what she earned as an independent attorney could not compare with the fortune she had raked in when she'd been the youngest and only female partner in the country's largest commercial law firm. Living in Vinderen had also been her idea. Not getting married was her choice. She had been married once and felt that was enough. Now that baby number two was on the way, he hoped that her attitude would soften. Håkon sighed heavily as he ran his fingers through his hair.

"Right now I'd give a lot to be able to sleep for twenty hours."

"Me too. Or even longer."

"What are your thoughts at present?"

Billy T. gave up on his seat and stretched himself out on the floor with his hands under his head and his feet propped up on the daybed.

"I'm trying to compile a profile of her," he said to the ceiling. "It's not so damn easy. I've now spoken to three cabinet ministers, four friends, office staff, political colleagues, as well as the devil and all his kin. It's strange, you know—"

Karen Borg stood in the doorway with a tray of coffee and cookies. Billy T. twisted his head around and opened his arms.

"Well, Karen, if you ever get tired of that guy over there, I'll move in. No hesitation."

"I'll *never* get tired of that guy over there," she said, placing the tray on the computer table. "At least not if you're threatening to take over."

"What that lady sees in you, I'll never understand," Billy T. muttered with a cookie in his mouth. "She could have me in a shot."

"What were you about to say?" Håkon asked, yawning. "Something was strange."

"Yes. It's strange how difficult it is to arrive at an opinion about somebody you've never met. People seem to—it's all so *different*, what people say. Some call her intelligent, hard working, friendly, pragmatic. Not an enemy in the world, that woman. Others point out that she could be bad tempered and obstinate and that she had several skeletons in the closet when it came to outmaneuvering competitors. A decade ago, they say, when she'd come to a critical juncture in her career, she would stop at nothing in order to position herself. And I mean *nothing*, nothing at all. Apparently she would jump into bed with the right person if that proved necessary. Others highlight how remarkable it was that she was never unfaithful. Never."

"Who are these other people?" For the first time, Håkon Sand showed something resembling interest in the topic under discussion.

"In fact it's the people who probably knew her best who maintain that she never got mixed up in anything like that. It seems as though . . ." Billy T. sat up and took a slurp of coffee. "It seems to me that the closer people were to her, the higher their opinion of her."

"That's probably only natural," Håkon commented. "It's the people closest to us who like us best."

"But are they the ones who *know* us best?"

They fell silent. From the floor above, they could hear the child squealing like an angry piglet.

"Hard work having toddlers, eh, Håkon?"

The Assistant Chief of Police rolled his eyes. "I had *no idea* it would be so much work. So much—so much of a *slog!*"

"Tell me about it." Billy T. grinned. "You should've done what I did. Have four children with four different mothers who look after them on an everyday basis, leaving me to take them now and again for fun and games. The best way to have children."

Håkon looked at him with what Billy T. thought might be something like forbearance. He lay down on the floor again and continued his painstaking examination of the ceiling.

"Okay," Håkon said softly. "That's why you're as happy as a clam every other Friday and sour as vinegar the following Monday, yes? Because you're so happy to hand them back, I mean."

"Drop it," Billy T. said tersely. "Let's drop it."

Håkon Sand stood up and poured more coffee for them both. "Watch you don't knock it over," he said, looking at the cup sitting unsteadily on the carpet. "So what do you think?"

Billy T. hesitated. "To start with, I'm placing most trust in those who knew her best. The problem is simply that . . ."

He got to his feet once more and stretched out his hands to touch the ceiling.

". . . the woman was actually extremely conventional, Håkon! It's *fucking* difficult to find anything in her life to indicate that someone might want her dead. At least to the point that they would actually *do* it. Murder her, I mean."

He sighed.

"For the time being, at least, we still have a great deal of work to do. To put it mildly."

He sighed again. This was a lousy day.

"But listen to this, Håkon."

Billy T. was towering over him, but suddenly he dropped forward to lean his hands on the table, giving Håkon a start.

"Actually there are only two possibilities. Either she was killed because she was Birgitte Volter. There was somebody who wanted *her* dead. As a person, I'm talking about. And in fact, so far there has been nothing, absolutely nothing, to indicate that. Or else someone killed her because she was the prime minister. They wanted to kill the *role* she occupied, so to speak. A plot against Norway. Against the policies of the Labor Party. Or something along those lines. And I have to admit—"

This was a difficult admission, and he swallowed.

"I have to admit that that's more likely. At the moment. And that means the guys on the eighth floor will have a field day. I don't like that idea at all."

The child in the room above had stopped howling, and now they could hear instead an even, rhythmic thumping, as though a toy was being banged on the floor.

"Tell me what you know about her, Billy T."

"Fuck, there's nowhere here that I can sit down!"

"Here. Take this."

Håkon Sand passed the chair over to him, and Billy T. smiled.

"It's her birthday on Friday. She's damn well going to have her funeral on her fifty-first birthday. She got married when she was only eighteen years old, to a childhood friend of the same age, Roy Hansen. They are still married. One child. Per Volter. Age twenty-two. Student at the military academy, stays at the Fredriksvern naval base in Stavern. Decent young man; the only sorrow he seems to have brought on his parents is that he's a member of the Young Conservatives. Fairly clever at school, vice chairman of a handgun club; he has inherited his mother's flair for organization."

"Handgun club? Does he have access to guns?"

"Yes, oh yes. Several guns. But that weekend he was on an expedition way up on the Hardanger Plateau; in fact there were problems trying to get in touch with him to inform him of his mother's death. And there's nothing to suggest that he had a strained relationship with his mother. On the contrary. Nice young man. Apart from all that stuff about the Young Conservatives. But, honestly, he is far beyond any suspicion."

"More," Håkon mumbled.

"Birgitte Volter was born in Sweden on April 11, 1946. Her father was Swedish; her mother had fled there during the war. They moved to Norway, to Nesodden, in 1950. She graduated from high school and moved quickly into the trade union movement. Became secretary or something of that nature at the State Liquor Monopoly in Hasle. Then on to the local authority in Nesodden, and gradually took more prominent positions in the Norwegian Civil Service Union. And so on and so forth. The rest is history, as they say. Great woman. Great favorite. All the same, it was a closely run thing in 1992."

"Friends?"

"That's strange too," Billy T. said, scratching his ear again. "I think I'm getting a bloody ear infection. That's all I need."

He stared at his forefinger, but could see nothing apart from an ink stain from the previous day.

"You know all that stuff we read in the newspapers. About these networks, you know. That this person knows that person and is best of friends with this one and that one. I don't think that can be right. Or else the newspapers are using an entirely different definition of *friendship* from that used by you and me. They're actually not *friends*. They're more like party colleagues, so to speak. They seem to have few proper friends, and those are almost always entirely outside politics: people they've met in ordinary workplaces, at school years ago, and that kind of thing. The only person inside politics I believe was really a friend of Birgitte's was the President of the Parliament."

"Enemies, then?"

"Same thing again. It depends what you mean by *enemies*. What is an enemy? If it's someone who speaks badly of you, then we've all got plenty of enemies. But is it right to call them that? It's obvious, Håkon, that when you reach so far inside a high-profile political party like the Labor Party—the governing party—you'll find many people who have on occasion felt aggrieved. But enemies? Not to mention, someone who would actually go so far as to *murder* you? No. Not that I can see. Not yet, at least."

"No." Håkon Sand crossed to the window and opened it a crack. "Actually we've got the same problem if we approach it all from a different angle," he said as he sat down again.

"A different angle?"

"Yes, if we view it as the actual—role? Was that what you called it? It seems really so . . . tame here. In Norway. It's as if it's not possible to think about Anne Enger Lahnstein plotting to kill Birgitte Volter, even though she's fanatical about stopping this Schengen agreement!"

Billy T.'s laughter was loud and booming.

"No, that would be something! That Lahnstein woman in combat gear sneaking through the air vents in the tower block with a knife in her mouth and a revolver in her belt!"

"Can you imagine it!"

Håkon Sand was still struggling to dry his hair. The atmosphere in the basement was ever so slightly damp, and so it was taking longer than usual, causing him to ruffle his grizzled locks repeatedly.

"It can't be anyone within the country. That's simply not how it *is* here. And the madman theory doesn't hold water either. He would have chosen another place. For God's sake, Norwegian government ministers get such minimal security, apart from in their offices. A madman would have attacked her *outside*. In a shop. At a handball game. Or something like that."

"Outside a movie theater," Billy T. said softly.

"Exactly. The murder of Olof Palme was a far greater challenge for the police, because anyone at all could have been the perpetrator! As far as Birgitte Volter is concerned, we have a totally different starting point."

They gazed at each other and suddenly raised their coffee cups simultaneously, as though at an invisible signal.

"Then *nobody* can have committed this murder," Håkon Sand said.

"Then we'll have to try to discover who this nobody is," Billy T. concluded. "Shall we go?"

That turned out to be a difficult task as the two-year-old clung to Billy T.'s left leg and would not let go, hanging on for dear life.

"Bath with Billitee! Bath with Billitee!"

He raised the roof when the two police officers clambered into the car outside the attractive white house at Holmenveien 12, but stopped abruptly when the exhaust pipe emitted a loud bang as the Volvo jolted out of the long driveway.

"Bye bye, Billitee and Daddy." He waved, thrusting his thumb into his mouth.

11:25 A.M., OSLO POLICE STATION

The colossal, curved police station at Grønlandsleiret 44 hummed with a constant low-frequency buzz, as though the building itself was alive: a hive of systematic, purposeful industry. Never before had the vast block—timeworn and gray, with its seven official floors, and secluded, wing-clipped Security Service division in the two-story attic—behaved like this. It was used to its sixteen hundred officers pursuing their own work individually, in exhausted battles against the criminals who ran ahead and thumbed their noses at all of them. But now, as a submissive April sun hung wearily in the sky above the hill at Ekebergåsen, the police station appeared to have renewed energy. The building itself seemed to stretch in length and height; the windows that usually looked like dull, half-closed eyes, staring out on a world the police would prefer not to acknowledge, sparkled vivaciously. The blinds were rolled up, the windows opened slightly, and inside, the people began almost imperceptibly to pull in the same direction. Even the two sequestered floors at the top dared to peep forward and upward, no longer clinging tightly to the roof in the hope of avoiding any more scandals, any more critical investigations.

"I'll grant him that, the Police Chief," Billy T. commented. "He's made quite a good job of organizing this."

A total of 142 police officers had been allocated full time to the investigation of Birgitte Volter's homicide, in addition to an unknown number of officers from the police division of the Security Service. Sixteen subgroups of varying sizes were operating out of Oslo Police Station. The smallest consisted of only three people, whose job it was to liaise with the Security Service; the largest, having commandeered the gymnasium on the sixth floor, had thirty-two police officers and was responsible for coordinating the tactical investigation. The whole of the police force's Criminal Intelligence Section was entirely preoccupied with pressing informants, analyzing information, and attempting to build a picture of everything that had occurred in Oslo's underworld in recent days. Billy T. had four people assisting him in compiling a profile of Birgitte Volter's life and times, a special assignment he regarded as far more exciting than the exhausting interviews he had conducted in the first days after the Prime Minister's death. Tone-Marit Steen was not a member of his group.

"Why on earth should *I* interview that guy? You've already done it pretty thoroughly, haven't you?" Billy T. was annoyed.

"I'd like you to have another go with him," Tone-Marit said quietly, handing Billy T. a slim, green folder.

"Listen," Billy T. said, pushing the folder back at the Police Sergeant. "We have to do everything properly. It's your job to do this kind of thing. That security guard can't have anything of significance to say about Birgitte Volter's private life."

"No. But honestly, Billy, can't you take this as a compliment? I think the man's lying, and you're one of the best interviewers we have. Please."

"How many times do I have to *say*—"

He banged his fists on the table.

"How often have I *told* you that I'm called Billy T.! T.! Not just Billy. Will you never *learn*!"

Tone-Marit nodded a furious and extravagant apology. "T. Billy T. What does the T stand for anyway?"

"That's none of *your* fucking business," he muttered, opening the window wider.

Tone-Marit Steen's appearance was deceptive. Her face was round, with sweet features that made her look as though she was about twenty, although in actual fact she was only two years shy of her thirtieth birthday. Tall and slim, she had narrow, slightly crooked eyes that disappeared when she smiled. She was a veteran player on the national women's soccer team, where she played left back. This was a role she had also adopted in her work in the police force, where she was a stalwart, solid defender of everything that was right and fair. She was strong, she was fit, and she was afraid of no one.

"You know, I'm just not putting up with this."

Her eyes flashed, and one corner of her mouth trembled.

"You always treat me like shit, and you couldn't care less about anything. I *will not put up with* you speaking to me like that. Understood?"

Billy T. looked like a fish out of water.

"Calm down, my dear girl! Calm down!"

"I'm not your dear girl! You're the one who needs to let up! You're nothing but a *male chauvinist pig*, Billy T.! You waltz around with all sorts of women and think you're sex on legs, but actually . . ."

Now she stamped on the floor, and Billy T. chuckled, making her even angrier.

". . . actually you don't even *like* women, Billy T. You're *scared* of them. I'm not the only one who notices that you treat female and male colleagues differently. It's the opinion of the whole team, I'm telling you. You're afraid of us, that's what you are."

"Now *you* really must give over. There are lots of girls here who—"

"Oh yes, yes. One girl. There is indeed one woman in this whole building who you *actually* do respect, Billy T. Her Royal Highness Hanne Wilhelmsen. And do you know why? Huh? Do you know?"

For a moment she seemed to hesitate, as though she did not dare; she licked her lips with the tip of her pink tongue, and inhaled deeply.

"Because you're never going to get her into bed! Because she's out of the question! The only woman you actually respect is a lesbian, Billy T. That's something you really should think about."

"NOW YOU GIVE OVER!"

He got to his feet and kicked the wastepaper basket so hard that it smacked against the wall; then silence descended on the room. Even the neighboring office, from where they had previously heard loud conversation, had fallen quiet. But Billy T. did not restrain himself.

"Don't you bloody dare come here and make nasty comments about Hanne Wilhelmsen! You—you don't even come up to her *ankles*! Not even to her ankles! And you never will!"

"I'm not saying anything nasty about Hanne," Tone-Marit said calmly. "Not in the slightest. I'm saying something nasty about you. If I had anything to say to Hanne, I would say it to her face. At the moment we're talking about you."

"To Hanne's face? To Hanne's face? You'd have needed to swim, then, wouldn't you? Eh?"

Tone-Marit tried to stop herself smiling, but her eyes gave her away.

"For heaven's sake, now you're being childish."

"For heaven's sake, for heaven's sake," he mocked, in a reedy, distorted voice.

Then Tone-Marit began to laugh. She made an effort to hold the laughter back, but it forced itself out, bubbling up, and eventually it erupted into a long, rippling burst. Tears flowed from the narrow slits below her eyebrows. She plopped on a chair, holding her stomach with the palm of her hand, rocking to and fro, and finally she began hiccuping so ferociously as she slapped herself on the thighs that Billy T. could not restrain himself either. He guffawed and swore under his breath.

"I'd better talk to the guy, then," he muttered at last as he took hold of the slim green folder. "Where is he?"

"I'll go and get him," Tone-Marit said, drying her eyes, still not quite able to compose herself.

"Get your damn carcass out of here, anyway," Billy T. said.

But he smiled as he said it.

"You really should speak to a psychologist," Tone-Marit mumbled inaudibly as she closed the door behind her.

11:30 P.M., OLE BRUMMS VEI 212

"I can't find it anywhere," Roy Hansen said to the trainee policewoman with braids and big blue eyes. "Sorry."

"And you've looked everywhere?" the epitome of Norwegian womanhood asked quite unnecessarily as she fiddled with her police cap.

"Of course. Everywhere. Handbags and closets and pockets. Drawers."

It had been an extremely painful experience. He had smelled the scent of her body in her clothes; the entire closet was redolent with Birgitte's fragrance, and the fragile, delicate scab that had formed over the bleeding wound since Friday night had been ripped away. Her handbags, full of familiar objects. The key ring he had made for her that summer they had turned twenty: a reef knot that had never untied and that she had used to joke was as solid and secure as the love they had for each other. A dark red lipstick that was almost used up; in a flash he had seen her in his mind's eye, the perfunctory, habitual way she applied the waxy color to her lips. A theater ticket, old and faded, from an evening he would remember for the rest of his life; it had caused him to pause in his search, standing alone in their bedroom as he sniffed at the ticket and wished himself back, far back, to the time before they became caught up in the Major Project: Birgitte's political career.

"Her pass is quite simply *not* here. Sorry."

A young man was sitting on the sofa, and the trainee police officer assumed he was the son of the house. He was wearing a uniform and was terribly pale. She tried to give him a smile, but he stared right past her.

"We'll have to leave it then. Perhaps she had actually lost it. I'm really sorry for disturbing you."

When she closed the front door behind her, she paused momentarily on the stairs, deep in thought. On Friday Volter had forgotten her pass. That had been clearly ascertained. All the same, they had examined her office thoroughly, and it wasn't there. The pass was apparently the size of a credit card, with a photo and a magnetic strip on the back. An ordinary government pass that was not in the widower's home either. Curious.

Well, the Prime Minister may have mislaid it. Simple as that. She could have put it somewhere in the town house apartment where her husband had not thought of looking. After all, he had just lost his wife and probably was not thinking straight.

The trainee officer settled in the driver's seat and inserted the key in the ignition. She then froze for a moment before arriving at a decision and starting the vehicle.

It bothered her that they could not find that pass.

12:07 P.M., OSLO POLICE STATION

Billy T. was in a bad mood, and the man on the opposite side of the desk was not much happier.

"Let's go over this one more time," Billy T. said briskly, attempting to make contact with the man's evasive eyes. "So an alarm sounded. From the conference room adjacent to the Prime Minister's restroom. At—"

"At twenty-three minutes to six. If you don't believe me, you can check the log."

"Why on earth would you suspect that I don't believe you?" Billy T. commented. "Hey! Look at me!"

The security guard did not lift his head, but raised his eyes ever so slightly.

"Why shouldn't we believe you?"

"Why else would I be called in here for a second time?" the man said sulkily. He was twenty-seven years and a few months old, according to the papers facing Billy T. on the desk.

The guard was a strange character. He was not exactly ugly, but he was certainly far from handsome. Though he was not quite repulsive, there was something indefinably unpleasant about his whole appearance. His face was pinched, his chin pointed, and his hair in need of a wash. His eyes might have been attractive if the man had looked more attentive; his eyelashes were long and dark. He could have been twenty, or just as easily approaching forty—Billy hadn't been able to guess his age until he'd checked the paperwork.

"You must appreciate and understand that your witness statement is fairly central to this inquiry, man!"

Billy T. grabbed a diagram of the fifteenth floor, a copy of the overhead acetate the Police Chief had shown them the previous day.

"Look at this!"

He pointed to the conference room, which quite clearly was separated from the Prime Minister's office by only a narrow restroom.

"You were here. At an extremely critical point in time. Tell me what took place."

The security guard snorted like a horse, spraying drops of spittle across the desk, and causing Billy T. to scowl.

"How many times do I have to tell you this?" the guard inquired crossly.

"Just as many times as I decide."

"Can I have something to drink? A glass of water?"

"No."

"Am I not even entitled to a glass of water?"

"You are not entitled to anything at all. If you want, you can stand up and leave the police station. You are a witness, and we require you to give a statement voluntarily. *But you'd damn well better do so! And without any more fuss!*"

He banged his fists on the table, at the same time snapping his teeth together ferociously. His hands were tender after his outburst half an hour earlier, and a stab of pain jolted through his forearms.

That helped. The security guard straightened up, literally, sitting bolt upright in his chair as he used his hands to brush his shoulders.

"I was sitting in the guardroom. Then an alarm sounded in the conference room. They are the silent type of alarms; you don't hear them in the actual location, only down in our office. They go off all the time, every other day at least, and we don't usually pay much attention to them."

He was speaking to the table edge.

"But we do have to check, of course. Always. So I went up then. That is to say, it's always supposed to be two of us who check, but we'd had quite a busy day because of the renovation work, and my partner had fallen asleep. So I went by myself."

Now he was trying to communicate with the ill-treated wastepaper basket in the corner.

"So I took the elevator to the fourteenth floor, because it was the other guy, the one who was asleep, who had the keys for the elevator to go all the way up. I said hello to the guard at the entrance and went upstairs to the fifteenth floor."

"Hold on a minute."

Billy T. waved with the flat of his hand.

"Can you take the elevator directly up to the fifteenth floor? Without passing the man in the glass booth?"

"Yes, to the sixteenth as well. But you need to have a key. Without the key, the elevator only goes as far as the fourteenth."

Billy T. pondered why this had not been mentioned when the Chief of Police had made his speech the previous day. He would let it lie for the moment, though they should all have been alerted to such an obvious method of accessing the Prime Minister's office. He quickly scribbled down "Elevator" on a yellow Post-it note and stuck it to the lampshade.

"Continue," he demanded.

"Yes, well, then I went into the conference room, but there was nobody there. A faulty connection as usual. They've never been able to sort out that system."

"Was the door to the restroom open?"

The security guard suddenly stared at him for the very first time. He hesitated, and Billy T. could have sworn that a minuscule tremor crossed the man's cheek.

"No. It was closed. I opened it and peeped inside the restroom, I had to do that, because someone could have hidden in there, but it was empty too. The door from the restroom to the Prime Minister's office was closed. I didn't touch it."

"And then?"

"And then—yes, well, then I went downstairs again. That was that."

"Why didn't you speak to the secretary in the anteroom?"

"The secretary? Why should I speak to her?"

Now the guard looked really surprised, but he had dropped his gaze and was studying something on Billy T.'s shirtfront instead.

"I don't usually—besides, she wasn't there."

"Yes, she was. She was there all afternoon and evening."

"No, she was not!"

The security guard shook his head vigorously.

"She might have been in the stall, for all I know, but she definitely wasn't there. I can see—"

He leaned across the diagram, pointing.

"Do you see? I would have seen her from there."

Billy T. chewed at his cheek.

"Mmmm—okay."

He removed the yellow note from the Anglepoise lamp, and jotted down "Toilet?" before replacing it.

"So then you went back down again. To—what was it you called it?"

"The guardroom."

"Oh yes."

Turning toward an enameled aluminum shelf at his back, Billy T. grabbed a thermos flask and poured steaming coffee into a cup decorated with a sketch of Puccini. The guard looked quizzically at the coffee cup but did not receive a response.

"I see you're interested in guns," Billy T. remarked, blowing noisily on the scalding hot drink.

"Is it that obvious?" the guard said querulously, glancing at the clock.

"Very funny. You do have a sense of humor, don't you? From the papers, you know. It's in there. I know most things about you, you see. I also have your security clearance here."

He waved a sheet of paper provocatively before replacing it at the bottom of the pile.

"You shouldn't have that," the guard said angrily. "That's not in accordance with the regulations!"

Billy T. grinned broadly and fixed his eyes on those of the guard. This time the man did not manage to avoid his gaze.

"Now just you listen to one little thing. Right now we're not exactly paying too much attention to the regulations, here at the station. If you've anything to complain about, just go ahead and try. Then we'll see if we can spare anyone to look into that kind of thing at the moment. I doubt it, actually. What kind of gun do you own?"

"I've got four guns. All of them registered. They're all at home, so if you want to come home with me, then—"

He stopped abruptly.

"Then what?"

"I can bring them here, if you want."

"Do you know, I think I would like you to do just that," Billy T. said. "But I emphasize that it's a voluntary action on your part. I'm not *ordering* you to bring them in."

The man muttered something under his breath that Billy T. could not catch.

"One more thing," the Chief Inspector said suddenly. "Do you know Per Volter?"

"The Prime Minister's son?"

"Yes. How did you know that, by the way?"

"I've read the newspapers, haven't I? Umpteen papers this past couple of days. No, I don't know him."

His entire body became increasingly agitated, and he fleetingly, unnervingly, crossed his left foot over his right.

"But," he added all of a sudden, "I know who he is, of course. A good shot. Competition marksman."

"Does that mean you've met him?"

The security guard took a conspicuously long time to consider this.

"No," he said, and for the second time looked directly into Billy T.'s icy blue eyes. "I've never met him. Never in my whole life."

2:10 P.M., MOTZFELDTS GATE 14

The loudspeaker on the computer piped its snappy electronic tune before progressing to a long-drawn-out, tense wail. Little Lettvik shuffled into her workroom, a voluminous apron wrapped around her body and a cigarillo in her mouth. The machine took its time to receive the message, and when the tiny envelope appeared at the bottom right-hand corner of the screen, she immediately clicked into her inbox.

The message had no sender. She directed the cursor at the top line, and double-clicked again.

The warrant.

Konrad Storskog had kept his promise.

She was not entirely sure whether she would keep hers.

4:30 P.M., OSLO POLICE STATION

"I'm starting to get bloody tired of these press conferences," Assistant Chief of Police Håkon Sand mumbled.

The public relations manager at the station had come from a well-paid post at *Dagbladet* newspaper and had surprised them all by taking on the thankless task of keeping society informed about everything the police were unable to achieve.

"Press *briefing*, Håkon. Not press conference," he said, holding open the door to the Police Chief's outer office.

"But four times a day? Is that really necessary?"

"It's the best way of avoiding speculation. You made a good job of it, by the way. The uniform suits you! And now there are four hours until the next one. You can look forward to that."

"And meanwhile, we've still nothing new to report," Håkon Sand commented, tugging at his infernal collar whose synthetic material made his neck red and sore.

There were six men in the Police Chief's office: one was setting up a slide projector while another was trying to find out how the venetian blinds worked. They had no success, and in the end the secretary had to be called in. She darkened the room in thirty seconds and switched on the light before closing the door again behind her.

"We've received a provisional autopsy report," the Chief of Police announced; by now his bluish shadow was in the process of becoming a full beard. "And it is in fact fairly specific. We were right as far as the time of the murder was concerned. Between half past five and seven. We cannot be more precise than that yet, since there were such extreme fluctuations in the temperature of the room, making it difficult to say."

He made a sign to Håkon Sand, who stood up and flicked the light switch.

An image appeared on the wall. A close-up of Prime Minister Birgitte Volter's head. In the blond hair, you could clearly see a hole, quite small, rather round, with black edges and a streak of dried blood in the strands. The Police Chief nodded to the Head of CID, who stepped into the projector beam and produced a folding pointer.

"As you see, the entrance wound is small. The bullet stopped here—"

He clicked the remote control, and a new image came into view. Underneath the hair you could clearly perceive a tiny bulge, almost like a painful, nasty pimple.

"It had entered the temple, passed through the brain and cranium on the other side, and in fact ended up across here, just under the skin. Birgitte Volter died instantly."

He clicked yet again.

"This is the bullet."

It looked modest, even though it was greatly enlarged: a black-and-white tape measure beside it indicated that the ammunition was small caliber.

"And the strange thing is—" he said, then interrupted himself. "No, let us first of all have the technicians' conclusions."

One more click brought up a drawing. A woman sat in an office chair with her hands on the desk. Behind her stood a faceless man with a gun in his hand, a revolver directed at the woman's temple.

"It must have happened something like this. It's quite obvious the gun must have touched the temple as the shot was fired. That can be deduced from the burn marks around the entrance wound. Which tells us that the perpetrator must have been standing behind her. There's certainly no room in front of her."

The pointer smacked the office desk in the picture.

"We won't speculate, of course, but it might be that—"

"A blackmail scenario," Håkon Sand declared.

The other men looked at him. The Security Service Chief, who was now wearing a charcoal suit and red tie, closed his eyes and took such a deep breath through his nose that it made a whistling noise.

The Head of CID continued. "Yes. It might well look like that. And in addition . . ."

He produced a new image, and now the wound in the Prime Minister's head was gaping at them, enlarged a thousand times.

". . . we see here fragments of material. Woolen fibers, it seems. We assume that they are from the shawl she was wearing, the one we have still not found. Black and red wool fibers. Which means that—"

"Was she shot *through* her own scarf?" Håkon Sand asked. "Was she wearing it on her head?"

The Head of CID seemed annoyed at the interruptions.

"I suggest we open this up for discussion afterward," he said truculently, swinging the pointer around until it suddenly became caught in a picture hook belonging to a painting that had been taken down for the occasion. "No, she was not wearing the shawl on her head, she was wearing it over her shoulder. But she may have had it over her head just then, almost as a—"

"A hood," Håkon Sand muttered. "She was blindfolded. By the perpetrator."

"Exactly," the Security Service Chief interjected, adjusting the knot of his tie as he leaned forward. "The man may have placed the shawl over her head to frighten her even more. That's a well-known tactic to prevent the victim from seeing anything at all. It makes people feel confused. Darkness, I mean."

"And then we come to the thing that strikes me as the most remarkable aspect of this case."

The Head of CID had obviously decided not to allow himself to be put off by the ill-timed interruptions.

"The caliber."

Again the photo of the bullet appeared on the wall.

"It's too small."

The Police Chief was now on his feet, standing at the window, gazing into the room as he rubbed his lower back.

"What do you mean by too small?"

"It's 7.62 millimeters. Small. By far the most common caliber for a handgun is 9 millimeters. Or .38 as they say in the USA. With small-caliber ammunition like this, it can't be guaranteed." Scratching his forehead, he hesitated just a touch too long.

"Can't be guaranteed that the woman would die!" Håkon Sand leaned forward eagerly in his seat.

"Exactly," the Head of CID mumbled despondently, looking up at the ceiling.

"I came across that once before," Håkon Sand continued. "A guy who had shot himself in the head twice. Twice! The first shot had entered his brain without doing much damage, at least not enough to kill him right away. But why . . ."

Now he was the one to hesitate, and the Head of CID took over.

"Yes, just so. Why should a person whose intention was to kill the

Prime Minister and who was cunning enough to enter what is probably the most carefully guarded office in all of Norway, bring with him
a gun that, strictly speaking, was not suitable for the job? And as if that
was not enough—"

He let the red tip of the pointer outline the bullet.

"This is an extremely *rare* caliber. In this country, at least. You can't
buy it over the counter, although they can be specially ordered, of
course."

"However, if"—the Chief of Police began, crossing over to the wall
that served as a screen—"if you are conducting some kind of extor-
tion—I mean, if he came to blackmail her and not to kill her—what
was it he was after? And why did he kill her if that was not his intention from the beginning?"

The room was silent and the atmosphere stuffy. The Police Chief
pressed a button on the telephone.

"Coffee," he said tersely, depressing the button again.

Two minutes later, the six men around the Police Chief's conference table were slurping coffee. Eventually the Security Service Chief
put down his white mug and cleared his throat.

"The King of Jordan was supposed to arrive here next Wednesday.
Incognito."

The others looked at one another, and the Police Chief stared
intently at the Head of the Criminal Intelligence Department, a mag-
nanimous red-haired man who, unusual for him, had not uttered a
word during the entire proceedings.

"An attempt to rescue the last vestiges of the Oslo Agreement," continued Ole Henrik Hermansen, the Security Service Chief, after a brief
pause during which he peered around, obviously searching for something. "Are we allowed to smoke in here?"

"Not really," the Chief of Police said, rubbing his head. "But we can
make an exception today."

He produced a glass ashtray from the desk drawer and placed it in
front of Hermansen, who had already lit a cigarette.

"Because of Prime Minister Volter's death, the visit will not now
take place, of course. That *could* be a lead. On the other hand, there
would be other far less dramatic ways of stopping the King of Jordan's
visit. If details of his trip had been leaked, a telephone threat to us
would have been sufficient."

Smoke rings formed a chain of haloes above his head.

"Then there are the right-wing extremists, of course. As you know, they've started to stir. The newspapers exaggerate, admittedly, but we know that at least two or three of the groups are committed enough in their beliefs to actually plan an assassination. Until now, we've regarded them as insignificant, not fanatical enough. It looks as though that's no longer the case."

"But . . ."

Håkon Sand waved his forefinger like an overenthusiastic exam candidate.

". . . if they're the ones behind it, why haven't they claimed responsibility for the murder? Wouldn't a great deal of the point in committing the murder be lost if none of us got to know that they're the ones who did it?"

"You've got a point," Ole Henrik Hermansen conceded, without looking in Håkon Sand's direction.

"We had expected a message. There hasn't been one. But if it's *true* that one or several of these groups are responsible for the killing, then we have a huge problem. On Friday."

"The funeral," the Police Chief said, with a note of fatigue in his voice.

"Exactly. The Prime Minister is at the very top of their so-called death lists. All the others on those lists, and I mean *every single one* of them, will be at the funeral."

"And that'll be hell on earth," commented the Head of the Anti-Terror Squad, a thick-set, dark-haired giant of a man.

"You could be right there," the Security Service Chief responded, stubbing out his cigarette with a crushing, resolute movement. "That may be why they have not yet issued any declaration. They're waiting. It's entirely possible, of course. Most definitely, entirely possible."

9:39 P.M., STOLMAKERGATA 15

Non potendo carezzarmi,
Le manine componesti in croce,
E tu sei morto senza sapere
Quanto t'amava questa tua mamma.

Billy T. stood in a little bedroom that seemed even smaller because of the bunk beds on either side, with the distance between them only about 20 inches. He took a break from making up the beds and held his head in his hands as he supported himself on the top bunk. The music blasted through the whole apartment: he had loudspeakers in every room. Even in the boys' room, though his persistent attempts to teach four young boys between six and eight years old to love opera had fallen on stony ground so far.

Sister Angelica cried over the loss of her dead son in the middle of the second part of Puccini's *Il trittico*, The Triptych, and Billy T. lifted the bedclothes up to his face, closing his eyes. There was a smarting sensation behind his eyelids. Since Friday morning, he had slept only five hours and that had been a restless sleep, during which he'd tossed from side to side and had woken feeling even more exhausted than when he had gone to bed. Soon he would have to capitulate to the Rohypnol tablets lying in the bathroom closet as a second life belt; he had not touched them for the past year.

He rubbed the sheets against his face. His eyes ached unrelentingly. The boys had been meant to stay the weekend. Demonstrating patience and a mature understanding beyond their years, the four half-brothers had found themselves being returned home to their respective mothers on Saturday morning after Billy T.'s sister had stepped in at short notice on Friday evening.

"Daddy is going to find the murderer," the eldest, Alexander, had explained to his youngest brother. "Daddy's going to find him. Isn't that right, Daddy?"

Now Daddy was tired. And sorry. He padded his way into the living room and threw himself down on the only good chair: a gigantic English wing chair in worn leather. He balanced his feet on the coffee table, an old, damaged piece of furniture from a second-hand store, and used the remote control to turn the volume on the enormous stereo system even higher.

> *M'ha chiamata mio figlio!*
> *Dentro un raggio di stelle*
> *M'è apparso il suo sorriso*
> *M'ha detto: Mamma, vieni in Paradiso!*

Addio! Addio!
Addio, chiesetta! In te quant'ho pregato!

He sat with the libretto booklet in front of him, although he knew most of the words by heart. The little book almost disappeared in his huge hands, and he sat there inert, staring into space.

He only just heard it ring. Irritated, he tried to ascertain the time; his eyes finally spotted the clock on the stove as he turned down the music.

"Okay, okay," he said as it rang once again before he reached the front door.

Fumbling with the security chain, he heard it ring yet again.

"Okay, *okay*," he snarled and opened the door wide.

The first thing he noticed was the enormous duffel bag, not properly closed at the top, with a big woolen sweater trying to push its way out. Then he spotted a pair of boots, beautiful boots, unusual, made of snakeskin and with real silver spurs. And then he lifted his eyes.

The woman standing before him smiled. She had mid-length brown hair and bright blue eyes with a distinctive black ring around the iris. Her pale leather jacket was new, with short fringes across the chest and Native American embroidery on the pockets. The woman was tan, a matte, golden color with no trace of redness, as though she had spent a long time in sunny climes. Above her eyes, a white line ran across each temple. She began to laugh.

"You look like a crazy loon! Can I come and stay with you?"

"Hanne," he whispered. "It can't be true! *Hanne!*"

"It's me all right," she said as he stepped over the duffel bag to put his arms around her in a bear hug, lifting her off her feet and walking backward with her into the apartment.

He dropped her into the armchair, flung out his arms, and roared, "Hanne! Why in the world are you here? When did you arrive? Are you staying long?"

"Bring in my bag, won't you?"

Billy T. collected the bag and switched off the opera.

"Do you want anything? Something to drink?"

He felt like a teenager and could feel himself blushing with pleasure, a totally unfamiliar sensation but not entirely unpleasant. Hanne

Wilhelmsen was back. She had come home again. She was going to stay with him. In the fridge, he had half a homemade pizza from Friday and five cans of Ringnes lager. Grabbing two, he switched on the oven and tossed one of the cans to the seated woman.

"Tell me," he said, sitting on the floor close by her, his arms hugging her knees, and staring directly into her eyes, "when did you get here?"

"Just now. Lots of delays and that sort of thing, and I'm dead tired. What is the time, actually?"

Without waiting for an answer, she suddenly caressed his bare head.

"It's so *good* to see you, Billy T.! How *are* you?"

"Fine, just fine," he said impatiently. "Are you starting back at work? At once?"

"No, I'm on sabbatical until Christmas, and I'm going back to California. In a while. But I just couldn't stay away. Cecilie understood. She realized that I would go crazy over there with all this."

She swept the beer can around in a semicircle, making it slosh about.

"I just couldn't leave you on your own with this case. I can help you as a sort of—freelancer? So you're not alone."

"Alone?"

He dug his head into her lap, clutching her legs tightly, and shook himself: shook them both.

"There are about two hundred of us, you know!"

"But nobody like me," Hanne Wilhelmsen said, laughing.

Her laughter. He sucked it in; it rippled, softly, genially, creeping inside his ears, into his brain, and spreading delightfully down his spine. Chief Inspector Hanne Wilhelmsen was back. In Norway. In Oslo. She was going to help him.

"I'm so glad you're here," he whispered. "I've—"

He stopped and scratched his back.

"You've missed me, have you? Likewise. Where shall I sleep? We've rented out our apartment, so I hope it's okay for me to move in here."

"That depends," said Billy T. "Will you take the risk of sharing the double bed with me, or do you want to take one of the boys' bunk beds?"

"The latter would be safer, I think," she said, yawning emphatically.

"But first we'll crack open some wine, okay?"

Hanne Wilhelmsen glanced at the almost untouched can of beer.

"There's nothing I'd rather do right now than share a bottle of wine with you. Nothing."

"And some pizza." Billy T. grinned. "That I made myself."

The clock on the bedside cabinet glowed green, telling her that the new day was four hours and five minutes old. Billy T. had thrown off the quilt and was lying diagonally across the specially built bed. Wearing boxer shorts and a soccer shirt, a present from Cecilie, San Francisco 49ers in size XXXL, he was snoring lightly with his mouth open. Hanne stood looking at him, and for a moment she nearly changed her mind. Then she sneaked over to him and snuggled down beside his huge body.

"I'm having such terrible nightmares," she whispered. "And the bed in there is so hard."

He smacked his lips slightly and stretched out closer to one side of the double bed. Then he rolled his left arm over her, as he mumbled, "I knew I could get you into bed with me."

Hanne giggled into the darkness before they both fell fast asleep.

MONDAY, APRIL 7

B enjamin Grinde stared at the Chief Justice and shook his head faintly.

"I honestly do not know what to say. As I told you on the phone yesterday, the police have admitted that this was all a huge mistake. I have simply no idea how the press got hold of it."

The Chief Justice raised the newspaper to eye level. His reading glasses were very strong and made his eyes appear so tiny that they virtually disappeared; now he was also squinting.

SUPREME COURT JUDGE CHARGED

Benjamin Grinde last person to see Volter alive

By Little Lettvik and Trond Kjevik (photo)

Though the police have spent the past three days denying that any arrests have been made in the Volter case, it appears that this is incorrect. The truth that both the police and Supreme Court Judge Benjamin Grinde have been desperately trying to hide is that Grinde was arrested at his home late on Friday evening.

Only half an hour after Prime Minister Birgitte Volter was found dead in her office, an arrest warrant was issued for Supreme Court Judge Grinde (see facsimile). The well-known lawyer, who is also chairman of the so-called Grinde Commission, appointed by Parliament last autumn, was seemingly the last person to see the Prime Minister alive. Grinde, who refused to make a statement on the matter to *Kveldsavisen*, asserts to the best of our knowledge that his visit to Birgitte Volter's office late on Friday afternoon was a purely routine appointment. However, the police will not confirm this as yet. As far as Oslo Police Station is concerned, a wall of silence surrounds the arrest warrant. Police Chief Hans Christian Mykland will say only that the warrant was withdrawn some time ago, when it emerged that an "error" had been made.

Reactions in police circles range from shock to anticipation. See pages 7, 8 and 9.

"Not good," the Chief Justice muttered. "Not good at all."

Benjamin Grinde stared at the table in front of him, fixing his gaze on a well-thumbed red statute book. The lion on the national coat of arms leered at him, arrogant and gloating, and Grinde blinked.

"It is not difficult to agree with that," he said softly. "What do you want me to do? Abstain from judicial activity until further notice?"

Putting down the newspaper, the Chief Justice rose and skirted the massive oak table in the judicial chambers before crossing to the window, which was framed by dark green velvet curtains. He peered at the facade directly opposite, where the opening words of the national anthem were carved into the stonework. Perhaps the Ministry of Finance wished to assure the outside world of their nationalistic inclinations at a time when everything was being done to hoard the fortune gushing in an uncontrollable, inexhaustible supply from the North Sea.

"Good photograph," he mumbled, placing his palm on the windowpane.

"What do you mean?"

"It's a really good photo of you. In the newspaper."

He wheeled around and sat down again quietly. For a while it looked as though he were on a journey, far away, but Benjamin Grinde knew that the Chief Justice was a man who thought before he spoke, and he ignored the lengthy pause.

"That would be unfair," the Chief Justice said at last. "The arrest warrant was obviously not genuine, and it would mean yielding to speculation if you were to relinquish your position. However, to be on the safe side, that ought to be raised with the advocates."

He stood up and held the door open for the four other Supreme Court judges, who were waiting outside in their black caps and purple velvet trim. He drew the eldest aside, and they conversed in subdued voices so that the others could not hear. As the Chief Justice opened the door to leave them, the Registrar stood in the doorway to make his ritual announcement: "Advocates stand at the bar!"

The eldest judge nodded to the other Supreme Court judges, who reacted by lining up behind him in a predetermined order, with Benjamin Grinde, the last to be appointed, at the rear.

The President of the Court sat down, and after a brief formal nod to the advocates, Grinde followed suit. But the sense of solemnity that normally suffused him on these occasions had deserted him. The high-backed chair felt uncomfortable, and his cap felt too warm.

"The court is in session. Today we shall consider appeal case number . . ."

Benjamin Grinde felt seriously unwell. He reached out for a glass of water, but his hands were shaking and he put them down.

"Are there any objections to the composition of the court?"

The President of the Court gazed from one advocate to the other as the two of them stood erect behind the bar directly opposite the horseshoe-shaped judges' table. The Adam's apple of the advocate whose first test case this was bobbed up and down like a yo-yo, preventing him from uttering a word. Instead he scratched his head feverishly, while his adversary, a female advocate aged about sixty, answered in a steady, clear voice: "No."

"I am aware that we are facing a special situation here today," the President of the Court continued, leafing fruitlessly through the papers in front of him, bundles of judicial abstracts of varying quality, for something he had spotted earlier. "I expect that the advocates are familiar with the substantial coverage in one of this morning's newspapers in which Judge Grinde . . ."

He nodded briefly to his left.

". . . was mentioned. He seems to have been charged in connection with this tragic murder case we are all familiar with. Well. For our part, we have made investigations and have received assurances from the Director General of Public Prosecutions that the entire situation was due to a misapprehension. I therefore cannot see that a speculative article in a—a tabloid newspaper . . ."

He looked as though he had sunk his teeth into a lemon.

". . . should lead to a Supreme Court judge relinquishing his position. However, as I said, this is a special situation, and I leave it to the advocates to express their viewpoints with regard to the extent to which Judge Grinde continues to enjoy the necessary confidence. I therefore repeat my question, and as I said, simply as a matter of form: Are there any objections to the composition of the court?"

"No!"

Now the two advocates replied in chorus, and the younger of them leaned toward the heavy teak bar. Swallowing repeatedly, he abruptly drew himself up to his full height again when the President of the Court called on him to speak.

A pause ensued, a lengthy pause. The man swayed. The view from the judges' table was restricted, so the judges did not see his female adversary make an encouraging gesture with her fist clenched and thumb pointing upward; she did this discreetly, hidden by the bar, but the man beside her was so lost that he did not notice it.

Benjamin Grinde was overcome by an uncontrollable urge to laugh. He stroked his fingers across his mouth, attempting to thrust the laughter back down where it had come from. This had never happened to him before; he had always had the greatest respect for the deference and gravity on which the country's highest court depended; it had to be solemn. He knew why the advocate was struggling.

The face of the advocate presenting the test case was chalk white, and his mouth was gaping like a fish out of water. Eventually he began. "Most remarkable court—"

The President of the Court cleared his throat, loudly and theatrically, and the advocate stopped abruptly. Now he looked as if he were on the brink of tears. The President of the Court knew the continuation of this string of words all too well: "the richest judges in the realm." He raised his hand discreetly toward the Registrar, who swiftly jotted down a few words on a yellow Post-it note and placed it before the unfortunate man; the man was now bright red in the face, his top lip lathered in a moustache of perspiration.

"Most honorable court, supreme judges of the realm," he commenced anew, and it seemed as though the entire room exhaled in relief, the dark walls no longer appearing so severe, not quite so overwrought.

Four of the judges smiled faintly and began to make notes.

Benjamin Grinde no longer felt the slightest inclination to laugh.

Nor did he notice Little Lettvik as she rose from the extreme rear of the public benches and left the chamber.

NOON, OSLO POLICE STATION

E ven the soft Kristiansand accent could not mask his fury. Chief of Police Hans Christian Mykland pounded on the table in front of him, and almost 150 police officers straightened up in their seats.

"I regard this matter *extremely* seriously. *Extremely* seriously. I thought I made myself clear when I addressed all of you here on Saturday. No leaks to the press. I was *crystal clear!*"

He thumped the table with the flat of his hand, and the room was so quiet that Billy T. did not dare even to breathe; his stomach was sore.

"That arrest warrant was a mistake. We all know that. Now we risk a juicy lawsuit for compensation for unjustifiable prosecution. Do you realize what it means to offend the judiciary, the third arm of government?"

No one felt called upon to answer; most of them were examining their own knees, in considerable detail.

"This will be followed up. Investigated. I will personally ensure that the person who leaked this warrant gets a thorough dressing-down. *From me!*"

The Police Chief had at last found time to shave, and there was something about him that indicated a new sense of determination; he seemed to have grown in stature in the course of the weekend.

"So. For the moment, we'll draw a line under that matter. At the next press conference, I shall . . ."

He glanced across at the public relations manager and corrected himself.

". . . at the next press briefing, I mean, I'll make it as clear as I possibly can that Benjamin Grinde cooperated with us as a witness. Then we'll see how big the fire actually is, and whether it is feasible to extinguish it. Now I'll hand over to the Head of CID."

The Head of CID looked startled, as though he had not been following the reprimand since it did not apply to him. "It would be useful to have a short summary," he began, as he placed an acetate on the overhead projector.

"Whoever has nothing to say, says it with an overhead," Billy T. muttered under his breath. He was once again sitting at the very back of the room, with Tone-Marit at his side.

She pretended not to hear him.

"As you know, we are working tirelessly on all fronts. First and foremost, it is important to discover how and why. As far as the latter is concerned, we have found it expedient to divide the possible motives into three main categories."

He turned to face the screen and pointed without getting to his feet. "One: the personal motive. Two: the international motive. Three: the extremist motive. In no particular order."

"It is quite extreme to kill the Prime Minister, regardless of the reason," Tone-Marit said softly, and Billy T. looked at her in surprise.

"Now you'd better be a good girl and sit quietly." He grinned.

"We've decided to be restrained as far as interviewing the closest family members are concerned, at least until after the funeral, which takes place on Friday. And that gives us a fresh problem."

He raised his hand toward the Head of the Terror Police, or the Anti-Terror Squad, as it was described more politely on paper. The thickset man with the raven-black hair and beard stood up stiffly.

"The funeral will require the very highest level of security measures. We are in the process of making a list of the groups that present a risk, that is to say, international terrorists, foreign agents, national extremists on both the right and left . . ."

He smiled in the direction of the Security Service Chief, who did not return the compliment. Obviously slightly offended, he continued. "And of course, mentally disturbed people. We know from previous experience, previous experience in the international arena, I should say, that crazy people crawl out of the woodwork when events like this take place. In addition, we are of course keeping an eye on those familiar to us within the criminal fraternity who are not suspected of having anything to do with the case. There will be a special talk about that tomorrow morning."

Resuming his seat, the Anti-Terror Squad Chief glanced at the Security Service Chief in anticipation of acknowledgment but still received no response.

The Head of CID started speaking again. "Right now, we're putting all our interviews with employees from the government tower block on to computer searches. We will attempt to uncover possible unauthorized access to the Prime Minister's office. It is therefore extremely important that all interviews are submitted on computer disk—"

"If we had better equipment, then that could be done with a few keystrokes," Billy T. sighed as he got to his feet.

"Are you leaving already?" Tone-Marit whispered.

"Got better things to do," Billy T. said.

Something was bothering him, but he could not quite put his finger on what it was. Something he had forgotten, a piece of information he had received but that he had lost somewhere up in his own hard disk, inside his head.

"Overload," he muttered to himself as he sneaked out the door toward the yellow zone on the third floor of the police station. "In fact, I do believe I can't handle any more information."

12:24 P.M., OSLO CITY CENTER

B rage Håkonsen was wearing jeans and an oversize rust-red college sweatshirt, its chest emblazoned with "Washington Redskins" and on the back a picture of a Native American chief in a feather headdress. The others found it odd that he wanted to go around with the image of a Native American man on his sweatshirt, but that was only because the others did not have a clue about anything. Native North Americans were a proud, majestic race. In contrast to their incompetent relations in the South—those small, dark-skinned creatures in gaudy clothing—the indigenous people of North America had a magnificent culture, were intelligent, and understood and respected nature and the animal kingdom. But the Jewish-infiltrated American government had ridden roughshod over them for several centuries, taking from them their self-evident right to water, land, and the prairies. The mere thought of it made his ears ring with rage.

The security guard momentarily glanced in his direction. Fast as lightning, Brage Håkonsen squeezed in behind an idling delivery truck full of clothes destined for the store at the end of Storgata.

When he tentatively peered out again, with his baseball cap pulled well down on his forehead, he could see the guard walking on: he appeared vigilant, with a nervousness that had not been evident previously. He wasn't behaving evasively or acting like a coward, as he usually did, but he seemed to have become more wary, like a wild animal during the hunting season. Now he slipped into a store, G-Sport, looking to left and right before he entered.

Brage Håkonsen scuttled past McDonald's and sprinted across the intersection, ignoring the warning red crossing man signal and forcing a Volkswagen Beetle to brake suddenly, though he did not so much as turn to face the driver.

Some considerable time passed before the security guard reappeared. He was carrying nothing, not even a bag from the store, so if he had purchased anything, it must have been small enough to cram into his pocket. He still seemed wary, and he scanned his surroundings continuously; now and again he would stop abruptly, wheel around, and then start to run, not far, only a few yards, before resuming his slow walking pace again, moving forward with almost exaggerated steadiness.

It had not been like this before. The security guard had been the easiest surveillance target in the world. He never looked at anybody, avoiding all eye contact, and Brage Håkonsen had been able to walk right behind him several times, in fact on occasion had even stood in front of him, only two or three yards away, in a delicious act of recklessness. The guard had never noticed him. Now he had eyes in the back of his head. Following him was tiresome, and Brage Håkonsen regretted wearing this sweatshirt. It would have been better to have put on something more neutral, a shirt and jacket, something in shades of brown or gray.

Eventually the guard crossed the bridge at Nybrua; it was more open here, and Brage Håkonsen was able to put a hundred yards between them without risking losing sight of him. All of a sudden, an ambulance siren sounded from the Accident and Emergency unit, and Brage saw that the security guard was startled. For a moment it looked as though he was considering jumping in the Akerselva River as he pressed against the railings and stared wildly around.

Brage Håkonsen smiled. He could not be mistaken. The only fly in the ointment was that the guard was behaving so suspiciously that he might be hauled in if anyone from the police caught sight of him. On the other hand, the police had most certainly already interviewed the man, perhaps more than once, and he was still a free man on the streets of Oslo.

When the security guard from the government complex rounded the corner of his own street and inserted his key into the front door without even chatting to the supervisor's daughter—who had appeared by his side and was staring at him indignantly, her hip thrust forward provocatively—Brage Håkonsen felt sure of his ground.

He remained on his feet, gazing at the run-down apartment block in Jens Bjelkes gate until the guard had clearly entered his own apartment.

Then Brage Håkonsen tried to hail a taxicab.

2:47 P.M., *KVELDSAVISEN* EDITORIAL OFFICE

The pain in Little Lettvik's left knee had subsided. She had refrained from indulging in anything unwholesome for the entire weekend, and her body seemed to have reacted to this unexpectedly considerate treatment by developing an aversion to cigarillos; she had not smoked for five hours. Little Lettvik felt exceptionally fit.

The police had not denied anything. It was true that they had rowed at breakneck speed at the press briefing less than an hour earlier—the water had positively splashed around the Chief of Police—but the information about the arrest warrant had not been contradicted. Little Lettvik thought warmly of Konrad Storskog and wondered fleetingly whether she should actually leave him in peace from now on.

Of course, they had been the only ones to cover the story. In recognition of this, the editor had given her the go-ahead to continue working on the connection between Birgitte Volter's murder and Benjamin Grinde's visit to the Prime Minister's office, though he was lukewarm about it.

"There's probably no more juice to be squeezed out of that lemon now," he had protested cautiously while biting his lip doubtfully. "A spicy story today, Little, but it's obvious that the police no longer suspect the guy. Jesus Christ, he was sitting in the Supreme Court again this morning!"

"Listen, Leif," Little Lettvik had argued, "the political guys have struck a gold mine. There's plenty to work on with that."

"They've got enough on their plates as it is. It's still totally unclear what kind of government we'll have on Friday. The political section hasn't had this much fun since the Furre case exploded."

"Exactly! And what was the most central aspect of the Furre case?"

The editor had not answered, but she had caught his attention, as his toying with the blotting pad on his desk revealed; it was worn and fluffy at the edges and the fingers picking at the border were the surest sign that chief editor Leif Skarre was interested in something.

"The criticism was directed first and foremost at the revelation that Berge Furre, a former Socialist Left politician, was secretly investigated by the Police Security Service. Isn't that right? Specifically, that he was investigated by them while he was serving on the Lund Commission, which had been set up to look into the activities of the self-same Security Service. Correct? Put simply, the argument was that it was *because* Furre was a member of the Lund Commission that he should not have been subject to such investigations. And then the defense counsel for the Security Service started to scream that no one is exempt in such cases, from a cat to a king. And now they've charged a Supreme Court judge! King Solomon himself, so to speak! Without a legal ruling! There's plenty there, you know. More than enough."

The editor had sat in silence for some time before grumpily nodding toward the door. That was all the consent she needed.

However, she had not discovered very much more about Benjamin Grinde. As she leafed through his folder, it struck her that hardly anyone seemed to actually know him. Even the friendly and exceptionally naive temp in the Supreme Court office that Little had enjoyed such success with on Friday afternoon had been unable to help her. Despite evidently finding it unbearably exciting that an Oslo journalist was interested in her opinions about this and that.

"No, Judge Grinde, he really *never* receives personal phone calls," she had chirped at the other end of the phone line.

Benjamin Grinde had innumerable acquaintances but obviously no friends, at least not in the judicial establishment. The descriptions she had been given in eleven wasted phone conversations were downright boring and totally unusable: Benjamin Grinde was clever, correct, and hard working.

"Advocate Fredriksen's office, how can I help you?"

Little Lettvik had finally lit a cigarillo, and she blew smoke out through her nose as she introduced herself and asked to speak to Frode Fredriksen. It took only a couple of seconds to get him on the line; Fredriksen was not the kind of person who passed up an opportunity to make use of his constitutional right to give a statement.

"A legal scandal!" he blustered, and Little Lettvik could virtually hear him brushing the dandruff from the shoulders of his suit, as he always did when he was emphasizing a point. "I'll tell you one thing, Little Lettvik: if the commission doesn't get to the bottom of this case, then I *personally* will ensure that the right people are brought to account. It is my damn *duty* as a spokesman for the powerless!"

Frode Fredriksen was able to use the most pompous expressions about the origins of a slice of bread, and Little Lettvik could not even be bothered to write this down. Instead she interrupted his tirade before he managed to get as far as "their inviolable human rights."

"But what is it actually that's so scandalous? What has happened?"

"The authorities want to hide something, Little. They are hiding something!"

"Yes, I realize that's what you mean. But what?"

"I don't know, obviously, but I'll tell you one thing: I've never come across anything like the wall of silence that the various authorities have built around this case. Never in my entire career. And that is, in all modesty, a very long time. As you know."

"What kind of silence, then?"

Little Lettvik lit another cigarillo with the old one.

"Records are missing," Frode Fredriksen continued. "They refused to release the records. The records were incomplete when I first received them. The hospitals in this country are the security police of the Public Health Service, I can tell you, Lettvik. Undue secrecy and the arrogance of power all the way. But we don't let that stop us."

"But you've applied for a postponement of the hearing into the demands for ex gratia compensation payments."

"Yes indeed. I'm hoping the Grinde Commission will shed fresh light on the case. The amounts might well be higher for that reason."

"But listen here, Fredriksen . . ."

Impatiently, Little Lettvik changed the receiver to her other ear.

". . . you must have some opinion about what might have happened. I mean, according to the commission's mandate, it is to report on both what possibly took place and to what extent the relatives have received adequate information from the Health Service. But honestly, this all happened more than thirty years ago, so can it really be so explosive? And why are you so outraged, given that you've received everything you've asked for? The commission was established, and wasn't that the very first thing you insisted on?"

The other end of the line went completely silent. Little Lettvik took a deep drag and held her breath, enjoying the comforting sensation as the nicotine pulsed through her bloodstream.

"Eight hundred too many children died in 1965, Little Lettvik," he eventually commented, softly and dramatically, his voice earnest; she heard the rustling of paper in the background. "At least 800 children! In 1964, 1,078 children under the age of one died in this country. In 1966, the figure was 976. The numbers for the years before and after this are relatively constant at around a thousand; these days it's dropped to around 300. But in 1965, Little Lettvik, 1,914 infants died! Such a fluctuation cannot be simply chance. They died of something. And the authorities will not investigate what that something was. A scandal. I repeat: a huge scandal."

Little Lettvik knew all this. She had read everything about the case. She had still not received an answer to her question, and for a moment she wondered whether she had the energy to continue the conversation. Then she suddenly changed tack. "What about Benjamin Grinde?"

Advocate Fredriksen gave a loud, booming laugh.

"You're certainly wide of the mark there! Or the police are, at least. And they have obviously realized that, as far as I understand it, even though you've hyped it all up. Benjamin Grinde is an outstanding man. Slightly boring, slightly pompous, but that comes with the territory. It's pervasive in that place. Oh no, Benjamin Grinde's an unusually talented lawyer and an irreproachable citizen. I was very pleased when they chose him to be chairman of the investigating commission. I have also taken the liberty of telling him so. On the quiet."

This was futile. Little Lettvik said thanks for the information without tangible enthusiasm and then she dialed a final phone number. She would have to eat something soon.

"Edvard Larsen," a pleasant voice answered.

"Hi, Teddy. Little Lettvik here. How's it going?"

"All right," the public relations manager in the Ministry of Health said tamely at the other end. Little Lettvik called at all hours and seemed to have limited understanding that he could not permit her a direct connection to Ruth-Dorthe Nordgarden. "How can I help you today?"

"Listen here. I really *must* speak to the Minister of Health."

"What's it about?"

"Unfortunately, I can't tell you. But it's important."

Teddy Larsen was usually the most patient of people, an invaluable talent in his post as the minister's spokesperson in the media world. But now he was about to run aground.

"You know very well that I need to know what it's about. We don't really have to go over all that yet again, do we?"

He tried to take the edge off his own irritation by laughing briefly. Little Lettvik groaned.

"Okay, then. It's completely harmless, but it is important. I want to ask her something in connection with the work of the Grinde Commission."

"Just give me your questions, and I'll make sure that you receive the answers as quickly as possible."

"Thanks for your help, but no thanks," Little Lettvik said, slamming down the receiver.

However, she was not so very discouraged. No member of the government was as easy to talk to as Ruth-Dorthe Nordgarden. It was only a matter of finding something with which she could scratch the cabinet minister's back. An exchange. Little Lettvik sat absentmindedly flicking through her Filofax, and of their own volition, her fingers found their way to Ruth-Dorthe Nordgarden's confidential home number.

It was just so damned annoying that she had to wait until tonight.

8:50 P.M., STOLMAKERGATA 15

"You could really try to make it a bit more attractive in here, you know. For the boys' sake, at least."

Hanne Wilhelmsen wore an apron around her middle, its aged leather spattered with wine and food stains. She waved the wooden spoon in the air, splashing the tomato sauce.

"You could at least try not to cover my entire kitchen in sauce, then," Billy T. replied, grinning. "That doesn't help make the place more attractive, does it?"

He wiped the fridge door with the back of his hand and licked off the red mess.

"Mmm, delicious. The boys should've been here. Spaghetti with ground beef and tomato is their favorite."

"Tagliatelle bolognese," she corrected him. "That's not spaghetti." She held up the packet in front of him.

"Flat spaghetti," he declared. "But what are you going to do with that?" Snatching up a stick of celery, he popped it into his mouth and pointed at a whole nutmeg.

"Don't touch!" She waved the wooden spoon again, and this time he got a long red stain across his once-immaculate white T-shirt.

"Look at this living room," she said dejectedly, securing the lid on the pan. "Those curtains must be from some time in the seventies!"

She was probably right. They were made of coarse-weave fabric, orange with brown stripes, and were hanging sadly crooked. In the folds you could see dust that must have been gathering there for years.

"At least you could have washed them. And meanwhile look at that." She peered between the upper and lower cabinets in the open-plan kitchen, at the stereo system on the bookshelf; it sparkled and shone in the light from a steel lamp with three bulbs and a raffia shade. "How much did that cost?"

"Eighty-two thousand kroner," Billy T. mumbled, attempting to reach the pan with a spoon.

"Don't *touch*, I said. Eighty-two thousand? If you had taken just half that sum and spent it at IKEA instead, you could have made it really nice in here. You don't even have a proper sofa!"

"The boys like sitting on the floor."

"You really are an oddball." She smiled. "I'll see what I can get done while I'm here."

Billy T. set the table and turned the television around so that they could watch Channel 21 while they were eating. Then he opened two beers and poured them as he adjusted the volume.

"By now people will be getting fed up with all these extra bulletins," Hanne Wilhelmsen muttered as she took off her apron. "I've watched two of them today, and they repeat the same thing every time. Very nearly, anyway."

The woman on screen was smart and inspired confidence, even though she reminded Hanne of a cartoon character.

"My goodness, she's had her hair cut," Hanne Wilhelmsen commented. "It looks lovely, actually."

"She must be almost as exhausted as us by now," Billy T. remarked, shoveling down his food. "She's had umpteen bulletins a day. And the news is not what it usually is, either. It's supposed to be news first, then sports, followed by commentary. Everything's been turned upside down now. Even them."

He used his spoon to point at the screen.

"Shh," Hanne signaled. "Keep quiet."

"And in the studio for this bulletin we have with us Chief of Police Hans Christian Mykland. Welcome, Sir!"

"Thanks."

"I'll come directly to the point, Sir, since I know you have far more important things to do than stand here with me. Can you give a straight answer as to whether the police are now any closer to solving the Volter case almost exactly three days after her murder?"

"Poor man," Hanne mumbled as she listened to the Police Chief's reply. "He's really got nothing to report, and yet he has to pad it out as though there was a great deal. Are you honestly so at a loss, Billy T.?"

"Just about."

He slurped the tagliatelle so that it formed a big red rose at the far corner of his mouth.

"Clown," Hanne muttered.

"We do have something more," Billy T. said, drying his mouth with his lower arm. "For instance, we've quite a rare caliber of weapon."

"Oh. How rare?"

"It's a 7.62 millimeter. We'll have the answer to what kind of gun was used quite soon, I think. But he can't say that there."

He nodded again in the direction of the television.

"I just can't understand the point of appearing in the studio because he can't really say anything at all. For fuck's sake, he's bloody furious about the nonsense that came out about the arrest warrant, and we've all had an extraordinary double-strength muzzle clamped on us."

"There's little hope of that being particularly effective," Hanne said as she took a slug of beer. "Oslo Police Station leaks like a sieve. Always has."

The Police Chief looked incredibly relieved when he was eventually allowed to leave. The red-haired newscaster transferred the viewers to another studio, where the leaders of the parties represented in Parliament were seated along a boomerang-shaped table. The program host in the center stared rather too long at the camera before starting to speak. He introduced a film clip that also appeared after a lengthy pause.

"Why can't they *ever* manage to get it together?" Hanne asked with a smile. "In the States, you never see that kind of thing. They're able to do things smoothly every time."

To the accompaniment of fairly meaningless images from Parliament, a commentator gave an account of the difficult game of solitaire that was now being played. Eventually the program host in the studio turned to an immaculately dressed and extremely solemn man in a light suit jacket.

"I thought it was that woman who was the leader of the Christian Democratic Party," Billy T. commented. "Not that guy there."

"She's the leader, but he's the parliamentary—shh!"

"It would be completely crazy if we were to make political capital out of this very tragic situation that has occurred with the murder of Prime Minister Volter."

"Does that mean that your centrist coalition—the Center Party; the Liberals; and your own party, the Christian Democrats—will not be seizing this opportunity to take power?"

The program host spoke in an odd mixture of dialects with a faint trace of a Trøndelag accent, and the strange lock of hair at the nape of his neck was bobbing up and down in time to his voice.

"As I said, a particularly tragic event has struck our country, and we parties of the center have decided that this is not the time to make changes. We must all stand together during this difficult period, and then the people will have the chance to decide the future government of the country at the election in September."

The Christian Democrat man was not finished, but the interviewer turned to the left and addressed a man with a full, well-maintained, mottled beard and a resigned expression.

"How do you in the Conservative Party interpret this?"

The man shook his head almost imperceptibly, with a discouraged air, and immediately fixed his gaze on the interviewer.

"Media course," Hanne said. "He's been on a media course."

"What?" Billy T. asked, helping himself yet again.

"Forget it. Shh."

"This is a difficult time, and certainly not the time for political game playing or mud slinging. Nevertheless, I take the liberty of saying that this clearly demonstrates just how unrealistic the centrist alternative is. For several months now, the three centrist parties have been promoting their coalition in readiness for the election this autumn, but now that an opportunity has arisen, they've dropped the idea like a hot potato. This shows that we Conservatives have been right all along. An alternative to the Labor Party *must* include the Conservatives."

"We won't receive an answer to that until this autumn, however." It was the Christian Democratic representative who intervened, but the interviewer resolutely cut him off.

Hanne laughed loudly. "They don't want power, any of them! They're damn well afraid!"

"Politics." Billy T. snorted, helping himself for a third time. "You can have a job here. As a cook."

"Chef," Hanne said absentmindedly, without taking her eyes from the TV screen.

"What?"

"As a chef. Really good cooks are called chefs, whether male or female. But I want to listen to this, if you don't mind."

"It would quite simply be wrong to take advantage of this extraordinary situation." This was the representative of the Center Party echoing his coalition partner in the Christian Democrats, and the Conservative shook his head again, this time more decidedly.

"But what's the difference?" he asked. "What exactly will be different come the autumn? The Labor Party is in a minority today and will still be so in September. As they have been throughout the postwar period. Do the Center Party, the Liberals, and the Christian Democrats really believe they'll gain a *majority* in Parliament after the election?"

"As I said, that remains to be seen," the Christian Democrat man said, trying to interject, but the program host waved his hand determinedly and the Conservative did not brook any interruption.

"Then it's really about time we got to know what your policies are on the important issues. The voters are entitled to hear. What's your position on the building of gas-fired power stations? What about the European Economic Area? Child benefits? And what do you genuinely believe with regard to the health care system? Are we going to find out anything about these matters before people go to the ballot boxes?"

They all began to speak at once.

"When the cat's away, the mice will play," Hanne commented.

"But that lot doesn't want to play," Billy T. said. "They're sitting stock-still, frightened that somebody will invite them out to the playground! Sick. They make me sick."

That did not seem to be holding him back any, and he piled his plate for a fourth time, scraping the bottom of the dish.

"Can't I put on some music instead?" he asked.

"No, honestly, this is important."

At last the men had stopped arguing, or at least they were not allowed to continue. Instead the viewers were transferred to the woman in the other studio, who had Tryggve Storstein standing at her side.

"Bloody hell, *he* looks exhausted, doesn't he?" Hanne said under her breath, as she put down her beer glass without touching another drop.

Tryggve Storstein was so drained that not even the makeup artists at the TV station had been able to do much for him. The dark shadows under his eyes were obvious in the strong light, and his mouth had taken on a sad, almost sullen expression that persisted throughout the interview.

"Yes, Tryggve Storstein, despite the tragic circumstances, may we now congratulate you on becoming the new Party Leader?"

He muttered something that might have been interpreted as thanks.

"You've been here with me listening to the discussion. Is it the case that you'll be the one who forms a new administration on Friday?"

Tryggve Storstein cleared his throat and nodded. "Yes."

The interviewer seemed perplexed by the terse response and made some vigorous arm movements before managing to pose another question. Storstein continued to be concise, sometimes seeming downright dismissive, and the interviewer struggled energetically to fill the time that the program schedule had obviously allocated to the interview.

"He doesn't exactly seem like the great white hope," Hanne Wilhelmsen said as she began to clear the table. "Coffee?"

"Yes, please."

"You can make it then."

The bespectacled man with the Trøndelag accent had taken over once again. Now his guests were three newspaper editors, who commented on the situation with great pathos and gravity.

"How are we to have a normal, healthy political process in the days ahead, as we move forward to the formation of a new government, when a police investigation is being conducted that could, and I emphasize *could*, lead to the discovery of murder suspects in the very circles from which the government will emerge?"

It was the program host who was posing the question.

"I really wish people would learn to speak using periods," Hanne said, almost to herself. Billy T. was whistling as he toiled over the coffee machine.

The editor of *Dagbladet* leaned forward eagerly, his beard almost touching the tabletop.

"Now, it's definitely of extreme importance for the police to keep out of the political process. It must be quite clear that no such considerations should hinder the police in their work. But, on the other hand, we can't have a situation where the party that is to form the government is emasculated by the fact that most of the candidates for the post of Prime Minister actually knew Birgitte Volter."

"Typical." Hanne Wilhelmsen sighed. "No one believes it could be someone close to her, despite statistics showing that murderers almost always belong to the victim's inner circle. But the entire political elite in Norway knew Birgitte Volter. Then it becomes too dangerous to believe in the statistics."

She stood up and switched off the TV set.

"Music?" Billy T. inquired optimistically.

"No! I want some silence, okay?"

For lack of a proper sofa, they lay down in the bedroom, head to toe in the double bed. Hanne's head was leaning against the wall, and her back was resting on a well-worn skinny pillow. She sipped the coffee he handed her.

"Yuck!"

She spluttered, spraying the coffee, and making a grimace.

"What on earth *is* this? Tar?"

"Too strong?"

Without waiting for a reply, he fetched milk from the fridge and poured a generous portion into her cup.

"There. Now we'll stay awake for a while."

He attempted to find a comfortable position on the bed, but there were no more cushions, so in the end he sat up.

"There's something about Ruth-Dorthe Nordgarden," he said, scratching his ear. "Fuck, there's something wrong inside here. It's bloody sore at times."

"What do you mean by something?"

"Well, an infection, or something like that."

"Idiot. I meant with Ruth-Dorthe Nordgarden."

"Oh."

Billy T. squinted at his fingertip, but there was still nothing visible.

"Strange lady," he said. "Lots of nervous hand movements and peculiar grimaces. At the same time, she gives the impression of being—cold!"

He waved his forefinger in the air.

"She seems cold as ice! Like a fish. There's something I'd like to investigate further, but I can't get hold of *what* it is, and there's absolutely no reason to think that she was anywhere near the PMO on the evening of the murder."

"PMO?"

"The Prime Minister's office. Now you'll have to learn the jargon."

"Was she a friend of the Prime Minister?"

"No, not according to what she herself says. They did not socialize, she told me. Bloody peculiar woman. There's something . . . spooky about her. I get damn nervous being in the same room as her!"

Hanne Wilhelmsen didn't answer. She warmed her hands on the steaming cup and stared at a child's drawing hanging on the bulletin board: a very advanced Batmobile with inlaid wings and cannons.

"And that—"

"Shh," Hanne interrupted noisily. Billy T. jumped and spilled his coffee.

"But what—?"

"Shh!"

Billy T. swore under his breath, though Hanne pretended not to notice. Instead she examined the wall behind him thoroughly, and Billy T. whirled around to find out what she was staring at with such concentration.

"Alexander," she said tentatively. "It was Alexander who drew that."

Suddenly she looked directly at him. Her eyes seemed larger than normal, and the black circles around the irises even more pronounced.

"Did she tell you they didn't socialize?"

"Yes. What about it?"

Hanne rose from the bed and placed her coffee cup on the floor before crossing to Alexander's drawing and peering at it searchingly.

"What *is* it about that drawing?" Billy T. asked.

"Nothing, nothing," Hanne said. "It's marvelous. But that's not what I'm thinking about."

She turned to face him, hands on hips and head canted to one side.

"Birgitte Volter's son, Per, is quite a good marksman. I've met him a few times at the Løvenskiold shooting range. When he was younger, his father often accompanied him. I can't say that I know him, but we've chatted now and again, and it would be natural to nod to each other if we met on the street. And . . ."

Billy T. stared at her, but his finger was still digging deep into his ear canal.

"If you have an infection coming, you really shouldn't pick at it like that," Hanne said, shoving his hand away. "But then, a year or so ago— no, actually, it was just before we left for the States in November, so it must have been around the time of the change of government—I caught sight of Roy Hansen and Ruth-Dorthe Nordgarden at Café 33 in Grnerløkka."

"At Café 33? *That* dive?"

"Yes, it struck me too. I went in to deliver something to someone who works there, and there they were sitting at the far end of the bar, with a glass of beer each. Yes, it must have been after the change of government, because before that, I hardly knew who Ruth-Dorthe Nordgarden was. She is really quite—pretty? Blond bimbo and all that, easy to notice. At first I thought of saying hello to Roy, but something held me back, and I left without him spotting me."

"But, Hanne, how can you remember this so clearly?"

"Because that same day I'd read an article in a newspaper. *Dagbladet*, I think, about these networks journalists are so fascinated by. About dynasties and such like. I think in fact I was carrying that newspaper when I was in Café 33."

"Fuck," Billy T. muttered, rubbing his earlobe. "I think I need to go to the doctor's."

"But isn't that quite odd, Billy T.?" Hanne remarked thoughtfully, again gazing at the Batmobile that she had now discovered had a television on its hood and "Il Tempo Gigante" on the trunk. "Isn't it really striking that Ruth-Dorthe Nordgarden says that she doesn't associate with Birgitte Volter outside work when she actually, just six months ago, was drinking beer with the woman's husband in a dingy joint in Grnerløkka?"

Billy T. stared at her, rubbing his head repeatedly.

"Yes," he finally said. "You're right. It's strange."

TUESDAY, APRIL 8

"And to think that you have stopped smoking, Hanne!"

"You're sharp; it took you only ten minutes to register that. Billy T. hasn't worked it out yet. And you've become an Assistant Chief of Police. Splendid!"

Håkon Sand, smiling from ear to ear, grasped her hand and squeezed it hard.

"You must come to visit us as soon as you can. Hans Wilhelm is growing so big!"

Håkon's little boy was named after Hanne Wilhelmsen, and she thanked the gods she did not believe in that she had remembered to bring a present. Strictly speaking, it was Cecilie who had remembered, in great haste at the airport, when Hanne had left California so abruptly. A soccer shirt for Billy T. and an enormous bright yellow alligator for Hans Wilhelm.

"Won't you stay with us?"

It was as though the brilliant idea had just dawned on him, and his entire face opened up in a sincere invitation.

"Karen might not be so happy to have a guest," Hanne said, brushing him aside. "Isn't she pregnant?"

"Next weekend," Håkon mumbled, and did not insist. "But you must visit us. Soon."

There was a faint knock at the door and a uniformed police officer entered. Taken aback, the man stood staring at Hanne.

"Heavens above! Have you come back? Welcome! When did you get here? Are you returning to work?"

As he gazed at Hanne in search of answers, he placed a folder in front of the Assistant Chief of Police.

"No, just a vacation." Hanne smiled stiffly. "Only a couple of weeks."

"Hah! I'll be surprised if you can keep away from the station now!"

110

They could hear the officer's laughter long after the door had closed behind him.

"What is it?" Hanne asked, pointing at the folder.

"Let's have a look."

Håkon Sand browsed through the contents of the folder, and Hanne Wilhelmsen had to steel herself not to stand up and read over his shoulder. She gave him two minutes, after which she couldn't bear it any longer.

"What is it? Is it something important?"

"The gun. We think we know what kind of gun the bullet came from."

"Let me see," Hanne said enthusiastically, trying to grab the papers.

"Hey, hey," Håkon protested, placing both hands flat on the bundle of papers. "Confidentiality, you know. You're on leave. Don't forget that."

"Duh!"

For a moment it looked as though he meant it, and she glared at him in disbelief.

"Once a police officer, always a police officer. Honestly!"

"Idiot!"

Laughing, he handed her the green folder.

"Nagant," Hanne Wilhelmsen mumbled, thumbing through the papers. "Probably a Russian model 1895. Strange. Bloody strange."

"Why so?"

She closed the folder but continued to cradle it on her lap.

"Interesting gun. Extremely unusual. Has an entirely unique patented device in the cylinder. The mechanism turns it when the hammer is cocked, and then moves it forward over a little projection on the barrel. A so-called gas seal between the cylinder and barrel. Curious, really, because the patent was once actually stolen from a Norwegian!"

"What?"

"Hans Larsen of Drammen. He invented a unique system for gas-sealed revolvers and sent it to Liège in Belgium to be produced. They didn't give a damn about the weapon, stole the patent, and it was developed into a revolver in Russia at the end of the nineteenth century. The czar and all that lot."

"You never cease to amaze me." Håkon Sand smiled. But he knew that Hanne's knowledge of marksmanship was such that many years earlier, several colleagues had tried to enter her as a contestant on the TV quiz show *Double or Quits*. She had protested vigorously when the station got in touch and nothing had come of it.

"And what's the point of having a—a gas-sealed barrel, was that what you called it?"

"Greater precision," Hanne explained. "The problem with a revolver is that there's a loss of pressure between the cylinder and the barrel, so precision is diminished. It doesn't usually matter too much because revolvers were never meant to be used at great distances. I saw one once."

She fell silent and read on.

"It says here that there are only five such guns listed in the gun register. But you have a big problem, Håkon. A huge problem."

She closed the folder again, and for a moment it looked as though she longed to slip it surreptitiously into the handbag beside her chair. However, she placed it instead on the table between them.

"As far as I know, we have more than one huge problem in this case," Håkon said, yawning. "There's a whole line of problems, so to speak. But what are you referring to?"

"This gun was mass-produced over a long period of time. You'll find it in a lot of countries, especially in regions that have been under Soviet influence. They sold them cheaply to all their allies in Europe and Africa in the fifties. For instance, you'll come across them in . . ."

She hesitated and passed her hand quickly over her eyes.

". . . in the Middle East. And there are in fact a number of them in Norway. More than five anyway. They tend to have arrived here in curious ways. The one I saw belonged to a Russian exile who had inherited it from his father, who had served in the Red Army during World War II."

"Unregistered weapon," Håkon said dejectedly under his breath, and puffed his cheeks. "That's all we need."

Hanne Wilhelmsen laughed and ran her fingers through her hair.

"But you weren't expecting anything else, were you, Håkon? Did you think the Norwegian Prime Minister would be killed with a gun that was listed in our totally useless gun register, full of holes as it is? Did you honestly think so?"

9:45 A.M., MINISTRY OF HEALTH

Actually, no one quite understood how she had become Health Minister. It struck Teddy Larsen, when she closed the meeting with a strange scowl—always these odd facial expressions, ticks, sudden, unprompted, and unexplained facial movements—that nobody actually understood why she was there. Hardly anyone outside the press-Parliament-government triangle had really known who she was when she was appointed Minister of Health, despite her having been joint Deputy Leader of the Labor Party for four years. The woman had a degree in history and had studied a couple of other insignificant subjects and had worked as a teacher at one time, long ago. She was divorced and had twin teenage daughters and had in fact stayed at home for a not inconsiderable period of time. Afterward, she had taken a step up here and there: had spent a short time in the Norwegian Confederation of Trade Unions, but not long, and some time in the Workers' Education Association, but there too she had not lasted long. Gradually she had attained more powerful positions while still managing to keep in the background to a remarkable degree. And she had never distinguished herself in health matters in any way. Until she became the minister.

Teddy Larsen did not like his new boss, and that bothered him intensely.

"We'll draw this morning's meeting to a close now."

The undersecretary, political adviser, and Senior Private Secretary stood up at the same time as Teddy Larsen.

"You!"

Startled, they all turned to face the minister.

"Gudmund! You stay behind."

The political adviser, a robust young man from Fauske, shrank and looked enviously at the others as they left the room in relief.

Ruth-Dorthe Nordgarden crossed from the conference table to her own large office chair. She sat there gazing at Gudmund Herland. She looked like a slightly worn Barbie doll: her face blank, her eyes like saucers as she made an odd gesture with her upper lip that forced the nervous young man to stare out the window.

"This Grinde case," she said vaguely.

The political adviser did not know whether to sit down, but did not receive any instructions to do so from his boss and therefore remained on his feet. He felt like an idiot.

"Yes," he ventured, tentatively.

"Why was I not informed that he wants more money?"

"But," Gudmund Herland began, "I tried to raise the subject—"

"Tried! I won't put up with not being kept informed about such important matters."

She was fiddling with a pen that threatened to disintegrate under her hard, stabbing movements.

"Ruth-Dorthe, I did tell you that he wanted a meeting to discuss this with you, but you—"

"You did *not* tell me what it was about."

"But—"

"That's an end to it."

She was determined and waved her hands wildly without looking at him.

"You need to sharpen up. You really must sharpen up. You can go now."

Gudmund Herland did not leave. He stood in the middle of the floor, feeling a wave of uncontrollable rage surge through his body, as he clamped his mouth shut and closed his eyes. The bloody bitch. The damn bastard harpy. Not only had he informed her that Benjamin Grinde wanted to talk to her, he had also advised her as earnestly as he could to meet the man. The health scandal was something she could use to make her name: she could demonstrate initiative. If there was one thing this government needed to do, it was to show exactly that kind of ability to take action. But she had listened to him with half an ear and brushed him aside. She did not have time. Maybe later. That was her perennial comment: "maybe later." This woman had no idea what it meant to be a government minister. She thought you could keep normal office hours, and she became completely pissed off if anything came between her and dinner with her gorgeous daughters.

He clenched his teeth so hard that there was a cracking sound, and he only just managed to hear what she said.

"Are you going to just stand there?"

He opened his eyes. Now she looked like a member of the Addams Family, her cheeks were drawn up in such a diabolical expression. She was not worth it. His political career would not run aground on this particular rock. Without uttering a word, he turned on his heel and walked out, seizing one minuscule scrap of pleasure, all the same, by slamming the door unnecessarily hard behind him.

Ruth-Dorthe Nordgarden lifted the phone and asked her secretary to invite the Senior Private Secretary to come in again. While she waited, she leaned back in the chair and rested her feet on the wastepaper basket as she studied the curtains. They were not to her taste, and it annoyed her that they had still not been replaced, despite her having given instructions about them several times.

She was nervous about this infant mortality case. If she was going to lose her ministerial job in the coming reshuffle, which she seriously doubted, it might turn out that she had overlooked something, something that might then be used against her. Perhaps. What was it Benjamin Grinde had wanted to discuss with her that he had chosen to take to Birgitte instead? Was it simply a fuss about money, or was there something more to it? Something else?

She dipped a sugar cube into her coffee cup and placed the sweet, brown lump on her tongue. Irritated, and not without a certain sense of anxiety, she reflected on her conversation with Little Lettvik the previous evening. She had not understood what the journalist was looking for. Nor had she given the woman anything. But the conversation had left Ruth-Dorthe Nordgarden with a gnawing feeling of unease, and she gulped sour reflux in the midst of all the sweetness.

The Senior Private Secretary stood in the doorway.

"You wanted to see me?"

"Yes." Ruth-Dorthe sniffled and sat properly in the chair, sugar crunching between her teeth, causing her to swallow several times. "I want all the papers concerning the infant mortality case here at once. Immediately."

The Senior Private Secretary nodded gently, aware that this actually meant she would have preferred to have been given the papers yesterday.

12:39 P.M., SECURITY SERVICE SECTION, OSLO POLICE STATION

When Ole Henrik Hermansen laughed, the sound was explosive and unfamiliar. The Security Service Chief was a buttoned-up man in every respect: his immaculate exterior and expressionless features made him the cliché of a secret agent. His face was impassive and lacked distinctive characteristics, from his graying, combed-back hair to his pale, watery eyes and his straight, thin-lipped mouth; this man could blend into any crowd of human beings, anywhere whatsoever in the Western world.

"Where did you get hold of that?"

The police officer facing him looked down at his chest and smiled self-consciously.

"I only wear it up here. Only at work. Never outside."

Bold black letters across the entire front of the gray T-shirt declared: "I've got your file."

"No, I certainly hope not. That sort of thing could bring us trouble."

"More trouble here, boss," the police officer said, placing a file on his desk and searching around for a chair.

"Sit down. What's this?"

"A report from the Swedish Security Police. Very troubling." Massaging his right shoulder with his left hand, he pulled a face.

The Security Service Chief did not touch the folder but gazed intently at his subordinate.

"Yesterday evening a small plane, a little six-seater Cessna, crashed in northern Sweden, in Norrland. In Västerbotten County, between Umeå and Skellefteå," the man in the T-shirt began.

Now he changed tack and brutally kneaded his left shoulder with his right hand.

"We sent a full emergency warning to all our neighboring countries on Friday evening, and security measures surrounding the Swedish Prime Minister, Göran Persson, and his Danish counterpart, Poul Nyrup Rasmussen, have been ramped up. Therefore this has not come out, fortunately—"

Hesitating, he stared at the folder he had placed before his boss. It would be better if his boss read it. But Ole Henrik Hermansen still made no sign of touching anything. Only an almost imperceptible raising of his eyebrows indicated his growing impatience to hear the rest.

"Prime Minister Göran Persson should have been on that plane. He was scheduled to open a major boat exhibition in Skellefteå, and because of the Social Democrats' national conference in Umeå, he had to take a small plane in order to manage both."

"He *should* have been on that flight," the Security Service Chief commented quietly, implying a question in his words.

"Yes. Fortunately, he had to cancel the trip. At the last minute. The pilot flew the plane alone. As far as I understand it, he lived there, in Skellefteå. The pilot, that is. Now he's dead."

At long last, Hermansen opened the folder. He leafed through it rapidly, so quickly that he could not possibly have absorbed much of its contents.

"And what are our Swedish friends saying? Sabotage?"

"They don't know. For the time being, they are mostly happy the story has not leaked out. But they have their own thoughts about it. As do we."

Ole Henrik Hermansen got to his feet and crossed over to a map of Scandinavia on the wall. It was covered in pushpins with red heads, clustered together in places. The map was well used. He let his finger run along the east coast of Sweden.

"Farther up," the police officer said. "Here."

He had followed his boss and now placed a stubby forefinger on the map.

"Right between Kvärnbyn and Vebomark."

Two pins spearing Malmö fell to the floor, though neither of the two men had touched them.

"I need to put up a new map," Hermansen said. "This must have been hanging here since the dawn of time. How many people knew that he was to make that journey?"

"Next to no one. Not even the pilot."

"Not even the pilot," the Security Service Chief repeated softly, using a finger to scratch his hairline. "How concerned are the Swedish Security Police?"

"Extremely."

The police officer hoisted his shoulders and rolled his head from side to side.

"And what's more, Göran Persson is coming here to Norway. For the funeral. Of course."

Ole Henrik Hermansen took a deep breath.

"Yes. Who's not coming!"

The police officer walked over to the door and was about to close it behind him when Hermansen suddenly called out.

"You!"

The police officer pushed his head around the door again.

"Yes?"

"Take off that shirt. On reflection, it's not so amusing after all. Take it off, please. And put it away somewhere."

3:30 P.M., PMO

"I sat here. I just—I just sat here!"

Wenche Andersen buried her face in her hands and started to cry, quietly and inconsolably. Her shoulders were shaking underneath her russet-colored jacket, and, crouching beside her, Tone-Marit laid her hand on Wenche Andersen's back. The Prime Minister's secretary had finally begun to reveal that the events of the past few days had left their mark: she seemed shrunken and much older.

"Can I get you something? Maybe a glass of water?"

"I just sat there. I didn't do a thing!"

She removed her hands from her face. Underneath her left eye, a black streak showed that her mascara had started to run.

"If only I had *done* something," she hiccuped. "Then I might have been able to save her!"

A reconstruction was never easy. Billy T. merely sighed, snatching a glimpse of Supreme Court Judge Benjamin Grinde, who also looked somehow diminished. His suit hung more loosely, and the pale tan of his complexion had completely vanished. Now he could see the slight pattern of broken veins on each of the man's cheeks, and his lips were pressed together in a tight, unattractive line.

"You couldn't have saved her," Tone-Marit consoled her. "She died instantly. We know that now. There was nothing you could have done."

"But who on earth *did* it, then? How did they get *in*? They must have gone past me somehow or other. Why did I just *sit* here?"

Wenche Andersen stretched out across the table, and Billy T. peered at the ceiling, trying to find the patience that he had lost long ago. It had taken an unnecessarily long time to complete the sound test: a police officer with blank cartridges had fired several shots in the Prime Minister's office. Although they could be heard only faintly through the double doors, Wenche Andersen had jumped just as high in her seat every time. From the toilet, nothing could be heard. The problem was that Wenche Andersen could not say with any certainty when she had left her post.

"Perhaps we should just try and get started," he suggested. "Wouldn't it be better to get this over and done with?"

The secretary sniffed loudly but did not stop weeping. However, she did at least straighten up and took the tissue that Tone-Marit offered her.

"Maybe so," Wenche Andersen whispered. "Maybe we should just begin."

Benjamin Grinde looked at Billy T., and after receiving a nod as a signal to leave, he stepped out into the corridor.

"Wait!" Billy T. shouted. "Don't come in until I tell you!"

Then he leaned across Wenche Andersen's desk, and said softly, "So the time was quarter to five. Around 5:45. Those who were still here were—"

He shuffled the papers in front of him.

"Øyvind Olve, Kari Slotten, Sylvi Berit Grønningen, and Arne Kavli," Wenche Andersen said helpfully, with a sniff between each name. "But they weren't here the whole time. They left in the course of the next half hour. All of them."

"Fine," Billy T. said. Turning toward the door, he yelled, "Come in!"

Benjamin Grinde strolled through the doorway, attempting to wrench a smile from the fixed grimace he had worn since his arrival. He nodded to Wenche Andersen.

"I have an appointment with the Prime Minister," he said.

"Stop," Billy T. commanded, scratching his ear. "There's no need to do any playacting here. Just tell me what you did."

"All right," muttered Benjamin Grinde. "So I came in, and said what I just said. Then I was asked to wait for a second, and then—"

He concentrated, and Wenche Andersen rushed to help once again.

"I stood up and went in to see Mrs. Volter, and she just waved him in, and I said to go ahead, and he went past me, just like that."

Benjamin Grinde moved tentatively toward Wenche Andersen. They could not agree on which side to pass each other, and stood on one spot, swaying from one side to the other like two fighting cocks unsure which was the stronger.

"Stop," Billy T. demanded again, with a deep sigh and meaningful look in the direction of the Head of CID, who had still not uttered a single word. "As I said a moment ago . . ."

He spoke in exaggeratedly slow, clear tones, as though faced with five-year-old children who still had no idea how to play Parcheesi.

". . . don't act it out. Try to relax. It's not particularly significant how you stood and where you walked in here. So—"

Placing a large fist on Benjamin Grinde's shoulder, he led him purposefully through the doors to the Prime Minister's office.

"You entered here, and then . . ."

Benjamin Grinde willingly allowed himself to be led past the conference table and out to the center of the floor. Billy T. released his shoulder warily and nodded forward. It was no use. The Supreme Court judge remained standing there, puzzled, and his complexion had turned even paler.

"You greeted her, I suppose," Billy T. suggested, aware that he was doing far more prompting than they had been taught to do at police college. "Did you give her a hug? Shake hands?"

Benjamin Grinde did not respond; he simply stared at the desk facing him, now clean and tidy, with no trace of the tragedy that had taken place last Friday evening.

"Did you shake hands, Grinde?"

The man flinched: it seemed to have suddenly dawned on him where he was and what was expected of him.

"We shook hands with a little hug. That was what she wanted. The hug, I mean. Personally, I found it a bit unnatural. I hadn't seen her for such a long time, many years."

His voice was low, intense, and totally flat.

"And then?"

Billy T. rotated his hand in the hope of encouraging Grinde to continue.

"Then I sat down. Here."

Sitting down on a chair, he placed the burgundy folder on the desk in front of him.

"Did you put that there?"

"What? Oh, yes. My folder. No."

He picked it up and set it down beside him, against the chair leg.

"I sat like this."

"For three-quarters of an hour," Billy T. said. "And you talked about . . ."

"Not necessary to bring that up here, Billy T.," the Head of CID interjected, clearing his throat. "This isn't an interview. Supreme Court Judge Grinde has already provided a statement. This is a reconstruction."

A servile smile was directed at Benjamin Grinde, but the judge's thoughts lay entirely elsewhere.

"Okay," Billy T. said, making no attempt to hide his irritation. "And then? When you had finished talking?"

"I stood up. I left. Nothing else happened."

He looked up at Billy T. His eyes were darker than before, the brown of the iris merging into the black pupils. The whites of his eyes were bloodshot, and his mouth was more pinched than ever.

"There's nothing more to tell. Sorry."

Momentarily, it appeared that Billy T. did not quite know what to do. Instead of continuing with the reconstruction, he crossed over to the window. In the daylight, the city seemed more sprawling and gray than it had the last time he'd stood here, when all the twinkling lights had made Oslo almost beautiful. Although the buildings directly opposite were new, a newspaper office adjacent to R5, there was something shabby about the view, something eternally incomplete. The construction projects on the corner beside the Hansen & Dysvik department store reinforced the impression that Oslo was a patchwork of old and new and would never in a million years reach the point of emerging as a fully finished project.

Abruptly, he wheeled around to face the room.

"What did she say as you left?"

Benjamin Grinde, still seated, stared straight ahead and answered, "She said, 'Have a good weekend.'"

"'Have a good weekend'? Nothing more, nothing less?"

"No. She wished me a good weekend, and I went out."

Then he got to his feet, tucking the folder underneath his arm, and walked toward the door.

"Can Judge Grinde be dismissed now?"

This was the Head of CID, and it was intended as more of an order than a question to Billy T.

"Fine," Billy T. mumbled.

But it certainly was not. This was not right. Benjamin Grinde was not telling the truth. The man was the worst liar Billy T. had ever encountered. His lies came with flashing blue lights and sirens:

obvious and conspicuous, though it was still impossible to interpret them.

"Get the security guard," he requested of a uniformed police officer as he followed Benjamin Grinde.

Halfway down the stairs, he again put his hand on the judge's shoulder. Grinde halted suddenly and stiffened, but did not turn around. Billy T. passed him, and stood two steps below him; when he turned to face him, their eyes were level.

"I think you're lying, Grinde," he said softly.

When the judge lowered his gaze, Billy T. surprised both of them by placing his hand under the man's chin, not roughly, not even in an unfriendly manner, but almost the way he did with his sons when they would not look him in the eye. It was extremely disrespectful, but for some reason, Benjamin Grinde accepted the indignity. Billy T. knew why. He lifted the judge's head and held his grip while he spoke.

"I don't believe you've told me the truth. And do you know what? I've no idea why. I'm fairly sure that you didn't kill Birgitte Volter. Don't ask me why, but I am. But you're hiding something. Something that was said, probably. Something that could help shed some light on this homicide."

Grinde had pulled himself together. With an abrupt motion, he jerked his chin out of Billy T.'s grasp and took a step back. Now he was looking down at the Chief Inspector.

"I've said all I'm going to say on this matter."

"So you admit there are things you have left *un*said?"

Billy T. did not relinquish eye contact.

"I've said all I'm going to say. Now I want to go."

He stepped past the tall police officer, and rounded the corner at the foot of the stairs without so much as a backward glance.

"Fuck," Billy T. whispered to himself. "Bloody hell."

"Now you really must get your act together, boy!"

The guard was not someone whose chin Billy T. felt inclined to hold in a friendly attempt to get some cooperation. Instead, he was the type you really wanted to put across your knee and spank: grouchy, surly, and apparently dreadfully nervous.

"Did you touch this door handle or did you not?"

Billy T. and the security guard were standing inside the small restroom between the Prime Minister's office and the conference room.

"I've told you a *thousand* times now," the guard replied angrily. "I did *not* touch that door."

"But how then can you explain why your fingerprints were found both here . . ."

Billy T. waved his forefinger in a circular motion around the doorframe.

". . . and here! On the handle!"

"I've been here about a hundred times before, of course," the guard answered, rolling his eyes. "Do you have time codes for these fingerprints, then?"

Billy T. closed his eyes and started to count. At ten, he opened them again.

"What is it with you, actually? Don't you appreciate the *seriousness* of this case, or what?"

He banged his clenched fist on the wall.

"Eh? Don't you understand anything, or what?"

"I understand that you believe I killed that Volter woman, and *I certainly did not!*"

His voice rose to a falsetto, and his bottom lip began to tremble. Billy T. stood staring at the man, without speaking a word, for a considerable time. Then he did it all the same. Placed his hand under the guard's chin and forced him to make eye contact. The guard tried to wriggle free, but the grip was too firm.

"You don't know what's in your own best interests," Billy T. said softly. "You don't understand that we two can help each other. If you can just tell me what happened that night, then both you and I will feel the better for it afterward. And one more thing: if you did kill Volter, then I'll find out. I can promise you quite sincerely: I am going to find out. But I don't think you did do it. Not at the moment. But you have to help me. *Do you understand that?*"

His grip around the man's face was so strong that red marks were forming on Billy T.'s fingers. The Head of CID muttered a warning behind his back.

But Billy T. did not hear. He stared into the security guard's brown eyes, which were encircled by unusually long lashes. The hairs on the back of Billy T.'s neck stood up when he recognized the gleam in the guard's eyes: pure anguish.

An unfathomable fear.

"I'm not the one you're bloody frightened of," Billy T. whispered, too quietly for anyone other than the guard himself to hear. "If you had your wits about you, you would have told me what's terrifying you. Because there is something. Just wait. I'll find out."

Then he released the guard's face with a brusque, angry gesture.

"You can go," he said irascibly.

"At least that woman isn't telling lies," Billy T. mumbled, mostly to himself.

Wenche Andersen had—with a lump in her throat the entire time— explained right down to the tiniest detail everything that she had done from the time she had last seen Birgitte Volter alive, up until she found the Prime Minister dead in her office. She had gone to the restroom three times, she related, and, crimson with embarrassment, she had clarified that once it had been a number two, and twice a number one. Tone-Marit smiled disarmingly as she emphasized that it was not necessary to go into so much detail.

"And then I phoned the police."

Now that she was finished, Wenche Andersen exhaled.

"Excellent," Tone-Marit praised her. The solid, nursery-school-teacher account was clearer than any other she had heard, and Billy T. closed his eyes and rubbed his face.

With a faint smile, Wenche Andersen thanked her for the compliment. Then she suddenly flushed bright red. Tone-Marit could literally see the agitation suffuse the woman: the carotid artery in her throat swelled and throbbed repeatedly.

"I've forgotten something," Wenche Andersen said. "I've forgotten something *yet again!*"

She immediately rushed into the Prime Minister's office and, uncharacteristically, did not even ask for permission.

"The box," she whispered, whirling around to face Billy T., who had followed her in. "The pillbox. Have you removed it?"

"Pillbox?"

Billy T. looked quizzically over at the officer in uniform, who produced a list of items that had been removed for closer examination.

"Nothing about that in here," the officer said, shaking his head.

"What kind of pillbox?" Billy T. inquired, tilting his head to one side as he placed the flat of his hand against his ear: it was aching terribly.

"An exquisite little ornament in enameled silver," Wenche Andersen explained.

She drew a tiny square shape in the air.

"Enameled and gilded—that's if it wasn't actually made of gold. It looked extremely old and always sat here on the table."

She pointed.

"I—"

Now she looked completely bewildered, but her bewilderment was mixed with something resembling shame, and she hesitated.

"I may as well just own up to it," she said at last, looking at the floor. "I once tried to . . ."

Again she put her head in her hands, and her voice became distorted, as though she were speaking with a damper depressed.

"I tried to open it. But the screw threads were sticky, and before I'd managed to unscrew it, the Prime Minister came into the room, and . . ."

Now she showed her face again; tears fell and she hiccuped as she tried to catch her breath.

"It's so awfully embarrassing," she whispered. "I had no business doing anything like that, and she simply—she simply took it from me and never mentioned it again."

Billy T. smiled warmly at the woman in the russet suit.

"You've done a brilliant job today," he comforted her. "Curiosity can get the better of all of us on occasion. You're free to leave now."

However, he continued to stand there in the Prime Minister's office after all the others had left.

"A pillbox," he said to himself at last. "Were there pills in it, I wonder?"

5:10 P.M., OLE BRUMMS VEI 212

"I'll be terribly discreet," Hanne Wilhelmsen said. "I'll blend in with the wallpaper."

"*You* blend in with the wallpaper? Impossible."

Billy T. was still unconvinced that it had been right to bring Hanne Wilhelmsen to Roy Hansen's house.

"Don't say a word," he muttered as they trudged up to the front door of the yellow-painted town house. "And under no circumstances say anything to anyone at work."

When they reached the door, Hanne thought she spied something. Something out of the corner of her eye: she wheeled around to face the waist-high hedge running down either side of the narrow front garden. There was nothing. Shaking her head, Hanne followed Billy T., who had already rung the doorbell.

No answer.

Billy T. pressed the bell again, but no one came to open the door this time either. Hanne descended the stairs to peer at the upper story.

"There's someone at home," she said softly. "The curtain twitched."

Billy T. hesitated for a moment before placing his finger on the button yet again.

"Yes?"

The man who stood facing them, who had just opened the door with an angry jerk, had toothpaste at the corners of his mouth and a three-day beard. His small eyes were blinking, as though he had just got out of bed. He had egg stains on his shirtfront: old, dark yellow yolk. Hanne hated eggs and had to turn away for a second. Breathing deeply through her nose, she smiled at a little apple tree immediately below the steps.

"Roy Hansen?" Billy T. asked, receiving a curt nod in response.

"Police," Billy T. announced, showing his ID card with his left hand while extending his right to shake hands in greeting. "Very sorry to disturb you. Can we come in?"

The man took a step toward them and looked sharply in both directions.

"Fine," he muttered. "The doorbell has rung four times today. Journalists."

Roy Hansen led them through a small hallway into a dimly lit living room where dust danced in the streak of light between the closed curtains. Collapsing onto the sofa with a faint groan, he gestured to the two police officers to sit down.

The air was stuffy and clammy, with a faint, cloyingly sweet scent of flowers and decomposing citrus fruits. Hanne stared at an enormous fruit bowl whose oranges had acquired greenish-gray spots of mold. Beside the bowl, on a pine sideboard along the gable wall, sat piles of unopened mail. In one corner of the living room was a mountain of floral bouquets that had not been touched either: forty or fifty huge parcels, most of them wrapped in gray paper, a few in blue cellophane wrappers. The pictures on the walls, popular but tasteful graphics, seemed dull and colorless, as though they had given up trying to bring pleasure to the occupants of this house, which was now on the brink of no longer being a home.

"Shall I help you with the flowers?" Hanne Wilhelmsen asked, without sitting down. "They shouldn't really just sit there."

Roy Hansen did not reply. He looked at the flower-filled corner, but the bouquets did not seem to concern him at all.

"At least we should cut out the cards," Hanne suggested. "So that you can thank them, I mean. Later. When you're feeling up to doing that."

Roy Hansen shook his head dejectedly and waved his arm toward the flowers.

"It doesn't matter. The garbage truck comes tomorrow."

Hanne sat down.

At one time, the living room had obviously been cozy. If the light had been allowed to flood in, the furnishings would have looked bright and cheerful, and the green potted plants alongside the large panorama window would have been impressive. Though the walls now appeared grayish white, they were actually pale yellow, and with illumination and fresh air in the room, they would have complemented the light pine flooring. Only four days ago, this room had been at the heart of a healthy, pleasant Norwegian home. Hanne shuddered at the thought of what death could do: it wasn't only the widower in front of her who seemed lost, but the actual house as well.

"I am so sorry about this," Billy T. said, and for once he sat completely still, with his legs stretched out politely in front of him. "You've been told that we would leave you in peace until after the funeral. However, something's come up that needs an immediate answer. As a matter of fact, before I mention what I've come for—"

A young man in his early twenties came down from upstairs, wearing a jogging suit and black sneakers. He was of medium height and fair, and his face was strikingly ordinary, almost anonymous.

"Going out for a run," he said quietly, heading for the hall door without even a glance in the direction of the two police officers.

"Per! Wait!"

Roy Hansen opened his arms wide, as though to detain his son.

"You know they'll try and talk to you," he said, looking helplessly at Billy T. "They stop us every time we go out!"

Irritated, Billy T. got to his feet.

"Damn journalists," he mumbled, crossing to the porch door. "Can't you go out this way? And then just jump over the hedge into the neighbor's garden?"

He opened the door and stared out.

"There," he said, pointing. "Over that fence there?"

Per Volter hesitated briefly; then, with a decisive air, and his eyes on the ground, he crossed the living room and made his exit through the porch door. Billy T. followed him.

"Billy T.," he said, offering his hand. "I'm from the police."

"I knew that," the young man said, without taking his hand.

"Condolences," Billy T. said. It was obvious he found the unfamiliar word difficult, but he could not think of anything better. "Dreadfully sorry."

The young man did not answer, but started jogging on the spot instead, as though he actually wanted to leave but was too well brought up to be more impolite than he already had been.

"Just one thing before you go," Billy T. continued. "While you're here. Is it true that you're a member of a gun club?"

"Marksmanship club," Per Volter said. "I'm the vice chairman of the Groruddalen Marksmanship Association."

For the first time, something approaching a smile crossed the young man's face.

"Do you know everyone there?"

"Virtually. At least all the ones who are fairly active."

"And you compete?"

"Yes. Though at the moment it's mostly military championships. I'm at military college."

Billy T. nodded before pulling out a photograph. A Polaroid picture, taken without authorization, and without the security guard from the government complex having had the chance to protest.

"Do you know this guy here?"

He held out the picture to Per Volter, who stopped running on the spot and examined the photograph for several seconds.

"No," he said hesitantly. "I don't think so."

"You're not sure?"

Per stared at the photo for a while longer. Then he shook his head vigorously, handed back the picture, and looked Billy T. directly in the eye.

"Quite sure. I've never seen that guy before."

Nodding briefly, he sprinted out into the garden and across to the five-and-a-half-foot-high fence, which he vaulted with an elegant hop before disappearing into the shrubbery on the other side.

Billy T. frowned as he watched him go, then returned to Hanne Wilhelmsen and Roy Hansen.

"Have you found the pass?" he asked as he sat down.

"No. Sorry. It can't be here."

Billy T. and Hanne exchanged a brief glance, and Billy T. could not manage to sit still any longer. He leaned forward, though the armchair was so low that his posture was painful, and he was almost squatting.

"Do you know whether Birgitte had a pillbox in silver or gold?"

"Enameled," Hanne added. "A little enameled box about this size." She crossed her thumbs and forefingers.

Roy Hansen looked from one to the other.

"A pillbox? What's that?"

"A tiny container," Hanne explained. "Probably very old. An heir-loom, perhaps?"

Cocking his head, Roy Hansen scratched his cheek, and the other two could hear a faint rasping sound. Then he stood up unexpectedly to fetch an album from a well-filled bookcase. When he sat down again, he leafed through it.

"Here," he said abruptly. "Could this be it?"

He bent over the coffee table and placed the photo album between himself and Hanne Wilhelmsen, pointing to one of the black-and-white photographs. An enlargement, it had obviously been taken by a professional photographer with large-format film: even the tiniest details were clear. A very young and extremely happy Birgitte Volter was standing in a bridal gown and veil beside a beaming Roy Hansen, who sported a fine head of hair and black horn-rimmed glasses. The bridal couple were standing beside a table laden with presents that included two irons, a large glass bowl, silverware, two tablecloths, a cream and sugar set made of something that might have been crystal, and a great many other objects difficult to distinguish. And right there, at the very front of the picture, a tiny box.

"It's almost invisible," Roy Hansen apologized. "And to be quite honest, I had forgotten about it. I haven't seen it for many, many years. I can't even remember who gave it to us."

"Do you recall the color?"

Roy Hansen shook his head.

"And not where it came from? Absolutely sure?"

The man continued to shake his head. His gaze was far away, as though trying to retrieve memories of the wedding from a forgotten, dusty corner of his brain. His eyes were fixed on the photograph, that happy photograph, and a tear lay trembling in the corner of his left eye.

"Well," Billy T. said, "we won't disturb you any longer."

The doorbell rang. Roy Hansen was clearly startled. The tear ran down his cheek and rushed toward the corner of his mouth; he wiped it away quickly with the back of his hand.

"Shall I answer it?" Hanne asked.

Roy Hansen rose slowly and laboriously, rubbing his hands several times over his face.

"No, thanks," he whispered. "I'm expecting my mother. It might be her."

It was as though the dust, the dim light, and the oppressive air had affected the acoustics. The flagging tick-tock from the old mantel clock made it sound as if the inner workings were wrapped in cotton wool; the entire room seemed padded. Everything was so soft and muffled that the voices from the hallway cut through sharply, like dissonant knives.

"Who are you?" the two police officers heard Roy Hansen say, almost yelling, like a cry for help.

Hanne Wilhelmsen and Billy T. promptly jumped up and rushed out to the hallway. Over Roy Hansen's stooped shoulders, Billy T. could see a tall man in his early forties with an untidy shock of hair. He was thrusting a gigantic, unwrapped bouquet of flowers at Birgitte Volter's widower, and the latter had moved a few paces back in confusion. Taking advantage of the opportunity, the man with the flowers was now almost inside the door. Billy T. pushed past Roy Hansen and placed a huge fist on the interloper's chest.

"Who are you?" he asked.

"Who am I? I'm from *Kikk og Lytt* magazine—we just want to offer our condolences, and maybe have a little chat?"

Billy T. wheeled around to look at Roy Hansen. The man had looked dreadful when they arrived and had wept in their presence. Billy T. had hated bothering him, but it had been so important to clear up the question of the pillbox that he hadn't seen any other option. Now Roy Hansen was ashen, and his forehead had broken out in a sweat.

"What the hell do you think you're doing, turning up like this!" Billy T. thundered. "Don't you understand *anything!*"

Hanne Wilhelmsen dragged Roy Hansen back with her into the living room and closed the door.

"Get out," Billy T. snarled. "Get out of here, for God's sake, and away from this whole area *right now!*"

"Heavens, what a ruckus. We were just trying to be nice!"

"*Nice*," Billy T. said, shoving the other man's chest so fiercely that he staggered and dropped the flowers. "Get out of here, I said!"

"Take it easy! I'm going. I'm on my way!"

The man bent down to retrieve the bouquet first, before taking a step back.

"Could you see that these are put in water?"

Billy T. did not strike him. Billy T. had destroyed many odds and ends in bouts of rage: wastepaper baskets and lampshades, windowpanes and car mirrors. However, Billy T. had not laid a hand on a single person since the time when, as a young boy, he had fought with his sister. He did not hit this man either, though a powerful swinging blow was only a hairbreadth away. But with his fists raised in the man's face, he continued to boom: "If I *ever* see you anywhere near here. If I as much as get *wind* of you or anyone else from that scandalous rag of yours, then . . ."

Closing his eyes, he counted to three.

"Get going. Now."

As he was about to slam the front door shut, the bouquet of flowers was thrust through the opening.

"Can you make sure that they get these flowers?" he heard the journalist say.

Billy T. used the door to whack the arm holding the bouquet. The man outside let go of the flowers, howling, "Goddamn it! Do you want to *kill* me?"

Billy T. opened the door for a second, and the arm was swiftly pulled away. He then slammed the door furiously, taking rapid deep breaths in an effort to regain his self-control.

"You can't stay here," he said to Roy Hansen when his head finally felt clear enough for him to reenter the living room. "Do they carry on like this all the time?"

"No, not all the time. Today's been the worst. It's as though—it's as though they expect me to have finished grieving now. As though three days was all I was granted, in a sense."

Leaning forward over his own knees, he burst into heartbreaking sobs.

Hanne Wilhelmsen wanted to leave. She felt an uncontrollable urge to go outside, away from this clammy, stuffy place and its two grieving occupants who could not talk to each other. Roy Hansen needed help, but neither she nor Billy T. could give him that.

"Can I call someone?" she said softly.

"No. My mother's coming soon."

The two police officers exchanged looks and decided to leave Roy Hansen to the despair it was impossible for them to share. However, they sat in their vehicle outside the house at Ole Brumms vei 212 for three-quarters of an hour, until an old woman made it safely to the front door with the help of a cabdriver. Without any journalists getting hold of her.

They had obviously been scared off by the blue light sweeping its warning from the roof of the patrol car all the way along the street.

On their way out, Billy T. had stuffed the beautiful bouquet from *Kikk og Lytt* into the garbage. It must have cost almost a thousand kroner.

6:30 P.M., BOMBAY PLAZA RESTAURANT

They sat at the far end of the Indian restaurant, munching papadum while they waited for the tandoori chicken. The thin, crisp crackers were spicy, bringing a touch of color to Øyvind Olve's face. He had hardly slept since Friday morning and felt his three gulps of beer go straight to his head.

"Lovely to see you," he said, raising his glass to Hanne Wilhelmsen. "When's Cecilie coming?"

Hanne Wilhelmsen was not sure whether to be insulted that everyone who knew both her and her partner inquired when Cecilie was coming home before they even asked about anything else. She decided not to let herself be riled.

"Not until Christmas. I'm going back to the States myself. In a while. This is just a kind of vacation, you might say."

At almost forty, the man facing her resembled a cuddly teddy bear. Not because he was particularly large, stout, or burly, but his flapping ears protruded cheerfully from a head that was round as a dishpan and crowned with a coal-black crew cut, and the eyes behind his small, circular glasses were warm and reassuring, as though they had never seen anything of the misery in the world. Which was an illusion, since he was an extremely experienced politician.

Until last Friday, he had been Birgitte Volter's Chief of Staff. State Secretary in the Prime Minister's office and a close friend of Cecilie Vibe. He came from Kvinnherad, where he had grown up on the farm beside Cecilie's parents' summer cottage. Cecilie's relationship with her past was less complicated than Hanne's, and she had included Øyvind and his sister, Agnes, the summer friends of her childhood, in her adult life. Hanne Wilhelmsen had cut all links with her own childhood. There was a distinct dividing line in her life marked by the day on which she and Cecilie had moved in together a very, very long time ago. To compensate for the loss of her own friends, she shared Cecilie's.

"What are you going to do now?"

He did not answer immediately but remained seated, staring at his beer glass as he spun it around repeatedly on its own axis. Then he stroked his head lightly and smiled.

"Only the gods know. Back to the party office, I expect. But first— first of all, I'll take a vacation."

"A well-earned one! How's it actually been going, the past six months?"

Before he had managed to reply, she beamed. "Go and see Cecilie, then! California's fabulous at this time of year! We've plenty of room, and it's only five minutes to the beach."

"I'll think about it. Thanks. But it might not be convenient—for Cecilie, I mean."

"Of course it'll be convenient! Honestly, she'll be so delighted. Everyone says they're going to come and visit us, but nobody does."

He smiled but dropped the subject.

"This has been the most turbulent six months of my life. Everything that could possibly go wrong has done so. But . . ."

He ran his hands through his hair once again, a bashful gesture he had been making for as long as they had known each other.

". . . it's really been thrilling as well. It builds solidarity. Believe it or not, all the negative criticism did not crush her. Birgitte, that is. She managed to hold us together. Us against them, in a sense. The responsible ones versus the lightweights."

A tall, dark man arrived with the food. The fiery red chicken in front of them steamed and gave off an enticing aroma, and Hanne Wilhelmsen realized that she had not eaten since breakfast. She grabbed a chunk of naan bread and talked with her mouth full.

"What was Birgitte Volter like? In real life, I mean. You've worked closely with her for many years, of course, isn't that right?"

"Mmm."

"What was she like?"

Øyvind Olve was a steady man from western Norway. He came from a working-class background and had progressed through the party ranks as a result of honest hard work and having the wit to keep his mouth shut when he should. Now he had no idea what to say. It was true that Hanne Wilhelmsen was a good friend, but she was also a police officer. He had already been interviewed twice, once by an enormous giant who, in other clothes, could have stepped out of a 1930s poster from Nazi Germany.

As he hesitated, Øyvind Olve could feel his head spinning from the alcohol.

"She was one of the most exciting people I have known," he said eventually. "She was considerate and capable; she had dreams and vision. The most remarkable thing was perhaps a quite extreme sense of accountability. She never let anything lie. She always took responsibility. And she was also very kind."

"Kind?" Hanne laughed. "Is there such a thing as a kind politician? What do you mean by *kind*?"

Øyvind Olve looked reflective for a moment before waving to the waiter to order another draft of beer. He looked quizzically at Hanne, but she waved her hand in a negative response.

"Birgitte wanted to do good. She was genuinely engaged by the idea that politics is concerned with creating a better society for as many people as possible. Not simply in her speeches. Not only on paper. She was really interested in people. For instance, she insisted on reading every single letter that came in, from anyone, anywhere in Norway, who wanted to bring their problems to her attention. And there were quite a lot of them, I can tell you. Not that we could do very much. But she read every single one of them, and some of the circumstances she read about made a real impression on her. On a couple of occasions she did intervene. To the great irritation of the bureaucrats. Boundless irritation."

"Was she unpopular with them? The bureaucrats, I mean."

Øyvind Olve stared at her for some time before resuming his meal.

"Do you know, it's almost impossible to say. I've never come across anyone as apparently loyal as the civil servants in the Prime Minister's office. It's quite honestly impossible to say whether they liked her. And maybe not of such great interest either."

He rubbed his eyes with his fingers bent at the knuckles, like a tired child.

"What about her personal life?" Hanne asked.

The question caught him off guard, and, removing his fingers from his face, he gazed at her with an almost shocked expression.

"Personal? I can't say I knew her personally."

"You didn't know her? But you've worked closely with the woman for years!"

"Worked, yes. That's not the same as knowing somebody personally. You ought to know that."

Smiling, he noticed that Hanne blushed slightly. She had worked at the Oslo Police Station for thirteen years, but only two of her colleagues had ever set foot in the apartment she shared with Cecilie Vibe.

"But you have social events and that kind of thing," Hanne insisted. "In the party, I mean. And you've traveled all around the world with her, of course, haven't you?"

"Not much. But what is it you actually want to know?"

Hanne Wilhelmsen put down her knife and fork and wiped her mouth with a large white linen napkin.

"Let me begin with something else," she said softly. "Was it Birgitte Volter who chose Ruth-Dorthe Nordgarden as Health Minister?"

Now it was Øyvind Olve whose cheeks were red. He fumbled with a piece of naan bread as he dipped it in the sauce, and red stains dripped on to his shirt.

"I wouldn't have told you this if it weren't for the fact that she's dead now," he muttered, trying to clean off the stain; it only increased in size from all his scrubbing with a dry napkin. "Perhaps it's difficult to understand."

"Try me." Hanne smiled.

"Putting together a government is a tremendously complicated jig-saw," Øyvind Olve began. "Naturally it's not up to the Prime Minister alone to choose cabinet members. A whole lot of different consider-ations have to be weighed. Geography, gender—"

He attempted to swallow a belch.

"The trade unions want to have their say. Central figures in the party. The Party Secretary. And so on and so forth."

He belched now, touching his chest.

"Heartburn," he mumbled apologetically.

"But what about Ruth-Dorthe Nordgarden?" Hanne asked again. She had pushed her plate aside and leaned her elbows on the table. "Who chose her?"

Øyvind Olve fished out an antacid from his pocket and took it.

"You shouldn't eat Indian food if you have stomach problems," Hanne advised. "What about Nordgarden?"

"It wasn't Birgitte who wanted her, in any case. Ruth-Dorthe was brought in over her head."

"By whom?"

He gave her a lingering look, and then shook his head.

"Honestly, Hanne. You're not even a party member."

"But I voted for you!" She grinned. "Every time!"

She understood all the same that she would obtain nothing more. Not about that. But perhaps about what interested her most.

"Did Ruth-Dorthe Nordgarden have an affair with Roy Hansen?" she ventured, so directly that Øyvind Olve belched violently again, and as a little streak of the antacid ran from the corner of his mouth, he picked up the ill-treated napkin once more.

"You of all people should be above listening to rumors, Hanne," he said quietly.

"Does that mean you've heard this before?"

Øyvind Olve rolled his eyes.

"If I were to tell you everything I've heard about who is sleeping with whom in Norwegian political circles, then we'd have to stay here for the rest of the week," he said, smiling faintly.

"No smoke without fire," Hanne replied.

"I'll tell you one thing, Hanne," Øyvind said, leaning toward her, his voice intense. "I've seen rooms thick with smoke but without so much as a tiny flame anywhere. I learned that long ago. You should also know that. How many men's names were linked with yours until people began to guess the truth? And how many women do you think you've been involved with according to the rumor mill?"

This was no longer pleasant. The remains of the tandoori smelled strong and pungent, and the beer had gone flat. The restaurant felt overheated, and she tugged at the neck of her sweater. Hanne Wilhelmsen had lived in faithful monogamy with Cecilie for almost nineteen years and was aware that at the Oslo Police Station, her name was mentioned in connection with the most unlikely sexual alliances. She glanced at the time.

"One thing, though," she said. "Did they know each other? Birgitte Volter and Ruth-Dorthe Nordgarden?"

"No," Øyvind Olve said, gesturing for the bill. "Not in the sense you would define knowing each other. Not outside politics. They were both party members."

"And you don't know anything about whether Ruth-Dorthe— What kind of name is that, by the way?"

With a smile, she continued. "Whether she knew Roy Hansen at all?"

"Not as far as I know."

Øyvind Olve shook his head.

"So if I tell you that I . . ."

The waiter appeared with the bill, and after a moment's hesitation placed it in front of Hanne, even though Øyvind had asked for it.

"There. You see what kind of authority you radiate." Øyvind grinned.

"If I tell you that I saw this Ruth-Dorthe woman and Roy Hansen sitting together, drinking beer in Café 33 about six months ago, would you be surprised?"

He looked at her with a furrow between his teddy bear eyes.

"Yes," he said, cocking his head. "It surprises me greatly. Are you quite sure that was who it was?"

"Quite sure," Hanne Wilhelmsen said, pushing the bill across to the other side of the table. "I'm not working at the moment!"

"That possibly applies to me too," Øyvind Olve muttered, but he picked up the bill all the same.

11:10 P.M., VIDARS GATE 11C

"Y ou have to help me," whispered the security guard. "Damn it,
    Brage, I need help!"

Brage Håkonsen, dressed in a brilliant white T-shirt and camouflage boxer shorts, could not believe his eyes. The guard from the government complex was standing outside his front door, looking
completely demented. His hair was sticking out in all directions, tan-
gled and uncombed, and his eyes were popping as if he had seen a
real-life vampire only a couple of minutes ago. He was wearing baggy
clothes and his shoulders had disappeared entirely underneath his
overlarge military jacket.

"Are you off your head?" Brage hissed. "Coming here! Now! Get
away with you, and *don't show your face here again!*"

"But, Brage," the guard grumbled. "Damn it all, I need *help*! I've—"

"I don't give a fuck what you've done!"

"But, Brage," the guard bleated again. "Listen to me at least! Let me
come in and talk to you!"

Brage Håkonsen placed a massive fist on the guard's chest. He was
a good head taller and towered over him.

"For the last time, get away from here."

Someone down below opened a door. Startled, Brage Håkonsen
gave the guard a forceful push across the landing, then slammed his
door; the guard could hear him making a racket with the security
chain.

A young man came up the stairs, and the guard pulled his jacket
lapels up under his ears, staring at the wall as the man walked past.
Then he stood listening to his footsteps all the way up to the fourth
floor.

What was he to do? His eyes filled with tears as his mouth trembled. He felt awful and had to sit down on the steps to avoid falling
over.

"I need to go away," he said to himself. "I fucking need to get away."

Finally he stood up and stumbled aimlessly out into the Oslo night.

WEDNESDAY, APRIL 9

The gun lay inside a padded envelope, addressed only to "Oslo Police Station" in thick black felt-tip pen. The consignment was not sent through the mail. The officer who stood at the door of Assistant Police Chief Håkon Sand's office was panting breathlessly.

"It was in a mail sack at the central post office," he gasped. "The mail sorters realized it might be important and have just delivered it."

Håkon Sand wore latex gloves. The envelope had already been opened, in itself a gross error of judgment: it could have been a bomb, of course. However, it was not an explosive device. Håkon Sand fished out the revolver and with extreme care placed it on a white sheet of paper in front of him.

"A Nagant," Billy T. whispered. "A Russian Model 1895."

"Not you too." Håkon sighed. "Do you and Hanne hold Saturday night quizzes, or what?"

"Guess," Billy T. said softly. "About guns and motorbikes. She knows all there is to know about both."

"Don't touch," Håkon Sand warned as Billy T. leaned toward the revolver.

"I'm not stupid, you know," Billy T. muttered, studying the gun from a distance of several inches. "Besides, it doesn't really matter anyway. I'll bet this gun has been clinically cleaned of any possible traces that might lead us to anything at all. It's been scrubbed and polished and looks good as new."

"You're probably right about that." Håkon sighed again. "But don't touch, regardless. Not the envelope either. It's all going to Forensics."

"But wait a minute!"

Billy T. suddenly brightened.

"If this was lying in one of the sacks at the central post office—what about videotape? Isn't that whole damn place crawling with cameras?"

"I've already thought of that," Håkon lied. "You!"

He was pointing at the officer who was still standing in the doorway, craning his neck.

"Instruct someone to go through the CCTV tapes for the last twenty-four hours. No, as a matter of fact, make it the past forty-eight hours."

"And then we'll find an insignificant, uncouth guy in a baseball cap who at least had the wit to turn away," Billy T. mumbled.

"Do you have a better suggestion, then?" Håkon said, slightly too loudly.

Billy T. only shrugged his shoulders as he headed back to his own office.

12:03 P.M., JENS BJELKES GATE 13

Of course, it had been crazy to say he was sick. Talk about stupidity. However, his boss had at least regarded him with concern and confirmed that he looked dreadful. About as dreadful as he felt, he assumed.

He had to get away. Preferably flee the country. But that would seem suspicious; he appreciated that. He could travel to Tromsø. He could go skiing. It would do him good. Morten was his best friend and had said many times that he should come. There was so much fucking snow up there this winter.

Packing a capacious rucksack, he made his way to Fornebu Airport without having bought a ticket. It was impossible for flights to be full on a Wednesday in April. Not in the middle of the day, anyway.

THURSDAY, APRIL 10

LATE MORNING, GOVERNMENT COMPLEX

"All predictions now center on the new government being similar to the old one, with the single change that Joachim Hellseth, currently spokesman for fiscal policy in Parliament, will be brought in as Finance Minister. Any further replacements in the government lineup would come as a great surprise."

The Minister of Agriculture switched off the radio and leaned back in his office chair. The reporter was probably correct. That was certainly the impression he'd gotten from Tryggve yesterday. He had smiled, although the smile had not appeared particularly sincere, and clapped him on the shoulder.

Not that it was so terribly important. Naturally he wanted to continue. He was enjoying it. The Ministry of Agriculture was an exciting place to be: he was doing a challenging and important job and would like to continue in the role. However, if it was not to be, then it was not to be. There were plenty of other jobs out there.

The phone rang.

For a moment he sat looking at it, smiling broadly; he felt calm and well, knowing that he would be fine regardless of what the message was. Then he lifted the receiver.

"Tryggve Storstein," the secretary intoned.

"Put him on," the Minister of Agriculture responded; then, after a short pause, "Hello, Tryggve. How's it going?"

"Better. Now at least I'm managing to get some sleep. Six hours last night. I feel like a new and better person."

Chuckling, the Minister of Agriculture took out his snuffbox.

"Churchill always managed with four. And he had a more peaceful time than you're having, didn't he?"

He thought he could hear the smile at the other end of the line.

"Well," Tryggve Storstein said. "You'll stay on in the team, won't you?"

The Minister of Agriculture felt the hand holding the receiver begin to shake. Had this been more important to him than he would admit? Swallowing, he coughed briefly.

"Of course. If you want me to."

"I do. The party does."

"I'm really pleased about that, Tryggve. Thank you very much."

His voice sounded genuinely happy.

The Culture Minister was leafing through four faxes that had just arrived on her desk. Lighting up a Prince Mild, she noticed with annoyance that she had smoked more than she usually permitted herself prior to lunchtime.

They were offers of employment, from two TV stations and one newspaper. And one from a large multinational company that required someone to deal with external communications. She let her gaze run over the sheets of paper without reading them thoroughly, then folded them and stuffed them into a drawer marked "Personal" in Dymo lettering.

The phone rang.

She took the call and the conversation that ensued lasted all of forty-five seconds.

When she replaced the receiver, she was smiling from ear to ear. She phoned through to her secretary, after having retrieved the faxes she had just filed away.

"Shred these, please," she said, handing the papers to her secretary.

The older woman sighed in relief.

"Congratulations," she whispered, winking with her right eye. "I'm so pleased!"

Health Minister Ruth-Dorthe Nordgarden could not get anything done. Every time the phone rang, she hurled herself at it, and every time she came away disappointed. Now she was no longer crestfallen. She was furious.

For a while she had considered phoning some of the others to discover whether they had heard anything. But it would be the greatest humiliation of all to have confirmed what she was finally beginning to suspect: that the others were to continue but she was not.

In a rage, she took hold of her large handbag and rummaged through its contents. She eventually found what she was looking for: a carrot wrapped in greaseproof paper.

A painful crunch seared through her head as she chomped on it.

1:46 P.M., SECURITY SERVICE SECTION, OSLO POLICE STATION

"This can't possibly be sheer chance. It's totally impossible."

The police officer who had burst into the Security Service Chief's office without knocking was agitated and out of breath as he slapped his right hand down on the papers he placed before Ole Henrik Hermansen.

"The Swedish Security Police are of the opinion that it was sabotage. A fuel pipe was damaged in a way they can't put down to either wear and tear or an operational fault. The entire plane was thoroughly examined only a few hours before departure, and they found nothing then."

Ole Henrik Hermansen had lost his inscrutable poker face. Now his expression was tense and alert; his brow wrinkled, and his eyes flashed with intense anxiety.

"Is this confirmed? Or to be more precise, how certain are they?"

"Naturally they don't know yet. They're making further investigations. But that's not all, Hermansen. There's much more!"

Producing a red folder from his own briefcase, the police officer flicked through to a large, grainy, color photograph of a young man with blond hair combed back; he was staring to one side of the camera lens, wore rimless glasses, and had a cigarette in the corner of his mouth.

"Tage Sjögren," the officer said. "Thirty-two years old, from Stockholm, leader of a group of right-wing extremists who call themselves White Struggle. They've been in trouble with the police before, but that's mostly been street protests on the anniversary of Karl the Twelfth's birthday and suchlike. In the past year, though, it seemed as if the group had gone underground. The Security Police had lost sight of them, though they know they're still active. And a week ago . . ."

Now the police officer was so enthusiastic that he laughed: he reminded the Security Service Chief of his own son when the boy came racing home with his report card before the summer recess.

". . . Tage Sjögren came to Norway!"

Ole Henrik Hermansen was holding his breath, but realized this only when his ears began to ring; he exhaled through tightly compressed lips, and a faint trumpeting sound underlined the sensational nature of the new information.

"Damn it," he said softly. "Do we know anything at all about his movements here?"

Leaning back in his chair, the police officer placed his hands behind his head.

"No. The devastating thing is that this Tage guy isn't of such interest to the Swedes that they would tell us as a matter of course. They only know that he traveled here and returned to Sweden on . . ."

By now the man was beaming; like a dog straining on a leash, he was in full cry and just waiting to be set free.

". . . on Saturday morning!"

Ole Henrik Hermansen stared at his subordinate for some considerable time.

"Get me the Head of the Swedish Security Police on the telephone," he snapped. "We need to ask them to bring the man in for an interview. Without delay."

10:30 P.M., MINISTRY OF HEALTH

The chauffeur had been waiting in the basement since five o'clock that afternoon. She knew that her use of chauffeur-driven cars annoyed everyone, including the Senior Private Secretary and her political colleagues, but then they couldn't know how irritating it was to have to make conversation with all kinds of taxicab drivers whose sole aim was to prove that they knew better than the nation's elected representatives. Anyway, you were entitled to some fringe benefits in this job.

Besides, it looked as though this would be the last day she would have use of her own chauffeur. Tryggve Storstein had still not phoned.

It had taken so long that the journalists had started to speculate. Little Lettvik had called on her confidential cell phone number, wanting to know if it was true that she had not been asked to continue. Ruth-Dorthe Nordgarden had slammed down the phone. The news roundup on television had been cautious, but nevertheless they had placed a question mark beside her photograph when they made their predictions for the new cabinet.

She needed another carrot. Peevishly, she rummaged in her hand-bag but found nothing. However, she knew there was a bag in the kitchen area.

She paused momentarily in the doorway leading to the outer office. Could she hear the phone from the kitchen? Before she had made up her mind, it rang. She had transferred all calls to her direct line and had sent the entire staff home. She did not want any witnesses to her great mortification.

"Hello," she yelled into the receiver; having dashed across to her desk, she was now standing at the wrong side, with nowhere to sit.

"Hello?" The voice sounded surprised. "Who am I speaking to?"

It was Tryggve.

"Hello, Tryggve. It's me. Ruth-Dorthe."

"Are you still working?"

"Just tidying things up."

A pause ensued.

"You can stop that. You're going to continue."

Another lengthy pause.

"Thank you so much, Tryggve. I'll never forget this. This day, I mean. Never."

At the other end of the phone, Tryggve Storstein felt the hairs stand up on the back of his neck.

Ruth-Dorthe's expression of gratitude sounded almost like a threat.

FRIDAY, APRIL 11

10:55 A.M., STORTORGET SQUARE

Not since the old king's funeral in January 1991 had Oslo city center been so crowded. The side streets leading to the main square were closed to vehicular traffic, and a phalanx of stern-looking uniformed police officers was trying to keep the road through Kirkegata open so that the cortège, which was expected in a few minutes, would have a clear route through. For the moment the line stayed firm, the gap between the bystanders on either side of the street no wider than a generous path. TV cameras were everywhere, and here and there Brage Håkonsen could see the ridiculously easy-to-recognize plainclothes police officers from the Security Service, who were wearing earplugs and sunglasses despite the overcast sky.

Two police horses rounded the corner adjacent to Karl Johans gate, trotting gracefully and nervously on either side of the road. It was effective: people pulled back in genuine alarm at the sight of the enormous animals frothing at the mouth and showing the whites of their eyes. All of a sudden four motorbikes raced around the corner from Karl Johans gate and across Kirkegata, followed by limousines in a cortège.

They advanced at top speed toward Oslo Cathedral, where they came to a sudden halt, forming a line. Prominent guests from far and near were quickly, and sometimes rather abrasively, hustled into the vestibule by uniformed and plainclothes police officers. Brage Håkonsen, from his lookout point at the intersection between Grensen and Kirkegata, grinned when he spotted German Chancellor Helmut Kohl protesting as he was led by the arm; he pushed aside the overeager officer—a whole head shorter—and took the time to turn to some acquaintance and greet him politely.

The musicians of the Royal Guards arrived, and Chopin's Funeral March fell like a cloak of silence on the thronging crowds. Brage

Håkonsen removed his cap, not out of respect but because he knew how important it was to behave like everyone else.

Behind the Guards swept a black hearse with Norwegian flags on the hood and mourning drapes at the windows, though these did not prevent the multitudes from seeing that Birgitte Volter's coffin was white. A wreath of deep-red roses, like a circlet of thick, coagulated blood, crowned the casket. Brage Håkonsen could hear people starting to sniff. For reasons he could not explain, and certainly would not admit to, he too became caught up in the solemnity of the occasion, in its ceremony and its sorrow.

He shook off the emotion, feeling annoyed, and moved to the front of the crowd, toward the actual square.

It happened all of a sudden.

Four men and seven women, yelling and shouting, pushed their way through the packed sidewalk and onto the road in front of the funeral cortège before any of the police had time to react.

"Stop the whaling," they screeched. "Killers! Killers!"

Brage stopped short; he found himself suddenly staring into the eyes of a colossal rubber whale that swelled and rose into the air, powered by an activist holding a helium pump between his legs.

"Stop the whaling NOW! Stop the whaling NOW!"

The rhythmic shouts almost drowned out the music played by the Royal Guards, the only people within earshot who paid no attention to the commotion. They played on, the somber cadences pounding out an accompaniment to the yells of the demonstrators and the wheezing of the whale, which had now grown to almost life size. It writhed and twisted as it expanded and seemed intent on swimming right into the cathedral. One of the activists—Brage had no idea where he'd come from, but he appeared to be in his late fifties, with a huge seaman's beard and a number of insignias on his shoulders—grabbed a bucket that had been hoisted to him by a young woman. In a flash, he prised the lid open with a Swiss army knife, and with a sweeping, unrestrained movement hurled red paint at the hearse. However, the chauffeur had grasped the situation and was now reversing at speed; the horses behind him whinnied in fear and trotted back. The red paint splashed on the asphalt, and only a few drops reached the vehicle conveying Birgitte Volter's earthly remains.

Though the police had been taken by surprise, it took them very little time to put a stop to the protest. Twenty police officers flung themselves at the demonstrators, and it took almost exactly five minutes to clap them in irons, puncture the whale, and cram both activists and deflated sperm whale into a Black Maria parked next to the H&M department store. The entire episode was dealt with speedily and efficiently, despite the actions of a group of male spectators who had felt called on to help the police but whose screaming, hot-tempered behavior had made the task considerably more onerous than it might have been.

"Hey!" Brage Håkonsen yelled, tugging and tearing at his handcuffs. "I'm not involved in this!"

He resisted as vigorously as he could as three men forced him into the vehicle.

"I'm not fucking involved in this! Can't you hear?"

"Shut your mouth," snarled a uniformed woman at the front of the van. "You lot lack all sense of decency. To wreck a—*wreck a funeral! Have you no shame!*"

She had turned to face him, and her words seemed almost to punch holes in the wire screen that separated off the space at the back where the detainees sat on benches.

"But I'm not bloody part of this!" Brage screamed again, banging his head repeatedly on the wall. "Let me go, for God's sake!"

The only response was the rumble of the engine as it started, and a mumbled mantra from his fellow prisoners: "Stop the whaling NOW! Stop the whaling NOW!"

12:13 P.M., OSLO CATHEDRAL

"I t was absolutely beautiful. So touchingly beautiful."

Birdie Grinde tried to keep her voice down, but it was so high-pitched that even when she whispered, she could be heard from a radius of several yards. She clung to her son's arm, dressed in the kind of black clothing that would be more suitable for a funeral in *The Godfather* than that of a Norwegian Social Democrat prime minister. Everything was black. And shiny. High-heeled shoes, fishnet stockings, dress, and cape. To round it off, she wore a glossy pillbox hat with a stiff black veil covering her face. What she did not yet know, but would take great pleasure in witnessing later that evening when she watched the footage of the ceremony on television, was that she was repeatedly captured by the TV cameras; this sobbing woman dressed in full mourning must surely be a close family member.

"Tone it down, Mother," Benjamin Grinde whispered. "Can you just tone it down a little?"

Roy Hansen and Per Volter were standing in the vestibule, both wearing dark suits. The son was half a head taller than his father; both had gray complexions and downcast eyes. They held out their hands at random intervals, and after a moment's hesitation, many people chose to walk past the two of them without offering their condolences. Others stood for a few seconds in quiet conversation, and most of the female government ministers gave them both long, heartfelt hugs.

Little Lettvik was with a group of journalists several yards away, scrutinizing the mourners. When Ruth-Dorthe Nordgarden stepped forward, last in the line of cabinet ministers, Little noticed that Roy Hansen turned away, apparently overcome by a wave of sobs, but the spasm did not subside until Ruth-Dorthe gave up and headed for the massive oak doors of the exit. Per Volter had been more obvious than his father: he refused to take her proffered hand and turned decisively toward the Bishop of Oslo, who towered over the mourners in full pontificals, looking like an old eagle in borrowed feathers.

"Roy," whispered Birdie Grinde when she finally reached him. "Roy! What a tragedy!"

Little Lettvik moved closer to the exit. Who was this old woman on Judge Grinde's arm?

"And Birgitte too," Birdie Grinde continued. People were beginning to turn and look at her. "What a dreadful thing to happen. Little Birgitte! Little, innocent, lovely Birgitte!"

She sniffed loudly as she turned toward Per Volter, who stared in surprise at this strange woman he had never clapped eyes on before.

"Per! So tall and handsome!"

She tried to embrace the young man, but he stepped back in alarm. Birdie Grinde was left hanging onto her son's arm, teetering dangerously because her high heels had got caught in a crack on the floor; she was on the verge of falling over.

"My God, I think I'm going to faint," she gasped.

Benjamin Grinde clutched his mother's arm tightly, and a police officer managed to grasp her around the waist and lift her upright.

"May I help you outside, madam?" he said politely, and without waiting for an answer, he escorted her out of the doors, through the crowds and across to the Parliament Building 100 feet away. Benjamin Grinde slinked after them, his lapels pulled up to conceal his face.

The journalists in the vestibule chortled at the incident. Everyone apart from Little Lettvik. Instead, she jotted down a few words on a spiral notepad: "Old woman with BG. Interesting?"

1:00 P.M., SLOTTSBAKKEN, THE SLOPE LEADING UP TO THE ROYAL PALACE

The journalists had been right. They had scored a bull's-eye in a total of sixteen ministerial posts. The preappointment talks had not produced a single surprise. Tryggve Storstein stood in the middle of the long row of ministers with a large bouquet of red roses and a preoccupied, aloof smile appropriate to the occasion. After all, only an hour had passed since his predecessor had been laid to rest. Fewer spectators than normal had gathered to greet the new cabinet, but more journalists and photographers.

It was drizzling, and the Minister of Transport and Communications appeared impatient to have the customary photo session over and done with. She continually looked at her watch and was premature in heading for the black government cars. Tryggve Storstein hauled her back.

Finally it was all over, and the crowd dispersed. Grabbing hold of Ruth-Dorthe's arm, Little Lettvik coerced her into an embrace. "Cell phone tonight," she whispered in her ear.

2:15 P.M., OSLO POLICE STATION

"First he invites the cops to look at his guns; then he vanishes into thin air! Don't you realize this stinks to high heaven, Håkon?"

Håkon Sand used his right hand to produce an exuberant drum roll on the desk.

"Not being at home when you're on sick leave is not what I call 'vanishing into thin air,' Billy T. He could be anywhere. At the doctor's. At his girlfriend's. At his mother's, for that matter."

"But he's not answering his phone either! I've phoned him several times since yesterday evening, and he can't be at the bloody doctor's for twenty-four hours!"

"At the hospital, then. Or at his girlfriend's, as I said."

"That guy doesn't have a girlfriend. Sure as shooting."

Running his hands through his hair, Håkon Sand invited Billy T. to take a seat.

"What do you actually think you've got on this guard?" he asked wearily.

"In the first place, he was definitely at the scene. Second, he owns guns. Four listed here in the gun register. And most suspicious of all—"

Reaching out for a half-empty bottle of cola, Billy T. guzzled the contents without asking the owner's permission.

"You're welcome," Håkon said sourly.

"But listen," Billy T. said, before his face changed into a grimace as he raised one buttock to emit a substantial, prolonged fart.

"For fuck's sake, Billy T., can't you cut that out?"

Standing up, Håkon waved one hand frantically as he held his nose with the other. Then he clumsily unlatched the window, throwing it open as wide as he possibly could. Billy T. guffawed and threw the cola bottle in the wastepaper basket.

"The most suspicious thing of all," Billy T. repeated, "is that the man changed his mind."

"What do you mean by changed his mind?"

Håkon was holding a box of matches, lighting them one at a time until the sulfur had burned out and he could light another.

"First of all, he said that I could come home with him to check his guns. Then he changed his mind and told me that he'd bring them here. I accepted gracefully. Since then, we haven't seen hide nor hair of him. And now he's supposed to be on sick leave!"

"So you think, then," Håkon said slowly, "that we should pull in a guy who we have nothing more on than that he did his job last Friday. A guy who has made the grave error of not coming running to Billy T. as he had promised, and what's more has made himself guilty in this particularly serious criminal case by falling ill!"

He threw the box of matches across the table, then tilted his head back and supported his hands on the armrests.

"Then you'll have to find a different lawyer. A search warrant implies there will be an arrest. We've had one overhasty warrant already.

Besides, this is not your job in fact. You have just as much a problem as Hanne! In sticking to what you're meant to do, I mean. The role of the security guard in all this is not up to you to judge."

"Bloody hell, Håkon!"

Billy T. slammed his fist down on the desk.

"It was Tone-Marit who insisted that I interview the guy!"

"It's no use." Håkon grinned. "Forget it. Just you shuffle back to your own office and find some more of Volter's friends to talk to."

Without uttering a word, Billy T. left the room and slammed the door behind him.

"Stop the whaling NOW," Håkon Sand said, giving a long and hearty chuckle.

Not until he had concluded two telephone conversations and was about to get down to work again did he discover that Billy T. had duped him completely.

The copy of the autopsy report that most certainly had nothing to do with Billy T. but that he had fussed like a child to be allowed sight of, was no longer on his desk.

Not to put too fine a point on it, Billy T. must have swiped it.

7:00 P.M., STOLMAKERGATA 15

"Don't you want to watch the news roundup, Hanne?"

Taking a cold beer from the fridge, Billy T. surveyed his living room with an air of satisfaction. Although he had never noticed the orange curtains that had hung there before, he could see that the new, air force blue ones were more attractive, especially now that Hanne had been to the Idé Skeidar furniture store to buy a sofa, also in blue. And she had found some old posters lying in the attic. He had no idea where she had got hold of the frames, but they looked very attractive on the wall behind the sofa. On the other hand, the potted plants were quite unnecessary. Even though the pots with their Indian patterns were fine themselves, the greenery would be dead within three weeks. He knew that only too well. He had tried it before.

Hanne, sitting engrossed in the copy of the autopsy report, chewing on a pen, did not reply.

"Hello! Earth calling Hanne Wilhelmsen! Do you want to watch *Dagsrevyen*?"

He tapped her head with his bottle and switched on the television. Funeral music thundered from the loudspeakers.

"Fine. But don't disturb me!"

Irritated, she rubbed her head where the bottle had thumped her, but did not even lift her eyes to the screen. Billy T. groaned and sat on the floor to watch the broadcast.

Without warning, he burst into gales of laughter.

"Look at those idiots! Look!"

An astonishing piece of footage captured the hotheaded protesters whose chief aim, quite literally, was to put an end to Norwegian whaling. A voice-over related that one Norwegian, three Dutch, two French, and six American citizens had been arrested after the demonstration in front of Oslo Cathedral.

"Those Americans who protest against whaling! The very people who grill and gas and poison *human beings*! And who have millions of citizens living below the poverty line! Hypocrites!"

He took a slug of the beer and farted again.

"You really need to cut that out," Hanne muttered, but she still didn't look up. "Didn't your mother teach you to go to the bathroom to do that sort of thing?"

"First it was my ear," Billy T. said testily. "Now that's better, but my stomach's playing up. I just *have to* get rid of that gas! Better out than in, as my grandmother used to say. Hush!"

There was no need to hush her, as Hanne was completely immersed in the autopsy report. The news bulletin about the demonstrators had finished, and the anchorman informed them that the Norwegian had been freed when it turned out that he had not had anything to do with the protest, while the foreigners had been remanded in custody.

"What is it you're actually looking for?" Billy T. asked, for the first time showing more than a passing interest in what Hanne was doing.

"Nothing." Hanne sighed, gathering the papers together before inserting them in a plastic wallet. "Absolutely nothing. I thought I'd had an ingenious idea that would have given us the answer to everything."

"What?"

"But as usual it wasn't so ingenious after all. The autopsy report precludes what I thought. But it was helpful to check it out. Thanks for getting it for me."

"I had to fool that nice boy of yours, Håkon. What was it you thought that was so ingenious?"

"Nothing," Hanne said with a smile. "It didn't add up. Shall we play?"

"Yes!"

Billy T. sprang up to fetch the bulky, old-fashioned table soccer set from the bedroom.

"I'm going to be England," he shouted as he maneuvered the table with its rubber figures impaled on eight steel rods into the living room.

"Fine. I'll be the Netherlands."

It did not bother either of them in the slightest that one team had pale green shirts and the other blue, neither color matching the national soccer teams. After all, they could have been old spare kits.

9:30 P.M., OLE BRUMMS VEI 212

A lone at last. His dark suit jacket, which looked just as tired and dejected as he did, was hanging on the back of a chair. Roy Hansen gazed at the photo of Birgitte on the sideboard. The candle beside it, the only source of light in the room, seemed almost hypnotic.

This past week had been unbelievable. He had never had any interest in new age or paranormal phenomena and was not religious either. However, the last few days had been as close to an out-of-body experience as he reckoned it was possible to have.

Tryggve Storstein had come to visit, embarrassed and exhausted but showing such empathy and sincere sorrow that in some strange way it had gratified Roy Hansen.

Tryggve had moved him. They had talked for a long time and had sat quietly together for even longer. The pair who had come from the Protocol Section of the Department of State had been less welcome. The woman had insisted on obtaining the services of City Maid: the flowers, dust, and darkness had to be swept away. At least now it was clean and tidy in here.

They had all tried to foist themselves on him this afternoon. They wished him well; he knew that. But he did not want anyone here. Only Per. But Per would not speak to him. He was either out jogging on endless long runs or sat in his room by himself, doing nothing, or talking on the phone, sometimes for ages, in conversation with somebody or other, though Roy had no idea who.

Some people had come home with him after the reception at the city hall. He had left as early as the Protocol Section had permitted. The Party Secretary and three others from the party office had accompanied him. Afterward a few more had arrived, but fortunately they had eventually realized that he wanted to be left alone. And they had cleaned up after themselves.

Roy Hansen had tried to switch on the television, but there was only endless coverage of the funeral. It seemed like a final, bitter defeat; he did not even have Birgitte's death to himself. Even as she lay there under a white wooden lid in a heavy coffin, she was not his. She belonged to the state. The general public. First and foremost, the party. Never to him. Not even today, when everything was over forever. Rather than being a quiet reunion of close family and friends, a chance to mourn in the company of others who were fond of the woman he had shared his life with, Birgitte's funeral had become a political summit. An adjunct.

He caught himself suddenly missing Birgitte's parents. They had both passed away at the end of the eighties, and that was probably for the best. They had been spared the experience of their daughter's murder. As they had been spared from witnessing the way Birgitte had steadily distanced herself from everyone around her, becoming increasingly alienated from all who loved her. But it would have been good to have them here today. Perhaps they could have shared this with him. It was obvious that Per could not.

Last Friday, Roy Hansen had longed more than anything for his son to come home, for him to be standing there in his uniform with his bulging backpack; the hours until Per returned on the Saturday morning had been unbearable. But when Per did finally arrive, he had in a sense disappeared. His face had been stony, closed, and locked.

Now, suddenly, he was standing there.

"Good night. I waited until Grandma fell asleep. Now I'm off to bed."

Roy Hansen had not even heard the car roll up. He stared at his son's contours in the doorway; the candlelight blurred his son's outline.

"But, Per," he whispered, "can't you sit down for a moment or two? Just for a little while."

The young man in the doorway did not move a muscle, and it was impossible to see his face.

"Sit down, do. Just for a short spell."

Suddenly light flooded from the ceiling. Per had switched it on, and when Roy's eyes had adjusted to the brightness and he had regained his sight, he got a shock.

Per, that decent boy. That well-brought-up, clever boy who had not once during his teenage years given his parents reason to worry. Per, who had been his boy, his comfort, and actually also his responsibility, since Birgitte had embarked on The Long Absence when the boy was hardly more than ten years old.

He was unrecognizable.

"If you're hell-bent on talking to me, *then I'll do that with pleasure!*"

His face was contorted, his eyes popping like those of a dead cod, and saliva sprayed from his mouth as he spoke.

"I hadn't intended to say anything! But do you really think that I don't *know*?"

He hovered threateningly over his father, his fists clenched.

"You're a—you're a bloody hypocrite! Do you know that, Dad, you're a—a—"

Now he was crying. He had not shed a tear during the funeral service, but now his eyes produced a flood of tears, and his face became blotchy: a strange malady had him in its grip, making him mean and repulsive. Roy leaned to one side of the sofa, almost reclining.

"Don't you think I know why Mum kept away? Why she couldn't bear to be at home any more?"

Roy Hansen attempted to draw even farther away from his son, but Per made a sudden movement with his fists that made him even more frightened, and he froze.

"And Ruth-Dorthe Nordgarden, of all people! That Dolly Parton look-alike! What do you think it did to Mum when she found that earring in the bed! *What do you think?*"

"But—"

Roy tried to sit upright. Again, Per raised his hands pugnaciously, his clenched fists poised in midair just a foot or so above him, pinning him to the spot.

"And I heard you! You thought I was out that evening, but in fact I came home!"

"Per—"

"Don't 'Per' me! I heard you both!"

The young man sobbed uncontrollably, coughing and sniffling and shrieking in a hysterical voice, and it became difficult to understand what he was saying.

"Calm down, Per! Tone it down!"

"Tone it down! Should I just, like, tone it down! It was you, Dad, who should have toned it down that night last autumn. You and that damn oversized whore!"

Suddenly, unexpectedly, he was drained. Per Volter lowered and unclenched his fists, which left him standing in something like a military at-ease pose and gasping for air.

"I'll never talk to you again!"

Per crossed to the door.

Roy Hansen stood up falteringly. He had lost his voice.

"But, Per," he whispered. "There's so much you don't know! So very much you don't know!"

He did not receive an answer, and immediately afterward heard the car race out of the driveway. The candle had gone out, leaving the living room bathed in a harsh and unforgiving light.

SATURDAY, APRIL 12

10:15 A.M., ODINS GATE 3

I t was impossible to get up. The double pillows under his head made it difficult to breathe. He peered down at his naked feet, looking for the hole through which all his strength had drained. He felt dead. The total emptiness was augmented by a sorrow he had never experienced before.

There was no way out of this. Benjamin Grinde's world was disintegrating. Last week had been one long journey to Golgotha, heading toward oblivion: the absolute end. The looks from his colleagues in the judiciary, as though something untouchable had wrapped itself like a sheet around him. They did not converse with him, and only occasionally, of necessity, did they speak to him. The newspaper headlines had destroyed everything. Even though the arrest warrant had not been legitimate. Even though the police had confirmed he was not a suspect. The warrant was there nonetheless, a written indictment that would in any case—now that this was all public knowledge—put his future career in jeopardy. But the other thing was worse.

Would he never escape a shared destiny with Birgitte? Would it never end? After all these years? They had each in their own way tried to move forward; they had both fled in different directions and ended up in the highest echelons, at the very pinnacle, but of their own individual trees.

With great effort, he pulled himself together, rolling his legs off the bed and struggling to sit upright. The bronze lion, frozen stiff, guarding the bedroom door, growled at him. Its mane was highly polished and shone like gold, its jaw black and coated in verdigris. He had bought it in a back street in Tehran. The big cat fascinated him, this foreign species of animal that had nevertheless been chosen as the most Norwegian of all: the symbol of Norwegian officialdom. It snarled on the coat of arms above the entrance to the government complex. There were two of them in front of the Parliament Building, tame and toothless lions that tried to look the part, without actually succeeding in scaring anyone. And most splendid of them all, the lioness with the ample breasts that guarded Room 9 in the Supreme Court: the conference and ceremonial room.

Benjamin Grinde stared at the bronze figure. It fixed him to the bed, as if a repellent stench of bad breath emanated from its mouth, and he longed to escape. From the bedroom. On wobbly legs, he padded out to the kitchen.

I've never looked inside it, he thought suddenly. He could not find more coffee. *What is actually inside it?*

The massive oak sideboard with its glass doors and relief pattern of bunched grapes appeared almost black in the gloom. The curtains were drawn; life went on outside, but in here there was nothing.

Underneath his great-grandmother's old tablecloth lay the tiny box he should have left where it was.

A beautiful little pillbox in enameled gold.

Drawing it out, he made an effort to open it.

**11:00 A.M., SECURITY SERVICE SECTION,
OSLO POLICE STATION**

"And you're saying we had this man in here yesterday? Here? At the police station?"

There was little sign of the formerly rigorous, unruffled Security Service Chief. Now he was trotting around the floor of his own office, combing his hair with his fingers.

"When was he released?"

"Yesterday afternoon. He had nothing to do with the demonstration. He was just in the wrong place at the wrong time."

"Brage Håkonsen," Ole Henrik Hermansen mumbled. "What previous do we have on him?"

"Nothing much."

The police officer tried to follow his boss with his eyes, but it was difficult: Hermansen was darting from side to side behind him.

"And what exactly is 'nothing much'?"

"He definitely belongs to extreme right-wing circles. He was once in Aryan Power, but that's a while ago now. These past couple of years he's been practically invisible. We suspect that he leads his own group, almost a cell. But we don't know anything about it."

The Security Service Chief came to an abrupt halt directly behind his subordinate.

"And Tage Sjögren paid him a visit as well. Last week."

The police officer made do with a nod, even though he was unsure whether it would be noticed.

"Find out everything," Ole Henrik Hermansen spluttered, crossing suddenly to the office chair. "Find out absolutely everything about this guy. If push comes to shove, arrest him."

3:32 P.M., TINDFOTEN IN TROMSDALEN NEAR TROMSØ

The snow was no longer white; it whipped around him in a shade of gray he had never seen before. All the gray specks floated together into a uniform nothingness; he could hardly see the tips of his skis ahead of him. They should not have left the shelter at Skarvassbu. He had told Morten it was crazy; the way the weather had closed in after they left Snarbydalen, they should have taken refuge at the shelter.

"But it's almost all downhill from here on," Morten had protested. "Twenty minutes of gentle uphill slopes, and then no more than half an hour of fabulous downhill skiing. There's beer at home. Do you really want to stay here?"

Morten had pointed at the shelves in the little tourist cabin. A few packets of cauliflower soup and four cans of the local stew were far less tempting than a rare beefsteak and cold beer at Morten's lodgings in Skattøra.

"But there's the risk of an avalanche, don't you think?" he had objected. "There could be an avalanche!"

"My God! I've skied this trail hundreds of times! There are no avalanches here. Come on!"

He had capitulated. Now he had no idea where Morten was. Stopping, he rested on his ski poles.

"Morten! Morten!"

It seemed as though the sound did not want to venture out into the gray blizzard. It about-turned just outside his mouth and forced itself back in again.

"Morten!"

He did not even know where he was. The terrain was still sloping gently uphill, but he had been skiing for nearly an hour. Morten had said that it would only take twenty minutes to reach the start of the downhill slopes. It must be these dreadful conditions. All this snow. Far more snow than usual: he knew from the weather forecasts that records were being broken almost daily in the north of Norway.

Wasn't it slightly flatter here?

He stopped and made an effort to check. The pelting, biting snow had begun to penetrate his clothes. Neither of them had been dressed for such horrendous weather.

"Morten!"

The security guard from the government complex felt dizzy: it was difficult now to know which way was up. He had lost his bearings regarding north, south, east, and west long ago. However, it was straight downhill now. The uphill slope had come to an end.

Suddenly he heard a noise. Different from the wailing, whistling wind and the rattling of the lock on his backpack. Low-frequency and threatening. He stood frozen stiff, feeling anxiety creep up through his legs.

There had to be six feet of snow below him. Was he standing on a bank? Was he alongside a rock face? Desperate, he began to head off: sharply, purposefully, although he had no idea of his locus on the route. Then he lost his balance.

The ground underneath him had started to move, slowly and insistently. The rumble had increased to a deafening roar, and before the guard had regained his footing, heaps of snow came tumbling down. As if the world was coming to an end. Flung hither and thither, he was soon lying on his back before being propelled onto his stomach. The snow forced its way everywhere: not only inside his clothing, onto his skin, but also inside his ears, eyes, mouth, and nose. All of a sudden he knew he was about to die.

The pressure on him increased. He was no longer sailing down the mountainside on top of the snow; he was underneath it. His surroundings were no longer gray; they were pitch-black. His eyes felt as if they were being hammered into his skull, and he panted for air that did not exist. His airways were full of snow.

Now they'll never find out about it.

He made a final effort to suck air down into his aching, flattened lungs, before everything went black. Only three minutes later he was dead.

4:10 P.M., KIRKEVEIEN 129

The fine French Empire–style antique chair looked chagrined beside the desk from IKEA. The Munch lithograph ought to have felt equally affronted, squeezed up beside a silkscreen print in a red picture frame that had been bought at auction in a gallery at Aker Brygge for two hundred kroner during the last economic upswing.

Ruth-Dorthe Nordgarden sat in the chair deep in thought. She stared at the cell phone in her right hand, then slammed it down and picked up the usual one instead: a cordless phone she had still not fully grasped how to operate.

She would get even. Perhaps not immediately, but at some point she would pay him back. Tryggve Storstein had not wanted her to continue in her job, and she knew that only other pressures had forced her name through.

It would certainly take time, but the opportunity would present itself, sooner or later.

"Hello?"

The receiver was as silent as the grave. Hesitating, she pressed a green button and smiled in relief when all at once she heard the dial tone, followed by a rapid squeaky tune.

"Hello?"

"Hello?"

"It's Ruth-Dorthe."

"Well, well. Congratulations."

The voice was noncommittal. However, she knew very well that she had him. Of course, he could not be relied on. No one could be relied on. But he was hers, all the same. He was the one who had looked after her in the first place; he had helped her, supported her, aware that their respective careers were interconnected: they were political Siamese twins. Gunnar Klavenaes also sat on the party's executive board.

"What on earth happened?" she asked.

"Don't concern yourself. It went okay. In the end."

Silence fell. She could hear the dishwasher: the program had jammed, and the machine was rinsing over and over again. She carried the phone with her to the kitchen.

"One moment."

It sounded like a tremendous rainstorm in there: a typhoon inside a tin can. Perplexed, she studied the buttons at the top of the panel without touching any of them. Eventually she resolutely pressed the off button. The wind speed inside dropped, and now there was a trickling sound, which grew fainter and fainter.

"Hello?"

"Yes, I'm still here."

"He won't last long," she said tonelessly.

"I think you're miscalculating, Ruth-Dorthe," was the response at the other end. "He is much stronger than you believe."

"Not if he inherits all the problems from Birgitte's time in office. And of course, he will. The election in the autumn will be the death of him."

"Not now. We're going to gain votes as a result of Birgitte's murder. That's what happened to the Social Democrats in Sweden."

She squinted at the tree in the backyard, on which tiny buds had started to sprout.

"We'll see," she muttered. "I phoned to ask if we could have dinner. Tonight."

"I can't manage today. I'm extremely busy at the moment. Can't I phone you again when I'm free?"

"Okay," she answered, offended. "I thought you might be interested to hear what I've got to tell you."

"Of course, Ruth-Dorthe. But another time, okay?"

Without replying, she pressed the green button with a tiny picture of a telephone again. It worked.

They thought she was on the way out. Even her supporters—some of them at least. It was only thanks to Gro Harlem Brundtland's resignation as Prime Minister the previous year that she had retained her post as joint Deputy Leader of the party. Her four-year tenure prior to that had not gone quite as expected; she had lost many friends, and the grumbling of those who did not wish her well had grown to a crescendo. At National Congress only two weeks after the change of government, everyone had been careful to ensure the least possible upset.

It was Birgitte's National Congress, and the leaders from the previous four-year period were to be left in peace. Ruth-Dorthe Nordgarden knew that she had been saved by the skin of her teeth. And she knew that Tryggve Storstein was her chief opponent. At that time he was only Deputy Leader and equal in status to her. Now he was Party Leader and Prime Minister.

However, she still knew which strings it was possible to pull.

She looked at the time. The girls would be out for a few hours longer. Ruth-Dorthe Nordgarden fixed herself a cup of coffee, but it was too strong. She screwed her nose up at it and shuffled out to the kitchen again for some milk. The fridge smelled rank when she opened it; the girls were shirking their chores more than ever these days. She was irritated to see that the milk was out of date. She poked her nose into the opening, sniffed, and decided to pour a generous amount into her cup all the same.

As she sipped the muddy brown beverage, she let her eyes roam from the cell phone to the cordless one. It was difficult to believe that cell phones could not be eavesdropped; it seemed remarkable that with current technology, it was possible to have a conversation and still be certain that no one else was listening. Cell phones *appeared* insecure: they crackled and crunched, and occasionally she had heard other voices on the line. Nevertheless, she decided to use the cell phone.

"You wanted to talk to me," she said listlessly once she was connected.

She ought to wash the windows. The weak spring sunshine struggled to reach her desk, and dust particles danced in the pale light. She listened to the voice at the other end for some considerable time.

"You're talking about internal documents," she said at last. "That's very difficult, of course. Not to say almost impossible."

That wasn't true. They both knew that. But Ruth-Dorthe Nordgarden wanted to be persuaded. She wanted to know what was in it for her.

Five minutes later, she disconnected the call.

She scribbled down a few words in the margin of her diary space for Monday. She would have to get hold of a repairman for the dishwasher as soon as possible. She would have to remember to ask the political adviser to arrange it.

6:00 P.M., JACOB AALLS GATE 16

"I am skeptical! I'm telling you, all the same, I am skeptical!" Birdie Grinde wrinkled her tanned forehead and puckered her lips. Nonetheless, Little Lettvik could discern a glimmer of curiosity in the old woman's eyes.

"After the dreadful things that newspaper of yours wrote about Ben, it's no wonder I'm not exactly delighted to see you. On the other hand..."

Birdie Grinde stepped back in the tiny hallway, indicating for Little Lettvik to follow.

"... if I can contribute in any way to people realizing that Ben had nothing to do with this terrible story, then that would be really splendid, of course."

The woman, who had to be in her late seventies, was wearing a tight-fitting pair of jeans that in a fascinating way illustrated what happened to an aging body. Her legs appeared frail and skinny and her calves as thin as pipecleaners. In the gap between the tight pants legs and her platform sandals, Little Lettvik could make out patches of taut, shiny brown skin and dark liver spots. Birdie Grinde's sweater, a loose-fitting pink angora, reached halfway down her posterior, below which Little could see that the ravages of time had removed all her buttock muscles.

Ten years ago, Little Lettvik thought. *Only ten years ago you would probably have got away with wearing such clothes.*

"You must sit down," Birdie Grinde commanded, and Little Lettvik noticed the disagreeable, vengeful eyes beneath the old woman's eyebrows, which formed two thin strands on her high forehead. "You'd probably appreciate a little snack, wouldn't you?"

When she returned from the kitchen, she was carrying a small plate of sandwiches in one hand and a stemmed cake stand in the other.

"Myself, I've kept my slim figure, as you can see. Just a glass of port for me! So!"

She poured herself such a generous amount that the reddish-brown liquid almost overflowed. Little Lettvik briefly nodded a "Yes, please" and received half a glass.

"You're driving, I expect," Birdie Grinde explained as she sat down. "Help yourself! Do tuck in!"

She pushed the two plates toward the journalist.

They looked good, and Little Lettvik was hungry. She was always hungry. Long ago she had read an article in a popular science magazine about hunger being a substitute for conscience. She had tried to forget that article. Picking up a sandwich filled with salmon and scrambled egg, she wondered whether this strange woman always had luxuries like this at hand, since she could not have been in the kitchen for longer than ten minutes.

It was unpleasant to eat under the eagle eye of the woman on the sofa. Her intense brown eyes glanced up at her from the glass of port, and Little Lettvik gave up when she'd finished only half the sandwich.

"How could you write such things?" Birdie Grinde resumed. "You already knew that the prosecution was a piece of nonsense!"

"Arrest warrant," Little Lettvik corrected. "It was an arrest warrant. And we also wrote that it had been rescinded. There was absolutely nothing in that article that wasn't true."

Birdie Grinde seemed preoccupied. She stared uninhibitedly at Little Lettvik, but her thoughts seemed not to revolve around her son having been wrongfully singled out as a murderer only a few days earlier. Some vague new expression was carved out on her raddled face: a mixture of amusement and embarrassment.

Little Lettvik found it disconcerting. "And of course it's been forgotten now," she continued. "Everybody forgets so quickly. I can reassure you on that point. But perhaps you could tell me something about your son's . . ."

Now the other woman's gaze was unbearable. She continued to stare while carefully wiping her mouth with a linen napkin, over and over again.

Little Lettvik shook her head gently. "Is there something wrong?"

"You have some scrambled egg on your chin," Birdie Grinde whispered, leaning across the coffee table. "Here!"

She pointed to her own chin, and Little Lettvik made a lightning movement with the back of her hand. A yellow lump was pushed across her skin, and Little Lettvik resorted to the other hand for assistance.

"You *do* have a napkin, you know," Birdie Grinde said pointedly.

"Thanks," Little Lettvik mumbled, fumbling to remove the roll of fabric from a large engraved silver ring.

"It's gone now." Birdie Grinde smiled in satisfaction. "What was it you wanted to ask me about?"

Little Lettvik seldom let others get the better of her. She never paid any attention to her own appearance. She just did not care. There was very little at all she did bother about, and privately she was extremely pleased that she was not particularly fond of anyone; she was not even especially concerned about other people. Perhaps about him, however. No, not him either. Her business, her crusade, her major project, was the truth. Truth was an obsession, and she laughed derisively at all the pathetic attempts by other journalists to engage in philosophical debates about ethics and journalism. Twice, only twice in a long and illustrious career, had she committed to print something that had turned out not to be true. It had been difficult. Those incidents had plagued her for months afterward. Running the gauntlet of official retractions and compensation payments had been sheer hell.

The truth could never be immoral. How you got hold of it, and what effect it had on other people, was entirely secondary. It made no difference whether she used lies and unscrupulous practices to get to the truth. The sole objective was to find out the truth. If every single word in an article she wrote was correct, then the article was legitimate.

Her certainty about her own eternal search for the truth made her invincible. But just then, facing this witch of a woman—this tiny, conceited, ludicrous squirrel who sat playing with her whiskers on the opposite side of a massive mahogany coffee table—just then, Little Lettvik felt an unaccustomed touch of insecurity.

She gave herself a shake and leaned back in the chair to try and reduce the size of her stomach. For the first time in ages, she peered down in annoyance at her own breasts. They spilled over like a solid balcony in front of her; she had not actually noticed before that they rested on her thighs when she was seated.

"I simply wondered whether you could tell me a little about your son," she said at last. "We would like to give our readers an accurate picture of him. He occupies an extremely prominent position, after all, and his life is of considerable public interest, wouldn't you agree?"

"Yes, very much so, that's my view exactly!"

Birdie Grinde laughed, a loud piercing ripple.

"To tell the truth, I'm surprised the press hasn't shown greater interest in him before. Do you know . . ."

Birdie Grinde leaned forward again, as if to inspire familiarity.

". . . Ben was the first person in Norway to achieve *both* a medical degree and a doctorate in law? The very first. Look at this!"

She rose from the sofa and crossed to a bookcase, continuing her flow of chatter. Crouching down stiffly for a moment, she produced a ring binder.

"Personally, I consider that the occasion received far too little attention."

She slapped the album down in front of the journalist.

"Only two little columns in *Aftenposten*," she fretted, pointing with a red-varnished fingernail. "It was quite an occasion, I tell you. But . . ."

She plumped down on her seat again.

". . . there was actually a longer article about Ben when he graduated from high school."

Birdie Grinde gestured with her hand to encourage Little Lettvik to leaf further back in the album.

"It was only in the local *Akershus Amtstidende*, of course, but all the same."

Little Lettvik flicked through the pages. Suddenly she spotted the young Benjamin Grinde in a large, yellowed, dog-eared newspaper picture. He was smiling faintly, shyly, at the photographer, and despite his thick head of hair and eyes as blank as any other eighteen-year-old's, he was easily recognizable. The man had grown more handsome over the years, admittedly, but even in this old newspaper image, she could see how good looking he was: immature, vulnerable, and engaging.

"My goodness," Little Lettvik muttered. "Did he get a distinction for his final grade?"

"Distinction in every subject." Birdie Grinde giggled delightedly. "At Oslo Cathedral School! The best in the city. Yes, I could almost say the best school in the country. At that time, anyway. Since then it has deteriorated, like so many other things."

Once again she pursed her mouth in disapproval.

"Who's this?"

Little Lettvik placed the heavy ring binder in front of Benjamin Grinde's mother. Producing a pair of half-moon glasses from a leather case on the table facing her, Birdie Grinde peered at the picture.

"Oh *that*," she shrieked. "That's Birgitte of course! Poor Birgitte, *look* how lovely she was!"

Birgitte Volter was standing with one arm around the eighteen-year-old Benjamin Grinde. The young man looked stiff as a board: his hands were dangling uncertainly in front of his thighs, and he was staring seriously at a point adjacent to the camera lens. Birgitte Volter, with mid-length hair and wearing a full skirt and pumps, and glasses with catlike frames, was laughing and holding a baby in her other arm. The infant was not lying comfortably; its head was hanging too far over the elbow. The caption written on the gray-black cardboard in white pen, neatly and legibly, was: "Little Liv's first day in the sun."

"Look at this," Birdie Grinde called eagerly, thumbing further through the album. "Here we are, all together on the beach! Birgitte Volter was a very close friend of our family, you understand. Her parents—brilliant people, they died several years ago, poor things—were our nearest neighbors. That was a *lovely* time."

She sighed, reclining on the sofa with a smile, staring longingly out the window.

"Such a *lovely* time," she repeated softly, more to herself than to Little Lettvik.

And Little Lettvik was not listening to her either.

"Who is this?" she asked loudly, pointing to another photograph.

Birdie Grinde did not respond. She continued to stare out the window, her face transformed. Something soft surrounded her eyes; her smile seemed to come from somewhere deep inside, from a place that had been locked away long ago.

"Excuse me," Little Lettvik called out. "Mrs. Grinde!"

"Oh." The old woman was startled. "I'm sorry. What was it you were asking?"

"Who is this?"

Little Lettvik did not want to draw attention to her own bitten nails, so instead tapped the photo of a baby with her knuckle. She was lying on her back on a terry towel, squinting unhappily at the sun, with her knees drawn up to her chest. Birgitte Volter was sitting on one side of the baby, still smiling flirtatiously. On the other side sat Benjamin Grinde, looking very solemn. Behind the child, crouching, handsome, broad shouldered, smiling widely, and with his hand under the baby's head, sat a man Little Lettvik recognized immediately. Roy Hansen.

"Who's the child?"

Birdie Grinde looked at her in confusion.

"The baby? That's Liv, of course!"

"Liv?"

"Yes, Birgitte and Roy's little daughter."

"Daughter? But they only have one child! A boy, isn't it? Per."

"But my dear woman . . ."

Birdie Grinde looked at her reproachfully.

". . . Per is only in his early twenties. This was taken in 1965. Little Liv *died*, you see. A terrible tragedy, the whole business. She died just like—"

She tried to snap her fingers.

"For no reason at all. Absolutely awful. It affected everybody so dreadfully. Poor Mr. and Mrs. Volter, they quite simply went into a decline. I would put it as strongly as that. They were never the same again. Thank God Birgitte was so young. And Roy too, of course, although I've never really understood how Birgitte could have fallen for that man. Young folk, you know. Young folk manage to get back on their feet. And Ben, that good boy. He was *shattered*. Poor Ben. He's so sensitive. His father was just the same. He was a photographer, you see, and actually had an artistic temperament. I always said that."

"And this was in 1965, you say?" Little Lettvik inquired, swallowing. "How old was the child?"

"Only three months, poor soul. A beautiful little baby. Enchanting. She wasn't exactly *planned*, if you understand what I mean . . ."

Birdie Grinde winked slightly with her right eye.

". . . but she was a little ray of sunshine. And then she just died. Crib death. Isn't that what they call it nowadays? We just called it a tragedy, we did. At that time we didn't have so many fine words, you see."

Little Lettvik coughed violently: a hacking, husky cough that came from somewhere around her knees. Clutching her mouth with both hands, she gasped, "Could I have some water, please?"

Birdie Grinde looked completely distracted as she scurried off to the kitchen.

Little continued to cough, at the same time grabbing the album and letting it slide into the voluminous depths of the bag she always carried. During one final, fierce explosion, she pulled the zipper closed.

"Here," Birdie chirped, appearing beside her with water in a stemmed crystal glass. "Please drink it carefully! Do you smoke, Miss Lettvik? You really ought to stop!"

Little Lettvik did not answer but downed all the water.

"Thanks," she murmured. "Now I really must go."

"Already?"

Birdie Grinde was unable to hide her disappointment.

"But maybe you'll come back again? Another time?"

"Of course," Little Lettvik assured her. "But I have to leave now."

She wondered fleetingly whether she should grab one of the tempting sandwiches on her way out. But then she pulled herself together.

There were limits, after all.

MONDAY, APRIL 14

I f Little Lettvik had possessed a tail, it would have been swishing contentedly from side to side. She was leaning over a computer screen, studying the draft of that day's front page. She was happiest of all with the picture: the wedding photograph of Birgitte Volter and Roy Hansen, taken by Benjamin Grinde's father, the photographer Knut Grinde. Birgitte Volter had a little bump at the waist of her dress, ever so slightly too big to be considered fashionable, two years after Marilyn Monroe's death.

"Where did you actually get hold of these pictures?" the editor mumbled.

He did not expect a reply, nor did he receive one. Little Lettvik simply smiled condescendingly as she asked for a printout.

"Get it yourself," the editor snapped.

However, nothing could spoil Little Lettvik's euphoric mood tonight. She trotted through to her own office, and clicked her way to that day's edition.

CHILDHOOD FRIEND INVESTIGATES FAMILY TRAGEDY

Previously unpublished photos
of Prime Minister Birgitte Volter

By Little Lettvik (Photo: private ownership)

Today, *Kveldsavisen* is able to reveal previously unknown aspects of late Prime Minister Birgitte Volter's life. These photographs from Volter's youth have never previously been published.

It has also never before come to light that, in 1965, Birgitte Volter and her husband lost their three-month-old daughter,

Liv, in tragic circumstances. Birgitte Volter was only nineteen years old when the baby was born, but she still managed to graduate from high school. As is well known, Birgitte Volter did not go on to university, and two months after Liv's death she began work as a secretary at the State Liquor Monopoly. She did not give birth to another child until 1975—Per Volter, who is now at military training academy.

The family has been extremely reticent about mentioning little Liv's demise. Sources in contact with this newspaper, and who claim to be very close to the Volter family, say that they had no idea about this tragic event. The newspaper has not succeeded in obtaining a comment from Roy Hansen, Birgitte Volter's widower.

Nor is it common knowledge that Birgitte Volter and Benjamin Grinde were extremely close friends in their youth. More than thirty years later, that same Benjamin Grinde has now been tasked with investigating what happened in 1965 when a remarkably high number of infants died in Norway.

See also pages 12 and 13.

Lighting another cigarillo, Little Lettvik clicked through to page 12.

EXTREMELY WORRYING, ACCORDING TO PROFESSOR

Fred Brynjestad aims strong criticism at Grinde

By Little Lettvik and Bent Skulle (photo)

"There is every reason to be skeptical about Supreme Court Judge Benjamin Grinde's impartiality as chair of the committee investigating what may have been a major health scandal in 1965." This is the assertion made by Fred Brynjestad, professor of public law and a doctor of law, to *Kveldsavisen*. The chair of the Parliamentary Standing Committee on Health and Social Affairs, Kari-Anne Søfteland of the Center Party, is deeply shocked by these new revelations, declaring that she and the rest of Parliament have been deceived.

"If it is the case that Birgitte Volter herself lost a daughter in the relevant year, and at that time had a close friendship with Benjamin Grinde, there is every reason for alarm bells to ring," Brynjestad says. "Prime Minister Volter should have realized, before Grinde was asked to undertake this task, that their relationship placed him in a compromising position," Brynjestad insists.

"It is far worse, however, that Grinde himself did not appreciate this," Professor Fred Brynjestad comments. "He is a very competent lawyer, and the problematic nature of this situation should have been most obvious to him."

Brynjestad adds that he is not necessarily accusing Grinde of prejudice, but there is a possibility that he *may* be biased, and that is sufficient reason for him to have refused to take on the role.

"This kind of thing has become worryingly common in our society," Professor Brynjestad continues. "Namely, that members of the social elite increasingly have links to one another, allowing them to operate beyond the usual boundaries and without being accountable to ordinary citizens. We end up with an invisible network of power we cannot control."

From the investigations carried out by this newspaper in recent weeks, it is clear that Benjamin Grinde is a prominent *éminence grise* in Norwegian society. He was a childhood friend of Birgitte Volter and has friends high up in both Parliament and the legal system.

Among other things, he was a member of the same choir as MPs Kari Buggeygarden (Labor Party) and Fredrik Humlen (Conservatives) from 1979 to 1984. During his student days, he counted among his friends Haakon Severinsen, who went on to become managing director of Orkla, one of the largest companies in Norway, and Ann-Berit Klavenaes, chief executive of the National Hospital in Oslo.

MP Kari-Anne Søfteland of the Center Party claims to be quite aghast that these connections have not come to light before now.

"Now we must sit down and decide on an entirely new commission," she told *Kveldsavisen* in a phone call from the Seychelles, where her committee is on a visit to study the operation of local infirmaries.

"This demonstrates how important it is for Parliament itself to retain control over such things. Obviously, this commission should have been appointed by Parliament. This setback is extremely unfortunate, as it will lead to major delays in the investigation," she concluded.

Logging out of the computer, Little Lettvik produced the photo album from the drawer and absentmindedly browsed through the pages. In several places she noticed empty holes where the tiny paper corners used to hold family photographs in place were displayed like meaningless frames around nothing.

Little Lettvik had only one problem. How was she to return the album?

She sat pondering this for a while, as the room slowly filled with light white tobacco smoke.

It doesn't really matter, she finally decided. I can just set fire to the whole shebang.

She took the album home with her. For safety's sake.

7:00 A.M., BOTANIC GARDENS, TØYEN

Hanne Wilhelmsen enjoyed the sensation of perspiration dripping off her and her heart protesting. On her way up the gentle slope of Trondheimsveien, she had stepped up a gear and sprinted through the gate to the Botanic Gardens and on up to the Zoological Museum. She chose a bench underneath a tree she did not recognize. The writing on the explanatory sign beside it was unreadable: some hooligan had sprayed his tag there.

She had never been so fit. Closing her eyes, she inhaled the scent of the trees that had embarked on the long journey into summer. Cecilie had been right: your sense of smell improved when you stopped smoking.

An old man approached her, with a rake in one hand and a spade in the other.

"Lovely weather." He nodded, smiling at the peevishly gray sky grumbling above them: it was drizzling.

Hanne Wilhelmsen chuckled. "Yes, you could say that!"

Peering down at her, the man made up his mind quickly. He sat beside her on the bench and fished out a plug of chewing tobacco that he carefully inserted under his tongue.

"This is the best weather," he muttered. "Rain now in the early morning, and then the sun will come out in the afternoon."

"Do you think so?" Hanne said skeptically, leaning her head back. The fine rain enveloped her face like a Japanese cloth face mask.

"Heavens above!" the man said, chortling. "Look over there!"

He was pointing to the west, where Sofienberg Church loomed against the gray-white sky.

"Do you see that chink of light over there?"

Hanne nodded.

"When there's a little chink over there, above Holmenkollen, slightly to the west-southwest, then there will be really good weather in a few hours."

"But that's not what was forecast," Hanne said, standing up to do some stretches. "They've forecast rain every day until Wednesday."

The old man's hearty laughter produced a spray of brown juice.

"I've worked here for forty-two years now," he said with satisfaction. "For forty-two years I've pottered around here with my plants. I know exactly what they need: water and sun and TLC. It's a grand job, so it is, young lady. People think that all these trees and plants require is scientific treatment, but these plants here, they need more than that."

He watched her in silence for some time, and she stopped doing her exercises to return his gaze. His face was lined and tanned. She was surprised that he was still in employment: he looked as if he should have been pensioned off long ago. He was a pleasant companion, as he had a kind of stillness that did not require her to say very much.

"It has to do with *instinct*, you see. They give me all these books and dissertations, or whatever they're called. But I don't need any of that. I know what each little flower and every bloody massive tree in this garden needs. I've got *instinct*, you see, young lady. I know what the weather is going to do, and I know what they need. Every tiny little flower."

He got to his feet and stepped across to a small plant just beyond the bench; Hanne could not quite decide whether it was a tree seed-ling or if it was meant to be so tiny.

"Look at this bush here, miss," the man said. "It comes all the way from Africa! I don't have to read books to understand that this little lady needs some extra warmth and care, you know. She sits there, poor thing, longing for home and the heat and her pals down in Africa."

He stroked the stem with his hand, and Hanne blinked fiercely when it struck her that it did in fact look as if the shrub enjoyed the contact. His hand was large and coarse, but he touched the plant with a soft, sensual sensitivity.

"You love these plants, I can see." Hanne smiled.

He straightened up proudly, leaning on his rake.

"Can't do a job like this otherwise," he said. "I've been doing this for forty-two years, you know. What do you do?"

"I'm in the police."

The man laughed loudly, a rousing, infectious rumble.

"Well, then you've got your hands full! With that poor Birgitte woman who kicked the bucket and all that! Have you got time to be running around the streets, eh?"

"I'm actually on leave," Hanne began, but checked herself. "But I have to keep fit, you know. Regardless."

The man produced a sizable pocket watch.

"My goodness, I have to get on now," he said. "This is my busiest time, you see, miss. The spring. Bye for now!"

Smiling, he lifted his rake in a parting gesture, but farther down the hill he turned on his heel and made his way back.

"Listen," he said earnestly. "I don't know much about these investi-gations. I just work in the garden. But it must be the same in your job too, mustn't it? That the most important thing is to follow your *instinct*?"

Hanne Wilhelmsen had sat down again. "Yes," she said softly. "I think you're right."

The old man raised his rake once more in farewell, and he shuffled off.

Hanne Wilhelmsen inhaled deeply. The air was cool and damp, a kind of internal cleansing cream. She felt light-headed and her thoughts seemed clearer, more ordered than in a long time.

She felt like Monsieur Poirot: dedicated to "the little gray cells." This situation was unfamiliar. Usually she was in charge. Usually all the information about a case was at her fingertips. But this time she knew only bits and pieces. Even Billy T. had expressed his frustration at having to be part of such a large team with only a very few people in possession of all the information. Unquestionably Håkon was better informed about the bigger picture, but he was in a spin, consumed with anxiety because Karen had not yet given birth.

The victim had two identities: Prime Minister Volter and Birgitte. Which one of these was the actual victim?

Hanne started running again. Downhill, past the old man, now on his knees digging up the earth; he did not even notice her. She increased her speed.

Neither identity was linked to a motive. At least not obviously so. Hanne was deeply skeptical about the international motive continually mooted in the newspapers. The angle of extremists seemed more likely, even though the Security Service did not seem to have anything specific to offer on that either. On the other hand, it was always difficult to know what the boys on the top floors were up to.

According to Billy T., Birgitte Volter's life seemed, not to put too fine a point on it, rather boring. Her personal life. Seemingly, there was no room for scandal; her public life was all-consuming. If she had been involved with a secret lover, then it must have been the most secret lover in all of history. The rumors that attached themselves to her, as to all other people in the public eye, were vague and had turned out to be totally unverifiable, and most of those were in the distant past anyway.

There was no real reason to murder the Prime Minister either. People did not assassinate Prime Ministers in Norway. Of course, Olof Palme had probably thought the same about his country when he refused to have bodyguards accompany him on his visit to a movie theater on that fateful February evening in 1986.

Hanne had reached Sofienberg Park, and it had now stopped raining. She peered toward the west. That chink in the clouds the old man had pointed out had increased in size, and now there was a whole little patch of blue over there. Sitting down on a swing, she swayed gently to and fro.

The few people with access to the Prime Minister's office seemed improbable perpetrators. Wenche Andersen would have had to have killed her boss in cold blood and then given a performance worthy of an Oscar for best supporting actress in her dealings with the police. Out of the question. Benjamin Grinde? Who had gone home to make preparations for his fiftieth birthday party and who, according to the police officers who had picked him up, had been completely calm until they told him that Volter was dead? It couldn't have been him. All the other coworkers at the office had watertight alibis. They had been at meetings, in radio studios, or at dinner engagements.

The answer had seemed so close when she'd asked to see the autopsy report. She had lain awake all night doing battle with the thought. Suicide. The simplest explanation of all. But how had a suicide victim been able to remove the gun she had used and then send it to the police several days later? Hanne Wilhelmsen did not believe in life after death. At least not such an active life. She had tossed and turned and come up with a number of theories. Fired up, she had begged to see the postmortem report. However, that shattered her theory with a simple little test. It was impossible to kill yourself without leaving forensic evidence. The pathologist had examined Birgitte's hands, partly to search for evidence of a struggle and partly as a routine procedure to exclude the possibility of suicide. Which he did. Her hands were chemically free of all traces of gunshot residue. Her theory had collapsed like a house of cards.

Hanne Wilhelmsen did not have the energy to jog any farther. She stood up from the car-tire swing and began to walk home to Billy T.'s strange hangout at Stolmakergata 15.

Did the answer lie in *why* the gun had been returned to the police? Was somebody trying to tell the police something?

Hanne shook her head in irritation. Her brain was getting clogged again; her thoughts whirled around noisily without finding a place within the vague pattern she had spent all weekend trying to put together.

The homicide of Birgitte Volter was a case that lacked a motive. Not an obvious one, at least. Not at present. What on earth did they have? Nothing but an eclectic collection of vanished objects and a dead body. They did have one returned, cleaned revolver of unknown origin. The ballistics tests had shown it *was* the murder weapon that had arrived in the envelope.

A shawl had disappeared. And a pillbox in enameled silver or gold. And a pass. Were these items connected?

Hanne Wilhelmsen's thoughts suddenly returned to the old man in the Botanic Gardens. Instinct. She stopped, closed her eyes, and attempted to check. She was used to trusting her instincts. Gut feeling. Spinal reflex. Now she could feel nothing but the start of a blister on her left heel.

All the same, she sprinted the rest of the way home.

9:10 A.M., OSLO POLICE STATION

"Anyhow, it can't be sheer chance, Håkon!"

Billy T. burst into the Assistant Police Chief's office, speaking far too loudly. He was carrying something huge; it was red and looked like some rubber creature that had deflated.

"What is that you've got?" Håkon Sand yawned.

"The whale," Billy T. said with a grin, propping the expired rubber whale in a corner. "My boys will love that this summer! The biggest floating toy on the beach."

"Bloody hell, Billy T. You can't just help yourself to confiscated property!"

"No? Should he just lie there then, this whale . . ."

As he kicked the toe of his boot in the direction of the red heap, it rustled softly, sadly.

". . . and stay all on his own down there in the dark basement? No, he'll have a better time with my boys."

Shaking his head, Håkon Sand yawned again.

"Listen to this, Håkon," Billy T. said, leaning over him. "This can't be sheer chance. The security guard from the government complex died in that avalanche out in the middle of nowhere on Saturday!"

"Tromsø is a university city with sixty thousand inhabitants. I doubt they'd appreciate you saying the place is in the middle of nowhere."

"It makes no difference, anyway. Don't you get it? Now the guy's dead, we can at least go into his apartment and take a look."

Billy T. slapped a blue sheet down on the desk in front of the police attorney. "Here. Fill out a search warrant."

Håkon Sand pushed the sheet away as though it were a box of scorpions.

"How long can they go past their due date before it becomes dangerous?" he mumbled.

"Eh?"

"Women. Pregnant women. How long can they go over their date?"

Billy T. grinned broadly. "Nervous, are we? You've been through all this before, Håkon. It'll be fine."

"But Hans Wilhelm arrived a week early."

Håkon tried to suppress yet another yawn.

"I thought Karen said she was due yesterday," Billy T. remarked.

"Yes," Håkon muttered, rubbing his face. "But no baby came."

"Jesus Christ, Håkon! They can go one or two weeks over the date without it being a problem. Anyway, the doctor might have made a mistake about the date. Relax. Fill out this instead."

Once more he tried to shove the paper across to Håkon.

"Give me a break!"

Håkon attempted first of all to push the paper back, but when this did not work, he grabbed hold of it and tore it to pieces with abrupt, angry movements.

"I don't know whether you recollect, Billy T. But I remember *fucking* well an episode a few years back when I tried to have that attorney, Jørgen Ulf, taken into custody, based on a witness statement from Karen. It was a real nightmare. The judge bit my head off because I had not acknowledged that the dead have the same rights as the living. I'm not bloody going down that road again."

Billy T. stared open-mouthed at Håkon.

"Stop catching flies," Håkon continued. "You might not learn from your mistakes, but I certainly do. What's more, and I'm saying this now for the last time: *the guard is none of your business!*"

Håkon slammed the flat of his hand on the table, and raised his voice yet another notch. "If you now go off to Tone-Marit to get her to run your errand, then I'll be furious! There's no legal authority for a warrant. And neither is there any reason at all to assume that there's anything at the security guard's house that we have legal authority to seize. Here!"

Turning around abruptly, Håkon took hold of one of four statute books on the shelf behind him. He smacked it down on the desk so vehemently that the windowpanes rattled.

"Criminal Procedure Act, section 194! Read it for yourself!"

Billy T. squirmed in his seat.

"What a bloody fuss you're making!"

Håkon Sand gave a deep sigh.

"I get so bloody *fed up*, Billy T."

He had dropped his voice, and he appeared to be directing his mutterings at the statute book.

"I get so fed up with you and Hanne sometimes. I know you're smart. I know you're usually right. It's just that . . ."

Leaning back in the office chair, he stared at the window. Two seagulls were sitting on the window ledge, peering in; they canted their heads as if they felt sorry for him.

". . . you're not the one who takes all the shit when the legal details don't add up. It's me. Do you know what the other attorneys in the building have started calling me?"

"Errand boy," Billy T. mumbled, trying not to smile.

"It doesn't bother me. Actually, I'm okay with it. I'm grateful for the relationship I have with you and Hanne. We have solved some major cases along the way, of course."

Now they were both smiling, and the seagulls hoarsely screeched their agreement outside the window.

"But is it not possible to show me a little—a little respect? Now and again?"

Billy T. looked solemnly at his colleague.

"Now you're really bloody mistaken, Håkon. I have to tell you . . ."

Leaning forward, he took hold of Håkon's hand. Håkon attempted to pull it back, but Billy T. would not let go.

". . . if there's one single lawyer in this building Hanne and I do have respect for, it's you. No one else. And do you know why?"

Håkon gazed at their two hands without offering a response. Billy T.'s was large and hairy, and surprisingly soft and warm. His own was bony and firm. He turned his hand over; now they were holding hands as if they were going to dance.

"We like you, Håkon. You show us respect. You're willing to bend the rules a little . . ."

Billy T. nodded in the direction of the large red book.

". . . when you realize they get in the way of catching the bad guys. You've stuck your neck out for Hanne and me loads of times. You are seriously wrong if you don't think we respect you. Completely wrong."

Håkon was suffused with a warm glow, and a pleasant feeling flooded through his abdomen; it felt like the long-lost childhood emotion of happiness. But he was also overwhelmed by an indescribable exhaustion. His eyes drifted shut, and he felt faint.

"Bloody hell, I'm so tired. Didn't sleep the whole night. Just lay there staring and staring at Karen's stomach. Are you sure it isn't dangerous?"

"Sure as shooting!" Billy T. said, releasing his hand. "But now you really must listen."

He rubbed his knuckles across his head.

"This might be really important. Birgitte Volter is dead. And then the security guard is killed in an avalanche. The person who was at her office at absolutely the most critical point. The guy who has been grouchy and surly, owns guns, and who fails to present them for inspection as he promised to. This could be a matter of life and death, Håkon! I've got to have that blue sheet!"

Håkon Sand got to his feet, stretched his arms up toward the ceiling, and rocked up and down on his toes.

"You can just let this drop, Billy T. You're not getting any search warrant. But if it's any consolation . . ."

He fell back onto his heels with a bump.

". . . last Friday a disclosure order was sent to the guard. In other words, he received a formal demand for the same thing that you had requested so nicely. It will now be up to his heirs to comply with it. He probably has parents somewhere. If Tone-Marit discovers that the guard needs further investigating, then I'll discuss that with her. With Tone-Marit. Not with you."

"But Håkon!"

Billy T. was not making any concessions.

"The guard's death is all too convenient! Can't you see that?"

Now Håkon Sand burst out laughing.

"So you think there's a terrorist organization that can arrange the blizzard of the century in northern Norway and then instigate an unexpected storm and an enormous avalanche? That avalanche was planned in November, you know! That was when it started snowing to such an amazing extent. An uncle of mine lives in Tromsø. He was hospitalized last week for a heart attack caused by too much snow clearing."

He laughed again, long and hearty.

"What an incredible show of weather to orchestrate! You're wrong about this, Billy T. For once in your life, you've got the wrong end of the stick."

He was right. Billy T. sulked. He stood up abruptly, then crouched down and embraced the rubber whale.

"I don't give a shit about any of it," he said angrily, and left the office.

"And put that whale back where you found it," Håkon Sand bellowed after him. "Do you hear? *Put it back!*"

12:15 P.M., SUPREME COURT

Five judges sat in their lunchroom enjoying tea and packed lunches in what was called "the long break." Two of them had still not become accustomed to skipping coffee. In the Supreme Court, people drank tea. The room was spacious and elegant, its two sets of pale birchwood sofas upholstered in apple-green wool to complement the warm gold of the walls. Several pictures hung around the room, attractive colorist works. The fine white porcelain cups rattled faintly, and now and again careful little sips could be heard.

"Has anybody seen Benjamin Grinde today?"

The furrow between the Chief Justice's eyes betrayed the slight unease he had felt since his discovery a couple of hours earlier that Judge Grinde was nowhere to be found.

"I dropped by his office a short time ago," the Chief Justice continued. "He was to be the first to consider the verdict in that social security case tried last Wednesday, wasn't he?"

Three of the other judges nodded feebly.

"That's what I thought. I am delivering a lecture to the social security tribunal next week and would like to be able to refer to the most recent decision."

"I haven't seen him either," Judge Sunde said, straightening his snow-white shirt collar.

"Nor me," another two said, almost in chorus.

"But he was supposed to have his opinion ready this afternoon," Judge Løvenskiold remarked. "We are having a meeting at four o'clock. So this is—"

"Odd." One of the others finished his sentence. "Really odd."

The Chief Justice stood up and stepped across to the telephone just beside the elegant kitchenette to the left of the entrance door. After a short, subdued conversation, he replaced the receiver and turned to face the others.

"This is very worrying," he said in a booming voice. "His office staff say he was expected as usual today, but he has not turned up. He hasn't left any messages either."

As the judges looked down into their teacups, they heard a truck engine idling in the street outside.

"I must look into this," the Chief Justice mumbled. "Immediately."

Had Benjamin Grinde been taken ill? It was extremely unlike him to be absent without explanation. The Chief Justice of the Supreme Court sat in his own office listening to the ring tone on the telephone receiver. He knew that the telephone at Odins gate 3 was now ringing, but it was evidently falling on deaf ears. He abandoned the attempt and replaced the receiver carefully.

In his employees' files, there were two numbers provided for Grinde's mother, his nearest relative. One was for overseas, though the Chief Justice was unable to identify the country code off the top of his head. The other one began with 22—Oslo. He dialed it, slowly and painstakingly.

"Hello, this is the Grindes' house," chirped the person at the other end. "How can I help you?"

The Chief Justice introduced himself.

Birdie Grinde was on top of the world. Yesterday she had received a visit from a journalist, and today the Chief Justice himself was calling.

"No, such a pleasure," she shrieked, forcing the Chief Justice to hold the receiver away from his ear. "How *can* I help you?"

He explained his business.

"I can only think that Ben just needs some rest," she reassured him. "He's exhausted, you know. This affair with the police has affected him dreadfully. I don't know if you have had the opportunity to notice, but he is very sensitive. It's a trait of the Grinde family. His father, for example—"

The Chief Justice interrupted her.

"So you think he may simply be asleep? But he hasn't left any messages."

"Both you and I know that's not like Ben. But perhaps he has just overslept. I can—"

Suddenly she stopped, but the pause did not last long.

"I can call in to his apartment this afternoon. I could just manage it before I go to the theater. I have a hairdresser's appointment right now, you understand, but this afternoon—"

"Thanks." He interrupted her again. "I would be grateful if you could do that."

"Of course," Birdie Grinde said, and the Chief Justice thought he could hear a touch of grievance in her voice.

"Goodbye," he said, replacing the receiver before she had a chance to reply.

5:30 P.M., MINISTRY OF HEALTH

"**B**ut I can do that, my dear!"

The Minister of Health's secretary looked alarmed when she found her boss bent over the fax machine, squinting in an effort to ascertain how it worked.

"This is personal," Ruth-Dorthe Nordgarden snapped, waving the nervous woman away.

Eventually the fax was sent, and Nordgarden brought the original back into her office.

"Send them in," she instructed one of the secretaries. Then she took her seat at the top of the conference table, half an hour after the meeting was actually supposed to have begun.

None of them made eye contact with her when they entered. The atmosphere was awkward, and there was a tension in the room that they all, except the minister herself, detected. She smiled anxiously and invited them to take their places around the table.

"First of all, I must just say that I don't have a good grasp of this kind of thing," she began. "So do your best to be extremely clear. Please. No, wait!"

Staring at the others, two men and three women, she opened her arms.

"Where is Grinde? Hasn't he arrived yet?"

She glanced at the clock.

The five others looked at one another in surprise.

"I had the impression," Ravn Falkanger, an elderly physician and professor of pediatrics, started to say. "I thought Judge Grinde was already here, for a preliminary meeting."

"Certainly not," Ruth-Dorthe Nordgarden broke in. "I haven't heard anything about a preliminary meeting."

Histrionically, she looked again at her watch, tugging at the sleeve of her jacket and holding her arm unnecessarily high.

"Well. If he hasn't arrived by now, then we'll just have to make a start. I have read this here."

She waved the eleven-page report that she had received that morning from the commission's secretary, a woman who looked unhappy and appeared far too young.

"And I have to say, you complicate it with all this medical jargon."

The oldest man present, Edward Hansteen, a professor of toxicology, cleared his throat quietly.

"It should be understood, Minister, that the work of the commission gradually took a different direction from the one set out in our original mandate. We would now like to travel abroad to examine the archives there. That was the reason Benjamin Grinde wanted to speak to the minister, which I understand—"

He cleared his throat again, more vigorously this time, and gazed down at his papers.

"I understand that the minister's pressure of work made it impossible to have such a meeting with Grinde. I assume that was why he sought help from Prime Minister Volter. The minister will appreciate that this is a delicate affair and Grinde wanted to raise it confidentially with our political masters."

The commission secretary began to blush in the painful pause that ensued. Perspiration appeared on her forehead, and she tried in vain to hide behind her long blond hair.

"Well," Ruth-Dorthe Nordgarden said. "All that is water under the bridge now. Let us keep to the here and now. Go ahead."

She nodded again to Dr. Hansteen.

The meeting lasted for three-quarters of an hour. The atmosphere did not improve. The discussion around the oval table was subdued, and only the minister's "I don't quite understand" and "Could you repeat that part?" cut through Edward Hansteen's even, pleasant tones. Synnøve von Schallenberg, a community medical practitioner, took over from her colleague occasionally; she too would look briefly at the minister as she clarified something, with a concerned expression on her face.

"As the minister undoubtedly understands," said Dr. Hansteen in his final summing-up, "we are faced with the probable conclusion that something highly irregular has taken place."

He emphasized the point by smacking the documents three times with his knuckles.

Ruth-Dorthe Nordgarden stared intently at the document facing her. The report she had received that morning. She *had* read it, but perhaps not very thoroughly. Not thoroughly enough. She should never have faxed it to Little Lettvik. And certainly not from this office. Could these things be traced? She had made a terrible mistake.

She made an incomprehensible grimace and tugged at her hair.

"Yes, but . . ."

The corner of her mouth twitched violently.

". . . is there anything here that could mean trouble from a purely political point of view?"

The four oldest members of the commission around the table exchanged uneasy glances. The young secretary intently studied a knot in the wooden tabletop. Health Minister Ruth-Dorthe Nordgarden realized just too late that she had overstepped the mark. The commission was not there to help her politically. It was their task to clarify the facts.

"You can go," she said quickly. "Thanks for—"

Her remaining words were drowned out by the scraping of chairs as the rest of them stood up. To cap it all, the commission secretary knocked her chair over. Ruth-Dorthe was left standing, immobile, her eyes full of tears. But none of the others noticed.

7:30 P.M., STOLMAKERGATA 15

Although it was fantastic that Hanne had moved in, Billy T. felt a powerful sense of well-being when he was entirely on his own. No one to foist the TV news program on him, and he could eat lukewarm meatballs and spaghetti out of the can without anyone wrinkling their nose at it. It was convenient. He simply let the can sit under the hot tap for a while and, presto, dinner was ready.

He had brought the beanbag in from the bedroom; he was still not entirely used to the blue sofa. The bag supported his body, and his legs and arms sprawled across the floor. He ignored the thumps on the wall from his ill-tempered neighbor and used the remote control to turn the volume up a notch.

Madame Butterfly was approaching the end. He empathized strongly with her in her great adversity. The man she loved and had waited many years for had returned at last, accompanied by another woman. And that woman, who had stolen her beloved, also wanted to take her single genuine treasure, her son. Her only child.

The music built to a crescendo: potent, dramatic. Billy T. closed his eyes, feeling the music flood through him; his toes were vibrating.

Con onor muore chi non può serbar vita con onore!

"Death with honor is better than life with dishonor," Billy T. whispered.

The telephone cut through the finale.

"*Goddamn it!*"

Leaping to his feet, he grabbed the phone and roared into it, "*Wait!*"

He laid the receiver down beside the phone, and crossed to the center of the room.

Madame Butterfly sang to her son in a heartfelt aria filled with pain: for his sake, she was willing to die.

It was over.

In a voice so soft that Tone-Marit Steen at the other end of the line wondered momentarily if she had dialed the wrong number, he said, "Hello, who is it?"

His voice had resumed its usual tone when, seconds later, he bellowed, "What the hell? Is Benjamin Grinde *dead*?"

TUESDAY, APRIL 15

Hanne Wilhelmsen chuckled as she read the Calvin and Hobbes comic strip. It was always the first thing she looked at. She had devoured everything that had been put in front of her: a hamburger with onions and roast potatoes, washed down by a glass of milk. She swallowed a belch and regretted eating the potatoes.

Billy T. did not subscribe to *Aftenposten*. It irritated Hanne that he was not even civilized enough to have a newspaper delivered to his door. She compensated for her friend's philistinism by eating breakfast in a café, surrounded by all the daily newspapers, after her morning run.

The coffee was not up to much, but it was strong. She wrinkled her nose, but that was as much in response to all the headlines about Benjamin Grinde's death. *Dagbladet* had gone for gigantic red lettering above their picture of Judge Grinde, and Hanne turned to page 4, as the front page requested her to. It screeched at her but contained only information she already knew. She couldn't be bothered to read any further.

For once, however, she had to admit that the newspapers had a point. It *was* striking that Benjamin Grinde had died eight days after Birgitte Volter. The Chief of Police's thundering exhortation for total silence had evidently borne fruit: as far as she could make out, none of the newspapers had discovered that the time of death had been established as Saturday afternoon. But it was an amazing coincidence. Government ministers and officials would probably go berserk if—or perhaps she should say when—they found out that the security guard from the government complex had shuffled off this mortal coil on the same day.

Something niggled at her, but she could not quite put her finger on it. The guard. Benjamin Grinde. Birgitte Volter. All dead within a single week. One had been murdered with a revolver. One had been killed in a natural disaster. And one had probably committed suicide; at least that was what Billy T. had whispered to her when he had tumbled into bed beside her at about four o'clock that morning. He told her that the man had been found stretched out in his bed with an empty pill bottle sitting neatly on the bedside table.

Fishing out a pen from her handbag, Hanne moved her dirty plate to a neighboring table and drew a triangle on her napkin. Grinde, the guard, and Volter were each allocated a corner. Underneath, she sketched a shawl, a revolver, a pass, and a pillbox. The answer lay there. She knew that the answer was right there.

She let the pen run from object to person, from person to object, and her head began to ache as the lines became an untidy and incomprehensible pattern. She had been prone to serious headaches since 1993, when she had been knocked unconscious outside her own office during an investigation into a scandalous case involving prominent politicians, attorneys, and members of the Intelligence Service, all of whom were mixed up in dealing narcotics.

She swallowed two painkiller tablets with the last drop of her milk.

Kveldsavisen had adopted a strident tone. The political section was at last beginning to take an interest in Little Lettvik's crusade, and out of everything in the six pages devoted to the case, the political comment was the most noteworthy.

CAN WE TOLERATE THE TRUTH?

Norway as a nation has been wounded in the past week by dramatic events unprecedented in our postwar history. Last Friday Prime Minister Birgitte Volter was found murdered in her office. Yesterday evening, a Supreme Court judge was found dead in his home, in mysterious circumstances.

Of course, we can look at these incidents from a variety of perspectives. Some might shrug them off, noting simply that even eminent people can be victims of violence in this increasingly violent society of ours, a trend our politicians seem powerless to stop. Such a conclusion would be naive and would appear to be covering matters up rather than shedding light on them.

During the past week, the Norwegian press has produced countless theories implying that international terrorist organizations could have picked out a Norwegian Prime Minister as a target. However, by focusing too much on this possibility, we are in danger of closing our eyes to explanations closer to home.

This newspaper was the only one to investigate the circumstances of Birgitte Volter's death. We have not contented ourselves with dutifully repeating the sparse details of the official press releases that the police have seen fit to share with the public.

Through our painstaking work, we have been able to reveal that Benjamin Grinde was probably the last person to see Volter alive. We have disclosed that for several hours, he was actually accused of the crime. Later, we were able to establish that there were very close ties between Judge Grinde and the Prime Minister.

Today we are able to reveal that the Grinde Commission has uncovered an extremely irregular situation in the Norwegian Health Service. The critical question now is: Are the politicians, press, and police brave enough to draw the necessary conclusions from these new revelations?

A situation like this is an important test for a state governed by the rule of law. If we are to pass this test, we have to take for granted the independence of the press, police, courts of law, and politicians. It requires, first and foremost, a press that is willing to seek the truth and to speak out, unconstrained by the established authorities.

We must learn from the experiences of other countries that have undergone similar national traumas. Eleven years ago, Sweden suffered a serious blow when Prime Minister Olof Palme was shot and killed on a public street. In the beginning, the investigation concentrated almost exclusively on the so-called Kurd lead. Other possibilities were not evaluated until it was too late. The investigation has suffered from a lack of professionalism and fixed theories. The result is that Sweden will probably never solve its national murder.

Recently, Belgium has been shaken by a pedophile scandal with connections that reach far inside the police force and in all likelihood into political circles as well. The powers that be have been so close to one another that it has been entirely possible to undermine the investigation of grotesque crimes. When it has been convenient to do so.

We must be on our guard to ensure that this does not also happen in our country.

The information that *Kveldsavisen* can today exclusively reveal to the Norwegian people indicates that the spike in infant mortality in 1965 was probably caused by a serious error on the part of the government. Vaccines dispensed by the National Institute of Public Health proved to be lethal, for perhaps many hundreds of children. Wholesale death was distributed and administered by a national directorate.

The top politician in the country and the chair of the investigating commission obviously had a meeting about this matter just over a week ago. Now they are both dead.

Are we willing to look the truth in the eye?

For the first time in ages, Hanne Wilhelmsen felt like a smoke. The proprietor of the little café where she sat had clearly never heard of the antismoking law, since its five other customers were all puffing cigarettes.

The health scandal had only just flared up in the press when she'd left for the United States. She knew of course that Grinde was to investigate the case and that he had paid Volter a visit on the day she died. But did this have anything to do with her homicide?

Once more she stared at her napkin. The pattern was more indistinct than before. She carefully drew a little cross above the security guard, then emphasized the line between Benjamin Grinde and Birgitte Volter, making a hole in the soft paper. However, it was as though the guard refused to disappear. She scribbled him out, but then the drawing was somehow wrong. There was something there. She simply could not work out what it was. Her headache returned, and she could not take any more painkillers.

"Hanne! Hanne Wilhelmsen!"

A man slapped her on the head with a newspaper. Quick as a flash, she shielded herself with her arm, before her face broke into an enormous smile.

"Varg! What are you doing here? Sit down!"

The man threw his voluminous, well-worn overcoat over the back of the chair with practiced ease as he sat down. Then he placed his forearms on the table, clasped his hands, and gazed at her.

"Unbelievable. You get prettier and prettier with every year that passes."

"What are you doing so far from Bergen? I thought you ventured away from the beautiful city of the seven mountains only with the greatest of reluctance."

"I'm on a case. A really strange case. A runaway boy nobody wants, but who seems to be extremely active in IT. The children's services are continually finding traces of him on the Internet, but they have no idea where he is. And he's only twelve years old."

Waving toward the café owner, he ordered coffee.

"Have tea instead," Hanne whispered.

"No way. I need my coffee in the morning. And what about you? What are you doing these days?"

Varg and Hanne did not recall how they had come to know each other. He was a private detective who seldom visited Oslo. They had some very distant acquaintances in common and had bumped into each other professionally on a couple of occasions. They had liked each other immediately, which had surprised them both.

"I'm actually on leave," Hanne said, without divulging anything further. "But I'm busy nevertheless and taking an interest in this Volter case. Impossible not to."

"Remarkable, all that stuff in the newspaper today," he said, nodding toward the disarray of papers on the table. "This health scandal really looks as though it will be major."

"I haven't actually managed to read much yet," Hanne responded. "What's it all about?"

"Well," he began, waving impatiently for his coffee, "it appears that an abnormal number of children died of so-called sudden infant death syndrome. In all probability, that's a kind of stock diagnosis used when all other causes of death have been excluded. All the children received

the same type of triple vaccine. It was given at the age of three months.
It turns out that this vaccine was—"

He fumbled to pick up the copy of *Kveldsavisen*, and leafed through
it eagerly, licking his finger at regular intervals.

"—contaminated. Here it is: 'It probably has to do with a derivative
that formed in the preserving agent. A derivative resembles the active
ingredient in the vaccine but has a totally different effect. It may have
attacked the children's hearts and caused them to stop beating.'"

"Let me see," Hanne said, grabbing the newspaper.

She was engrossed for a few minutes, and Varg was halfway through
his cup of coffee before she looked up again.

"This is really terribly serious," Hanne said softly, folding up all the
newspapers. "They don't even know where the vaccine was purchased."

"No, that's the main point. This commission has obviously asked
that it be allowed to undertake investigations in foreign archives to try
to get to the bottom of it. The records here in Norway seem to be
deplorably deficient. The likelihood is that the vaccine was produced
in some uncivilized country where they did not have satisfactory
hygiene procedures."

He drank the rest of his coffee, then stood up abruptly.

"I have to go. But, Hanne—" He hesitated for a second before saying
with a smile, "I'll be fifty in August. Why don't you make a trip over the
mountains? I've decided to have a bit of a celebration."

"I'll be in the States," Hanne replied apologetically, opening her
arms. "But congratulations all the same! See you sometime!"

He threw on his coat and headed off. Hanne tore out a sheet of
paper from her diary and drew her triangle again. Volter–Grinde–
guard. In the article it had stated that Health Minister Ruth-Dorthe
Nordgarden had given assurances that the matter would be taken
extremely seriously and that the necessary authorization and resources
for the investigations into foreign leads would be forthcoming. Hanne
hesitated slightly before putting the initials RDN between Grinde and
Volter. Suddenly the guard did not seem so important: his presence on
the paper interfered with a new triangle connecting the other three. If
Benjamin Grinde had killed himself, why had he done so? If it had
something to do with the health scandal, she could not see the logic in
it. He should really have considered it a feather in his cap that he had

discovered the root cause. It was true that the headlines in recent days must have been extremely uncomfortable for him, but to commit suicide . . .

Now her headache was unbearable. Suddenly she drew a large X through the whole picture and tore it to shreds.

"There's really no rhyme or reason to this," she said to herself as she headed out the door to see if some fresh air would do the trick.

Once outdoors, she tapped a number into her cell phone. Without introducing herself, she asked, "Can we meet up tonight?"

Only seconds later, she wrapped up the conversation. "Fine. Seven o'clock. At Tranen restaurant in Alexander Kiellands plass."

Then she pressed Billy T.'s number.

"Hi, it's me. You'll be on your own again tonight. I've got a dinner date."

"Is this off the record or on the record if Cecilie phones and asks for you?" Billy T. laughed at the other end.

"Idiot. I've a meeting with Deep Throat. You can tell *that* to Cecilie."

Now her headache was excruciating. Holding her fingers to her forehead, she decided to go home to Stolmakergata and try to get some sleep.

11:15 A.M., ODINS GATE 3

The technical team had been there for several hours yesterday evening. There were minuscule traces of them everywhere, almost imperceptible signs that the apartment had been turned upside down by people who did not live there, even though everything had been put back tidily. Everything apart from an empty plastic container of amitriptyline 25 milligram tablets that had been sitting on Grinde's bedside table beside half a glass of water, and the bedclothes, which had also been removed for closer inspection.

Billy T. was standing in the middle of the room, holding a brief report from the crime scene technicians. The body had been found in bed, wearing only boxer shorts. There was no sign of forced entry; the door was locked from the inside and the security chain was in place. The mother of the deceased had phoned a locksmith in order to get into the apartment, but the locksmith had demonstrated the presence of mind to call the police first.

Billy T. folded the paper twice and stuffed it into his back pocket. He had argued to be allowed to attend; after all, Tone-Marit owed him something after that interview with the guard.

"Amitriptyline," he remarked to Tone-Marit. "Was the guy using antidepressants?"

"There's nothing to indicate that," she replied. "He just knew what he needed to take. He took two Valium tablets to calm himself and then a fistful of amitriptyline. The tablets were bought on Friday. He issued the prescription himself, in his mother's name, and fooled the pharmacy staff by saying that his mother was recently widowed and needed some tranquilizers during the transition period. The guy was a doctor. They know what's required, and they can get most of it at an ordinary pharmacy."

The kitchen was the most glamorous room in the apartment, with cherrywood cabinets and counters in something that looked like black marble.

"Larvikite," Tone-Marit Steen said, stroking the hard, polished surface. "Lovely. And look at this!"

A wide American refrigerator had been integrated into the reddish-brown cherrywood panels; it had a freezer on one side and fridge compartment on the other, and an opening in the middle of the freezer dispensed water with ice cubes in it. He opened the freezer door. Neat parcels marked "Elk tenderloin 1996," "Lingonberries 1995," and "Homemade fettuccine March 20" suggested that the contents of the fridge would be equally exotic. But that was not the case. It contained only a wedge of brie that had begun to go moldy, a shriveled pepper, three bottles of Farris mineral water, and two bottles of white wine. Billy T. stuck his nose into the single carton of skimmed milk on the shelf in the door and recoiled with a grimace. Grinde had not eaten for a while. A lithograph hung above a little table for two under the window and the food processor was exactly the same as the one Billy T. had seen in the canteen kitchen at the police station. The room was stunning, if somewhat sterile.

In that respect, the living room was more pleasant. Bookcases lined an entire wall and contained every genre of literature. Billy T. pressed the button to eject the CD from the player: Benjamin Britten's *Peter Grimes*. Not exactly Billy T.'s taste; he shook his head slightly at the thought of the fisherman Peter Grimes, who went out in all weather and tormented the life out of the workhouse boys apprenticed to him. Powerful stuff, and certainly not suitable for someone in suicidal anguish.

He saw that Tone-Marit was looking at some tiny figurines. He took one of them down from the shelf in the massive, heavy sideboard, and wondered what it could be.

"Japanese netsuke," Tone-Marit said with a smile. "Little miniatures that were originally made as belt toggles but were later used as ornaments and collectibles."

Astonished, Billy T. stared from the tiny, scary-looking Shinto-god he held in the palm of his hand to Tone-Marit.

"These are truly beautiful," she continued. "They're probably genuine. They were made before 1850, which means they're exceptionally valuable."

Carefully, she replaced the figures on the shelf, lining them up behind the polished glass doors.

"My grandfather ran a Japanese agency," she explained, almost embarrassed.

Billy T. knelt down and opened the double doors embossed with decorative bunches of grapes. Inside lay starched, ironed tablecloths, all neatly folded.

"A methodical person, this guy Grinde," he mumbled as he closed the doors.

Then he went into the bedroom. It was tidy, but the bed was stripped. A pair of trousers hung neatly in an electric trouser press on the wall, and a shirt and tie were draped over a little wing chair. The bathroom opened off the bedroom, and was decorated in a masculine style with dark blue floor tiles. Its white walls were broken at shoulder height by a border of blue and yellow in some kind of Egyptian pattern that ran around the room. A faint, fresh, masculine odor was evident. A toothbrush. An old-fashioned shaving brush and shaving soap. Billy T. picked up the razor: it looked like silver and had the initials BG on the handle.

He felt like an intruder and suddenly imagined a fearful scenario: Imagine if *he* were the one who had been found dead! Imagine some police officer going through *his* bathroom, touching his things, peering at his most intimate belongings. He gave himself a shake, hesitating before he opened the cabinet door.

That was it.

He did not doubt it for a moment.

"Tone-Marit," he roared. "Bring an evidence bag and come here!"

She appeared in the doorway almost instantly.

"What is it?"

"Look."

She approached him slowly, her eyes following his forefinger down to a little, gilded, enameled pillbox.

"Oy," she said, her eyes like saucers.

"Yes, you could say that." Billy T. grinned as he put it in a plastic bag and closed the zipper.

3:45 P.M., OSLO POLICE STATION

The Security Service Chief looked like a funeral director. His suit was too dark, his shirt too white. The narrow black tie ran like an exclamation mark down the front of his inappropriate outfit. Admittedly, they planned to meet Birgitte Volter's next of kin, but it was now four days since the funeral had taken place.

None of those assembled in the Police Chief's conference room had experienced anything like this before. Naturally, most of them had at least once in their career spoken to the bereaved relatives of a murder victim, but never in such an official way. And certainly not after the murder of a prime minister.

"Well," the Chief of Police said.

He stared in disbelief at Billy T., who was wearing gray flannel pleated trousers, a white shirt, and an unbuttoned dark gray jacket. The colors on his tie were mellow and autumnal, and he looked like a completely different man. Even the inverted cross in his earlobe had been removed, and in its place twinkled a tiny diamond.

The Superintendent rushed breathlessly into the room, red in the face.

"The elevators are out of order," he groaned, rubbing his hands over the seat of his trousers.

Roy Hansen stood in the doorway, having been ushered in solicitously by the Police Chief's secretary. He greeted each person in turn, and the round of handshakes became so lengthy and complicated in the confusion of chairs that Billy T. sensibly abstained from adding to the awkwardness. Instead he sat down, nodded to the widower, and avoided asking what had happened to Per Volter.

Per Volter arrived five minutes late. His clothes looked as though they had been slept in, which they probably had; there was a whiff of stale perspiration combined with the unmistakable stench of earlier intoxication masked at daybreak with green mouthwash. His eyes were evasive, and he raised his hand in a collective greeting instead of accepting the hands hesitantly extended toward him. He did not condescend to give his father so much as a glance.

"I'm late," he muttered, collapsing unceremoniously onto a chair, his back half-turned on his father. "Sorry."

The Chief of Police stood up without quite knowing what to say. It did not seem appropriate to actually "welcome" people to the investigation into the homicide of their wife and mother. He gazed in the direction of Roy Hansen, who had his eyes trained on his son's back; his expression was so surprisingly naked and full of despair that the Police Chief momentarily lost his courage and considered postponing the entire session.

"I'm quite sure this will be unpleasant," he finally ventured. "And I'm really sorry about that. However, I—and my colleagues—thought you would prefer to get a firsthand account of where we stand. In the investigation, I mean."

"We know a lot less than the guys outside the door downstairs," Per Volter broke in loudly and abruptly.

"I beg your pardon?"

The Police Chief laid his hand on Per's shoulder and looked him in the eye.

"Outside the door?"

"Yes. Journalists. I had to run the gauntlet of them to make my way through. Do you think I'm happy to have my photograph taken like this?"

He tugged at his shirtfront, as if to demonstrate his grubby condition.

The Police Chief examined something immediately in front of his feet and swallowed several times. His Adam's apple chafed against his chin, which was red with shaving rash.

"I can only apologize. It was not our intention for anyone to know you were coming. Sorry."

"Sorry here and sorry there!"

Per Volter pushed back his chair and stretched out like a defiant teenager, his backside on the edge of his seat, his shoulders against the backrest, and his legs splayed out across the floor.

"To serve and protect. Isn't that what they say? Until now, you've neither served nor protected. Agreed?"

He slammed a fist onto the wall beside him, then buried his face in his hands.

Roy Hansen cleared his throat. His face was now ashen, and his eyes were perilously moist. The other men in the room sat quiet as mice, and only Billy T. dared to look at father and son.

"Per," Roy Hansen said softly. "You know you can—"

"Don't speak to me," Per Volter bellowed. "Haven't I told you that? Haven't I told you that I never want to speak to you again?"

He covered his face once more.

The Chief of Police was crimson. Fumbling with a cigarette he could not light, he continued to stare at one of his knees. The Superintendent's mouth was gaping, although he was unaware of it, and it was only when a dribble started to run down his chin that he clamped his jaw shut and promptly used his arm to wipe his face.

The Police Chief peered studiously through the window, as though evaluating a possible escape route.

"Per Volter!"

It was Billy T., his voice deep and penetrating.

"Look at me!"

The young man on the opposite side of the table stopped rocking from side to side, though he still kept his face hidden.

"Look at me," Billy T. roared, slapping the palm of his hand on the teak table so forcefully that the windows juddered.

Startled, Per took his hands away.

"We know you're feeling dreadful. Everyone in this room understands that you must be going through a terrible ordeal."

Billy T. leaned further across the table.

"But you're not the first person in the history of the world to lose his mother! Now you really must pull yourself together!"

Per Volter sat up angrily in his chair.

"No, but I'm the only one to have his family's whole life history laid bare in every newspaper in the country afterward!"

Now he was sobbing, quietly and with little sniffs, and rubbing his eyes repeatedly, to no avail.

"You're right there," Billy T. said. "I certainly can't imagine what that must be like. But you have to let us get on with our jobs all the same, which right now involves telling you and your father how things stand. If you would like to listen, that's fine. If not, I suggest you leave. I can get someone to accompany you out the rear exit so you can avoid the press out there."

The young man did not answer; he was still weeping.

"Hello," Billy T. said softly. "Per!"

Per Volter looked up. The police officer's eyes were a peculiar pale, matte ice-blue color, the sort you might see on a dangerous dog or in a horror movie. However, his mouth was extended in a faint smile that suggested an understanding that Per Volter felt no one had shown him since his mother had been shot.

"Do you want to go, or would you rather stay? Or would you perhaps like to wait in my office, so that you and I can have a chat by ourselves afterward?"

Per Volter forced a smile.

"Sorry. I'll stay."

Then he blew his nose on a tissue offered by the Police Chief. He straightened up completely and placed one foot over the other, staring at the Police Chief as though wondering, with impatience and amazement, why the report had ended before it had begun.

It did not take long. After a brief report, the Chief of Police handed the meeting over to the Security Service Chief, who was equally concise. Billy T. was aware that the information being imparted had been methodically filtered, and that in fact Ole Henrik Hermansen was relating everything and nothing. The most interesting aspect was that when he spoke in general terms about the extremist lead, an odd expression crossed his lips, and his gaze was not as steady as usual.

The security guard, Billy T. thought. *They've found something on the guard.*

"What?" he exclaimed all of a sudden: the Police Chief had spoken his name three times without him hearing. "Oh, sorry. The pillbox, yes."

Retrieving a little plastic bag from his jacket pocket, he placed it in front of Roy Hansen. The widower had not uttered a word since Per had shrieked at him, and he still did not open his mouth. He peered at the plastic bag with a poker face.

"Do you recognize this?" Billy T. asked. "Is this Birgitte's pillbox?"

"Never seen it before," Per Volter said before his father had gotten around to answering.

The young man leaned forward to pick up the bag. Billy T. swiftly placed his hand over the object.

"Not yet. Do you recognize it?"

He removed the box from the bag and held it up to Roy Hansen.

"It's ours," the widower whispered. "We received it at our wedding. Birgitte and I. A wedding present. It's the one I showed you in the photograph."

"Certain?"

Roy Hansen nodded slowly, without taking his eyes off the box.

"*I've* not seen it before," Per Volter repeated.

"Where did you find it?" Roy Hansen asked, holding out his palm to Billy T.

"In Benjamin Grinde's apartment," Billy T. replied, placing the box in Roy Hansen's hand.

"What?"

Per Volter looked from one to the other.

"At that Supreme Court judge's place?"

All the police officers nodded enthusiastically, as though to make the assertion even more credible.

"At Benjamin Grinde's," Roy Hansen said. "Why on earth—?"

He looked up from his thorough inspection of the little pillbox.

"Yes, well, that was what we were hoping one of you might be able to tell us," Billy T. said, fingering the diamond on his earlobe.

"No idea," Roy Hansen mumbled.

"Not a single theory?"

Despair had given way to aggression, and the widower raised his voice. "Maybe Benjamin Grinde stole it? Swiped it! Some time or other. What do I know! He could have taken it years ago, for that matter, since I haven't seen it for as long as I can remember."

"No. It must have been on the day he met Birgitte, before she was killed," Billy T. said calmly. "Her secretary remembers that the box always used to sit on her desk."

He glanced at Per Volter, who shrugged and shook his head.

"Haven't a clue," he reiterated. "Never seen it before."

"You probably noticed it was difficult to open," Billy T. said, address-ing Roy Hansen. "But we managed it. There was a lock of hair inside the box. It looks as if it came from a baby."

Per gasped, obviously forcibly steeling himself to prevent another bout of tears.

"We thought," Billy T. began. "We thought perhaps—it isn't easy to ask about this, Mr. Hansen, but—"

Roy Hansen looked as if he had shrunk, and his eyes were closed.

"We have emphasized that every single piece of information about Birgitte may be of relevance to the case, and so it is necessary to ask . . ."

Billy T. placed the flat of his hand on his shaved head and rubbed it pensively to and fro. He considerately neglected to look at the Police Chief, knowing what his superior officer would say.

"Why did you not tell us about this dead baby?" he asked quickly. "About your daughter?"

"Billy T.," the Police Chief said sharply, and waited. "This is not an interrogation! You certainly don't need to answer that right now, Mr. Hansen."

"But I want to!"

He got to his feet and crossed stiffly to the window, then turned abruptly to face the others.

"You just admitted that you have no idea what it's like to have your life dissected in the newspapers. You're *completely* correct about that. You haven't a clue! The whole of Norway is preoccupied with Birgitte. You are preoccupied with Birgitte. I have to put up with it. But there is one thing that actually belongs only to me! *Me! Do you understand that?*"

Now he was standing at Billy T.'s side; one hand rested on the table as he looked into Billy T.'s eyes.

"Why haven't I said anything about Liv, you ask. *Because it's none of your business!* Okay? Liv's death was *our* tragedy. Birgitte's and mine!"

His fury abated just as swiftly as it had erupted. Suddenly it appeared that he did not quite know where he was or why he was there, and he gazed around the room in astonishment before returning to his seat.

The silence lasted for some considerable time.

"Well," Billy T. said, returning the pillbox gently to the little bag and stuffing it into his jacket pocket again. "We'll leave that, then. I'm sorry if I've said something that might have caused offense. There's just one more thing."

He looked at the Police Chief, who, with a resigned nod, invited him to continue.

"We have something that absolutely must not come out. We have managed to keep the press at bay until now, and we'd really like to keep this information to ourselves for a while yet. We have . . ."

He produced an envelope from a folder and placed the contents in front of the two relatives.

"We know that this is the gun that was used in the murder," he said, pointing to the two photographs. "This is a Russian—"

"Nagant," Per Volter interrupted. "A Russian Nagant. Model 1895."

He stared at the picture.

"Where is the gun?"

"Why do you ask?" Billy T. asked.

"Where is the gun?" Per Volter repeated his question, the roses in his cheeks making him look feverish. "I want to see the gun."

Within just a few minutes, an officer knocked on the door, handed a revolver to Billy T., and left again.

"Can I touch it?" Per asked quietly, looking at Billy T., who nodded.

With practiced movements, Per Volter examined the gun that had killed his mother. He inspected the barrel, found it empty, aimed at the floor, and pulled the trigger.

"Are you familiar with this type of gun?" Billy T. inquired.

"Yes," Per Volter said. "I know this gun very well. It's mine."

"Yours!"

The Security Service Chief was almost shouting.

"Yes. This Nagant belongs to me. Can anyone tell me how it ended up here?"

5:30 P.M., STENSPARKEN PARK

It worried him greatly that he had not insisted on a different meeting place. He hated Stensparken Park. He could barely walk through the little green oasis between Stensgata and Pilestredet without getting insulted by one of the scum who usually roamed there, repulsive homosexuals who always mistook him for one of their own, no matter how he dressed or acted. Once a man had ingratiatingly compared him to Jonas Fjeld, the fictional detective, and that was what had saved the guy from being knocked to the ground. Brage Håkonsen had the complete works of crime writer Øvre Richter Frich on his bookshelf, and Fjeld was his hero.

They should have arranged to meet later in the evening. It was still light now. The supplier had, however, been insistent, saying that he was going abroad and wanted this over and done with.

Brage Håkonsen had strolled through the park three times: it was impossible to stand still. That was when they crept out. The vermin of society.

At last. The man with the dark ankle-length coat made an almost imperceptible gesture toward him. Surveying his surroundings as discreetly as possible, Brage began to approach the other man. As they passed each other, he felt something drop into the bag he was carrying, a nylon bag with some training gear at the bottom. He had released his grip on one handle just in time.

Now he clutched it again and jogged across to two trash cans at the other end of the little park. He opened one and dropped a padded envelope inside, together with an ice cream wrapper he had found half an hour before.

Five thousand was not so bad. Not for an unregistered, efficient handgun. Untraceable. As Brage Håkonsen left the park, he saw out of the corner of his eye the man in the long coat heading for the trash cans. Smiling, Brage held the bag extra tightly.

Suddenly an icy sensation raced down his spine. That man over there, the one standing under a tall tree reading a newspaper, he had seen before. Today. Not long ago. He made a strenuous effort to remember where. In the kiosk? On the tram? Picking up his pace, he glanced over his shoulder to see whether the man with the newspaper was following, but he was not. He just stared after him and then stooped over his newspaper again.

He must be one of them. The homosexuals. Relieved, Brage breathed out and scuttled across toward the veterinary college.

However, he could not let go of the thought of the man with the newspaper. He would travel out to the cabin and hide the gun there. For the time being. Until the plan was completely ready. It was almost, but not quite. He was unsure who to take with him, since the project could not be accomplished alone. But he wanted only one assistant.

The more people involved, the greater the likelihood of it all going down the drain.

Now that the Prime Minister had been taken out, it was the turn of the President of the Parliament. The symbolic value would be enormous. However, something made him hesitate as he unlocked the door to his apartment: he could not travel out to the cabin. Hardly anyone knew he had it. Only the old woman on the ground floor, for whom he did some shopping and washed the stairs, and who had given him the keys to her cabin by way of thanks. She was childless and as old as the hills, and knew hardly anyone apart from the council care workers who brought her hot food three times a week. But she was quite charming too. He had not actually had any ulterior motive when he'd started chatting to her about this and that, but when it emerged that her husband had been a Norwegian soldier in the Waffen-SS and that he had died during the war, he had begun to help her out. After all, you had to look after your own. It was a matter of honor.

He wanted to go to the cabin. Something told him that he could not. Something told him that the gun ought not to remain in his apartment or in his own storeroom.

Padding down to the basement, he unlocked the storeroom belonging to Mrs. Svendsby and placed the wrapped pistol behind four jars of preserves dated 1975. He did not even look at the gun before he locked up again and replaced the key between two joists under the ceiling.

Mrs. Svendsby had trouble with her hips and had not visited the basement for more than fifteen years.

7:10 P.M., TRANEN RESTAURANT

The Tranen restaurant had made no effort to be trendy. While all the other gloomy cafés in Oslo had begun attracting crowds of taxi-riding tourists from the West End, the Tranen remained quite simply *too* gloomy. Few of its customers had ever ventured west of the Bislett Stadium at any point in their lives, and now most of them were in no condition to toddle even that far. They sat there with their few kroner from social security, their florid, reddish-purple faces, and their life stories that no one wanted to hear. Hanne Wilhelmsen knew that they were desperately sad: they just sat there shouting, so thoroughly pickled in alcohol that they were never going to be listened to by anyone.

Glancing at the time, she tried to suppress her irritation.

Øyvind Olve rushed breathlessly through the door. He scanned the room in confusion and looked as though he thought he had come to the wrong place. A cowboy sat at the table just inside the door. Actually, it was a woman, and in truth she looked as if she had never sat her broad backside on anything resembling a horse, but the accessories were all in place. She was wearing a shiny red leather jacket with long fringes of luminous nylon and studs on the back spelling out the words "Divine Madness" in script. On her head she wore a white replica Stetson, and her jeans were three sizes too small, making it difficult for her to sit down. Perhaps that was why she was half standing, leaning over a man who was obviously refusing to pay her bill. Or perhaps she simply wanted to show off her boots: shiny, brilliant white, and clearly made of plastic.

"You said you would pay," she slurred, snatching at the collar of a man with thin strands of hair draped over his crown. "Really, Tønna, you *promised* to treat me!"

The man attempted to wriggle out of the alleged agreement, quite literally, but ended up knocking over an almost untouched glass of beer. All five people seated around the table stared in shock as the expensive droplets spilled across the table and flowed in a wide waterfall onto the floor.

"Fuck, Tønna, what *are* you doing?" the cowgirl whined. "Now you owe me another one at least!"

Øyvind Olve did not spot Hanne Wilhelmsen until she waved at him. Relieved to escape from the rodeo near the door, he planted himself on a seat opposite her before slapping his briefcase on the table.

"Øyvind, at last," she said, smiling reproachfully. "When are you going to get yourself something better than that?"

Feeling hard done by, he gazed at the briefcase, a small valise-type affair in red and black nylon with the Labor Party logo in one corner.

"But I think this one's fine!"

Hanne Wilhelmsen put her head back and laughed uproariously.

"Fine? It's downright awful! Did you get it at a conference or something?"

Taken aback, Øyvind Olve nodded as he placed his bag at his feet, out of the policewoman's line of vision.

Hanne nodded toward the glass of beer on the table in front of him; she had ordered for them both.

"Why on earth did you want to meet here?" he whispered, rolling his eyes.

"Because it's the only place in Oslo you can be absolutely sure nobody's listening to what you say," she whispered back, peering conspiratorially around the room. "Even the Security Service folk don't poke their noses in here!"

"But," he muttered, staring at the grease-spattered menu, "is it okay to *eat* in here?"

"We'll eat somewhere else afterward," she said brusquely. "The beer is just as good here as any other place. Now, do tell."

Sipping from her glass, she leaned her elbows on the table as she licked her lips.

"What on earth is this health scandal all about? What's actually going on?"

"When this sort of thing happens, it usually has to do with a power struggle. And leaks to the press."

"You mean someone's leaking information?"

"The stuff that was in the newspapers today," Øyvind said, drawing a circle in the condensation on his beer glass, "they didn't even know about in the Prime Minister's office. It looks as if somebody is out to frame us."

"Frame you? But isn't it true, then, what's in the papers?"

"It may well be. And if it is true, it would have been made public. The point is that this is something that the investigations committee needs to look into, and since so much has already come out, it becomes difficult for us to respond to it rationally."

"Us? Do you mean the party?"

Øyvind Olve smiled, almost anxiously.

"Yes, to some extent. But mainly the government. I keep forgetting that I'm no longer working in the Prime Minister's office. Sorry."

"How can this damage the present government, though? It all happened more than thirty years ago!"

"Everything attaches itself to the government. You must see that. It's the government that has taken responsibility for investigating this, and it was only by the skin of our teeth that we avoided having the whole of Parliament take control of the inquiry. Fortunately Ruth-Dorthe was quick off the mark and managed to put together a committee of government appointees before the MPs got themselves organized. The case was evidently not of sufficient importance at that point. But now, as you can see—"

He took a slug of beer and groaned.

"Look at the Security Service scandal, when there was all that heat about them allegedly doing illegal surveillance on Communist activists," he continued, lowering his voice further. "When the Lund Commission's report was finally published . . ."

After raising his glass once more, he downed half the contents.

". . . didn't you notice how they tried to turn it into *their* victory?"

"Who did?"

"The opposition. The Socialist Left and the Center Party. Among others. As if Parliament itself was responsible for all the investigation work, and not an exceptionally competent Supreme Court judge with a good crew on board! As if we in the government were not also interested in a thorough investigation into any possible corruption!"

"But," Hanne objected, "the government had completed its investigation by then, and very little action had been taken!"

"Yes," Øyvind Olve said, smacking his glass down on the table. "But that wasn't the *government's* fault, you know! Confound it, it wasn't Prime Minister Gro herself who'd gone searching through files looking for dirt on Communist activists and all that stuff!"

He waved irritably for another beer. Instead of the waiter, they were suddenly faced with a man four and a half feet tall, dressed in a tuxedo, and with a nose that had most definitely seen better days but had probably never been any larger. His mouth was not visible until he opened it, and, with a sweeping motion of his top hat, declared, "Your Excellencies! It gives me great pleasure for this debauched establishment to receive a visit from upstanding folk like yourselves! May I, on behalf of the proprietor and Tranen's regular customers, wish you a most sincere welcome!"

Using both hands to replace his hat on his head, he made a stiff little bow.

"My name is The Penguin, and you good people can probably understand why!"

Laughing heartily, he grabbed the edge of their table with his chubby little fingers. His tuxedo was old and worn, and the silky gray cummerbund was stretched precariously around his pudgy torso; his arms and legs were too short for the rest of his body.

Hanne began to search for her purse.

"But, my good woman," the man exclaimed in exasperation, "how could Your Excellencies come to the presumptuous conclusion that my little expedition to your table has a selfish motive? My wretched task is to offer you both a warm welcome!"

As the little man stared furiously at Hanne's purse, she swiftly returned it to her bag.

"So, yes." The man nodded contentedly. "Then I'll leave you to your pleasant conversation and the golden elixir, while expressing a sincere wish to see you good folks here again."

He clicked his fingers lightly, and the waiter appeared carrying two glasses of beer without either Hanne or Øyvind having ordered.

"Now you really must stop bothering the customers, Penguin," the waiter said crossly. "Off you go."

"He's not bothering us," Hanne said, but it was futile.

The waiter pushed the little man in front of him and over to the other side of the room.

"Where were we?" Hanne asked, pouring the small amount left in her old glass into the new one.

"What in the world was that all about?" Øyvind wondered, unable to stop staring at the figure in the tuxedo.

"It's just city life!" Hanne grinned broadly. "You don't have such things out in the countryside!"

"Oh yes we do," Øyvind mumbled. "But they don't wear tuxedos."

"You were in the middle of a story."

Øyvind gazed at the peculiar man for some time.

"The art of government is an uncomfortable balancing act," he said finally. "In every sense. Especially when the wear and tear is as great as it is in our party. Everything is laid at our door. Everything that's negative, that is. The country is overflowing with milk and honey, but everyone still curses the Labor Party. This health scandal—"

Looking at his watch, he placed his hand on his stomach.

"Hungry?" Hanne Wilhelmsen inquired.

"Mmm."

"Afterward. Tell me more first."

"Well," Øyvind Olve continued. "If it is true that something went wrong in 1965, then of course we're interested in having it brought to light. We all are. For a number of reasons. Responsibility has to be apportioned, and most important of all, we need to learn from any mistakes that were made, even if they happened a long time ago. But it is important that things are well timed. Now that so much of this affair seems to have leaked out to the press, the government has been put on the defensive. Damn it all, Hanne, the Prime Minister's office didn't even *know* about this until it was printed in today's newspaper!"

"I still don't understand," Hanne said. "It would eventually. Who was in government in '65?"

"Gerhardsen was replaced by Borten that year," Øyvind murmured. "But that's not the point! The point is that this makes the government look negligent; it makes us seem uninformed with respect to what the newspapers have found out, and that's always a sign of weakness. Or it's perceived to be. At least by people in political circles. And that's what matters."

He gave a beery belch.

"You'll have to do something about your digestive system," Hanne commented.

"And now that they've linked the health scandal to Birgitte's homicide, we *really are* in trouble." He leaned across the table, his face only inches from Hanne's.

"But it's very likely just nonsense," Hanne protested.

"Nonsense? Yes, sure, but that doesn't matter! As long as the newspapers spice this up by conflating it into a single issue, then people will regard it as a single issue. Especially when it looks as though—"

He leaned back abruptly and stared at the bar counter. It did not appear as if he intended to continue.

"Looks as though what?"

Hanne was whispering now.

"Looks as though the police don't have a clue what happened in the Volter case," Øyvind enunciated slowly. "Or do you?"

Hanne outlined a heart in the condensation on the table where her beer glass had been sitting.

"You mustn't include me in the police," Hanne said. "I don't work there."

Abruptly Øyvind Olve bent down to lift his ridiculous nylon briefcase onto the table. He struggled with the zipper, then presented Hanne with three sheets.

"Exactly. You don't work there. Then you can tell me what I should do with this."

He pushed the documents across to her.

"What is it?" she asked, turning the printed page to take a look.

"It's something I found in Birgitte's office. I had to go through all the documents; many of them were of a delicate political nature. This was shoved in between two red folders."

"Red folders?"

"Classified documents, top secret."

The sheets contained a list of names, printed in ten-point characters, followed by some sort of information about dates.

"Dates of birth and death," Øyvind Olve clarified. "Obviously, it must be a list of the sudden infant deaths in 1965. And look at this."

Retrieving the papers, he flicked through to the third sheet, and his eyes scanned the page before he presented it to Hanne, pointing.

"'Liv Volter Hansen. Born March 16, 1965, died June 24, 1965.'"

"But what is this?"

"By various circuitous means and a hell of a lot of white lies, I've discovered that this overview was produced by the Grinde Commission. The parents of these children were chosen at random by computer and were to be interviewed in depth about their children's health, behavior, feeding patterns, and so on prior to the time of death. A random selection, in other words. Sheer chance. And by chance the Prime Minister landed in this group. But the most interesting aspect is that the list was prepared on April 3. The day before Birgitte was murdered. The only way she could have obtained it would have been if Benjamin Grinde had given it to her. I've checked every other possibility. Mail records, minute books, absolutely everything. She must have received it from Grinde. And look at this."

He pointed at something else on the sheets: a few handwritten words in the margin of the first page: *"New person???"* and *"What should be said?"*

"What on earth does that mean?" Hanne wondered, more to herself than to her companion.

He answered all the same. "I don't know. But it's Birgitte's writing. What'll I do?"

"You'll do what you should have done right away," Hanne said, in a loud, reproving voice. "You have to hand these papers to the police. Now, immediately."

"But we were just about to eat," Øyvind Olve complained.

8:00 P.M., OSLO POLICE STATION

Per Volter was just beginning to lose his hair. Billy T. could see that clearly: it was thinning at the crown, and in time the young man would have an actual bald patch.

Billy T. did not quite know what to do. Per Volter had been stretched out across the desk in the Chief Inspector's office, his head in his arms, crying like a baby, for almost ten minutes. It had all been brought on by a few simple words of speculation from Billy T.

"I think you have a few things to tell me."

"Do you think I killed Mum?" Per Volter had yelled, before breaking down in a paroxysm of tears.

Nothing had helped. Billy T. had reassured him that this was not the case. In the first place, his alibi was absolutely watertight: twenty soldiers and three officers could swear that he had been in a tent on the Hardanger Plateau when the shot was fired in the Prime Minister's office. Second, there was not a single iota of motive. And third, he would hardly have offered up the information that the unregistered murder weapon belonged to him, if he really was the murderer.

Billy T. had told him this repeatedly, but to no avail. In the end he gave up and decided to let Per cry himself out. It appeared that this would take some time.

Billy T. inspected his nails and wondered whether to pay a visit to the restroom. Just as he was making up his mind, rising from his chair, Per Volter sniffed noisily and sat up halfheartedly, his features blurred, his face red and swollen.

"Do you feel a bit better?" Billy T. asked him, sliding back down into a sitting position.

Per Volter did not reply but dried his face with his sleeve, which was at least a start.

"Here," Billy T. said, offering him a paper towel. "Your guns and equipment are remarkably well organized."

The compliment was emphasized by a smile of acknowledgment, but it did not appear particularly encouraging to Per.

"Have you been there?" he muttered, staring down at the wet paper towel.

"Yes. Two police officers went home with your father, and they've written a report stating that the storage arrangements are exemplary. Guns kept separately in a locked cabinet, ammunition in another. All five guns registered with us."

"That register of yours is such a joke," Per Volter mumbled. "As far as I know, it's only for this area, and it's not even computerized."

"We're waiting for new gun legislation," Billy T. said, pouring coffee from a steel thermos flask into two mugs and pushing one across to Per; he gave him the one with the picture of Franz Kafka. "But why?" he asked, with a note of hesitation.

Looking up, Per made a grimace after burning his tongue. "Why what?"

"Why hadn't you registered the Nagant?"

Per sat blowing into his mug. The coffee was still too hot, and he put it down gingerly on the desktop.

"I just didn't get around to it. The other guns were bought. But the Nagant was a gift. On my eighteenth birthday. It belonged to my grandmother. She was quite active during the war, was in Finnmark and all that kind of thing, and we used to say that the Nagant was her war medal."

Now the young man smiled faintly, and there was a touch of pride in his expression.

"She operated on a wounded Russian and saved his life. She wasn't even a doctor! The autumn of '43, that was, and the man had nothing to give her apart from his gun. Kliment Davidovich Raskin was his name."

He was smiling broadly now.

"When I was a child, I thought the name was so cool. After the war, Grandma spent years trying to find him. Through the Red Cross and the Salvation Army and suchlike. She never located him. Grandma died when I was sixteen. Lovely lady. She . . ."

His tears threatened to spill again, and Per made a fresh attempt with the coffee.

"I got the Nagant as a present from my mum on my eighteenth birthday," he murmured into his cup. "It was the best present I had ever received."

"Have you ever used it?"

"Yes. The ammunition's quite unusual, so it has to be specially ordered. I've used the gun six or seven times, I think. Mostly just for the sake of it. It's not a very precise weapon. Old as well. Grandma had never used it."

Once more he was overwhelmed by the memory of someone who was no longer alive. Tears ran from the corner of his left eye, but he remained upright.

"Why are you so angry with your father, Per?"

Just as Billy T. asked the question, his inner alarm bells rang loudly. Per should be informed that he did not have a duty to testify against members of his own family. Nevertheless, Billy T. did not withdraw the question.

Per Volter gazed out the window, holding the mug of coffee up to his mouth, without drinking it. The steam seemed to do him good; he closed his eyes and it was obvious that the moisture on his red, streaky face felt pleasant.

"Angry is just the start of it," he said softly. "The man's a shit. He was unfaithful to Mum and he lied to me."

Suddenly he made eye contact with Billy T. His eyes were deep blue, and for an uncomfortable moment, Billy T. felt that he was looking at a ghost: Per looked so like his mother.

"Dad was having an affair with Ruth-Dorthe Nordgarden."

He spat out the name as if it were an effort to enunciate it at all.

Billy T. said nothing, but felt his heart beat faster: a disagreeable fluttering, and, closing his mouth, he involuntarily touched his chest.

"I've no idea how long it lasted," Per continued. "But I caught them at it at home last autumn. Dad didn't know. That I heard them, that is. I told him the other day. For fuck's sake—"

Slamming his coffee mug on the table, he put his head in his hands, and leaned his elbows on his thighs, rocking slowly to and fro as he continued to speak into his hands.

"I don't even know if Mum knew about it."

There was no more. It was too warm in the little room; the heat pressed against his skin, and Billy T. could still feel a frightening stitch under his left rib. He tried to raise his arm, but the pain increased so much it made him stop.

"I wish I belonged to an ordinary family," Per whispered, only just audibly. "I wish I didn't have to read about us in the papers. About—"

"About your sister," Billy T. finished for him.

The pain had diminished somewhat, but his heart was still thumping in an unfamiliar rhythm.

Per Volter took his hands away from his face and again stared into Billy T.'s eyes. Now the likeness to his mother was disturbing.

"I knew nothing about my sister until I read it in the newspaper," he said in a dull voice. "Nothing! I didn't even know that I had a sibling! Didn't I have a right to know that? Don't you think they should have told me that I once had a sister?"

He was almost shrieking, his voice slipping into falsetto from time to time.

Billy T. nodded, but did not utter a word.

"I always thought that Mum worked so hard out of—some sort of sense of duty. The party and the country and all that. Now I think . . ."

He began to cry yet again. He tried to resist, swallowing and rubbing his eyes, his body really too exhausted to withstand a fresh bout. But it was all in vain. Snot and tears ran down his face, and his sleeves were too wet to be of any use when, time after time, he pressed his face against his forearms.

"I think she wasn't really that fond of me. If she could forget a baby so easily that she was never spoken of, then it's not so strange that she forgot about me now and again. She didn't love any of us."

"I think you're quite wrong there," Billy T. ventured, though even he could tell that his voice sounded reedy and unconvincing. "Not talking about someone doesn't mean that you're not fond of the person. You must remember that."

"Can you imagine what it's like to read about things like that in the newspaper?" Per Volter interrupted. "To read innermost family secrets that you didn't even know about? I *hate* Dad. *I hate that guy!*"

Billy T. did not reply. There was nothing to say. The pain this young man was feeling was so immense and unmanageable that there was insufficient space for it anywhere. The room where they were sitting was overheated and stuffy; it felt as if it might explode at any minute.

Billy T. knew he ought to let him continue his rant. He ought to keep him with him, give him food and drink, then take him to a place where he could continue to talk to someone he could confide in; Per Volter needed the opportunity to spew out all the pain now that he had begun the huge task of letting it all out.

But Billy T. was too weary. He could not cope with any more. Closing his eyes, he tried to think about how he was going to get to bed.

"I'll get someone to drive you home," he said quietly.

"I don't want to go home," Per Volter answered. "I don't know where I want to go."

11:30 P.M., VIDARS GATE 11C

He could not sleep. He thought about the gun behind the jam jars in Mrs. Svendsby's basement storeroom. Even though it was safer there than in his own storeroom, he was not happy about it. It should really be at the cabin.

The man with the newspaper bothered him too. He had not looked like the others. He looked uninterested; not interested in that way. But all the same he had kept his eye on him. It bothered him intensely.

Brage Håkonsen twisted around; in his anxiety he had made the sheet damp. He groaned unhappily and got out of bed. Most of all, he wanted to phone Tage. He needed outside help. That would be the safest thing. But he could not phone. Heaven only knew whether the phone was bugged. His cell phone was a reliable alternative, but although the police couldn't eavesdrop it, they could find out what number he had phoned. That was why they stuck to phone boxes. And cryptic letters that were always burned as soon as the contents had been read.

His body felt as though it were covered in ants. His skin crawled and itched, and he scratched his stomach as he roamed restlessly around the small living room. In the end he sat down on the stationary bicycle in his bedroom and pulled the foot straps very tight. He pedaled and pedaled, and after a mile felt his muscles start to loosen up. Sticky perspiration clung to his half-naked body, and his breathing was heavy and rhythmic.

The doorbell rang.

Brage Håkonsen stiffened; he released his feet from the straps, leaving the pedals to turn the last few revolutions by themselves.

He did not want to open the door. He had no idea who it was, but his anxiety and the mysterious, uncomfortable tension had returned, sitting like a twinge in his diaphragm and making him tremble all of a sudden. He sneaked slowly back to bed, but did not dare switch off the light. Any change would be noticed from outside the apartment, betraying the fact that someone was at home.

It rang again, harsh and insistent.

He lay stiff and silent, refusing to open the door. No one should be calling so late. He was entirely within his rights not to open up. Suddenly he noticed his porn magazines. Unobtrusively he propped himself up on his elbow: the sight of the thick bundle of magazines on his bedside table worried him more than the gun in the basement. Swiftly, softly, he stood up again, lifted the mattress, and stuffed the magazines between the wooden slats on the bed base.

Now the doorbell rang for the third time, briskly and nonstop for one whole minute.

He had nothing here he could be hauled in for. He had no unfinished business with anyone.

He had to open up.

Throwing on a navy blue dressing gown with black stripes, he tied the belt as he approached the door.

"Okay, okay," he muttered, sliding back the security chain to open the door.

Two men stood outside, both around forty: one dressed in a gray-brown suit and tie, the other in jacket and trousers with an open-necked shirt.

"Brage Håkonsen?" the man in the suit inquired.

"Yes?"

"We're from the police."

They each held out a little plastic card with a photo and the lion of the national coat of arms.

"You are under arrest."

"Arrest? What for?"

Instinctively Brage Håkonsen stepped back, and the two men moved quickly inside. The casually dressed man closed the door quietly behind them.

"For unlawful possession of a gun."

The man held out a blue sheet, but Brage refused to take it.

"Gun? I don't have a bloody gun!"

"You don't have a firearms license," the taller police officer said. "But you still bought a pistol in Stensparken Park this afternoon."

Fuck. Damn and blast it. The man with the newspaper was not a bloody homo. He was from the police.

"I did not," Brage Håkonsen said, but all the same he went to put on his clothes.

He was not even allowed to go into the bedroom on his own; the tall man followed him, staring intently at him until he was ready to accompany them to the police station at Grønlandsleiret 44.

WEDNESDAY, APRIL 16

"Long time no see," Billy T. said, grinning at Severin Heger as he bent down to help him retrieve the folder he had just dropped.

"You should look where you're going," Police Inspector Heger responded, though he returned the smile.

"What are you doing these days?" Billy T. asked, looking quizzically at his colleague.

Severin Heger had been working in the Security Service for nearly four years. He was the only Security Service officer Billy T. was on good terms with, and there was a reason for that. They were the same age, they had been in the same year at police college, both were well over six feet tall, and both rode Honda Goldwing motorbikes. When Billy T. had become unofficial national champion in full-contact karate in 1984, Severin had been runner-up. The day they received their diplomas and became proud owners of a single gold stripe on the epaulettes of their uniform jackets, they had ended up, in company with many others, in the city center. That night, Severin made a clumsy and fairly drunken pass at Billy T. With tact and delicacy, Billy T. had rejected him, but when Severin Heger then suddenly broke down in convulsive sobs, Billy T. had put his arm around his shoulders and seen him home. Billy T. had made three pots of coffee in the course of that long night filled with despair and reassuring words. When the sun broke through the clouds in the east and they were both stone-cold sober, sitting with their feet propped up on the balcony of the tiny apartment in Etterstad, Severin had suddenly stood up, produced a little engraved silver cup, and exclaimed, "I want you to have this, Billy T. This was my very first trophy, and it's the best one I have. Thank you very much."

Since then they had not had much to do with each other, barring a hello now and again and a clap on the shoulder in the corridors, though on very rare occasions they met for a chilled summer beer. Neither of them ever mentioned that spring evening many years ago. The silver cup sat on a shelf in Billy T.'s bedroom, together with an egg-cup he had received at his christening and a silvered child's shoe that had belonged to his eldest son. From what Billy T. could understand, Severin had made his decision that night, contrary to the advice Billy T. had given him. Severin Heger lived in celibacy, and Billy T. had never heard so much as a spiteful rumor about his old pal.

"I'm probably working on the same as you, I expect," Severin Heger replied. "That's what almost everybody is working on, is it not?"

"I suppose so. Are you doing okay?"

Severin Heger bit his lip and scanned his surroundings. People were rushing past them, some raising a hand in greeting, others calling out a cheerful hello as they went by.

"Have you time for a cup of coffee?" Severin suddenly asked.

"Not really, but yes please," Billy T. answered with a grin. "The canteen?"

They sat at the innermost table, beside the doors leading to the roof terrace. The weather was cool and the sky threatened rain, so they were left to sit in peace.

"You must all be in your element up there now," Billy T. remarked, nodding toward the ceiling. "Never had it so good, eh!"

Severin looked at him earnestly.

"I don't understand why you have such a negative view of us," he said. "My colleagues are decent, hard-working people, exactly like the rest of you."

"I don't have anything against *you*. It's just that I can't stand all that secrecy and scaremongering. Right now, for instance, I have a strong sense that not even the leaders of this investigation know exactly what theories you are working on. The most frustrating aspect of being on this case is that it seems as though nobody has a complete overview. But the rest of us at least try to keep one another informed."

Severin did not answer but continued to gaze at Billy T. as he scratched the back of one hand with the other.

"What's on your mind?" Billy T. asked, pouring cola into his glass so hastily that it fizzed over and dark froth streamed across the table.

"Damn and blast," he muttered, wiping the tabletop with his hand and drying it on his trousers.

Severin leaned toward him, looking at the spillage.

"We took in an extremist yesterday," he said quietly. "A guy who bought an unregistered gun in a suspicious fashion in a park, and we believe he's the leader of a group of neo-Nazis. He is definitely in regular contact with a Swede with the same interests, and the Swede . . ."

After fishing a handkerchief from his pocket, Severin started to dry the table.

". . . this Swede came to Norway three days before Birgitte Volter's murder, visited friends here in Oslo, and disappeared back to his homeland the day after the homicide."

Billy T. looked as if Severin Heger had told him that he was going to marry Princess Märtha Louise.

"What the hell are you saying?"

Severin Heger flashed Billy T. a warning look as two women passed them to see if it might be possible to sit outside, regardless. Having poked their heads outside, they changed their minds and vanished back in the direction of the counter, on the other side of the canteen.

"And as if that wasn't enough," Severin continued, now almost whispering, "we have reason to believe this guy we hauled in yesterday somehow knew the security guard in the government complex. The one who died recently in the avalanche. Do you know about him?"

"Know about him?"

Billy T. tried to lower his voice, but his eagerness distorted his tone as he hissed, "I don't only *know about* him! I've interviewed the guy, damn it! And I've continually hassled for the need to take a closer look at him! Is it true? Is there really a connection there?"

"We don't know for sure," Severin said, gesturing with his hand to persuade Billy T. to calm down. "But we have reason to believe there might be. Isn't that what you say when you can't reveal how you know something?"

"But did you get anything out of the guy?"

"Zilch, zero, nothing. We searched his apartment. There was nothing there apart from suspect literature on a shelf and porn magazines under his bed. No gun. Nothing criminal."

"But can you hold him?"

"Doubtful. Progress is so bloody slow on this new gun legislation. At the moment the penalties are so minimal that we'll have problems holding him much longer than today. Then we'll put in surveillance and all that kind of thing. Heaven knows what that might lead to. The Swedish Security Police have interviewed Tage Sjögren, the Swede I mentioned, and they held him for two days. Pushed him really hard, but the guy said nothing, and they were forced to let him go."

Suddenly he glanced at his watch, and ran his thumb over his glass. "Need to go."

"But, Severin!"

Billy T. grabbed Severin's arm as he was leaving.

"How's life?" he asked softly.

"I don't have a life. I work in the Security Service."

Smiling briefly, Severin withdrew his arm and scurried out of the canteen.

5:19 P.M., VIDARS GATE 11C

Brage Håkonsen knew that in the days ahead, his life would not be his own. There would be eyes everywhere, and everything he did would be duly noted and then filed in a folder on the top floors of the police station. He would have to live with it somehow. He did not feel nearly as upset as he had thought he would; it had been worse when he was mistakenly arrested as an antiwhaling demonstrator. Now at least it was to do with something he believed in, and it would be naive to think he would never come under suspicion for his activities. He simply had to be even more careful.

It had been sensible to keep his mouth shut. His attorney had advised that; the old guy had actually seemed like a wimp, but Brage Håkonsen was aware that they shared opinions on various issues. The cop had been damn grouchy about his choice of attorney, and it had taken several hours before they finally allowed them to have a discussion. The last thing the lawyer had said was that he had to be careful in the future. He had winked his right eye from under his bushy eyebrows as he said it.

The cops hadn't found the gun. Not that he had dared to go to the basement to check, but they would obviously have confronted him with the pistol if they had known where it was. It could stay there. For a while.

First and foremost, his arrest meant that the assassination attempt would have to be postponed. That was regrettable, for a number of reasons. One, they would lose some of the impact the longer they left it between the Volter woman's death and the new attack. Two, it was always a fucking nightmare to alter a fairly detailed plan. On the other hand, he had already decided to change his partner in crime. Reidar could be depended on, of course, but it had not taken Brage very long to realize that the boy was not particularly bright. So when Tage had said as he'd left that he could be called on at any time, stressing the importance of cross-border cooperation, it had dawned on him that they should do it together, he and Tage. It might be an advantage to postpone it, since Tage might have ideas about how to amend the plan.

Just the thought of it made him ecstatic, and he laughed when he peeped out the window and saw two men in an old Volvo on the opposite side of the street.

He knew how he could get to the cabin without being seen. He just had to wait for a couple of days.

FRIDAY, APRIL 18

12:07 P.M., PRESS CONFERENCE ROOM
IN THE GOVERNMENT COMPLEX

"We only just made it."

Edvard "Teddy" Larsen had to engage his brain to avoid heaving a sigh of relief as he passed the flock of photographers crowding around the door to the large room as they waited for the minister to appear.

He had had to draw on his many years of finely honed ingenuity and cunning to make her understand that they had to do this his way. Ruth-Dorthe Nordgarden had persisted in her intransigence: Teddy should read out a statement on her behalf, and then she would turn up to answer questions for ten minutes.

"But Ruth-Dorthe," he had tried to explain, "it would look really strange if *I*, an employee in the ministry, were to read out a statement from *you*, a politician! It would look extremely peculiar!"

"But I can't just stand there reading aloud with loads of people in front of me, watching," she had complained. "Does it actually matter if it looks slightly irregular? The most important thing is for them to hear what action we're taking."

It had taken half an hour to convince her, and strictly speaking, that was the thirty minutes he should have used to prepare. Anyhow, at least she had come to her senses.

Teddy Larsen zigzagged through the throng of assembled journalists to mount the podium. His tie was crooked, and one of his shirttails had crept out of his trouser waistband. He made a discreet attempt at tucking it in again after a close friend, a TV reporter in the second row, made frantic grimaces to persuade him to look down.

The daily newspapers were arrayed on the table in front of him. He had read them already. Extremely thoroughly. They were all crammed full of material on the health scandal. The *Kveldsavisen* editor had cleared the entire front page for a color photo of a married couple in their early sixties who sat crouched on either side of a little white marble gravestone with an angel on top. On the stone, the name "Marie" was engraved in gold, and underneath, the lettering read: "Born May 23, 1965, died August 28, 1965. We will never forget you." The headline above the picture screamed: WHO IS RESPONSIBLE FOR LITTLE MARIE'S DEATH?

As he took his seat, Teddy Larsen looked at the doorway. Ruth-Dorthe Nordgarden eventually made her entrance in a tremendous blaze of flashbulbs. She was holding her arm up in front of her face, as if she were on her way to court and about to be remanded in custody for a serious crime, reluctant to be recognized.

My God, Teddy Larsen thought. *Those will be terrific photographs.*

He rubbed his eyes momentarily and then helped Ruth-Dorthe to her place. She peered at the audience, gesturing at them to stop the bombardment of flashes, then cleared her throat and looked down at the papers in front of her.

"Welcome to the press conference," Teddy Larsen began, having gotten to his feet. "Health Minister Nordgarden will first give a brief statement on what we currently know about the infant deaths in 1965. That will take approximately ten minutes. Afterward, you'll have an opportunity to ask questions."

He nodded encouragingly to Ruth-Dorthe, but she was engrossed in the papers. Taking a couple of steps toward her, he placed a reassuring hand on her shoulder.

"Go ahead, Minister."

Her voice was frail and obviously nervous when she started. Her big baby-blue eyes fluttered around the audience, but when they finally came to rest on the manuscript in front of her, the words flowed more smoothly.

"In light of the press headlines of the past few days, I find it necessary to give an account of the historical circumstances with regard to the government's purchase of the triple vaccine in 1964 and 1965. I emphasize that this account will not affect the work of the investigation commission—which, as you know, is almost completed. I will merely provide a purely factual account."

She suddenly glanced up from her papers, a practiced gesture that failed to have the desired effect, as she then had difficulty finding her place in the text.

"The government wishes the entire matter to be brought into the open," she continued when she finally found her place. "A considerable amount of work has been undertaken on this matter by the Ministry of Health, and within a short period of time, in order to avoid further speculation. I hope that this is an issue we will soon be able to put behind us so that we can return our focus to more pressing current problems on the agenda."

Teddy Larsen closed his eyes in despair. He had deleted that sentence when he had read through the speech, politely telling Ruth-Dorthe that the last thing she should do was minimize the importance of the issue. She evidently didn't give a shit for his advice.

"A limited quantity of triple vaccine was purchased for the cohort of 1965. The supplier was the reputable Dutch pharmaceutical company Achenfarma. The National Institute of Public Health was listed as the importer. Toward the end of 1965, reports were coming in about an unusually high infant mortality rate that year. The triple vaccine was then withdrawn, although I emphasize . . ."

Her voice was now a screeching falsetto and she had to clear her throat twice before she managed to continue.

". . . I emphasize that no causal relationship was demonstrated between the triple vaccine and the deaths. Therefore this action was taken to be on the safe side. Closer investigation has shown that the preserving agent in the vaccine was contaminated. For the following year's cohort, an arrangement was made to buy the vaccine from an extremely reputable American pharmaceutical company."

Ruth-Dorthe increased her pace, now reading so fast that some of the journalists had problems following what she said, and a murmur of protest spread through the room. Teddy Larsen wrote two words on a Post-it note, which he placed as discreetly as possible in front of the minister.

Though she completely lost her thread, she digested his message and read more slowly when she resumed her speech.

"This was the first the government knew of the damaging effects of Achenfarma's vaccine. Public health authorities caution that it is of crucial importance that the vaccination program retains the confidence of the populace. If more than 10 percent of the population stops receiving vaccinations, then the program loses its protective efficacy. I would remind you that the vaccines routinely administered in Norway are intended to provide protection against serious and some-times life-threatening illnesses, and there is *no* reason . . ."

She emphasized the gravity of her point by striking the table.

". . . no reason at all not to trust the vaccines that are administered to babies and children now."

Total silence descended on the room before the storm broke. Teddy Larsen had to think on his feet, and after a minute's struggle, shouting assurances that they would all get a chance to speak, he brought the rows of journalists to some semblance of order. The questions rained down about everything from demands for compensation to whether this Achenfarma company was still in existence. *Dagbladet* wanted to know if the Ministry of Health had been aware of the connection between the deaths and the triple vaccine for years, or if they had just found out about the scandal through the work of the commission. *Bergens Tidende* was represented by a hothead whose questions were unnecessarily detailed, unnecessarily provocative, and, at least for the time being, unnecessarily conspiratorial.

Ruth-Dorthe astonished Teddy by responding with a calmness and clarity that he had never witnessed before. She did not allow herself to be knocked off her perch, and she answered more precisely than any-one would have expected. Teddy began to relax his shoulders, think-ing that this was not going too badly, when all was said and done. The only thing giving him slight cause for concern was that Little Lettvik was sitting perfectly still in the front row, without writing a single note. Only when the hailstorm of questions had subsided somewhat did she stand up brusquely and ask to speak. Ruth-Dorthe shot her a friendly smile and told her amiably to go ahead, before Teddy had a chance to do so.

"I have noted with interest that the minister wishes to bring all the historical facts out into the open," she began, noticing with satisfaction that the other journalists kept their mouths completely shut as all eyes swiveled in her direction.

Even the photographers paused; they all wanted to hear what Little Lettvik had to say, since she was the one who had broken the story in the first place.

"And all this information about the purchase of the vaccine is interesting. Is the minister certain it was Achenfarma that manufactured this vaccine?"

Ruth-Dorthe appeared confused: a tiny tic twitched up and down on the left side of her face.

"Yes," she replied. "Yes indeed, that was where it was bought."

"But I'm not asking where the vaccine was *bought*," Little Lettvik said, standing with legs apart, her wiry hair sticking out in all directions, her entire body seeming eager, like a much too old and overweight elkhound trying to show the puppies how things should be done. "I'm asking who *manufactured* it."

"No, yes," Ruth-Dorthe Nordgarden responded, riffling through her papers.

She found nothing, and looked at Teddy for assistance, but he shook his head and shrugged before commenting, "No, manufactured. Might that have been another subcontractor in the pharmaceutical industry?"

"Is that intended as a question on behalf of the government minister?" Little Lettvik inquired. "In that case, I can shed light on the matter: the vaccine that took the lives of perhaps a thousand infants in 1965 was made in the GDR. By a company called Pharmamed. It is still in existence, but is now privatized."

After a moment's silence, the buzz erupted. TV journalists pushed their way forward and thrust microphones at Little Lettvik, giving breathless instructions to their camera operators about alternating between the journalist and the minister.

"In fact, we at *Kveldsavisen* have done what the Grinde Commission failed to do," Little Lettvik continued, smiling broadly. "We have examined the overseas archives. It was very simple."

She smiled again, indulgent and malicious, as she crossed to the podium and threw a document down on the table in front of the minister.

"The East German company Pharmamed was granted an export license in 1964 for a batch of vaccines destined for Achenfarma. But the triple vaccine never went on to the Dutch market. The only thing that was processed there was the packaging, as the entire deadly consignment was sold to Norway."

A young man rushed in through the door, where he remained standing for a few seconds, frantically scanning the room. Then he spotted Little Lettvik and crashed forward to hand her a newspaper.

"Thanks, Knut," she said, permitting herself an arrogant little bow before she held up the paper.

"This is *Kveldsavisen's* special edition, which is hitting the streets as we speak," she said, peering around at her colleagues. "You can read all about it there."

Chuckling softly, she took a couple of deep breaths before continuing. "I have also come across a letter. From the Norwegian Ministry of Health to Achenfarma, dated April 10, 1964. The letter concerns a reminder about the vaccine consignment. However, right at the very end, it says, and for simplicity's sake I'm translating this: 'The Ministry of Health confirms that part payment will be made directly to the subcontractor.'"

Ruth-Dorthe Nordgarden looked as though she had stopped breathing. Teddy Larsen felt a burning desire to bring the session to a halt, but he knew that doing so would only make a bad situation worse.

"I would remind you all," Little Lettvik said, and now she was speaking to her colleagues as much as to the minister, "that this happened in the very coldest year of the Cold War. Three years after the Berlin Wall was built. When the GDR was politically isolated and all NATO countries were implementing trade restrictions. Six years *before* Willy Brandt launched his politics of reconciliation."

Little Lettvik was queen of the castle, and everyone knew it. She paused for effect.

"Can the minister tell us why none of these facts were included in the statement she has just given, the statement that was supposed to bring the historical facts out into the open?"

Ruth-Dorthe Nordgarden stiffened.

"It is not my remit to respond to completely unsubstantiated information."

"Unsubstantiated? Read *Kveldsavisen*, Minister. And I'll give the government a piece of friendly advice, if I may. Start to look more closely at the countries to which iron ore was exported from Narvik in 1965. Look very closely at that. Because *we* already have."

She resumed her seat.

None of the others composed themselves sufficiently to ask further questions, and Teddy Larsen quickly took advantage of the opportunity to declare the press conference over.

Ruth-Dorthe darted from the room, followed by a posse of

photographers who tripped over one another, screaming and swearing, but none of them was quick enough to spot that Ruth-Dorthe Nordgarden was in floods of tears.

11:51 P.M., EIDSVOLL

"Are you asleep, darling?" he whispered from the doorway. His wife sat up in bed.

"No," she sniffed. "I'm not sleeping. I'm thinking."

It distressed him when he heard her voice. Its despair. Sorrow. They had spent so many years learning to live with this. Somehow they had managed to make it into something that bound them together, something serious and weighty that was theirs and theirs alone. The picture of little Marie hung on the wall above the sofa; she was naked on a sheepskin rug, with a look of surprise on her little face, mouth open and a tiny dribble suspended from her bottom lip, and enormous eyes like saucers. It was the only professional photograph they had of the child, and it had lost its color with the passage of time, just as their lives had faded after Marie's death, and for some reason, no more children had come to Kjell and Elsa Haugen. One year after the child had died, he had refurbished her room as a workroom, and Elsa had tacitly accepted that. However, he knew that she had a shoebox filled with the baby's effects: a pale pink sleeper, a terry-towel diaper, her rattle, and a lock of hair they had snipped off after she had gone. The box was kept at the bottom of the wardrobe, and Elsa had never shared it with him, but he did not regard this as a reproach. It was a mother's thing, a mother's memories; he understood and accepted that. Over the years they had stopped marking Marie's birthday, and little by little life had become tolerable. They visited her grave on Christmas Eve, but not otherwise. They both thought it best that way.

He stared at his own hands, at his wedding ring embedded on his finger.

"Come on, let's make some coffee," he said. "We're not going to get any sleep anyway, either of us."

She gave him a tentative smile, drying her tears with a big, crumpled handkerchief, and padded after him down to the kitchen. They sat on opposite sides of the dining table, an everyday table with only one chair on either side.

"It's so peculiar," she said softly. "I always think of Marie as a baby. But she would have been a grown-up. Thirty-two years old. Maybe we—"

The tears cascaded down her exhausted cheeks, and she squeezed his hand.

"Maybe we would have had grandchildren, even. Someone to take over the farm."

She gazed at her husband. He was fifty-four years old. They had met at the community hall at the age of fifteen and had been faithful to each other ever since. If it hadn't been for Kjell, her life would have been over the morning she woke to find Marie dead in her crib. For four hours, she had held the baby tight, rocking her, and refusing to be parted from her when the local doctor arrived. In the end, it was Kjell who persuaded her to let go. It was Kjell who lay down beside her, keeping her alive for the next three days. It was Kjell who, over the years, had made it possible for her to smile at the thought of their child—the child who, despite everything, they had been able to keep for a few months.

"Well," Kjell said, looking out the window. The darkness was no longer winter black, and a gray glimmer in the night sky promised that spring would soon arrive in earnest. "There's no point thinking like that, Elsa. There's just no point."

"You shouldn't have let that journalist come, Kjell," she whispered. "You shouldn't have let her come. Everything's become—everything's become—"

He pressed her hands more tightly.

"There, there," he said, trying to elicit a smile.

"It's as if it's all come flooding back." She sobbed quietly. "All the awfulness. What we've managed to—"

"Hush, hush," he whispered. "I know, sweetheart. I know. It was stupid. But she seemed so decent on the phone. It seemed so important to—what was it she said? To turn the spotlight on this vaccine scandal. I felt it was the right thing to do, the way she put it. She seemed so interested and sympathetic."

"She wasn't particularly sympathetic when she came," Elsa said, raising her voice and releasing his hands in order to blow her nose. "Did you see how she stared at Marie's photograph? What cheek she had, asking to borrow it. What cheek."

She stood up angrily and removed the pot from the coffee machine.

She poured for them both, but instead of sitting down again, she remained standing with her back to the kitchen counter.

"And that other woman, the photographer. The way she pushed us around in the cemetery. Did you see how she trampled on the flowers? *Sorry*, was all she said, as she stamped all over Herdis Bråttom's brand-new grave. What a way to carry on!"

Kjell Haugen did not say a word. He sipped his coffee and let Elsa have her rant. For a short time, it made her less sorrowful. He was desperately full of remorse. The woman from *Kveldsavisen* had been there for barely half an hour and hadn't listened to what they had to say. She was not interested in them; she only wanted the details and jotted them down on a notepad in a tearing hurry, without making eye contact. She hadn't even accepted coffee and cake, though Elsa had baked a cream layer cake before they came.

"She didn't even pick up that Dr. Bang understood what had happened," Kjell said suddenly. "We didn't get to tell her about that. That he wrote letters to the authorities for many years afterward."

Elsa was staring out the window. The sky had begun to brighten. Faint rays of morning sun seemed to be creeping up from the field, from every furrow in the newly ploughed soil.

"It's like a knife," she whispered. "It's as if someone has sliced open a scar that has taken so many years to heal."

Kjell Haugen stood up stiffly and headed for the living room, where he lifted the copy of the newspaper off the coffee table. All of a sudden, he tore it to shreds and threw the pieces into the stove. He took hold of a matchbox, but his hands were trembling so violently that he could not succeed in setting the paper ablaze.

"I'll do it," his wife said softly from behind his back. "I'll light it."

"It was stupid," he whispered into the flames when they flared up, coloring his face a golden red. "But she seemed so sympathetic when she phoned."

SATURDAY, APRIL 19

He had fooled them, and it had been so easy that it was laughable. Admittedly, it had taken a while to find out where they were positioned. He now had six cartons of milk in the fridge after four unnecessary trips to the little corner shop. It would sour, but that didn't matter. It was almost too good to be true. The police were keeping an eye on the entrance to Vidars gate. Period. They had obviously not discovered that it was possible to go through the basement and across into the neighbor's garden, where a cellar flap into the backyard allowed him to jump over the fence and out through the door three blocks farther down. No one had spotted him. To be entirely on the safe side, he had taken three buses and one tram in different directions, leaping off suddenly at the last minute. Finally he had gone into a sports store and had bought a cheap bicycle.

He had cycled all the way to the cabin, not arriving until late evening, after darkness had really closed in. The final stretch had been totally deserted; the dismal spring weather was evidently insufficiently tempting, even for the most committed walkers. He had read for a while and had struggled to fall asleep, getting out of bed several times to reassure himself that there was nobody lurking outside. An occasional animal noise came sweeping across the lake, and for an hour or so a light spring shower had whispered softly around the cabin. Otherwise, all was silent.

He was still tired after only three hours of fitful sleep, but he did not want to sleep any more. He had swum all the way across the lake twice, and his body was wide awake even though his head felt sluggish. He made some coffee and spread a few slices of bread with fish roe.

He switched on the radio, but there was nothing worth listening to:

just lots of noisy pop music, and Brage Håkonsen was not keen on that. Instead he took out a book by David Irving and read as he ate.

He had probably lost his job. He had been absent for four days now without getting in touch, and the bad-tempered warehouse boss would certainly bite his head off if he returned. But he didn't want to go back. In any case, he didn't want to think about that at the moment. After all, he had money in the bank and lived modestly.

He snatched a glimpse out the window and saw that it was bright outside now; it would be sensible to head for the potato cellar while it was still early. People occasionally wandered past on weekends, even though the path was more than two hundred yards from the cabin. The lake seemed enticing to the few walkers with the energy to venture this far, and he had given up trying to frighten them off with a "Fishing and Swimming Forbidden" sign. The forestry authority removed them after a while anyway.

The safest course of action would be to go now.

He pulled a sweatshirt over his head and pushed his feet into a pair of sneakers without tying the laces. He needed a new pair, but he had to be careful now. The bike had cost three thousand kroner, and it was annoying to have spent so much money when he had a good, expensive bicycle in the backyard. However, it hadn't been worth the risk. It would have been tricky to haul it through the basement, and he wasn't sure if he would have managed to drag it with him over the fence.

The morning air had a pungent odor of earth and forest, making him dizzy, even though he had already been outside. He jogged the forty yards over to the little hillock located to the east. The door to the potato cellar was covered in spruce branches and twigs, and would have been invisible if he had not known it was there.

Removing the camouflage and stacking it beside the entrance, he fished out the key to the hefty padlock from a pocket in his sweatshirt. The lock was well oiled, and it was a simple matter to lift off the heavy cellar flap. The hinges squeaked a little, and Brage paused for a second, stiffening as he strained to listen. Then he exhaled, placing the flap cautiously all the way down on one side of the opening, and entered the pitch-black cave. It always took time for his eyes to adjust to the dark, and he switched on a flashlight.

Now he could hear something. Something other than the occasional small animal. Something more than the wind toying tentatively and ineffectually with last year's rotting leaves. A twig snapped. Several twigs fractured. He heard footsteps.

"Come out of there," he heard a loud voice call out imperiously.

For a second or two, he considered his options. He had the newly purchased revolver in his pocket and was holding ammunition in his hands. In front of him lay four AG-3s and two shotguns, as well as four saloon rifles. Ammunition for all of them was on the shelf. He would have time to load. He could shoot his way out.

"Come out right now!" the man roared from the entrance.

Brage Håkonsen felt anxiety crush his ribs. He attempted to open the package of bullets for the revolver, but his fingers seemed swollen and uncooperative.

I don't dare do it, it suddenly dawned on him. *For fuck's sake, I just don't dare.*

With gritted teeth, he backed out of the potato cellar. His eyes were filled with tears, but he swallowed repeatedly to retain a degree of control.

Once he emerged from the opening, they threw themselves on him. He lay flat as a pancake on his stomach and could taste the forest floor as spruce needles forced their way into his nose and mouth. A stab of pain jolted through him as the handcuffs were slammed around his wrists.

"They're too tight!" he screamed, and spat. "For fuck's sake! They're too bloody tight!"

One of the men had been inside the potato cellar already.

"Look at this," he said as his colleague yanked Brage to his feet. "What have we here, then?"

He was holding an AG-3 in one hand and in the other the box of documents. The plans. The great ideas.

"We fooled you completely," the man said, with a loud guffaw. "You thought we were rank amateurs, only watching the door, didn't you?"

His laughter echoed across the water, and a large bird screeched as it took off in fright at the opposite side of the lake.

"Fucking homo," Brage growled.

The police officer holding him, a big, strong guy in his fifties, grinned broadly.

"It takes one to know one," he said, pulling Brage firmly and purposefully in the direction of the cabin.

Severin Heger ran ahead to call for reinforcements.

9:40 A.M., KIRKEVEIEN 129

This headache was killing her. A drill was boring into each temple, her eyes were smarting, and she had no idea why. She hadn't drunk any alcohol the night before; in fact, she hadn't touched a drop since that fatal evening when Birgitte Volter was killed. Even so, she had difficulty keeping herself upright; this pain was new and different and really terrifying. Two painkillers had not helped, and she rummaged around in her bag in search of something more effective.

The newsprint on the page danced in front of her eyes when she sat down at the kitchen table. The coffee tasted acrid, but after half a cup, she felt her headache subsiding slightly. Whether due to the coffee or the tablets covered in dust and fluff from her handbag, she was not quite sure.

The story was no longer a *Kveldsavisen* exclusive. Although *Kveldsavisen* had the edge, all the other newspapers in Oslo and the major regions had now thrown their hats into the ring as well. That created a demand for new angles, fresh theories, and a great deal of pessimistic conjecture. There was now, effectively, no limit to what commentators could speculate about. Even though nobody had yet dared identify a murderer, not a single voice in government circles had refrained from expressing the opinion, if you read between the lines, that the health scandal was obviously closely connected to Birgitte Volter's death.

The specter of Benjamin Grinde permeated the pages of every newspaper, despite there being hardly a mention of his name. They all homed in on the friendship between Volter and Grinde, holding it up as an example of the unacceptable culture of influence within central government that had been established by the Labor Party over many years. Buying vaccines from an Eastern bloc country during the frostiest period of the Cold War was far and away the worst scandal in Norwegian postwar history, greater than the Lund Commission's revelations about the Security Service, infinitely more serious than the debate over government responsibility regarding the Kings Bay coal-mining disasters. Even through her intense headache, Ruth-Dorthe Nordgarden had to admit that on this point, the newspapers were probably not entirely out in left field: several hundred lives may have been lost because of the vaccines—if all of this was true, of course, something no one actually knew for certain yet.

Strictly speaking, the other newspapers had no new facts to add to the revelations contained in yesterday's extra edition of *Kveldsavisen*. However, the *Kveldsavisen* story had been so comprehensive that it spawned innumerable pages of commentary from the learned and the not-so-learned, from politicians and indefatigable spokespeople. As was his wont, Fred Brynjestad, professor of public law, made a number of vitriolic attacks, though the more observant reader might have struggled to figure out who he was aiming at. Since Einar Gerhardsen, who had served as Prime Minister from 1963 to 1965, was long dead, and his last Minister of Social Affairs also, the intensity of the criticisms seemed rather reckless. Especially as it had in no way been clarified how high up the political ladder responsibility for the vaccine purchase went or who had profited by the transaction.

There were also a couple of comments about Ruth-Dorthe Nordgarden's role in all this. Not that she was singled out as the killer, far from it—in 1965 she had been twelve years old and a Girl Guide— but nevertheless *Kveldsavisen*, *Dagbladet*, and *Aftenposten* all went so far as to set a question mark against her handling of the issue. It was particularly galling that they had "reliable sources" who maintained that she had refused to meet Benjamin Grinde only days before he visited Birgitte Volter. The speculations about why she had not been willing to meet him were as fantastic as they were crazy.

"I simply didn't have time," she muttered to herself. "I couldn't fit it in."

Many MPs had also stuck their oars in, some lamely and hesitantly, others rushing in with no other target in sight than the election, now only five months off. As usual, to a greater or lesser degree, they all prefaced their remarks with meaningless provisos. Meaningless, because they then went on to express themselves with the greatest confidence about absolutely everything: the Labor Party's relationship to the Eastern bloc in the sixties, the role of politics in the investigation of Volter's homicide, the work and composition of the Grinde Commission. The opposition also made one hell of a racket about what the murder had done to Norwegian society in general, and Norwegian politics in particular. The closed season was definitely over, and it was time for the opposition to ensure that the Labor Party would not benefit from too powerful a Palme effect during the early summer polls.

"As if the murder is an indication of how incompetent the Labor Party is." Ruth-Dorthe Nordgarden sighed, touching her forehead as she squeezed her eyes shut. "As if the murder says anything at all about the Labor Party. Six months ago we were accused of persecuting Communists in the sixties. Now we stand accused of being in cahoots with them."

Furious and dejected, she used the newspaper to clobber an audacious fly, dizzy with spring and crawling in the direction of the marmalade spoon.

"I'm off, Mum," said a head of tousled blond hair that suddenly appeared around the doorframe.

"Have you had breakfast?"

"Bye!"

"Breakfast!"

Sighing histrionically, she leaned back in her chair. Outside the window, the massive larch had really started to put on its summer clothing: it would be vibrant green by May 17, Norway's Constitution Day.

"Has Astrid *gone*?"

Another, if possible even more rumpled, head stared crossly at her.

"You're *not* going until you've eaten some breakfast!"

"But I just *have to* run."

Bang.

The front door left a vacuum of silence she was not sure she liked, or wanted to fill with something else. She did not need to consider this for long. Her cell phone sitting in its charger was glaring at her with an evil green eye, as though it knew what a trial it was for her to use it.

She had memorized the number by heart.

"I hope you slept well," she said petulantly when someone at the other end eventually picked up.

"Thanks, the same to you," came the saccharine reply. "I have slept the sleep of the just."

"You can't *write* all that stuff," Ruth-Dorthe exploded. "To think *you* could write such things about me, after—"

"After what? After being given so much help, do you mean? But wasn't that in the service of freedom of expression, Ruth-Dorthe?"

"You know *perfectly* well what I mean!"

"No, honestly, I don't. You sent me the commission's document. Entirely voluntarily. There were no promises from me involved in that."

"But you have—you have *destroyed* me! And not only me, but also perhaps the whole government. Just look at what *Aftenposten* wrote today. To think—"

She made an angry, rustling noise with the newspapers.

"Here. 'It is regrettable that it does not seem possible to eradicate the "you scratch my back and I'll scratch yours" culture that exists within our largest political party. The only difference here is that the back-scratching seems to have extended to former GDR leader Walter Ulbricht. We honestly do not know which is worse.'"

She threw the newspaper away.

"In the editorial! What have you done, Little Lettvik? We had an *agreement!*"

"Wrong. We did not have an agreement. I have helped you when it has been expedient. You have helped me. If it is no longer possible to return favors, we'll just have to put that down to the free press and a vibrant democracy. We both support that, don't we?"

"I—"

She had to compose herself and be restrained. Her headache was back, pounding mercilessly, and she felt nauseous.

"I will never, ever speak to you again," Ruth-Dorthe whispered into the receiver.

But there was only a dial tone, and that seemed completely uninterested in her promises, given far too late.

The phone rang, startling her.

"Hello?"

Though the cell phone was stone-dead, the ringing continued.

Bewildered, she looked around the living room, keeping her cheek pressed to the cell phone as if it were a security blanket bringing comfort in difficult times.

It was the ordinary cordless phone that was ringing.

"Hello," she ventured again, this time into the right phone. "No, hello, Tryggve. I was just about to call you. I need to talk to you about this health— Okay?"

She began to chew the nail on her left pinkie.

"I understand. Four o'clock on Monday. At your office. But then I'll be—never mind. I'll be there. Four o'clock."

She had bitten her nail down to the quick, and a jag of pain passed through her finger. A little drop of blood trickled out, and she put her fingertip into her mouth before traipsing off to find a Band-Aid.

2:27 P.M., SECURITY SERVICE SECTION, OSLO POLICE STATION

"Look at this, look at this," Severin Heger said jauntily, his voice conveying a hint of satisfaction.

He tried to make eye contact with the prisoner facing him, but the young man was staring down at his own hands, muttering something impossible to catch.

"What did you say?" the police officer asked.

"Surely these aren't necessary?" the man repeated, lifting his wrists toward him. "Handcuffs in here!"

"If you hadn't tried to run off umpteen times between your cabin and the station, then we could have discussed it. But not now."

Smiling broadly, he served Brage Håkonsen a cola.

"How will I manage to drink this with these on?" the young man complained, now almost sniveling.

"It's quite easy," Severin Heger said. "I've tried it myself. So what have we here?"

The pages he was reading were sheathed in plastic wraps, every one of them. They were typewritten, in fairly pompous language peppered with spelling mistakes that might have led one to assume that the author was rather elderly. Perhaps they were merely typos.

"You wrote this, did you?"

The police officer was still smiling, and his tone was friendly, bordering on cheerful.

"None of your fucking business," the prisoner murmured softly.

"What was that?"

Severin Heger was no longer smiling. He leaned unceremoniously across the desk and grabbed hold of Brage's flannel shirt.

"One more word of that kind, and this will become *very* much harder for you," he snarled. "Just you sit up straight and answer all my questions politely. *Understood?*"

"I want to speak to a lawyer," Brage said. "I'm saying nothing until I get to speak to an attorney!"

Severin Heger stood up and remained there staring at Brage Håkonsen for such a long time that the young man began to squirm in his seat.

"Of course," the police officer said finally. "Of course you can speak to a lawyer. That's your right. It'll take some time, and I can assure you that in a few hours I'll be considerably less amiable and patient than I am now. We've a great deal here, you know. These papers. And those guns. Enough to let you roast for a really long time. But okay, you're the one to decide. It goes without saying that a quick, easy round with me now would be best for you, but of course you can have an attorney if you want one. They're usually off on weekends, you know, but by tomorrow morning we should probably have organized something."

Brage Håkonsen gazed at his glass of cola and attempted to raise it to his mouth using both hands.

"See! It's quite easy after all. Now I'll send you back to your cell so that we can wait for that attorney of yours."

"No," Brage said quietly.

"What was that?"

"No. We can just talk for a bit now. If I can have an attorney later, I mean."

"Quite sure? No whining afterward that you didn't know your rights and so on?"

The young man shook his head almost imperceptibly.

"Very wise," Severin Heger commented, sitting down again. "Born March 19, 1975, is that right?"

Brage nodded.

"Warehouse worker and unmarried, living at 11c Vidars gate?"

Another nod.

"So can you tell me something about these papers, then?"

Brage Håkonsen cleared his throat and sat upright.

"What's the penalty for this sort of thing?" he asked quietly.

Severin Heger waved his left hand dismissively.

"Forget that for the moment. You are charged with contravening Criminal Code paragraph 104a: 'Anyone who blah blah organization of military character blah blah has as its purpose the use of sabotage, force, or other unlawful means to disrupt the established order blah blah.' You ought to know it quite well. You're so well read."

He peered down at the inventory of books, nodding in acknowledgment.

"From two to six years. Depends a little," Severin Heger explained, having realized that Brage Håkonsen would not say anything further until he had an answer. "But don't worry about that now. Just answer my questions. Are you the person who wrote this stuff?"

Ashen, Brage Håkonsen stared straight ahead. His eyes, which didn't look blue anymore, stared colorlessly into the room; they had stopped blinking.

"Six years," he whispered. "Six years!"

"But," the police officer insisted, "aren't you running ahead of yourself now?"

"They are my papers," Brage interrupted. "I was the one who wrote them. Just me and me alone."

"That was stupid, then," Severin Heger said drily, then added immediately, "but it's quite smart of you to admit everything. Extremely smart, I would say. Killing the President of the Parliament? *That* would not have been so smart, on the other hand."

He leafed through another three pages.

"Even more unfortunate, this here," he said, placing the paper in front of Brage. "A cut-and-dried plan on how to kill Prime Minister Volter. At the supermarket checkout!"

"She shops there. Shopped, I mean."

Brage Håkonsen stared straight ahead in a way that reminded Severin Heger of a B-movie he had seen in a hotel room in England when he couldn't sleep: *The Plague of the Zombies*. It was obvious that the young man did not want to cry; on the contrary, he seemed relaxed, almost like a sleepwalker, sitting there. If his hands had not been reluctantly held together by the handcuffs, they would probably have dangled at his sides, conscious of nothing, just registering the passage of time.

"But it didn't happen at the supermarket," Severin Heger said. "She was murdered at her office."

"And it wasn't me who did it either," Brage Håkonsen said evenly. "It was someone else."

Severin Heger could hear the blood rushing to his brain, as if his entire body understood this was the crucial moment. The noise in his ears was so loud that he involuntarily tipped his head to one side so that he could hear better. Then he asked, "And you know who it was?"

"Yes."

He heard someone outside the door, and regretted for one terrible second that he had forgotten to display the "Interview—Do Not Disturb" sign. He breathed a sigh of relief when the steps passed by and disappeared along the corridor.

"And who was that, then?"

He tried to make his question sound low-key. He took hold of his own glass of cola, as if to emphasize how mundane all this was. As if he routinely sat there listening to right-wing extremists with information on people who had killed prominent members of society. The soft drink fizzed over when he tried to top up his tumbler.

For the first time, something resembling a smile crossed Brage Håkonsen's face.

"I know who did it. I also know who sent the gun back to you. In a large, brown envelope, isn't that right, with black letters and no stamp? It was slipped into a mailbox at the central post office, wasn't it? What I can tell you right now is that these two actions were carried out by two different people."

This information had not been made public. There were very few people in the police station who knew about it. They all knew the gun had been returned; there had been huge headlines in the newspapers about it. But not that it had been mailed at the central post office. And certainly not that it had arrived in a brown envelope with no stamp.

"And have you thought about giving me some names?"

"No."

Brage was smiling properly now, and Severin Heger had to clutch the edge of the table to avoid punching him.

"No. I know who killed Volter. And who sent the gun. I have two names to offer. But you'll get nothing out of me until we've cut a deal."

"You've watched too many movies," Severin Heger hissed. "We don't make deals of that kind in Norway!"

"Well," Brage Håkonsen said, "there's a first time for everything. And *now* I'd really like to speak to that attorney."

7:00 P.M., STOLMAKERGATA 15

Billy T.'s four sons, Alexander, Nicolay, Peter, and Truls, were charming when they were in their pajamas. And asleep. But only then. The rest of the time, they were lively and entertaining, cocky and inventive, and extremely boisterous. Hanne Wilhelmsen touched her forehead discreetly, swiftly, and imperceptibly, or so she thought.

"Worn out now?" Billy T. asked, depositing a wooden ladle of oatmeal porridge in each of the bowls in front of his four offspring. The boys had taken Hanne's hint and were now sitting reasonably quietly, apart from Peter, who was pinching Truls's thigh with a pair of tongs he had taken from the bottom drawer in the kitchen.

"Not really," she smiled. "Maybe just a little worn out."

The children had tumbled through the door yesterday evening, whooping in anticipation. Truls was dressed as a Native American, having come straight from a costume party; the three older boys wore tracksuits over their wet bathing shorts.

"Honestly, Billy T.," Hanne had exclaimed. "It's only *April!*"

Shamefaced and muttering darkly, he had made them change into dry clothes and had hung Truls's feather headdress on the wall. After that the action had been nonstop. The worst of it was probably when Billy T. had embarked on a major project to install hooks in the ceiling with short lengths of rope attached to see how far the boys could swing. Alexander got all the way from the bathroom to the kitchen and back using only his arms and without letting go, to the tremendous, noisy admiration of his little brothers and thunderous applause from his father. Truls fell off after three attempts; they had been to the emergency room to have his arm set in a cast that morning.

All that high-voltage activity had made them dead tired. Truls did not even have the energy to react to the tongs; his eyelids were sliding shut as he chewed on his porridge to the point that it looked as though he had fallen asleep.

"Hey there, young man," Billy T. roared. "You need to brush your teeth!"

Half an hour later they were all fast asleep.

"Three names from the Russian royal family, and then *Truls?*" Hanne said in a whisper when they had checked that everything was as it should be. "I've always wondered why."

"His mother thought he should have a proper, indisputably Norwegian name."

"It's Danish, actually."

"Eh?"

"Truls. It's not Norwegian. It's Danish!"

"Well. He's not quite the same as the others. So he had to have something liberal and Norwegian. So that he wouldn't feel left out. It was his mother who chose it. I didn't even know of his existence until he was three months old. I had to go through a hell of a battle to get visitation rights. But now it's all worked out fine."

Truls was not like the others. He was black. Billy T.'s two eldest sons looked a lot like their father, with blond hair, good complexions, and big ice-blue eyes. Peter, the second youngest, had fiery red hair and a face covered in freckles. Truls was black—so black that you would not have believed his father was white were it not for his smile. When he drew back the corners of his mouth in a crooked grin, he was the spitting image of his father.

"Beautiful children, Billy T. I'll grant you that. You've a talent for making children."

Hanne Wilhelmsen carefully patted Nicolay's quilt cover and tried to drag Billy T. out of the room.

He held back and sat down on one of the lower bunks, where Truls was sleeping open-mouthed, with his new cast like a shield over his eyes.

"Is he in pain, do you think?" Billy T. whispered. "Does he feel it? Should I have given him some painkillers?"

"You heard what the doctor said. A nice clean break, it will heal within three weeks, and he shouldn't need anything unless he's in obvious pain. Now he's sleeping peacefully. It can't be that sore."

"But he doesn't usually do that with his arm."

Billy T. attempted to place Truls's arm down alongside the quilt, but it popped back, and the boy whimpered softly.

"I should have given him something for the pain," Billy T. said despondently.

"What I think is that you shouldn't have started that race across the ceiling. At least you could have put something underneath. Mattresses on the floor or something like that. Can't you see that Truls is much more delicate than the others? He's going to be nowhere near as big as you."

"It's just that he's the youngest," Billy T. said stubbornly. "He's so small because he's only six years old. He'll grow taller. Just you wait."

"He's smaller than the others, Billy T. He is your boy even though he doesn't have your athletic prowess. Now you need to let up."

"His mother's going to kill me about that arm," he murmured, rubbing his hand over his face. "She thinks I'm too rough with him."

"Maybe you are," Hanne whispered. "Come on now."

He did not want to leave. He remained there on the edge of the bed, crouching uncomfortably because the gap between the top and bottom bunk was not big enough. His hand fell tentatively from his face onto the boy's head; he stroked the wiry, curly hair over and over again.

"If anything serious were to happen to him—" he said softly. "If anything were to happen to any of my children, then I don't know . . ."

Hanne sat down warily on Peter's bed, pushing the boy carefully to one side. A pale white arm with multiple brown spots lay on top of the quilt; he coughed in his sleep and wrinkled his brow.

"Think how it must have been for Birgitte Volter," she said, tucking the boy's arm underneath the quilt; it was cool in the bedroom and his skin felt cold.

"Volter?"

"Yes. First when her baby died. Then when everything was brought up again more than thirty years later. I think—"

Alexander turned over on the top bunk.

"Daddy!"

Billy T. stood up and asked the boy what he wanted. Alexander blinked his eyes and grimaced at the light flooding in from the hallway.

"Thirsty," he mumbled. "Cola."

Grinning, Billy T. made a sign to Hanne that she should go back to the living room. He fetched a glass of water for the boy and shortly afterward sat down beside her on the blue sofa.

"What were you saying just now?" he said, grasping the can of beer she handed him. "You were talking about Volter."

He belched quietly and dried his mouth with the back of his hand.

"The baby who died. I can't get it out of my head. Think how it must have been for her. For some reason I can't get it out of my head that the actual *death* has something to do with the case. But then—"

Billy T. grabbed the remote control in front of them to put on some music. Hanne got hold of it just in time and moved it out of Billy T.'s reach.

"Honestly, Billy T.," she said in annoyance. "It must be possible, even for you, to conduct a conversation without any screeching from the loudspeakers at two hundred decibels."

He did not reply but instead took a long slug from his can of beer.

"Perhaps we should spend some time thinking about how it was for Birgitte," Hanne said quietly. "How was she feeling in those final days of her life? You should look into that. Instead of searching wildly around to find out what everyone else was doing at the time of the murder! We should really spend some time working out what those words on the paper mean. 'New person' followed by a question mark. Wasn't that it? And what was the other thing again?"

Billy T. did not appear to be really listening.

"But the security guard," he said into the room. "Given what Severin told me yesterday, I'm more certain than ever that the guard's involved somehow. And if that's the case, then it doesn't bloody matter how that Birgitte woman was feeling!"

"Now you're being nasty. A moment ago you were tearing yourself apart at the thought of anything befalling your own child, and now you're suddenly cold as ice regarding the fact that Birgitte Volter actually experienced what gives you nightmares. That's what's called lack of empathy. You should seek help."

"Not at all!" He pinched her on the thigh. "Don't kid! I've got loads of empathy; it's just that we won't get any fucking place if we get bogged down in that kind of thing during the investigation."

"Yes, you will," Hanne Wilhelmsen said, pushing his hand away. "I think this is the only way we can get to the bottom of this. We have to discover how things were going for her, how she was really feeling at that particular time, what her life was like on that particular day. April 4, 1997. Then we find out what role the guard played in all this."

"And how has Her Majesty arrived at this methodology?" he asked, standing up to get a slice of bread. "Do you want a mackerel sandwich?"

She did not reply and said instead, "I do have a strong feeling that the death of Birgitte Volter's baby is more relevant to the murder case than the actual health scandal. I think we've got lost in the detail of all the other babies who died. And I think you're right about the guard. Something links him in too. Was he born in 1965?"

"No. He's far younger."

"The old man was right."

"What?" Billy T. said, his mouth full of mackerel and tomato sauce.

"The old man in the park. Forget it. I think I'll have a sandwich after all. But I'd like a glass of milk with it."

"Suit yourself," Billy T. muttered, opening another can of beer.

11:25 P.M., OLE BRUMMS VEI 212

"Can't you sit down, Per?"

His voice was husky from whiskey and far too many cigarettes, and he had to use the armrest for support as he stood up. He shouldn't have been drinking. But he was searching for some way out of all his pain, and nothing else had helped. The doctor who had visited two days ago had given him a prescription for Valium, but there were limits. He did not want to use pills. A good drink was far less dangerous. There had been six of them now.

Per glared at him contemptuously; he was wearing a jogging suit even though he could not possibly have been out running, not as late as this, not for such a long time. It was six hours since Roy Hansen had heard the front door slam behind his son.

"Are you drinking?" Per spat out. "That's all we need now. For God's sake, Dad."

That was enough. Roy Hansen thumped his fist into the wall and knocked over a lamp beside the sofa; the glass shade smashed into a thousand pieces.

"Will you just sit down! Now!" he screamed, rubbing his chest as though trying to straighten up inside his clothes; he had worn them for two days and they were crumpled and creased. "Just sit down and talk to me!"

Staring in surprise at his father, Per Volter shrugged his shoulders and dropped down into the armchair opposite. Roy, sober all of a sudden and running his fingers through his hair, sat perched on the very edge of the sofa, as if about to take off.

"When are you going to stop punishing me?" he asked. "Don't you think I'll soon have been punished enough?"

His son did not answer; as he fiddled with a large pewter table lighter that was out of gas, the flint emitted meaningless little rhythmical hissing sounds.

"I'm having a dreadful time, Per. Just the same as you. I can see that you're suffering, and I'd give anything to be able to do something for you. But you just lash out and punish me and push me away. Both you and I know this can't continue. We need to find some—some way to talk to each other."

"And what would you say then?" the boy asked suddenly and unexpectedly, banging the lighter down on the table.

Roy leaned back in the sofa, placing his hands on his lap. He appeared to be praying to a higher authority, with his chin on his chest and his fingers folded.

"I would say how sorry I am. I would beg for forgiveness. For what happened last autumn. With—"

"Ruth-Dorthe Nordgarden," Per said venomously. "It's not me you need to beg for forgiveness. It's Mum! She's the one you should have said sorry to. But she didn't know about it, of course."

"You're wrong."

Roy Hansen lit another cigarette, grimacing with displeasure as he did so, as if he only now realized how unpleasant it was. Nevertheless, he did not extinguish it.

"Your mother knew everything. It was the only time in all our married life that I'd done anything like that. I don't know why it happened, it just . . ."

He exhaled smoke through his nose, looking his son directly in the eye.

"I don't think it's right to explain this to you. But I would like you to know that I told Mum all about it. The day she returned home from that meeting in Bergen. I sat here on the sofa the entire time until she came home, late in the evening. Night. It was two o'clock, because she'd been to the office first, and when she returned, I told her everything."

Per stared at his father with an expression suggesting he doubted the veracity of what he had just been told.

"But—what did she say, then?"

"That's a matter between your mother and me. But she forgave me. After a while. Long before she died. You should too. I really wish you could forgive me, Per."

They sat for some time in the gloom without uttering a word. The rain was pouring down outside. A gutter was obviously leaking, and a flood of water was cascading down the northwest corner of the exterior wall. Far in the distance, they could hear a dog's bark. The noise was fierce and alarming, cutting through the relentless sound of the foul spring weather. The deafening barking reminded them both that there was a world out there, a world they were part of, and that soon it would be time for them to resume contact with it once again.

"When I move back home this autumn, I'd like to get myself a dog," Per said impetuously.

Roy felt overwhelmed by an unspeakable tiredness. He felt dizzy and could hardly keep his eyes open.

"Of course, you can have a dog," he said, attempting a smile; even this was an almost insurmountable challenge. "A hunting dog?"

"Mmm. A setter, I thought. Are you being straight with me?"

"Yes! Of course you can have a dog. You're grown up and can decide for yourself."

"I didn't mean that. Did you really tell Mum?"

Roy coughed as he stubbed out his cigarette.

"Yes. Your mother and I—we didn't have many secrets from each other. A few, naturally. But not many. Not like that."

Per got to his feet and shuffled through to the kitchen. Roy remained seated, with his eyes closed. His boy had come back. He was going to move home again in the autumn, after all. Here, to the house where his little family had lived and quarreled and loved ever since Per was born.

Perhaps he had fallen asleep. It seemed as though only a second or two had passed when he suddenly heard the rattle of a plate being placed on the table.

"Can I have one?" Roy asked.

Per did not reply, but pushed the plate forward a few inches.

"What was she really like?" he asked.

"Mum? Birgitte?"

He was confused.

"No. Liv. My sister. What was she like?"

Roy Hansen put down his sandwich, untouched, on the table. He scratched his midriff and felt wide awake all of a sudden.

"Liv was wonderful."

He laughed lightly, softly.

"That's what everybody says about their children. But she was so— so little! So tiny and petite. Completely different from you; you were— you were such a boy. Big and strong and screaming like a stuck pig when you were hungry, right from the very first day. Liv was—she had dimples and blond hair. Yes, I think—yes, it was blond. Almost white."

"Do we have a photograph of her anywhere?"

Roy shook his head slowly.

"There were loads of photos," he said after a while. "Benjamin Grinde's father, yes, you know him. Well, his father was a photographer, and they lived right beside Grandma and Grandpa, and Mum and I lived there too, the first few years, before we got—there were lots of photographs. I think Mum burned them all. I haven't seen any since then, anyway. But . . ."

He glanced across at his son, who had not touched his food either, but who sat watching him with a marveling, almost shy expression.

". . . there may be some in the attic," Roy continued. "I'll go through everything someday. Tidy up a little. I think I'll start work again as well. On Tuesday or Wednesday, maybe. When are you going back to college?"

"Soon."

In the silence, they ate four sandwiches each and drank milk and coffee, occasionally glancing at each other; Roy smiled every time, and Per quickly looked away. But the malice was no longer there. The spiteful expression disappeared as the storm outside picked up, and the rain drummed heavily, furiously, against the enormous panorama windows overlooking the garden.

"Where is she buried, Dad? Liv. Is there a gravestone?"

"At Nesodden. I'll take you there sometime."

"Don't make it too long? Soon?"

"Soon, my boy. We can go there fairly soon."

When his son went to bed, he did not say goodnight. But it would not take so very long until he got around to that once again.

MONDAY, APRIL 21

In a peculiar way, Billy T. had begun to enjoy these large meetings. Normally he hated such things, but there were advantages, in fact, in getting the leaders of the numerous investigation teams together twice a week. It was the best way of gathering the threads and coordinating the group effort; equally important, the meetings now also allowed time for discussion. Everyone was present, even Tone-Marit Steen, although nobody quite knew why, since she did not actually lead a team, at least not formally; but somehow she had assumed a role that suited her. Eloquent, thorough, and with a comprehensive overview, she showed up every time without anyone objecting.

The only person who made a habit of being cursory and who always seemed to be holding something back from everyone else was the Security Service Chief. This was probably to be expected. Today the meeting was given extra weight by the presence of the Senior Public Prosecutor, but Billy T. was determined not to let himself be affected by the appearance of this surly, ill-tempered person, whom he considered to be the most obstinate woman in the world. She was capable, boring, and headstrong and had made a virtue out of being totally unreceptive to the opinions of any other living creature, at any time, and about any matter whatsoever. Regardless. Now she sat browsing through a sheaf of papers and looked crossly at Billy T. when he entered the room, not even expending so much as a nod. Fine, he would not grovel to such trash and did not say hello to her either.

He helped himself to water from a thermos flask, pouring it into a white cup bearing a National Catering logo. The teabag was allowed to remain in the cup for exactly a minute and a half, and he checked his watch before he used his fingers to press it dry and dispose of it in the wastepaper basket in the corner. The water was not hot enough, however, and the tea was tasteless.

Finally everyone had arrived, apart from Assistant Chief of Police Håkon Sand. No one had heard or seen anything of him, and it was already ten minutes past the appointed starting time. The Chief of Police had no wish to wait any longer.

"This past week has brought us some surprises," he began. "Billy T.! Would you make a start?"

Putting his teacup down, Billy T. strode to the head of the table, where he leaned against the wall with his arms behind his back.

"We think we've ruled out the family from the case," he began. "Per, the son, has a completely watertight alibi. Obviously we also looked into the possibility of a conspiracy, since strictly speaking he would not have needed to be present in person in the Prime Minister's office when the shot was fired, but there is absolutely no basis for anything of that nature. As far as the weapon is concerned, we had another look at the conspiracy theory angle when it turned out to belong to Per, but the only conclusion we can come to is that it was somehow stolen from the family. No . . ."

Pushing his hands against the table edge, he stood rocking on his toes as he looked down at the floor for a second.

". . . Per Volter is an extremely unhappy young man whose life has been turned upside down in the space of a very short time. But a murderer—I refuse to believe that. Roy Hansen can also be ruled out. I have explained this before."

He glanced at the Police Chief, who nodded briefly.

"He would have had difficulty sneaking past the guards, murdering his wife, and later sending us his son's gun. And we know that he received a phone call from his mother at 4:40 at his home. That is confirmed by the phone company's records. That in itself ought to exclude him. As you know, they live in Groruddalen. The homicide must have happened around that time. Even though . . ."

Once more he made eye contact with the Chief of Police, who nodded again, irritated now.

". . . I take no pleasure in spreading dirt that doesn't need to be spread, it should be mentioned that it has come to our attention that last autumn, Roy Hansen had a little—affair. With Ruth-Dorthe Nordgarden, the Health Minister."

A subdued murmur rippled through the room, and an expression of interest crossed even the Senior Public Prosecutor's face behind her unbecoming, old-fashioned, steel-rimmed glasses.

"However, it was short-lived. And I think it highly unlikely that such a relationship could have been a motive for murder. No."

Billy T. started to head back to his own seat but stopped halfway.

"The Volter/Hansen family is a normal Norwegian family. With their joys and sorrows, and their dark secrets. Like all the rest of us. And as far as this health scandal is concerned . . ."

He ran his fingers over his head, a habitual gesture when he felt discouraged.

". . . it's probably for others to judge that."

The conversation he'd had with Hanne Wilhelmsen on Saturday after the children had gone to bed raced like a video on fast-forward somewhere inside his brain.

"Personally, I doubt this murder has to do with the health scandal as a whole. Birgitte was at a tender age then and the mother of a young baby. And no matter how much those politicians yell and shout—no, *if*, and I stress *if*, the high rate of infant mortality in 1965 has anything to do with the murder, then I believe we must search for something concerning her own little baby girl. But taking all things into consideration, I'm not convinced."

Sitting down, he mumbled a postscript. "The guard. He did it."

He had covered his mouth with his hand and did not intend others to hear. The guard was not his business. Tone-Marit Steen, sitting beside him, could not stop smiling.

"You don't give up," she whispered, getting to her feet at a signal from the Police Chief.

"Billy T. did not mention the gun," she continued, aloud this time. "The Nagant used in the homicide, which we know for certain belongs to Per Volter. We have inspected the gun cabinet in the family home and it has fingerprints from every member of the family, which seems entirely natural. I should also add that the rest of the house was very nearly completely free of prints. Not surprising, since the Department of State had performed the smart trick of employing the city's most efficient cleaning agency to clean the house *before* we had examined it."

Tone-Marit paused meaningfully.

"That was a mistake, you might say. In the meantime we will just have to work on the assumption that by some means or other, the gun was stolen from the family residence even though there is no sign of forced entry. Unfortunately, we cannot establish the timing of the theft with any accuracy, as Per had not looked inside the gun cabinet since Christmas."

From her perch at one end of the table, she twisted around to face her fellow investigators.

"Billy T. has locked himself on to this security guard from the government complex," she said, smiling at her colleague. "And, in fact, I agree with him. There is something there, something I haven't yet been able to grasp. None of us has. I'm convinced that the guy was lying about something. It was like a curse that he went off and died the way he did. Inconsiderate, to say the least."

Some of the others chuckled, but the Senior Public Prosecutor shot her a murderous look, so she adopted a serious expression, winking at Billy T.

"In contrast with the majority of others in this case, we know that the guard was in fact present at the crime scene. Which is not insignificant, since our biggest problem, apart from constructing anything resembling a motive, is to establish the *possibility* of someone having murdered Volter. We are therefore continuing to work on discovering whether he was linked to any particular group. In that respect I could do with some closer cooperation—some additional assistance from—"

Tone-Marit shot a challenging look across at the Security Service Chief, who for his part continued to sit like a sphinx. Billy T. was impressed. Tone-Marit was not bloody afraid of anyone or anything.

"And then we come to this Benjamin Grinde," she said, shifting her gaze to the Police Chief. "Do you want me to cover this as well, or perhaps the Superintendent?"

The Chief of Police rotated his right hand impatiently, and Tone-Marit continued. "To take the pillbox first: it has fingerprints from Birgitte Volter, Wenche Andersen, and Benjamin Grinde. On the outside. Which means that the box *probably* came into Grinde's possession relatively recently. That fits, of course, with Wenche Andersen's witness statement. On the inside, there are actually no prints. It is impossible to say what is the significance of the box or whether it even has any significance at all."

She smoothed her forehead with her finger and looked at the Police Chief.

"I would give a great deal to see a suicide letter from that man, because there's not a shred of doubt that Benjamin Grinde did commit suicide. There's no sign of a break-in in the apartment, absolutely nothing to suggest the use of force or coercion. The apartment was clean and tidy, and there were ashes in the fireplace indicating that he had the presence of mind to get rid of his most personal papers. The cases he had brought home to work on were neatly laid out so that they would not present any difficulties for the person taking over responsibility for them. However, there was no suicide note, which in itself is quite unusual."

"Perhaps he did not owe anyone an explanation," the Chief of Police said softly.

Tone-Marit glanced up from her notes, a small index card with key words she held in her left hand.

"We come across that occasionally," the Police Chief continued, placing his elbows on the table. "We might call them *orderly* suicides. Clean. Everything organized tidily, no loose ends. Only the end of a life. It's erased, in a sense. As though it had never been. Sad. Terribly sad."

"But what about his mother? And the man had friends. Very close friends."

"But did he owe them anything?"

The Chief of Police seemed emphatic, and Billy T. tried to conceal his own astonishment. When the Chief had taken over, roughly six months earlier, Billy T., in common with most others, had been deeply skeptical. The man had very little experience of operational work and had hardly been in the police service at all, only two years in the early seventies as a lowly attorney up north in Bodø. He'd ended up as a judge in the Court of Appeal for eleven years, hardly ideal training for heading up the country's largest and most anarchic police station. However, he had grown into the post and had impressed them all during the past two weeks. He held them together and enabled them all to function as a team. They were all working 'til they dropped, but no one had yet complained about unpaid overtime, in itself a testament to exemplary management skills.

"Suicide is an extremely interesting subject," the Police Chief continued, now leaning back in his chair, knowing that everyone was following intently. "Depressing and fascinating. You could say, roughly speaking, that the difference between those of us who, now and again, at difficult times, consider taking our own lives—"

He smiled, a different, boyish smile: it suddenly dawned on

Tone-Marit that he was attractive, in his freshly ironed uniform shirt, the sleeves of which he had rolled up, contrary to regulations. There was something youthfully masculine about him, yet at the same time something dashing and extremely strong.

"The difference between us and the others is that we think about how such a death would devastate those closest to us," he said softly. "We see what a terrible tragedy it would be for those left behind. So we grit our teeth, and after a few months, life seems better and brighter. The . . ."

Now he rose from his seat and crossed to the window. Outside, the rain had started to subside, but the heavy clouds lay gray and moist above the enormous, pearly green lawn in the triangle formed by the police station, Oslo Prison, and the street at Grønlandsleiret. He appeared to be searching for a hidden code in the pattern of the raindrops on the windowpane as he continued.

". . . what we might call the *genuine* suicide candidate thinks the opposite. He or she believes that things will be *better* for those who love them if they choose death. They feel that they are a burden. Not necessarily because they have done anything wrong but perhaps because the pain they are carrying has become so—so intolerable that it has spilled over onto their loved ones, making life unbearable for everybody. Or so they think. So they take their own lives."

"My goodness," Billy T. exclaimed involuntarily; never before had he heard the word *love* from the mouth of a superior officer.

"Look at this man Grinde," the Chief of Police went on, paying no attention to the minor interruption. "A successful man. Extremely competent. Highly respected in many circles. He has many interests and good friends. Then something happens. Something so dreadful that he—he must have taken the decision with a degree of calm deliberation: he collected the medication himself and tidied up after himself. The pain was unbearable. What caused that pain?"

He wheeled around abruptly, opening out his arms as if collectively inviting them to suggest why a man they knew little about, strictly speaking, would have committed suicide.

"You did not mention honor," Billy T. murmured.

"What did you say?"

The Police Chief stared intently at him; there was fire in his eyes, and Billy T. regretted opening his mouth.

"Honor," he mumbled all the same. "Like in *Madame Butterfly*."

The Police Chief sat open-mouthed, looking as if he had no idea
what Billy T. was talking about.

"'Death with honor is better than life with dishonor.' Or something
like that," Billy T. said.

When he realized that he was expected to continue, he raised his
voice.

"When prominent people are caught with their fingers in the till or
their pants down, it sometimes happens that they kill themselves.
Usually we have our own thoughts about that, don't we? That the guy
was embarrassed, that the disgrace would be too great, and so on and
so forth. Normally we regard such suicides as proof of guilt. Someone
has done something terribly wrong and can't bear having to face the
world. But that isn't—that isn't always the only explanation, you know!
It's possible that the person just couldn't stand the thought of living
with dishonor, even if he was innocent!"

"Or, for example," Tone-Marit Steen dared to interrupt, "the suicide
victim may have done something that was—perhaps it could be called
morally reprehensible but not necessarily criminal. Seen in that light,
an incident might be judged quite differently by different people; some
might not give so much as a shrug, whereas for this particular person,
maybe someone of especially high moral standards, the—"

"With all due respect, Chief of Police!"

Ole Henriksen Hermansen, the Security Service Chief, who until
that point had been sitting almost motionless, examining his own
cuticles, slammed his fist on the table.

"I consider it hardly appropriate to sit here discussing more or less
empty ideas about the mystery of suicide in the middle of a highly
pressured working day. There are limits!"

The corner of his mouth twitched, and his complexion had acquired
a darker hue than normal. The sole of his foot was moving to and fro,
and he stared provocatively at the Chief of Police.

The Chief of Police smiled, a grimace so filled with tolerance that
not even the Superintendent was in any doubt that it was a reprimand,
and a very arrogant one at that. The Security Service Chief's face was
now puce, and he stood up to continue speaking. He grasped the edge
of the table with both hands, as though he, the only person in the room
in full control of his wits, needed to hold on tightly to solid reality.

"If we can now put these high-flown theories to one side," he said harshly, his voice almost at falsetto pitch, "then in fact I have a great deal to report."

The others looked at one another. This had a new and unexpected ring to it. Perhaps that was what had been required, a philosophical analysis of the deeper facets of suicide. Now Ole Henriksen Hermansen was suddenly going to speak!

"Go ahead," the Chief of Police invited, but the smile remained on his face.

"Then I'll begin by offering an apology," Hermansen said, using his fingers to tidy a few strands of hair. "I am aware that some of you have felt somewhat—underinformed, let's put it that way. I'm sorry that was necessary. We all know that this station has an unfortunate tendency to leak information to the press. Quite ruthlessly. We have had to keep a lot to ourselves."

Pushing his chair back, he stepped across to the head of the table.

"The reason I now find it essential to give a comprehensive briefing is because it seems as if the investigation is going in—in all directions, so to speak. Whereas we actually have what we regard as a break-through."

"Oh, jeez," Billy T. blurted out. The Police Chief's foray into philosophical matters had been fascinating, but there was nothing like tangible evidence.

"However, that means," Hermansen continued, "that the very greatest care must be exercised in regard to the information you are about to hear. If this gets out, we risk the entire investigation collapsing like a house of cards, and we'll be left high and dry."

"Much as we have been all along," muttered Billy T., but he shut his mouth when Tone-Marit kicked him hard on the shin.

"On our side, we found it interesting that the last conversation Birgitte Volter had before she died was apparently a discussion of the case that has now been christened the health scandal. We have read the newspapers in the last few days with not inconsiderable interest."

That's what you do, of course, Billy T. thought. *You don't do anything other than read newspapers and cut and paste and join things together.*

But he wisely kept his mouth shut; Tone-Marit's glare was unmistakable.

"However, most of what has been written about that day, we know from before. And we know a lot more besides."

Hermansen paused for effect, enjoying the situation. Everyone was giving him full attention. At last someone had something. Something specific.

"A number of allied countries had limited trade connections with the German Democratic Republic in 1964 and 1965," Hermansen said loudly, starting to pace back and forth in front of his audience, like a pedantic professor. "It was one link in a major operation orchestrated by the Americans, tied in with the exchange of prisoners between East and West. The East Germans insisted on a condition that consignments of goods in short supply could be imported and that some of their export goods should be accepted in the West. In that way, they could obtain both goods and foreign currency."

Not understanding where this was heading, Billy T. began drumming his fingers impatiently on the table, but the Chief of Police caught his eye, and he stopped immediately.

"Norway placed itself at their disposal by exporting iron ore and importing, among other things, pharmaceutical products. In fact there were a number of different goods that crossed the border between East and West at that time, but it's not necessary to go into all that. What is important is to remember that this was done in cooperation with our close ally, the United States of America, and with an extremely positive objective: the return of Western agents and diplomats who were under arrest. The USA operated this kind of trade on a far larger scale than us, understandably, even though it was contrary to the Truman Doctrine, and of course it was not something you talked about in public. It is especially critical to remember . . ."

The Security Service Chief sat down on a chair back, with his feet on the seat: he looked like a young show-off.

". . . that the GDR was not even recognized as a separate state at that time. That didn't happen until 1971. East Germany was a tremendously closed system, and from our point of view, the worst thing was that they actually could not pay their way."

Now the Police Chief raised his eyebrows.

"But," he objected tentatively, "surely they had a monetary system?"

"Of course they did. But what was an East German mark worth? Zero point zilch! For us, the solution was a straightforward exchange of goods. For the Americans, it was worse. The East Germans demanded cash. In many ways it is correct to say that the Americans quite simply bought the freedom of their own people. Very expensively, and perhaps also at the cost of one of their most important principles of foreign policy, namely that they should trade only with states that pay reasonable regard to political rights and universal human rights."

"As if they've ever followed that," Billy T. muttered, but once again he was completely ignored. "What the hell has this to do with the murder of Birgitte Volter?"

"The Security Service was not involved in the trade arrangements, of course," Hermansen continued, unperturbed. "But we were kept informed. That was essential, since we had to keep a number of East German citizens under surveillance. I don't need to tell you that we still have quite a few files from that time lying about."

Jumping down from his perch, he again began to pace the floor.

"Right now, though, it's more interesting to look at one of the East German citizens on whom we did *not* have a file. Or more precisely: he was a *former* East German citizen. Kurt Samuelsen. Born in Grimstad in southern Norway in 1942 to a Norwegian mother called Borghild Samuelsen. His father was an unnamed Wehrmacht soldier, stationed in Norway during the Nazi occupation. The boy was put in a children's home immediately after his birth and one year later was sent to the Third Reich as part of its Lebensborn Program. So—"

Suddenly Hermansen halted his restless traipsing to and fro across the room. He planted his feet firmly on the floor, slightly apart, as if adopting a military at-ease pose, even putting his hands behind his back.

"Kurt Samuelsen ended up in the Eastern bloc after the war. No one had news of him, and no one asked about him. That is to say, his mother made some cursory inquiries around 1950, but few people were willing to offer assistance to a woman deemed a collaborator for having become pregnant by a Nazi soldier, a woman whose head had been shaved in retribution and who had been sentenced to three months' imprisonment in 1945. But in 1963, during a study visit to Paris, our friend Kurt Samuelsen jumps ship. He is twenty-one years old and a very promising chemistry student, and he troops up to the Norwegian embassy to tell them he is Norwegian."

"Norwegian?"

No one looked at the Superintendent; everyone wanted Hermansen to continue.

"Yes. He has papers and other proof that he really *is* Kurt Samuelsen. He is allowed to travel to Norway and is reunited with his mother amid great celebration. Even the most hardened members of the Norwegian Home Guard were able, by 1963, to take pleasure in such a touching reunion of mother and son. Well. Kurt Samuelsen enrolled at Oslo University, in the Pharmaceutical Institute. He was an extremely able student and gained his master's degree at the young age of twenty-four. And in pharmaceutical chemistry, not just pharmaceutics, mind. He spoke perfect Norwegian after only six months in the country, which in a strange way supported the mother's belief that this really was her long-lost son."

The Security Service Chief suddenly stopped, and without asking any of the others, lit a cigarette. He carried a portable ashtray, with lid, in his pocket, and he placed it on the table in front of him. Inhaling deeply, he smiled in satisfaction as he pressed on.

"So far, all is sweetness and light. But Kurt Samuelsen traveled back to East Germany as early as 1968 without telling his mother. And no one has heard of him since."

Now not even Billy T. uttered a word; he contented himself with quietly clucking his tongue.

"I'm really bothered by your smoking," Tone-Marit commented bluntly. "Could you put it out, please?"

The Security Service Chief looked at her crossly but did as she asked.

"When his mother died in 1972, it proved impossible for the family to find him. The matter was investigated eventually, and Western intelligence services finally found him by chance in Bulgaria in 1987. Then it was revealed that the man was *not* Kurt Samuelsen. His name is Hans Himmelheimer. The genuine Kurt Samuelsen has always lived in Karl-Marx-Stadt, now Chemnitz, and has never set foot outside the former East Germany. Not even since reunification. And now we get to the most important part of all."

He fished out yet another cigarette, but caught himself just in time and neglected to light up.

"Hans Himmelheimer was brought to our attention by our German sister organization. They found his name when they opened the STASI archives. Hans Himmelheimer is today the chief pharmacist in a giant German corporation. Perhaps you'd like to guess which one?"

"Pharmamed," Tone-Marit, Billy T., and the Police Chief chorused.

"Exactly. No less. Like all other industries in the former East Germany, Pharmamed was owned by the state, but, unusually, it has since made a brilliant success of privatization. Among other things, it's the sole trader of a type of disposable syringe that breaks after a single use; the patent is worth its weight in gold, not least because of the AIDS epidemic. And Hans Himmelheimer was in Norway as recently as March this year."

"What!" The Police Chief opened his arms wide, but was quieted by Hermansen.

"Wait. He was here at a conference at the Oslo Plaza Hotel; he stayed there for four nights. Under his real name. Fairly reckless, if you ask me, as there must have been a sizable risk of somebody recognizing him. After all, he lived in Norway for five years."

Until now, Ole Henrik Hermansen had been enjoying himself. That had been obvious to everyone. But it was well deserved. What he had to relate was truly sensational, and he related it with style.

However, all of a sudden, a touch of uncertainty washed over him. His eyes wandered and he toyed anxiously with his cigarette.

"Our analysts claim that it is exceptionally damaging for Pharmamed that this vaccine case has leaked out. Not so much because the company may be held accountable—it's likely that from a legal point of view, the current company would be seen as an entirely separate entity after privatization and all that. But there is the matter of the name."

No one asked what he meant, even though none of them understood.

"The name Pharmamed. The company has experienced phenomenal growth since the Berlin Wall came down. Today it is worth billions. And it is still called Pharmamed. I must admit I don't quite understand why they can't simply change the name, at least in a worst-case scenario, but apparently that would cost enormous sums and pose additional difficulties in the bargain. Reputable names are invaluable, I'm told. This scandal might stick to the entire company, and that would be catastrophic in such an *exceptionally* demanding industry as pharmaceuticals. So if we keep to our original theory, regarding . . ."

Hermansen rubbed his face roughly; his skin became red and angry and, for the first time, he looked exhausted.

". . . this matter of the shawl."

Indicating to the Police Chief to dim the lights, he placed an acetate on the overhead projector. The sketch of the headless man behind Birgitte Volter, with the shawl over her face and a revolver directed at her temple, the one they had all seen on the very first Saturday of the investigation, suddenly took on a new meaning.

"Let us for the moment assume that we were right. The intention was not to kill Birgitte Volter. The intention was to threaten her. And what could be more effective than to—"

"To demonstrate to her that they had managed to enter her house and steal the Nagant without anyone noticing anything!"

Billy T. was almost shouting.

"But," the Chief of Police stammered, "she had the scarf over her face! She couldn't see the Nagant!"

The Security Service Chief looked at him with a resigned expression in his eyes.

"The perpetrator may have shown it to her first. As I said last time we looked at this drawing, this thing with the shawl was meant to frighten her even more. Viewed in the context of this theory, she was killed by accident. The intention must have been to get her either to stop or perhaps simply tone down the work of the Grinde Commission."

"You could be right," Billy T. said. "You could indeed be right."

The level of noise increased as his audience turned to one another, eager to discuss the new and, to put it mildly, astounding turn the case had taken. Hermansen looked unsettled as he scanned the room and did not seem to derive any pleasure from interrupting their chatter.

"However—and, I might almost say, unfortunately—this is not the only lead we're following. The case took yet another remarkable turn yesterday."

The room fell silent.

"What!" Tone-Marit Steen exclaimed. "Does it have something to do with this?"

"With the murder of Prime Minister Volter, yes. With Pharmamed, no."

He gave a quick and concise review of Brage Håkonsen's intrusion into the case. The whole story was over and done with in about seven minutes, including the crashed light aircraft that no one could yet say for certain had been an act of sabotage directed at Göran Persson, the Swedish Prime Minister; Tage Sjögren's trip to Norway at a crucial time; and Brage Håkonsen's relatively impressive store of weapons and the fact he had in his possession cut-and-dried plans for assassination attempts on sixteen named, distinguished, Norwegian citizens, whose only apparent connection was that they either occupied an extremely high position on the social ladder or had a broad-minded attitude toward immigrants.

Finally, he sighed loudly and added, "I would like to write the guy off as a romantic fool. My boys claim he's far too cowardly to ever make a serious attempt at murder. He had the opportunity to shoot his way to freedom when he was arrested, for God's sake; he was in a place where there were substantial piles of guns, enough to equip a respectable troop of commandos. But he didn't dare. Nonetheless . . ."

He got to his feet again. He seemed stiff. Everybody was beginning to feel tired; the meeting had lasted for nearly three hours and all of them were longing for coffee and a smoke.

". . . he says he knows who did it. And he seems to know what he's talking about."

Hermansen recounted the story of how Brage Håkonsen could relate in detail how the revolver had been returned.

"In that case, he knows more than we do," Tone-Marit asserted. "We've stared for hours at the video from the central post office, and it's been impossible to find anything of interest. When they had that CCTV installed, they should have made sure the quality was good enough to be of some use!"

"So Brage claims he knows. But he wants to make an exchange."

"An exchange?" The Senior Public Prosecutor had not opened her mouth for the entire interminable meeting. Now there was a sudden flash from underneath the thick glasses. "Should we let him go in exchange for a name? Out of the question."

"In the meantime, we've explained to him that's not the way our system works," the Security Service Chief said tersely. "He knows it's not normal practice."

"And neither is the murder of a prime minister in this country," Billy T. murmured. But he didn't have the appetite to argue with the Senior Public Prosecutor. From bitter experience, he knew that nothing good ever came of that.

"Well, we'll take a break now," the Police Chief announced. "Half an hour, then we'll sit down again and run another lap. I think it would be sensible to amalgamate Billy T.'s group with Tone-Marit's."

"Yesss!" Billy T. exulted, giving Tone-Marit a smacking kiss.

"Half an hour," the Police Chief reiterated. "Not a minute longer."

"Sometimes you really are so *childish*, Billy T.," Tone-Marit said angrily, fiercely drying her cheek.

12:30 P.M., PMO

She couldn't settle properly. In many ways, it seemed like spreading gossip, and nothing could be more foreign to her. She had worked as secretary to the Prime Minister for eleven years, and her lifestyle reflected her responsibilities: she was quiet and circumspect, with no indulgences and a social circle smaller than most. Plenty of people had tried to pump her for information over the years—friends and acquaintances and a journalist or two—but she was well aware of how she should conduct herself. The post had its own code of honor. Even if everybody else disregarded old-fashioned conventions, she would not betray her ideals.

The uncertainty had been painful to endure. For several days she had mulled it over, without coming any closer to a decision about what she should do. She was no longer entirely certain what had persuaded her. Perhaps it had been her friend's genuine despair and confusion. Probably, though, it was knowing that the disloyalty she was about to disclose was many times more reprehensible than the indiscretion she would be committing by confiding everything in the Prime Minister.

Tryggve Storstein had been attentive and obliging and had thanked her with a warmth in his voice that contrasted sharply with the discouraged, almost sorrowful expression that had crossed his face when she had stepped back through the door, was still not convinced that she had done the right thing.

She liked the new Prime Minister. Of course, it was too early to say for sure, and she did not wish to have a definitive view about whether she liked her boss. But it was impossible not to feel comfortable in his company. Although he could appear absentminded, almost out of place behind the massive, curved desk where he sat with a constant frown and the fleeting, odd, and embarrassed little tug on his mouth when he cleared his throat or asked her about something. Usually he fetched everything for himself. It was as though he found it awkward to have servants; he had admitted as much one day when they had bumped into each other at the coffee machine in the kitchen: "I feel so stupid when someone does this sort of thing for me. People ought to be able to make and get coffee for themselves."

Her friend had actually wept. She had whispered and sobbed quietly, her flame-red nails dancing nervously like big, spotless ladybirds across her face as she stutteringly blurted out what was on her mind. When she had approached her, it was because she too felt totally bewildered, and because Wenche Andersen was not only an old friend, but also in a position of some authority—if not formally, then at least by virtue of her experience and competence. Her friend had worked in the Minister of Health's office for only four years. In fact, she had gotten the job on Wenche Andersen's recommendation, which added to her sense of responsibility.

"He was very pleased that we told him," she reassured her in a low voice on the phone, but she put the receiver down abruptly when one of the undersecretaries entered.

Prime Minister Storstein had explicitly asked that the episode not be mentioned to anyone else. That had been on Friday, and since then nothing had happened. Not as far as Wenche Anderson knew at any rate, and that was probably as it should be.

The phone rang again as soon as she replaced the receiver.

"Prime Minister's office."

It was the car leasing company. She listened attentively for several seconds.

"Put it in a plastic bag, and whatever you do, don't touch it any more than you already have. Drive it across to the police station immediately. Ask for Tone-Marit Steen. Steen, yes. With two e's. I'll phone and let them know you're on your way."

The pass. They had found Birgitte Volter's pass. It had been lying trapped in a crevice of the seat in one of the government limousines and had not turned up until today's thorough vacuuming.

Wenche Andersen lifted the receiver once again to contact the pleasant young officer who had interviewed her what now seemed like eons ago. As she dialed the number, she noticed her hands. It looked as if everything but the skin had shriveled; the skin itself lay in delicate folds, but the tendons and tissue beneath appeared to have lost all their strength. As Wenche Andersen slowly stroked the back of her hand, it struck her for the first time in ages that she was growing older.

Yet again she felt that stab, the longing to turn back the clock.

1:00 P.M., SECURITY SERVICE SECTION, OSLO POLICE STATION

"If we bring him before the court now, all hell will break loose, don't you understand that?"

Severin Heger had never raised his voice to his boss before, but right now he was desperate.

"If this gets out, then we will have burned all our bridges! I've never heard of anyone managing to process a remand application without the press getting hold of it. For God's sake, Hermansen, you're worried enough about things leaking out downstairs in this building, but that's *nothing* compared to what happens in a courtroom."

The Security Service Chief began thrusting his lower jaw back and forth, making a clicking noise—a bad habit his wife thought she had managed to wean him of several years earlier. Then he started crunching his teeth together from side to side. He was ruminating so intently that it sounded as though he might literally crack up.

"I appreciate your point," he mumbled, tearing at a corner of the desk blotter. "But we can't hold him without a custody order. He's been languishing here since Saturday morning as it is, and strictly speaking, we can't keep him beyond today."

Severin Heger clasped his hands and tried to sit still.

"Can't we ask one of the permanent judges?" he asked quietly. "One of the ones we usually use. And then we can process the custody hearing quietly sometime late this evening, when the courthouse is empty."

Ole Henrik Hermansen gazed at a spider constructing a beautiful abode in a corner of the ceiling by the door. The enthusiastic insect rushed to and fro, then suddenly hung in midair, held by a thread so gossamer fine that it was invisible to the naked eye. A midge was battling for its life in the center of the web, to no avail; the spider had caught sight of it and was approaching threateningly, climbing its imperceptible, self-built funicular.

"Spring will be here soon," the Security Service Chief grunted. "I'll see what I can arrange. We can't choose our judges, Severin. But we can go through the documents with a fine-tooth comb. I'll ring the Chief Justice and see what I can do with regard to the timing. Late afternoon would at least be better than now."

"You really *must* manage to fix it," Severin Heger said, leaving his boss's office to prepare the paperwork.

4:03 P.M., PMO

Tryggve Storstein had not yet settled in to his new office. There was not a single personal item in the spacious, rectangular room overlooking the city. Not even a photograph of his wife and children. Not even a coffee cup with "Dear Dad" or "Good Boy" on it. Even though he was entitled to both. At least, his children thought so; but the mug with "World's Greatest Dad" in green writing on an orange background was lying inside the drawer marked "Private." He did not feel comfortable; this did not feel like his domain. Not the office. Not the job. Not all these people running around who were supposed to be his administrative machinery. The office was too large, the view over the checkered clamor of the city too splendid. It made him dizzy. However, he had accepted, and he had meant it. He was the right person for this job, even though the suits so far had seemed too roomy, and he sometimes floundered, getting his wife to knot three ties in readiness for him every Sunday night. He would get used to everything. He just needed enough time. Who knew, he might even get used to nobody any longer using his first name.

"Send her in," he muttered into the intercom when Wenche Andersen quietly declared that the Health Minister had arrived.

"Tryggve!"

Trotting determinedly across the floor toward him, she opened her arms for a hug. He avoided this by sitting down to concentrate on some insignificant papers. He did not look up until she was seated.

"I think you know why I want to speak to you," he said, looking up without warning.

Ruth-Dorthe Nordgarden had never noticed Tryggve Storstein's eyes before. They made contact with hers like an unexpected shower of arrows. They were unpleasant, candid; for some reason he no longer had that half-sad, half-embarrassed fold above his eyes that meant you did not fix too specifically on his actual gaze or the eyes inside those deep hollows. He had changed. His eyes *were* his face now. A wide, green-gray expression of something she reluctantly—but immediately—recognized: open and undisguised contempt.

A blush of shame spread through her; she felt it prickling the skin on her hands, and without wanting to, she fell into her very worst nervous habit: scratching her neck.

"What do you mean?"

Ruth-Dorthe forced a smile, but the nerves in her face would not cooperate, contorting her mouth into a revealing grimace; he understood that.

"Let's not make this unnecessarily awkward, Ruth-Dorthe," he said, getting to his feet.

Taking up position beside the window, he spoke to his own reflection in the glass, the reinforced pane with a greenish tint that was supposed to protect him from external attack. He gave a thin smile, since it had not helped Birgitte one iota.

"Do you know what the point is of being a politician?" he asked. "Have you ever stopped and asked yourself what's the purpose of it all?"

She did not move a muscle. He watched her reflection, frozen stiff except for her hand running up and down her slender neck, up and down.

"You should at least have done that. I've observed you for a long time, Ruth-Dorthe. Longer than you have observed me. I've never liked what I've seen. That hasn't been much of a secret, either."

All at once, he wheeled around and looked at her, trying to make eye contact. But she couldn't even manage that, just stared intently at a point on the side of his shoulder.

"You don't have any ideals, Ruth-Dorthe. I wonder if you ever have. That is dangerous. Without ideals, we lose sight of the actual aim—the fundamental reason for getting involved in politics. Damn it all, you're a member of the Labor Party!"

Now he raised his voice, his cheeks inflamed and his eyes even larger.

"What is it we really stand for? Can you answer me that?"

Leaning forward, he placed his hands on her armrest, with his face now only a foot from hers. She could smell the faint fragrance of his aftershave, but she did not want to look. Could not manage to, or bear to.

"The public out there—voters, the majority, call them what you will—why should they vote for us rather than anyone else? Because we want to *distribute* wealth, Ruth-Dorthe. We're no longer revolutionaries. We're not even particularly radical. We manage a market-driven society and enjoy a good quality of life in an international arena largely controlled by capital. That is fine by us. A great deal has changed. Perhaps we should even change our name. But what—"

She could feel the warmth of his face; microscopic droplets of spittle sprayed over her flushed countenance and she blinked repeatedly but did not dare turn away.

"Fairness," he whispered. "A reasonable, fair division of all that milk and honey floating around out there. That can never—"

Abruptly, he drew himself up to his full height, as though he had suddenly felt a pain in his back.

At the window, he turned around again. Darkness was creeping across the city; together with the rain, it had lain in wait behind the stark hills, biding its time until evening. Two cars had collided on Akersgata, and he saw angry figures waving their arms and an impatient bus trying to mount the sidewalk in order to drive past.

"We can never achieve total fairness," he said bluntly. "Never, except being able to do *something*, trying to level things out. Have you ever been to the East End?"

He looked at her reflection in the glass; her complexion had acquired a greenish hue.

"Have you even *been* out there? Have you visited an immigrant family in Tøyen with five children and a toilet on the landing and rats as big as kittens in the basement? And then gone over there . . ."

He waved the palm of his hand toward the western hill.

". . . and seen what their living conditions are like?"

Ruth-Dorthe had to bite the inside of her cheek to avoid breaking down entirely. She continued to blink, all of a sudden aware that her left hand was on the verge of seizing up with cramp, her knuckles livid as she tried to release her grip on the chair arm.

"You don't often have the time," Tryggve Storstein said.

His tone had altered and softened, as though he were talking to an obstinate little child who needed a fatherly admonition.

"All too seldom do we have time to consider why. Why we keep going. But now and again we need to make time."

Without warning, his voice shifted yet again as he sat down heavily in his own office chair and his words lashed across the desktop.

"You're in politics for yourself, Ruth-Dorthe. For your personal benefit. You are deadly. You don't think about others. Not about the party, and not about most other people. Only yourself."

She could not endure this. Her life was about to collapse around her; it was like standing in an earthquake zone, not knowing whether the ground was secure under her feet or if an abyss would open in the next second. She would not put up with this. Furious, she thrust herself forward across the desk, grabbing a paperweight and hefting it threateningly.

"Now you're really overstepping the mark," she hissed. "Don't forget that I'm the Deputy Leader of—"

He burst out laughing, throwing his head back with a loud guffaw. "And it's a mystery how that came about."

"But—"

"*Shut up!*"

She sank back into her seat, still holding the paperweight, clutching it tightly, clinging to the bulky cobalt glass ornament as if it were her last chance for something or other, she did not quite know what.

"You are a fool," Tryggve Storstein said, his voice dripping with contempt. "Don't you know anything about modern appliances? Didn't you know that a fax machine keeps a record of all communications and stores the numbers of all recipients?"

The room was whirling. What could she do? She had something on him. Didn't she? Some old stories about his liaisons with women, something about an inheritance issue. She had heard something; she could look it up, throw it back at him, right in his face; he couldn't do this, he mustn't.

"You're so egotistical that you don't see other people, Ruth-Dorthe. You don't understand them. They suddenly turn on you when you least expect it, because you never take the time to put yourself in other people's shoes, to think about how they feel and how they experience the world. That's why you can never be a politician. You've never been a politician. You desire power for its own sake. Power is your aphrodisiac. The problem is that you're in love only with yourself. You can't behave any differently because you don't like anyone else. Do you understand what you've done by leaking this commission report to *Kveldsavisen*?"

"But," she ventured, in a dull, metallic voice, "I—it contained nothing but the *truth*!"

It seemed as though she had suddenly and surprisingly discovered a weapon, and she grasped it with both hands.

"But you're afraid of the truth, you know, Tryggve. And you hate people like me, who actually believe we need greater press freedom. Yes, people like us who believe that free speech and an open society should mean more than franking 'Withheld from the Public' on government documents!"

He laughed uproariously, swiveling his chair to and fro, to and fro, chortling all the while.

"The truth! Are you so power crazed and arrogant that you think you have the right to control access to the truth as if it were your own servant? Do you believe—"

Throwing back his head, he laughed hysterically.

"Do you believe the truth is something you can parcel out among your own press contacts in order to get your back scratched now and again? I wondered about that, you see."

Now he was no longer amused, his voice trembling as he struggled not to shout.

"I wondered why someone like you—a disloyal, incompetent, unpopular, and scheming character like you—was dealt with so *incredibly* lightly by the press. Why they haven't hung you out to dry long ago has been something of a mystery. Not only to me. Now I know the reason why. You have paid them. Paid them with information."

He stretched out his hand peremptorily.

"Give me that paperweight!"

She dropped her gaze, hesitating slightly, before setting it down at the far edge of the desk. It was in danger of tipping onto the floor, and he had to rise from his seat in order to rescue it.

"I never thought—I *never* thought that I would have to instruct a minister in my own government about the fundamental democratic rules of the game. Don't you understand, Ruth-Dorthe, that you are tasked with managing the Health Service on behalf of *the Norwegian people*? Instead, you have used your authority to pursue a personal vendetta against me. You leaked information to the press so that you could beat me by being first with statements, and so I would be caught off guard, totally ignorant. It's such a crass breach of trust that I simply don't have words to describe it. A breach of my trust and a breach of the trust invested in you by the people on whose behalf you have been appointed to govern. And with these *scraps* of truth that you have allowed to leak out, you have succeeded in not only undermining confidence in the government and our credibility, but you have also contributed to the spread of fear and speculation. Fear and speculation! There you have your truth!"

He shut his eyes briefly, and his old face returned: the anxious, half-embarrassed expression was in place again. It gave her courage, and she tried afresh.

"But the truth can *never* be damaging! It is only by—"

"I'll tell you something about the truth," he said wearily in a quiet voice. "Of course it should come out. Fully and completely. So I'll give my report to Parliament. Not to the Akersgata press pack. They'll receive everything, naturally, in the fullness of time, but Parliament is the appropriate forum for this extremely important matter. Only then can this be tackled with the—with the decorum a matter such as this demands. And in the meantime . . ."

Leaning forward, he dialed a four-digit number on the phone.

". . . would you be kind enough to bring in two cups of tea, Wenche?" He disconnected the call and waited.

Neither of them said a word until Wenche Andersen entered. Little blotches of lilac colored her cheeks, but her hand movements were steady and familiar as she set out cups and saucers and poured generous servings for them both.

"Sugar?" she asked Ruth-Dorthe Nordgarden. "Milk?"

The Health Minister made no response, and Wenche Andersen did not consider it appropriate to press for an answer. She tiptoed lightly back to her own domain but managed to catch an encouraging smile from her boss as she closed the door.

"You are being put under supervision," he said softly, stirring a spoonful of sugar into the golden-brown tea. "With immediate effect. Not a single decision of any significance is to be taken without consulting me. Understood?"

"But—"

Something was happening to Ruth-Dorthe Nordgarden. Her face had adopted a different expression, as though all her features had become magnified; her mouth grew, her nose seemed swollen, her eyes appeared too coarsely carved, too large for her face, which was actually quite narrow. The shadows cast by the desk lamp emphasized the irregular proportions: a thin face with overlarge details.

"You can't do that! In fact, you haven't got the right to do that! Vote me down at the next cabinet meeting, go ahead and do that, but you're not entitled to take control away from me!"

Tryggve Storstein continued to stir his tea, with an unnecessary circular rhythm that gave him something to look at. Suddenly he stopped, licked the spoon, and blew on the hot tea.

"The alternative is that you resign now," he said softly. "You can choose between the two evils. Either you do as I say, and then I replace you some time after the election. Nice and quietly, and nobody will be any the wiser. Or else you resign now, and I announce the reason for your departure. All of it."

"But you can't—the party—Tryggve!"

"The party!"

He laughed again, even more heartily, as though he really did find the situation entertaining.

"You have never thought of the party," he said, drained. "Now you get to choose. The devil or the deep blue sea."

They sat in silence for fully five minutes. Tryggve drank his tea, stretched his legs out in front of his chair, and looked as if he were thinking of something else entirely. Ruth-Dorthe seemed to have been turned to stone. A lonely teardrop ran down her scarlet, inflamed cheek. Seeing it, he momentarily felt a touch of something resembling compassion but swiftly brushed it aside.

"The devil or the deep blue sea, Ruth-Dorthe. The choice is yours."

At that instant, the phone rang, startling them both, and Tryggve Storstein hesitated before grabbing the receiver.

"It's for you," he said curtly, surprised, and passed the phone across the desk.

The Minister of Health clutched it mechanically, like a mannequin in a shop window, with stiff limbs and staccato movements.

"Okay," she said a moment later and handed back the phone. "I'm required at Oslo Police Station. Immediately."

And so Ruth-Dorthe Nordgarden left her Prime Minister without saying which option she would take.

It did not matter.

He knew that she would never in her wildest moments opt for a public humiliation.

He had crushed her. It astonished him that he did not feel even a scintilla of regret or sorrow. When he took stock, he realized that he felt pity for her, but that was all.

Someone should have destroyed her long ago.

11:10 P.M., OSLO POLICE STATION

"I don't bloody know."

Rubbing his face quickly and roughly, Billy T. made a sound with his lips as if he had just emerged from ice-cold water.

"But her explanation actually sounds credible. There's something about that woman—"

He shivered and now tried to reach a point on his back with his fingers, wriggling in desperation.

"Scratch me, Hanne, give me a scratch! There! No, no, further up, to the side. Yes, there."

Rolling her eyes, Hanne Wilhelmsen scratched the same spot, quite savagely, for several seconds.

"So. Sit down."

She smiled at Håkon Sand, who seemed unable to focus on anything except the fact that the new baby had still shown no sign of wanting to emerge from its mother's womb. He dialed a short number and indicated to the other two to keep quiet.

"Oh, I'm sorry," he said, pulling a grimace into empty space. "Were you sleeping?"

He listened for a short while before making a kissing noise into the receiver and putting down the phone.

"She thinks my solicitude is going too far when I keep on waking her." He grinned sheepishly. "But all this is making me so bloody nervous! I missed the big meeting today just because I thought I saw some spasms in Karen's stomach when we got up this morning. My God, this is so tiresome."

"Relax," the other two chorused. "He'll arrive when he's ready."

"It's a girl," Håkon Sand muttered, gazing at Birgitte Volter's pass, enclosed in a plastic wallet and already examined for prints.

Ruth-Dorthe Nordgarden's had been extremely distinct. Two instances. One of her thumb and one of her right middle finger. The expression on her face when she was confronted with this had indicated absolute, total bewilderment. With some assistance and given time to think, she had stammeringly arrived at the conclusion that Birgitte had mislaid it in the Cabinet Room of the Parliament Building about a month earlier. Ruth-Dorthe had picked it up, chased a few steps after her, and handed it back. That was the only reason she could come up with for her fingerprints having turned up on Birgitte Volter's government pass.

"If she really had used it, she would have ensured the prints were removed before placing it in the vehicle for someone to find," Hanne said wearily. "As far as I understand, government ministers don't have personal cars, and Tone-Marit said that both Birgitte and Ruth-Dorthe used the same vehicle several times during the fortnight prior to the murder."

"I believe the woman," Billy T. agreed. "As I said, there's something altogether nasty about her, but it seems that her neighbor saw her going out with the garbage at half past six on the evening in question. I have to admit I became slightly curious when it turned out that nobody managed to get hold of her on the phone all that evening, but she claims that she simply wanted a quiet night at home and had disconnected everything."

"Ruth-Dorthe is just a serpent in Paradise," Hanne said quietly. "The sort who screws up every investigation because she has so many secrets and forces us to dislike her. What in the world can Roy Hansen have seen in a bitch like her?"

"Slip of the dick," Billy T. said with a grin.

"Yes, you know all about that," was Hanne's rejoinder. "But honestly! What was that all about?"

"At the risk of you calling me a male chauvinist pig, Hanne, I do believe that it was a little intrigue on the part of our friend Ruth-Dorthe. That woman collects secrets and sexual entanglements the way other people collect stamps. She has both the ingenuity and the looks to do it. In any case, it's none of our business who she sleeps with. Not unless it has any relevance to the case, and in this instance, it hasn't. I'm convinced of that."

Yawning, Håkon glanced at the time.

"I must go home now. If the baby hasn't arrived within twenty-four hours, I'm going to insist on a cesarean section."

A man was standing at the door of Håkon's office: he had arrived so quietly that no one had noticed him.

"Severin the Supreme," Billy T. greeted him enthusiastically. "Did you get up late too?"

"I'm awake around the clock these days," he said. Then, nodding in Hanne's direction, "My goodness, what a tan you've got! Back from vacation, or what?"

"Sort of," she answered. "How are things?"

"Okay, thanks. I'd like a word with you, Billy T.," he said, with a toss of his head.

"Of course," Billy T. replied. "We'll go to my office."

He extricated himself noisily from the cramped room, stepping over Hanne and knocking over a container filled with pens.

"See you in the hallway in ten minutes, then," he said to Hanne as he slapped Severin Heger on the back.

Then he turned around, thrust his torso into the room again, and whispered so loudly that everyone could hear, "She's sleeping in my double bed, Håkon. With me!"

"Kiss and tell," Hanne Wilhelmsen muttered, making up her mind to spend the night at the house of a female friend.

However, on second thought, it was too late to call.

TUESDAY, APRIL 22

J ens Bjelkes gate 13 was located in the middle of no-man's-land. Too far east to be called Grnerløkka and too far west for Tøyen. It was a block both God and the urban regeneration program had forgotten. Modern technology had yet to reach this gray, peeling apartment building: there was no intercom system, so Hanne Wilhelmsen and Billy T. were able to walk straight into the dark entryway.

"This is madness," Hanne whispered. "I can't see how you intend to go about this. And why couldn't the Security Service guys follow it up themselves?"

"They're totally paranoid up there at the moment," Billy T. said, coming to a halt. "The way they've been turned upside down and inside out these last few years, it's a wonder they survive at all."

"Heavens," Hanne said, "are you siding with the Security Service now?"

"Nah! But we all agree, don't we, that we need to have a security section?"

"Do we? All of us?" Hanne mumbled, eager to walk on.

"Wait," Billy T. said. "Severin knows something he's not allowed to know officially. I've no idea why. Maybe it has something to do with illegally acquired information. What do I know? Anyway . . ."

Lowering his voice, he put his arm around Hanne and thrust his face almost directly into hers.

". . . they remanded that Brage guy I was telling you about. Yesterday afternoon. Provisionally, he's only accused of 104a, but they're hoping for a breakthrough with regard to Volter's homicide. The problem is that the guy has an alibi for the evening of the murder: he was at The Scotchman with some Swedish Nazi cretin, and about twenty people can vouch for their presence there."

"Which in itself doesn't exclude the possibility of a conspiracy," Hanne said reflectively.

"Exactly! And what Severin also can't know officially is that this Brage guy can somehow be linked to the security guard!"

"*What?*"

"Don't ask me how. I'm guessing there are a few illegal files up there on the top floors. Anyway, I've insisted *all along* that there was something about that guard. *All along!*"

Unexpectedly, a girl ambled through the entranceway. She was slim and gangly, and she stared at them with ill-concealed inquisitiveness. As she passed, she blew a huge bubble of bright pink bubble gum: it burst and lay like a torn, wet tissue across her face.

"Hi," Hanne said, with a smile.

"Hi," the girl mumbled, picking the remains of the bubble gum from her skin.

"Stop a minute," Billy T. said as amiably as he could, but it was no use—the girl looked at him in alarm and headed for the street.

"Hold on," Hanne said, rapidly following her and clutching at her arm. "We'd like to ask you something. Do you live here?"

"Who the fuck are you?" the girl said angrily. "Let me go!"

Hanne released her immediately, but she still caught the little glimmer of curiosity in the girl's eye and knew she would not leave.

"Did you know the man on the first floor? The slim guy with brown hair?"

As the girl stared at them, it struck both police officers that they had never before seen anyone's complexion change color so swiftly.

"No," she said abruptly, and made to go.

But Billy T. had walked past her and was now blocking the exit.

"Did he have many visitors?" he asked.

"Don't know."

She was a strange mixture of child and woman. Her body was skinny, but her breasts had begun to fill out, no longer just pointed intimations of something yet to emerge. Her hips were boyishly narrow, but she had already learned to move with a challenging, clichéd gait. Her hair was unevenly streaked with shades ranging from dirty red to chocolate brown, and her left nostril sported a silver ball. But the eyes below her penciled eyebrows were those of a child: big, blue, and rather anxious.

"How old are you?" Hanne asked, again trying to adopt a friendly tone; she flung out her arms and opened her palms in an inviting, unthreatening fashion.

"Fifteen," the girl whispered.

"What's your name?"

Suddenly her adult side gained the upper hand.

"Who the fuck are you?" she asked, trying to sneak past Billy T. yet again.

"We're from the police," he said, moving sideways.

Without warning, her top lip began to tremble, and she hid her face in her hands.

"Let me past," she sobbed. "Let me leave!"

Placing a hand on her shoulder, Hanne tried to persuade the girl to take her hands away from her face. The nails she could discern under her hairline were bitten down to the quick.

"He hadn't done anything wrong," the girl whispered. "That's the honest truth!"

11:00 A.M., OSLO POLICE STATION

It did not take long for Billy T. to realize that he would not get one single word closer to the facts, at least not while Kaja's father remained in the room. The man had to be around fifty years old, but alcohol, cigarettes, and poor diet had resulted in a complexion that was open-pored and flaccid, giving him the appearance of being in his late sixties. When he coughed, it was obvious that he had one foot planted well inside a wide-open grave, and Billy T. found himself placing his hand over his mouth in a futile attempt to keep the apparently life-threatening bacteria at a distance.

"Bloody hell," the caretaker panted. "I demand a lawyer, I'll have you know!"

"Listen here," Billy T. said, staring at Kaja, who sat like a flower that had withered all too soon, unable to decide which of the two men in the room she feared more. "Either you stay here while I have a chat with Kaja, or else I'll contact the child welfare service to find a substitute guardian. Your choice."

"Child welfare? They've got nothing to do with us. I'm staying."

The man folded his arms over his belly. A huge red stain on his undershirt made it look as though he had placed his hands on a map of Norway. He hawked vigorously, and for a second Billy T. thought he was about to spit on the floor. Instead, he struggled to swallow.

"But I told you, I need an attorney."

"No, you don't. I'm going to talk to Kaja, not accuse her of anything."

"No, you're no' fucking doin' that. Kaja's no' done anythin' wrong. At least, nothin' the police need to poke their noses into."

Billy T. looked from Kaja to her father.

"Does Kaja have a mother?" he asked optimistically. "Perhaps she could be here instead of you if it's difficult to spare the time and such-like?"

"Her mother's dead. I'm staying. I can't just leave my daughter and let the cops sink their claws into her."

It seemed the man was now beginning to enjoy being at the police station. A different expression, one of contentment, spread across his ashen, sweaty face, and he fumbled in the lining of his trousers for a pack of rolling tobacco.

"No smoking here, sorry," Billy T. murmured. "But listen—"

He produced a notepad from his desk drawer, and as he filled something out, he continued.

"I'm writing you a chit for something to eat. The canteen's on the sixth floor. They have a separate smoking section there. So I'll have a chat with Kaja while you're away, but of course, I won't write anything down until you're back. How does that suit?"

He assumed his most winning smile. The caretaker hesitated, his eyes alternating between the chit and Kaja.

"What can I have to eat, then?" he asked, mumbling.

"Whatever you like. Just help yourself to whatever you want."

The caretaker came to a decision and rose to his feet, puffing.

"But no' a fuckin' word down on paper until I'm back again! D'you hear? No' a word!"

"Of course not. Take all the time you need. And here," said Billy T., handing the man a copy of a men's magazine as well as the chit. "Take all the time you need."

The void left by Kaja's father's departure was palpable. The spartan office seemed to grow larger, finally affording space to the fragile girl. She had at last stopped biting her nails and now gazed out the window, screwing up her eyes; she looked as if she had forgotten where she was.

"Sorry to hear about your mother," Billy T. said softly. "Very sorry."

"Mmm," the girl responded, apparently unmoved.

"Were you afraid of him?"

She turned abruptly, focusing on the room.

"Of my dad?"

"No. Of him."

She shook her head gently.

"Maybe you were in love with him, then?"

It crossed Billy T's mind that the security guard—who had sat in the very same seat where Kaja was now ensconced almost exactly a fortnight earlier, a grouchy, feeble, and thoroughly stubborn character—must have been enormously difficult to have any feelings for other than loathing. However, there was something in the girl's eyes. Something in the slight hand movements, as she clasped her fingers and tugged at a little ring of plain metal. Still saying nothing.

"I realize you're feeling sad," Billy T. said softly. "But what is it you're so scared of?"

Something happened, something Billy T. later found difficult to describe; it occurred so quickly and came to pass so unexpectedly. Kaja underwent a total metamorphosis, opening out her arms, looking him straight in the eye, half standing up from the chair, and almost shouting. "You think it was him, but you're wrong. You always want to believe the worst about people and it wasn't so strange that he didn't dare talk to you and you just think he did it and it—it wasn't Richard! Richard didn't do it! And now he's dead, and you think that . . ."

Now she really did throw herself across the desktop, burying her head in her hands and sobbing inconsolably.

"It wasn't Richard, he only—it's at home in my closet, but it wasn't him, he just—it's in my closet and I don't know—Richard—"

Billy T. closed his eyes, aware of how tired he was. How bloody fed up he was. For some reason, he thought of Truls. The picture of his little boy, bravely trying not to cry as the doctor prepared to realign his bone before setting his arm in a cast, had fixed itself in his mind's eye; he rubbed his hand over his face to brush the image away. Opening his eyes again, he looked at the girl without uttering a word.

How many young people would weep bitter tears in this horrible, unpretentious office on the second floor of the police station before this case was solved?

Billy T. thought about his youngest son and reflected on how life would never be the same again. Norway would never be the same. He sat facing a young girl—a poor, neglected little scrap of humanity—who apparently held the key to it all. She could tell him what had actually happened on the evening of April 4, 1997, on the fifteenth floor of the government tower block; she knew the answer, and if he coaxed a little here and cheated a little there, she would share everything she knew with him. However, Billy T. was not sure if he had the energy to cope with it.

He thought about Hanne Wilhelmsen's imminent departure. She had mentioned it that morning, in passing, with her mouth full of cornflakes. She was missing Cecilie; she would be leaving soon.

In a flash he strenuously attempted to suppress, he had a vision of the enraged look on Truls's mother's face when she had caught sight of the brilliant white cast covered in the scrawled black autographs of his three older brothers. His little son had proudly held up his arm to his mother, the woman with the black, reproachful eyes.

"What's in the closet, Kaja?" he asked.

"The shawl," she muttered, getting to her feet. "The shawl that prime minister woman was wearing when she was killed!"

Billy T. stood up abruptly. The chair rolled toward the wall, and he momentarily forgot that he was actually too exhausted. Too fed up. Too tired of everything.

"The shawl! Do you have the shawl? Did the security guard murder Volter? Listen to me, Kaja! Was it Richard who killed the Prime Minister?"

"Aren't you listening to what I'm saying?" she sobbed. "It wasn't Richard. He was only going to—that alarm went off, and he went up there on his own, his buddy was sleeping, I think."

She dried her eyes with the back of her hand, but the flood of tears would not cease.

"He took the revolver. He's crazy about guns, but the lady was dead when he got there. He does loads of shooting, and has piles of magazines and books and all that sort of stuff. Richard's just nuts about guns and that kind of thing. He—the revolver was lying there, wasn't it, and the woman was dead, and it was lying on top of this shawl, you see, so he took the whole lot and—bloody hell, he was scared to death afterward. I noticed he was behaving really oddly and all that, one evening when I was—"

Now she blushed, and her blue eyes looked younger than ever.

"Don't tell Dad," she begged weakly. "I'm not allowed to go to Richard's place. Promise you won't say anything to Dad!"

"To hell with your father," Billy T. barked. "Are you telling me that Richard just took the gun that was lying beside a shot Prime Minister? Was he *crazy* or what?"

"It was my idea to mail it back. I thought if you got that revolver, then you could find out who had done it, somehow. We polished it 'til it shone, and then I went down to the central post office with it, and I forgot—stamps. But I was wearing mittens."

"But the shawl?" Billy T. almost yelled. "Why didn't you send that back as well?"

Squirming in her seat, Kaja looked longingly at the pack of cigarettes she had fished out of a backpack shaped like an artless baby panda clinging to her back.

"Just have a smoke," Billy T. said, slapping a massive ashtray made of orange-glazed lava down on the table in front of her. "Why didn't you send the shawl too?"

"Richard said—a shawl is much more difficult to wipe clean. He was afraid he might have left traces on it that we wouldn't be able to remove. He said it was possible to get fingerprints from skin, so we couldn't be sure whether it was possible to get fingerprints from fabric and that kind of thing. And we couldn't just throw it in the garbage, because—in the movies, the cops always examine the garbage, you know, and so it would be safer to look after it for a while. Richard was going to go to Germany, and then he was going to come home and get me when— Dad hated Richard, you see."

The thought of her father brought back the convulsive sobs, and her face contorted into a painful grimace.

"Calm down," Billy T. said, more quietly now. "I'll sort things out with your father. I promise he won't give you any grief."

He did not know whether his attempt at a reassuring smile had any effect, but he was short of time. Now at least he could insist on that search warrant he had been agitating for. And he would be sure to get it. He grabbed the phone to contact Assistant Chief of Police Håkon Sand.

"Sorry," his secretary said cheerfully. "He's gone to the hospital. The baby's on its way!"

Billy T. swore vehemently, then glanced apologetically at the girl. But she hadn't heard and was obviously used to worse language anyway.

"Tone-Marit," he snapped into the receiver. "Get the duty officer and come in here on the double. Now! At once!"

Kaja had lit her second cigarette.

"Can I come with you?" she asked quietly, blowing smoke out of the corner of her mouth. "Can I come with you and show you the shawl?"

4:05 P.M., A REMAND CELL AT OSLO POLICE STATION

The attorney was certainly not stupid: he understood everything. Negotiating two days' imprisonment had been smart. Brage had gone along with the proposal that he be kept in custody until Wednesday in order to give the cops time to consider. And they had managed to keep it out of the press. The lawyer had hassled them, threatening to sue them for compensation if they didn't keep the short sentence secret. Two days. That was how long they had to think about it. Whether they wanted to make a deal. They probably would. He had something they wanted. Two names. That idiot Richard and his girlfriend. Richard was an oddball: involving your girlfriend in something like that! Brage had seen her and followed her all the way to the post office. He had no idea why Richard had not wanted to keep the gun. Perhaps the girl had panicked. A damn child; she couldn't be more than fourteen or fifteen.

The cops had their hearts set on the names. That Heger guy had been quite amazed when he had been able to provide accurate details. They knew that he had two big fat names.

Brage Håkonsen strode to the center of the hot, stuffy cell, and stretched himself out on the concrete floor. He did sit-ups without a break, and at the same steady pace. The entire time. Ninety-eight, ninety-nine.

A hundred.

He sat up with his arms around his knees, not even particularly sweaty.

As long as he had the names, the cops would make a deal. He was going to be freed.

10:30 P.M., MOTZFELDTS GATE 14

As Little Lettvik sat in the old armchair, having poured herself a stiff Jack Daniels, she experienced the disappointing taste of success. It was always like that. A brief, intense feeling of triumph, followed by emptiness. You had to go on. Nothing was as dead and meaningless as yesterday's newspaper. In a few months, almost no one would remember that she had been the one who had uncovered it all. It had been wonderful for a few hours. Especially during the press conference. Demolishing Ruth-Dorthe in front of a crowded room was one of her greatest achievements. Her colleagues' half-appreciative, half-envious looks had done her good. Some of them, the youngest, the ones with less to protect as yet, had been quite open. They had approached her, slapping her back enthusiastically, and wanting to know how she had unearthed Pharmamed at such lightning speed.

If only they knew.

When she thought about it, she felt a jab under her breastbone. Distaste. She peered accusingly at the glass in her hand and pressed her left fist against her stomach.

Perhaps she should not have done it. She had exploited something of long standing that was, in a way, invaluable. The word made her cough, and she slammed down her glass.

Of course she should have done it. No one would find out, because no one ever had. Never. Not once in all these years. Thirty-two years.

The doorbell rang.

As the piercing pain under her solar plexus struck, she was forced to curl up in discomfort.

Once again, the bell rang impatiently. She tried to straighten up, but had to walk to the door crouching forward slightly and with perspiration breaking out on her forehead.

"Little Lettvik?"

She had no need to ask the identity of the two men. She recognized one of them. He worked for the Police Security Service.

"Yes," she moaned.

"We'd like you to accompany us to the station for an interview."

"Now? Half past ten at night?"

The tall man smiled, and, sensing the contempt in his eyes, she quickly transferred her gaze to the younger, shorter one, but he did not look down.

"Yes. You're probably well aware of why it's so urgent."

She thought she was going to faint. Fumbling to hold the door frame, she closed her eyes to stop the room spinning.

They knew. Fucking hell, they knew.

Once she had packed her capacious handbag and shrugged on her coat, a dawning realization popped fleetingly into her head. She pushed it aside as quickly as possible.

A realization about what it must have been like for Benjamin Grinde.

WEDNESDAY, APRIL 23

Hanne Wilhelmsen peered into the tiny, wrinkled face. The newborn baby girl screwed up her features, her eyes becoming two supercilious lines. She resembled a baby dormouse, except that she meowed. She mewled almost inaudibly, like a kitten, her lips twisting toothlessly, quivering in displeasure. Her complexion was blotchy and her face asymmetrical, with tufts of downy red hair above her ears. The fontanel—seemingly way too open—was beating rapidly and rhythmically and made it look as if her head was not fully formed. It was downright terrifying.

"Isn't she beautiful?" Karen Borg whispered. "Isn't she just the most gorgeous baby you've ever seen?"

"Weeell, yes," Hanne Wilhelmsen lied. "She's lovely. All babies are lovely."

"Indeed they are not," Karen protested, still in a whisper. "Have you seen that little boy over there? He looks like—a monkey!"

Karen giggled, but had to wipe away tears that flowed from her left eye.

"I'm sorry I'm the only one who could come," Hanne said. "Håkon's in court, and it's so absurdly important to make sure this custody case gets wrapped up. He'll come the minute he's finished. He promised—"

"Here," Karen interrupted, passing the little cotton parcel containing a twenty-four-hour-old baby to the Chief Inspector. "Feel how delightful she is!"

"No, no," Hanne Wilhelmsen insisted, but she was forced to accept the bundle. Karen did not seem strong enough to hold the baby like that, with arms extended, for very long.

She was really not a pretty sight. Hanne carefully, and actually without thinking too much about it, laid her own face on the baby's. The scent was sublime. A lovely, sweet fragrance that gave Hanne goose bumps. Suddenly the baby opened its eyes: deep, colorless wells with undefined irises.

"She looks so wise," Hanne whispered. "Her eyes are like my grandmother's. What's her name to be?"

"We're not entirely sure. We can't agree. Håkon wants a double name, since Hans Wilhelm has one, but I don't like double names for girls. We'll see."

"Dyveke," Hanne said softly, kissing the infant's forehead, light as a feather, the baby skin tickling her lips. "She looks as if she's called Little Dove."

"We'll see." Karen laughed. "Sit down here."

Hanne cautiously inched her way along the edge of the bed and handed the baby back to her mother.

"Was it difficult?"

"Can you put her in the crib?" Karen asked, grimacing. "It was a cesarean in the end, and trying to bend is excruciating."

Hanne placed the bundle down carefully in the plastic tub, which was on tall legs and had wheels, and to be on the safe side, she rocked it.

"You don't look too strong," she said dubiously. "Cesarean?"

"Yes, they lost the fetal heartbeat."

Karen Borg burst into tears. She sobbed convulsively. From time to time, she laughed apologetically and tried to dry her tears. But they continued to fall in copious amounts, and she could not find a way to stop them.

"I can't understand why I'm behaving like this, but I've been weepy all day long. Fortunately, I managed to pull myself together when Mum and Hans Wilhelm were here earlier. He was so sweet, he—"

Hanne stood up and wheeled a folding screen across to the bedside, then sat down again, clutching Karen's hand.

"On you go; cry if you like."

"I'm so glad you came." Karen sniffed. "But it's Håkon who should have been here. *We* were the ones who nearly lost her. She's healthy and fine and I shouldn't cry, but—"

Damnable police station, Hanne thought. *Couldn't they have sent another lawyer to deal with this custody case?* She got to her feet again and crossed to a little basin on the gable wall beside the door. Underneath was a shelf with cloths; she soaked one in cold water, wrung it out, and placed it on Karen's forehead.

"She could have died," Karen said sotto voce. "She's okay now, but she could have. If she had died, it would have been my fault. Håkon was nagging for ages to have the birth induced, but I—it would have been my fault. I wouldn't have managed—"

The rest was lost in a bout of vigorous sniffling, and she put her hands on the cold cloth, hiding her face.

It struck Hanne so unexpectedly that she had to look away. She let her eyes rest on the little baby girl in the pink blanket. She was fast asleep, and a miniature yellow rabbit with saucer eyes was beside her head, keeping watch. But that did not seem to be helping much: it was not enough to set her mother's mind at ease.

This must have been what it was like for Birgitte Volter. On Midsummer's Eve 1965. Exactly like this. But with the massive difference that her baby did not survive. She had died. At the age of only three months.

"Liv Volter Hansen," Hanne muttered to the yellow rabbit. Its improbably large front teeth were made of toweling and curled gaily and unnaturally at the bottom.

"What did you say?" Karen hiccuped, slightly calmer now. "Liv what's-her-name?"

Smiling, Hanne shook her head.

"I was thinking about Birgitte Volter's baby. The one who died. Birgitte Volter must have gone through such a—"

"Dreadful time," Karen completed, struggling to sit up more comfortably in the bed. "I can't think of anything worse."

Smiling wanly, she seemed to succeed in composing herself.

"I understand all hell has broken loose," she said. "I just heard it on the news."

"Yes. I was down at the courthouse before I came here, and there's a press furor such as I've *never* seen before. The first person remanded in the murder case—they're going berserk. You should take it as a compliment that Håkon had to take the case. Next time you give birth, let's hope there's no interference from a prime minister's homicide."

"There won't be a next time," Karen groaned, and now she gave a genuine smile. "Out of the question! But does this mean the case is—is it solved?"

"That would be an exaggeration. But it's certainly a breakthrough. I would agree with that."

Hanne scanned the room quickly. The woman in the neighboring bed was being visited by the baby's father; their faces were close together in murmured conversation over a pale blue bundle—the monkey, obviously. The woman across from her was dark-skinned and had five adults and two toddlers visiting, crawling over the quilt and making a tremendous noise. Hanne stood up, crossed to the other side of the bed, and with her back to the others in the room, gave a half-whispered account of the events of the previous day.

"Billy T. was bloody disappointed by the search. They found loads of literature about guns and a number of suspect magazines, as well as four registered weapons. But nothing more. Apart from one little detail that wasn't enough for Billy T., but that Håkon was delighted about. An address book. The guard's little red book. And under H for Håkonsen, there was Brage's name listed, with his address, though no phone number. So we have—"

She leaned close to her friend, and could see, despite the dull exhaustion in Karen's eyes, that she was extremely interested. Hanne counted on her fingers.

"First, we have Brage's assassination plans and enormous collection of weapons. Second, although he flatly denied knowing the security guard, he has claimed, in the presence of a police officer, to know things he could not possibly know unless he had some kind of connection to the guy. He thought he was being smart, but instead he has gabbed his way right into the middle of the case!"

Chuckling, she drew her hair behind her ear and tapped a third finger on the quilt cover.

"Third, the address book proves there is some connection between the two. And the guard is . . ."

She stopped and straightened her back.

". . . the guard, in fact, has been the most promising line of inquiry all along. If he killed Birgitte Volter, we can forget the problem that has been causing the police so much grief: How could anyone sneak into a room that was as good as sealed shut? He was there. He had the gun."

"But how would he have got hold of a revolver that actually belonged to Volter's son?"

"Yes," Hanne said. "You have a point there. I'm impressed! I've no idea. But in any case, the guard's the best lead, and right now . . ."

She smiled as she looked at the time.

". . . and right now Brage Håkonsen is sitting quaking in the court-house while your brilliant husband—while Håkon persuades a judge that there are reasonable grounds for suspicion."

"But there's certainly more than *that*," Karen said, removing the cloth from her forehead.

"Do you want me to wring it out again?"

"No thanks, Hanne. Surely with all that evidence, you'll soon be moving toward a conviction? Especially if you get Brage Håkonsen remanded in custody now, and then have the opportunity to investigate further while he's behind bars?"

"No," Hanne responded. "We're some distance away from a conviction. You should know that! Because—"

"Kaja might actually be right," Karen said quietly. "She could be telling the truth."

Hanne stretched toward the baby's crib and picked up the protective rabbit. As she slowly stroked its ears, she nodded and stared into space, breathing in the combined scent of baby and strong detergent. "Precisely. Kaja may have told the truth."

THURSDAY, APRIL 24

"Hanne! You must wake up!"

Billy T. shook Hanne's arm warily; she was lying diagonally across the bed, making the most of having the space to herself. Two quilts were bundled up underneath her hips and legs, and she was stretched out on her back with her hands above her head.

"Where have you been?" she muttered, turning onto her front. "Turn off the light, please."

"We've had such a diabolical amount to clear up. Paperwork and all that shit."

He pulled the quilts brutally away, and rapidly folded them into two enormous pillows that he placed against the headboard. He then put Hanne into a sitting position, to the accompaniment of soft, murmured objections.

"Coffee and breakfast," he said with feigned good cheer, nodding toward the bedside table.

"And newspapers. Hell and damnation. They *all* cover Brage's arrest."

With a lingering yawn, Hanne gave herself a shake, then carefully kept her coffee cup level all the way to her mouth, scowling momentarily as she burned her upper lip.

The copy of *Dagbladet* was on top. The entire front page was emblazoned with a picture of Brage Håkonsen being moved from the courthouse to a police car. In the usual fashion, his jacket was pulled up over his head.

"Look at this," Billy T. said, having crept up beside her. "That's me!"

He slapped his hand on the photograph.

"My goodness, that guy Brage must be some size," Hanne said. "He looks almost as tall as you and Severin!"

She flicked through to page 4.

NEO-NAZIS MURDERED VOLTER

Right-wing extremist imprisoned for six weeks

By Steinar Grunde, Vebjørn Klaas, and Sigrid Slette

Late yesterday afternoon, the Oslo police force were successful in their application to have a 22-year-old man remanded in custody, accused of involvement in the homicide of Prime Minister Volter. Chief of Police Hans Christian Mykland confirmed to *Dagbladet* that police consider the arrest of the 22-year-old, who has long-standing links to neo-Nazi groups, to be a breakthrough in the investigation of the murder of the late Prime Minister, Birgitte Volter. The chief suspect, however, is a man killed in an avalanche in Tromsdalen outside Tromsø on Saturday April 12.

"Nevertheless, it should be emphasized that there is still a great deal to investigate in this case, and that police are also following a number of other leads," Police Chief Mykland insists.

Suspect Dead

At a press conference late yesterday evening, it emerged that, ever since the night of the murder, police have harbored suspicions about a 28-year-old man employed as a security guard in the government complex. This man was interviewed several times, but police did not consider that they had sufficient evidence for an arrest. The man died in an avalanche that took the lives of two men near Tromsø earlier this month. Police believe this man had a connection to the 22-year-old now remanded in custody. The latter is thought to be the leader of a neo-Nazi action group.

Assassination Plans

When searching the accused's cabin in Nordmarka, the police found a cache of weapons, together with detailed plans to assassinate a number of prominent spokespeople on social issues. Police will not comment on the degree to which Birgitte Volter was mentioned in these plans, but from what this newspaper has learned, her name was at the top of a list of sixteen named people.

Conspiracy

The remanded 22-year-old is charged with a number of offenses, including illegal possession of weapons and plotting to "disrupt the established order." Police deny that this has been done for tactical reasons. The court also agreed that there were reasonable grounds for suspecting the 22-year-old of involvement in the actual murder of Birgitte Volter. Although the accused has a solid alibi for the evening of the homicide itself, police believe he may be one of possibly several involved behind the scenes in the case.

"We have reason to suspect a conspiracy," Hans Christian Mykland asserts, refusing to rule out a number of further arrests in the case.

"Poor boy," Hanne said, scratching the bridge of her nose. "He'll be banged up for a while. Regardless."

"What do you mean by 'regardless'?" Billy T. said crossly. "The guy's as guilty as fuck!"

Without replying, Hanne leafed further through the paper.

PARLIAMENT PARALYZED

Extraordinary security measures implemented

By Kjellaug Steensnes

MPs from most political parties have expressed grief, sorrow and shock at the latest twist in the Volter case. "This was bound to happen. We have been warning against right-wing extremists for some considerable time, but the Security Service, as is well known, is more concerned with monitoring lawful political activity," says Kaare Sverdrup, the Socialist Left Party spokesperson for Justice and the Police.

He was fully supported by the Red Election Alliance's parliamentary representative.

The parliamentary leaders of the Labor Party, Conservatives, Center Party, Liberals and Christian Democrats have all expressed their satisfaction at the news that within such a short space of time, the police seem to have come close to solving Birgitte Volter's shocking murder.

The security measures surrounding our elected members have now been considerably reinforced. The administrative leadership in Parliament refuses to give details, and it will neither confirm nor deny whether such precautions were already in place when Birgitte Volter was killed. Nonetheless, *Dagbladet* has reason to believe that the Parliamentary President and Vice Presidents, as well as the more prominent MPs, are now guarded twenty-four hours a day, with some personnel provided by the police, and others hired in from a security services company.

Protection Refused

Frederik Ivanov of the Conservative Party has told *Dagbladet* that he personally has refused the extra protection.

"If we organize our lives around the antidemocratic elements in our society, then we have lost the battle against all forms of extremism," he declares, adding that he has nevertheless found it necessary to send his wife and family to a secret destination elsewhere in the country. Ivanov is best known as the Conservatives' most vocal spokesman on the need for generosity toward new immigrants.

"For me, the tragic events of the past few weeks only underscore the eternal need to focus on humanity, philanthropy and tolerance," he says.

Cooperation

Annema Brøttum of the Labor Party feels uncertain, insecure and sad. "Something valuable has been taken from us," she said in a statement.

"Norway can no longer claim to be some kind of peripheral place of innocence; we are no longer a haven on the fringes of the world. This proves how important it is to seek cooperation across national borders; only by consistent commitment and openness between countries can such forms of politicized violence be fought."

Satan

Cora Veldin (Christian Democrats) points out that right-wing extremists are the product of a society in decline. "As long as we politicians are unwilling to take moral stand-points, society will crumble," she declares.

"The gospel of love has vanished, due to materialistic values that provide fertile soil for such Satanic deeds," Veldin concludes.

Innocent

"As far as I am aware, judgment has not yet been passed in this case. The man is innocent until the opposite has been proven."

Vidar Fangen Storli (Progress Party) refused to give any further comment.

"For once I agree with the Progress Party," Hanne said, cramming the remainder of a slice of bread into her mouth. "Why do you *always* cut the slices so thick?"

"Don't speak with your mouth full," Billy T. said fractiously, struggling to prevent the newspaper dipping into the jam.

"Have you noticed anything strange?" Hanne asked as she grabbed the copy of *Kveldsavisen*, brimming with material about Brage Håkonsen as were all the other newspapers.

"Yes," Billy T. said, sweeping the sheet with his hand. "You drop so many bloody crumbs! Soon I'll have to use the vacuum cleaner on the bed."

"Billy T., you either need to accept the consequences of breakfast in bed, or else stop serving it. Honestly!"

Hanne thumped him hard on the arm with her fist.

"Ow! Stop that! What did you ask me?"

"A few days ago, the newspapers were convinced there was a connection between the health scandal and Volter's homicide. They hyped
it up; obtained statements left, right, and center; wrote editorials
about confusion and all that sort of stuff. And then, hey, presto!"

She tried to click her fingers but had butter on her thumb, so they
just slid toward each other with a little squish.

"An ever so tiny arrest, and they do a complete about-turn. Now
they have—one, two, three, four, five . . ."

She riffled quickly through the pages.

". . . nine pages! Taking it for granted that the guard and Brage
Håkonsen committed the crime! *Nine pages!* The guy's miles away
from a conviction. Don't they have memories?"

"Who?"

"Journalists, of course. Don't they *remember* what they were writing
a week ago?"

"Yes, but—"

Billy T. scratched his crotch vigorously and seemed disgruntled.

"Are you siding with these *journalists* now?" Hanne asked, chuckling. "You're damn well jumping about just as much as they are, anyway. Don't *scratch* yourself there, for heaven's sake. Go to the bathroom
if you've got lice."

She thumped him again, this time on the hand.

"Will you pack it in! Damn it, that hurt!" He rubbed the back of his
hand, and moved farther over to the left. "Now I'm starting to feel
really happy that you're leaving soon."

"You don't mean that!"

She crawled over to him and put his arm around her shoulders.

"Actually I'm not really so keen to leave. This is where I feel at home.
But I miss Cecilie so terribly, and she— I'm going on Saturday."

He hugged her tightly.

"I know that. If we really are close to solving this case, then I'll soon
be able to come and visit," he said.

"Great. Can you bring the children with you?"

Billy T. threw his head back, banging it against the wall, and laughed
heartily.

"Very clever! I don't think Cecilie would get much done if the house
was filled with that gang of mine!"

Hanne turned to face him, enthusiastic.

"She's at work all day! Think what fun it would be! Sunshine, sum-mer, and swimming in the sea. We can go to Disneyland!"

He shook his head.

"I can't afford it."

"Just bring Truls, then!"

He pushed her away.

"We'll see. But as a matter of fact—"

He got to his feet and disappeared. Hanne could hear sounds from the kitchen: rattling followed by a whining, droning screech.

"Håkon's having a goodbye party for you tomorrow," he shouted above the racket from the hand-held vacuum cleaner.

"Cut that out," Hanne said, rolling out of bed just in time. "Who's going?"

"Håkon and you and me. And Tone-Marit, I think. If you don't have any objections, I'll invite Severin as well."

"What?"

She reached for the vacuum cleaner. Billy T. stretched his hand above his head and launched himself at the other side.

"Turn that off!"

"Okay, okay," Billy T. said sulkily, pressing the button. "Is it okay if Severin and Tone-Marit come, then?"

Hanne drew herself up to her full height and shook her head gently. Then she began to scratch one foot against the other.

"You know that I don't associate with police officers in my free time," she said softly. "So why are you asking?"

Throwing the vacuum cleaner down on the mattress, Billy T. opened his arms in a gesture of resignation.

"But Cecilie isn't even here, and anyway . . ."

He crept over to Hanne and tried to take her hand in his. She pulled back in a flash, beyond his reach, without even looking him in the eye.

". . . how long are you planning to keep this up?" he murmured. "How long are you going to continue with this game of hide-and-seek?"

"I'm *not* hiding," she spluttered. "But I'm quite entitled to choose my own friends."

She slammed the bedroom door noisily behind her, and soon Billy T. could hear the whooshing sound of the shower; even the rushing water seemed angry. He padded after her and opened the bathroom door a crack.

"Is it okay for them to come?" he called out with his mouth against the gap. "Can Tone-Marit and Severin come to your party?"

His voice was as distorted as a little child's, and he hunkered down. *"Please!"*

Hearing a faint, reluctant burst of laughter, he closed the door and headed off to phone Håkon Sand.

11:45 P.M., MOTZFELDTS GATE 15

Little Lettvik was feeling awful. This was a new, unfamiliar experience. It was as if her whole body was agitated, consumed with an inexplicable anxiety. Something had clamped onto the upper part of her back, somewhere behind her shoulder blades, and was shooting arrows throughout her body, filling her with a pain that nothing could relieve. She had tried most things, God knows, but there were limits to what she could get hold of, given that she would not seek medical assistance. Alcohol did not help and did not even make her intoxicated. As a last resort, she had tried to swim the pain away.

At least twenty years had elapsed since she had paid a visit to Tøyen swimming pool. The place had not changed very much. She had managed to swim two hundred meters before her heavy, out-of-condition body cried out for her to stop, but when she was slumped in the sauna, eyes closed and with a towel wrapped around her stomach, the pain returned.

Humiliation. That was what it was. The pain of being humiliated. They had looked at her, seen through her, and bit by bit revealed what they knew. Had they had cameras watching the two of them? Some of what they had said suggested they were aware of exactly what the two of them had been up to, and in some detail. The mere thought caused the pain to escalate and her face to blush a fiery red. Worst of all, however, was that they had known for ages. Perhaps for a number of years.

She had been naive. Repeatedly naive. Little Lettvik, exceptionally talented journalist, prize winning and highly honored, with a special reputation for holding the powers that be to account. Despite all that, she had not realized that they knew.

Perhaps she had dropped her guard because it was all such a long time ago. Mostly. A few times in recent years, admittedly, and then again in March.

The pain was unbearable now, and her eyes welled up with tears. As Little Lettvik leaned forward, she fished out a short letter that had arrived that day, the handwriting elegantly cursive, and the stamp placed neatly in the top right-hand corner, with all the perforations intact. At first she could not think who the woman was. Elsa Haugen. Not until she had run her eyes over the sheet of paper a couple of times did it dawn on her. Little Marie's mother. The woman in Elverum. Or was it Eidsvoll? The letter described her sorrow and pain and a wound that had been ripped open. Sleepless nights and insulting behavior.

Little Lettvik sighed deeply and tore the letter to shreds.

Her own pain was enough to cope with.

FRIDAY, APRIL 25

Øyvind Olve sat at the head of the enormous pine dining table, rocking a tiny infant. The baby was making inexplicable movements with her hands, and Øyvind stared in fascination at the tiny fingers. As Karen Borg leaned over him to take hold of the bundle, he realized that he really did not want to let go.

"Beautiful girl." He smiled broadly. "What's her name to be?"

"We don't know yet," Karen answered. She addressed the room: "Everybody!"

Clutching the baby to her shoulder, she looked exhausted and drawn. It bothered Hanne Wilhelmsen, who had quite simply not spared a thought for Karen, hadn't even considered that it might be too much for her to have to entertain a house full of people the day she returned home from hospital with a new baby and a fresh surgical scar.

"I'm off to bed. I can't hear anything up there, so just go ahead and enjoy yourselves. I'd appreciate it, though, if you'd try not to make too much noise when you leave, okay?"

Håkon Sand jumped to his feet.

"I'll help you!"

"No, no, you sit down. Have a good time. But remember, you have to take Hans Wilhelm early tomorrow morning."

"I can take him!" Billy T. roared. "Just send the boy over to me, Karen."

Karen did not reply, but made a slight movement with the baby as a goodnight salute before vanishing into the upstairs area of their spacious, comfortable wooden house.

Billy T. took hold of the sixth bottle of red wine and opened it with a worldly flourish.

"Hope you've got enough of this in your cellar, Håkon." He grinned, and did the rounds of refilling glasses.

"No thanks, I've had enough," Øyvind Olve said, placing his hand over his glass.

"What kind of wimp is this you've brought with you today, Hanne? Doesn't even drink!"

Øyvind Olve still felt like an outsider. He could not quite understand why Hanne had insisted on him accompanying her. It was true that he had met Billy T. a couple of times before, with Hanne and Cecilie at their apartment, but the gigantic, boisterous man had obviously forgotten him. He had never met any of the others.

"I have to drive in the morning," he mumbled, refusing to relinquish the glass.

"Drive! He's going to *drive* a car! What's all that about?"

"You need to behave, Billy T.," Hanne said, patting him reassuringly on the back to make him sit down. "Not everybody can match your pace, you know."

"Go on, Tone-Marit," Billy T. said as he resumed his seat. "What did he say then?"

Tone-Marit was still seated; she was laughing and had tears in her eyes. Lowering her voice, she mimicked a halting, broad Kristiansand dialect.

" 'Perhaps he did not owe anyone anything.' And then Billy T. started talking about *Madame Butterfly* and honor! You should have seen the Superintendent's face! He looked like somebody just released from a mental institution!"

The others screamed with laughter, and even Øyvind Olve smiled, despite not having any idea what was so amusing about Billy T. and Tone-Marit's account of Monday's plenary meeting.

"And then," Billy T. bellowed, waving his glass of red wine, narrowly missing knocking over the entire bottle as he stood up without warning to slam his fist on the tabletop. "Then the wit had gone too far for His Excellency the Security Service Chief. He—"

Billy T. cleared his throat, and when he resumed speaking, he had suddenly turned into Ole Henrik Hermansen. "With all respect, Chief of Police! I'm not spending my demanding workday listening to this nonsense!"

Now Hanne had to hush the others, as they were laughing so loudly it would be impossible for Karen to get any sleep. Tone-Marit had a chunk of potato salad stuck in her throat and her face was rapidly turning puce. Billy T. hammered her back mercilessly.

"But it's really quite impressive that the Chief is so preoccupied by such things, don't you think?" Hanne said.

"His son committed suicide two years ago," Tone-Marit said, having retrieved the piece of potato and wiped her tears. "So really, we shouldn't laugh."

"I didn't know that," Hanne said, pressing her glass against her cheek. "How do you know?"

"I know everything, Hanne! Absolutely everything!" Tone-Marit whispered loudly and dramatically, holding eye contact for so long that Hanne suddenly felt the need to help herself to more grilled meat.

"But why were you talking about honor in that context?"

This was Øyvind Olve, only the third time he had said anything all evening.

Billy T. regarded him for some time, adopting a reflective pose.

"To be honest, I don't quite know why I brought that up. When we talk about 'integrity,' we all know what that means. We're focused on that all the time. But 'honor,' on the other hand—it's become a word that makes us look down at the floor in embarrassment. But really, they're two sides of the same coin, if you think about it."

He shoved his plate of leftover food and barbecue sauce to one side and leaned his elbows on the table.

"Consider Benjamin Grinde. Clever boy all his life. Really *fucking* clever boy. Everything goes well for him. Judge and doctor and God knows what. Then he's smeared in the newspapers and dragged down into the dirt. One week later, he takes his own life. We should be allowed to think about *honor* in those circumstances, don't you agree?"

Hanne Wilhelmsen stared down into her glass of red wine. It almost glowed, sending little rays of light toward her eyes as she slowly rotated the glass.

"It could be as straightforward as that, as far as Benjamin Grinde is concerned," she said, sipping the wine. "But for the sake of the hypothesis, let's look more closely at the order of events. If Benjamin Grinde had committed suicide in a *different* situation, no one other than his closest relatives would have raised an eyebrow. The police would have put their heads around the door to establish that it was suicide and closed the file. But Grinde's sudden and probably self-inflicted death occurred—"

She unfolded a large paper napkin and leaned across the table to steal a pen from Øyvind Olve's breast pocket.

"Birgitte Volter was murdered on April 4."

She drew a little dot and wrote the number 4 above it.

"We know that she was shot in the head, with a gun the murderer could *not* have been entirely sure would actually kill anyone, even if it was fired at short range. There's no trace of a perpetrator. A total of three people had business either *at* or in extremely *close* proximity to the crime scene—at the time of the murder, I mean. The secretary, the guard, and Grinde. Within one short week, two of them are dead, even though they were both in the prime of life. Strange, don't you think?"

She emphasized the point by sketching two tiny crosses on the paper.

"And then there's a—"

"But Hanne," Tone-Marit interrupted.

Håkon felt his muscles tense; cutting in on Hanne Wilhelmsen's train of thought was normally punished by an icy look that shut most people up for a very long time. He dipped into his plate of food, hoping to avoid witnessing the humiliation. To his great surprise, he saw Hanne lean back in her chair, look amiably at Tone-Marit, and wait for her to continue.

"Sometimes we *overinterpret* aspects of cases," Tone-Marit said eagerly. "Don't you agree? I mean, the guard died in a natural catastrophe, and no one other than the Good Lord has control of that."

She blushed slightly at the religious reference, but moved on swiftly. "And quite honestly, I think it sounds strange that Benjamin Grinde should have taken his own life because he regretted having killed the Prime Minister of the country, who, what's more, was an old friend. Maybe the suicide doesn't have anything to do with the case at all! Maybe he'd been feeling depressed for a long time? Besides, since we can now state with certainty that the gun was at the guard's home, we can entirely exclude Benjamin Grinde from the case. Can't we?"

"Yes, we are doing that, in a sense. At least, I think we can rule out the possibility that he killed her. But the suicide may still have a connection to the case. *In a different way!*"

No one uttered a word, and they had all stopped eating.

"My point is," Hanne said, clearing more space in front of her. "My point is that the order of events can sometimes confuse us. We're searching for a pattern, for a logical connection, where nothing of the kind exists!"

Drumming the pen on the table, she tilted her head to one side. Her hair fell across her face, and Billy T. turned to her and coiled the strands behind her ear.

"You look so sweet when you're enthusiastic," he murmured, kissing her on the cheek.

"Idiot. Listen to this, then. If you're still sober enough. In addition to two dead people and a number of peculiar items that have led us astray but have now been located, we have also almost experienced a government crisis. Isn't that true, Øyvind?"

Øyvind Olve's eyes blinked behind his small glasses. He had listened to the conversation with interest, but it came as a surprise that he was expected to contribute something.

"Well," he said hesitantly, toying with his fork. "Actually there have been two. The first had to do with forming the new government. And that went tolerably well. From a political point of view, we have obtained a lot of ammunition for the election. Our friends in the political center weren't exactly falling over themselves to take over the reins of power."

He paused for a moment, and Severin took advantage of the opportunity. He had drunk too much and knew it was not wise. He was not used to alcohol, and took a big slug of Farris mineral water.

"But you said *two* crises," he insisted. "What was the other one?"

"The health scandal, of course. Not exactly a government crisis, but it has been tough. All the same, we've ridden that one out now. Tryggve made a fairly good job of the preliminary report to Parliament. In addition, it acted like pure Valium on our good friends in the opposition that there were nonsocialist as well as social-democratic governments in power in '64 and '65. We gave the East Germans good iron ore and got bad vaccines in return. As far as I'm concerned, the entire vaccine issue is an example of the cynicism that reigned supreme during the Cold War. No one escaped it. Not even a few hundred babies."

The table went completely quiet and they could hear little toddling steps descending the stairs.

"In a way, those babies were war victims." Øyvind sighed, suddenly thirsty for more wine. "They are war victims as much as anybody."

A two-year-old stood in the doorway beside the huge, impressive soapstone fireplace. He was wearing blue pajamas adorned with footballs, and rubbing his eyes.

"Daddy! Hansillem can't sleep."

"I'll tell Hansillem some lovely bedtime stories," Billy T. volunteered, getting to his feet.

"Billitee." The child smiled, holding out his arms.

"It'll take five minutes, max," Billy T. said before he disappeared. "Don't say anything important!"

"Hanne," Håkon said quickly; it stung him slightly that the little boy had been so easily pacified by Billy T. "Of the two theories—if you had to choose between the Brage–guard line of inquiry and the Pharmamed one, which would you choose? Because one really rules out the other, doesn't it? And to be honest, I've—"

He began to clear away the plates. "Anyone for dessert?"

"What have you got?" Hanne said, giving him a hand.

"Ice cream and Spanish strawberries."

"Yes, please," Severin responded. "Both! You said you had a problem?"

"Hanne, of course, has said that the Security Service Chief's original theory is too over the top," Håkon said, standing in the center of the room with three plates in each hand. "And we're actually agreed on that. It sounds too much like a cops-and-robbers story. To think that a large company in a democratic country would send a team of killers to visit the prime minister of a friendly country, and a close ally in the bargain!"

"It's true, you have a point," Hanne said, after placing strawberries and ice cream on the table and handing around the dessert plates. "But you should never let yourself be constrained by your imagination. I have to confess that I had problems when the Mannesmann affair came to light."

She anticipated Tone-Marit's question.

"As you'd expect, Statoil, being a key player in both the national and international oil industry, spends billions buying goods and services. These contracts are worth their weight in gold, and the company directors put a great deal of time and effort into preventing corruption in their own ranks. Nevertheless, there was one person who allowed himself to be bribed by an enormous German conglomerate. The Statoil employee received generous gifts, and the Mannesmann company was awarded contracts to supply steel pipes for oil platforms. I didn't think such things were possible, at least not in Norway. Not in Germany either, for that matter. The moral is: there are no morals. Other than making money. And if we take, for example, the thalidomide case—"

She could have bitten off her tongue. As she said it, she recalled something Billy T. had told her many years earlier: Severin Heger's sister had been born without arms or legs. And only one ear.

"It's okay," Severin said, taking another drink. "It's quite all right, Hanne."

Embarrassed, she stirred her ice cream, which had started to melt.

"Didn't you hear me, Hanne? I said it's all right."

"Well. Thalidomide, which was sold in Norway under the brand-name Neurodyn, was a medicine for pregnancy sickness. Among other things. I seem to remember that it also had a certain sedative effect. It was produced in West Germany in the fifties, and only after more than ten thousand children had been born with significant disabilities did a German geneticist discover a connection between the medicine the mothers had taken and the serious damage caused to the fetuses."

"How on earth do you know all this stuff?" Tone-Marit murmured.

"I know *everything*," Hanne whispered, looking her straight in the eye. "Absolutely everything!"

Øyvind laughed heartily, but Hanne did not allow herself to be knocked off course.

"Naturally, it was a catastrophe for the producers. Lawsuits for huge compensation sums, followed by bankruptcy. Even though the company produced a number of other quite excellent medicines, no one would touch the organization afterward. And don't you think, my dear friends . . ."

Her hand gesture included them all, even a big yellow alligator sitting on the chair beside the window.

". . . that they're quaking in their boots down at Pharmamed right now! Even though it was a long time ago. *Even* though they're under different ownership. The name is tarnished. For a long time to come, the word *Pharmamed* will be linked with the wicked, tragic deaths of infant children."

For some time, the only sound to be heard was the scraping of spoons against the household's expensive glass bowls.

"But," Severin said unexpectedly, "although in principle—"

He slurred slightly: *principle* was a difficult word.

"Although I really agree with you, that is to say that you should never exclude anything at all and that money is a powerful motive for most things, but—"

Billy T. came crashing into the room.

"Have I missed anything?"

"Is he asleep?" Håkon asked.

"Like a log. I told him two scary stories. He was paralyzed with fear, and now he's sleeping soundly. Where are you?"

"I have to tell you, unfortunately, that the Pharmamed line of inquiry has to be shelved," Severin said. "At least, there was nothing suspicious about Himmelheimer being in Oslo this spring. He was busy with—other things, so to speak."

"No more, Severin," Billy T. said softly, sending him a warning look. "We're not all police officers here, you know."

"That guy there," Severin said, pointing to Øyvind Olve, "is well used to big secrets. He's worked with the Prime Minister. But listen to this then—"

He took an enormous gulp of red wine.

"When we were checking out this Hans Himmelheimer guy, we went to the SAS Hotel. Staff, room service, telephone records—everything. He didn't make any suspicious calls. Two home to his dear wife in Germany, four to the Pharmamed office. But do you know what, his wife at home did not know that there were *two* people staying in Herr Himmelheimer's hotel room. As well as himself, this guy Hans had signed in a *frau!*"

"His mistress," Billy T. muttered.

"Exactly! And now you'll have to guess. I can tell you that she's Norwegian. But then you'll probably name two million one hundred and eighty-seven other Norwegian women before you arrive at the right one."

No one felt compelled to participate in a guessing game, and Billy T. frowned with impatience.

"His *frau* was Little Lettvik!"

"That can't be true," Billy T. said.

"That woman at *Kveldsavisen*?" Øyvind asked.

"It's just not possible," Hanne murmured.

"Little Lettvik," Håkon repeated.

Tone-Marit burst out laughing, her eyes again becoming two narrow lines above her cheekbones.

"Shhhh," Severin said, moving his palms up and down on the tabletop. "I must ask you to be really quiet. They have known each other for years. Met at university here in Oslo, at Blindern, in 1964, at a time when Little Lettvik's name suited her rather better. Since then they've met up every so often, when Hans has been at conferences abroad. At home in Leipzig he has a wife and three teenage children, but when he's abroad having fun, his companion has been Little Lettvik. Sweet, really."

He emptied his glass and held it out to Billy T., who eagerly poured him another.

"We pulled her in for an interview. She hummed and hawed a great deal about protecting her sources and all that shit, so we didn't get very much out of her. But there's absolutely no doubt that she somehow got the information from him. Probably fooled him completely. Perhaps a little bit of pillow talk?"

"So that's how her newspaper managed to crack the case so bloody fast," Hanne said thoughtfully. "I wondered about that. To be quite honest, I was ever so slightly impressed."

"Anyway," Severin said with a deep sigh. "Hans Himmelheimer didn't do anything in Oslo other than attend two meetings and spend the rest of his time in bed with Little Lettvik. We've managed to discover that much. And we're not one iota closer to substantiating that Pharmamed had anything whatsoever to do with the murder."

It had started raining. Håkon stood up to put a log on the fire. The blue streak of lightning that suddenly illuminated the window overlooking the dark, wet spring garden was followed immediately by a clap of thunder that startled them all. Huddling closer together, they all leaned in toward the table to create an intimate atmosphere that made them feel like better friends than they actually were. Even Tone-Marit smiled when Billy T. stroked her back in a friendly gesture after she was startled by the deafening crash.

"I hate thunder," she said, almost apologetically.

"But why at a hotel? Little Lettvik lives on her own, surely?" Håkon Sand scratched his head.

"Lettvik said that, as a matter of principle, she never lets a man step across her threshold," Severin explained. "After meeting her, that seems entirely convincing."

Hanne began. "But if Pharmamed is no longer a useful line of inquiry—"

"The bottom line is, there is quite simply *nothing* to build on there," Severin interrupted. "Which doesn't mean, of course, that we shouldn't make further inquiries. But I . . ."

He gulped, and swallowed.

". . . I don't believe there's anything to find there. The gun was at the guard's apartment—we know that—but how would the guard have come into contact with Pharmamed? If they were behind the murder, it would all have been far more professional. A different gun, and at the very least a different sort of accomplice from that scruffy guy. No, forget about Pharmamed."

"Forget the guard as well," Billy T. broke in. "I've been obsessed by him for three weeks, but, think about it—he's an odd character. He lets his girlfriend, who is *fifteen*, persuade him to send the gun back to us. He goes on holiday to Tromsø—*Tromsø*! He'd have fled to Bolivia or somewhere like that if he had really killed Volter. I think the guard was telling the truth, in fact, when he told Kaja what happened. Why would he lie to her? He obviously relied on her so much that he entrusted her with the shawl and the gun. If he had murdered Volter, he would *never* have sent back the revolver. It sounds quite incredible that he could have stolen it from a dead prime minister, but on the other hand—he's one of the most repulsive characters I've ever encountered. If anyone could have done such a thing, it would be him. But he was a fucking coward. Just like that Adonis, Brage. No. Forget the guard. I hate to say it, but it wasn't him."

"But listen to this, everyone."

Hanne had switched to Farris, and as she raised the glass to her face, she could feel the bubbles in the mineral water tickling her skin.

"If we're going to shelve Benjamin Grinde—and that old hag Ruth-Dorthe Nordgarden, who has kicked up a fuss but clearly done nothing else. And Pharmamed. And the guard. And him too, that poor Nazi fucker who's cooped up down in our backyard, then—then there's nobody left!"

"Some personal enemy that we just haven't discovered yet," Billy T. said. "It means days and months of hard slog, and probably we'll never get to the bottom of it. We're not good enough. Pure and simple. Now I'd like some music. Real music."

He stood up to prod Håkon in the back.

"Opera, Håkon, do you have anything like that? Puccini?"

"I think we have *Tosca* over there. You'll need to look."

"*Tosca's* fine! She killed for the sake of love. That's why most people commit murder, I have to tell you, ladies and gentlemen."

"Is that why you're so fond of opera?" Tone-Marit asked. "Because they all kill one another? Don't you get enough of that at work?"

Billy T. let his fingers run up and down the CD rack at the other end of the room. Eventually he found what he was looking for. When he placed it in the player, he was momentarily moved to tell Håkon what he thought of his inferior stereo system, but decided against it. Instead he stood up with a sigh of satisfaction as the *Tosca* overture poured out from the loudspeakers.

"I'll tell you one thing, Tone-Marit."

He closed his eyes as he began to conduct the invisible orchestra.

"Opera!" he yelled. "Opera is actually a load of garbage. But Puccini, you understand, he creates women the way women really should have been. Tosca, Liú, Madame Butterfly, the whole bunch—when they're faced with the ultimate tragedy, they take their own lives. They make such great demands of life and of themselves that they no longer wish to live once something has gone really wrong."

His arm movements became increasingly energetic, and the others sat mesmerized, watching his strange demeanor.

"They are uncompromising," Billy T. thundered. "Completely uncompromising!"

Then, without warning, he stopped, in the middle of a vigorous swoop from floor to ceiling. As his arms dropped to his sides, he opened his eyes and crossed the room quietly to reduce the volume.

"Just like you, Hanne," he said as he sat down beside her and gave her a smacker of a kiss on the cheek. "Totally uncompromising. But—"

He stared at her, and the others had obviously noticed it as well. Chief Inspector Hanne Wilhelmsen appeared to be in a trance. Her mouth had fallen open, and she had apparently stopped breathing. Her eyes, big as saucers, were shining and seemed to be peering into something somewhere else entirely, perhaps in another time as well. On her neck, a pulse was beating quite clearly, with a steady rhythm.

"What's up with you?" Billy T. asked. "Hanne, are you sick?"

"I'm thinking about the Volter murder," she whispered. "We have eliminated all the possible murderers. So we are faced with—"

The CD began to stutter, the player spitting out three staccato notes, over and over again. But not even Billy T. made a move to do something about it.

"The truth is, it's impossible for the murder of Prime Minister Birgitte Volter to have been committed," Hanne Wilhelmsen said. "Nobody could have done it."

Inexplicably and entirely automatically, the CD player pulled itself together. The music gushed once again from the loudspeakers, pure and flowing, filling the house where a newborn baby lay sleeping together with her mother upstairs. Tone-Marit Steen stole a glance at her bare arm and saw that she had goose bumps. It was as though an angel had just flown through the room.

SUNDAY, APRIL 27

The ray of light that fell from the skylight onto the dirty timber floor put him in mind of a seal. The darkness was almost black around the sharp white gash in all the grayness. The air was distended with dust and old memories, and he stumbled over Per's first pair of blue-painted skis as he approached the opening ahead of him. He recalled a holiday long ago—before Per. He and Birgitte had gone to Bergen and they had watched the seals in the aquarium there, at Nordnes. As he had looked at them from the window in the pool, down in some kind of basement, the seals had twirled around in the water, round and round, until all of a sudden they shot up toward the light that fanned out from the sky; the seals had veered upward, up toward the light, toward the air.

Roy Hansen stood in the middle of the attic floor. He had not been up there for three years, and he was thinking about seals. It was about time the place had an airing.

For several days, he had thought about moving away. After the funeral, when everything had been at a slight distance but the road ahead seemed impossible to travel. He did not want to live there any longer, not with Birgitte's belongings, her stamp everywhere: a fridge magnet she had made once, before Christmas; the sofa that he had not wanted but she had insisted on—she thought it matched the walls so well, and he had capitulated. Per had cleared out her clothes in private one evening when he had been visiting his mother; she had become so terribly old. When he returned home, Per had said nothing, only given a little smile, and Roy had tried to thank him, but it was impossible. The clothes were gone, and with them something of her scent. He had already thrown out the sheets on which she had slept on the last night of her life.

But in recent days these things had gained new meaning. They were no longer a burning, cruel reminder of something he would never regain. Birgitte permeated the walls, the objects, the pictures she had chosen, and the books she had read. It was okay. He wanted it to be like that. But he wanted to know what was there.

That was why he was standing in the attic. Birgitte had not come up here often either. But far more often than he had. When she came downstairs again, there was always something incandescent and dreamy about her, not for long, but it lasted for a day or so. A faraway look in her eyes, something he had never attempted to break through. He had loved her too long to do that. There must be something up here, and he had never been able to muster the strength to come and look, until now.

It was painful, skirting around things. An old loom with damaged shuttles made him laugh. That had been a phase too. Birgitte, heavily pregnant with Per, wearing hand-woven jackets by Sigrun Berg and consumed by an irrepressible desire to learn to weave—though she lacked the time to do anything more than take an introductory course at the Workers' Education Association. He touched the yarn: it was so dusty that it was impossible to make out the color in this dim light. The pattern on the wall hanging, barely begun, was almost invisible, and he ran his finger over its grimy surface, outlining a heart with the letter B inside it. The loom could stay. He would never get rid of that.

A massive trunk sat at the edge of the beam of light. He groaned as he dragged it all the way across to take a better look. The key was missing. He straightened his back and looked around. The hiding place was obvious; he spotted it at once, and it crossed his mind that perhaps Birgitte had wanted him to. He ran his fingers over the joist that divided the attic into two sections. The key—large, heavy, and black—was there, where it had to be.

The lid was heavy but did not creak when he opened it. The trunk was empty, apart from a smallish round box; a hatbox, he thought—his mother had owned ones like it. The color was ashes of rose, and a large bow was tied around it. Birgitte had knotted that, he thought, as he let the heavy silk slide through his fingers.

He hesitated before opening the box. A peculiar taste spread through his mouth: iron or blood. His posture was uncomfortable. With great care, he lifted the box, closed the lid of the trunk, and sat down.

On top lay a pair of baby socks that must at one time have been brilliant white. They were tiny, for a newborn infant, with delicate lace edging around the ankles. He placed the socks on his knees and stroked them gently with his thumb before taking up the photograph. The very first photo of Liv, lying naked with her knees drawn up to her chest and her fists clenched: she was crying. Underneath the picture was a pink book. Opening it, he leafed through it cautiously, afraid the pages would disintegrate in his hands. Birgitte had recorded so much. Birthweight, length; the little linen bracelet from the maternity unit, inscribed with Birgitte's name and Liv's date of birth, glued onto the first sheet of paper. The glue was almost completely desiccated, and when he stroked the bracelet, it fell out; he reinserted it right at the back, where it was held fast between the pages. The very last entry was dated June 22, 1965: "Liv was given her triple vaccine today. She cried bitterly, and it was painful for both mother and baby, but it was soon over and done with." After that, there was nothing.

Roy could not breathe. Abruptly, he put down the box, and the baby socks dropped from his knees onto the dirty floor as he stood up. The skylight was stiff and difficult to budge, but he managed to open it in the end. He remained for a while in the draft of fresh air, with the light dazzling his face.

Birgitte would not even have pictures on display. Once, a year after Liv's death, he had put a photo of her on their bedside table in a silver frame he had just purchased. In a fury, Birgitte had told him to remove it. She would never talk about Liv. She would not keep anything of hers. After Per was born, Roy had tried to raise the issue on a couple of occasions. Per ought to have been told about her. There was an obvious risk that he would find out about his sister from someone else, and that would be so much worse. Again, Birgitte was furious. Eventually it had become impossible. Liv was a no-go subject, and Roy had found it even more difficult to tell Per about her when he became older. And so the baby had simply disappeared, gradually and slowly. He would think of her now and again; it could catch him fiercely, mostly around midsummer, when the sun shone brightly in the sky and everything had that fresh odor of new summer life. Liv. Birgitte would not hear of her, or speak of her, or be reminded of her. That was what he had always thought.

There was only one child in Birgitte's life: Per. That was the impression she had given. That was what they had all thought. She had accepted Per with gravity and responsibility. That playful, youthful joy that had danced between them when Liv was born had vanished. A constant, anxious concern had replaced it and had not relinquished its grip until Birgitte had finally come to accept that Per was a robust, healthy ten-year-old.

He sat down gingerly on the trunk once more, balancing the hatbox on his lap. There was the silver spoon they had bought when she had been christened. And her pacifier: he smiled when he saw how old-fashioned it was, plain and baby pink, the rubber brittle with age. Underneath everything, right at the bottom of the box of memories, lay a letter. It felt substantial, inside the envelope. On the outside, his name was penned in Birgitte's elegantly flowing handwriting.

As he opened it, his hands were shaking so violently that the envelope fell to the floor. Straightening up, he turned his face to the light again and took a deep breath. Then he unfolded the letter and smoothed it out several times with the edge of his hand.

It had been written thirty-two years earlier.

Nesodden, August 2, 1965

Dearest Roy,

I've thought for a long time about writing this letter, but it's only now that I think I can manage to do so. If I don't, I'm afraid I'll never be able to pluck up the courage. The only way this letter will ever fall into your hands is if I have to leave you. And I don't think I'll ever do that. You have lost enough, and I love you, but God knows I've barely known how to go on living during these past few weeks. It seems so impossible. I drag myself through one day after another, and all I want to do is sleep. What I have done can never be forgiven. Not by you, and certainly not by me.

I see that you are carrying just as much pain as I am, but at least you escape the guilt. You are not at fault, but I have done something wrong, and the shame is unendurable. Every time you try to make me talk about Liv and everything that has happened, I feel the guilt and shame overwhelm me completely. The hurt in your eyes when you think I'm angry is just unbearable, that too, and I try, I really try, but it's all so impossible. Perhaps it would be best to tell you the truth. Then you could hate me and leave me, and I would receive the punishment I deserve. But I don't have the strength. I don't dare. I'm too cowardly. Too much of a coward to die, too much of a coward to go on living in an honorable manner.

And so, tonight, I'm writing this letter.

These past weeks I have wracked my brain continually: How could it have happened?

I loved her so dearly! Even though she arrived at such an inconvenient time. I remember so well how you reacted when I told you I was pregnant. I had been dreading it for a couple of weeks, since you had just started at teacher training college and nothing could have been worse than having a baby just at that time. You laughed so heartily! You swung me around and said that everything would be fine, and the next day you had made all the plans and had gone around telling everyone you were going to be a daddy. I'll never, ever forget how well you took it.

I was so scared that something might happen to her. Mum teased me and said that plenty of babies had come into the world before this and managed to survive. Now, tonight, I see that my love for Liv was not worth a button. I thought I was a good mother because I loved and looked after my baby, but I was irresponsible. A sense of responsibility is more important than all the love in the world; if I had shown responsibility, Liv would still be with us.

I was supposed to have some time off on midsummer's eve. I was so looking forward to it! At last we would be just Roy and Birgitte, the way we had been before Liv arrived, the way we had been last year, that wonderful summer. Of course I know we should never have left such a little baby in the care of a babysitter, but we were only going down to the jetty, and Benjamin was so good with Liv. I should never have gone, but it was so lovely to have some time off. Mum and Dad were in Oslo, and I think if they had been at home, all those terrible events would never have happened. Mum would not have let me go. Or she would have looked after Liv.

You were so dashing when I set off for the house around eleven o'clock to breast-feed Liv. You laughed when I waved and made a sign to let you know I would be back soon. You were slightly drunk, but you were so handsome and funny and I was happy as I stumbled back home; I had drunk too much as well. The alcohol went straight to my head that night. You know how seldom I touch liquor, and my head was a bit muddled. That's my only explanation for what took place: my head was a bit muddled.

I told both you and all the others that I was tired and fell asleep when I came home. That this was why I did not come back.

That's a lie.

Roy rubbed his nose and felt the moisture on his fingertips. The next lines on the sheet of paper were crossed out, firmly, in black ink, twice making holes in the paper. He continued to the next page.

Everything is a big black lie. I can feel how difficult it is, this, just the actual writing of the truth. It's as if it doesn't want to be committed to paper.

Benjamin met me at the door. He was quite flustered and had been about to run down to fetch me. Liv was restless and making gurgling noises, he said, and she was running a fever: her temperature was nearly 104. I didn't realize that this might be dangerous, Roy. She had been feverish a few times before; it came upon her quickly and disappeared just as fast. Right then, I felt quite fed up with the whole idea of a child. We'd been going to have such an enjoyable evening. I was having some time off! So I told him it probably wasn't serious, that she just needed some breast milk, and then she'd probably fall asleep again.

And she did settle down when I put her to the breast. She really did, I'm sure this is not something I imagined! Admittedly, she can't have taken very much, but she wasn't particularly restless when I tucked her up in her crib again. She still had a fever, I could see that from her eyes and the feel of her skin, but babies do sometimes become feverish, don't they?

Suddenly I was overcome by the notion that Benjamin was so sweet. It's so awful to think about it, since I had just left you down at the jetty and had felt that you were the most handsome guy of them all down there! Cross my heart, I'd never looked at Benjamin that way before, after all he's still in high school and always so solemn. But it was something that happened; maybe it was stupid of me to breast-feed Liv in Benjamin's presence.

Sorry! It just happened. He was wet behind the ears and hesitant, and we drank wine, even though I knew you would notice that the bottle was gone. It was probably the first bottle we'd been able to afford in six months. Why did you never ask about that?

The wine on top of all the beer I'd drunk was too much, and when I woke up on the sofa at five o'clock in the morning, Benjamin had left. You still hadn't returned home. I had a dreadful headache, and felt so ashamed. I searched for the headache pills but couldn't find any. Then I went in to see to Liv. She was completely cold. Her eyes were closed, and her skin was icy. I lifted her up, and it really took me a minute or so to realize that she was dead.

I don't remember very much after that. Just that I washed the wineglasses and put them back. And you came home immediately afterward, happy and roaring drunk.

I have only exchanged a word or two with Benjamin since all this happened, but I can see it in him as he walks down the road, that he feels awful. He is moving to the city at the end of the month; he's been accepted to study medicine, Mrs. Grinde told me. She seems worried. He has lost weight and speaks less than ever, she said. I hope I never have to see him again. He will always, always, remind me of betrayal, my great betrayal of you and my unforgivable betrayal of our daughter.

I think of her all the time. Every single second of the day, and at night I dream of her skin, her honey-colored hair, the tiny fingernails no larger than a dot. Now and again, in the briefest of glimpses, I forget that she is dead.

But she is.

I was irresponsible, and I failed her. I have decided to go on living, but I need to push Liv completely out of my life, out of our lives. For the remainder of my time on earth, I will never, ever forget that the most important thing in life is to show responsibility. I will take responsibility, and I'll never lose sight of that again.

Now I can't bear to write any more. If you ever read this letter, Roy, then I will no longer exist.

Then you'll know that I'm not worth grieving for.

Your Birgitte

The dust danced in the shaft of light. The draft from the skylight blew the minuscule particles up and down in unpredictable movements, glimmering like microscopic floodlights, floating aimlessly here and there. Stiffly, Roy folded the letter. When he looked at his hands, they seemed to belong to another person, someone he had never met. He replaced the letter in the hatbox, which was sitting at his feet with its lid askew. Slowly, he stretched out his hands, palms upward, into the beam of light.

It was as though someone was sprinkling gold dust over them, and he fancied that he could feel the particles against his skin; he needed to feel something, something painful, and suddenly he gave himself a violent slap.

Those last hours with Birgitte were crystal clear to him. That last night. He had slept badly. Every time he woke, he'd see her staring out into the darkness with her eyes wide open, not even blinking. The wall between them was too enormous; he did not know what tormented her, but knew her well enough not to try to creep across, to break his way through. He said nothing then, and nothing later either. Not to the police. Their questions—about Birgitte, about the pillbox, about Liv— had been so distressing. Suddenly he knew why. There was something inside him that had lain hidden and forgotten for so long that it refused to emerge. He would not let it. It should stay where it was, far from all consciousness. He had forgotten it all.

But actually he had never forgotten.

The truth struck him, almost like a revelation. The sun had just reached its zenith above the roof, and the bright diffused light illuminated the whole attic. Once more, Roy thought about the seal. The image was amazingly clear in his mind's eye, like a well-preserved photograph, or a film clip that had never aged; the shiny seal, at ease in the water, twisting and turning in a turquoise pool in Bergen in 1970, sending him an agonizing look before shooting up toward the light, toward life on the surface, toward the air.

No one had murdered Birgitte. Birgitte had taken her own life.

FUGUE
FRIDAY, APRIL 4

6:30 P.M., PMO

When Benjamin closed the door behind him, it was as though he were closing down life itself.

He was just as handsome as ever. Just as serious. But he was no longer her junior; the twelve months that separated them had been wide as an ocean when they were youngsters, but now he was her equal. Their conversation had been low-key. In a way, it was as if the past thirty-two years had not happened; when she looked at his face, she could smell lilacs and mother's milk. She saw herself in a princess-style dress, tight at the waist, tailored across the bust, the skirt flaring wide and daringly short to her knees. She had sewn it herself, so happy that her body had quickly returned to its former shape and weight after the birth. His eyes, brown eyes with girlish lashes, were the eyes of midsummer, the eyes of youth; Liv lay in his gaze, and Birgitte Volter knew that the decision she had made was irrevocable.

"I have to withdraw from this," he had said, toying with the little pillbox, the one she and Roy had received from his parents as a wedding present, the one nobody was allowed to touch, but that she could not take from him, could not stop him from examining; perhaps he would open it, and she could not do anything to prevent that. "I have spent so many years forgetting, and I *had* forgotten. It's unbelievable that I could forget. Perhaps it was because I was so young. I console myself with that, Birgitte. I was so very young. But I cannot keep silent again, Birgitte. If I am asked, I will have to tell the truth. Even if it harms us both."

She had not attempted to dissuade him. Mechanically, she had scribbled a few words on the list of data he had given her, the list with Liv's name on it. The name jumped out at her and meant Liv's death could no longer be forgotten, could no longer be hidden in a year far back in time that she had spent the rest of her life trying to erase.

Benjamin had been gentle. His voice sang, and his eyes made contact with hers every time she sought them. They conversed for a while, and remained silent even longer. Eventually he stood up. He did not even make an effort to conceal that he was taking the pillbox with him. He held it up, looked at it, and, without a word, stuffed it into his pocket.

"It's so long ago, Birgitte. We have to learn to live with it now, to stop trying to pretend it didn't happen. We both made a mistake. But it's such a long time ago."

Then he left her, and as the door closed behind him, life closed down for Birgitte Volter.

It was not the humiliation she feared. Or the dishonor. The downfall that might follow was something she could accept. She did not fear the judgment of others. Perhaps they would not even reproach her. She had Roy, and Per. She deserved to lose everything else, only not them, and they would still be there.

At night, certainty had come to her. The decision had really been taken many years before.

Thirty-two years was not enough. Time had not healed the wounds, only brought a mature awareness of the enormity of her betrayal. Her little girl had died alone, even though her mum could have been with her. There was both the shame of her betrayal and a longing for Liv's world.

Her life was over because Liv had returned. Liv was in the room. Birgitte could smell the scent of the baby girl's neck; she felt the tiny, fine hairs on her nose. Birgitte felt her breast press against the little mouth as it drew into a hungry pout. She experienced the powerful, unfamiliar, frightening feeling of responsibility that had surged through her when at the age of only eighteen, almost nineteen, she had held her firstborn in her arms. She had sobbed for hours; she could hear that sobbing now, it came from all around her, filling the room right up to the heavens, almost as high as it was possible to reach in Oslo, this city where she had hidden herself from Liv, working, and struggling to escape her youthful catastrophe. She had taken on great responsibilities since then, and she had felt the weight of those great responsibilities, but she had never really been able to run away from her abysmal betrayal. Now it had seized her again: it stood like a grinning, slobbering lion in front of her, and this was the place where everything would be brought to a close. This was where Liv's death had led her, all the way to this point, and it was here her own life must end.

Slowly, she wrapped the revolver in the shawl. She could not bear to see the gun. The revolver was an accusation in itself. She had chosen her mother's Nagant precisely because her mother would have stopped her from doing what she did; Mum would never have let Liv die.

As she aimed the swaddled gun at her temple, she heard someone making a noise in the restroom behind her.

It did not prevent her from pulling the trigger.

ABOUT THE AUTHOR

A nne Holt has worked as a journalist and a news anchor, and she spent two years working for the Oslo Police Department before founding her own law firm and serving as Norway's minister for justice from 1996 to 1997. Since her first book in 1993, Holt's work has been published in thirty languages and sold more than seven million copies. She is the recipient of several awards, including the Riverton Prize and the Norwegian Booksellers' Prize, and she was short-listed for an Edgar Award in 2012. She was also short-listed for the 2012 Shamus Award and the 2012 Macavity Award. In October 2012, Anne Holt was awarded the Great Calibre Award of Honor in Poland for her entire authorship. She lives in Oslo with her family.

STUDIES IN APPLIED MECHANICS 2

NONLINEAR DIFFERENTIAL EQUATIONS

STUDIES IN APPLIED MECHANICS

1. Mechanics and Strength of Materials (Skalmierski)

2. Nonlinear Differential Equations (Fučík and Kufner)

3. Mathematical Theory of Elastic and Elastico-Plastic Bodies. An Introduction (Nečas and Hlaváček)

STUDIES IN APPLIED MECHANICS 2

NONLINEAR DIFFERENTIAL EQUATIONS

SVATOPLUK FUČÍK

Department of Mathematics, Faculty of Mathematics
and Physics, Charles University, Prague

ALOIS KUFNER

Mathematical Institute of the Czechoslovak Academy of Sciences,
Prague

ELSEVIER SCIENTIFIC PUBLISHING COMPANY

Amsterdam — Oxford — New York 1980

Published in co-edition with SNTL Publishers of Technical Literature, Prague

Distribution of this book is being handled by the following publishers:

for the USA and Canada
Elsevier/North-Holland, Inc.
52 Vanderbilt Avenue
New York, 10017

for the East European Countries, China, Northern Korea, Cuba, Vietnam and Mongolia
SNTL Publishers of Technical Literature, Prague

for all remaining areas
ELSEVIER SCIENTIFIC PUBLISHING COMPANY
335 Jan van Galenstraat
P. O. Box 211, 1000 AE Amsterdam, The Netherlands

Library of Congress Cataloging in Publication Data

Fučík, Svatopluk.
    Nonlinear differential equations.

    (Studies in applied mechanics ; 2)
    Bibliography: p.
    Includes index.
    1. Differential equations, Nonlinear.
I. Kufner, Alois, joint author. II. Title.
III. Series.
QA371.F86   515'.36   79-19877
ISBN 0-444-99771-7

Series ISBN 0-444-41758-3

Translation © 1980 by Dr. Michal Basch
Copyright © 1980 RNDr. Svatopluk Fučík, CSc and Doc. RNDr. Alois Kufner, CSc

Printed in Czechoslovakia

CONTENTS

PREFACE 7

LIST OF SYMBOLS 11

CHAPTER I. SOME EXAMPLES TO BEGIN WITH 15

Section 1. Various Notations. Linear Equations 15
Section 2. Nonlinear Equations 19
Section 3. Nonlinear Systems 24
Section 4. Further Nonlinear Problems 27
Section 5. A Free Boundary Problem. The Plate Equation 30

CHAPTER II. INTRODUCTION 33

Section 6. Second Order Equations 33
Section 7. Higher Order Equations 37
Section 8. Spaces of Continuous Functions. Solution of a Differential Equation 43
Section 9. Boundary Conditions 46
Section 10. Solution of a Boundary Value Problem 60
Section 11. On an Integral Identity 69

CHAPTER III. THE WEAK SOLUTION OF A BOUNDARY VALUE
             PROBLEM 73

Section 12. The Carathéodory Property and the Němyckiĭ Operators 73
Section 13. Sobolev Spaces 85
Section 14. Differential Operators 94
Section 15. Boundary Value Problems 101
Section 16. Various Generalizations 131
Section 17. Regularity of the Weak Solution 160

CHAPTER IV. THE VARIATIONAL METHOD 169

Section 18. First Derivative of a Functional 169
Section 19. Potentials of Boundary Value Problems 179

Section 20. The Euler Necessary Condition 179
Section 21. Second Derivative of a Functional 182
Section 22. Lagrange Conditions 184
Section 23. Convex Functionals 187
Section 24. Weak Convergence and Weak Compactness 191
Section 25. Reflexive Spaces 195
Section 26. Existence Theorems 198
Section 27. Minimal Surfaces 218
Section 28. Excursion on Numerical Methods 225

CHAPTER V. THE TOPOLOGICAL METHOD 239

Section 29. Existence Theorems 239
Section 30. The Brouwer and the Leray-Schauder Degree of a Mapping 248
Section 31. General Boundary Conditions for Second Order Ordinary Differen-
            tial Equations 262
Section 32. Summary of Chapters IV and V. Some Additional Remarks 267

CHAPTER VI. NONCOERCIVE PROBLEMS 274

Section 33. Vanishing Nonlinearities. Regular Case 274
Section 34. Vanishing Nonlinearities. Singular Case...................... 281
Section 35. Jumping Nonlinearities with Finite Jumps 290
Section 36. Jumping Nonlinearities with Infinite Jumps 299
Section 37. Rapid Nonlinearities 307
Section 38. Periodic Problems 309

CHAPTER VII. VARIATIONAL INEQUALITIES 312

Section 39. Formulation of the Problem................................. 312
Section 40. More on the Definition of the Solution of a Variational Inequality.. 318
Section 41. Examples 324
Section 42. Some Special Results 338
Section 43. Existence Theorems 343

REFERENCES 353

INDEX 357

PREFACE

This book owes its origins to our friend and respected colleague Prof. Dr. Karel Rektorys, DrSc. His book "Variational Methods in Mathematics, Science and Engineering" represents a highly successful attempt of presenting to a broad range of readers a textbook devoted to modern methods of solution of boundary value problems in linear partial differential equations; a textbook based upon deep results of functional analysis and yet intended not only for mathematicians but also (indeed principally) for engineers.

We had the opportunity to acquaint ourselves with the book of Prof. Rektorys — which covers an immense amount of material, both theory and applications — in manuscript form; it inspired us to try to write a sort of loose "nonlinear continuation" of his "Variational Methods".

Our book starts where "Variational Methods" ends. Concluding his book, Prof. K. Rektorys writes (p. 553): "Nonlinear problems have remained entirely aside in our book. Their investigation is based, in essentials, on the theory of the so-called monotone operators and is in the center of interest of outstanding mathematicians at present." Let us add that the investigation of boundary value problems in nonlinear differential equations is also of central interest to physicists, engineers and practitioners in general; in Chapter I, we mention several nonlinear problems which have their origins in practical applications.

The increased interest in the field of nonlinear problems among the "technical public" was partly due to the fact that mathematics had developed, in (nonlinear) functional analysis, a powerful tool for the solution of such problems. The vigorous expansion of the study (more precisely: mathematical study) of nonlinear problems dates from the sixties and is principally associated with the following names: G. Minty and F. E. Browder (U.S.A.), M. M. Vajnberg and M. A. Krasnoselskiĭ (U.S.S.R.), J. Leray and J.-L. Lions (France). In connection with the development of the methods of solution of nonlinear differential equations, one must mention Prof. Dr. Jindřich Nečas, DrSc., who contributed significantly to this development, in particular to its growth in Czechoslovakia, and trained and educated a number of collaborators among whom the present authors number themselves.

The number of papers on nonlinear problems — theoretical papers as well as papers biased towards applications — published annually in journals is immense. The number of published books is relatively much smaller — one might mention the books by M. M. Vajnberg [89], [90], J.-L. Lions [58], [59], H. Gajewski, K. Gröger, K. Zacharias [38], V. Barbu [4]. However, all these publications are of a slightly different character and are aimed at a readership different from that envisaged for the present book. Bearing in mind the example set by Prof. Rektorys, our aim was to write a text which would appeal to a broad range of readers, to mathematicians as well as to engineers. This aim influenced the style of exposition employed. Modern methods of solving nonlinear differential equations require modern mathematical tools and devices. However, we did not consider it useful to collect all the applied, and thus in view of the principal aim of the book merely auxiliary, mathematical apparatus together into a separate chapter. We therefore try to explain all the necessary material from other mathematical disciplines (as far as possible) always at the point of its actual application. We believe that this will not leave readers with the impression that functional analysis plays only a subservient role in the theory of differential equations. On the contrary, we hope that the readers will become aware of the mutual interconnections of the various mathematical disciplines.

Originally, we planned to relegate all the auxiliary apparatus to footnotes. It soon became apparent, however, that we had underestimated the importance of the "auxiliary" tools: at some points of the text, the footnotes would have outweighed the text proper. Therefore we adopted this approach mainly in the opening parts of the book when recalling the elements of functional analysis. In fact, we assume that the reader has a working knowledge of analysis up to the elements of the theory of the Lebesgue integral, whilst everything else should be found in the book, albeit without proofs but with adequate references to the literature.

Proofs are not always given in full. The reason is that the declared aim of this book was the exposition of the principal ideas and methods, not an exhaustive survey and presentation of assertions in the greatest possible generality. Because of this, illustrations are given instead of proofs at some points, elsewhere the assertion is proved under simplifying conditions, and elsewhere again reference to the available literature is made. Uppermost in our thoughts is the promotion of a discipline which we consider useful, not a monograph presenting the most general assertions of the theory of nonlinear equations. (Nevertheless, we indicate several possible generalizations in the remarks, with references to the literature.)

As mentioned already, the book is meant for mathematicians as well as for engineers. Since "one cannot serve two masters", both groups will have their objections to the book. The mathematician will miss detailed proofs — in this we were limited by the size of the book as well as by its accessibility to other groups of readers. On the other hand, the engineer will miss the discussion of specific equations of mathematical physics; here the authors lack the experience and close contact with applications which is so pleasingly apparent in the book of Prof. Rektorys. Nevertheless, we hope that this deficiency will be rectified by the publication of the book being prepared by J. Nečas and I. Hlaváček [74] which is, in a sense, an "application" of the methods presented here. Similarly, we did not feel competent to embark on a detailed exposition of numerical methods. Indeed, these methods could serve as material for a completely new book (see, for example, J. Céa [8]). At least we have included the informative Section 28 for which the material was kindly prepared by RNDr. J. Haslinger, CSc., to whom we express our gratitude.

A few words now concerning the contents of the book. Following Chapter I, which serves as "bait" in a sense, we deal – in Chapters II and III – with the question of what we understand, in essence, by the solution of a differential equation and by the boundary value problem in a differential equation. Two types of solutions are introduced: the classical solution and the weak solution. From the point of view of this book, the concept of the classical solution is merely auxiliary. The weak solution is illustrated by means of a considerable number of examples. In this context, we direct the reader's attention to difficulties which arise with the definition of the weak solution. Since knowledge of the concept of weak solution is necessary for the understanding of the subsequent chapters, the exposition here is at a fairly easy pace. The main results of the book are presented in Chapters IV and V. There, two basic methods are given which make it possible to single out a class of differential equations for which there exists a weak solution of the boundary value problem. So-called coercive elliptic problems form the class in question and it can be said that the questions of the existence of the weak solutions of these problems are settled, essentially, even from the point of view of numerical methods. The material of Chapter VI differs substantially from the problems investigated in Chapters IV and V. So-called non-coercive problems are studied in more detail there and new, mostly as yet unpublished, results are presented. There is a multitude of open problems in this field which we submit to the reader here; the numerical processing of these problems is still in its infancy.

Chapter VII is devoted to a brief introduction to the very interesting and important field of problems concerning the so-called variational inequalities whose main application is in mechanics. From this brief outline, it is clear that by far not all types of nonlinear differential equations are discussed. For instance, evolution equations (i.e., equations representing phenomena dependent on time) are not included in the book at all. At this point, we refer to the extensive monograph by O. Vejvoda et al. [92], to the books by J.-L. Lions which include an immense amount of material, as well as to the book by H. Gajewski, K. Gröger and K. Zacharias mentioned above. On the other hand, we wish to stress that using the concept of weak solution, the difference between an ordinary and a partial differential equation, which is so striking in the classical approach, is suppressed. We have exploited this especially in the illustrative examples where it is possible to use clearer and simpler apparatus for ordinary equations.

Now, brief instructions on how to read the book: The text is divided into sections numbered consecutively. The sections are then arranged into paragraphs labelled by pairs of numbers so that, e.g., 13.12 stands for the twelfth paragraph of the thirteenth section. When referring to paragraphs we use this notation frequently. Formulas are numbered in each section separately. In the current section, we refer to a formula simply by its number. When referring to a formula appearing in some other section, we denote it by a pair of numbers placed in parentheses so that, e.g., (13.12) stands for the twelfth formula of the thirteenth section. Figures have the same number as the paragraph to which they belong. The exposition is completed by a number of illustrative examples. Not all of these are elaborated in detail; a considerable number are, rather, exercises calling for the reader's active participation.

In writing the text, we made use of the experience gained while lecturing and working in seminars at the Faculty of Mathematics and Physics of the Charles University and at the Mathematical Institute of the Czechoslovak Academy of Sciences, as well as from the activities of the seminar at the Technical University of Plzeň. We therefore wish to express our thanks to all those who took part in the work of these seminars as well as to those who have in some other way contributed to the elimination of mistakes and to the general improvement of this text. Among all these colleagues, we thank particularly Dr. Milan Kučera, CSc., and the referees of this book, Prof. Dr. Karel Rektorys, DrSc., and Dr. Oldřich John, CSc.

Prague, April 1979

S. FUČÍK
A. KUFNER

LIST OF SYMBOLS

1. Note that throughout this book we work in the real field only, i.e., with real numbers and with real functions of one or more real variables.
2. The numbers in the first column stand for the number of the paragraph in which the symbol considered can be found.

	$\{v \in V;\ \mathscr{P}(v)\}$	set of all elements v from V which possess property $\mathscr{P}(v)$
	$\mathbb{R}^N$	N-dimensional Euclidean space
	$\mathbb{R} = \mathbb{R}^1$	set of all real numbers
	$\mathbb{N}$	set of all positive integers
	$\mathbb{N}_0$	set of nonnegative integers
	Ω	domain in $\mathbb{R}^N$ (bounded, in most cases)
	$\partial\Omega$	boundary of domain Ω
	$x = (x_1, x_2, \ldots, x_N)$	point in $\mathbb{R}^N$
	(x, y)	point in $\mathbb{R}^2$
	$[a, b]$	closed interval: $\{t \in \mathbb{R};\ a \leq t \leq b\}$
	(a, b)	open interval: $\{t \in \mathbb{R};\ a < t < b\}$
	$[a, b)$	half-open interval: $\{t \in \mathbb{R};\ a \leq t < b\}$
	$(a, b]$	half-open interval: $\{t \in \mathbb{R};\ a < t \leq b\}$
	$\overline{M}$	closure of set M
1.4	$v\big|_S$	restriction of function v to set S
26.27 34.2	u^+, u^-	positive and negative parts of function u
14.1	$<,>$	symbol of duality ($<F, v>$ stands for the value of the functional F at the point v)
20.7	$<,>$	inner product in Hilbert space
15.7	$<,>_\Omega$	symbol of duality
15.7	$<,>_\Gamma$	symbol of duality
24.5	$\rightharpoonup$	symbol denoting weak convergence
12.8	$\subset\!\subset$	symbol denoting continuous imbedding
26.24	$\subset\!\subset\ \subset\!\subset$	symbol denoting compact imbedding

6.1 **7.3**	$\left.\begin{array}{l} a_i \\ a_\alpha \end{array}\right\}$	coefficients of differential operators
14.1	A	formal differential operator
14.1 **14.2**	$\left.\begin{array}{l} \\ \mathbb{A} \\ \end{array}\right\}$	operator determined by differential operator A
14.1	$a(u, v)$	form determined by differential operator A
7.2	$\alpha = (\alpha_1, \alpha_2, \ldots, \alpha_N)$	multi-index
7.2	$|\alpha| = \sum_{i=1}^{N} \alpha_i$	length of multi-index α
15.7	(A, V, Q)	boundary value problem
30.1 **33.14**	$\left.\begin{array}{l} \\ B(r) \\ \end{array}\right\}$	sphere with radius r and center at the origin
9.2 **17.8**	$\left.\begin{array}{l} \mathscr{C}^{0,1} \\ \mathscr{C}^\infty \end{array}\right\}$	classes of domains in $\mathbb{R}^N$
8.2	$C^k(\Omega)$	space of smooth functions
8.2	$C^k(a, b)$	space of smooth functions
8.2	$C^0(\bar{\Omega})$	space of smooth functions
8.2	$C^k(\bar{\Omega})$	space of smooth functions
8.2	$C^k_0(\Omega)$	space of smooth functions
8.2	$C^\infty(\Omega)$	space of smooth functions
8.2	$C^\infty(\bar{\Omega})$	space of smooth functions
8.3	$C^{0,1}(\bar{\Omega})$	space of smooth functions
17.8	$C^{k,\lambda}(\bar{\Omega})$	space of smooth functions
12.2	**CAR**	class of functions
12.13	**CAR**(p)	class of functions
16.15	**CAR**$*(p)$	class of functions
16.20	**CAR**(G)	class of functions
18.5	$dF(u)$	differential of functional F
18.5	$dF(u, v)$	derivative of functional F
21.2	$d^2F(u, v, w)$	second derivative of functional F
30.1	$d[F(x); B(r), 0]$	Brouwer degree of mapping F
30.14	$d[Tu; B(r), \Theta]$	Leray-Schauder degree of operator T
6.2 **16.28**	$\left.\begin{array}{l} \\ \text{div } v \\ \end{array}\right\}$	divergence of vector function v
10.4	$\mathscr{D}(A)$	domain of operator A
7.2	$D^\alpha u$	derivative of function u
13.2	$D^\alpha u$	generalized derivative of function u
7.2	$\delta_k u$	
7.2	$\hat{\delta}_k u$	
1.2	Δ	Laplace operator
1.2	Δ^2	biharmonic operator

16.20	$E_G(\Omega)$	Orlicz space
	$\|\cdot\|_G$	norm in E_G
15.7	**f**	functional on space Q
18.8	$F'(u)$	differential of functional F
15.7	**g**	functional on space V
2.1	grad u	gradient of function u
20.7	H	Hilbert space
12.5	$\mathscr{H}$	Němyckiǐ operator
7.2	$\varkappa = \varkappa(N, k)$	
12.7	$L_p(\Omega)$	Lebesgue space
12.7	$L_p(a, b)$	Lebesgue space
	$\|\cdot\|_p$	norm in L_p
12.8	$L_\infty(\Omega)$	
	$\|\cdot\|_\infty$	norm in L_∞
16.20	$L_G(\Omega)$	Orlicz space
	$\|\cdot\|_G$	norm in L_G
12.8	meas M	measure of set M
1.5	Mu	operator on $\partial\Omega$
1.5	Nu	operator on $\partial\Omega$
1.1	v	vector of outward normal (to $\partial\Omega$)
	$q = \begin{cases} p/(p-1) \\ \infty \end{cases}$	for $p > 1$ for $p = 1$
15.7	Q	special Banach space
2.3	sgn a	sign of number a
8.2	supp u	support of function u
31.1	$T'(u)$	Fréchet derivative of mapping T
15.7	$\mathscr{V}$	special linear set of functions
15.7	$V = \overline{\mathscr{V}}$	special Banach space
13.3	$W^{k,p}(\Omega)$	Sobolev space
13.4	$W^{k,p}(a, b)$	Sobolev space
13.3	$\|\cdot\|_{k,p}, \|\|\cdot\|\|_{k,p}$	norms in $W^{k,p}$
13.5	$W_0^{k,p}(\Omega)$	Sobolev space
13.6	$W_0^{k,p}(a, b)$	Sobolev space
13.7	$\|\cdot\|_{k,p,0}$	norm in $W_0^{k,p}$
16.18	$W^{1;p,q}(\Omega)$	anisotropic Sobolev space
16.18	$W_0^{1;p,q}(\Omega)$	anisotropic Sobolev space
16.22	$W^k E_G(\Omega)$	Sobolev-Orlicz space
16.22	$W^k L_G(\Omega)$	Sobolev-Orlicz space
16.22	$W_0^k E_G(\Omega)$	Sobolev-Orlicz space
	$\|\cdot\|_{k,G}$	norm in $W^k L_G$

16.24 $W^k E_{\vec{G}}(\Omega)$ anisotropic Sobolev-Orlicz space

        X Banach space

        $\|\cdot\|_X$ norm in X

        X^* dual space to space X

CHAPTER I

SOME EXAMPLES TO BEGIN WITH

SECTION 1. VARIOUS NOTATIONS. LINEAR EQUATIONS

1.1. In what follows, Ω is a bounded domain in N-dimensional Euclidean space $\mathbb{R}^N$, $N \geq 1$. Points in $\mathbb{R}^N$ are denoted by

$$x = (x_1, x_2, \ldots, x_N);$$

in the two-dimensional case, where $N = 2$, the coordinates of a point are denoted by x and y:

$$(x, y).$$

We denote by the symbol $\partial\Omega$ the *boundary* of the domain Ω. We assume that at every point $x \in \partial\Omega$ (with the possible exception of a finite number of points) the unit vector of the *outward normal* v to $\partial\Omega$ is defined, namely

$$v = (v_1, v_2, \ldots, v_N).$$

For a function u, the *derivative in the direction of the outward normal* is given by

$$\frac{\partial u}{\partial v} = \frac{\partial u}{\partial x_1} v_1 + \frac{\partial u}{\partial x_2} v_2 + \ldots + \frac{\partial u}{\partial x_N} v_N. \tag{1}$$

In the case of the plane, where $N = 2$, $\partial\Omega$ will most frequently be a curve; the components of the vector of the outward normal will be denoted by v_x, v_y, thus

$$v = (v_x, v_y).$$

Besides the derivative in the direction of the outward normal

$$\frac{\partial u}{\partial v} = \frac{\partial u}{\partial x} v_x + \frac{\partial u}{\partial y} v_y \tag{2}$$

we introduce the *derivative in the direction of the tangent*:

$$\frac{\partial u}{\partial \tau} = -\frac{\partial u}{\partial x} v_y + \frac{\partial u}{\partial y} v_x. \tag{3}$$

1.2. In this chapter, we present a number of boundary value problems in differential equations, most of which describe some specific physical situation. In doing this, we formulate no precise assumptions. It is to be understood that all concepts we shall work here with have some reasonably defined meaning. Thus, e.g., for the function $u = u(x)$ defined on Ω, we introduce the *Laplace operator* Δ by the formula

$$\Delta u = \frac{\partial^2 u}{\partial x_1^2} + \frac{\partial^2 u}{\partial x_2^2} + \dots + \frac{\partial^2 u}{\partial x_N^2} \; ; \tag{4}$$

here, it is (tacitly) assumed that the function u actually possesses all second order partial derivatives which appear in formula (4). Furthermore, we introduce the *biharmonic operator* Δ^2 by means of the formula

$$\Delta^2 u = \Delta(\Delta u) = \sum_{i,j=1}^{N} \frac{\partial^4 u}{\partial x_i^2 \, \partial x_j^2} \; .$$

In particular, for $N = 2$ we have

$$\Delta^2 u = \frac{\partial^4 u}{\partial x^4} + 2 \frac{\partial^4 u}{\partial x^2 \, \partial y^2} + \frac{\partial^4 u}{\partial y^4} \; . \tag{5}$$

Here, we assume once again that the function u has (continuous) partial derivatives of the fourth order.

Precise formulations of the conditions and assumptions are presented in subsequent chapters.

1.3. The equation of a bar. Consider a bar of length 1 which we assume is placed along the interval $[0, 1]$. The deflection of this bar (in general, of variable cross-section or, rather, of variable modulus of elasticity, on an elastic subsoil and vertically loaded) is expressed by the function $u = u(x)$, defined for $x \in [0, 1]$, which satisfies the following fourth-order ordinary differential equation:

$$\frac{d^2}{dx^2} \left[E(x) \, I(x) \frac{d^2 u}{dx^2} \right] + Q(x) \, u = f(x), \quad x \in (0, 1). \tag{6}$$

Here, $E(x)$ is the modulus of elasticity in tension (Young's modulus), $I(x)$ is the cross-sectional moment of inertia about the bending axis, $Q(x)$ the yielding coefficient of the subsoil, and $f(x)$ the function representing the vertical load.

If the bar is clamped at both ends, then the situation is described by the conditions

$$u(0) = 0, \quad u'(0) = 0 \; ; \quad u(1) = 0, \quad u'(1) = 0 \; ; \tag{7}$$

if it is simply supported, then the situation is described by the conditions

$$u(0) = 0, \quad u''(0) = 0 \; ; \quad u(1) = 0, \quad u''(1) = 0 \; . \tag{8}$$

Consequently, to solve the problem of a clamped or a simply supported bar means to find a function $u = u(x)$ satisfying equation (6) and conditions (7) or (8), respectively.

1.4. The Poisson equation. Let Ω be a plane domain and let $f = f(x, y)$ be a given function on Ω. We seek the function $u = u(x, y)$ defined on $\bar{\Omega} = \Omega \cup \partial\Omega$ and satisfying the equation

$$-\Delta u = f \text{ on } \Omega.$$

This — the so-called *Poisson — equation* describes a number of physical phenomena: E.g., u might stand for the deflection of a membrane (of a homogeneous isotropic material) having the shape Ω, loaded by vertical forces; or, u could be the distribution of temperature under stationary heat conduction in a plate of shape Ω with constant heat conductivity and with internal sources of heat independent of time (here, the function f represents either the vertical load or the heat sources).

Various conditions may join the Poisson equation on $\partial\Omega$. For instance, the condition

$$u|_{\partial\Omega} = 0 \text{ †)}$$

means that the membrane is clamped along its edge, or that the edge of the considered plate is kept at zero temperature; the condition

$$\frac{\partial u}{\partial n} = g \quad \text{on} \quad \partial\Omega,$$

where $g = g(x, y)$ is a given function defined on $\partial\Omega$, means that the emission of heat along the edge of the plate is prescribed; the condition

$$\frac{\partial u}{\partial n} + cu = d \quad \text{on} \quad \partial\Omega,$$

where $c = c(x, y)$, $d = d(x, y)$ are given functions defined on $\partial\Omega$, means that heat exchange occurs (in a prescribed manner) between the plate and its environment.

1.5. The equation of a plate. Let Ω again be a plane domain, $f = f(x, y)$ a given function on Ω, and let us look for the function $u = u(x, y)$ which satisfies the equation

$$\Delta^2 u = f \quad \text{on} \quad \Omega. \tag{9}$$

---

†) The symbol $v|_S$ denotes the restriction of the function $v = v(x)$ (defined on some set $M \subset \mathbb{R}^N$) to the set $S \subset M$, i.e.,

$$v|_S(x) = v(x), \quad x \in S.$$

However, we will not always be consistent; frequently, we shall write

$$v \quad \text{on} \quad S$$

instead of $v|_S$.

The function u describes the deflection of a thin plate (of constant thickness, homogeneous, isotropic), vertically loaded by forces characterized by the function f.

Further, by

$$Mu = \sigma \, \Delta u + (1 - \sigma) \frac{\partial^2 u}{\partial v^2} \tag{10}$$

and

$$Nu = -\frac{\partial}{\partial v} (\Delta u) + (1 - \sigma) \frac{\partial}{\partial \tau} \left[\frac{\partial^2 u}{\partial x^2} v_x v_y - \frac{\partial^2 u}{\partial x \, \partial y} (v_x^2 - v_y^2) - \frac{\partial^2 u}{\partial y^2} v_x v_y \right] \tag{11}$$

we denote operations prescribed on $\partial \Omega$ [see $(2), (3)$ for the notation]; σ is the so-called Poisson constant.

Equation (9) together with the conditions

$$u\big|_{\partial \Omega} = 0 \, , \quad \frac{\partial u}{\partial v}\bigg|_{\partial \Omega} = 0$$

describes the deflection of a plate clamped along its edge. In connection with the conditions

$$u\big|_{\partial \Omega} = g \, , \quad Mu\big|_{\partial \Omega} = h \, ,$$

where $g = g(x, y)$, $h = h(x, y)$ are given functions defined on $\partial \Omega$, equation (9) describes the deflection of a plate which has prescribed settling of supports along its edge and a prescribed moment (in the case when $g = h = 0$, a simply supported plate is in question). Finally, the conditions

$$Mu\big|_{\partial \Omega} = 0 \, , \quad Nu\big|_{\partial \Omega} = 0$$

describe a plate with a free edge.

1.6. The differential equations discussed in the above paragraphs were linear. However, it is nonlinear equations that we want to treat here and the linear problems were discussed as an easy introduction to the problems of the field.

The differential equations mentioned up till now represent certain physical phenomena. However, the mathematical description of physical phenomena necessarily entails some simplification: were all the factors to be included in the representations, mathematically unsolvable problems would frequently arise. Consequently, the mathematical description is actually no more than an approximation to physical reality. The description involving linear equations is a sort of first approximation whose advantage lies in that it leads to mathematical problems solvable by given mathematical techniques at the given moment. A more exact representation of the physical phenomenon would lead to nonlinear equations; thus, the nonlinear representation is a further approximation which makes it possible to take additional factors into consideration. We try to illustrate this on the following example: The

Poisson equation from Paragraph 1.4 is a special case of the equation

$$-\frac{\partial}{\partial x}\left(k(x, y)\frac{\partial u}{\partial x}\right) - \frac{\partial}{\partial y}\left(k(x, y)\frac{\partial u}{\partial y}\right) = f(x, y) \quad \text{on} \quad \Omega, \tag{12}$$

where the given function $k = k(x, y)$ characterizes, e.g., the heat conductivity of the material at the point (x, y) while the function $u = u(x, y)$ represents the distribution of temperature. If the material is such that the conductivity is constant, we obtain the Poisson equation

$$-k\, \Delta u = f \quad \text{on} \quad \Omega$$

($k = \text{const.}$). However, we know that the conductivity of the material may vary not only with location, but also with the temperature to which the material is exposed, i.e., we know that the function k may also depend on the function u and, eventually, on its derivatives as well:

$$k = k\left(x, y; u, \frac{\partial u}{\partial x}, \frac{\partial u}{\partial y}\right).$$

The problem of temperature distribution is then described by an equation of the type of (12), i.e., by the equation

$$-\frac{\partial}{\partial x}\left(k\left(x, y; u, \frac{\partial u}{\partial x}, \frac{\partial u}{\partial y}\right)\frac{\partial u}{\partial x}\right) - \frac{\partial}{\partial y}\left(k\left(x, y; u, \frac{\partial u}{\partial x}, \frac{\partial u}{\partial y}\right)\frac{\partial u}{\partial y}\right) =$$

$$= f(x, y) \quad \text{on} \quad \Omega. \tag{13}$$

However, this equation is already nonlinear.

We discuss nonlinear equations in more detail below.

SECTION 2. NONLINEAR EQUATIONS

2.1. Let $u = u(x_1, x_2, \ldots, x_N)$ be a function defined on a domain $\Omega \subset \mathbb{R}^N$. The *gradient* of u is an N-dimensional vector function denoted by the symbol grad u and defined as follows:

$$\text{grad } u = \left(\frac{\partial u}{\partial x_1}, \frac{\partial u}{\partial x_2}, \ldots, \frac{\partial u}{\partial x_N}\right).$$

In what follows, we deal with functions defined on plane domains in the first place, i.e., for $N = 2$. Thus, for the function $u = u(x, y)$ we have

$$\text{grad } u = \left(\frac{\partial u}{\partial x}, \frac{\partial u}{\partial y}\right) \tag{1}$$

and

$$|\text{grad } u|^2 = \left(\frac{\partial u}{\partial x}\right)^2 + \left(\frac{\partial u}{\partial y}\right)^2. \tag{2}$$

2.2. The nonlinear equation (1.13) mentioned at the end of Paragraph 1.6 was a special case of the equation

$$-\frac{\partial}{\partial x}\left(a_1(x, y; u, \text{grad } u)\frac{\partial u}{\partial x}\right) - \frac{\partial}{\partial y}\left(a_2(x, y; u, \text{grad } u)\frac{\partial u}{\partial y}\right) +$$

$$+ a_0(x, y; u, \text{grad } u) = f(x, y) : \dagger) \tag{3}$$

equation (1.13) is obtained from equation (3) by putting

$$a_1(x, y; \xi_0, \xi_1, \xi_2) = a_2(x, y; \xi_0, \xi_1, \xi_2) = k(x, y; \xi_0, \xi_1, \xi_2),$$

$$a_0(x, y; \xi_0, \xi_1, \xi_2) = 0. \tag{4}$$

In equation (3), $a_i = a_i(x, y; \xi_0, \xi_1, \xi_2)$ are given functions defined for $(x, y) \in \Omega$, $(\xi_0, \xi_1, \xi_2) \in \mathbb{R}^3$, and $f = f(x, y)$ is a given function defined on Ω.

In practice, equations of the form of (3) occur frequently. Let us note a few special cases for which conditions (4) are always satisfied.

(i) In (4), put

$$k(x, y; \xi_0, \xi_1, \xi_2) = m(\xi_1^2 + \xi_2^2),$$

where $m = m(t)$ is a given function of one variable $t \geq 0$. Thus, we have the equation

$$-\frac{\partial}{\partial x}\left(m(|\text{grad } u|^2)\frac{\partial u}{\partial x}\right) - \frac{\partial}{\partial y}\left(m(|\text{grad } u|^2)\frac{\partial u}{\partial y}\right) = f(x, y) \quad \text{on} \quad \Omega. \tag{5}$$

Equation (5) describes, e.g., the elasto-plastic deformation of a plane body of shape Ω; the function m characterizes the properties of the material of the body, the function f the load. If, moreover, we prescribe the condition

$$u|_{\partial\Omega} = 0,$$

we are dealing with a body clamped along its edge.

$\dagger$) The symbol

$$\frac{\partial}{\partial x}\left(a_1(x, y; u, \text{grad } u)\frac{\partial u}{\partial x}\right)$$

is to be understood as the partial derivative of the composite function $v = v(x, y)$ defined as follows:

$$v(x, y) = a_1(x, y; u(x, y), \text{grad } u(x, y))\frac{\partial u}{\partial x}(x, y).$$

Similarly for the expression

$$\frac{\partial}{\partial y}\left(a_2(x, y; u, \text{grad } u)\frac{\partial u}{\partial y}\right).$$

(ii) The same equation (5) describes the stationary magnetic field in an electrical machine: The function $u = u(x, y)$ is the magnetic potential, and the function m is the so-called permeability of the environment.

Let us divide the boundary $\partial\Omega$ into two parts Γ_1 and Γ_2. Furthermore, let us introduce the conditions

$$u|_{\Gamma_1} = g , \quad m(|\text{grad } u|^2) \frac{\partial u}{\partial v}\Big|_{\Gamma_2} = h ,$$

where $g = g(x, y)$ and $h = h(x, y)$ are given functions defined on Γ_1 and Γ_2, respectively. This means that the potential on Γ_1 and the density of the induction flow on Γ_2 are given.

(iii) Consider equation (5) again, but now with a rather special function m:

$$m(t) = (1 + t)^{-1/2} .$$

Thus, we have the equation

$$- \frac{\partial}{\partial x} \left[\frac{1}{\sqrt{\left[1 + \left(\frac{\partial u}{\partial x}\right)^2 + \left(\frac{\partial u}{\partial y}\right)^2 \right]}} \frac{\partial u}{\partial x} \right] - \frac{\partial}{\partial y} \left[\frac{1}{\sqrt{\left[1 + \left(\frac{\partial u}{\partial x}\right)^2 + \left(\frac{\partial u}{\partial y}\right)^2 \right]}} \frac{\partial u}{\partial y} \right] =$$
$$= f(x, y) \quad \text{on} \quad \Omega , \tag{6}$$

which can be reduced to the following form for $f = 0$:

$$\left(1 + \left(\frac{\partial u}{\partial y}\right)^2 \right) \frac{\partial^2 u}{\partial x^2} - 2 \frac{\partial u}{\partial x} \frac{\partial u}{\partial y} \frac{\partial^2 u}{\partial x \partial y} + \left(1 + \left(\frac{\partial u}{\partial x}\right)^2 \right) \frac{\partial^2 u}{\partial y^2} = 0 .$$

This last equation together with the condition

$$u|_{\partial\Omega} = g$$

describes the so-called minimal surface problem (the Plateau problem): The function $u = u(x, y)$ describes just that surface in $\mathbb{R}^3$ whose projection into the (x, y) plane is the domain Ω with the prescribed shape (given by the function g) above $\partial\Omega$, and with the smallest area of all possible surfaces of this type.

However, equations of the above type (6) also describe, e.g., the flow of fluids or gases, or problems from the theory of elasto-plastic deformations.

(iv) Consider equation (5) again, this time with the function

$$m(t) = 1 - \frac{\gamma - 1}{2} t^{1/(\gamma - 1)} ,$$

where $\gamma > 1$ is a given constant. The corresponding equation characterizes then the potential flow of gases. If

$$\left(\frac{\partial u}{\partial x}\right)^2 + \left(\frac{\partial u}{\partial y}\right)^2 \leqq \frac{2}{\gamma - 1},$$

we have subsonic flow.

2.3. The nonlinear Laplace operator. We again consider a plane domain Ω and the function $u = u(x, y)$ which satisfies the equation

$$-\frac{\partial}{\partial x}\left(\left|\frac{\partial u}{\partial x}\right|^{p-2}\frac{\partial u}{\partial x}\right) - \frac{\partial}{\partial y}\left(\left|\frac{\partial u}{\partial y}\right|^{p-2}\frac{\partial u}{\partial y}\right) = f(x, y) \quad \text{on} \quad \Omega, \tag{7}$$

where $f = f(x, y)$ is a given function defined on Ω again and p is a real number satisfying the condition

$$p > 1. \; \dagger)$$

We are not aware whether equation (7) has any physical meaning. Nevertheless, it is useful from the methodological point of view and we use it frequently to illustrate various concepts and assertions. Since, for $p = 2$, the Laplace operator appears on the left-hand side of equation (7) and equation (7) reduces to the Poisson equation,

---

†) If

$$\frac{\partial u}{\partial x}(x) = 0 \quad \text{and} \quad 1 < p < 2,$$

then the expression

$$\left|\frac{\partial u}{\partial x}(x)\right|^{p-2}$$

is meaningless; in such cases we define

$$\left|\frac{\partial u}{\partial x}(x)\right|^{p-2}\frac{\partial u}{\partial x}(x)$$

as equal to zero. This is reasonable, since for every real number a we have

$$a = |a| \operatorname{sgn} a,$$

where

$$\operatorname{sgn} a = \begin{cases} 1 & \text{for} \quad a > 0, \\ -1 & \text{for} \quad a < 0, \\ 0 & \text{for} \quad a = 0, \end{cases}$$

and thus

$$|a|^{p-2} a = |a|^{p-1} \operatorname{sgn} a,$$

where the right-hand side is meaningful even for $p < 2$.

we may call the expression

$$\frac{\partial}{\partial x}\left(\left|\frac{\partial u}{\partial x}\right|^{p-2}\frac{\partial u}{\partial x}\right) + \frac{\partial}{\partial y}\left(\left|\frac{\partial u}{\partial y}\right|^{p-2}\frac{\partial u}{\partial y}\right)$$

the "nonlinear Laplace operator".

Note that equation (7) is again a special case of equation (3): It is obtained by putting

$$a_1(x, y; \xi_0, \xi_1, \xi_2) = |\xi_1|^{p-2},$$
$$a_2(x, y; \xi_0, \xi_1, \xi_2) = |\xi_2|^{p-2},$$
$$a_0(x, y; \xi_0, \xi_1, \xi_2) = 0.$$

If we choose the functions a_1 and a_2 as above and, moreover, if we put

$$a_0(x, y; \xi_0, \xi_1, \xi_2) = |\xi_0|^{p-2}\xi_0,$$

we obtain the equation

$$-\frac{\partial}{\partial x}\left(\left|\frac{\partial u}{\partial x}\right|^{p-2}\frac{\partial u}{\partial x}\right) - \frac{\partial}{\partial y}\left(\left|\frac{\partial u}{\partial y}\right|^{p-2}\frac{\partial u}{\partial y}\right) + |u|^{p-2}u = f(x, y) \quad \text{on} \quad \Omega.$$

On account of the (methodological) significance of this equation, we now give its one-dimensional analogue: If $N = 1$, we seek the function $u = u(x)$ defined on an interval $[a, b]$ and satisfying the equation

$$-\frac{d}{dx}\left(\left|\frac{du}{dx}\right|^{p-2}\frac{du}{dx}\right) + |u|^{p-2}u = f(x) \quad \text{for} \quad x \in (a, b), \tag{8}$$

or, otherwise,

$$-\left(|u'|^{p-2}u'\right)' + |u|^{p-2}u = f(x) \quad \text{for} \quad x \in (a, b). \tag{9}$$

2.4. The Monge-Ampère equation. The problem of finding the surface represented by the function $u = u(x, y)$ for $(x, y) \in \bar{\Omega}$, which has a prescribed form on the boundary $\partial\Omega$ and a prescribed curvature, is a typical nonlinear problem. This problem leads to the equation

$$\frac{\partial^2 u}{\partial x^2}\frac{\partial^2 u}{\partial y^2} - \left(\frac{\partial^2 u}{\partial x \partial y}\right)^2 = f(x, y) \quad \text{on} \quad \Omega$$

with the condition

$$u\big|_{\partial\Omega} = g.$$

2.5. Equations of the fourth order. In the problems investigated in this section up till now, we encountered equations of the second order which were nonlinear analogues of the Poisson equation. We now discuss equations which are analogues of the equation of the plate from Paragraph 1.5.

(i) Consider once more a plane domain Ω and put

$$H(u) = \left(\frac{\partial^2 u}{\partial x^2}\right)^2 + \left(\frac{\partial^2 u}{\partial y^2}\right)^2 + \left(\frac{\partial^2 u}{\partial x\, \partial y}\right)^2 + \frac{\partial^2 u}{\partial x^2}\frac{\partial^2 u}{\partial y^2}$$

for the function $u = u(x, y)$. The equation

$$\frac{\partial^2}{\partial x^2}\left[g(H(u))\left(\frac{\partial^2 u}{\partial x^2} + \frac{1}{2}\frac{\partial^2 u}{\partial y^2}\right)\right] + \frac{\partial^2}{\partial x\, \partial y}\left[g(H(u))\frac{\partial^2 u}{\partial x\, \partial y}\right] +$$

$$+ \frac{\partial^2}{\partial y^2}\left[g(H(u))\left(\frac{\partial^2 u}{\partial y^2} + \frac{1}{2}\frac{\partial^2 u}{\partial x^2}\right)\right] = f(x, y) \quad \text{on} \quad \Omega \tag{10}$$

with the conditions

$$u\big|_{\partial\Omega} = 0, \quad \frac{\partial u}{\partial v}\Big|_{\partial\Omega} = 0 \tag{11}$$

represents the elasto-plastic deformation of a rigidly clamped plate. The function $g = g(t)$ of the variable $t \geq 0$ is given and it characterizes the material of the plate; the function $f = f(x, y)$ characterizes the load. Conditions (11) express the fact that the plate is clamped along its edge (naturally, it is possible to consider a simply supported plate, etc. − just as in Paragraph 1.5).

The function

$$g(t) = t^{(\gamma-1)/2},$$

where γ is a positive constant, corresponds to a plate under conditions of creep.

The reader will undoubtedly have noted that the choice

$$g(t) = 1$$

leads to the equation $\Delta^2 u = f$ which has already been encountered in Paragraph 1.5.

(ii) In Paragraph 2.3, the "nonlinear Laplace operator" was introduced. Similarly, it is possible to introduce the "nonlinear biharmonic operator"

$$\Delta(|\Delta u|^{p-2}\, \Delta u), \tag{12}$$

where $p > 1$ and where we obtain the biharmonic operator $\Delta^2 u$ for $p = 2$. As before, we do not know whether the equation with the operator (12) has any physical interpretation. However, it can be used to model various theoretical considerations.

SECTION 3. NONLINEAR SYSTEMS

3.1. Hitherto we have discussed problems where it was necessary to find a single function which satisfies an equation on Ω and additional conditions on $\partial\Omega$. In this section, we discuss problems in which several unknown functions are to be found.

3.2. The von Kármán equations. Consider again the plane domain Ω and let us introduce the following notation:

$$[u, v] = \frac{\partial^2 u}{\partial x^2} \frac{\partial^2 v}{\partial y^2} - 2 \frac{\partial^2 u}{\partial x\, \partial y} \frac{\partial^2 v}{\partial x\, \partial y} + \frac{\partial^2 u}{\partial y^2} \frac{\partial^2 v}{\partial x^2}.$$

This time, we look for a pair of functions

$$u = u(x, y), \quad v = v(x, y)$$

defined on $\bar{\Omega}$ and satisfying the following system of two equations:

$$\begin{aligned} \Delta^2 u &= [u, v] + f \\ \Delta^2 v &= -[u, u] \end{aligned} \quad \text{on} \quad \Omega. \tag{1}$$

This system represents the deformation of an elastic thin plate subject to a vertical load. The load is characterized by the function f; the function u represents the displacement in the direction perpendicular to the plate (deflection of the plate), and v is the so-called Airy function which characterizes the distribution of tension in the plane of the plate.

Let us divide the boundary $\partial \Omega$ into three parts $\Gamma_1, \Gamma_2, \Gamma_3$ and impose the following conditions on $\partial \Omega$ (i.e., along the edge of the plate):

$$v|_{\partial \Omega} = g_0, \quad \frac{\partial v}{\partial v}\bigg|_{\partial \Omega} = g_1, \tag{2}$$

where g_0, g_1 are given functions and, further,

$$u|_{\Gamma_1} = \frac{\partial u}{\partial v}\bigg|_{\Gamma_1} = 0 ;$$

$$u|_{\Gamma_2} = 0, \quad Mu|_{\Gamma_2} + h_0 \frac{\partial u}{\partial v}\bigg|_{\Gamma_2} = h_1 ;$$

$$Mu|_{\Gamma_3} = 0, \quad Nu|_{\Gamma_3} = 0 \tag{3}$$

[the symbols Mu and Nu are defined in Paragraph 1.5, see formulas (1.10) and (1.11); h_0 and h_1 are given functions]. These conditions mean that the plate is rigidly clamped along Γ_1, elastically clamped along Γ_2, and free along Γ_3.

3.3. The Navier-Stokes equations. Let Ω be a domain in $\mathbb{R}^N$, $N \geq 2$. In hydrodynamics, the problem frequently occurs of finding an N-tuple of functions

$$u_1(x), u_2(x), \ldots, u_N(x)$$

defined on $\bar{\Omega}$ (in the cases of $N = 2$ and $N = 3$, these are the components of the velocity of the fluid along the axes) and a function

$$p(x)$$

(pressure of the fluid) so that the so-called Navier-Stokes system of equations

$$-v\,\Delta u_i + \sum_{j=1}^{N} u_j \frac{\partial u_i}{\partial x_j} = f_i(x) - \frac{\partial p}{\partial x_i} \quad (i = 1, 2, \ldots, N),$$

$$\frac{\partial u_1}{\partial x_1} + \frac{\partial u_2}{\partial x_2} + \ldots + \frac{\partial u_N}{\partial x_N} = 0 \tag{4}$$

and the conditions

$$u_i\big|_{\partial\Omega} = 0, \quad i = 1, 2, \ldots, N, \tag{5}$$

be satisfied in Ω.

3.4. Further examples. (i) The equilibrium state of a thin rotating rod is represented by a pair of functions $u(x)$, $v(x)$ defined for $x \in [0, 1]$ and satisfying the system of ordinary equations

$$\left.\begin{array}{l} \dfrac{d^2 u}{dx^2} = \lambda \sin v(x) \\[2mm] \dfrac{d^2 v}{dx^2} = \lambda\, u(x) \cos v(x) \end{array}\right\} \quad \text{for} \quad x \in (0, 1)$$

(λ is a constant) and the conditions

$$u'(0) = v(0) = u(1) = v'(1) = 0 \tag{6}$$

or the conditions

$$u'(0) = v'(0) = u(1) = v(1) = 0. \tag{7}$$

(ii) In all the problems hitherto presented in this section, the physical phenomenon was represented by a system of differential equations on Ω and by conditions on $\partial\Omega$. These conditions on $\partial\Omega$ were formulated in such a way that each of the individual unknown functions satisfied its own conditions and there was no connection with the other functions — the interconnection of the functions was manifested only by way of the system of differential equations. However, there also exist problems where the unknown functions are connected in a certain way even in the conditions on $\partial\Omega$.

We present no actual physical problem with boundary conditions of this type here as we shall not discuss this question. Let us note, merely, that in the case of a system of two equations with two unknown functions $u = u(x, y)$, $v = v(x, y)$, defined on Ω, boundary conditions of the types

$$(au + bv)\big|_{\partial\Omega} = 0$$

or

$$v\big|_{\partial\Omega} + \left(a\,\frac{\partial u}{\partial x} + b\,\frac{\partial v}{\partial y}\right)\bigg|_{\partial\Omega} = g\,,$$

where a, b, g are given functions on $\partial\Omega$, can be considered. Thus, in this case, the functions u and v are connected in the boundary condition in contradiction to conditions (2) and (3) or (6) and (7), where a condition is imposed separately on each of the functions u and v.

SECTION 4. FURTHER NONLINEAR PROBLEMS

4.1. Ordinary differential equations. With the exception of system (i) in Paragraph 3.4 and of the equation of the bar in Paragraph 1.3, we have up till now encountered problems represented by partial differential equations. We now mention briefly several problems leading to ordinary differential equations.

(i) The rotation of a heavy string is represented by the equation

$$\frac{d^2u}{dx^2} + \omega^2\,\frac{u}{\sqrt{(x^2 + u^2)}} = 0 \quad \text{on} \quad (0, 1)$$

together with the conditions

$$u(0) = u'(1) = 0\,,$$

where ω is angular velocity.

(ii) In the theory of chemical reactors, one encounters the problem of finding a function $u = u(x)$, defined for $x \in [0, 1]$, which satisfies the equation

$$\beta\,\frac{d^2u}{dx^2} - \frac{du}{dx} + F(u) = 0 \quad \text{on} \quad (0, 1)$$

and the conditions

$$-u'(0) + \alpha\,u(0) = 0\,, \quad u'(1) = 0\,;$$

here, F is a given function, β and α are given constants.

(iii) In the preceding problem, the nonlinearity of the equation was determined by the function F. However, the nonlinearity can also be concealed in integral form as demonstrated in the following problem describing the processes in the helium atom: We look for a function $u = u(x)$ defined for $x \geq 0$ which satisfies the equation

$$-\frac{1}{2}\,\frac{d^2u}{dx^2} - \frac{2u}{x} + u\,R(u) = \lambda u \quad \text{on} \quad (0, \infty)$$

and the condition

$$u(0) = 0\,,$$

while

$$R(u) = \frac{4\pi}{x} \int_0^x u^2(t)\, dt + 4\pi \int_x^\infty \frac{u^2(t)}{t}\, dt \,.$$

4.2. Nonlinearities hitherto encountered have mostly been of the "power type". However, in chemistry and nuclear physics one often finds problems represented by equations of the type

$$\Delta u + u\, e^u = f \quad \text{on} \quad \Omega$$

or

$$\Delta u + e^u = f \quad \text{on} \quad \Omega \,,$$

where the nonlinearity is of the "exponential type". The investigation of these non-linearities is more difficult by far than the investigation of the "power" nonlinearities. More on these problems will be found in Chapters 3 and 5 (see Paragraphs 16.19 through 16.23 and 32.4).

4.3. The transmission problem. Consider again a plane domain Ω and the problem already discussed in Section 2:

Find the function $u = u(x, y)$, defined on $\bar{\Omega}$, which satisfies on Ω the equation

$$-\frac{\partial}{\partial x}\left(k(x, y; u, \text{grad } u)\, \frac{\partial u}{\partial x}\right) - \frac{\partial}{\partial y}\left(k(x, y; u, \text{grad } u)\, \frac{\partial u}{\partial y}\right) = f(x, y) \qquad (5)$$

and on $\partial\Omega$ the condition

$$u\big|_{\partial\Omega} = 0 \,. \qquad (6)$$

Here $k = k(x, y; \xi_0, \xi_1, \xi_2)$ is a given function defined for

$$(x, y) \in \Omega \quad \text{and} \quad (\xi_0, \xi_1, \xi_2) \in \mathbb{R}^3 \,.$$

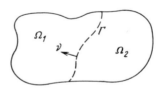

Fig. 4.3

Assume now that the domain Ω is divided into two parts Ω_1, Ω_2 by a curve Γ (see Fig. 4.3), and that the function k is given in different ways on Ω_1 and on Ω_2, i.e.,

$$k(x, y; \xi_0, \xi_1, \xi_2) = \begin{cases} k_1(x, y; \xi_0, \xi_1, \xi_2) & \text{for} \quad (x, y) \in \Omega_1 \,, \\ k_2(x, y; \xi_0, \xi_1, \xi_2) & \text{for} \quad (x, y) \in \Omega_2 \,. \end{cases} \qquad (7)$$

In this case, we formulate a rather different problem instead of the problem (5), (6): Find a function u_1, defined on $\bar{\Omega}_1 = \Omega_1 \cup \partial\Omega_1$, which solves the equation

$$- \frac{\partial}{\partial x}\left(k_1(x, y; u_1, \operatorname{grad} u_1)\frac{\partial u_1}{\partial x}\right) - \frac{\partial}{\partial y}\left(k_1(x, y; u_1, \operatorname{grad} u_1)\frac{\partial u_1}{\partial y}\right) =$$

$$= f_1(x, y) \quad \text{on} \quad \Omega_1 \tag{8}$$

and satisfies, on $\Gamma_1 = \partial\Omega_1 - \Gamma$, the condition

$$u_1|_{\Gamma_1} = 0, \tag{9}$$

and find, further, a function u_2, defined on $\bar{\Omega}_2 = \Omega_2 \cup \partial\Omega_2$, which solves the equation

$$- \frac{\partial}{\partial x}\left(k_2(x, y; u_2, \operatorname{grad} u_2)\frac{\partial u_2}{\partial x}\right) - \frac{\partial}{\partial y}\left(k_2(x, y; u_2, \operatorname{grad} u_2)\frac{\partial u_2}{\partial y}\right) =$$

$$= f_2(x, y) \quad \text{on} \quad \Omega_2 \tag{10}$$

and satisfies, on $\Gamma_2 = \partial\Omega_2 - \Gamma$, the condition

$$u_2|_{\Gamma_2} = 0; \tag{11}$$

f_i stands for the restriction of the function f to Ω_i $(i = 1, 2)$. To these conditions, still further conditions are then added which make possible the "binding" of the two solutions u_1 and u_2 along the line of connection Γ of the two domains Ω_1 and Ω_2. These additional conditions are called the transmission conditions and have the form

$$u_1|_\Gamma = u_2|_\Gamma,$$

$$k_1(x, y; u_1, \operatorname{grad} u_1)\frac{\partial u_1}{\partial v}\bigg|_\Gamma = k_2(x, y; u_2, \operatorname{grad} u_2)\frac{\partial u_2}{\partial v}\bigg|_\Gamma, \tag{12}$$

where v is the vector of the normal to Γ oriented, e.g., into the interior of the domain Ω_1.

The problem of finding the functions u_1 and u_2 which satisfy equations (8) and (10), conditions (9) and (11) and the transmission conditions (12) is sometimes called the transmission problem.

4.4. Multidimensional problems. We have so far mostly discussed one-dimensional $(N = 1)$ and two-dimensional $(N = 2)$ problems the only exception being the Navier-Stokes equations in Paragraph 3.3. However, the reader will certainly be able to generalize, in most cases without difficulty, the problems formulated for the plane domain Ω to cases involving more variables. For the sake of illustration alone, we formulate below the "multidimensional analogue" of problem (iii) from Paragraph 2.2.

Let Ω be a domain in an N-dimensional Euclidean space $\mathbb{R}^N$ $(N \geq 2)$. Let $f = f(x)$ be a function defined on Ω, $g = g(x)$ a function defined on $\partial\Omega$, and let us look for the function $u = u(x)$ defined on $\bar{\Omega}$ which satisfies the equation

$$-\sum_{i=1}^{N} \frac{\partial}{\partial x_i} \left(\frac{1}{\sqrt{(1 + |\text{grad } u|^2)}} \frac{\partial u}{\partial x_i} \right) = f \quad \text{on} \quad \Omega \tag{13}$$

and the condition

$$u = g \quad \text{on} \quad \partial\Omega ; \tag{14}$$

we have

$$|\text{grad } u|^2 = \left(\frac{\partial u}{\partial x_1} \right)^2 + \left(\frac{\partial u}{\partial x_2} \right)^2 + \cdots + \left(\frac{\partial u}{\partial x_N} \right)^2$$

here.

If we put $f = 0$, then problem (13), (14) becomes a minimal surface problem again; however, the "surface" is now in the space $\mathbb{R}^{N+1}$.

SECTION 5. A FREE BOUNDARY PROBLEM. THE PLATE EQUATION

5.1. In the problems above, the domain Ω was always given beforehand and we looked for a function defined on $\bar{\Omega}$ which satisfied a differential equation on Ω as well as an additional condition on $\partial\Omega$.

In the problem presented below, not even the shape of the domain Ω is (completely) known and the problem thus involves one additional "unknown". Problems of this type are called free boundary problems.

5.2. The seepage problem. In essence, our next problem is the problem of fluid flow through a porous medium. Imagine a dam on an inpervious basis. For the sake of simplicity, let us assume that the dam (or rather its cross-section) has the shape of a rectangle of width a and height b. The height of water above the dam is $y_1(y_1 < b)$ and the height of water below the dam is $y_2(y_2 < y_1)$. We assume that the material of the dam is homogeneous and isotropic and that the permeability coefficient of the material is equal to one. The seepage of water through the dam takes place inside the domain bounded from above by the curve $y = \varphi(x)$ which starts at the point E, is decreasing, and terminates at the point G with coordinates $(a, \varphi(a))$ where $\varphi(a) \geq y_2$.

Our problem is to determine the distribution of the velocity of fluid flow through the body of the dam, i.e., to determine a vector function $v = v(x, y)$ on the "curvilinear rectangle" $ABGE$. The function v is determined by the potential of velocity $u = u(x, y)$; we then have

$$v = -\text{grad } u .$$

However, as can be seen, we have to determine not only the function u on $ABGE$ but also the function φ which defines this curvilinear rectangle.

In line with the notation in the figure, point A has coordinates $(0, 0)$, B has co-ordinates $(a, 0)$, C has coordinates (a, b), D has coordinates $(0, b)$, E has coordinates $(0, y_1)$ and F has coordinates (a, y_2). We denote the rectangle $ABCD$ by Q.

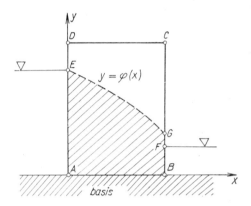

Fig. 5.2

The problem is now the following: We have to find the function $y = \varphi(x)$ defined for $x \in [0, a]$ and the function $u = u(x, y)$ defined on $\bar{\Omega}$, where

$$\Omega = \{(x, y) \in Q; \ 0 < x < a, \ 0 < y < \varphi(x)\} \,,$$

where

(i) the function φ is decreasing and

$$\varphi(0) = y_1 \,, \quad \varphi(a) \geq y_2 \,;$$

(ii) the function u satisfies the equation

$$\Delta u = 0 \quad \text{on} \quad \Omega$$

and the following conditions along the boundary of the domain Ω:

$$\frac{\partial u}{\partial v} = 0 \quad \text{on the segment } AB \text{ and on the arc } EG,$$

$$u = y_1 \quad \text{on the segment } AE,$$

$$u = y_2 \quad \text{on the segment } BF,$$

$$u = y \quad \text{on the segment } FG \text{ and on the arc } EG.$$

[The first of the above conditions represents the fact that there is seepage neither along the subsoil nor in the direction of the crown of the dam; the last of the above conditions can be written as follows:

$$u(x, \varphi(x)) = \varphi(x) \quad \text{for} \quad x \in (0, a),$$
$$u(a, y) = y \qquad \text{for} \quad y \in (y_2, \varphi(a)).]$$

Thus, if the function φ is known, we are dealing with a familiar (even linear) problem; the function φ characterizes the "free boundary".

5.3. A problem of the Signorini type. Recall now the equation of a thin plate as discussed in Paragraph 1.5 and consider the following problem from the theory of elasticity: A function $u = u(x, y)$ is to be found, defined on a plane domain $\bar{\Omega} = = \Omega \cup \partial\Omega$, which satisfies the equation

$$\Delta^2 u = f \quad \text{on} \quad \Omega \tag{1}$$

and the boundary conditions

$$Mu = 0 \qquad\qquad \text{on} \quad \partial\Omega$$
$$u \geq 0 \quad \text{and} \quad Nu \geq 0 \quad \text{on} \quad \partial\Omega$$
$$u \cdot Nu = 0 \qquad\qquad \text{on} \quad \partial\Omega. \tag{2}$$

[As far as the symbols M and N are concerned, see (1.10) and (1.11).] The solution of the equation for a thin plate is in question; here, the plate is supported along its edge in such a way that it can only deflect upwards ($u \geq 0$ on $\partial\Omega$) and the shearing force Nu can be nonzero only for zero deflection [i.e., for $u(x) \neq 0$, we have $Nu(x) = = 0$ or, in other words $u \cdot Nu = 0$ on $\partial\Omega$].

This boundary value problem differs from the previous problems in that the boundary conditions are given in the form of inequalities (see, e.g., the problem of a plate with free edge in Paragraph 1.5).

5.4. Remark. It appears that the two problems discussed in this section have nothing in common. What is more, the two problems are actually linear problems although we stated that it is nonlinear problems that we are principally interested in here. In Chapter VII, we shall show that there is no inconsistency: We shall see that the two problems do have something in common and that they are actually of a non-linear nature, and so they were duly presented here.

CHAPTER II

INTRODUCTION

SECTION 6. SECOND ORDER EQUATIONS

6.1. Let Ω be a domain in $\mathbb{R}^N$, $N \geq 1$, and let

$$a_i = a_i(x; \xi_0, \xi_1, ..., \xi_N), \quad i = 0, 1, ..., N, \tag{1}$$

be functions of $2N + 1$ variables defined for

$$x \in \Omega, \quad (\xi_0, \xi_1, ..., \xi_N) \in \mathbb{R}^{N+1}.$$

Furthermore, let $f = f(x)$ be a function defined on Ω.

In what follows, we investigate differential equations of the form

$$-\sum_{i=1}^{N} \frac{\partial}{\partial x_i} a_i(x; u, \operatorname{grad} u) + a_0(x; u, \operatorname{grad} u) = f(x), \text{ †)} \tag{2}$$

i.e., we look for a function $u = u(x)$ defined on Ω which satisfies equation (2) for all $x \in \Omega$.

Equation (2) is called a differential equation of the second order (in divergent form); the functions a_i are called the coefficients of equation (2), and the function f is called the right-hand side of equation (2).

The term "coefficient of equation" does not correspond to the term which is current for linear differential equations [see Paragraph 6.3 (i)]. Nevertheless, we hope that this will not give rise to any misunderstanding.

6.2. Remarks. (i) For the time being, we understand the expression on the left-hand side of equation (2) to be a formal symbol, since nothing has yet been assumed about the functions a_i. This will be made up for in Section 8.

---

†) The expression

$$\frac{\partial}{\partial x_i} a_i(x; u, \operatorname{grad} u)$$

is to be understood as the partial derivative (with respect to x_i) of the composite function $v = v(x)$ defined as follows:

$$v(x) = a_i(x; u(x), \operatorname{grad} u(x)).$$

(ii) We have called equation (2) an equation in divergent form. This has its origin in the fact that the left-hand side of the mentioned equation is (but for its sign and the function a_0), actually, the divergence of the vector

$$a = (a_1, a_2, ..., a_N)$$

the components of which are the coefficients of equation (2)†); equation (2) can then be written as

$$-\operatorname{div} a + a_0 = f,$$

where, naturally, the vector a as well as the function f also depend on the desired function u and its derivatives.

6.3. Examples. (i) If we choose the a_i in (1) as follows:

$$a_i(x; \xi_0, \xi_1, ..., \xi_N) = \xi_i \quad \text{for} \quad i = 1, ..., N,$$
$$a_0(x; \xi_0, \xi_1, ..., \xi_N) = 0,$$

then equation (2) will take the form

$$-\sum_{i=1}^{N} \frac{\partial}{\partial x_i}\left(\frac{\partial u}{\partial x_i}\right) = f(x)$$

or, in other words,

$$-\Delta u = f(x),$$

where Δ is the Laplace operator (see Paragraph 1.2). Thus, equation (2) is the so-called Poisson equation already encountered (for $N = 2$) in Paragraph 1.4.

This equation is a special case of a second order linear differential equation. A general second order linear differential equation is obtained if all the functions a_i in (1) are linear functions of the variables $\xi_0, \xi_1, ..., \xi_N$, i.e., if they have the form

$$a_i(x; \xi_0, \xi_1, ..., \xi_N) = \sum_{j=0}^{N} a_{ij}(x)\,\xi_j, \quad i = 0, 1, ..., N,$$

with given functions $a_{ij}(x)$ defined on Ω. An equation with such coefficients will then be of the form

$$-\sum_{i=1}^{N}\sum_{j=1}^{N} \frac{\partial}{\partial x_i}\left(a_{ij}(x)\frac{\partial u}{\partial x_j}\right) - \sum_{i=1}^{N} \frac{\partial}{\partial x_i}(a_{i0}(x)\,u) + \sum_{j=1}^{N} a_{0j}(x)\frac{\partial u}{\partial x_j} + a_{00}(x)\,u = f(x).$$

---

†) If $v(x) = (v_1(x), v_2(x), ..., v_N(x))$ is a vector function defined on an N-dimensional domain Ω, i.e., for $x = (x_1, x_2, ..., x_N) \in \Omega$, we define the divergence of the vector v as the function

$$\operatorname{div} v = \frac{\partial v_1}{\partial x_1} + \frac{\partial v_2}{\partial x_2} + ... + \frac{\partial v_N}{\partial x_N}.$$

(ii) If we choose the functions a_i in (1) as follows:

$$a_i(x; \xi_0, \xi_1, ..., \xi_N) = |\xi_i|^{p-1} \operatorname{sgn} \xi_i, \quad i = 1, ..., N,$$

$$a_0(x; \xi_0, \xi_1, ..., \xi_N) = 0,$$

where p is a real number, $p > 1$, then equation (2) will have the form

$$-\sum_{i=1}^{N} \frac{\partial}{\partial x_i} \left(\left| \frac{\partial u}{\partial x_i} \right|^{p-1} \operatorname{sgn} \frac{\partial u}{\partial x_i} \right) = f(x).$$

On the left-hand side we have the so-called "nonlinear Laplace operator" encountered (for $N = 2$) in Paragraph 2.3.

(iii) Consider a plane domain Ω, i.e., let $N = 2$, and choose the functions a_i in (1) as follows:

$$a_1(x, y; \xi_0, \xi_1, \xi_2) = m(\xi_1^2 + \xi_2^2) \, \xi_1,$$

$$a_2(x, y; \xi_0, \xi_1, \xi_2) = m(\xi_1^2 + \xi_2^2) \, \xi_2,$$

$$a_0(x, y; \xi_0, \xi_1, \xi_2) = 0,$$

where $m = m(t)$ is a function of one real variable defined for $t \geqq 0$. Then equation (2) assumes the form

$$-\frac{\partial}{\partial x} \left(m(|\operatorname{grad} u|^2) \frac{\partial u}{\partial x} \right) - \frac{\partial}{\partial y} \left(m(|\operatorname{grad} u|^2) \frac{\partial u}{\partial y} \right) = f(x, y).$$

We have already encountered this equation in Paragraph 2.2 (for the notation, see Paragraph 2.1).

(iv) We recommend the reader to go through the specific equations discussed in Chapter I (first of all, the equations from Paragraphs 2.2, 4.1, 4.2, 4.3, 4.4) and derive the concrete form of the coefficients a_i for the individual equations.

6.4. General form of an equation of the second order. For the moment, consider a plane domain Ω, i.e., $N = 2$. Equation (2) then takes the form

$$-\frac{\partial}{\partial x} a_1 \left(x, y; u, \frac{\partial u}{\partial x}, \frac{\partial u}{\partial y} \right) - \frac{\partial}{\partial y} a_2 \left(x, y; u, \frac{\partial u}{\partial x}, \frac{\partial u}{\partial y} \right) +$$

$$+ a_0 \left(x, y; u, \frac{\partial u}{\partial x}, \frac{\partial u}{\partial y} \right) = f(x, y), \tag{3}$$

where the coefficients $a_i(x, y; \xi_0, \xi_1, \xi_2)$ $(i = 0, 1, 2)$ are defined for $(x, y) \in \Omega$, $(\xi_0, \xi_1, \xi_2) \in \mathbb{R}^3$. If the derivatives indicated in (3) are worked out (see the footnote on p. 33), then this equation will assume (after some simple modifications) the form

$$- \frac{\partial a_1}{\partial \xi_1} \frac{\partial^2 u}{\partial x^2} - \frac{\partial a_2}{\partial \xi_1} \frac{\partial^2 u}{\partial x \, \partial y} - \frac{\partial a_1}{\partial \xi_2} \frac{\partial^2 u}{\partial y \, \partial x} - \frac{\partial a_2}{\partial \xi_2} \frac{\partial^2 u}{\partial y^2} -$$

$$- \frac{\partial a_1}{\partial \xi_0} \frac{\partial u}{\partial x} - \frac{\partial a_2}{\partial \xi_0} \frac{\partial u}{\partial y} + a_0 - \frac{\partial a_1}{\partial x} - \frac{\partial a_2}{\partial y} = f, \tag{4}$$

where, naturally, the functions $a_0, \partial a_i/\partial \xi_0, \partial a_i/\partial \xi_1, \partial a_i/\partial \xi_2$ $(i = 1, 2)$ also depend on the desired function u and its derivatives $\partial u/\partial x, \partial u/\partial y$ [we tacitly assume that the derivatives of the functions a_1, a_2, u which appear in formula (4) do actually exist].
   The Monge-Ampère equation (see Paragraph 2.4) has the form

$$\frac{\partial^2 u}{\partial x^2} \frac{\partial^2 u}{\partial y^2} - \frac{\partial^2 u}{\partial x \, \partial y} \frac{\partial^2 u}{\partial y \, \partial x} = f;$$

the reader will easily discover that this equation cannot be written in the divergent form (3), or (4), i.e., that there do not exist any functions a_0, a_1, a_2 such that equation (4) reduces to the Monge-Ampère equation.
   Consequently, this means that an equation of the form (3) is by far not the most general second order differential equation (in two variables); in the most general form, such an equation can be written as follows

$$F \left(x, y; u, \frac{\partial u}{\partial x}, \frac{\partial u}{\partial y}, \frac{\partial^2 u}{\partial x^2}, \frac{\partial^2 u}{\partial x \, \partial y}, \frac{\partial^2 u}{\partial y \, \partial x}, \frac{\partial^2 u}{\partial y^2} \right) = 0,$$

where $F = F(x, y; \xi_0, \xi_1, \xi_2, \xi_3, \xi_4, \xi_5, \xi_6)$ is a given function of nine variables defined for

$$(x, y) \in \Omega, \quad (\xi_0, \xi_1, ..., \xi_6) \in \mathbb{R}^7.$$

[We obtain the Monge-Ampère equation by choosing

$$F(x, y; \xi_0, ..., \xi_6) = \xi_3 \xi_6 - \xi_4 \xi_5 .]$$

   Equation (3) is thus a special case of a second order equation in two variables and, similarly, equation (2) is a special case of a second order equation in N variables $(N \geq 1)$. However, as already seen when discussing the examples of Chapter I, equations of type (2) or (3) appear frequently in applications; therefore, it is reasonable to investigate them in detail.
   Although we deal principally in this book with equations which have the form (2) (i.e., with equations in the divergent form), it is sometimes possible to apply some methods used in the sequel, with certain modifications, to general equations as well.

6.5. Euler equations. The so-called Euler equations encountered in variational calculus belong to the class of equations of the form (2): Let the functional

$$I(v) = \int_\Omega F\left(x; v(x), \frac{\partial v(x)}{\partial x_1}, \ldots, \frac{\partial v(x)}{\partial x_N}\right) dx$$

be given $[F = F(x; \xi_0, \xi_1, \ldots, \xi_N)$ is a given function of $2N + 1$ variables], and let the derivatives $\partial F/\partial \xi_i$, $i = 0, 1, \ldots, N$, exist. The equation

$$-\sum_{i=1}^N \frac{\partial}{\partial x_i}\left(\frac{\partial F}{\partial \xi_i}(x; u(x), \text{grad } u(x))\right) + \frac{\partial F}{\partial \xi_0}(x; u(x), \text{grad } u(x)) = 0 \quad \text{on} \quad \Omega$$

is called the Euler equation of the functional I. It is immediately seen that this is an equation of the form (2) with $f = 0$ and with the coefficients

$$a_i = \frac{\partial F}{\partial \xi_i}, \quad i = 0, 1, \ldots, N .$$

We note that the relation of equations of the form (2) to the problem of the minimum of a functional is discussed in Chapter IV.

6.6. Examples. (i) The minimal surface equation

$$-\sum_{i=1}^N \frac{\partial}{\partial x_i}\left(\frac{1}{\sqrt{(1 + |\text{grad } u|^2)}} \frac{\partial u}{\partial x_i}\right) = 0$$

(see Paragraph 4.4) is an Euler equation of the functional

$$I(v) = \int_\Omega \sqrt{(1 + |\text{grad } v|^2)} \, dx ,$$

i.e., the function F of the preceding paragraph has the form

$$F(x; \xi_0, \xi_1, \ldots, \xi_N) = (1 + \xi_1^2 + \ldots + \xi_N^2)^{1/2} .$$

(ii) The equation

$$-\frac{\partial}{\partial x}\left(m(|\text{grad } u|^2)\frac{\partial u}{\partial x}\right) - \frac{\partial}{\partial y}\left(m(|\text{grad } u|^2)\frac{\partial u}{\partial y}\right) = f(x, y)$$

(see Paragraph 2.2) is an Euler equation of the functional

$$I(v) = \int_\Omega \left[\frac{1}{2} M\left(\left(\frac{\partial u}{\partial x}\right)^2 + \left(\frac{\partial u}{\partial y}\right)^2\right) - f(x, y) \, u(x, y)\right] dx \, dy ,$$

i.e., the function F of the preceding paragraph has the form

$$F(x, y; \xi_0, \xi_1, \xi_2) = \tfrac{1}{2}M(\xi_1^2 + \xi_2^2) - f(x, y)\,\xi_0,$$

where the function $M = M(s)$ is determined by means of the function $m = m(t)$ as follows:

$$M(s) = \int_0^s m(t)\, ds.$$

SECTION 7. HIGHER ORDER EQUATIONS

7.1. In the preceding section, the notion of the equation of the second order was introduced. However, equations of higher order — namely the fourth order — were encountered in Chapter I (see Paragraph 4.4). Such equations will therefore be discussed in this section and the notion of equation of order $2k$ will be introduced. First of all, we introduce some new symbols.

7.2. Notation. Let N be a positive integer. The vector

$$\alpha = (\alpha_1, \alpha_2, \ldots, \alpha_N)$$

whose components are nonnegative integers α_i is called a *multi-index* (more precisely: an *N-dimensional multi-index*); the number

$$|\alpha| = \sum_{j=1}^{N} \alpha_j$$

is called the *length of the multi-index α*.

If α is a multi-index and $u = u(x)$ a function defined on the domain $\Omega \subset \mathbb{R}^N$, we denote by the symbol

$$D^\alpha u$$

the partial derivative

$$\frac{\partial^{|\alpha|} u}{\partial x_1^{\alpha_1} \partial x_2^{\alpha_2} \ldots \partial x_N^{\alpha_N}}.$$

The number of all N-dimensional multi-indexes of length at most k is denoted by $\varkappa$; we have

$$\varkappa = \varkappa(N, k) = \frac{(N + k)!}{N!\, k!}.$$

At the same time, this is the number of all (partial) derivatives of a function of N variables, from order zero through order k inclusive — in so much, of course, as we do not pay heed to the order of differentiation in the case of mixed derivatives and identify, e.g., the derivatives

$$\frac{\partial^2 u}{\partial x_1 \, \partial x_2} \quad \text{and} \quad \frac{\partial^2 u}{\partial x_2 \, \partial x_1} \, . \quad \dagger)$$

Furthermore, we introduce the symbol

$$\delta_k u$$

for the vector function whose components are all the derivatives of the function u of orders 0, 1, 2, ..., k:

$$\delta_k u = \{D^\alpha u\}_{|\alpha| \leq k} = \left\{ u, \frac{\partial u}{\partial x_1}, \ldots, \frac{\partial u}{\partial x_N}, \frac{\partial^2 u}{\partial x_1^2}, \ldots, \frac{\partial^k u}{\partial x_N^k} \right\}. \tag{1}$$

Thus, the vector $\delta_k u$ has $\varkappa$ components (the order of differentiation is immaterial). The components of $\delta_k u$ are ordered lexicographically, i.e., in the following way: The first component is the function u (i.e., the derivative of order zero), followed by derivatives of first order, then by derivatives of second order, etc., and, finally, by derivatives of order k. Derivatives of the same order s ($s \leq k$) will be arranged as follows: If $\alpha = (\alpha_1, \ldots, \alpha_N)$, $\beta = (\beta_1, \ldots, \beta_N)$ are two multi-indexes of length s, then the derivative $D^\alpha u$ precedes the derivative $D^\beta u$ if for some n from the set $\{1, 2, \ldots, N\}$ we have

$$\alpha_n > \beta_n, \quad \alpha_i = \beta_i \quad \text{for} \quad i = 1, \ldots, n-1 .$$

For $k = 1$, we have, e.g., $\varkappa = N + 1$ and

$$\delta_1 u = \{u, \text{grad } u\} = \left\{ u, \frac{\partial u}{\partial x_1}, \frac{\partial u}{\partial x_2}, \ldots, \frac{\partial u}{\partial x_N} \right\}.$$

For $k = 2$ and $N = 2$, we have $\varkappa = 6$ and

$$\delta_2 u = \left\{ u, \frac{\partial u}{\partial x}, \frac{\partial u}{\partial y}, \frac{\partial^2 u}{\partial x^2}, \frac{\partial^2 u}{\partial x \, \partial y}, \frac{\partial^2 u}{\partial y^2} \right\}.$$

$\dagger)$ Let us recall a classical result from differential calculus of functions of several variables which says: If a function $u = u(x)$ defined on the domain $\Omega \subset \mathbb{R}^N$ has the derivatives

$$\frac{\partial^2 u}{\partial x_1 \, \partial x_2} = \frac{\partial}{\partial x_1} \left(\frac{\partial u}{\partial x_2} \right) \quad \text{and} \quad \frac{\partial^2 u}{\partial x_2 \, \partial x_1} = \frac{\partial}{\partial x_2} \left(\frac{\partial u}{\partial x_1} \right)$$

and if these derivatives are continuous on Ω, then the order of differentiation is immaterial, i.e.,

$$\frac{\partial^2 u}{\partial x_1 \, \partial x_2} (x) = \frac{\partial^2 u}{\partial x_2 \, \partial x_1} (x)$$

holds for every $x \in \Omega$. Naturally, a similar assertion holds for derivatives of higher order as well.

In what follows, it will be seen that we are dealing with functions for which the order of differentiation is immaterial.

Denoting, further, by the symbol

$$\hat{\delta}_k u$$

the vector of all k-th derivatives of the function u, i.e.,

$$\hat{\delta}_k u = \{D^\alpha u\}_{|\alpha|=k}, \tag{2}$$

it is possible to split the vector $\delta_k u$ into two parts:

$$\delta_k u = \{\delta_{k-1} u, \hat{\delta}_k u\}.$$

The vector $\hat{\delta}_k u$ is sometimes called the principal part of the vector $\delta_k u$; in what follows, we will see that this is a reasonable definition.

If we wish to emphasize that the value of the vector function $\delta_k u$ at the point $x \in \Omega$ is concerned, we write

$$\delta_k u(x).$$

7.3. Equations of order $2k$. Let Ω be a domain in $\mathbb{R}^N$, $N \geq 1$, $k \in \mathbb{N}$, and let

$$a_\alpha = a_\alpha(x; \xi) \quad (\alpha \text{ are multi-indexes, } |\alpha| \leq k) \tag{3}$$

be functions of $N + \varkappa$ variables defined for

$$x \in \Omega, \quad \xi \in \mathbb{R}^\varkappa$$

[the number $\varkappa = \varkappa(N, k)$ was defined in Paragraph 7.2]; the components of the vector ξ are denoted by ξ_β, where the subscript β runs over the set of all multi-indexes of length at most k, and the components ξ_β are ordered lexicographically as above (see Paragraph 7.2). Thus, we have

$$\xi = \{\xi_\beta, |\beta| \leq k\}.$$

Furthermore, let $f = f(x)$ be a function defined on Ω.

Below, we investigate differential equations of the form

$$\sum_{|\alpha| \leq k} (-1)^{|\alpha|} D^\alpha a_\alpha(x; \delta_k u(x)) = f(x), \tag{4}$$

i.e., we look for a function $u = u(x)$ defined on Ω which satisfies equation (4) for all $x \in \Omega$.

Equation (4) is called a differential equation of order $2k$ (in divergent form); the functions a_k will be called the coefficients of equation (4) and the function f the right-hand side of equation (4).

7.4. Remarks. (i) In formula (4), summation in $\sum\limits_{|\alpha| \leq k}$ is over all the multi-indexes α of length at most k. The expression on the left-hand side of equation (4) represents a purely formal symbol here, since nothing has as yet been assumed about the functions a_α.

(ii) The reader will certainly have observed that the notation used for writing the equation in Paragraph 7.3 differs from the notation in Paragraph 6.1: We now deal with multi-indexes while in formula (6.2) "ordinary" summation subscripts were used. Naturally, equation (6.2) could be written in the form of (4) as well — it is a special case of equation (4) for $k = 1$; however, this will not be done in most cases, since the application of multi-indexes might confuse rather than clarify the matter for second order equations.†)

Thus, we make the convention that for second order equations the notation of Paragraph 6.1 will be used, as a rule; the notation using "ordinary" summation subscripts will also be used for equations of higher orders in cases where the number of variables remains small, i.e., for $N = 1$ or $N = 2$. Multi-indexes will be used in all cases when general considerations concerning equations of order $2k$ with large or unspecified k are in question.

7.5. Examples. (i) If all functions $a_\alpha = a_\alpha(x; \xi)$ from (3) are linear functions of the variables ξ_β, $|\beta| \leq k$, then equation (4) will be a linear differential equation of order $2k$.

Let us put, e.g., $N = 2$ [then $\varkappa = \frac{1}{2}(N + 1)(N + 2)$], and let us denote by M the set of the following N-dimensional multi-indexes:

$$(2, 0, 0, \ldots, 0, 0) ; \quad (0, 2, 0, \ldots, 0, 0) ; \quad \ldots; \quad (0, 0, 0, \ldots, 0, 2) .$$

Now, let us define the functions $a_\alpha = a_\alpha(x; \xi)$ for $|\alpha| \leq 2$ as follows:

$$a_\alpha(x; \xi) = \sum_{\beta \in M} \xi_\beta \quad \text{for} \quad \alpha \in M ,$$

$$a_\alpha(x; \xi) = 0 \quad \text{for} \quad \alpha \notin M, \ |\alpha| \leq 2$$

(thus, in particular, $a_\alpha = 0$ for multi-indexes α such that $|\alpha| = 0$ and $|\alpha| = 1$). Equation (4) which corresponds to this choice of the coefficients a_α has the form

$$\sum_{\alpha \in M} D^\alpha (\sum_{\beta \in M} D^\beta u) = f(x) \tag{5}$$

[for $\alpha \in M$ we have $|\alpha| = 2$ and, consequently, $(-1)^{|\alpha|} = 1$]. Equation (4) is thus written in terms of multi-indexes. However, it can also be written using "ordinary" summation subscripts:

$$\sum_{i=1}^{N} \frac{\partial^2}{\partial x_i^2} \left(\sum_{j=1}^{N} \frac{\partial^2 u}{\partial x_j^2} \right) = f(x) , \tag{6}$$

---

†) The notation which makes use of multi-indexes can be "rewritten" using ordinary summation subscripts and vice-versa; this is rather complicated, however, and not very helpful. As far as technical problems arising here are concerned, the reader may learn more in Chapter 31 of the book [80]. See also the next paragraph.

i.e., we have the equation $\Delta^2 u = f$ where $\Delta^2 = \Delta(\Delta)$ is the so-called biharmonic operator already encountered (for $N = 2$) in Paragraph 1.5.

Formulas (5) and (6) represent the same equation. Comparing them shows that the notation using multi-indexes is, in specific cases, not always the most advantageous: The notation of (6) is clearer and does not call for the introduction of the multi-index set M.

(ii) Let $k = 2$, and let M be the set of multi-indexes from Example (i). Let $p > 2$, and let us define the functions a_α for $|\alpha| \leq 2$ as follows:

$$a_\alpha(x; \xi) = \left| \sum_{\beta \in M} \xi_\beta \right|^{p-2} \left(\sum_{\beta \in M} \xi_\beta \right) \quad \text{for} \quad \alpha \in M,$$

$$a_\alpha(x; \xi) = 0 \qquad\qquad\qquad \text{for} \quad \alpha \notin M, \; |\alpha| \leq 2.$$

Equation (4) which corresponds to this choice of the coefficients a_α assumes the form

$$\sum_{\alpha \in M} D^\alpha \left(\left| \sum_{\beta \in M} D^\beta u \right|^{p-2} \sum_{\beta \in M} D^\beta u \right) = f(x);$$

it is the equation

$$\Delta(|\Delta u|^{p-2} \Delta u) = f(x),$$

where we find the so-called nonlinear biharmonic operator (see Paragraph 2.5) on the left-hand side.

(iii) Let $k = 2$ and $N = 2$ (and, thus, $\varkappa = 6$). Then we have to define altogether 6 functions,

$$a_\alpha(x, y; \xi), \quad (x, y) \in \Omega, \quad \xi = (\xi_0, \xi_1, ..., \xi_5) \in \mathbb{R}^6$$

(recall that the components $\xi_0, \xi_1, \xi_2, \xi_3, \xi_4, \xi_5$ of the vector ξ correspond, respectively, to the functions $u, \partial u/\partial x, \partial u/\partial y, \partial^2 u/\partial x^2, \partial^2 u/\partial x\, \partial y, \partial^2 u/\partial y^2$). †) Let us define the functions a_α as follows:

$$a_{(2,0)}(x, y; \xi) = g(\xi)(\xi_3 + \tfrac{1}{2}\xi_5),$$
$$a_{(0,2)}(x, y; \xi) = g(\xi)(\xi_5 + \tfrac{1}{2}\xi_3),$$
$$a_{(1,1)}(x, y; \xi) = g(\xi)\,\xi_4,$$
$$a_\alpha(x, y; \xi) = 0 \quad \text{for} \quad |\alpha| = 0, |\alpha| = 1,$$

where $g(\xi) = G(\xi_3^2 + \xi_4^2 + \xi_5^2 + \xi_3\xi_5)$, $G = G(t)$ is a given function of the variable $t \geq 0$.

---

†) We are guilty of a certain inconsistency here: The components of the vector ξ are not numbered by means of multi-indexes although there are α multi-indexes with the coefficients a_α. To be consistent, we would have to write the components of the vector ξ as follows:

$$\xi_{(0,0)}, \xi_{(1,0)}, \xi_{(0,1)}, \xi_{(2,0)}, \xi_{(1,1)}, \xi_{(0,2)}.$$

Equation (4), corresponding to this choice of the coefficients a_α and written using "ordinary" summation subscripts, has the following form:

$$\frac{\partial^2}{\partial x^2}\left[\mathscr{G}(u)\left(\frac{\partial^2 u}{\partial x^2} + \frac{1}{2}\frac{\partial^2 u}{\partial y^2}\right)\right] + \frac{\partial^2}{\partial x\,\partial y}\left[\mathscr{G}(u)\,\frac{\partial^2 u}{\partial x\,\partial y}\right] +$$

$$+ \frac{\partial^2}{\partial y^2}\left[\mathscr{G}(u)\left(\frac{\partial^2 u}{\partial y^2} + \frac{1}{2}\frac{\partial^2 u}{\partial x^2}\right)\right] = f(x, y),$$

where

$$\mathscr{G}(u) = G\left(\left(\frac{\partial^2 u}{\partial x^2}\right)^2 + \left(\frac{\partial^2 u}{\partial y^2}\right)^2 + \left(\frac{\partial^2 u}{\partial x\,\partial y}\right)^2 + \frac{\partial^2 u}{\partial x^2}\frac{\partial^2 u}{\partial y^2}\right);$$

it is thus equation (2.10) describing the elasto-plastic deformation of a plate — see Paragraph 2.5, where $g(H(u))$ was used in place of $\mathscr{G}(u)$.

SECTION 8. SPACES OF CONTINUOUS FUNCTIONS. SOLUTION OF A DIFFERENTIAL EQUATION

8.1. Hitherto, we have not stated what it is that we understand by the solution of equation (7.4) or (6.2). In this book, the concept of solution will be encountered in various senses; in this section, we shall define the so-called classical solution. However, certain appropriate sets of functions will first be introduced.

8.2. The spaces $C^k(\Omega)$. (i) Let Ω be a domain in $\mathbb{R}^N$, $N \geq 1$, and let k be a non-negative integer. By the symbol

$$C^k(\Omega)$$

we denote the set of all functions $u = u(x)$ defined on Ω all of whose derivatives $D^\alpha u$ of order $|\alpha| \leq k$ are continuous in Ω.

(ii) By the symbol

$$C^0(\bar{\Omega})$$

we denote the set of all functions $u = u(x)$ defined on $\bar{\Omega} = \Omega \cup \partial\Omega$ which are continuous on $\bar{\Omega}$. Obviously, we have

$$C^0(\bar{\Omega}) \subset C^0(\Omega) ;$$

moreover, the functions from $C^0(\bar{\Omega})$ are continuous on the boundary $\partial\Omega$ as well.

(iii) For a positive integer k, we denote by the symbol

$$C^k(\bar{\Omega})$$

the set of all those functions $u \in C^k(\Omega)$ whose derivatives $D^\alpha u$ have the following property: For every derivative $D^\alpha u$ $(|\alpha| \leq k)$ there exists a function $v_\alpha \in C^0(\bar{\Omega})$ for which

$$D^\alpha u(x) = v_\alpha(x) \quad \text{holds for} \quad x \in \Omega . \tag{1}$$

[In other words: The function u belongs to $C^k(\bar{\Omega})$ if all its derivatives of at most the k-th order are continuous inside $\bar{\Omega}$, i.e., in Ω, and if it is possible to extend each of these derivatives continuously to $\bar{\Omega}$, i.e., to the boundary $\partial\Omega$.]

If $u \in C^k(\bar{\Omega})$, we shall say for short that $D^\alpha u \in C^0(\bar{\Omega})$ for $|\alpha| \leq k$ although — strictly speaking — we can define the derivative of the function u at the point x for $x \in \Omega$ but not for $x \in \partial\Omega$. By the value of $D^\alpha u(x)$ for $x \in \partial\Omega$ we mean the value of $v_\alpha(x)$, where v_α is the function from (1).

Let us note that for $N = 1$, when Ω is an interval (a, b), the boundary $\partial\Omega$ consists of the points a and b and the derivative at these points is then the left-hand derivative (at the point b) and the right-hand derivative (at the point a).

(iv) Let $u = u(x)$ be a function defined on $\Omega \subset \mathbb{R}^N$, and let M be the set of those points $x \in \Omega$ for which $u(x) \neq 0$. The closure of the set M (in the space $\mathbb{R}^N$) is denoted by

$$\text{supp } u$$

and is called the *support* of the function u.

By the symbol

$$C_0^k(\Omega)$$

we denote the set of all functions $u \in C^k(\Omega)$ for which

$$\text{supp } u \subset \Omega .$$

The function $u \in C_0^k(\Omega)$ is then identically equal to zero in some neighbourhood of the boundary $\partial\Omega$.

(v) We put

$$C_0^\infty(\Omega) = \bigcap_{k=0}^{\infty} C_0^k(\Omega) ,$$

$$C^\infty(\bar{\Omega}) = \bigcap_{k=0}^{\infty} C^k(\bar{\Omega}) .$$

8.3. The space $C^{0,1}(\bar{\Omega})$. Let $u = u(x)$ be a function defined on $\bar{\Omega} = \Omega \cup \partial\Omega$. We say that this function satisfies the *Lipschitz condition* on $\bar{\Omega}$ if a constant $c > 0$ exists such that for all $x, y \in \bar{\Omega}$ the inequality

$$|u(x) - u(y)| \leq c|x - y|$$

is satisfied.

By the symbol

$$C^{0,1}(\bar{\Omega})$$

we denote the set of all functions $u \in C^0(\bar{\Omega})$ which satisfy the Lipschitz condition on $\bar{\Omega}$.

(i) The Lipschitz condition implies that the function u is continuous on $\bar{\Omega}$. Moreover, it implies that the difference quotient of the function u is bounded on $\bar{\Omega}$: For $x, y \in \bar{\Omega}$, $x \neq y$, we have

$$\frac{|u(x) - u(y)|}{|x - y|} \leqq c .$$

The existence of the derivative of the function u does not, however, follow from this; nevertheless, the following important assertion holds, the proof of which can be found, e.g., in [81]:

(ii) If u is a function from $C^{0,1}(\bar{\Omega})$, then the first order partial derivatives

$$\frac{\partial u}{\partial x_i} , \quad i = 1, ..., N ,$$

exist for almost all $x \in \bar{\Omega}$ †); for these x, we have

$$\left| \frac{\partial u(x)}{\partial x_i} \right| \leqq c .$$

8.4. The classical solution of a differential equation. Assume that the functions $a_\alpha = a_\alpha(x; \xi)$ from (7.3), defined for $x \in \Omega$ and $\xi \in \mathbb{R}^\varkappa$, have continuous derivatives of order $|\alpha|$ with respect to all variables, i.e., that

$$a_\alpha \in C^{|\alpha|}(\Omega \times \mathbb{R}^\varkappa) .$$

Furthermore, let $f = f(x)$ be a given function from $C^0(\Omega)$.

We say that the function $u = u(x)$ defined on Ω is *the classical solution* of the equation

$$\sum_{|\alpha| \leqq k} (-1)^{|\alpha|} D^\alpha a_\alpha(x; \delta_k u(x)) = f(x) \quad \text{on} \quad \Omega \tag{2}$$

if

$$u \in C^{2k}(\Omega)$$

and if equation (2) is satisfied for all $x \in \Omega$.

8.5. Remark. The concept of classical solution introduced in the preceding paragraph is quite a natural concept. As far as this chapter is concerned, it is an auxiliary concept; for this reason, we are not going to pursue its detailed analysis. In fact, it can

---

†) We say that a property is satisfied *almost everywhere in* $\bar{\Omega}$ if it is satisfied for all x in the set $\bar{\Omega} - M$, where the set $M \subset \bar{\Omega}$ has zero Lebesgue measure.

The reader may find the properties of Lebesgue measure discussed, e.g., in the book [51].

immediately be seen that the assumptions are unnecessarily strong: For equation (2) to make reasonable ("classical") sense, it is sufficient that the derivative $D^\alpha a_\alpha$ exist [this derivative need not be continuous and we do not need the other derivatives of order $|\alpha|$ — see, e.g., Paragraph 6.2, formula (6.4), from where it is clear which derivatives of the coefficients of the equation are needed]; similarly, we could drop the requirement of continuity of the derivatives of order $2k$ of the function u and make do with their existence (naturally, for mixed derivatives the order of differentiation need not then be immaterial); it is even possible to drop the requirement of continuity of the function f.

In what follows (see Chapter III), we will deal with yet another concept of solution which is more general.

SECTION 9. BOUNDARY CONDITIONS

9.1. Recalling the examples of Chapter I, we see that there we looked not just for any, arbitrary, solution of the differential equation, but for a solution which satisfied, in addition, certain conditions on the boundary $\partial\Omega$. These conditions possessed reasonable physical meaning: For instance, a given equation describes the deflection of a plate, but it does not take into account whether the plate is clamped along its edge or not, and does not take into account the type of fixing (clamped, supported, hinge-connected, etc.). These specific conditions express the requirements on the behaviour of the solution u on $\partial\Omega$ — the so-called *boundary conditions*.

For instance, put $N = 1$ and choose the interval $(0, 1)$ as the domain Ω. The ordinary differential equation

$$-\frac{d}{dx}\left(\left(\frac{du}{dx}\right)^2\right) = 0 \quad \text{for} \quad x \in (0, 1) \tag{1}$$

is an equation of the type (6.2): Its coefficients are of the form

$$a_1(x; \xi_0, \xi_1) = \xi_1^2, \quad a_0(x; \xi_0, \xi_1) = 0.$$

The solution of this equation is easily found: It is the function

$$u(x) = ax + b,$$

where a, b are arbitrary real constants. Thus, we have found the classical solution of differential equation (1), but not a unique one. If we require now that the solution u of equation (1) satisfy, on the boundary $\partial\Omega$ (which consists in this case of the points $x = 0$ and $x = 1$), conditions of the type

$$u(0) = c_0, \quad u(1) = c_1, \tag{2}$$

where c_0, c_1 are given constants, then the solution is now determined uniquely, indeed: The boundary conditions (2) lead to the system of equations

$$a \cdot 0 + b = c_0 ,$$
$$a \cdot 1 + b = c_1$$

for the unknowns a, b. We find that $b = c_0$ and $a = c_1 - c_0$, so that the function $u = u(x)$ which satisfies equation (1) with boundary conditions (2) has the form

$$u(x) = (c_1 - c_0) x + c_0 .$$

Boundary conditions are thus given on the boundary $\partial \Omega$ of the domain $\Omega \subset \mathbb{R}^N$. On the whole, in order to be able to formulate the boundary conditions, certain requirements have to be imposed on the boundary $\partial \Omega$. Therefore, we now proceed to describe the type of domain which we shall work with below; they are those domains whose boundaries are "reasonable" in a certain sense.

9.2. Domains with a "Lipschitz boundary". Let Ω be a bounded domain in $\mathbb{R}^N$, and let us assume that for every point $x \in \partial \Omega$ there exist numbers $r > 0$ and $\varepsilon > 0$, both dependent on x, and a Cartesian coordinate system $(y_1, y_2, ..., y_{N-1}, y_N)$, also dependent on x, with the following properties:

If we denote by $K = K(x, r)$ the closed ball in $\mathbb{R}^N$ with center at the point x and radius r, by Γ the "surface" $\partial \Omega \cap K$, and by Δ the projection of the "surface" Γ onto the hyperplane given by the equation $y_N = 0$, then there exists a function $a = a(y_1, y_2, ..., y_{N-1})$ defined on Δ such that

(a) $\qquad\qquad\qquad\qquad a \in C^{0,1}(\Delta)$

(see Paragraph 8.3);

(b) the "surface" Γ is given by the equation

$$y_N = a(y_1, y_2, ..., y_{N-1})$$

[in other words:

$$\Gamma = \{(y_1, ..., y_{N-1}, y_N); \quad y_N = a(y_1, ..., y_{N-1}), (y_1, ..., y_{N-1}) \in \Delta\}] ;$$

(c) the set

$$M_1 = \{(y_1, ..., y_{N-1}, y_N); (y_1, ..., y_{N-1}) \in \Delta ,$$
$$a(y_1, ..., y_{N-1}) - \varepsilon < y_N < a(y_1, ..., y_{N-1})\}$$

is a part of the domain Ω;

(d) the set

$$M_2 = \{(y_1, ..., y_{N-1}, y_N); (y_1, ..., y_{N-1}) \in \Delta ,$$
$$a(y_1, ..., y_{N-1}) < y_N < a(y_1, ..., y_{N-1}) + \varepsilon\}$$

lies outside the set $\bar{\Omega}$.

The set of all the domains of the above type is denoted by the symbol

$$\mathscr{C}^{0,1}.$$

Roughly speaking, it is the set of those domains whose boundaries $\partial\Omega$ are (locally) describable by means of a function which satisfies the Lipschitz condition, while the domain Ω lies "on one side of the boundary $\partial\Omega$" and the outside of the domain Ω "lies on the other side"; see also Fig. 9.2a.

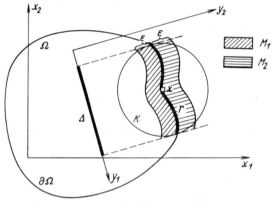

Fig. 9.2a

Now, let us illustrate the various possibilities using some more figures (all of them for a plane domain, i.e., for $N = 2$).

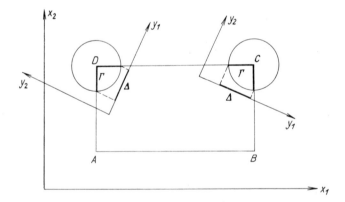

Fig. 9.2b

1) If Ω is the rectangle $ABCD$ of Fig. 9.2b, then Ω belongs to $\mathscr{C}^{0,1}$. Indeed, if the point $x \in \partial\Omega$ is some point lying within anyone of the sides, then the corresponding surface Γ will always be described by a constant function if we, moreover, choose the coordinate system in a suitable way: For points along the segment CD we choose

as the coordinate system (y_1, y_2) the original system (x_1, x_2), for points along segment AB we choose the system (y_1, y_2) in such a way that $y_1 = -x_1$, $y_2 = -x_2$, for points along the segment BC we choose the system so that $y_1 = -x_2$, $y_2 = x_1$, etc. Naturally, none of the above systems is applicable to any of the vertices A, B, C, D; the choice of the systems for the points C and D is shown in Fig. 9.2b and the corresponding "surface" Γ will be described there by a piecewise linear function.

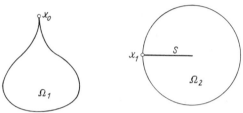

Fig. 9.2c

2) The domains shown in Fig. 9.2c do not belong to the class $\mathscr{C}^{0,1}$: The boundary of the domain Ω_1 can indeed be represented by a function in the neighbourhood of the point x_0, but this function will not satisfy the Lipschitz condition. As far as the domain Ω_2 is concerned (Ω_2 is a circle with the segment S removed), it is precisely the points of the segment S which are the source of trouble: In the neighbourhood of the point x_1, the boundary $\partial\Omega$ cannot be described by a function at all; the points on S can no doubt be described, but the corresponding sets M_1 and M_2 will both be parts of the domain Ω_2.

Domains of the type of $\mathscr{C}^{0,1}$ are introduced, among other reasons, because of the fact that they enable the introduction of the surface integral and the vector of the outward normal to $\partial\Omega$. In fact, a function $a \in C^{0,1}(\Delta)$ which describes a part Γ of the boundary $\partial\Omega$ has — in accordance with Paragraph 8.3 (ii) — derivatives

$$\frac{\partial a}{\partial y_j}, \quad j = 1, 2, ..., N - 1,$$

almost everywhere in Δ. Therefore, the outward normal to $\partial\Omega$ exists almost everywhere on Γ: Indeed, if

$$y = (y_1, ..., y_{N-1}, a(y_1, ..., y_{N-1}))$$

is a point on Γ at which the function a has first order partial derivatives, then the vector of the outward normal $v = (v_1, v_2, ..., v_N)$ to $\partial\Omega$ has the following components at the point $y \in \Gamma$:

$$v_i = \left(1 + \sum_{j=1}^{N-1} \left(\frac{\partial a}{\partial y_j}\right)^2\right)^{-1/2} \frac{\partial a}{\partial y_i}, \quad i = 1, 2, ..., N - 1,$$

$$v_N = \left(1 + \sum_{j=1}^{N-1} \left(\frac{\partial a}{\partial y_j}\right)^2\right)^{-1/2}. \tag{3}$$

The vector of the outward normal is not defined for all points $y \in \Gamma$ but only for those at which partial derivatives of the function a exist. However, since these derivatives exist almost everywhere on Δ, the vector of the outward normal exists almost everywhere on Γ. However, we may assume that the vector ν exists everywhere on Γ: It is enough to give its definition on the set of measure zero upon which it is not given by formulas (3).

If u is a function defined on $\partial\Omega$, it is possible to define the surface integral: We define

$$\int_{\Gamma} u(x) \, dS = \int_{\Delta} u(y_1, \ldots, y_{N-1}, a(y_1, \ldots, y_{N-1})) \cdot$$

$$\cdot \left[1 + \sum_{i=1}^{N-1} \left(\frac{\partial a}{\partial y_i} (y_1, \ldots, y_{N-1}) \right)^2 \right]^{1/2} dy_1 \ldots dy_{N-1}$$

and the integral

$$\int_{\partial\Omega} u(x) \, dS$$

can then be introduced by suitably "combining" the integrals over the individual "areas" Γ which cover the boundary $\partial\Omega$. We will not go into the details of this problem here; readers interested in these details are referred to the book [80], Chap. 28.

9.3. Boundary conditions. In what follows, we shall assume throughout that the domain Ω is of the $\mathscr{C}^{0,1}$ type. Now, it is possible to introduce the concept of boundary condition, whose physical as well as mathematical meaning was mentioned in Paragraph 9.1.

The boundary condition is again nothing other than a requirement that the function u satisfy a certain "differential equation", this time not on Ω but in fact on $\partial\Omega$. Here, the equation may even be a "differential equation of order zero" as illustrated, e.g., by conditions of the type of

$$u|_{\partial\Omega} = g \,,$$

encountered in Chapter I.

In Paragraph 6.4, we exhibited the most general form of a second order differential equation $(N = 2)$; analogously, the boundary condition can be expressed most generally as follows:

Let s be a nonnegative integer and σ the number of multi-indexes of length s (see Paragraph 7.2); let the function

$$\Phi(x; \eta) \,, \tag{4}$$

defined for $x \in \partial\Omega$ and $\eta \in \mathbb{R}^\sigma$, be given, and let the function $u \in C^s(\overline{\Omega})$ satisfy the condition

$$\Phi(x; \delta_s u(x)) = 0 \quad \text{on} \quad \partial\Omega \tag{5}$$

[i.e., the values of the vector function $\delta_s u(x)$ are considered for $x \in \partial\Omega$; the values of the derivatives of the function u on $\partial\Omega$ are understood here in the sense of its continuous extension — see Paragraph 8.2 (iii)]. At the same time, we assume that the function Φ does indeed depend upon at least one of those components of the vector η for which we substitute derivatives of the s-th order in (5), i.e., we assume that at least one s-th derivative of the function u occurs in (5).

Condition (5) is then called a *boundary condition of the s-th order*.

9.4. Boundary value problem. We speak of a boundary value problem if we are given

1) a differential equation [of the form (7.4)];
2) a certain number of boundary conditions (independent in a certain sense).

(What we understand by the solution of a boundary value problem will be discussed in Paragraph 10.2.)

The number of boundary conditions, their order and the actual form of the corresponding functions Φ need generally bear no relation to the differential equation, i.e., to its order $2k$ and to the actual form of the functions a_α, $|\alpha| \leq k$. However, there is a close relation between the differential equation and the boundary conditions in particular physical problems (examples of which were given in Chapter I). Because of this, we are not going to prescribe boundary conditions entirely arbitrarily here; we shall observe several principles which reflect physical reality and which are also advantageous for the mathematical investigation of the problem. The principles are the following:

(a) For a differential equation of order $2k$ we shall consider k boundary conditions, i.e., we shall give k functions

$$\Phi_1, \Phi_2, ..., \Phi_k .$$

(b) The function Φ_i will express a boundary condition of order s_i; the numbers $s_1, s_2, ..., s_k$ will all be different here and we will have

$$0 \leq s_i \leq 2k - 1 ,$$

i.e., we shall consider boundary conditions of order at most $(2k - 1)$.

Boundary conditions of order at most $(k - 1)$ are called *stable* boundary conditions (for an equation of order $2k$), while boundary conditions of higher order are called *unstable* boundary conditions.†)

As a rule, we shall not work with boundary conditions in their general form (5). We present below several examples with typical boundary conditions as they occur in practical problems and as encountered predominantly in the sequel.

---

†) The reasons for using the terms "stable" and "unstable" are explained, e.g., in the book [80], Chap. 32.

9.5. The Dirichlet problem. Let φ_0, φ_1, ..., φ_{k-1} be given functions defined on $\partial\Omega$ and consider an equation of order $2k$. Boundary conditions expressed by

$$\frac{\partial^i u}{\partial v^i} = \varphi_i \quad \text{on} \quad \partial\Omega \quad (i = 0, 1, ..., k-1)$$

or, in other words, by

$$u = \varphi_0 \qquad \text{on} \quad \partial\Omega\,,$$

$$\frac{\partial u}{\partial v} = \varphi_1 \qquad \text{on} \quad \partial\Omega\,,$$

$$\frac{\partial^2 u}{\partial v^2} = \varphi_2 \qquad \text{on} \quad \partial\Omega\,,$$

$$\vdots$$

$$\frac{\partial^{k-1} u}{\partial v^{k-1}} = \varphi_{k-1} \quad \text{on} \quad \partial\Omega\,, \tag{6}$$

where derivatives of the i-th order in the direction of the outward normal v to $\partial\Omega$ appear on the left-hand sides, are stable boundary conditions: Namely, we have

$$\frac{\partial u}{\partial v} = \sum_{r=1}^{N} v_r \frac{\partial u}{\partial x_r}\,,$$

$$\frac{\partial^2 u}{\partial v^2} = \sum_{r=1}^{N} \sum_{s=1}^{N} v_r v_s \frac{\partial^2 u}{\partial x_r \, \partial x_s}\,,$$

etc., and generally,

$$\frac{\partial^i u}{\partial v^i} = \sum_{|\alpha|=i} \frac{i!}{\alpha!} v_1^{\alpha_1} \dots v_N^{\alpha_N} D^\alpha u$$

(where α is a multi-index, $\alpha!$ denotes the number $\alpha_1! \, \alpha_2! \dots \alpha_N!$, v_j is the j-th component of the vector of the outward normal v and the values of the derivatives are considered on $\partial\Omega$), so that conditions (6) are in fact of the form (5), i.e., of the form

$$\Phi_i(x; \hat{\delta}_i u(x)) = 0 \quad \text{for} \quad x \in \partial\Omega$$

(the symbol $\hat{\delta}_i u$ was introduced in Paragraph 7.2), where the function $\Phi_i = \Phi_i(x; \eta)$ depends, appart from x, only on those η_α for which $|\alpha| = i$ and the dependence is moreover linear: We have

$$\Phi_i(x; \eta) = \sum_{|\alpha|=i} \frac{i!}{\alpha!} v_1^{\alpha_1}(x) \dots v_N^{\alpha_N}(x)\, \eta_\alpha - \varphi_i(x)\,, \quad i = 0, 1, ..., k-1$$

$[v_j = v_j(x)$ is the j-th component of the vector of the outward normal v to $\partial\Omega$ at the point $x \in \partial\Omega]$. We also see that conditions (6) actually include derivatives of order at most $(k-1)$.

The boundary value problem which consists of looking for the solution of equation (7.4) of order $2k$ with boundary conditions (6) is called the *Dirichlet problem* for equation (7.4).

Assume that all the functions φ_i $(i = 0, 1, ..., k - 1)$ are identically equal to zero (on $\partial\Omega$). Then the boundary conditions (6) assume the form

$$u\big|_{\partial\Omega} = \frac{\partial u}{\partial \nu}\bigg|_{\partial\Omega} = \ldots = \frac{\partial^{k-1}}{\partial \nu^{k-1}}\bigg|_{\partial\Omega} = 0 \;\dagger) \tag{7}$$

(we call them homogeneous boundary conditions). Let us note that conditions (7) can be reformulated in the form

$$D^\alpha u\big|_{\partial\Omega} = 0 \quad \text{for all } \alpha \text{ such that } |\alpha| \leq k - 1 . \tag{8}$$

The number of boundary conditions in (8) is

$$\varkappa(k - 1, N) = \frac{(k + N - 1)!}{(k - 1)! \, N!} ,$$

thus — in general — larger than k and larger than in (7). This is, essentially, in conflict with principle (a) of Paragraph 9.4. However, the conflict is illusory; indeed, the conditions in (8) are dependent in a certain sense and it can be shown (under certain assumptions concerning the domain Ω) that conditions (7) and (8) are equivalent.

Let us try to illustrate this equivalence for $k = 2$, $N = 2$: In this case, conditions (7) reduce to

$$u\big|_{\partial\Omega} = 0 , \quad \frac{\partial u}{\partial \nu}\bigg|_{\partial\Omega} = 0 , \tag{$*$}$$

while conditions (8) are as follows:

$$u\big|_{\partial\Omega} = 0 , \quad \frac{\partial u}{\partial x}\bigg|_{\partial\Omega} = 0 , \quad \frac{\partial u}{\partial y}\bigg|_{\partial\Omega} = 0 . \tag{$**$}$$

Since

$$\frac{\partial u}{\partial \nu} = \nu_x \frac{\partial u}{\partial x} + \nu_y \frac{\partial u}{\partial y} \quad \text{and} \quad \frac{\partial u}{\partial \tau} = -\nu_y \frac{\partial u}{\partial x} + \nu_x \frac{\partial u}{\partial y} ,$$

$\dagger)$ As a matter of fact, the symbol $(\partial^i u/\partial \nu^i)\big|_{\partial\Omega}$ is illogical for $i \geq 1$, since the normal ν is defined on $\partial\Omega$ only and, therefore, the derivative in the direction of the normal is defined on $\partial\Omega$ only and it is not necessary to discuss its restriction to $\partial\Omega$. However, we hope the reader will bear with this illogicality, commited in the interests of brevity so that we may write

$$\text{``}\frac{\partial^i u}{\partial \nu^i}\bigg|_{\partial\Omega} = 0\text{''} \quad \text{instead of} \quad \text{``}\frac{\partial^i u}{\partial \nu^i}(x) = 0 \quad \text{for} \quad x \in \partial\Omega\text{''} .$$

where v_x, v_y are the components of the vector of the outward normal to $\partial\Omega$ and $\partial u/\partial\tau$ is the derivative in the direction of the tangent to $\partial\Omega$, we have

$$\frac{\partial u}{\partial x} = \frac{\partial u}{\partial v}\,v_x - \frac{\partial u}{\partial\tau}\,v_y\,, \qquad \frac{\partial u}{\partial y} = \frac{\partial u}{\partial v}\,v_y + \frac{\partial u}{\partial\tau}\,v_x\,.$$

From this, we see at once that conditions (∗) and (∗∗) are equivalent: Indeed, the condition $u|_{\partial\Omega} = 0$ implies $(\partial u/\partial\tau)|_{\partial\Omega} = 0$.

Conditions (8) are discussed here because they are precisely the conditions we shall work with later and because they are "more tractable" than conditions (7) (e.g., they do not include the concept of the normal to $\partial\Omega$).

For more details on the equivalence of conditions (7) and (8) see [68].

9.6. Boundary value problem for a second order equation. Consider a differential equation of the second order — e.g., in the form (6.2). We then impose just a single boundary condition in line with principle (a) of Paragraph 9.5.

(i) Consider the boundary condition

$$u = \varphi \quad \text{on} \quad \partial\Omega\,, \tag{9}$$

where φ is a given function defined on $\partial\Omega$. In fact, this is condition (6) of the preceding paragraph, so that the boundary value problem for which (6.2) is to be solved under condition (9) is the *Dirichlet problem* for equation (6.2). (We have already discussed such problems in Chapter I — see Paragraph 1.4.)

(ii) Consider the boundary condition

$$\frac{\partial u}{\partial v} = \varphi \quad \text{on} \quad \partial\Omega\,, \tag{10}$$

i.e.,

$$v_1\frac{\partial u}{\partial x_1} + v_2\frac{\partial u}{\partial x_2} + \ldots + v_N\frac{\partial u}{\partial x_N} = \varphi \quad \text{on} \quad \partial\Omega\,,$$

where φ is again a given function on $\partial\Omega$. This condition is unstable since we are considering a second order equation, i.e., $k = 1$, and condition (10) is of first order, i.e., of order $2k - 1$.

The boundary value problem in which equation (6.2) is to be solved under condition (10) is called the *Neumann problem* for equation (6.2). (Such problems were discussed in Chapter I as well — see Paragraph 1.4.)

(iii) Consider the condition

$$\frac{\partial u}{\partial v} + hu = \varphi \quad \text{on} \quad \partial\Omega\,, \tag{11}$$

where $h = h(x)$ and $\varphi = \varphi(x)$ are given functions defined on $\partial\Omega$, $h(x) \geq h_0 > 0$. This is again an unstable boundary condition.

The boundary value problem with condition (11) is called the *Newton problem* for equation (6.2).

(iv) Consider the condition

$$s_1(x)\frac{\partial u}{\partial x_1} + s_2(x)\frac{\partial u}{\partial x_2} + \ldots + s_N(x)\frac{\partial u}{\partial x_N} = \varphi(x), \quad x \in \partial\Omega, \tag{12}$$

where $s_i = s_i(x)$, $\varphi = \varphi(x)$ are given functions on $\partial\Omega$,

$$\sum_{i=1}^{N} s_i^2(x) = 1.$$

Condition (12) is again unstable; it can be written in the form

$$\frac{\partial u}{\partial s} = \varphi \quad \text{on} \quad \partial\Omega,$$

where the derivative in the direction of the vector $s = (s_1, s_2, \ldots, s_N)$ appears on the left-hand side; naturally, the vector s varies with $x \in \partial\Omega$.

The boundary value problem with the boundary condition (12) is called the *problem with oblique derivative* for equation (6.2). In the special case of $s_i(x) = v_i(x)$ $(i = 1, \ldots, N)$, the problem with oblique derivative reduces to the Neumann problem.

(v) Let us assume that the boundary $\partial\Omega$ is divided into two parts Γ_1 and Γ_2, and consider the boundary condition of the form

$$u = \varphi_1 \quad \text{on} \quad \Gamma_1,$$

$$\frac{\partial u}{\partial v} = \varphi_2 \quad \text{on} \quad \Gamma_2, \tag{13}$$

where φ_1 and φ_2 are given functions defined on Γ_1 and Γ_2, respectively. The boundary value problem in which equation (6.2) has to be solved under conditions (13) is called the *mixed problem* for equation (6.2).

In fact, condition (13) is a condition of type (5): Indeed, it may be written in the form

$$a(x)\, u + b(x)\frac{\partial u}{\partial v} = a(x)\, \varphi_1(x) + b(x)\, \varphi_2(x), \quad x \in \partial\Omega,$$

i.e., with the aid of the function

$$\Phi = \Phi(x; \eta_0, \eta_1, \ldots, \eta_N) = a(x)\left[\eta_0 - \varphi_1(x)\right] + b(x)\left[\sum_{i=1}^{N} v_i(x)\, \eta_i - \varphi_2(x)\right]$$

defined for $x \in \partial\Omega$ and $(\eta_0, \eta_1, \ldots, \eta_N) \in \mathbb{R}^{N+1}$, while the functions a and b are defined as follows:

$$a(x) = \begin{cases} 1 & \text{for} \quad x \in \Gamma_1, \\ 0 & \text{for} \quad x \in \Gamma_2, \end{cases} \qquad b(x) = 1 - a(x)$$

[as before, $v_i(x)$ is the i-th component of the vector of the outward normal v to $\partial\Omega$ at the point $x \in \partial\Omega$].

9.7. Nonlinear boundary conditions. The boundary conditions discussed in Paragraphs 9.5 and 9.6 were linear — i.e., the appropriate function $\Phi = \Phi(x; \eta)$ was a linear function of the variables η_α. We now present yet another — generally nonlinear — boundary condition.

Consider again the second order differential equation of the form (6.2), i.e., consider the equation

$$-\sum_{i=1}^{N} \frac{\partial}{\partial x_i} a_i(x; u(x), \text{grad } u(x)) + a_0(x; u(x), \text{grad } u(x)) = f(x) \quad \text{on} \quad \Omega, \quad (14)$$

the coefficients of which, i.e., the functions

$$a_i = a_i(x; \xi_0, \xi_1, \ldots, \xi_N),$$

are this time defined for $x \in \bar{\Omega}$ and $(\xi_0, \xi_1, \ldots, \xi_N) \in \mathbb{R}^{N+1}$, thus — in particular — even for $x \in \partial\Omega$.

The boundary condition

$$\sum_{i=1}^{N} a_i(x; u(x), \text{grad } u(x)) v_i(x) = \varphi(x) \quad \text{on} \quad \partial\Omega, \quad (15)$$

where $v_i(x)$ are the components of the vector of the outward normal and $\varphi = \varphi(x)$ is a given function on $\partial\Omega$, is important for it is closely related to the differential equation: Indeed, it is determined directly by the coefficients of equation (14).

Condition (15) is not very intuitive; we therefore illustrate it using the following three rather concrete examples:

(i) Put

$$a_i(x; \xi_0, \xi_1, \ldots, \xi_N) = F_i(\xi_0, \xi_1, \ldots, \xi_N) \xi_i, \quad i = 1, 2, \ldots, N,$$

$$a_0(x; \xi_0, \xi_1, \ldots, \xi_N) = 0 \quad (16)$$

[i.e., the coefficients a_i do not depend on x and depend on ξ_i in a special way — see, for instance, Paragraph 2.3 where an equation of this type with $F_i(\xi_0, \xi_1, \ldots, \xi_N) = |\xi_i|^{p-2}$ was investigated]. Condition (15) then takes the form

$$\sum_{i=1}^{N} F_i(u(x), \text{grad } u(x)) \frac{\partial u}{\partial x_i} v_i(x) = \varphi(x) \quad \text{on} \quad \partial\Omega.$$

In fact, this is a condition of type (12): On the left-hand side we have actually a multiple of the derivative of the function u in the direction of the vector

$$s = (v_1 F_1, v_2 F_2, ..., v_N F_N);$$

the difference, which is, incidentally, substantial, as compared with condition (12) obviously lies in the fact that the direction of the vector s as well as its magnitude depend not only on the point $x \in \partial\Omega$ but also on the values of the function u and of its first derivatives at this point.

(ii) Let us put

$$a_i(x; \xi_0, \xi_1, ..., \xi_N) = F(\xi_0, \xi_1, ..., \xi_N) \xi_i, \quad i = 1, 2, ..., N$$

[i.e., assume that all the functions F_i in (16) are identical and equal to the function F; see, for instance, Paragraph 2.2 where $F(\xi_0, \xi_1, ..., \xi_N) = m(\xi_1^2 + ... + \xi_N^2)$]. Condition (15) then takes the form

$$\sum_{i=1}^{N} F(u(x), \operatorname{grad} u(x)) \frac{\partial u}{\partial x_i} v_i(x) = \varphi(x) \quad \text{on} \quad \partial\Omega$$

or, in other words,

$$F(u(x), \operatorname{grad} u(x)) \frac{\partial u}{\partial v} = \varphi(x) \quad \text{on} \quad \partial\Omega.$$

(iii) Let us put

$$a_i(x; \xi_0, \xi_1, ..., \xi_N) = \xi_i, \quad i = 1, 2, ..., N$$

[i.e., put $F_1 = F_2 = ... = F_N \equiv 1$ in (16)]. The differential equation (14) is then the Poisson equation

$$-\Delta u = f \quad \text{on} \quad \Omega$$

(Δ is the Laplace operator) and condition (15) takes the form

$$\frac{\partial u}{\partial v} = \varphi \quad \text{on} \quad \partial\Omega,$$

i.e., we have here the Neumann problem [see Paragraph 9.6 (ii)].

With regard to the above analogy, the boundary value problem consisting of solving equation (14) under condition (15) is sometimes also called (even for the case of general coefficients a_i) the Neumann problem for equation (14).

Let us note that even the nonlinear boundary condition of type (16) has a physical meaning. In case (iii), it was the linear condition

$$\frac{\partial u}{\partial v} = \varphi \quad \text{on} \quad \partial\Omega,$$

which describes, e.g., the heat flow through the boundary (see Paragraph 1.4). The general boundary condition (15), too, has a similar meaning: Thus, e.g., in Paragraph 2.2 (ii), we had a condition of the type

$$m(|\mathrm{grad}\ u|^2)\frac{\partial u}{\partial v} = \varphi \quad \text{on}\quad \partial\Omega\,,$$

describing the induction flow density on the boundary of the domain Ω. It can be seen that this is condition (15) for coefficients of the form

$$a_i(x; \xi_0, \xi_1, \ldots, \xi_N) = m(\xi_1^2 + \ldots + \xi_N^2)\,\xi_i\,, \quad i = 1, 2, \ldots, N\,,$$

$$a_0(x; \xi_0, \xi_1, \ldots, \xi_N) = 0\,.$$

9.8. Boundary value problem for an ordinary differential equation. Consider the case $N = 1$. The interval $(0, 1)$ is chosen as the domain Ω, so that the boundary $\partial\Omega$ consists of two points: $x = 0$ and $x = 1$.

(i) Put $k = 1$, i.e., consider an equation of the second order. The differential equation (6.2) has the form

$$-(a_1(x; u(x), u'(x)))' + a_0(x; u(x), u'(x)) = f(x) \quad \text{for}\quad x \in (0, 1)\,,$$

where $a_i(x; \xi_0, \xi_1)$ $(i = 0, 1)$ are functions defined for $x \in [0, 1]$ and for $(\xi_0, \xi_1) \in \mathbb{R}^2$. In general, the boundary condition is expressed by

$$\Phi(x; u(x), u'(x)) = 0 \quad \text{for}\quad x = 0 \quad \text{and}\quad x = 1$$

[where $\Phi(x; \eta)$ is a function defined for $x = 0$, $x = 1$ and $\eta \in \mathbb{R}^2$], i.e.,

$$\Phi(0; u(0), u'(0)) = 0\,, \quad \Phi(1; u(1), u'(1)) = 0$$

[note that the derivatives $u'(0)$ and $u'(1)$ are, essentially, the left-hand and the right-hand derivatives, respectively]. Now observe the analogues of the boundary value problems investigated in Paragraphs 9.6 and 9.7.

The boundary conditions

$$u(0) = c_0\,, \quad u(1) = c_1\,,$$

where c_0, c_1 are given constants, correspond to the case 9.6 (i); the conditions

$$u'(0) = c_0\,, \quad u'(1) = c_1$$

correspond to the case 9.6 (ii) [in fact, we should write $-u'(0)$ in the first condition to express the circumstance that the derivative "in the direction of the outward normal to $\partial\Omega$" is considered; however, the sign is obviously not essential here].

The conditions

$$u'(0) + h_0\, u(0) = c_0\,, \quad u'(1) + h_1\, u(1) = c_1\,,$$

where h_0, h_1, c_0, c_1 are given constants, correspond to the case 9.6 (iii). Finally, the conditions

$$u(0) = c_0\,, \quad u'(1) = c_1$$

or the conditions

$$u'(0) = c_0\,, \quad u(1) = c_1$$

correspond to the case 9.6 (v) (in the first eventuality, we choose $\Gamma_1 = \{0\}, \Gamma_2 = \{1\}$ in the second, we choose, conversely, $\Gamma_1 = \{1\}, \Gamma_2 = \{0\}$).

Boundary conditions (15) from Paragraph 9.7 are — for $N = 1$ — as follows:

$$a_1(0; u(0), u'(0)) = c_0\,, \quad a_1(1; u(1), u'(1)) = c_1\,.$$

(ii) Put $k = 2$, i.e., consider the differential equation of the fourth order of the form

$$(a_2(x; u, u', u''))'' - (a_1(x; u, u', u''))' +$$

$$+ a_0(x; u, u', u'') = f(x) \quad \text{for} \quad x \in (0, 1)\,. \tag{17}$$

Since $k = 2$, we give, in accordance with principle (a) of Paragraph 9.4, two boundary conditions which define, generally, the relation between $u(x)$, $u'(x)$, $u''(x)$ and $u'''(x)$ for $x = 0$ and $x = 1$. For instance, the boundary conditions

$$u(0) = c_{00}\,, \quad u'(0) = c_{10}\,,$$

$$u(1) = c_{01}\,, \quad u'(1) = c_{11}$$

are stable and represent the Dirichlet problem for equation (17) (the c_{ij} represent given constants here as well as in the sequel).

On the other hand, the boundary conditions

$$u''(0) = c_{20}\,, \quad u'''(0) = c_{30}\,,$$

$$u''(1) = c_{21}\,, \quad u'''(1) = c_{31}\,.$$

are unstable.

These conditions can now be combined in various ways. However, this is left to the reader.

9.9. Partial differential equations of the fourth order.

Put $k = 2$ and $N = 2$; thus, we consider a plane domain Ω and a function $u = u(x, y)$ of two variables. For an equation of the fourth order of the form (7.4) we give — in accordance with Paragraph 9.4 — two boundary conditions which are of at most third order and have the general form

$$\Phi(x, y; \delta_3 u(x, y)) = 0 \quad \text{for} \quad (x, y) \in \partial\Omega\,. \tag{18}$$

Here, $\Phi(x, y; \eta)$ is a function defined for $(x, y) \in \partial\Omega$ and for $\eta = (\eta_0, \eta_1, ..., \eta_9) \in \mathbb{R}^{10}$. For the variables η_i we substitute as follows:

$$\eta_0 = u, \quad \eta_1 = \frac{\partial u}{\partial x}, \quad \eta_2 = \frac{\partial u}{\partial y}, \quad \eta_3 = \frac{\partial^2 u}{\partial x^2}, \quad \eta_4 = \frac{\partial^2 u}{\partial x\, \partial y}, \quad \eta_5 = \frac{\partial^2 u}{\partial y^2},$$

$$\eta_6 = \frac{\partial^3 u}{\partial x^3}, \quad \eta_7 = \frac{\partial^3 u}{\partial x^2\, \partial y}, \quad \eta_8 = \frac{\partial^3 u}{\partial x\, \partial y^2}, \quad \eta_9 = \frac{\partial^3 u}{\partial y^3}.$$

We note two special cases:

(i) The conditions

$$u\big|_{\partial\Omega} = \varphi_0, \quad \frac{\partial u}{\partial v}\bigg|_{\partial\Omega} = \varphi_1 \tag{19}$$

(where φ_0, φ_1 are given functions defined on $\partial\Omega$) are stable boundary conditions and represent the Dirichlet problem for the equation of the fourth order.

(ii) The conditions

$$Mu\big|_{\partial\Omega} = \varphi_0, \quad Nu\big|_{\partial\Omega} = \varphi_1, \tag{20}$$

where the expressions Mu and Nu were defined in Paragraph 1.5, are unstable since they represent boundary conditions of the second and third orders: The first of the conditions (20) is of the form (18) with the function

$$\Phi(x, y; \eta) = \sigma(\eta_3 + \eta_5) + (1 - \sigma)(v_x^2\eta_3 + 2v_x v_y \eta_4 + v_y^2\eta_5),$$

and the second of the conditions (20) is also of the form (18), with a still more complicated function Φ; in the most simple case of $\sigma = 1$, we have

$$\Phi(x, y; \eta) = -v_x(\eta_6 + \eta_8) - v_y(\eta_7 + \eta_9).$$

SECTION 10. SOLUTION OF A BOUNDARY VALUE PROBLEM

10.1. A boundary value problem consists of a differential equation and boundary conditions. Hitherto, however, we have only introduced, in Paragraph 8.4, the concept of the solution of an equation. Therefore, we now introduce the concept of the classical solution of a boundary value problem and briefly discuss the methods of finding this solution.

10.2. The classical solution of a boundary value problem. Consider the boundary value problem determined by the differential equation of order $2k$

$$\sum_{|\alpha| \le k} (-1)^{|\alpha|}\, D^\alpha a_\alpha(x; \delta_k\, u(x)) = f(x) \quad \text{on} \quad \Omega \tag{1}$$

and by the boundary value conditions

$$\Phi_i(x; \delta_{s_i} u(x)) = 0 \quad \text{on} \quad \partial\Omega \quad (i = 1, 2, \ldots, k),\tag{2}$$

where

$$0 \le s_1 < s_2 < \ldots < s_k < 2k.\tag{3}$$

Assume that the functions $a_\alpha = a_\alpha(x; \xi)$ defined for $x \in \Omega \subset \mathbb{R}^N$ and $\xi \in \mathbb{R}^\varkappa$ belong to $C^{|\alpha|}(\bar\Omega \times \mathbb{R}^\varkappa)$, that f belongs to $C^0(\Omega)$, and that the functions $\Phi_i(x; \eta)$ are defined for $x \in \partial\Omega$ and $\eta \in \mathbb{R}^{\sigma_i}$ (σ_i is the number of multi-indexes of length s_i).

We say that the function $u = u(x)$ defined for $\bar\Omega = \Omega \cup \partial\Omega$ is the classical solution of the boundary value problem (1), (2) if

(a) $u \in C^{2k}(\bar\Omega)$;
(b) equation (1) is satisfied for all $x \in \Omega$;
(c) boundary value conditions (2) are satisfied for all $x \in \partial\Omega$.

10.3. Remarks. (i) In accordance with the condition $u \in C^{2k}(\bar\Omega)$ of the preceding paragraph, the derivatives $D^\beta u$, for $|\beta| \le 2k$, are defined not only in Ω but even on $\partial\Omega$ and boundary conditions (2) then make sense: According to condition (3), we substitute into the i-th boundary condition the values of $D^\beta u(x)$ for $x \in \partial\Omega$ and $|\beta| \le s_i < 2k$.

(ii) Considering the definition of the classical solution of a boundary value problem we see that condition (a) of Paragraph 10.2 is an essentially superfluous luxury. Namely, for condition (b) of Paragraph 10.2 to be satisfied it is sufficient for the function to have the appropriate derivatives inside Ω, i.e., it suffices to assume that

$$u \in C^{2k}(\Omega)$$

(in other words, it suffices to assume that u is the classical solution of the differential equation — see Paragraph 8.4); for condition (c) from Paragraph 10.2 to be satisfied it is sufficient that derivatives of order s exist up to the boundary $\partial\Omega$, where

$$s = \max(s_1, s_2, \ldots, s_k) = s_k,$$

i.e., the condition

$$u \in C^s(\bar\Omega).$$

is sufficient.

The classical solution of the boundary value problem (1), (2) is sometimes defined, therefore, as the function $u = u(x)$ for which

$$u \in C^{2k}(\Omega) \cap C^s(\bar\Omega)\tag{4}$$

holds and which satisfies, further, conditions (b) and (c) of Paragraph 10.2. [Condition (4) is sometimes verbally expressed as follows: "The classical solution u has continuous derivatives in Ω of those orders which appear in the equation, and continuous derivatives in $\bar{\Omega} = \Omega \cup \partial\Omega$ of those orders which appear in the boundary conditions."]

Since $s < 2k$ in accordance with conditions (3), condition (4) is weaker than condition (a) of Paragraph 10.2 and the classical solution introduced in this remark is more general. However, it has already been mentioned in Remark 8.5 that the concept of classical solution will be merely auxiliary for the purposes of this book, and the definition of Paragraph 10.2 will therefore be used in the sequel.

10.4. The boundary value problem as an operator equation. If the function $a_\alpha = = a_\alpha(x; \xi)$ for $|\alpha| \leq k$ belongs to $C^{|\alpha|}(\bar{\Omega} \times \mathbb{R}^\varkappa)$, then the function $v = v(x)$ defined for $x \in \bar{\Omega}$ by the formula

$$v(x) = \sum_{|\alpha| \leq k} (-1)^{|\alpha|} D^\alpha a_\alpha(x; \delta_k u(x)) \tag{5}$$

is continuous on $\bar{\Omega}$, i.e., $v \in C^0(\bar{\Omega})$, if $u \in C^{2k}(\bar{\Omega})$. Thus, formula (5) defines a differential operator $\mathscr{A}$ which to the function $u \in C^{2k}(\bar{\Omega})$ assigns the function $v = \mathscr{A}u$ from $C^0(\bar{\Omega})$.

The spaces $C^s(\bar{\Omega})$ are linear spaces for every $s \in \mathbb{N}_0$ if the sum of two functions u, v and the c-multiple of a function u are defined in the usual way:

$$(u + v)(x) = u(x) + v(x), \quad (cu)(x) = c\,u(x)$$

for every $x \in \bar{\Omega}$.

As mentioned already in the preceding section, we assume throughout that the domain Ω belongs to the class $\mathscr{C}^{0,1}$. In particular, the domain Ω is thus bounded and the expressions

$$\max_{x \in \bar{\Omega}} |D^\beta u(x)| \quad \text{for} \quad u \in C^s(\bar{\Omega}) \text{ and } |\beta| \leq s$$

therefore make sense. *The formula*

$$\|u\|_{C_s(\bar{\Omega})} = \sum_{|\beta| \leq s} \max_{x \in \bar{\Omega}} |D^\beta u(x)|$$

defines a norm on $C^s(\bar{\Omega})$; *the space* $C^s(\bar{\Omega})$ *with this norm is a Banach space.*†)

---

†) Let us recall a few concepts from functional analysis:

(i) Let X be a linear space with zero element Θ, and let us assign to every element $u \in X$ a number $\|u\|_X$ with the following properties:

(a) $\|u\|_X \geq 0$; $\|u\|_X = 0$ if and only if $u = \Theta$;

(b) $\|cu\|_X = |c|\,\|u\|_X$ for every element $u \in X$ and for every real number c;

(c) $\|u + v\|_X \leq \|u\|_X + \|v\|_X$ for every two elements $u, v \in X$.

Then we say that $\|u\|_X$ is the *norm* of the element $u \in X$ and the space X with this norm is called a *normed linear space*.

Consequently, the operator $\mathscr{A}$ given by formula (5) maps the Banach space $C^{2k}(\overline{\Omega})$ into the Banach space $C^0(\overline{\Omega})$. ††)

However, we limit somewhat the domain of the differential operator $\mathscr{A}$: We choose as $\mathscr{D}(\mathscr{A})$ the set of all those functions $u \in C^{2k}(\overline{\Omega})$ which satisfy the boundary conditions (2).

To find the (classical) solution of the boundary value problem (1), (2) [where we now assume that the functions $a_\alpha = a_\alpha(x, \xi)$ are from $C^{|\alpha|}(\overline{\Omega} \times \mathbb{R}^\varkappa)$ and that $f = f(x)$ is a given function from $C^0(\overline{\Omega})$] then means, essentially, to find the solution of the operator equation

$$\mathscr{A}u = f, \tag{6}$$

i.e., to find, for the given function $f \in C^0(\overline{\Omega})$, a function $u \in \mathscr{D}(\mathscr{A})$ such that (6) is valid.

The requirement $u \in \mathscr{D}(\mathscr{A})$ expresses that the function u is to satisfy the boundary conditions. Taking account of the definition of the operator $\mathscr{A}$ — see (5) — equation (6) then says that the function u is the classical solution of the differential equation (1).

10.5. On the operator equation (6). Following the clarification of questions concerning the concept of the (classical) solution of the boundary value problem in non-

---

(ii) The sequence $\{u_n\}_{n=1}^\infty$ of elements of a normed linear space X is called *fundamental* if the following is true: For every $\varepsilon > 0$ there exists a number $k = k(\varepsilon) \in \mathbb{N}$ such that for $m > k$ and $n > k$ we have

$$\|u_m - u_n\|_X < \varepsilon.$$

(iii) A normed linear space X is called *complete* if every fundamental sequence of elements from X has a limit in X, i.e., if for a given fundamental sequence $\{u_n\}_{n=1}^\infty$ an element $u_0 \in X$ exists with the following property: For every $\varepsilon > 0$ there exists a number $k = k(\varepsilon) \in \mathbb{N}$ such that for $n > k$ we have

$$\|u_n - u_0\|_X < \varepsilon.$$

A complete normed linear space is called a *Banach space*.

For more details concerning the concepts introduced in this footnote and also in other footnotes which refer to functional analysis, see, e.g., [51], pp. 82 and the following.

The assertions concerning the spaces $C^s(\overline{\Omega})$ which were given above are proved, for instance, in [54].

††) Let X, Y be two Banach spaces. We say that *an operator $\mathscr{A}$ from X into Y is defined* if we are given

(a) a set $M \subset X$;

(b) a rule which assigns to every element $u \in M$ a uniquely determined element $v \in Y$; this element is denoted by $\mathscr{A}u$, i.e.,

$$v = \mathscr{A}u.$$

The set M is called the *domain* of operator $\mathscr{A}$ and is denoted by $\mathscr{D}(\mathscr{A})$.

Instead of the operator $\mathscr{A}$ we shall speak also of the *mapping* $\mathscr{A}$.

linear differential equations, we now find ourselves confronted with basic theoretical problems:

a) the problem of the existence of the solution of a boundary value problem,
b) the problem of determining this solution.

As far as problem b) is concerned, we note immediately that an explicit formula giving the solution of a boundary value problem in nonlinear differential equations can be found only in quite exceptional cases. For this reason, numerical methods find broad application here (see Chapter IV).

Essentially, the present book is devoted to problem a). Methods will be described here which have been developed in the past few decades on the basis of new mathematical tools, which are dealt with in the coming chapters. Below, we present the so-called linearization method which is based on more profound results concerning the solvability of boundary value problems in linear differential equations and on the so-called fixed point principles. By means of this method we obtain (in a special case) results concerning the existence of a solution, naturally under assumptions which are rather restrictive as compared with the methods discussed in Chapters IV and V. Even from the point of view of the (at least approximate) determination of the concrete form of the solution, the procedure mentioned above is fairly complicated.

These and further difficulties, which occurred and still do occur when trying to find the solution of nonlinear problems, were probably among the reasons why a number of problems were formulated in "linear" language — though at the price of certain simplifications.

Before explaining the method of linearization on a simple example one of the classical fixed point principles is given.

10.6. The fixed point of an operator. The Banach contraction principle. Let B be an operator mapping a subset M of the Banach space X into the same Banach space X. The element $u \in M$ is called a *fixed point* of the operator B if

$$Bu = u ,\tag{7}$$

i.e., if the element u is mapped by the operator B into itself.

By the *fixed point principle* we mean a theorem which states sufficient conditions under which a fixed point of an operator exists. The simplest of these principles is the *Banach contraction principle* (see, e.g., [51]) which says:

(i) *Let B be an operator defined on the Banach space X with values in X. Assume that B is a so-called contractive operator, i.e., that a number c, $0 \leqq c < 1$, exists such that for all pairs of elements $u, v \in X$ we have*

$$\|Bu - Bv\|_X \leqq c\|u - v\|_X .\tag{8}$$

Then there exists precisely one fixed point of the operator B.

The Banach contraction principle is not only the oldest and simplest fixed point principle, but it also has the advantage that the method of its proof includes instructions as to how to find that fixed point. It even indicates the error associated with its approximating sequence. Namely, the fixed point is determined as the limit of a sequence $\{u_n\}_{n=0}^{\infty}$ (called the sequence of *successive approximations*) of elements from X constructed by the following iterative method: We choose arbitrarily an element $u_0 \in X$ (the so-called zero-th approximation) and construct the element $u_1 = Bu_0$, then the element $u_2 = Bu_1$, etc. Generally, the element u_n is determined by the formula

$$u_n = Bu_{n-1}, \quad n \in \mathbb{N}.$$

The sequence $\{u_n\}_{n=0}^{\infty}$ converges in the space X to the fixed point $\hat{u}$ of the operator B and

$$\|u_n - \hat{u}\|_X \leq \frac{c^{n-1}}{1-c} \|u_1 - u_0\|_X, \quad n \in \mathbb{N}.$$

10.7. The linearization method. Consider the case of $N = 1$, $\Omega = (0, 1)$, and look for the classical solution of the boundary value problem

$$-\frac{d^2 u}{dx^2} + g(u(x)) = f(x) \quad \text{for} \quad x \in (0, 1), \tag{9}$$

$$u(0) = u(1) = 0, \tag{10}$$

i.e., for the solution of the (homogeneous) Dirichlet problem for equation (9), where $f = f(x) \in C^0([0, 1])$ and $g = g(t)$ is a function defined for $t \in \mathbb{R}$ which satisfies the Lipschitz condition: A constant $C \geq 0$ exists such that for all $t, s \in \mathbb{R}$ we have

$$|g(t) - g(s)| \leq C|t - s|. \tag{11}$$

The operator equation (6) is then in question, where the operator $\mathscr{A}$ is defined as follows: We have

$$\mathscr{D}(\mathscr{A}) = \{u \in C^2([0, 1]); u(0) = u(1) = 0\}$$

and

$$(\mathscr{A}u)(x) = -u''(x) + g(u(x)).$$

(The nonlinearity of this boundary value problem is concealed in the function g.)

Now, let v be a fixed chosen (but arbitrary) function from the space $C^0([0, 1])$ and let us look for the function $u \in C^2([0, 1])$ which solves the linear boundary value problem

$$-\frac{d^2 u}{dx^2} = f(x) - g(v(x)) \quad \text{for} \quad x \in (0, 1),$$

$$u(0) = u(1) = 0. \tag{12}$$

Equation (12) is indeed linear: It is an equation of the form

$$-\frac{d^2u}{dx^2} = F(x) \quad \text{for} \quad x \in (0, 1),$$

(13)

where $F(x) = f(x) - g(v(x))$.

Equation (13) with boundary conditions (10) can be solved rather easily for any arbitrary function $F \in C^0([0, 1])$: The solution is given by the formula

$$u(x) = \int_0^1 K(x, t)\, F(t)\, dt,$$

where $K(x, t)$ is the so-called *Green's function* of the boundary value problem (13), (10) defined as follows:

$$K(x, t) = \begin{cases} (1 - x)\, t & \text{for} \quad 0 \le t \le x, \\ x(1 - t) & \text{for} \quad x < t \le 1 \end{cases}$$

(14)

(see, e.g., [79]). Thus, the boundary value problem (12) has the solution

$$u(x) = \int_0^1 K(x, t)\, [f(t) - g(v(t))]\, dt.$$

This defines an operator B on the space $C^0([0, 1])$:

$$(Bv)(x) = \int_0^1 K(x, t)\, [f(t) - g(v(t))]\, dt \quad \text{for} \quad v \in C^0([0, 1]).$$

(15)

Obviously, $Bv \in C^0([0, 1])$ for $v \in C^0([0, 1])$. But we have, moreover [since Bv is a solution of problem (12)], for arbitrary $v \in C^0([0, 1])$,

$$Bv \in \mathscr{D}(\mathscr{A}).$$

Hence, it is readily seen that to find the solution of the boundary value problem (9), (10) is the same as to find the fixed point of the operator B in the space $C^0([0, 1])$, i.e. to find the function $u \in C^0([0, 1])$ for which

$$Bu = u$$

holds, or — in other words —

$$\int_0^1 K(x, t)\, [f(t) - g(u(t))]\, dt = u(x), \quad x \in [0, 1].$$

Then $u \in \mathscr{D}(\mathscr{A})$ will be automatically true, since $Bu \in \mathscr{D}(\mathscr{A})$.

Consequently, problem (9), (10) will be solved if we manage to find the fixed point of the operator B, i.e., if we are able to show, in view of the Banach contraction principle — see 10.6 (i), e.g. — that B is a contractive operator. We show that the following assertion is valid:

(i) *If the function g satisfies condition* (11) *with C < 1, then the operator B defined by formula* (15) *is a contractive operator on the Banach space* $C^0([0, 1])$.

Proof. The norm of the difference $Bv - Bw$ in the space $C^0([0, 1])$ is to be estimated. From (15) it follows, first of all, that for $v, w \in C^0([0, 1])$

$$(Bv)(x) - (Bw)(x) = \int_0^1 K(x, t) [g(w(t)) - g(v(t))] dt .$$

Exploiting the fact that $|K(x, t)| \leq 1$ and that the function g satisfies condition (11), we obtain

$$|(Bv)(x) - (Bw)(x)| \leq C \int_0^1 |w(t) - v(t)| dt \leq C\|w - v\|_{C^0([0, 1])} \qquad (16)$$

for arbitrary $x \in [0, 1]$ $[\|u\|_{C^0([0, 1])} = \max_{x \in [0, 1]} |u(x)| -$ see Paragraph 10.4]; thus,

$$\|Bv - Bw\|_{C^0([0, 1])} \leq C\|w - v\|_{C^0([0, 1])} .$$

From assertion (i) and from 10.6 (i), the next assertion then follows immediately:

(ii) *Let the function g(t) satisfy condition* (11) *with C < 1. Then the boundary value problem* (9), (10) *has one and only one classical solution for any arbitrary right-hand side f* $\in C^0([0, 1])$.

(iii) Using the boundary value problem (9), (10), we clarify the construction of the sequence of successive approximations introduced in Paragraph 10.6. Arbitrarily, we choose a function $u_0 \in C^0([0, 1])$ and find the function $u_1 = Bu_0$ where the operator B is defined by formula (15). This means, in other words, that we find the solution u_1 of the boundary value problem (for a linear differential equation)

$$-\frac{d^2u}{dx^2} = f(x) - g(u_0(x)), \quad x \in (0, 1),$$

$$u(0) = u(1) = 0 .$$

We then find the solution u_2 of the boundary value problem

$$-\frac{d^2u}{dx^2} = f(x) - g(u_1(x)), \quad x \in (0, 1),$$

$$u(0) = u(1) = 0 .$$

Generally: If u_n is determined, we find the solution u_{n+1} of the boundary value problem

$$-\frac{d^2u}{dx^2} = f(x) - g(u_n(x)), \quad x \in (0, 1),$$

$$u(0) = u(1) = 0 .$$

The solution of the boundary value problem (9), (10), the existence of which is ensured by assertion (ii), is then obtained as the limit of the sequence $\{u_n\}_{n=0}^{\infty}$. (Also, the estimate of the distance of the approximate solution u_n from the exact solution as given in the conclusion of Paragraph 10.6 is often useful.) In point of fact, we have thus reduced the question of the solvability of the nonlinear boundary value problem to the solution of a sequence of boundary value problems for a linear differential equation of the type of (12).

(iv) As an exercise, the reader can now formulate and prove the existence of the (classical) solution of the boundary value problem

$$-\frac{d^2u}{dx^2} + g(x, u(x), u'(x)) = f(x), \quad x \in (0, 1),$$

$$u(0) = u(1) = 0,$$

where $f \in C^0([0, 1])$ and where the continuous function $g = g(x, t, \tau)$ satisfies the following Lipschitz condition: A number C, $0 \leq C < 1$, exists such that for all $x \in [0, 1]$ and all $t, \tau, s, \sigma \in \mathbb{R}$ we have

$$|g(x, t, \tau) - g(x, s, \sigma)| \leq C(|t - s| + |\tau - \sigma|).$$

[Note that in this case the operator B defined by the formula

$$(Bv)(x) = \int_0^1 K(x, t)[f(x) - g(x, v(x), v'(x))]\,dx$$

has to be considered on the Banach space $C^1([0, 1])$!]

10.8. More on the solution of the operator equation (6). The existence of the classical solution of the boundary value problem (9), (10) was quite easily proved in the preceding paragraph. However, let us not be misled: The relative simplicity was also due to the fact that the solution of the linear problem (12), (10) to which the former problem was reduced exists for any arbitrary right-hand side F and can easily be expressed by means of the operator B.

Were we to consider, e.g., the domain Ω in $\mathbb{R}^N$, $N > 1$, and the nonlinear problem

$$-\Delta u + g(u(x)) = f(x) \quad \text{on} \quad \Omega,$$

$$u|_{\partial\Omega} = 0,$$

then the corresponding linear problem

$$-\Delta u = F(x) \quad \text{on} \quad \Omega,$$

$$u|_{\partial\Omega} = 0,$$

where $F(x) = f(x) - g(v(x))$ and v is a fixed function from $C^0(\overline{\Omega})$, would cause considerably more serious problems than in the case of $N = 1$: For instance, as the linear problem does not generally have a solution for $F \in C^0(\overline{\Omega})$, stronger assumptions on f, g and v are necessary than for $N = 1$. Also, the concrete form of Green's function, which is an analogue of the function K from (14) and with the aid of which the operator B can be defined, is known only for very special types of domains (see. e.g., [79]) and does not have properties as good as those of the function K of (14).

Difficulties of this and of similar type form the reason why the application of the method of linearization together with the Banach contraction principle is not very suitable for the proof of the existence of the (classical) solution of boundary value problems in nonlinear partial differential equations.

It has already been mentioned several times that in this book we start not from the concept of the classical solution but from the concept of the weak solution which is based on a certain integral identity and works with a rather different class of function spaces. Even in the case of this concept of solution, the boundary condition is reduced to a certain operator equation again solved (although in rather more camouflaged form) with the aid of a certain fixed point principle. However, we shall see, e.g., that it will be possible to prove the existence of the solution of the boundary value problem (9), (10) even for functions g which do not satisfy condition (11), and thus for more general classes of nonlinear equations. For this reason, the closing paragraphs of this section should be understood only as a supplement allowing comparison with methods investigated later and laying emphasis on their significance.

SECTION 11. ON AN INTEGRAL IDENTITY

11.1. Theorem. (Green's Formula.) *Let Ω be a domain in $\mathbb{R}^N$ which is of the class $\mathscr{C}^{0,1}$, and let v, w be two functions from $C^1(\overline{\Omega})$. Then the relation*

$$\int_\Omega \frac{\partial w(x)}{\partial x_i} v(x)\, dx = -\int_\Omega w(x) \frac{\partial v(x)}{\partial x_i}\, dx + \int_{\partial\Omega} w(x)\, v(x)\, v_i(x)\, dS \tag{1}$$

holds, where v_i is the i-th component of the unit vector of the outward normal v to $\partial\Omega$.

This theorem belongs to the fundamental theorems of mathematical analysis. It is true under even weaker conditions on the functions v, w (see Paragraph 13.12). The last of the integrals in (1) is a surface integral (in the case of $N = 2$ it is a line integral) understood, e.g., in the sense indicated in Paragraph 9.2.

Formula (1) is called *Green's formula*. Sometimes it is also called the formula for integration by parts for functions of several variables: Namely, if $N = 1$ and Ω is, e.g., the interval (a, b), then the boundary $\partial\Omega$ consists of the points $x = a$ and $x = b$ and formula (1) takes the form

$$\int_a^b w'(x)\, v(x)\, dx = -\int_a^b w(x)\, v'(x)\, dx + [w(b)\, v(b) - w(a)\, v(a)],$$

which is actually the formula for integration by parts.

11.2. Green's formula for higher order derivatives. (i) Let v, w be two functions from $C^2(\overline{\Omega})$, where $\Omega \in \mathscr{C}^{0,1}$. Let us apply formula (1) with the function w replaced by the function $\partial w / \partial x_j$ which belongs to $C^1(\overline{\Omega})$. Then we have

$$\int_\Omega \frac{\partial^2 w(x)}{\partial x_i \, \partial x_j} v(x) \, \mathrm{d}x = -\int_\Omega \frac{\partial w(x)}{\partial x_j} \frac{\partial v(x)}{\partial x_i} \, \mathrm{d}x + \int_{\partial\Omega} \frac{\partial w(x)}{\partial x_j} v(x) \, v_i(x) \, \mathrm{d}S . \qquad (2)$$

Now, formula (1) is applied once more, this time for the subscript j and for the pair $w, \partial v / \partial x_i$ (i.e., the function v is replaced by the function $\partial v / \partial x_i$). One obtains

$$\int_\Omega \frac{\partial w(x)}{\partial x_j} \frac{\partial v(x)}{\partial x_i} \, \mathrm{d}x = -\int_\Omega w(x) \frac{\partial^2 v(x)}{\partial x_j \, \partial x_i} \, \mathrm{d}x + \int_{\partial\Omega} w(x) \frac{\partial v(x)}{\partial x_i} v_j(x) \, \mathrm{d}S . \qquad (3)$$

Substituting now from formula (3) for the first integral on the right-hand side of formula (2) — still remembering that for $v \in C^2(\overline{\Omega})$ the derivatives $\partial^2 v / \partial x_i \, \partial x_j$ and $\partial^2 v / \partial x_j \, \partial x_i$ are equal — the following formula is obtained:

$$\int_\Omega \frac{\partial^2 w(x)}{\partial x_i \, \partial x_j} v(x) \, \mathrm{d}x =$$

$$= \int_\Omega w(x) \frac{\partial^2 v(x)}{\partial x_i \, \partial x_j} \, \mathrm{d}x + \int_{\partial\Omega} \left[\frac{\partial w(x)}{\partial x_j} v(x) \, v_i(x) - w(x) \frac{\partial v(x)}{\partial x_i} v_j(x) \right] \mathrm{d}S . \qquad (4)$$

Formula (4) could be called Green's formula for derivatives of the second order.

(ii) Now it is possible to continue: If v, w are two functions from $C^3(\overline{\Omega})$, then (1) (with the function w replaced by the function $\partial^2 w / \partial x_j \, \partial x_k$) implies

$$\int_\Omega \frac{\partial^3 w(x)}{\partial x_i \, \partial x_j \, \partial x_k} v(x) \, \mathrm{d}x = -\int_\Omega \frac{\partial^2 w(x)}{\partial x_i \, \partial x_k} \frac{\partial v(x)}{\partial x_i} \, \mathrm{d}x + \int_{\partial\Omega} \frac{\partial^2 w(x)}{\partial x_j \, \partial x_k} v(x) \, v_i(x) \, \mathrm{d}S .$$

The first integral on the right-hand side is then modified employing formula (4) — where, naturally, the subscript i is replaced by the subscript j, the subscript j by the subscript k, the function v by the function $\partial v / \partial x_i$, and, finally, Green's formula for derivatives of the third order is obtained:

$$\int_\Omega \frac{\partial^3 w(x)}{\partial x_i \, \partial x_j \, \partial x_k} v(x) \, \mathrm{d}x = -\int_\Omega w(x) \frac{\partial^3 v(x)}{\partial x_i \, \partial x_j \, \partial x_k} \, \mathrm{d}x +$$

$$+ \int_{\partial\Omega} \left[\frac{\partial^2 w(x)}{\partial x_j \, \partial x_k} v(x) \, v_i(x) - \frac{\partial w(x)}{\partial x_k} \frac{\partial v(x)}{\partial x_i} v_j(x) + w(x) \frac{\partial^2 v(x)}{\partial x_i \, \partial x_j} v_k(x) \right] \mathrm{d}S \qquad (5)$$

(the equality of the derivatives was again exploited).

(iii) It is now immediately seen that for $m \in \mathbb{N}$ and for functions $v, w \in C^m(\overline{\Omega})$ the following formula holds:

$$\int_\Omega D^\alpha w(x)\, v(x)\, \mathrm{d}x = (-1)^{|\alpha|} \int_\Omega w(x)\, D^\alpha v(x)\, \mathrm{d}x + \int_{\partial\Omega} G(v, w)\, \mathrm{d}S,\qquad (6)$$

where α is an N-dimensional multi-index of length m, $|\alpha| = m$, and where $G(v, w)$ is a sum of products of the type

$$\pm\, D^\beta v(x)\, D^\gamma w(x)\, v_i(x),\quad x \in \partial\Omega,$$

with $|\beta| < m$, $|\gamma| < m$, and $v_i = v_i(x)$ is a component of the vector of the outward normal to $\partial\Omega$ at the point $x \in \partial\Omega$.

11.3. Special case of formula (6). If $v = v(x)$ is a function from $C_0^m(\Omega)$ [see Paragraph 8.2 (iv)], then $v(x) = 0$ for $x \in \partial\Omega$, and even for those $x \in \Omega$ which are "near $\partial\Omega$". Therefore, we also have $D^\beta v(x) = 0$ for $|\beta| \leq m$ and $x \in \partial\Omega$. In particular, the expression $G(v, w)$ is equal to zero for such a function. The surface integral in formula (6) then vanishes and we obtain the following important assertion:

Let $\Omega \subset \mathbb{R}^N$, $\Omega \in \mathscr{C}^{0,1}$, $m \in \mathbb{N}$. If $v \in C_0^m(\Omega)$ and $w \in C^m(\overline{\Omega})$, then

$$\int_\Omega D^\alpha w(x)\, v(x)\, \mathrm{d}x = (-1)^{|\alpha|} \int_\Omega w(x)\, D^\alpha v(x)\, \mathrm{d}x\qquad (7)$$

for all multi-indexes α such that $|\alpha| \leq m$.

11.4. Remark. Let $v \in C_0^m(\Omega)$, and denote by K_1 the support of the function v:

$$K_1 = \operatorname{supp} v$$

[see Paragraph 8.2 (iv)]. Then $K_1 \subset \Omega$ and $v(x) = 0$ for $x \in \Omega - K_1$. Consequently, it is possible to consider integrals over K_1 in formula (7) instead of integrals over Ω. For this reason, the values of the function w are irrelevant for $x \in \Omega - K_1$. In particular, formula (7) then holds if

$$v \in C_0^m(\Omega),\quad w \in C^m(\Omega),$$

since functions from $C^m(\Omega)$ belong to $C^m(\overline{\Omega}_0)$ for every domain Ω_0 such that $\overline{\Omega}_0 \subset \Omega$, and it suffices to choose Ω_0 so that $\Omega_0 \supset \operatorname{supp} v_0$.

This fact will be exploited in the next paragraph.

11.5. An integral identity. Let the function $u \in C^{2k}(\Omega)$ be the classical solution of the differential equation of order $2k$

$$\sum_{|\alpha|\leq k} (-1)^{|\alpha|}\, D^\alpha\, a_\alpha(x;\, \delta_k\, u(x)) = f(x)\quad \text{on}\quad \Omega\qquad (8)$$

(see Paragraph 8.4).

Further, let

$$v \in C_0^k(\Omega) .$$

Equation (8) holds for all $x \in \Omega$; let us then multiply equation (8) by the number $v(x)$ and integrate the resulting equality over the domain Ω:

$$\sum_{|\alpha| \leq k} (-1)^{|\alpha|} \int_\Omega D^\alpha a_\alpha(x; \delta_k u(x)) \, v(x) \, dx = \int_\Omega f(x) \, v(x) \, dx . \qquad (9)$$

We now use formula (7) where we choose

$$w(x) = a_\alpha(x, \delta_k u(x)) .$$

We obtain

$$\int_\Omega D^\alpha a_\alpha(x; \delta_k u(x)) \, v(x) \, dx = (-1)^{|\alpha|} \int_\Omega a_\alpha(x; \delta_k u(x)) \, D^\alpha v(x) \, dx .$$

Applying the above relation, equality (9) can be written as follows:

$$\sum_{|\alpha| \leq k} \int_\Omega a_\alpha(x; \delta_k u(x)) \, D^\alpha v(x) \, dx = \int_\Omega f(x) \, v(x) \, dx ; \qquad (10)$$

this relation is valid for every function $v \in C_0^k(\Omega)$.

We have thus proved the following assertion:

If u is the classical solution of equation (8), *then integral identity* (10) *holds for every function* $v \in C_0^k(\Omega)$.

Naturally, this assertion is not reversible: identity (10) can be satisfied even for functions u which have derivatives only up to and including order k but do not have derivatives of higher orders. Consequently, such a function cannot be the classical solution of equation (8).

Thus, identity (10) can hold for a broader class of functions u than equation (8). This fact also serves as the basis of our considerations in the sequel: The function u is called the weak (generalized) solution of equation (8) if identity (10) is satisfied for all functions $v \in C_0^k(\Omega)$. However, more details on this topic will be found in the next chapter where identity (10) will be analyzed thoroughly.

CHAPTER III

THE WEAK SOLUTION OF A BOUNDARY VALUE PROBLEM

SECTION 12. THE CARATHÉODORY PROPERTY AND THE NĚMYCKIĬ OPERATORS

12.1. In Chapter II, we mentioned that the concept of the weak solution of the differential equation

$$\sum_{|\alpha| \leq k} (-1)^{|\alpha|} \, D^\alpha a_\alpha(x; \delta_k u(x)) = f(x) \quad \text{on} \quad \Omega$$

will be based, primarily, on the integral identity

$$\sum_{|\alpha| \leq k} \int_\Omega a_\alpha(x; \delta_k u(x)) \, D^\alpha v(x) \, dx = \int_\Omega f(x) \, v(x) \, dx \qquad (1)$$

valid for every $v \in C_0^k(\Omega)$.

When deriving this identity in Paragraph 11.5, we started from the following assumptions:

$$u \in C^{2k}(\Omega), \quad v \in C_0^k(\Omega), \quad f \in C^0(\Omega),$$

$$a_\alpha(x; \xi) \in C^{|\alpha|}(\Omega \times \mathbb{R}^\times). \qquad (2)$$

Under these assumptions, all the expressions in (1) are meaningful. However, if we ignore the fact that the identity (1) was obtained from some differential equation and study it quite independently, we immediately see that assumptions (2) are unnecessarily strong: Nowhere in (1) do we need derivatives of u of order higher than k; we do not even need the differentiability of the functions a_α; moreover, not even the continuity of the functions appearing in (1) is necessary.

Let us therefore investigate identity (1) in more detail and try to make clear under exactly how "weak" assumptionsconcerning the functions $a_\alpha(x; \xi)$, $u(x), v(x)$ do the expressions appearing in (1) make sense.

We first analyse the left-hand side of the identity. For a chosen fixed function v, this side can be written in the form

$$\int_\Omega h(x; u_1(x), \ldots, u_m(x)) \, dx , \qquad (3)$$

where $u_1(x), \ldots, u_m(x)$ are replaced by all the derivatives of the function u up to and including order k.

When then is the integral (3) meaningful? Recall that throughout this book Lebesgue integrals are used. Therefore, it is necessary that for admissible functions $u_1(x), \ldots, u_m(x)$ the composite function

$$g(x) = h(x; u_1(x), \ldots, u_m(x))$$

be measurable on Ω and, moreover, that it be Lebesgue integrable.†)

In the sequel, we assume that the functions $u_1(x), \ldots, u_m(x)$ are measurable on Ω. The class of all measurable functions is very broad: "Almost every" function defined on an open set Ω is measurable. In spite of this, it is not true that every function composed of two measurable functions need itself be measurable — and the function $g = g(x)$ mentioned above is a composite function. For this reason, we introduce one very useful concept which makes it possible to formulate better the results concerning the measurability of the composite function g.

12.2. Definition. Let Ω be a domain in $\mathbb{R}^N$ and let

$$h = h(x; \xi)$$

be a function defined for almost all $x \in \Omega$ and for all $\xi \in \mathbb{R}^m$. We say that the function h has the *Carathéodory property* if

(i) for all $\xi \in \mathbb{R}^m$, the function

$$h_\xi(x) = h(x; \xi)$$

(as function of the variable x) is measurable on Ω;

(ii) for almost all $x \in \Omega$, the function

$$h_x(\xi) = h(x; \xi)$$

(as a function of the variable ξ) is continuous on $\mathbb{R}^m$.

The fact that a function h has the Carathéodory property is denoted, for the sake of brevity, symbolically by writing

$$h \in \textbf{CAR} .$$

---

†) By saying that a function $g = g(x)$ is Lebesgue integrable we mean that the Lebesgue integral

$$\int_\Omega g(x) \, dx$$

is a finite number. The reader may find more on the Lebesgue integral, e.g., in [51].

12.3. Remarks. (i) Measurability is a very broad concept. However, since every continuous function is measurable, Definition 12.2 implies directly the following very useful criterion for the Carathéodory property:

If the function $h = h(x; \xi)$ is continuous on $\Omega \times \mathbb{R}^m$, then $h \in$ **CAR**.

Symbolically, this can be written as

$$C^0(\Omega \times \mathbb{R}^m) \subset \textbf{CAR}.$$

The reader to whom the class **CAR** appears too abstract may, with negligible loss of generality, think of the function $h \in$ **CAR** as a function which is continuous in all variables, i.e., $h \in C^0(\Omega \times \mathbb{R}^m)$.

(ii) In Paragraph 12.2, we assumed that the function $h(x; \xi)$ was defined for almost all $x \in \Omega$, i.e., for $x \in \Omega - M$ where the set M is of measure zero. In what follows, sets of measure zero will play no role in our considerations; therefore, it is possible to define the function h in an entirely arbitrary manner also for $x \in M$ (e.g., in such a way that the function $h_x(\xi)$ be a continuous function of the variable ξ; the simplest thing is to put

$$h_x(\xi) = 0 \quad \text{for} \quad x \in M).$$

In Definition 12.2, it is then possible to write "all $x \in \Omega$" instead of "almost all $x \in \Omega$". This convention of completing the definition of functions defined almost everywhere will be also used further in the text.

The significance of the Carathéodory property is brought out by the following theorem.

12.4. Theorem. *Let N, m be positive integers and let Ω be a domain in $\mathbb{R}^N$. Let the function $h = h(x; \xi)$ be defined for $x \in \Omega$ and $\xi \in \mathbb{R}^m$, and let $h \in$* **CAR**. *Let $u_i = u_i(x)$, $i = 1, \ldots, m$, be measurable functions on Ω. Then the composite function*

$$g(x) = h(x; u_1(x), \ldots, u_m(x))$$

is again a measurable function on Ω.

The proof of this theorem can be found, e.g., in [37], [52], [89]. Note that the proof is not at all simple and that it exploits classical theorems from the theory of measurable functions, in particular the so-called Lusin theorem (see [51]) which gives necessary and sufficient conditions for a given function to be measurable.

We introduce yet another useful concept:

12.5. Definition. Let $h = h(x; \xi)$ be a function defined for $x \in \Omega$ and $\xi \in \mathbb{R}^m$, and let $h \in$ **CAR**. The operator $\mathscr{H}$ defined for m-tuples of measurable functions $u_i = u_i(x)$ $(x \in \Omega, i = 1, \ldots, m)$ by the formula

$$\mathscr{H}(u_1, \ldots, u_m)(x) = h(x; u_1(x), \ldots, u_m(x)) \quad \text{for} \quad x \in \Omega,$$

is called the *Němyckiĭ operator* (determined by the function h).

12.6. Remark. Theorem 12.4 thus guarantees that the Němyckiĭ operator maps an m-tuple of measurable functions onto a measurable function again. If we choose $m = \varkappa = \varkappa(N, k)$ and if we assume that the function $a_\alpha = a_\alpha(x; \xi)$ from (1) belongs to **CAR**, then the function

$$b_\alpha(x) = a_\alpha(x; \delta_k u(x))$$

is measurable on Ω if the function u and its derivatives $D^\gamma u$ $(|\gamma| \leq k)$ are measurable on Ω (thus, e.g., if they are continuous).

Moreover, if also the functions $D^\alpha v$ $(|\alpha| \leq k)$ are measurable functions on Ω, then also the function

$$g(x) = \sum_{|\alpha| \leq k} a_\alpha(x; \delta_k u(x)) D^\alpha v(x)$$

is measurable on Ω since the sum and the product of measurable functions is again a measurable function.

This solves the first problem: We know when the function in the integral on the left-hand side of identity (1) is measurable. It remains to solve the second problem, namely the problem of the integrability of the function $g(x)$: We have to find a sufficient condition for the functions $a_\alpha(x; \xi)$, $u(x)$, $v(x)$, which would guarantee that the Lebesgue integral

$$\int_\Omega \sum_{|\alpha| \leq k} a_\alpha(x; \delta_k u(x)) D^\alpha v(x) \, dx$$

be finite. To solve this problem, more must first be said about certain classes of Lebesgue integrable functions.

12.7. The space $L_p(\Omega)$. Let p be a real number,

$$p \geq 1,$$

and let Ω be a domain in $\mathbb{R}^N$. By the symbol

$$L_p(\Omega)$$

we denote the set of all measurable functions $u = u(x)$ on Ω for which the integral

$$\int_\Omega |u(x)|^p \, dx$$

is finite.

If $N = 1$ and the domain Ω is an interval (a, b), we denote the space $L_p(\Omega)$ by the symbol

$$L_p(a, b).$$

In the sequel, we regard two functions $u_1(x)$ and $u_2(x)$ as *equal* if they only differ on a set of measure zero. (The usefulness of this new idea of equality introduced on the set of functions is obvious from what immediately follows.)

The set $L_p(\Omega)$ is a linear set, first of all. *The expression*

$$\|u\|_p = \left[\int_\Omega |u(x)|^p \, dx\right]^{1/p}$$

defines a norm on $L_p(\Omega)$ †), and the space $L_p(\Omega)$ with this norm is a Banach space.

We now summarize several important properties of the spaces $L_p(\Omega)$:

(i) *The set $C_0^\infty(\Omega)$ is dense††) in the space $L_p(\Omega)$.*

(ii) *The space $L_p(\Omega)$ is separable.†††)*

(iii) The so-called *Hölder inequality* holds: *Let $p > 1$, and let us define the number q by the formula*

$$\frac{1}{p} + \frac{1}{q} = 1, \quad \text{i.e.,} \quad q = \frac{p}{p-1}. \tag{4}$$

Let $u \in L_p(\Omega)$ and $v \in L_q(\Omega)$. Then

$$\int_\Omega |u(x)\,v(x)| \, dx \leqq \left[\int_\Omega |u(x)|^p \, dx\right]^{1/p} \left[\int_\Omega |v(x)|^q \, dx\right]^{1/q} \tag{5}$$

[in other words: *If $u \in L_p(\Omega)$ and $v \in L_q(\Omega)$, then their product $u \cdot v$ is an element of the space $L_1(\Omega)$ and*

$$\|uv\|_1 \leqq \|u\|_p \, \|v\|_q. \tag{6}$$

The proofs of all the assertions of this paragraph can be found, e.g., in [54]

12.8. The space $L_\infty(\Omega)$. We denote by the symbol

$$L_\infty(\Omega)$$

the set of all functions $u = u(x)$ on Ω for which the number

$$\|u\|_\infty = \inf_{\text{meas } M = 0} \ \sup_{x \in \Omega - M} |u(x)| \tag{7}$$

---

†) Here, we make use of the new equality between functions: The zero element Θ of the space $L_p(\Omega)$ is the function equal to zero everywhere in Ω, which is identical with any function equal to zero almost everywhere. For this reason, the implication

$$\|u\|_p = 0 \Leftrightarrow u = \Theta,$$

holds without which the expression $\|\cdot\|_p$ would not define a norm.

††) We say that a subset M of a normed linear space X is *dense in X* if for every element $u \in X$ and every number $\varepsilon > 0$ there exists an element $v \in M$ such that

$$\|u - v\|_X \leqq \varepsilon.$$

†††) A normed linear space X is said to be *separable* if there is a dense subset M in this space which is at most countable, i.e., $M = \{v_1, v_2, \ldots, v_n, \ldots\}$ where $v_i \in X$.

is finite [recall that the symbol

$$\text{meas } M$$

denotes the Lebesgue measure of the set M; the infimum in (7) is then taken over all subsets $M \subset \Omega$ which are of measure zero]. Thus, $u \in L_\infty(\Omega)$ if there exists a set M of measure zero such that u is bounded on $\Omega - M$.

Formula (7) defines a norm on $L_\infty(\Omega)$, and $L_\infty(\Omega)$ with this norm is a Banach space.

Some assertions of Paragraph 12.7 can be transferred, but the analogue of assertion 12.7 (ii) does not hold: *The space $L_\infty(\Omega)$ is not separable.*

(i) The following analogue of the *Hölder inequality* is valid: *If $u \in L_1(\Omega)$ and $v \in L_\infty(\Omega)$, then*

$$\int_\Omega |u(x)\, v(x)|\, \mathrm{d}x \leqq \|u\|_1 \|v\|_\infty . \tag{8}$$

(ii) *If the domain Ω is bounded and if $1 < r < s < \infty$, then we have*

$$L_\infty(\Omega) \subsetneqq L_s(\Omega) \subsetneqq L_r(\Omega) \subsetneqq L_1(\Omega) . \,\dagger)$$

12.9. Remark. The Hölder inequality (6), or (8), implies immediately that the integral

$$\int_\Omega a_\alpha(x; \delta_k\, u(x))\, \mathrm{D}^\alpha v(x)\, \mathrm{d}x$$

is finite if, e.g.,

$$\mathrm{D}^\alpha v \in L_p(\Omega), \quad a_\alpha(x; \delta_k\, u(x)) \in L_q(\Omega), \tag{9}$$

where the numbers $p > 1$, $q > 1$ are linked by relation (4), or where either $p = 1$, $q = \infty$ or $p = \infty$, $q = 1$ holds. At present, we do not in fact know which assumptions on the functions a_α and u guarantee that the second of conditions (9) be satisfied. Therefore, we present the following theorem.

12.10. Theorem. *Let $p_1, p_2, \ldots, p_m$ and r be real numbers, $p_i \geqq 1$ $(i = 1, \ldots, m)$, $r \geqq 1$. Let $h = h(x; \xi)$ be a function defined for $x \in \Omega$ and $\xi \in \mathbb{R}^m$, and let $h \in$ CAR. Denote by $\mathcal{H}(u_1, \ldots, u_m)$ the Němyckiĭ operator determined by the function h.*

$\dagger)$ If X is a normed linear space with the norm $\|\cdot\|_X$ and Y a normed linear space with the norm $\|\cdot\|_Y$, then the notation

$$X \subsetneqq Y$$

means that

(a) $X \subset Y$,

(b) there exists a constant $c > 0$ such that for all $u \in X$

$$\|u\|_Y \leqq c\|u\|_X$$

holds.

We say that *the space X is continuously imbedded into the space Y.*

(i) *Then, for an arbitrary m-tuple of functions $u_i \in L_{p_i}(\Omega)$ $(i = 1, ..., m)$,*

$$\mathscr{H}(u_1, ..., u_m) \in L_r(\Omega)$$

holds if and only if the following condition is satisfied: (a) *A function $g \in L_r(\Omega)$ and a number $c \geq 0$ exist such that for almost all $x \in \Omega$ and for all $\xi \in \mathbb{R}^m$*

$$\left| h(x; \xi_1, ..., \xi_m) \right| \leq g(x) + c \sum_{i=1}^{m} \left| \xi_i \right|^{p_i/r} . \tag{10}$$

(ii) *If condition* (a) *is satisfied, then the Němyckiǐ operator $\mathscr{H}$ is a continuous operator from the Cartesian product*

$$L_{p_1}(\Omega) \times L_{p_2}(\Omega) \times ... \times L_{p_m}(\Omega)$$

into the space $L_r(\Omega)$.†)

12.11. Comments on Theorem 12.10. (i) In the sequel, only the following assertion of Theorem 12.10 will be used:

If condition (a) *is satisfied, then the operator $\mathscr{H}$ is a continuous operator from $L_{p_1}(\Omega) \times ... \times L_{p_m}(\Omega)$ into $L_r(\Omega)$.*

(ii) If condition (a) is satisfied, then it can be proved easily that the operator $\mathscr{H}$ maps the Cartesian product $L_{p_1}(\Omega) \times ... \times L_{p_m}(\Omega)$ into $L_r(\Omega)$: As a consequence of

---

†) (i) Recall that the operator A which maps the Banach space X (with the norm $\|\cdot\|_X$) into the Banach space Y (with the norm $\|\cdot\|_Y$) is called a *continuous operator* if the following is true: If $\{u_n\}_{n=1}^{\infty}$ is a sequence of elements from X, $u_n \in \mathscr{D}(A)$, $u_0 \in \mathscr{D}(A)$, and

$$\lim_{n \to \infty} \left\| u_n - u_0 \right\|_X = 0 ,$$

then we have

$$\lim_{n \to \infty} \left\| A u_n - A u_0 \right\|_Y = 0 .$$

(ii) Let $X_1, X_2, ..., X_k$ be Banach spaces. The set X of all k-tuples

$$(u_1, u_2, ..., u_k), \quad \text{where} \quad u_i \in X_i, \quad i = 1, 2, ..., k ,$$

is called the *Cartesian product* of the spaces $X_1, X_2, ..., X_k$ and is denoted by

$$X = X_1 \times X_2 \times ... \times X_k .$$

The space X is again a Banach space if the norm on X is defined, e.g., by

$$\left\| (u_1, u_2, ..., u_k) \right\|_X = \left(\sum_{i=1}^{k} \| u_i \|_{X_i}^s \right)^{1/s} ;$$

the symbol $\|\cdot\|_{X_i}$ stands for the norm in the space X_i and s is an arbitrary but fixed number in the interval $[1, \infty)$.

the familiar inequality

$$(d_1 + \ldots + d_n)^r \le n^{r-1}(d_1^r + \ldots + d_n^r)$$

$(d_i \ge 0,\ r \ge 1)$, we have, in view of (10),

$$\left| h(x; u_1(x), \ldots, u_m(x)) \right|^r \le \left[|g(x)| + c \sum_{i=1}^{m} |u_i(x)|^{p_i/r} \right]^r \le$$

$$\le (m + 1)^{r-1} \left[|g(x)|^r + c^r \sum_{i=1}^{m} |u_i(x)|^{p_i} \right].$$

The integral of the last expression is finite since $g \in L_r(\Omega)$ and $u_i \in L_{p_i}(\Omega)$ $(i = 1, \ldots, m)$, and thus also the function

$$\mathscr{H}(u_1, \ldots, u_m)(x) = h(x; u_1(x), \ldots, u_m(x))$$

belongs to $L_r(\Omega)$. At the same time, for every m-tuple $(u_1, \ldots, u_m) \in L_{p_1}(\Omega) \times \ldots$ $\ldots \times L_{p_m}(\Omega)$, the following estimate is obtained:

$$\left\| \mathscr{H}(u_1, \ldots, u_m) \right\|_r \le c_1 + c_2 \sum_{i=1}^{m} \|u_i\|_{p_i}^{p_i/r}, \tag{11}$$

where c_1, c_2 are nonnegative constants $\left[c_1 = (m + 1)^{(r-1)/r} \|g\|_r,\ c_2 = (m + 1)^{(r-1)/r} c \right]$.

(iii) The proof of the continuity of the operator $\mathscr{H}$ as well as the proof of the reverse implication of that of Remark (ii) above is substantially more difficult and exploits more involved results from measure and integration theory; the proof can be found, e.g., in [37] or in the books [52], [89].

(iv) The reader will certainly have noted that Theorem 12.10 actually says, among other things, the following: If the Němyckiǐ operator $\mathscr{H}$ maps the Cartesian product $L_{p_1}(\Omega) \times \ldots \times L_{p_m}(\Omega)$ into $L_r(\Omega)$, then the operator $\mathscr{H}$ is in fact continuous.

We wish to emphasize that this situation is quite exceptional in the theory of operators (unfortunately!).

12.12. Example. As the function h, choose the function $a_\alpha(x; \xi)$ from identity (1); thus, $m = \varkappa = \varkappa(N, k)$.

(i) Let $p > 1$, choose all the p_i in Theorem 12.10 the same and equal to the number p, and as r choose the number $q = p/(p - 1)$. Then, we have $p_i/r = p/q = = p - 1$ and inequality (10) takes the form

$$|a_\alpha(x; \xi)| \le g_\alpha(x) + c_\alpha \sum_{|\beta| \le k} |\xi_\beta|^{p-1}, \tag{12}$$

where g_α is a given function from $L_q(\Omega)$ and c_α is a nonnegative constant. According to Theorem 12.10, the function

$$w(x) = a_\alpha(x; \delta_k u(x))$$

· will then be an element of the space $L_q(\Omega)$ if $a_\alpha \in$ **CAR**, if inequality (12) is satisfied for almost all $x \in \Omega$ and for all $\xi \in \mathbb{R}^\varkappa$, and if

$$D^\beta u \in L_p(\Omega) \quad \text{for} \quad |\beta| \leq k.$$

Inequality (11) then says that

$$\left\| a_\alpha(x; \delta_k u(x)) \right\|_q \leq c_{\alpha 1} + c_{\alpha 2} \sum_{|\beta| \leq k} \left\| D^\beta u \right\|_p^{p-1}.$$

The integral

$$\int_\Omega a_\alpha(x; \delta_k u(x)) \, D^\alpha v(x) \, dx$$

will now be finite if

$$D^\alpha v \in L_p(\Omega):$$

The numbers p and q are connected by the relation $1/p + 1/q = 1$; thus, we can use the Hölder inequality (5), or (6), by which

$$\left| \int_\Omega a_\alpha(x; \delta_k u(x)) \, D^\alpha v(x) \, dx \right| \leq \left\| a_\alpha(x; \delta_k u(x)) \right\|_q \left\| D^\alpha v \right\|_p \leq$$

$$\leq \left(c_{\alpha 1} + c_{\alpha 2} \sum_{|\beta| \leq k} \left\| D^\beta u \right\|_p^{p-1} \right) \left\| D^\alpha v \right\|_p \tag{13}$$

holds (with nonnegative constants $c_{\alpha 1}$, $c_{\alpha 2}$ which do not depend on the functions u, v).

(ii) Choose $p = 1$ and $q = \infty$. Inequality (12) then takes the form

$$\left| a_\alpha(x; \xi) \right| \leq g_\alpha(x) + \varkappa \cdot c_\alpha, \tag{14}$$

where g is a given function from $L_\infty(\Omega)$ and c_α is a nonnegative number. Thus, it is immediately seen that the function

$$w(x) = a_\alpha(x; \delta_k u(x))$$

will be an element of the space $L_\infty(\Omega)$ if $a_\alpha \in$ **CAR** and $D^\beta u \in L_1(\Omega)$ for $|\beta| \leq k$ (it would even suffice if all the functions $D^\beta u$ were simply measurable). Inequality (13) now obviously holds again if we put $p = 1$ in it: In fact, it suffices to use the Hölder inequality (8) according to which

$$\left| \int_\Omega a_\alpha(x; \delta_k u(x)) \, D^\alpha v(x) \, dx \right| \leq \left\| a_\alpha(x; \delta_k u(x)) \right\|_\infty \left\| D^\alpha v \right\|_1.$$

12.13. Coefficients with polynomial growth. Condition (12) will assume a very important role in our further considerations. In fact it tells us how must the function $a_\alpha(x; \xi)$ behave with respect to the variable ξ by setting certain limits on its growth: The function a_α cannot grow faster, in the variable ξ, than the polynomial $c_1 + c_2 |\xi|^{p-1}$.

For this reason, we call the functions a_α which satisfy the condition (12) functions with polynomial growth. Since we will always consider only functions a_α which have the Carathéodory property, we introduce the following notation: Let $p \geq 1$; then

$$a_\alpha \in \textbf{CAR}(p) \tag{15}$$

means that

(a) $a_\alpha \in \textbf{CAR}$,

(b) a function $g_\alpha \in L_q(\Omega)$ and a constant $c_\alpha \geq 0$ exist such that a_α satisfies condition (12), where either $q = p/(p-1)$ for $p > 1$, or $q = \infty$ for $p = 1$.†)

For the sake of completeness, we note that condition (12) can be expressed in a number of other equivalent forms; e.g., it is possible to replace (12) by the condition

$$\left| a_\alpha(x; \xi) \right| \leq \tilde{g}_\alpha(x) + \tilde{c}_\alpha \big(\sum_{|\beta| \leq k} |\xi_\beta|^p \big)^{1/q}$$

with $\tilde{c}_\alpha \geq 0$ and $\tilde{g}_\alpha \in L_q(\Omega)$.

12.14. Examples. Condition (15) will play an important role in our further considerations; we, therefore, illustrate it using the following examples.

(i) Let $p > 1$, and put

$$a_\alpha(x; \xi) = |\xi_\alpha|^{p-2} \xi_\alpha = |\xi_\alpha|^{p-1} \operatorname{sgn} \xi_\alpha, \quad |\alpha| \leq k .$$

Then, obviously,

$$a_\alpha \in \textbf{CAR}(p) :$$

First of all, the reader verifies easily that $a_\alpha \in \textbf{CAR}$; thus, the problem is to verify that the growth condition (12) is satisfied. In fact, condition (12) is actually satisfied, since it suffices to choose $g_\alpha \equiv 0$ and $c_\alpha = 1$ and we have

$$\left| a_\alpha(x; \xi) \right| = |\xi_\alpha|^{p-1} \leq \sum_{|\beta| \leq k} |\xi_\beta|^{p-1} .$$

In particular, for

$$a_\alpha(x; \xi) = \xi_\alpha^2$$

we then have

$$a_\alpha \in \textbf{CAR}(3) .$$

---

†) If not otherwise stated, the following convention will be adhered to in the sequel: The pair of numbers p, q, where $p \geq 1$, is determined thus:

$$\text{for} \quad p > 1 \quad \text{we have} \quad q = p/(p-1),$$
$$\text{for} \quad p = 1 \quad \text{we have} \quad q = \infty .$$

(ii) Put

$$a_\alpha(x; \xi) = e^{\xi_\alpha} ;$$

then

$$a_\alpha \notin \mathbf{CAR}(p) \quad \text{for arbitrary} \quad p > 1 ;$$

indeed, if $c \geq 0$, $d \geq 0$, and $p > 1$ are given constants, then a number $t_0 \geq 0$ exists (dependent on c, d, and p) such that

$$e^t > ct^p + d \quad \text{for} \quad t \geq t_0 .$$

Therefore, an estimate of the type of (12) cannot be valid.

(iii) Choose $k = 1$ and use "ordinary" indexes instead of multi-indexes here. Condition (12) then assumes the form

$$\left| a_i(x; \xi_0, \xi_1, ..., \xi_N) \right| \leq g_i(x) + c_i \sum_{j=0}^{N} \left| \xi_j \right|^{p-1} \tag{16}$$

$(i = 0, 1, ..., N)$ with $g_i \in L_q(\Omega)$ and $c_i \geq 0$.

In particular, if we choose

$$a_i(x; \xi_0, \xi_1, ..., \xi_N) = \frac{\xi_i}{\sqrt{(1 + \xi_1^2 + ... + \xi_N^2)}} , \quad i = 1, ..., N, \tag{17}$$

then

$$a_i \in \mathbf{CAR}(2) :$$

Indeed, we have

$$\sqrt{(1 + \xi_1^2 + ... + \xi_N^2)} \geq 1 ,$$

and thus

$$\left| a_i(x; \xi_0, \xi_1, ..., \xi_N) \right| \leq \left| \xi_i \right| \leq \sum_{j=0}^{N} \left| \xi_j \right|^{p-1} \quad \text{with} \quad p = 2$$

holds, which is condition (16) with $g_i \equiv 0$ and $c_i = 1$.

Of course, it can also be shown that

$$a_i \in \mathbf{CAR}(p) \quad \text{for arbitrary} \quad p > 1 :$$

Namely, we have

$$\left| \xi_i \right| \leq \sqrt{(1 + \xi_1^2 + ... + \xi_N^2)} ,$$

and thus

$$\left| a_i(x; \xi_0, \xi_1, ..., \xi_N) \right| \leq 1$$

holds, which is condition (16) with $g_i(x) \equiv 1$ and $c_i = 0$ [we assume that the domain Ω is bounded and, therefore, $g_i \in L_q(\Omega)$ for arbitrary $q > 1$].

(iv) Let $k = 1$ again and put

$$a_i(x; \xi_0, \xi_1, ..., \xi_N) = \xi_i^2 , \quad i = 0, 1, ..., N .$$

It was already shown that $a_i \in CAR(3)$ in Example (i). However,

$$a_i \notin CAR(2) \ ;$$

indeed, if $c \geq 0$ and $d \geq 0$ are given constants, then a number $t_0 \geq 0$ (dependent on c and d) exists such that

$$t^2 > ct + d \quad \text{for} \quad t \geq t_0 \, ,$$

and the reader can now easily prove that one arrives at a contradiction from here with the growth condition in the assumption $a_i \in CAR(2)$.

The last example shows that if a function a_α belongs to the class $CAR(p)$ it still need not belong to the class $CAR(r)$ with $r < p$. Therefore, we pursue the investigation of the relation between the classes $CAR(p)$ for different values of p. We have the following lemma:

12.15. Lemma. *Let Ω be a bounded domain in $\mathbb{R}^N$, $r > p \geq 1$. If $a_\alpha \in CAR(p)$, then $a_\alpha \in CAR(r)$.*

We leave the proof of this assertion to the reader; it is based on the following fact: There exist nonnegative numbers c and d (dependent on p and r) such that

$$t^p \leq ct^r + d \quad \text{for all} \quad t \geq 0 \, .$$

12.16. Remark. As already stated, condition (15) will be essential in the sequel. If then the coefficients $a_\alpha = a_\alpha(x; \xi)$ are given, we ask whether a number $p \geq 1$ exists such that

$$a_\alpha \in CAR(p) \, .$$

The examples in Paragraph 12.14 as well as Lemma 12.15 show, however, that there is some freedom in choosing the number p: *If $a_\alpha \in CAR(p)$, then also $a_\alpha \in CAR(p + \varepsilon)$ for every $\varepsilon > 0$.*

We therefore emphasize at this point that, roughly speaking, we will be interested in the "least possible" $p \geq 1$ such that (15) holds. So, for instance, for the functions a_α of the type

$$a_\alpha(x; \xi) = \xi_\alpha \, , \quad |\alpha| \leq k \, ,$$

the number $p = 2$ is precisely the desired "optimal" parameter [see Example 12.14 (i)]; for the coefficients a_α given by formula (17) this "optimal" parameter is $p = 1$, etc. The reasons for precisely this choice of the parameter p will be discussed in the sequel — see, e.g., Paragraph 14.5 (iii).

12.17. More on the identity (1). Identity (1) was the starting point of all the considerations of this section. We now return to that identity: From Example 12.12, we see that the left-hand side of the identity is a finite number if

$$a_\alpha \in \mathbf{CAR}(p) \quad \text{for} \quad |\alpha| \leq k$$

with a number $p \geq 1$, under the assumption, of course, that

$$D^\alpha v \in L_p(\Omega) \quad \text{for} \quad |\alpha| \leq k \, ,$$
$$D^\beta u \in L_p(\Omega) \quad \text{for} \quad |\beta| \leq k \, . \tag{18}$$

As far as the right-hand side of identity (1) is concerned, we see immediately that it is finite if

$$f \in L_q(\Omega) \, , \quad v \in L_p(\Omega) \, ;$$

it suffices to apply the Hölder inequality (6), or (8).

SECTION 13. SOBOLEV SPACES

13.1. Let us examine further condition (12.18) which was of importance for identity (12.1): This condition is certainly satisfied if we assume that Ω is a bounded domain in $\mathbb{R}^N$ and if we then choose both u and v from the space $C^k(\bar{\Omega})$. However, this is an unnecessarily "special" space — it turns out that a broader class of functions is sufficient, namely functions from the so-called *Sobolev space* discussed in the paragraphs which follow.

Recall once more that we assume throughout that

$$\Omega \in \mathscr{C}^{0,1} \, ;$$

in particular, the domain Ω is thus bounded.

13.2. The generalized derivative. Let k be a positive integer, and let $p \geq 1$. Consider the set $C^k(\bar{\Omega})$ and define, for $u \in C^k(\bar{\Omega})$, the norm of a function u by the formula

$$\|u\|_{k,p} = \sum_{|\beta| \leq k} \left[\int_\Omega |D^\beta u(x)|^p \, dx \right]^{1/p} = \sum_{|\beta| \leq k} \|D^\beta u\|_p \tag{1}$$

[which is, indeed, a norm since the expressions $\|D^\beta u\|_p$ are norms in the space $L_p(\Omega)$].

(i) The space $C^k(\bar{\Omega})$ with the norm (1) is not complete. Now, let $\{u_n\}_{n=1}^\infty$ be a sequence of functions $u_n = u_n(x)$ from $C^k(\bar{\Omega})$ which is fundamental [with respect to the norm (1)], i.e., for which

$$\lim_{m,n \to \infty} \|u_m - u_n\|_{k,p} = 0 \, .$$

It follows, from formula (1), that for an arbitrary multi-index β, $|\beta| \leq k$, we have

$$\|D^\beta u_m - D^\beta u_n\|_p \leq \|u_m - u_n\|_{k,p} \, . \tag{2}$$

If the multi-index $(0, 0, \ldots, 0)$ is chosen for β, we see that the sequence $\{u_n\}_{n=1}^{\infty}$ is fundamental in $L_p(\Omega)$. However, the space $L_p(\Omega)$ is complete (see Paragraph 12.7) and, therefore, there is an element w in the space $L_p(\Omega)$, determined uniquely by the sequence $\{u_n\}_{n=1}^{\infty}$, such that

$$w = \lim_{n \to \infty} u_n \quad \text{in} \quad L_p(\Omega).$$

Now choose some other multi-index β, $1 \leq |\beta| \leq k$. Formula (2) implies that the sequence $\{D^{\beta} u_n\}_{n=1}^{\infty}$ is fundamental in $L_p(\Omega)$, and since this space is complete a uniquely determined element $w_{\beta} \in L_p(\Omega)$ exists such that

$$w_{\beta} = \lim_{n \to \infty} D^{\beta} u_n \quad \text{in} \quad L_p(\Omega).$$

It might possibly be thought that the element $w_{\beta} \in L_p(\Omega)$ constructed above depends upon the choice of the fundamental sequence $\{u_n\}_{n=1}^{\infty}$. But this is not the case. In fact, if $\{v_n\}_{n=1}^{\infty}$ is some other sequence of functions from $C^k(\overline{\Omega})$ which is again fundamental with respect to the norm (1) and which has as its limit $\left[\text{in } L_p(\Omega)\right]$ the same element w as the sequence $\{u_n\}_{n=1}^{\infty}$, i.e., if

$$\lim_{n \to \infty} v_n = w \quad \text{in} \quad L_p(\Omega),$$

then we also have

$$\lim_{n \to \infty} D^{\beta} v_n = w_{\beta} \quad \text{in} \quad L_p(\Omega).$$

Thus, the element w_{β} is in fact determined uniquely by the element w; we call this element the generalized derivative (of order $|\beta|$) of the function u and denote it by the usual symbol $D^{\beta} w$:

$$w_{\beta} = D^{\beta} w . \dagger)$$

The index β was arbitrary (save for $|\beta| \leq k$, of course). Therefore, the $\varkappa$-tuple of functions

$$\{w_{\beta}\}_{|\beta| \leq k}, \quad \text{where} \quad w_{(0,0,\ldots,0)} = w,$$

is uniquely determined by the function w. Following the notation of Paragraph 7.2, we can denote this $\varkappa$-tuple by the symbol

$$\delta_k w ;$$

it consists of the function $w \in L_p(\Omega)$ together with all its generalized derivatives $D^{\beta} w$ of order $|\beta| \leq k$, with $D^{\beta} w \in L_p(\Omega)$.

---

†) The fact that we use the same notation for the generalized derivatives as for the "classical" derivatives is no problem. In fact, it can be shown that whenever the function w defined by the sequence $\{u_n\}_{n=1}^{\infty}$ belongs to the space $C^{|\beta|}(\overline{\Omega})$, the generalized derivative of w_{β} is identical with the "classical" derivative $D^{\beta} w$.

(ii) The generalized derivative $D^\beta w$ of the function $w \in L_p(\Omega)$ can also be characterized by the relation

$$\int_\Omega D^\beta w(x)\, v(x)\, dx = (-1)^{|\beta|} \int_\Omega w(x)\, D^\beta v(x)\, dx , \qquad (3)$$

valid for every function $v \in C_0^\infty(\Omega)$. Let us prove this assertion: If $u_n \in C^k(\overline{\Omega})$ and $v \in C_0^\infty(\Omega)$, then

$$\int_\Omega D^\beta u_n(x)\, v(x)\, dx = (-1)^{|\beta|} \int_\Omega u_n(x)\, D^\beta v(x)\, dx$$

holds for $|\beta| \leq k$ according to Green's theorem (see Paragraph 11.3). Since $D^\beta u_n$ converges to $w_\beta = D^\beta w$ and u_n converges to w as $n \to \infty$, in both cases in the sense of convergence in the norm of the space $L_p(\Omega)$, relation (3) follows from the preceding relation on passing to the limit as $n \to \infty$.

(iii) So far, the concept of the generalized derivative $D^\beta w$ has been established for a function $w \in L_p(\Omega)$ which is the limit [in the norm of the space $L_p(\Omega)$] of a sequence of functions $u_n \in C^k(\overline{\Omega})$ which is fundamental with respect to the norm (1). We now establish this concept for arbitrary functions from $L_p(\Omega)$; to this end, we just use relation (3) which characterizes the generalized derivative of our — hitherto special — function w.

Let then $w \in L_p(\Omega)$ and let w_β (where β is an N-dimensional multi-index) be a function defined on Ω and such that $w_\beta \in L_1(K)$ for every closed set $K \subset \Omega$. We say that the function w_β is the *generalized derivative* of the function w and denote it by $D^\beta w$ if for every function $v \in C_0^\infty(\Omega)$ the relation

$$\int_\Omega w_\beta(x)\, v(x)\, dx = (-1)^{|\beta|} \int_\Omega w(x)\, D^\beta v(x)\, dx \qquad (4)$$

holds.

From part (i) of this paragraph it follows that the concept of the generalized derivative makes sense. The reader can easily verify that the generalized derivative possesses the properties we are familiar with in the case of "classical" derivatives. In particular, the relations

$$D^\beta(u + v) = D^\beta u + D^\beta v , \quad D^\beta(cu) = c\, D^\beta u \quad \text{for} \quad c \in \mathbb{R}$$

and

$$D^\gamma(D^\beta u) = D^{\gamma + \beta} u$$

are valid.

(iv) The reader who is familiar with the concept of distribution will certainly have recognized that the function w_β is the so-called derivative of the function w in the sense of distributions. We will not make use of the concept of distribution ourselves, however, but refer the interested reader to the book [85].

13.3. The Sobolev space $W^{k,p}(\Omega)$. Let k be a positive integer and let $p \geq 1$. By the symbol

$$W^{k,p}(\Omega)$$

we denote the set of all functions $u \in L_p(\Omega)$ all of whose generalized derivatives $D^\beta u$ of order at most k exist and again belong to $L_p(\Omega)$:

$$D^\beta u \in L_p(\Omega) \quad \text{for} \quad |\beta| \leq k \,.$$

The Sobolev space $W^{k,p}(\Omega)$ has the following properties:

(i) *The expression*

$$\|u\|_{k,p} = \sum_{|\beta| \leq k} \|D^\beta u\|_p \tag{5}$$

serves to define the norm on the space $W^{k,p}(\Omega)$. *The space* $W^{k,p}(\Omega)$ *with this norm is a separable Banach space.*

(ii) *The set* $C^\infty(\overline{\Omega})$ *is dense in the space* $W^{k,p}(\Omega)$.

(iii) *The expression*

$$\|\|u\|\|_{k,p} = \|u\|_p + \sum_{|\beta| = k} \|D^\beta u\|_p$$

defines another norm on the space $W^{k,p}(\Omega)$ *which is equivalent to the norm* (5).†) *Another norm on the space* $W^{k,p}(\Omega)$, *which is also equivalent to the norm* (5), *is given by the expression*

$$\left(\sum_{|\beta| \leq k} \|D^\beta u\|_p^p \right)^{1/p} \,.$$

The proofs of the assertions of this paragraph can be found, e.g., in [54], [68]; for $p = 2$, see also [80].

13.4. Example. Consider the case $N = 1$ and $\Omega = (a, b)$. Moreover, put $k = 1$ and consider the Sobolev space $W^{1,p}(\Omega)$, denoted in this special case by

$$W^{1,p}(a, b) \,.$$

A function $u = u(x)$ from $L_p(a, b)$ belongs to $W^{1,p}(a, b)$ if its generalized derivative $u'(x)$ also belongs to $L_p(a, b)$. Define the function $U = U(x)$ for $x \in [a, b]$ by the formula

$$U(x) = \int_a^x u'(t) \, dt \,.$$

---

†) Let X be a normed linear space and let $\| \cdot \|_X$ and $\|\| \cdot \|\|_X$ be two norms on X. We say that these norms are *equivalent* if there exist positive numbers c_1 and c_2 such that for all elements $u \in X$ we have

$$c_1 \|u\|_X \leq \|\|u\|\|_X \leq c_2 \|u\|_X \,.$$

The integral exists since $u' \in L_p(a, b)$, and thus $u' \in L_1(a, b)$. The function $U(x)$ is not only continuous but even absolutely continuous on $[a, b]$ and has, therefore, a derivative, which is equal to $u'(x)$, almost everywhere in (a, b). Integration by parts yields

$$\int_a^b U(x)\, v'(x)\, \mathrm{d}x = [U(b)\, v(b) - U(a)\, v(a)] - \int_a^b u'(x)\, v(x)\, \mathrm{d}x \qquad (6)$$

for every function $v \in C^\infty([a, b])$ [we have $U' = u'$ almost everywhere in (a, b)]. If we choose $v \in C_0^\infty(a, b)$, the first expression on the right-hand side vanishes since $v(a) = v(b) = 0$.

Since u' is the generalized derivative of the function u, relation (4) is valid, i.e.,

$$\int_a^b u'(x)\, v(x)\, \mathrm{d}x = -\int_a^b u(x)\, v'(x)\, \mathrm{d}x \qquad (7)$$

for every function $v \in C_0^\infty(a, b)$.

Comparing formulas (6) and (7), we see that

$$\int_a^b [u(x) - U(x)]\, v'(x)\, \mathrm{d}x = 0 \quad \text{for every} \quad v \in C_0^\infty(a, b)\,,$$

whence it follows that $u(x) - U(x) = \text{const.}$ for almost all $x \in [a, b]$. Thus, we have shown that the function $u \in W^{1,p}(a, b)$ is equal to the absolutely continuous function

$$\int_a^x u'(t)\, \mathrm{d}t + \text{const.}$$

almost everywhere in $[a, b]$ and that the generalized derivative u' is actually equal to the "classical" derivative of the function u which exists almost everywhere in $[a, b]$.

We can exploit the above fact to formulate another — equivalent — definition of the space $W^{1,p}(a, b)$: We say that a function u defined on $[a, b]$ is an element of the space $W^{1,p}(a, b)$ if it is absolutely continuous on $[a, b]$ and if its derivative [which exists almost everywhere in (a, b) by absolute continuity] belongs to $L_p(a, b)$.

Similarly, it can be shown that, for $k > 1$, $W^{k,p}(a, b)$ is the space of those functions u whose $(k - 1)$-st derivative $u^{(k-1)} = v$ is absolutely continuous in $[a, b]$ and whose k-th derivative $u^{(k)}$ [which exists almost everywhere in (a, b), since the absolutely continuous function v has the derivative $v' = u^{(k)}$ almost everywhere in (a, b)] belongs to $L_p(a, b)$.

13.5. The space $W_0^{k,p}(\Omega)$. Obviously, the set $C_0^\infty(\Omega)$ is a subset of the Sobolev space $W^{k,p}(\Omega)$. We denote the closure of this set with respect to the norm (5) by

$$W_0^{k,p}(\Omega)\,.$$

This is again a Banach space, under the norm (5), and a subspace of the Sobolev space $W^{k,p}(\Omega)$.

13.6. Example. Let $N = 1$ and $\Omega = (a, b)$ again. It can be shown that $W_0^{k,p}(a, b)$ is just the subspace of all the functions u of $W^{k,p}(a, b)$ which satisfy:

$$u(a) = u'(a) = u''(a) = \ldots = u^{(k-1)}(a) = 0 \,,$$

$$u(b) = u'(b) = u''(b) = \ldots = u^{(k-1)}(b) = 0 \,.$$

It is meaningful to discuss the values of the functions $u^{(i)}(x)$ at the points $x = a$ and $x = b$, for $i = 0, 1, \ldots, k - 1$, since these functions are even absolutely continuous in $[a, b]$. As far as the derivatives at the end-points of the interval $[a, b]$ are concerned, the values of the left-hand and right-hand derivatives are to be considered.

In particular, then

$$W_0^{1,p}(a, b) = \{u \in W^{1,p}(a, b); u(a) = u(b) = 0\} \,.$$

13.7. Lemma. *The expression*

$$\|u\|_{k,p,0} = \sum_{|\beta|=k} \|D^\beta u\|_p \tag{8}$$

defines a norm on the space $W_0^{k,p}(\Omega)$, equivalent to the norm (5).

The proof of the above assertion will be carried out for $N = 1$, i.e., for $\Omega = (a, b)$; for general N, we refer to [54], [68]. Recall that in (5) the summation is over all the generalized derivatives of order $|\beta| \leq k$ while in (8) it is only over derivatives of order k.

Obviously,

$$\|u\|_{k,p,0} \leq \|u\|_{k,p} \,;$$

thus it suffices to prove that a number $c > 0$ exists such that for all $u \in W_0^{k,p}(a, b)$ we have

$$\|u\|_{k,p} \leq c\|u\|_{k,p,0} \,. \tag{9}$$

The Hölder inequality, applied to the product of the function $u^{(i)}$ and the function identically equal to one, implies that

$$\left| \int_a^b u^{(i)}(x)\, dx \right| \leq (b - a)^{(p-1)/p} \|u^{(i)}\|_p \,, \quad i = 0, 1, \ldots, k \,.$$

Further, for $i = 0, 1, \ldots, k - 1$, we have

$$u^{(i)}(x) = \int_a^x u^{(i+1)}(t)\, dt \quad \text{for} \quad x \in [a, b] \,,$$

since $u^{(i)}(a) = 0$ by Example 13.6. Therefore,

$$\left|u^{(i)}(x)\right|^p = \left|\int_a^x u^{(i+1)}(t)\,dt\right|^p \leq \left(\int_a^b \left|u^{(i+1)}(t)\right|\,dt\right)^p \leq (b-a)^{p-1}\left\|u^{(i+1)}\right\|_p^p.$$

Integration of this inequality over the interval (a, b) then yields

$$\int_a^b \left|u^{(i)}(x)\right|^p\,dx \leq (b-a)^p \left\|u^{(i+1)}\right\|_p^p$$

or, in other words,

$$\left\|u^{(i)}\right\|_p \leq (b-a)\left\|u^{(i+1)}\right\|_p, \quad i = 0, 1, ..., k-1.$$

Thus, we have $\left\|u^{(i)}\right\|_p \leq c_i\left\|u^{(k)}\right\|_p$, where $c_i = (b-a)^{k-i}$, and, finally,

$$\left\|u\right\|_{k,p} = \left\|u\right\|_p + \left\|u'\right\|_p + ... + \left\|u^{(k-1)}\right\|_p + \left\|u^{(k)}\right\|_p \leq$$

$$\leq (c_0 + c_1 + ... + c_k)\left\|u^{(k)}\right\|_p = (c_0 + c_1 + ... + c_k)\left\|u\right\|_{k,p,0},$$

which is inequality (9).

13.8. The trace of a function from the space $W^{k,p}(\Omega)$ on the boundary $\partial\Omega$. Let $u \in W^{k,p}(\Omega)$. Then the symbol

$$u\big|_{\partial\Omega}, \quad \text{or} \quad \text{``}u(x) \quad \text{for} \quad x \in \partial\Omega\text{''}$$

is not meaningful in general, since $\partial\Omega$ is a set of measure zero and the function u is — as a function from $L_p(\Omega)$ — defined almost everywhere on $\bar{\Omega}$. †)
   In Example 13.4, we have seen, however, that it is sometimes possible to speak of "values of the function (and of its derivatives) on the boundary $\partial\Omega$": For $N = 1$ and $\Omega = (a, b)$, the boundary $\partial\Omega$ consists of the points a and b and the values

$$u(a), u(b), u'(a), u'(b), ..., u^{(k-1)}(a), u^{(k-1)}(b)$$

are well-defined for a function $u \in W^{k,p}(a, b)$, since the functions $u(x), u'(x), ...$ ..., $u^{(k-1)}(x)$ are even absolutely continuous on $[a, b]$.
   This leads to the concept of the trace of a function u on $\partial\Omega$ which is a generalization of the concept of the restriction $u\big|_{\partial\Omega}$.
   First, we present a theorem, the proof of which may be found, e.g., in the books [54], [68].

---

†) Actually, the function u was only defined on Ω. However, we may assume that it was in fact defined on $\bar{\Omega} = \Omega \cup \partial\Omega$: The set $\delta\Omega$ is of measure zero and such sets are irrelevant to our considerations.

13.9. Theorem. *There exists one and only one continuous linear operator T which assigns to every function* $u \in W^{1,p}(\Omega)$ *a function* $Tu \in L_p(\partial\Omega)$ †) *and has the following property: For* $u \in C^\infty(\bar{\Omega})$, *we have*

$$Tu = u|_{\partial\Omega} . \tag{10}$$

13.10. Convention. The function Tu defined on $\partial\Omega$ is called the *trace* of the function $u \in W^{1,p}(\Omega)$ on $\partial\Omega$. Since, by formula (10), the concept of the trace on $\partial\Omega$ is a natural generalization of the concept of the restriction on $\partial\Omega$, the trace of the function u will be denoted, in the sequel, by the same symbol u, or by the symbol $u|_{\partial\Omega}$ (instead of Tu). If $\varphi = \varphi(x)$ is a function defined on $\partial\Omega$, then the statement

$$u = \varphi \quad \text{on } \partial\Omega \text{ in the sense of traces}$$

will express the fact that $Tu = \varphi$.

If $u \in W^{2,p}(\Omega)$, then

$$D^\beta u \in W^{1,p}(\Omega)$$

for the generalized derivative $D^\beta u$ with $|\beta| = 1$. Thus, it is also possible to define the trace of the first (generalized) derivative of the function $u \in W^{2,p}(\Omega)$ as

$$T(D^\beta u) ,$$

where T is the operator of Theorem 13.9. — Similarly, for a function $u \in W^{k,p}(\Omega)$, it is possible to define (on the basis of Theorem 13.9) traces of all the derivatives $D^\beta u$ of order $|\beta| \leq k - 1$.

Naturally, the trace of the k-th derivative cannot be defined. Indeed, there does not exist a continuous mapping T from $L_p(\Omega)$ into $L_p(\partial\Omega)$ such that $Tu = u|_{\partial\Omega}$ for $u \in C^0(\bar{\Omega})$.

---

†) A function $u = u(x)$, defined for $x \in \partial\Omega$, belongs to $L_p(\partial\Omega)$ if

$$\|u\|_{p,\partial\Omega} = \left[\int_{\partial\Omega} |u(x)|^p \, \mathrm{d}S \right]^{1/p} < \infty . \tag{*}$$

The surface integral was introduced in Paragraph 9.2; applying the notation of Paragraph 9.2, we see that in the integral in (*) we actually have a combination of integrals of the type

$$\int_{\Delta} |u(y_1, \ldots, y_{N-1}, a(y_1, \ldots, y_{N-1}))|^p .$$

$$\cdot \left[1 + \sum_{i=1}^{N-1} \left(\frac{\partial a}{\partial y_i} (y_1, \ldots y_{N-1}) \right) \right]^{1/2} \mathrm{d}y_1 \ldots \mathrm{d}y_{N-1} ,$$

i.e., the space $L_p(\partial\Omega)$ reduces to a space of the type $L_p(\Delta)$, where Δ is a domain in $\mathbb{R}^{N-1}$.

13.11. Traces of functions from $W_0^{k,p}(\Omega)$. The following assertion holds:

$$W_0^{k,p}(\Omega) = \{u \in W^{k,p}(\Omega); \ D^\beta u = 0 \quad \text{on } \partial\Omega \text{ in the sense of traces for all}$$
$$|\beta| \leq k - 1\} .$$

(This fact is confirmed also by Example 13.6.) In particular, $W_0^{1,p}(\Omega)$ is thus the set of all the functions of $W^{1,p}(\Omega)$ for which $u|_{\partial\Omega} = 0$ in the sense of traces.

For this reason, the spaces $W_0^{k,p}(\Omega)$ are sometimes called spaces with zero traces, for short.

Applying the concept of the trace, we can now generalize Green's theorem (see [68]):

13.12. Theorem. *Let $u \in W^{1,p}(\Omega)$, $v \in W^{1,q}(\Omega)$, where $p > 1$, $q > 1$, $1/p + 1/q = = 1$. Then we have*

$$\int_\Omega \frac{\partial u}{\partial x_i}(x) \, v(x) \, dx = - \int_\Omega u(x) \frac{\partial v}{\partial x_i}(x) \, dx + \int_{\partial\Omega} uvv_i \, dS, \tag{11}$$

where $\partial u/\partial x_i$, $\partial v/\partial x_i$ are generalized derivatives, v_i is the i-th component of the vector of the outward normal to $\partial\Omega$, and the functions u, v in the surface integral are understood to be traces of the functions u, v on $\partial\Omega$.

13.13. Remarks. (i) If either $u \in W_0^{1,p}(\Omega)$ or $v \in W_0^{1,q}(\Omega)$, then the trace on $\partial\Omega$ of the respective function is equal to zero and the surface integral in formula (11) vanishes.

(ii) Just as in Paragraph 11.12, Green's Theorem 13.12 can be generalized to derivatives of higher order. For illustration only, we give one of the simpler assertions: *If $u \in W^{k,p}(\Omega)$ and $v \in W_0^{k,q}(\Omega)$, where $1/p + 1/q = 1$, then*

$$\int_\Omega D^\beta u(x) \, v(x) \, dx = (-1)^{|\beta|} \int_\Omega u(x) \, D^\beta v(x) \, dx \tag{12}$$

holds for $|\beta| \leq k$.

Since the Sobolev spaces are now at our disposal, it is possible to present the following assertion which is a direct consequence of Theorem 12.10, with reference to Example 12.12.

13.14. Theorem. *Let $a = a(x; \xi)$ be a function defined for $x \in \Omega$ and $\xi \in \mathbb{R}^\varkappa$, and let $a \in \mathbf{CAR}(p)$ with $p \geq 1$. Then the Němyckiĭ operator which is determined by the function a, and which assigns to every function $u \in W^{k,p}(\Omega)$ the function*

$$a(x; \delta_k u(x)),$$

is a continuous operator from $W^{k,p}(\Omega)$ into $L_q(\Omega)$ [where $q = p/(p-1)$ for $p > 1$, and $q = \infty$ for $p = 1$].

This assertion will be substantially exploited in the sequel. For the moment, we merely recall that for $a_\alpha \in CAR(p)$ and $u \in W^{k,p}(\Omega)$ we have

$$a_\alpha(x; \delta_k u(x)) \in L_q(\Omega)$$

according to this theorem, so that, by the Hölder inequality, the left-hand side of identity (12.1) is a finite number if also $v \in W^{k,p}(\Omega)$.

SECTION 14. DIFFERENTIAL OPERATORS

14.1. The formal differential operator. Let k be a positive integer, $p > 1$†), and consider the differential operator of order $2k$

$$(Au)(x) = \sum_{|\alpha| \leq k} (-1)^{|\alpha|} D^\alpha a_\alpha(x, \delta_k u(x)), \tag{1}$$

already encountered in Chapter II. Naturally, for the functions $a_\alpha = a_\alpha(x; \xi)$ defined for $x \in \Omega$ and $\xi \in \mathbb{R}^\varkappa$ we will now assume that

$$a_\alpha \in CAR(p) \quad \text{for} \quad |\alpha| \leq k \tag{2}$$

(see Paragraph 12.13).

The operator A defined by formula (1) will be called a *formal differential operator* since formula (1) merely represents a certain formal symbol [under our assumptions it is impossible to cary out, e.g., the differentiation indicated in (1)].

To the operator A we assign a form $a(u, v)$ defined by the formula

$$a(u, v) = \sum_{|\alpha| \leq k} \int_\Omega a_\alpha(x; \delta_k u(x)) D^\alpha v(x) \, dx . \tag{3}$$

In the sequel, we will work primarily with the form $a(u, v)$; the operator A mainly serves the purpose of showing with which differential operator this form is associated. We now examine the properties of the expression $a(u, v)$ in more detail.

From the considerations of Sections 12 and 13, especially those of Paragraphs 12.12, 12.13, 12.16 and 13.14, it follows that under assumption (2) the number $a(u, v)$ will be finite if

$$u \in W^{k,p}(\Omega), \quad v \in W^{k,p}(\Omega) .$$

Indeed, by the Hölder inequality we then have

$$|a(u, v)| \leq \sum_{|\alpha| \leq k} \|a_\alpha(x; \delta_k u(x))\|_q \|D^\alpha v\|_p \leq \Big(\sum_{|\alpha| \leq k} \|a_\alpha(x; \delta_k u(x))\|_q \Big) \|v\|_{k,p} . \tag{4}$$

---

†) We confine ourselves here to values of the parameter p from the interval $(1, \infty)$, although it is possible — as the reader will easily see in the following paragraphs — to consider $p = 1$ as well (with the convention from the footnote on p. 82 concerning the value of q). However, the choice of $1 < p < \infty$ has its own justification, as the reader will appreciate in Section 16.

Now, let u be a fixed element from $W^{k,p}(\Omega)$. If v_1, v_2 are functions from $W^{k,p}(\Omega)$ and c_1, c_2 real numbers, then

$$a(u, c_1 v_1 + c_2 v_2) = c_1\, a(u, v_1) + c_2\, a(u, v_2)\,;$$

this relation together with the estimate (4) says that for fixed u expression (3) defines a continuous linear functional Φ over the space $W^{k,p}(\Omega)$ †), namely by the relation

$$a(u, v) = \,<\!\Phi, v\!> = v \quad \text{for every} \quad v \in W^{k,p}(\Omega)\,.$$

The functional $\Phi \in \big(W^{k,p}(\Omega)\big)^*$ is determined uniquely by the $\varkappa$-tuple

$$\{a_\alpha(x;\, \delta_k\, u(x))\}_{|\alpha| \le k}\,,$$

i.e., more precisely: For given fixed coefficients a_α, the functional Φ is actually given by the function $u \in W^{k,p}(\Omega)$. Symbolically, we write

$$\Phi = \mathbb{A}u\,.$$

---

†) (i) Let X be a normed linear space. A continuous linear operator Φ, with the domain $\mathscr{D}(\Phi) = X$, which maps the space X into the space $\mathbb{R}$ is called a *continuous linear functional* over X. For the linear functional Φ to be continuous it is necessary and sufficient that a constant $c \ge 0$ exist such that

$$|\Phi u| \le c\|u\|_X \quad \text{for all elements} \quad u \in X\,.$$

The set of all continuous linear functionals Φ over the space X is denoted by X^* and called the *dual* (or adjoint) *space* of the space X. The space X^* is again a normed linear space if the norm of the functional Φ is defined by the formula

$$\|\Phi\|_{X^*} = \sup_{u \in X,\, u \neq \theta} \frac{|\Phi u|}{\|u\|_X}\,.$$

For the value of the functional Φ at the "point" $u \in X$ we often use the notation

$$<\!\Phi, u\!>$$

instead of the symbol Φu.

(ii) We will not discuss the characterization of all the continuous linear functionals over the space $W^{k,p}(\Omega)$. We present two examples only, which happen to be very important in what follows:

(a) *Let $f \in L_q(\Omega)$ and put*

$$<\!\Phi, u\!> = \int_\Omega f(x)\, u(x)\, \mathrm{d}x\,, \quad u \in W^{k,p}(\Omega)\,.$$

Then $\Phi \in (W^{k,p}(\Omega))^*$.

(b) *Let $f_\beta \in L_q(\Omega)$ for $|\beta| \le k$ and put*

$$<\!\Phi, u\!> = \sum_{|\beta| \le k} \int_\Omega f_\beta(x)\, D^\beta u(x)\, \mathrm{d}x\,, \quad u \in W^{k,p}(\Omega)\,.$$

Then $\Phi \in (W^{k,p}(\Omega))^*$.

From the above, from the definition of the Sobolev spaces, and from Theorem 12.10, follows the next important assertion:

14.2. Theorem. *The formal differential operator A from* (1) *with the coefficients* $a_\alpha \in \mathbf{CAR}(p)$ *defines the operator* $\mathbb{A}$ *from the space* $W^{k,p}(\Omega)$ *into the dual space* $(W^{k,p}(\Omega))^*$, *which is given by*

$$<\mathbb{A}u, v> = \sum_{|\alpha| \leq k} \int_\Omega a_\alpha(x; \delta_k u(x)) \, D^\alpha v(x) \, dx; \quad v \in W^{k,p}(\Omega). \tag{5}$$

Moreover, the operator $\mathbb{A}$ *is continuous.*

14.2$\frac{1}{2}$. Remark. Let V be a subspace of the space $W^{k,p}(\Omega)$ (again with the norm $\|\cdot\|_{k,p}$). The reader will easily verify — just as in the preceding paragraphs — that under the assumptions of Theorem 14.2 the relation

$$<\mathbb{B}u, v> = \sum_{|\alpha| \leq k} \int_\Omega a_\alpha(x; \delta_k u(x)) \, D^\alpha v(x) \, dx, \quad u \in W^{k,p}(\Omega), \quad v \in V,$$

again defines a continuous operator $\mathbb{B}$, now mapping the space $W^{k,p}(\Omega)$ into the space V^*. The following relation holds between the operators $\mathbb{B}$ and $\mathbb{A}$:

$$<\mathbb{A}u, v> = <\mathbb{B}u, v> \quad \text{for all} \quad u \in W^{k,p}(\Omega) \quad \text{and for all} \quad v \in V.$$

I.e., the functional $\mathbb{B}u \in V^*$ is a restriction of the functional $\mathbb{A}u \in (W^{k,p}(\Omega))^*$ to the subspace V. This fact should formally be expressed by

$$(\mathbb{A}u)|_V = \mathbb{B}u \, ;$$

However, we do not use this notation in what follows and we simply identify the operators $\mathbb{A}$ and $\mathbb{B}$. If, e.g., $\mathbf{f} \in V^*$, then the equality

$$\mathbb{A}u = \mathbf{f}$$

will mean that $(\mathbb{A}u)|_V = \mathbf{f}$.

14.3. Differential equations. In the above paragraphs, the formal differential operator A was "identified", in a certain sense, with the operator $\mathbb{A}$ from the space $W^{k,p}(\Omega)$ into the dual space $(W^{k,p}(\Omega))^*$.

Now let $\mathbf{f} \in (W_0^{k,p}(\Omega))^*$ be a given functional on $W_0^{k,p}(\Omega)$ and consider the operator equation

$$\mathbb{A}u = \mathbf{f} \tag{6}$$

[i.e., look for an element $u \in W^{k,p}(\Omega)$ which satisfies relation (6); equation (6) is understood in the sense of the conclusion of Remark 14.2$\frac{1}{2}$, where the space $W_0^{k,p}(\Omega)$ is chosen for V].

The equality of the functionals in (6) means that

$$<\mathbb{A}u, v> = <\mathbf{f}, v> \quad \text{for all} \quad v \in W_0^{k,p}(\Omega).$$

In view of formula (5), this relation can be written as follows:

$$\sum_{|\alpha| \leq k} \int_\Omega a_\alpha(x; \delta_k u(x)) \, D^\alpha v(x) \, dx = <\mathbf{f}, v> \tag{7}$$

for every function $v \in W_0^{k,p}(\Omega)$.

Consider now the rather more special functional **f**: Put

$$<\mathbf{f}, v> = \int_\Omega f(x) \, v(x) \, dx, \tag{8}$$

where f is a fixed function from $L_q(\Omega)$ $[q = p/(p-1)]$. Relation (7) will then reduce to the relation

$$\sum_{|\alpha| \leq k} \int_\Omega a_\alpha(x; \delta_k u(x)) \, D^\alpha v(x) \, dx = \int_\Omega f(x) \, v(x) \, dx.$$

This is, however, nothing other than identity (12.1) obtained in Section 11 when investigating the differential equation

$$\sum_{|\alpha| \leq k} (-1)^{|\alpha|} \, D^\alpha a_\alpha(x; \delta_k u(x)) = f(x) \quad \text{on} \quad \Omega,$$

under considerably stronger conditions than in the present paragraph, of course. Here, it is the formal differential equation

$$Au = f \quad \text{on} \quad \Omega,$$

which is a rather more intuitive version of the operator equation (6) [with the functional **f** given by relation (8)].

14.4. Weak solution of a differential equation. Let A be the formal differential operator defined by relation (1), **f** a functional on the space $W_0^{k,p}(\Omega)$.

We say that the function

$$u \in W^{k,p}(\Omega)$$

is a *weak solution* of the (formal) differential equation

$$Au = \mathbf{f} \tag{9}$$

if for all $v \in W_0^{k,p}(\Omega)$ the relation

$$<\mathbb{A}u, v> = <\mathbf{f}, v> \tag{10}$$

holds, where $\mathbb{A}$ is the operator from $W^{k,p}(\Omega)$ into the dual space $(W^{k,p}(\Omega))^*$ determined by the differential operator A by means of formula (5).

14.5. Remarks. (i) We emphasize again that relation (9) is just a particular formal expression which can also be expressed in the form

$$Au = f \quad \text{on} \quad \Omega$$

if the functional **f** is determined by formula (8) with the function $f \in L_q(\Omega)$.

(ii) In the definition of the weak solution of a differential equation, we actually require that the "integral" identity (10) be satisfied for all $v \in W_0^{k,p}(\Omega)$. Note that this condition is equivalent to the requirement that (10) hold for all functions

$$v \in C_0^\infty(\Omega) \,.$$

[This is implied by the density of the set $C_0^\infty(\Omega)$ in the space $W_0^{k,p}(\Omega)$ — see Paragraph 13.5.]

(iii) We look for the weak solution of a differential equation in the space $W^{k,p}(\Omega)$ determined by the formal differential operator A: The number k determines the order of this operator, the number p the growth of its coefficients a_α.

If then a formal differential operator is given, we have to investigate its coefficients a_α and to find out whether they belong to a suitable class **CAR**(p). Thus, we have to find the value of the parameter p. As mentioned above in Remark 12.16, the parameter p is not determined uniquely, in general, since if $a_\alpha \in$ **CAR**(p), then also $a_\alpha \in$ **CAR**(r) for every $r > p$ and, therefore, we could equally look for the weak solution in the space $W^{k,r}(\Omega)$. However, we will always try to find the least possible value $p > 1$, for two reasons namely: On the one hand, for $1 < p < r$ we have

$$W^{k,r}(\Omega) \subset W^{k,p}(\Omega) \,,$$

so that for a smaller p a "larger" space is at our disposal. On the other hand, for reasons of the solvability of a boundary value problem which will be discussed in subsequent chapters, we are interested in as accurate as possible an estimate of the coefficients a_α: In fact, we will require not only an estimate from above of the type of (12.12), but also an estimate from below. There, it will be important that the parameter p be as small as possible.

If, e.g., a linear differential operator is considered, it is appropriate to look for the weak solution in the space $W^{k,2}(\Omega)$, i.e., to put $p = 2$: For a linear operator A the coefficients a_α have the form

$$a_\alpha(x; \xi) = \sum_{|\beta| \leq k} a_{\alpha\beta}(x)\, \xi_\beta$$

[see Paragraph 7.5 (i)]. Assuming that the coefficients $a_{\alpha\beta}$ are bounded functions, one obtains

$$\left| a_\alpha(x; \xi) \right| \leq c_\alpha \sum_{|\beta| \leq k} \left| \xi_\beta \right|$$

which is a special case of condition (12.12) for $p = 2$, thus $a_\alpha \in \textbf{CAR}(2)$ [and it can be shown that $a_\alpha \notin \textbf{CAR}(s)$ for $1 < s < 2$].

This means, essentially, that the theory of the weak solutions of linear differential equations as discussed, e.g., in [80], will constitute a special case in our considerations.

14.6. Relation between the classical and the weak solutions. We now compare the conditions under which we have defined (in Paragraph 8.4) the classical solution and (in Paragraph 14.4) the weak solution of the differential equation

$$\sum_{|\alpha| \leqq k} (-1)^{|\alpha|} D^\alpha a_\alpha(x; \delta_k u(x)) = f(x) \quad \text{on} \quad \Omega. \tag{11}$$

The difference is made apparent in the following table:

Formulation	Classical	Weak
Coefficients	$a_\alpha \in C^{|\alpha|}(\Omega \times \mathbb{R}^\varkappa)$	$a_\alpha \in \textbf{CAR}(p)$
Right-hand side	$f \in C^0(\Omega)$	$f \in L_q(\Omega)$; generally $\textbf{f} \in (W_0^{k,p}(\Omega))^*$
Solution	$u \in C^{2k}(\Omega)$	$u \in W^{k,p}(\Omega)$

We shall show that every classical solution is also a weak solution. Or, more precisely: *If*

$$a_\alpha \in C^{|\alpha|}(\Omega \times \mathbb{R}^\varkappa) \cap \textbf{CAR}(p), \quad f \in C^0(\Omega) \cap L_q(\Omega),$$

then every classical solution u of equation (11) *which is such that* $u \in W^{k,p}(\Omega)$ *is at the same time a weak solution.* In fact, the proof of this assertion has already been given in Paragraph 11.5: It suffices to multiply equation (11) by the function $v \in C_0^\infty(\Omega)$, apply Green's theorem and — as in Paragraph 11.5 — we obtain identity (12.1), which is the relation (10) with the operator $\mathbb{A}$ given by formula (5) and with the functional $\textbf{f}$ given by formula (8). The fact that relation (10) is valid "merely" for $v \in C_0^\infty(\Omega)$ does not matter [see Remark 14.5 (ii)]. Since, by assumption, we also have $u \in W^{k,p}(\Omega)$, u is the weak solution of the differential equation (11).

However, it can be shown conversely that under certain conditions the weak solution could be the classical solution as well:

14.7. Theorem. *Let the function* $u \in W^{k,p}(\Omega)$ *be the weak solution of the (formal) differential equation* (9) *and let the following conditions be satisfied:*

(a) *the function u belongs to* $C^{2k}(\Omega) \cap W^{k,p}(\Omega)$;

(b) *the functional* **f** *is determined by the function* $f \in C^0(\Omega) \cap L_q(\Omega)$ *by means of formula* (8);

(c) *the function* a_α *belongs to* $C^{|\alpha|}(\Omega \times \mathbb{R}^\varkappa) \cap$ **CAR**(p).

Then the function u is the classical solution of the differential equation (11).

Proof: Since u is the weak solution, relation (10) is satisfied for every $v \in C_0^\infty(\Omega)$. With regard to condition (b) it is possible to write this relation in the form

$$\sum_{|\alpha| \leq k} \int_\Omega a_\alpha(x; \delta_k u(x))\, D^\alpha v(x)\, dx = \int_\Omega f(x)\, v(x)\, dx$$

$[u \in W^{k,p}(\Omega),\ v \in C_0^\infty(\Omega)]$. Applying Green's theorem to the integrals on the left-hand side of this equality we obtain, by formula (13.12), the relation

$$\sum_{|\alpha| \leq k} \int_\Omega (-1)^{|\alpha|}\, D^\alpha a_\alpha(x; \delta_k u(x))\, v(x)\, dx = \int_\Omega f(x)\, v(x)\, dx$$

or, in other words,

$$\int_\Omega \Big[\sum_{|\alpha| \leq k} (-1)^{|\alpha|}\, D^\alpha a_\alpha(x; \delta_k u(x)) - f(x) \Big] v(x)\, dx = 0\,.$$

This relation holds for every function $v \in C_0^\infty(\Omega)$. Therefore, the expression in the square brackets must itself be equal to zero almost everywhere in Ω, i.e.,

$$\sum_{|\alpha| \leq k} (-1)^{|\alpha|}\, D^\alpha a_\alpha(x; \delta_k u(x)) = f(x) \quad \text{for almost all} \quad x \in \Omega\,. \text{†)}$$

However, we are dealing with continuous functions throughout. Therefore, the last relation holds for all $x \in \Omega$. This implies that u is the classical solution of equation (11).

14.8. Remark. The above considerations indicate that the concept of the weak solution of a differential equation generalizes in a reasonable manner the concept of the classical solution. We will return to the connections between the two concepts later on when dealing with the so-called *problem of the regularity* of the solution in Section 17.

---

†) We have here made use of the following assertion: *If* $w \in L_p(\Omega)$ $(p > 1)$ *and if*

$$\int_\Omega w(x)\, v(x)\, dx = 0$$

for all functions $v \in C_0^\infty(\Omega)$, *then* $w(x) = 0$ *for almost all* $x \in \Omega$.

Assertions of a similar type will be used repeatedly in this book. For the proof for $p = 2$, see, e.g., [80].

SECTION 15. BOUNDARY VALUE PROBLEMS

15.1. The practical problems discussed in Chapter I show that it is important to look for those solutions of differential equations (on Ω) which satisfy specific conditions on $\partial\Omega$, i.e., to look for solutions of boundary value problems. For this reason the concept of the classical solution of a boundary value problem was introduced in Chapter II and, similarly, we now also introduce the concept of the weak solution of a boundary value problem.

However, the definition of the weak solution of a general boundary value problem is rather confused. For this reason, we begin with the discussion of a simpler particular boundary value problem, namely the Dirichlet problem.

15.2. The weak solution of the Dirichlet problem. Let A be the formal differential operator of order $2k$ given by formula (14.1) with coefficients

$$a_\alpha \in \mathbf{CAR}(p), \quad |\alpha| \leq k, \quad p > 1.$$

Furthermore, let $\mathbf{f}$ be a continuous linear functional on the space $W_0^{k,p}(\Omega)$, and let φ be a function from $W^{k,p}(\Omega)$.

We say that the function

$$u \in W^{k,p}(\Omega)$$

is the *weak solution of the Dirichlet problem* (for the operator A) if

(i) $u - \varphi \in W_0^{k,p}(\Omega)$;

(ii) for every $v \in W_0^{k,p}(\Omega)$ we have

$$\sum_{|\alpha|\leq k} \int_\Omega a_\alpha(x; \delta_k\, u(x))\, D^\alpha v(x)\, dx = \langle \mathbf{f}, v \rangle .$$

15.3. Remark. Condition (ii) of the definition above is already familiar from Paragraph 14.7: It says that the function u is the solution of the "formal differential equation"

$$Au = \mathbf{f} \quad \text{on} \quad \Omega .$$

We therefore investigate condition (i). This condition states — see Paragraph 13.11 — that for $|\beta| \leq k - 1$

$$D^\beta(u - \varphi)\big|_{\partial\Omega} = 0 \quad \text{or, in other words}, \quad D^\beta u = D^\beta\varphi \quad \text{on} \quad \partial\Omega$$

in the sense of traces. Since the function φ is given, so also are the traces $D^\beta\varphi\big|_{\partial\Omega}$. Condition (i) then says that the desired solution u and its derivatives $D^\beta u$ of order up to and including $(k - 1)$ "assume the prescribed values on $\partial\Omega$". Comparison with Paragraph 9.5 shows that it is reasonable to speak, in this case, of the Dirichlet problem.

The relation between the function φ and the functions φ_i from the boundary conditions (9.6) will be discussed below (see Paragraph 15.5). Note that although the function φ is given on Ω it is the traces of the functions $D^\beta \varphi$ ($|\beta| \le k - 1$) on $\partial\Omega$ which will be important for our purposes (see the conclusion of Paragraph 15.4).

15.4. Example. Consider the case $N = 1$, $\Omega = (0, 1)$, and $k = 1$. Then the formal differential operator A is the following ordinary differential operator of the second order:

$$(Au)(x) = - \frac{d}{dx} a_1(x, u(x), u'(x)) + a_0(x, u(x), u'(x))$$

where it is assumed that $a_i \in \mathbf{CAR}(p)$ ($i = 0, 1$), i.e., that

$$|a_i(x; \xi_0, \xi_1)| \le g_i(x) + c_i(|\xi_0|^{p-1} + |\xi_1|^{p-1}) \quad (i = 0, 1)$$

with constants $c_i \ge 0$ and functions $g_i \in L_q(\Omega)$.

The function $u \in W^{1,p}(0, 1)$ is the weak solution of the Dirichlet problem (for the operator A) if

(i) $u - \varphi \in W_0^{1,p}(0, 1)$;

(ii) for every function $v \in W_0^{1,p}(0, 1)$ we have

$$\int_0^1 [a_1(x; u(x), u'(x)) v'(x) + a_0(x; u(x), u'(x)) v(x)] \, dx = <\mathbf{f}, v> ,$$

where φ is a given function from $W^{1,p}(0, 1)$ and $\mathbf{f}$ is a given functional from $(W_0^{1,p}(0, 1))^*$.

In Paragraph 9.8, the Dirichlet problem for the operator A in the classical formulation was investigated: We sought the function $u \in C^2([0, 1])$ such that

$$- \frac{d}{dx} a_1(x; u(x), u'(x)) + a_0(x; u(x), u'(x)) = f(x) \quad \text{for} \quad x \in (0, 1),$$

$$u(0) = c_0, \quad u(1) = c_1 .$$

If we wish to formulate the problem weakly, we choose the functional as follows:

$$<\mathbf{f}, v> = \int_0^1 f(x) v(x) \, dx \quad \text{for} \quad v \in W_0^{1,p}(0, 1)$$

and give the function φ, e.g., in the form

$$\varphi(x) = c_0 + (c_1 - c_0) x .$$

Condition (i), i.e., the condition $u - \varphi \in W_0^{1,p}(0, 1)$, then says that $u(0) - \varphi(0) = 0$, $u(1) - \varphi(1) = 0$ (see Paragraph 13.6) which means that $u(0) = c_0$, $u(1) = c_1$ or, in other words, that the function u satisfies the given boundary conditions.

It is seen here that the concrete form of the function φ is not important; what is important is simply that φ belong to $W^{1,p}(0, 1)$ and that the conditions $\varphi(0) = c_0$, $\varphi(1) = c_1$ be satisfied.

15.5. Connection between the weak and the classical solutions of the Dirichlet problem. (i) Consider the classical solution of the Dirichlet problem for the operator A of (14.1), i.e., let $f \in C^0(\bar{\Omega})$, $\varphi_i \in C^0(\partial\Omega)$ $(i = 0, 1, ..., k - 1)$, and let the function $u \in C^{2k}(\bar{\Omega})$ satisfy the equation

$$\sum_{|\alpha| \leq k} (-1)^{|\alpha|} D^\alpha a_\alpha(x; \delta_k u(x)) = f(x) \quad \text{on} \quad \Omega \tag{1}$$

and the boundary conditions

$$\frac{\partial^i u}{\partial v^i} = \varphi_i \quad \text{on} \quad \partial\Omega, \quad i = 0, 1, ..., k - 1. \tag{2}$$

It can easily be shown that condition (ii) of Paragraph 15.2 is then satisfied; the steps are the same as in Paragraph 14.6.

In a sense, there are more problems with condition (i) of Paragraph 15.2: This condition will be satisfied if we manage to find a function $\varphi \in W^{k,p}(\Omega)$ such that

$$\varphi_i = \frac{\partial^i \varphi}{\partial v^i} \quad \text{on} \quad \partial\Omega \quad \text{(in the sense of traces)} \tag{3}$$

for $i = 0, 1, ..., k - 1$. It is then possible to write conditions (2) as follows:

$$\frac{\partial^i u}{\partial v^i} = \frac{\partial^i \varphi}{\partial v^i} \quad \text{or, in other words,} \quad \frac{\partial^i}{\partial v^i} (u - \varphi) = 0 \quad \text{on} \quad \partial\Omega \quad \text{in the sense of traces};$$

this is equivalent — see Paragraph 9.5 — to

$$D^\beta(u - \varphi) = 0 \quad \text{on} \quad \partial\Omega \quad \text{in the sense of traces for} \quad |\beta| \leq k - 1,$$

and these conditions mean further that

$$u - \varphi \in W_0^{k,p}(\Omega)$$

(see Paragraph 13.11).

In Example 15.4, the function φ was constructed rather easily; generally, it is by no means a simple problem. In fact, we have here the problem of extending a function from $\partial\Omega$ to $\bar{\Omega} = \Omega \cup \partial\Omega$ in such a way that the extension possess some stipulated properties, e.g., that it be an element of the space $W^{k,p}(\Omega)$. We will not treat this problem here, noting only that for a domain Ω with a "sufficiently smooth" boundary $\partial\Omega$ and for functions φ_i continuous on $\partial\Omega$ it may be proved that a function φ satisfying conditions (3) actually exists. Naturally, this function is not determined uniquely and its construction is also not easily accomplished in general. (For the details, see [54], [68].)

For $N = 1$, it is of course possible to construct the function φ without any trouble: In this case, the boundary conditions (2) are of the form

$$u^{(i)}(0) = c_{i0}, \quad u^{(i)}(1) = c_{i1}, \quad i = 0, 1, \ldots, k - 1,$$

where c_{ij} $(i = 0, 1, \ldots, k - 1; j = 0, 1)$ are given constants. The function φ can in this case be given in the form of a polynomial

$$\varphi(x) = d_0 + d_1 x + d_2 x^2 + \ldots + d_{2k-1} x^{2k-1}$$

whose $2k$ coefficients $d_0, d_1, \ldots, d_{2k-1}$ are determined from the $2k$ conditions

$$\varphi^{(i)}(0) = c_{i0}, \quad \varphi^{(i)}(1) = c_{i1}, \quad i = 0, 1, \ldots, k - 1.$$

Obviously,

$$\varphi \in W^{k,p}(0, 1),$$

and thus

$$u - \varphi \in W_0^{k,p}(0, 1).$$

If a function $\varphi \in W^{k,p}(\Omega)$ exists which satisfies conditions (3), then the classical solution of the Dirichlet problem for equation (1) [with boundary conditions of the form (2)] is simultaneously the weak solution.

(ii) Now, let us assume conversely that $u \in W^{k,p}(\Omega)$ is the weak solution of the Dirichlet problem. Just as in Theorem 14.7, it could be proved that the function u is the classical solution of the Dirichlet problem if, in addition, the following conditions are also satisfied:

(a) the function u belongs to $C^{2k}(\bar{\Omega})$;
(b) the functional $\mathbf{f}$ is determined by the function $f \in C^0(\bar{\Omega})$ by means of formula (14.8) [it would be enough for $f \in L_q(\Omega) \cap C^0(\Omega)$];
(c) the functions a_α belong to $C^{|\alpha|}(\Omega \times \mathbb{R}^\varkappa) \cap \mathbf{CAR}(p)$;
(d) the function φ belongs to $C^{k-1}(\bar{\Omega})$.

The proof is quite simple. In the first place, we show — as in Theorem 14.7 — that the function u satisfies equation (1). We then apply condition (i) from Paragraph 15.2, i.e., the relation

$$u - \varphi \in W_0^{k,p}(\Omega).$$

This relation says that $D^\beta(u - \varphi)|_{\partial\Omega} = 0$ for $|\beta| \leq k - 1$, not only in the sense of traces but also in the sense of the normal restriction which is meaningful since we have $u - \varphi \in C^{k-1}(\bar{\Omega})$ on account of conditions (a) and (d). However, we then also have

$$\frac{\partial^i(u - \varphi)}{\partial v^i} = 0 \quad \text{on} \quad \partial\Omega \quad \text{for} \quad i = 0, 1, \ldots, k - 1,$$

and the function u satisfies the boundary conditions (2) in which the derivatives $\partial^i \varphi / \partial v^i$ are chosen for the functions φ_i.

15.6. From the above paragraphs, it is, we hope, clear that the concept of the weak solution of the Dirichlet problem is an appropriate generalization of the concept of the classical solution: Under sufficiently strong conditions, the two concepts are equivalent, while under weak conditions (when we can no longer speak of the classical solution) it is possible to introduce the weak solution.

We now pass to the formulation of the concept of the weak solution for relatively general boundary value problems. This concept is formally more complicated than the concept of the classical solution and is not altogether easy. We ask the reader, therefore, not to allow himself to be discouraged, to bear with the authors, and to return to the definition again having studied it along with the remarks and examples which follow. We believe that he will then be able to understand it and also appreciate that the definition is indeed a reasonable one.

15.7. Weak solution of a boundary value problem. Let A be the formal differential operator of order $2k$ given by formula (14.1) with the coefficients

$$a_\alpha \in \mathbf{CAR}(p), \quad |\alpha| \leq k, \quad p > 1. \tag{4}$$

Let, further, $\mathscr{V}$ be a linear set of functions defined on Ω such that

$$C_0^\infty(\Omega) \subset \mathscr{V} \subset C^\infty(\bar{\Omega}).$$

Denote by V the closure of the set $\mathscr{V}$ in the norm $\|\cdot\|_{k,p}$ of the Sobolev space $W^{k,p}(\Omega)$; then

$$W_0^{k,p}(\Omega) \subset V \subset W^{k,p}(\Omega). \tag{5}$$

Furthermore, let a Banach space Q of functions defined on Ω be given, with the norm $\|\cdot\|_Q$, such that the set $C_0^\infty(\Omega)$ is dense in Q and

$$V \subset Q . \; \dagger) \tag{6}$$

Finally, let

(a) a function $\varphi \in W^{k,p}(\Omega)$,

(b) a functional $\mathbf{g} \in V^*$ such that for every $v \in W_0^{k,p}(\Omega)$ we have

$$<\mathbf{g}, v>_V = 0 , \tag{7}$$

---

†) For the notation, see the footnote on p. 78.

(c) a functional $\mathbf{f} \in Q^*$

be given. †)

We say that the function $u \in W^{k,p}(\Omega)$ *is a weak solution of the boundary value problem* (A, V, Q) if

(i) $u - \varphi \in V$;

(ii) for every $v \in V$ we have

$$\sum_{|\alpha| \le k} \int_\Omega a_\alpha(x; \delta_k u(x)) D^\alpha v(x) \, dx = <\mathbf{f}, v>_Q + <\mathbf{g}, v>_V. \tag{8}$$

15.8. Remarks. (i) It is not yet clear to what (classical) boundary value problem the problem (A, V, Q) just introduced corresponds, in what relation the boundary value problem in the weak formulation is to the boundary value problem in the classical formulation, and how the different boundary value problems discussed in Chapter II (the Dirichlet, Neumann, mixed, etc., problems) are distinguished in the weak formulation. Therefore, it will first be shown (in Paragraph 15.9) which choice of prescribed spaces, functions and functionals in Paragraph 15.7 leads to the Dirichlet problem discussed in Paragraph 15.2; after that, we shall explain what the individual prescribed elements mean (from the point-of-view of the classical solution) for the general boundary value problem.

(ii) In the formulation of a boundary value problem a number of distinct parameters appear:

the domain Ω,

the formal differential operator A [which determines the values k and p and thus also the space $W^{k,p}(\Omega)$],

the spaces V, Q,

the function φ,

the functionals $\mathbf{f}, \mathbf{g}$.

All these parameters are called, collectively, the *data of the boundary value problem.*

---

†) Two functionals appear here: The functional $\mathbf{g}$ on the space V and the functional $\mathbf{f}$ on the space Q. To distinguish between them we will denote the value of the functional $\mathbf{g}$ at "the point" v by the symbol

$$\langle \mathbf{g}, v \rangle_V$$

and the value of the functional $\mathbf{f}$ at "the point" v by the symbol

$$\langle \mathbf{f}, v \rangle_Q.$$

In view of inclusion (6), both the value $\langle \mathbf{f}, v \rangle_Q$ as well as the value $\langle \mathbf{g}, v \rangle_V$ are defined for arbitrary $v \in V$. Thus, the sum

$$\langle \mathbf{f}, v \rangle_Q + \langle \mathbf{g}, v \rangle_V \quad \text{for} \quad v \in V$$

which will be exploited in the sequel is also well-defined.

To make possible a certain identification of different boundary value problems we speak of the "boundary value problem (A, V, Q)" thus emphasizing at least the formal differential operator A together with the spaces V and Q. Strictly speaking, we should speak of the "boundary value problem $(\Omega, A, ..., \mathbf{g})$", i.e., we should enumerate all the data. We hope, however, that the abbreviated notation will be sufficient.

(iii) Note that obtaining the weak solution of a boundary value problem (A, V, Q) requires the solution of a certain operator equation, namely the equation

$$\mathbb{A}u = \Phi$$

on the set

$$\{u \in W^{k,p}(\Omega); \, u - \varphi \in V\} \, .$$

Here, $\mathbb{A}$ is the operator defined by means of the formal differential operator A in Paragraph 14.2, Φ is a functional from V^* defined by

$$<\Phi, v> \, = \, <\mathbf{f}, v>_Q + <\mathbf{g}, v>_V \, ,$$

and the equation $\mathbb{A}u = \Phi$ is understood in the sense of Remark $14.2\tfrac{1}{2}$.

15.9. Example. The Dirichlet problem for the formal differential operator A which was formulated in Paragraph 15.2, is obtained by choosing the data in Paragraph 15.7 as follows:

$$\mathscr{V} = C_0^\infty(\Omega) \quad [\text{and thus } V = W_0^{k,p}(\Omega)] \, ,$$
$$Q = V = W_0^{k,p}(\Omega) \, .$$

In this special case, we need not specify the functional $\mathbf{g}$ at all. Indeed, this functional has to satisfy condition (7) and since $V = W_0^{k,p}(\Omega)$ holds in our case we have $<\mathbf{g}, v>_V = 0$ for every $v \in V$ and $\mathbf{g}$ does not then appear in (8) at all.

Thus, the Dirichlet problem is the boundary value problem $[A, W_0^{k,p}(\Omega), W_0^{k,p}(\Omega)]$.

15.10. The significance of the space Q and of the functional f. We now turn our attention to condition (ii) of Paragraph 15.7, i.e., to the identity (8).

This identity is supposed to hold for every $v \in V$. In particular, since $W_0^{k,p}(\Omega) \subset V$ according to (5), relation (8) has to hold for every function $v \in W_0^{k,p}(\Omega)$. For such v we have $<\mathbf{g}, v>_V = 0$; condition (ii) from Paragraph 15.7 then means, in particular, that

$$\sum_{|\alpha| \leq k} \int_\Omega a_\alpha(x; \delta_k \, u(x)) \, D^\alpha v(x) \, \mathrm{d}x \, = \, <\mathbf{f}, v>$$

for every function $v \in W_0^{k,p}(\Omega)$.

However, this last condition was encountered, e.g., in Paragraph 14.4. It says that the weak solution u of the boundary value problem (A, V, Q) is at the same time the weak solution of the (formal) differential equation

$$Au = \mathbf{f} \quad \text{on} \quad \Omega,$$

which is not at all surprising. The fact is particularly stressed here because in the sequel it allows us to concentrate primarily on the question of the interpretation of distinct types of boundary conditions in the definition of the weak solution.

The notation "$Au = \mathbf{f}$ on Ω" is purely formal. If we assume that the functional $\mathbf{f}$ has the form (14.8) for some function f, it is possible to write

$$Au = f \quad \text{on} \quad \Omega$$

instead of our former notation. This latter notation is also formal, of course, but it more closely "resembles" a differential equation and under the conditions of Theorem 14.7 it actually is a differential equation as well.

Thus, it is now possible to interpret some of the data given in Definition 15.7:

(a) The left-hand side of (8) actually "represents" the formal differential operator

$$(Au)(x) = \sum_{|\alpha| \leq k} (-1)^{|\alpha|} D^\alpha a_\alpha(x; \delta_k \, u(x)).$$

(b) The space Q and the functional $\mathbf{f}$ from Q^* "represent" the right-hand side of the formal differential equation

$$Au = \mathbf{f} \quad \text{on} \quad \Omega.$$

Usually, we choose for the space Q the space $L_r(\Omega)$ with a suitable parameter $r \geq 1$ [according to assertion (i) of Paragraph 12.7, the set $C_0^\infty(\Omega)$ is then dense in Q and in what follows we shall see that the condition $V \subseteq Q$ is satisfied as well], and the functional $\mathbf{f}$ is chosen in the special form (14.8), i.e.,

$$<\mathbf{f}, v>_Q = \int_\Omega f(x) \, v(x) \, dx, \quad v \in L_r(\Omega),$$

with the function $f \in L_s(\Omega)$, $1/r + 1/s = 1$.

With respect to the last formula, the symbol

$$<\mathbf{f}, v>_\Omega$$

is often used in the literature in place of the symbol $<\mathbf{f}, v>_Q$. The symbol $<\mathbf{f}, v>_\Omega$ emphasizes the fact that the value of the functional $\mathbf{f}$ could be given by means of an integral over Ω.

The mentioned special form of the functional $\mathbf{f}$ (and of the space Q associated with it) is very natural and at the same time sufficiently general. For the purposes of this book as well as for practical needs this form is sufficient, the general form being of more or less theoretical significance only. For this reason, the space Q will not be specified in most of the examples below.

15.11. The significance of the space V, of the function φ and of the functional g. Since, according to the preceding paragraph, the data Q and $\mathbf{f}$ represent in the definition of the weak solution of a boundary value problem that part which corresponds to the differential equation, it is to be expected that the remaining data will correspond to the boundary conditions. This is actually the case:

(a) The set $\mathscr{V}$ which determines the space V "represents" the so-called *stable boundary conditions* (i.e., boundary conditions containing derivatives of order at most $k - 1$); the function φ then represents the "right-hand sides" of these boundary conditions.

(This type of boundary conditions has already been encountered when discussing the weak solution of the Dirichlet problem where only stable boundary conditions appear.)

Note that the set $\mathscr{V}$ actually plays an auxiliary role in the definition of the weak solution; the space V is of prime importance. In the sequel, we will start by presenting the set $\mathscr{V}$ as a class of smooth functions satisfying certain conditions on $\partial\Omega$; the experience gained in doing this will help us later to give the space V directly.

(b) The functional $\mathbf{g}$ "represents" the so-called *unstable boundary value conditions* (i.e., boundary value conditions containing derivatives of order higher than $k - 1$). Very often, this functional is chosen in the form

$$<\mathbf{g}, v>_V = \int_{\partial\Omega} g(x)\, v(x)\, \mathrm{d}S$$

where the function g is from the space $L_t(\partial\Omega)$ for a suitably chosen subscript $t \geq 1$.

With respect to the above formula, the symbol

$$<\mathbf{g}, v>_{\partial\Omega}$$

is frequently used instead of the symbol $<\mathbf{g}, v>_V$, thus emphasizing that the values of the functional $\mathbf{g}$ can be given by means of a surface integral over $\partial\Omega$ and that $\mathbf{g}$ represents a boundary condition.

(The role of the functional $\mathbf{g}$ will be illustrated in examples which follow below; for the moment, we note that the functional $\mathbf{g}$ actually represents the "right-hand side" of an unstable boundary condition; its concrete form is determined by the formal differential operator A.)

15.12. An ordinary differential equation of the second order. Put $N = 1$, $k = 1$, and for the domain Ω choose the interval $(0, 1)$. Then the space

$$W^{1,p}(0, 1)$$

will be the initial space and the function $u \in W^{1,p}(0, 1)$ will be the weak solution of the boundary value problem (A, V, Q) if

$$u - \varphi \in V \tag{9}$$

and if

$$\int_0^1 [a_1(x; u(x), u'(x)) v'(x) + a_0(x; u(x), u'(x)) v(x)] \, dx =$$

$$= <f, v>_Q + <g, v>_V \tag{10}$$

holds for all $v \in V$. (The conditions on the spaces V, Q, the functionals $\mathbf{f}$, $\mathbf{g}$, and the functions φ, a_1, a_0 were given in Paragraph 15.7; see also Example 15.4.)

We already know that relation (10) means that the function u "satisfies the ordinary second-order differential equation" in the form

$$-\frac{d}{dx} a_1(x; u(x), u'(x)) + a_0(x; u(x), u'(x)) = f(x) \quad \text{for} \quad x \in (0, 1) \tag{11}$$

[under the assumption, of course, that the functional $\mathbf{f}$ is given by the function f in accordance with formula (14.8)]. Thus, let us examine how distinct boundary value problems can be expressed by specific choice of the space V.

(I) As the set $\mathscr{V}$ of Paragraph 15.7 choose the set $C_0^\infty(\Omega)$; we then have $V = W_0^{1,p}(\Omega)$ and the boundary value problem corresponds to the Dirichlet problem, i.e., to equation (11) with the boundary conditions

$$u(0) = c_0, \quad u(1) = c_1,$$

where the constants c_0 and c_1 are determined by the function φ from condition (9): $c_0 = \varphi(0)$ and $c_1 = \varphi(1)$ (see Paragraphs 15.2 and 15.4). (The functional $\mathbf{g}$ need not be given in this case — see Paragraph 15.9.)

(II) Choose $\mathscr{V} = C^\infty([0, 1])$, i.e., $V = W^{1,p}(0, 1)$. In this case, condition (9) is satisfied automatically, for arbitrary choice of φ [from $W^{1,p}(0, 1)$, of course!]. For this reason, the function φ need not be given in this case at all. Assume that the function $a_1(x; \xi_0, \xi_1)$ is defined for $x \in [0, 1]$ — thus also at the points $x = 0$ and $x = 1$ — and define the functional $\mathbf{g}$ by the relation

$$<g, v>_V = d_0 v(0) + d_1 v(1), \tag{12}$$

where d_0, d_1 are given constants. [Note that the functional $\mathbf{g}$ is well-defined since for $v \in V$ we have $v \in W^{1,p}(0, 1)$ and the values $v(0)$ and $v(1)$ are defined (see Paragraph 13.4). At the same time, condition (7) is satisfied, i.e., $<g, v>_V = 0$ for $v \in W_0^{1,p}(0, 1)$, since for such functions v we have $v(0) = v(1) = 0$.]

In the next paragraph, we shall prove that the boundary value problem (A, V, Q) then corresponds to the problem of solving equation (11) with the boundary conditions

$$a_1(0; u(0), u'(0)) = -d_0,$$

$$a_1(1; u(1), u'(1)) = \quad d_1 \tag{13}$$

[see Paragraph 9.8 (i) and Paragraph 9.7; in fact, this is the Neumann problem for equation (11)].

(III) Choose $\mathscr{V} = \{w \in C^\infty([0, 1]); w(0) = 0\}$; hence, V is the set of those functions $v \in W^{1,p}(0, 1)$ for which $v(0) = 0$. Assume that the function $a_1(x; \xi_0, \xi_1)$ is also defined for $x = 1$ and that the functional $\mathbf{g}$ again has the form (12).

The boundary value problem (A, V, Q) then corresponds to the problem of solving equation (11) with the boundary conditions

$$u(0) = c_0, \quad a_1(1; u(1), u'(1)) = d_1, \tag{14}$$

where the constant c_0 is determined by the function φ from condition (9): $c_0 = \varphi(0)$. †)

(IV) In fact, all types of boundary conditions are represented in the three cases above: In Example (I), stable boundary conditions on the "entire boundary $\partial\Omega$" were considered, i.e., at both end-points of the interval $(0, 1)$; in Example (II), we had unstable boundary conditions at both end-points; in Example (III), we had a stable boundary condition at one end-point and an unstable boundary condition at the other one.

At the same time, we see that the form of the unstable boundary conditions – see, e.g., (13) – is determined by the form of the coefficient $a_1(x; \xi_0, \xi_1)$ for $x = 0$ and $x = 1$.

---

†) (i) We see that the constant d_0 from (12) plays no role here; the functional $\mathbf{g}$ could have been given in the form

$$<\mathbf{g}, v>_V = d_1 v(1).$$

Similarly, only the value (more precisely, the trace) $\varphi(0)$ is of importance as far as the function $\varphi \in W^{1,p}(0, 1)$ is concerned.

(ii) If we choose $\mathscr{V} = \{w \in C^\infty([0, 1]); w(1) = 0\}$ and $\mathbf{g}$ again according to (12), the boundary value problem (A, V, Q) corresponds to the problem of solving equation (11) with the boundary conditions

$$a_1(0; u(0), u'(0)) = -d_0, \quad u(1) = c_1,$$

where c_1 is again determined by the function φ from condition (9): $c_1 = \varphi(1)$. The functional $\mathbf{g}$ could have been given here in the form

$$<\mathbf{g}, v>_V = d_0 v(0)$$

as before, and for the function φ only the trace $\varphi(1)$ is of importance.

If, for instance

$$a_1(0; \xi_0, \xi_1) = a_1(1; \xi_0, \xi_1) = \xi_1, \qquad (15)$$

conditions (3) assume the form

$$-u'(0) = d_0, \quad u'(1) = d_1,$$

i.e., we have the Neumann problem for equation (11) [see 9.6 (ii)], while conditions (14) take the form

$$u(0) = c_0, \quad u'(1) = d_1,$$

i.e., we have a mixed problem for equation (11) [see 9.6 (v)]. Condition (15) is satisfied, e.g., if the coefficient $a_1(x; \xi_0, \xi_1)$ is given by the formula

$$a_1(x; \xi_0, \xi_1) = \xi_1 \quad \text{for all} \quad x \in [0, 1], \quad (\xi_0, \xi_1) \in \mathbb{R}^2.$$

In this case, equation (15) takes the form

$$-\frac{d^2 u}{dx^2} + a_0(x; u(x), u'(x)) = f(x) \quad \text{for} \quad x \in (0, 1).$$

On the other hand, we see that the boundary conditions cannot be prescribed arbitrarily. For instance, the boundary value problem for equation (11) with the boundary conditions

$$\alpha\, u(0) + \beta\, u'(0) = -d_0, \quad \alpha^2 + \beta^2 \neq 0,$$
$$\gamma\, u(1) + \delta\, u'(1) = \quad d_1, \quad \gamma^2 + \delta^2 \neq 0,$$

can be formulated in the weak form if the coefficient $a_1(x; \xi_0. \xi_1)$ is such that

$$a_1(0; \xi_0, \xi_1) = \alpha\xi_0 + \beta\xi_1, \quad a_1(1; \xi_0, \xi_1) = \gamma\xi_0 + \delta\xi_1$$

[thus, e.g., it is possible to consider a coefficient in the form

$$a_1(x; \xi_0, \xi_1) = [\alpha(1 - x) + \gamma x]\,\xi_0 + [\beta(1 - x) + \delta x]\,\xi_1\,].$$

However, the differential equation (and thus the coefficient a_1) is given in advance in most cases and cannot be "adapted" to the boundary conditions.

This is something of a drawback of the weak solutions. It will be shown in Chapter V, however, that this snag can be eliminated under certain conditions [see Section 31; see also Paragraph 15.16 (I-4)].

15.13. Remark concerning Paragraph 15.12. In Paragraph 15.12, we have assigned, somewhat mechanically, to a certain choice of the space a certain type of boundary conditions; we will show now that this assignment has a logical basis, namely by exhibiting the connection between the classical and the weak solutions of the boundary value problem. The discussion will be given for the boundary value problem of Example 15.12 (II). It will be clear, however, that one could proceed analogously in Example 15.12 (III) equally well.

(i) *Assume that the function* $u \in C^2([0, 1])$ *is the classical solution of the following boundary value problem:*

$$-\frac{d}{dx} a_1(x; u(x), u'(x)) + a_0(x; u(x), u'(x)) = f(x) \quad \text{for} \quad x \in (0, 1), \qquad (11)$$

$$a_1(0; u(0), u'(0)) = -d_0, \quad a_1(1; u(1), u'(1)) = d_1, \qquad (13)$$

where $a_1 \in C^1([0, 1] \times \mathbb{R}^2) \cap \textbf{CAR}(p)$, $a_0 \in C^0([0, 1] \times \mathbb{R}^2) \cap \textbf{CAR}(p)$, $f \in C^0([0, 1])$, d_0 *and* d_1 *are constants.*

Then the function u *is also the weak solution of the boundary value problem* (A, V, Q) *of Example 15.12 (II)* [*i.e., with* $V = W^{1,p}(0, 1)$], *with the functionals* **f** *and* **g** *in the form*

$$<\textbf{f}, v>_Q = \int_0^1 f(x) v(x) \, dx, \quad <\textbf{g}, v>_V = d_0 v(0) + d_1 v(1). \qquad (16)$$

We prove this assertion: Multiply equation (11) by the function $v \in W^{1,p}(0, 1) = V$ and integrate the equality obtained from 0 to 1. Since Green's theorem (which is just the theorem on integration by parts in this case) yields

$$-\int_0^1 \frac{d}{dx} a_1(x; u(x), u'(x)) \, v(x) \, dx = -[a_1(x; u(x), u'(x)) v(x)]_0^1 +$$

$$+ \int_0^1 a_1(x; u(x), u'(x)) v'(x) \, dx, \text{†}) \qquad (17)$$

we obtain the relation

$$\int_0^1 a_1(x; u(x), u'(x)) v'(x) \, dx + \int_0^1 a_0(x; u(x), u'(x)) v(x) \, dx =$$

$$= \int_0^1 f(x) v(x) \, dx + a_1(1; u(1), u'(1)) v(1) - a_1(0; u(0), u'(0)) v(0).$$

Applying the boundary conditions (13), it is possible to write the above equation in the form

$$\int_0^1 [a_1(x; u(x), u'(x)) v'(x) + a_0(x; u(x), u'(x)) v(x)] \, dx =$$

$$= \int_0^1 f(x) v(x) \, dx + d_1 v(1) + d_0 v(0). \qquad (18)$$

---

†) The symbol $[w(x)]_0^1$ denotes the difference $w(1) - w(0)$.

But this is nothing other than identity (10) with the functionals **f** and **g** from (16) so that u is actually the weak solution.

(ii) Let us now assume that u is the weak solution of our boundary value problem, i.e., that it satisfies relation (18) for every $v \in W^{1,p}(0, 1)$. We shall prove that u is the classical solution as well, i.e., that it satisfies equation (11) and boundary conditions (13) subject, naturally, to the assumption that the functions $u = u(x)$, $a_i = a_i(x; \xi_0, \xi_1)$, $i = 1, 2$, and $f = f(x)$ are as smooth as in part (i):

We start from relation (18) and modify the first integral on the left-hand side according to formula (17); this yields the relation

$$- \int_0^1 \frac{d}{dx} a_1(x; u(x), u'(x))\, v(x)\, dx + \int_0^1 a_0(x; u(x), u'(x))\, v(x)\, dx +$$

$$+ \left[a_1(1; u(1), u'(1))\, v(1) - a_1(0; u(0), u'(0))\, v(0) \right] =$$

$$= \int_0^1 f(x)\, v(x)\, dx + d_1\, v(1) + d_0\, v(0). \tag{19}$$

As already shown in Theorem 14.7, the function u is the classical solution of differential equation (11) under the above assumption. But this means that all the integral terms in (19) will vanish since

$$\int_0^1 \left[- \frac{d}{dx} a_1(x; u(x), u'(x)) + a_0(x; u(x), u'(x)) - f(x) \right] v(x)\, dx = 0.$$

Consequently, relation (19) assumes, after modification, the form

$$\left[a_1(1; u(1), u'(1)) - d_1 \right] v(1) = \left[a_1(0; u(0), u'(0)) + d_0 \right] v(0).$$

This equality is to hold for every $v \in V = W^{1,p}(0, 1)$. If, in particular, we choose the function v so that $v(1) = 0$ and $v(0) = 1$, we obtain the first of the boundary conditions (13); if we choose v so that $v(0) = 0$, $v(1) = 1$, we obtain the second of the boundary conditions (13). This concludes the proof of the assertion.

15.14. An ordinary differential equation of the fourth order. Put $N = 1$ and $k = 2$, and again choose the interval $(0, 1)$ as domain Ω. We thus have in mind a boundary value problem for the formal differential operator of the fourth order

$$(Au)(x) = \frac{d^2}{dx^2} a_2(x; u(x), u'(x), u''(x)) -$$

$$- \frac{d}{dx} a_1(x; u(x), u'(x), u''(x)) + a_0(x; u(x), u'(x), u''(x)), \tag{20}$$

where we assume that the coefficients $a_i = a_i(x; \xi_0, \xi_1, \xi_2)$ belong to **CAR**(p) with $p > 1$, thus, in particular, that

$$\left|a_i(x; \xi_0, \xi_1, \xi_2)\right| \leq g_i(x) + c_i\left(\left|\xi_0\right|^{p-1} + \left|\xi_1\right|^{p-1} + \left|\xi_2\right|^{p-1}\right), \quad i = 0, 1, 2,$$

for $x \in (0, 1)$ and $(\xi_0, \xi_1, \xi_2) \in \mathbb{R}^3$, with $c_i \geq 0$ and with the functions $g_i \in L_q(0, 1)$, $q = p/(p - 1)$.

In the definition of the weak solution of the boundary value problem (A, V, Q), we begin with a space V such that

$$W_0^{2,p}(0, 1) \subset V \subset W^{2,p}(0, 1),$$

and look for a function $u \in W^{2,p}(0, 1)$ for which

$$u - \varphi \in V \tag{21}$$

$- \varphi$ is a given function from $W^{2,p}(0, 1)$ †$)$ $-$ and which satisfies the relation

$$\int_0^1 a_2(x; u(x), u'(x), u''(x))\, v''(x)\, dx + \int_0^1 a_1(x; u(x), u'(x), u''(x))\, v'(x)\, dx +$$

$$+ \int_0^1 a_0(x; u(x), u'(x), u''(x))\, v(x)\, dx = <\mathbf{f}, v>_Q + <\mathbf{g}, v>_V \tag{22}$$

for all $v \in V$.

As we already know, relation (22) expresses the fact that the function u "satisfies the ordinary fourth-order differential equation"

$$(Au)(x) = f(x) \quad \text{for} \quad x \in (0, 1) \tag{23}$$

with the operator A of (19) [and with a function f determining the functional $\mathbf{f}$ by means of the first formula in (16)]. We therefore discuss the question: To which boundary value problems do the different spaces V correspond?

(I) The space $V = W_0^{2,p}(0, 1)$ corresponds to the Dirichlet problem, i.e., to equation (23) with the boundary conditions

$$u(0) = c_{00}, \quad u(1) = c_{01}; \tag{24}$$

$$u'(0) = c_{10}, \quad u'(1) = c_{11}, \tag{25}$$

---

†$)$ The function φ is, of course, given on the interval $[0, 1]$ but, as will be seen in the sequel, we will be interested mainly in the traces of the function φ and its derivatives φ' on $\partial\Omega$, i.e., in the values $\varphi(0)$, $\varphi(1)$, $\varphi'(0)$ and $\varphi'(1)$ (these values are defined in view of Paragraphs 13.4 and 13.8). See also Remark 15.3.

where the constants c_{ij} are determined by the function φ from condition (21): We have $c_{00} = \varphi(0)$, $c_{01} = \varphi(1)$, $c_{10} = \varphi'(0)$, $c_{11} = \varphi'(1)$. (The functional $\mathbf{g}$ need not be given in this case — see Paragraph 15.9.)

(II) Choose $V = W^{2,p}(0, 1)$; in this case, condition (21) is automatically satisfied for every function $\varphi \in W^{2,p}(0, 1)$. Therefore, the function φ need not be given at all, just as in Example (II) of Paragraph 15.12.

Assume, further, that the functions $a_i(x; \xi_0, \xi_1, \xi_2)$ $(i = 1, 2)$ are defined for $x \in [0, 1]$, thus also for $x = 0$ and $x = 1$, and that the function $a_2(x; u(x), u'(x), u''(x))$ has a derivative at the points $x = 0$ and $x = 1$. The functional $\mathbf{g}$ is determined by

$$<\mathbf{g}, v>_V = d_{10}\, v'(0) + d_{11}\, v'(1) + d_{00}\, v(0) + d_{01}\, v(1),\qquad(26)$$

where the d_{ij} are given constants. [The condition $<\mathbf{g}, v>_V = 0$ for $v \in W_0^{2,p}(0, 1)$ is satisfied since for such functions v we have $v(0) = v(1) = v'(0) = v'(1) = 0$.]

This choice of the space V and the functional $\mathbf{g}$ corresponds to the boundary conditions

$$a_2(0) = -d_{10}, \quad a_2(1) = d_{11}\qquad(27)$$

and

$$\frac{d}{dx}\, a_2(0) - a_1(0) = d_{00}, \quad \frac{d}{dx}\, a_2(1) - a_1(1) = -d_{01}.\ \dagger)\qquad(28)$$

The assumptions concerning the functions a_1, a_2 and the functional $\mathbf{g}$ will persist throughout the following examples.

(III) If V is chosen to be the closure of the set

$$\mathcal{V} = \{w \in C^\infty([0, 1]);\ w(0) = 0,\ w(1) = 0\}$$

[i.e., $V = W^{2,p}(0, 1) \cap W_0^{1,p}(0, 1)$ will hold here], then this choice corresponds to equation (23) with the boundary conditions (24) and (27). [The constants c_{ij} are

---

$\dagger$) To shorten the notation we shall use the following symbols: $a_i(0)$ to stand for the number $a_i(0; u(0), u'(0), u''(0))$, $a_i(1)$ to stand for the number $a_i(1; u(1), u'(1), u''(1))$ $(i = 1, 2)$. Further, the expression $da_2(0)/dx$ will mean the derivative of the function $h(x) = a_2(x; u(x), u'(x), u''(x))$ with respect to x at the point $x = 0$, similarly for the expression $da_2(1)/dx$. Recall that these last expressions contain derivatives of the third order u''', if this derivative exists: We have, in fact,

$$\frac{dh}{dx} = \frac{\partial a_2}{\partial x}\, (x; u(x), u'(x), u''(x)) + \frac{\partial a_2}{\partial \xi_0}\, (x; u(x), u'(x), u''(x))\, u'(x) +$$

$$+ \frac{\partial a_2}{\partial \xi_1}\, (x; u(x), u'(x), u''(x))\, u''(x) + \frac{\partial a_2}{\partial \xi_2}\, (x; u(x), u'(x), u''(x))\, u'''(x).$$

determined by the function φ from condition (21), the constants d_{ij} by the functional **g** from (26).] †)

(IV) If we choose V to be the closure of the set

$$\mathscr{V} = \{w \in C^{\infty}([0, 1]);\ w'(0) = 0,\ w'(1) = 0\},$$

then this corresponds to equation (23) with the boundary conditions (25) and (28).

(V) If we choose V to be the closure of the set

$$\mathscr{V} = \{w \in C^{\infty}([0, 1]);\ w(0) = 0\},$$

then this corresponds to equation (23) with the boundary conditions

$$u(0) = c_{00},\quad \frac{d}{dx}a_2(1) - a_1(1) = -d_{01}$$

and with the boundary conditions (27).

(VI) If we choose V to be the closure of the set

$$\mathscr{V} = \{w \in C^{\infty}([0, 1]);\ w'(0) = 0\},$$

then this corresponds to equation (23) with the boundary conditions

$$u'(0) = c_{10},\quad a_2(1) = d_{11}$$

and with the boundary conditions (28).

(VII) If we choose V to be the closure of the set

$$\mathscr{V} = \{w \in C^{\infty}([0, 1]);\ w(0) = 0,\ w'(0) = 0\},$$

then this corresponds to equation (23) with the boundary conditions

$$u(0) = c_{00},\quad a_2(1) = d_{11},$$

$$u'(0) = c_{10},\quad \frac{d}{dx}a_2(1) - a_1(1) = -d_{01}.$$

(VIII) If we choose V to be the closure of the set

$$\mathscr{V} = \{w \in C^{\infty}([0, 1]);\ w(0) = 0,\ w'(1) = 0\},$$

---

†) Just as in Paragraph 15.12 (III), we see that the constants d_{00} and d_{01} in (26) play no role here; the functional **g** could have been given in the form

$$<\mathbf{g}, v>_V = d_{10}\, v'(0) + d_{11}\, v'(1).$$

An analogous remark (with different combinations of the constants d_{ij}, of course) could also be made for Examples (IV)—(X) below.

then this corresponds to equation (23) with the boundary conditions

$$u(0) = c_{00}, \quad u'(1) = c_{11},$$

$$a_2(0) = -d_{10}, \quad \frac{d}{dx} a_2(1) - a_1(1) = -d_{01}.$$

(IX) If we choose V to be the closure of the set

$$\mathscr{V} = \{w \in C^\infty([0, 1]); \ w(0) = 0, \ w'(0) = 0, \ w(1) = 0\},$$

then this corresponds to equation (23) with the boundary conditions (24) and with the boundary conditions

$$u'(0) = c_{10}, \quad a_2(1) = d_{11}.$$

(X) If we choose V to be the closure of the set

$$\mathscr{V} = \{w \in C^\infty([0, 1]); \ w(0) = 0, \ w'(0) = 0, \ w'(1) = 0\},$$

then this corresponds to equation (23) with the boundary conditions (25) and with the boundary conditions

$$u(0) = c_{00}, \quad \frac{d}{dx} a_2(1) - a_1(1) = -d_{01}.$$

(XI) If we choose V to be the closure of the set

$$\mathscr{V} = \{w \in C^\infty([0, 1]); \ \alpha \, v(0) + \beta \, v'(0) = 0, \ \gamma \, v(1) + \delta \, v'(1) = 0\},$$

where $\alpha, \beta, \gamma, \delta$ are constants (non-zero, in general), then this corresponds to equation (23) with the boundary conditions

$$\alpha \, u(0) + \beta \, u'(0) = c_{20}, \quad \gamma \, u(1) + \delta \, u'(1) = c_{21},$$

$$\beta \frac{d}{dx} a_2(0) + \alpha \, a_2(0) - \beta \, a_1(0) = d_{20},$$

$$\delta \frac{d}{dx} a_2(1) + \gamma \, a_2(1) - \delta \, a_1(1) = d_{21}. \tag{29}$$

[The constants c_{20}, c_{21} are determined by the function φ from condition (21), the constants d_{20} and d_{21} are determined by the functional $\mathbf{g}$ from (26); to be precise, we have

$$c_{20} = \alpha \, \varphi(0) + \beta \, \varphi'(0), \quad c_{21} = \gamma \, \varphi(1) + \delta \, \varphi'(1),$$

$$d_{20} = \beta d_{00} - \alpha d_{10}, \quad d_{21} = \gamma d_{11} - \delta d_{01}.]$$

15.15. Remarks concerning Paragraph 15.14. (i) If we subject the individual examples of the preceding paragraph to a more detailed analysis, we discover that in every case [with the exception of Example (XI)] four out of eight conditions were available: They were the conditions of order zero (24) and the conditions of the first order (25) (which are the stable boundary conditions), the conditions of the second order (27) and the conditions of the third order (28) (which are the unstable boundary conditions). These conditions were combined in various ways. In Examples (I)–(IV), the conditions were always of the same type at the left-hand end-point $(x = 0)$ and at the right-hand end-point $(x = 1)$ while in Examples (V)–(X) there was one set of conditions for $x = 0$ and another for $x = 1$. But in all these cases, two conditions were always prescribed for $x = 0$ and two for $x = 1$. The situation was more complicated to some extent in Example (XI) where certain linear combinations of the preceding conditions were constructed.

[It should be noted that Examples (I)–(XI) do not exhaust all the possibilities: In (V)–(X) it is possible, e.g., to interchange the roles of the points $x = 0$ and $x = 1$, etc.]

The analysis of the examples presented also shows that, e.g., conditions (24) and (28) or the conditions (25) and (27) did not appear simultaneously (i.e., together in one example). This was not accidental. On the one hand, boundary value problems with such conditions cannot be described in the language of weak solutions (the mathematical arguments supporting this assertion will be given in the second part of this remark); on the other hand, the mathematical formulation does not reflect any realistic physical situation.

Finally, we recall what was previously discussed in part (IV) of Paragraph (15.12), namely the fact that the form of the unstable boundary conditions is given by the form of the differential operator or, stated more precisely, by the form of its coefficients $a_i(x; \xi_0, \xi_1, \xi_2)$ for $x = 0$ and $x = 1$. This is immediately seen from conditions (27) and (28).

Example (XI) then shows that there can also be some close relationship between the stable and the unstable conditions: This is manifested by the presence of the same constants α, β, γ and δ in the two types of condition.

(ii) From the assertions of Paragraph 15.14, it is by no means obvious why a given choice of the space V yields precisely the boundary conditions discussed in the corresponding examples. We now carry out some modifications which will make clear the relation between the space V and the boundary conditions.

Let us assume, therefore, that the weak solution $u \in W^{2,p}(0, 1)$ of the problem (A, V, Q) determined by relations (21) and (22) is sufficiently smooth, e.g., that $u \in C^4([0, 1])$, and that the same is true of the coefficients $a_i = a_i(x; \xi_0, \xi_1, \xi_2)$ $(i = 0, 1, 2)$ and for the right-hand side f; for instance, let $a_i \in C^i([0, 1] \times \mathbb{R}^3) \cap CAR(p)$ $(i = 0, 1, 2)$ and $f \in C^0([0, 1])$. Finally, assume that the functional **g** is given by formula (26) and the functional **f** by the formula

$$<\mathbf{f}, v>_Q = \int_0^1 f(x)\, v(x)\, \mathrm{d}x\,. \tag{30}$$

We start from identity (22) and make use of the fact that by Green's theorem (i.e., the theorem on integration by parts) we have

$$\int_0^1 a_2(x; u(x), u'(x), u''(x))\, v''(x)\, dx = \int_0^1 \frac{d^2}{dx^2} a_2(x; u(x), u'(x), u''(x))\, v(x)\, dx +$$

$$+ \left[a_2(x; u(x), u'(x), u''(x))\, v'(x) - \frac{d}{dx} a_2(x; u(x), u'(x), u''(x))\, v(x) \right]_0^1$$

and

$$\int_0^1 a_1(x; u(x), u'(x), u''(x))\, v'(x)\, dx =$$

$$= - \int_0^1 \frac{d}{dx} a_1(x; u(x), u'(x), u''(x))\, v(x)\, dx + \left[a_1(x; u(x), u'(x), u''(x))\, v(x) \right]_0^1 .$$

These relations together with formulas (26) and (30) make it possible to write identity (22), after obvious modification, in the form

$$\int_0^1 \left[(Au)(x) - f(x) \right] v(x)\, dx = v'(0) \left[d_{10} + a_2(0) \right] + v'(1) \left[d_{11} - a_2(1) \right] +$$

$$+ v(0) \left[d_{00} - \frac{d}{dx} a_2(0) + a_1(0) \right] + v(1) \left[d_{01} + \frac{d}{dx} a_2(1) - a_1(1) \right]. \quad (31)$$

Here, A is the differential operator of (20) and v is an arbitrary function from the space V.

We already know (see, e.g., Theorem 14.7) that under our assumptions the function u satisfies the equation $Au = f$ on Ω so that the integral on the left-hand side of equality (31) is equal to zero. This means that identity (22) reduces to the relation

$$v'(0) \left[d_{10} + a_2(0) \right] + v'(1) \left[d_{11} - a_2(1) \right] +$$

$$+ v(0) \left[d_{00} - \frac{d}{dx} a_2(0) + a_1(0) \right] + v(1) \left[d_{01} + \frac{d}{dx} a_2(1) - a_1(1) \right] = 0, \quad (32)$$

which is to hold for every $v \in V$.

From equality (32) and from the form of the space V we are now able to work out which boundary conditions correspond to the appropriate boundary value problem in the weak formulation. We proceed according to the following general guidelines:

If any of the conditions $v(0) = 0$, $v(1) = 0$, $v'(0) = 0$, $v'(1) = 0$ appears in the definition of space V, stable boundary conditions are thus defined [e.g., if $v(1) = 0$ and $v'(0) = 0$ is to hold for $v \in V$, this corresponds to the boundary conditions

$$u(1) = c_{01}, \quad u'(0) = c_{10},$$

where $c_{01} = \varphi(1)$, $c_{10} = \varphi'(0)$]. Under these conditions some of the summands in

(32) vanish. However, if relation (32) is to hold for all $v \in V$, the remaining summands have to vanish as well; this is achieved by putting equal to zero the coefficients of those of the numbers $v(0), v(1), v'(0), v'(1)$ in (32) which we did not assume to be equal to zero beforehand [e.g., for the case when $v(1) = 0, v'(0) = 0$ this means that we have to set equal to zero the coefficients of $v(0)$ and $v'(0)$; this yields the unstable boundary conditions

$$\frac{d}{dx} a_2(0) - a_1(0) = d_{00}, \quad a_2(1) = d_{11}].$$

[The example quoted above corresponds to Example (VIII) of Paragraph 15.14, with the roles of the end-points $x = 0$ and $x = 1$ interchanged, of course.]

To illustrate these "guidelines", we return once more to the individual examples of Paragraph 15.14: In Example (I), we assumed that $v(0) = v(1) = v'(0) = v'(1) = 0$; relation (32) is then satisfied with no additional assumptions. — In Example (II), on the contrary, nothing definite was assumed about the numbers $v(0), v'(0), v(1)$ and $v'(1)$. It is therefore necessary to put all four coefficients in (32) equal to zero; this yields the boundary conditions (27) and (28). — In Example (III), it was assumed that $v(0) = 0$ and $v(1) = 0$ for $v \in V$; it is necessary to put the coefficients of $v'(0)$ and $v'(1)$ equal to zero which yields the boundary conditions (27). — We could proceed further along the same lines; however, we leave this to the reader who will easily establish the procedure leading from the conditions imposed on the functions $v \in V$ in Example (XI) together with relation (23) to the boundary conditions (29).

From relation (32) it is also seen why certain boundary conditions cannot appear simultaneously: Should, e.g., the conditions

$$u'(0) = c_{10}, \quad a_2(0) = -d_{10}$$

be imposed at the end-point $x = 0$ [the first condition meaning that $v'(0) = 0$ has to hold for $v \in V$], then no further condition could be imposed at this point to ensure that the term $v(0) [d_{00} - da_2(0)/dx + a_1(0)]$ vanish in (32).

15.16. Partial differential equations of the second order. Consider boundary value problems in partial differential equations of the second order, i.e., put $k = 1$ and let Ω be a domain in $\mathbb{R}^N$ with $N > 1$. The formal differential operator A is defined in the usual way:

$$(Au)(x) = -\sum_{i=1}^{N} \frac{\partial}{\partial x_i} a_i(x; u(x), \operatorname{grad} u(x)) + a_0(x; u(x), \operatorname{grad} u(x)). \quad (33)$$

For the coefficients $a_i = a_i(x; \xi_0, \xi_1, \ldots, \xi_N)$ we assume here that they belong to the class $\mathbf{CAR}(p)$ with a parameter $p > 1$; this means, among other things, that the functions a_i satisfy the growth conditions

$$|a_i(x; \xi_0, \xi_1, \ldots, \xi_N)| \leq g_i(x) + c_i \sum_{j=0}^{N} |\xi_j|^{p-1}, \quad i = 0, 1, \ldots, N, \quad (34)$$

for $x \in \Omega$ and $(\xi_0, \xi_1, ..., \xi_N) \in \mathbb{R}^{N+1}$, with non-negative numbers c_i and with the functions $g_i \in L_q(\Omega)$, $q = p/(p-1)$.

The basic space in which we look for the weak solution of the boundary value problem (A, V, Q) is the space

$$W^{1,p}(\Omega) .$$

(I) Choose the coefficients a_i as follows:

$$a_0(x; \xi_0, \xi_1, ..., \xi_N) = \xi_0 |\xi_0|^{p-2} \quad (p \geq 2) ,$$

$$a_i(x; \xi_0, \xi_1, ..., \xi_N) = \xi_i \quad \text{for} \quad i = 1, ..., N .$$

The growth conditions (34) are obviously satisfied†); for this choice of the coefficients a_i, the formal differential operator A from (33) has the form

$$Au = -\Delta u + |u|^{p-2} u .$$

We look for the weak solution of the boundary value problem (A, V, Q), i.e., for the function $u \in W^{1,p}(\Omega)$ such that we have

$$u - \varphi \in V \tag{35}$$

[where φ is a given function from $W^{1,p}(\Omega)$ and V is a space for which

$$W_0^{1,p}(\Omega) \subset V \subset W^{1,p}(\Omega)]$$

and such that

$$\sum_{i=1}^{N} \int_{\Omega} \frac{\partial u}{\partial x_i} \frac{\partial v}{\partial x_i} dx + \int_{\Omega} u(x) |u(x)|^{p-2} v(x) dx = \langle f, v \rangle_Q + \langle g, v \rangle_V \tag{36}$$

holds for all $v \in V$.

(I-1) Choose $V = W_0^{1,p}(\Omega)$. Then the functional $\mathbf{g}$ need not be given since for $v \in V$ we have $\langle g, v \rangle_V = 0$. We still define the functional $\mathbf{f}$ by the formula

$$\langle f, v \rangle_Q = \int_{\Omega} f(x) v(x) dx , \quad \text{where} \quad f \in L_q(\Omega) . \tag{37}$$

The boundary value problem (A, V, Q) then corresponds to the Dirichlet problem

$$-\Delta u + |u|^{p-2} u = f \quad \text{on} \quad \Omega ,$$

$$u = \varphi \quad \text{on} \quad \partial\Omega .$$

---

†) According to Example 12.14(i), we have $a_0 \in \mathbf{CAR}(p)$, $a_i \in \mathbf{CAR}(2)$ for $i = 1, ..., N$. Since $p \geq 2$, Lemma 12.15 also implies $a_i \in \mathbf{CAR}(p)$.

(I-2) Choose $V = W^{1,p}(\Omega)$; let us define the functional $\mathbf{f}$ by the relation (37) and the functional $\mathbf{g}$ by the formula

$$<\mathbf{g}, v>_V = \int_{\partial\Omega} g(x)\, v(x)\, dS, \quad \text{where} \quad g \in C^0(\partial\Omega).\tag{38}$$

The function φ need not be given since condition (35) is satisfied automatically.

The boundary value problem (A, V, Q) then corresponds to the Neumann problem

$$\begin{cases} -\Delta u + |u|^{p-2}\, u = f & \text{on} \quad \Omega, \\[2mm] \dfrac{\partial u}{\partial v} = g & \text{on} \quad \partial\Omega. \end{cases}$$

(I-3) Divide the boundary $\partial\Omega$ into two parts Γ_1 and Γ_2 and choose for the space V the closure $\left[\text{in } W^{k,p}(\Omega)\right]$ of the set

$$\mathscr{V} = \{w \in C^\infty(\bar{\Omega}); w(x) = 0 \quad \text{for} \quad x \in \Gamma_1\};$$

thus, $V = \{v \in W^{1,p}(\Omega); v|_{\Gamma_1} = 0 \text{ in the sense of traces}\}$. The functionals $\mathbf{f}$ and $\mathbf{g}$ are chosen as in (I-2) and φ is a given function from $W^{1,p}(\Omega)$.

The boundary value problem (A, V, Q) then corresponds $\left[\text{see part (III) of this paragraph}\right]$ to the mixed problem

$$\begin{cases} -\Delta u + |u|^{p-2}\, u = f & \text{on} \quad \Omega, \\[2mm] u = \varphi & \text{on} \quad \Gamma_1, \\[2mm] \dfrac{\partial u}{\partial v} = g & \text{on} \quad \Gamma_2. \end{cases}$$

[Note that there is some freedom in the choice of the function φ and the functional $\mathbf{g}$: As far as φ is concerned, we are actually interested only in its trace on Γ_1, while the functional $\mathbf{g}$ can be chosen, e.g., in the form

$$<\mathbf{g}, v>_V = \int_{\Gamma_2} g(x)\, v(x)\, dS \quad \text{with} \quad g \in C^0(\Gamma_2).]$$

(I-4) If we were to try to express the Newton problem in the weak form, i.e., the boundary value problem

$$\begin{cases} -\Delta u + |u|^{p-2}\, u = f & \text{on} \quad \Omega, \\[2mm] \dfrac{\partial u}{\partial v} + cu = g & \text{on} \quad \partial\Omega, \end{cases}$$

we would find out that it is not possible: No choice of the space V or of the functional $\mathbf{g}$ corresponds to the boundary condition $\partial u/\partial v + cu = g$ on $\partial\Omega$.

(Note that a similar problem was previously encountered for ordinary differential equations — see the end of Paragraph 15.12.)

It should be added, of course, that it is possible to introduce the concept of the weak solution of the Newton problem. However, this requires a certain modification: Instead of condition (36) we will require that for all $v \in V$ the identity

$$\sum_{i=1}^{N} \int_{\Omega} \frac{\partial u}{\partial x_i} \frac{\partial v}{\partial x_i} \, dx + \int_{\Omega} u(x) \, |u(x)|^{p-2} v(x) \, dx + \int_{\partial\Omega} c(x) \, u(x) \, v(x) \, dS =$$
$$= \langle f, v \rangle_Q + \langle g, v \rangle_V \tag{39}$$

be satisfied [in other words, we complete the form $a(u, v)$ which corresponds to the formal differential operator A — see Paragraph 14.1 — in this concrete case by the surface integral

$$\int_{\partial\Omega} c(x) \, u(x) \, v(x) \, dS \,].$$

Naturally, it has to be shown that the left-hand side of identity (39) represents the value of the functional $Au \in V^*$ at the point $v \in V$ even in this modified form (see Paragraph 14.2$\frac{1}{2}$).

We leave the proof of this assertion as well as the proof that condition (35) together with identity (39) actually correspond to the Newton problem to the reader. We merely add that by means of similar "tricks" it is also possible to introduce the concept of the weak solution for various other boundary value problems not covered by the definition in Paragraph 15.7.

(II) Choose the coefficients a_i as follows:

$$a_i(x; \xi_0, \xi_1, \ldots, \xi_N) = \xi_i |\xi_i|^{p-2} , \quad i = 0, 1, \ldots, N .$$

The growth conditions (34) are again obviously satisfied. When looking for the weak solution of the boundary value problem (A, V, Q), the aim is to find a function $u \in W^{1,p}(\Omega)$ which is to satisfy both condition (35) and the identity

$$\sum_{i=1}^{N} \int_{\Omega} \left|\frac{\partial u}{\partial x_i}\right|^{p-2} \frac{\partial u}{\partial x_i} \frac{\partial v}{\partial x_i} \, dx + \int_{\Omega} |u(x)|^{p-2} u(x) \, v(x) \, dx =$$
$$= \langle f, v \rangle_Q + \langle g, v \rangle_V$$

for all $v \in V$.

Choose the functionals f and g as in (I-2) and the set V as in (I-3). The boundary value problem (A, V, Q) then corresponds [see part (III) of this paragraph] to the following (mixed) boundary value problem:

$$-\sum_{i=1}^{N} \frac{\partial}{\partial x_i} \left(\left|\frac{\partial u}{\partial x_i}\right|^{p-2} \frac{\partial u}{\partial x_i}\right) + |u|^{p-2} u = f \quad \text{on} \quad \Omega ,$$

$$u = \varphi \quad \text{on} \quad \Gamma_1 ,$$

$$\sum_{i=1}^{N} \left|\frac{\partial u}{\partial x_i}\right|^{p-2} \frac{\partial u}{\partial x_i} v_i = g \quad \text{on} \quad \Gamma_2 , \tag{40}$$

where v_i is the i-th component of the vector of the outward normal to Γ_2. Note that we exclude neither the case when $\Gamma_2 = \emptyset$ [and thus $\Gamma_1 = \partial\Omega$; we then have the Dirichlet problem for equation (40)], nor when $\Gamma_1 = \emptyset$ [and thus $\Gamma_2 = \partial\Omega$; we then have the Neumann problem for equation (40) and the first boundary condition disappears].

(III) We no longer specify the coefficients $a_i = a_i(x; \xi_0, \xi_1, ..., \xi_N)$ so that we are now dealing with the general formal differential operator A of the second order of formula (33). To find the weak solution of the boundary value problem (A, V, Q) then means to find a function $u \in W^{1,p}(\Omega)$ such that

$$u - \varphi \in V$$

and that

$$\sum_{i=1}^{N} \int_{\Omega} a_i(x; u(x), \operatorname{grad} u(x)) \frac{\partial v(x)}{\partial x_i} \, dx + \int_{\Omega} a_0(x; u(x), \operatorname{grad} u(x)) \, v(x) \, dx =$$

$$= <\mathbf{f}, v>_Q + <\mathbf{g}, v>_V \tag{41}$$

be true for all $v \in V$.

Similarly as in Paragraph 15.15 part (ii), we will now show how it is possible, from the form of the space V and of the functional $\mathbf{g}$, to "guess" to which boundary condition (in the classical formulation) the boundary value problem (A, V, Q) corresponds.

Assume that the weak solution $u \in W^{1,p}(\Omega)$ of the problem (A, V, Q) exists and, further, that it belongs to $C^2(\bar{\Omega})$. Assume further that the coefficients a_i belong to $C^1(\bar{\Omega} \times \mathbb{R}^*) \cap \mathbf{CAR}(p)$ for $i = 1, 2, ..., N$, that $a_0 \in C^0(\bar{\Omega} \times \mathbb{R}^*) \cap \mathbf{CAR}(p)$ (in particular, the coefficients are then defined for $x \in \partial\Omega$ as well), that the functional $\mathbf{f}$ is of the form (37) with the function $f \in C^0(\bar{\Omega})$, and that the functional $\mathbf{g}$ is of the form (38). By Green's Theorem 13.12 we have

$$\int_{\Omega} a_i(x; u(x), \operatorname{grad} u(x)) \frac{\partial v(x)}{\partial x_i} \, dx = - \int_{\Omega} \frac{\partial}{\partial x_i} a_i(x; u(x), \operatorname{grad} u(x)) \, v(x) \, dx +$$

$$+ \int_{\partial\Omega} a_i(x; u(x), \operatorname{grad} u(x)) \, v(x) \, v_i(x) \, dS$$

$(i = 1, ..., N)$ and identity (41) can therefore be written as

$$- \sum_{i=1}^{N} \int_{\Omega} \frac{\partial}{\partial x_i} a_i(x; u(x), \operatorname{grad} u(x)) \, v(x) \, dx + \int_{\Omega} a_0(x; u(x), \operatorname{grad} u(x)) \, v(x) \, dx =$$

$$= \int_{\Omega} f(x) \, v(x) \, dx + \int_{\partial\Omega} g(x) \, v(x) \, dS - \sum_{i=1}^{N} \int_{\partial\Omega} a_i(x; u(x), \operatorname{grad} u(x)) \, v(x) \, v_i(x) \, dS$$

or, in other words, as

$$\int_\Omega \left[(Au)(x) - f(x)\right] v(x)\,dx =$$

$$= \int_{\partial\Omega} \left[g(x) - \sum_{i=1}^N a_i(x; u(x), \text{grad } u(x)) v_i(x)\right] v(x)\,dS, \tag{42}$$

where A is the operator from (33). However, our assumptions guarantee that $Au = f$ on Ω (see Theorem 14.7); the integral on the left-hand side of (42) is therefore equal to zero. Finally then, condition (41) has the following form: For every $v \in V$ we have

$$\int_{\partial\Omega} \left[g(x) - \sum_{i=1}^N a_i(x; u(x), \text{grad } u(x)) v_i(x)\right] v(x)\,dS = 0. \tag{43}$$

Assume now that the space V is given in the same way as in (I-3) (the case $\Gamma_1 = \partial\Omega$ or $\Gamma_2 = \partial\Omega$ is also allowed). The condition

$$u - \varphi \in V$$

then says that the function u satisfies, on Γ_1, the stable boundary condition

$$u = \varphi \quad \text{on} \quad \Gamma_1. \tag{44}$$

If $v \in V$, then $v(x) = 0$ on Γ_1 (in the sense of traces) and it suffices to integrate in (43) over Γ_2 so that this condition takes the form

$$\int_{\Gamma_2} \left[g(x) - \sum_{i=1}^N a_i(x; u(x), \text{grad } u(x)) v_i(x)\right] v(x)\,dS = 0.$$

Since the function $v \in V$ is arbitrary here, the expression in the brackets has to be equal to zero. In this way, we obtain the unstable boundary condition

$$\sum_{i=1}^N a_i(x; u, \text{grad } u) v_i = g \quad \text{on} \quad \Gamma_2. \tag{45}$$

The boundary value problem (A, V, Q) then corresponds to the problem of solving the equation

$$Au = f \quad \text{on} \quad \Omega$$

with the boundary conditions (44) and (45). All these data were obtained from formula (43) which is the "appropriately rewritten" identity (41) from the definition of the weak solution. We recommend the reader, in his own interest, to work through the steps performed in part (III) in the cases of the particular differential operators investigated in parts (I) and (II).

15.17. We have thus presented certain "rules" according to which it is possible to describe to what concrete boundary value problem (in the classical formulation) a boundary value problem formulated in terms of the weak solution corresponds. We have investigated, in a relatively very detailed way, ordinary differential equations of the second and fourth orders and partial differential equations of the second order. Now, we recommend the reader to work out the case of partial differential equations of the fourth order, eventually of higher orders as well. Observing the similarities of Paragraphs 15.12 and 15.16, he will be in a position to exploit the analogies with Paragraph 15.14.

15.18. Another example (the transmission problem). Put $N = 2$, i.e., consider a plane domain Ω, and consider the boundary value problem for the formal differential operator A of the second order given by the formula

$$(Au)(x, y) = -\frac{\partial}{\partial x}\left(k(x, y; u(x, y))\frac{\partial u}{\partial x}(x, y)\right) - \frac{\partial}{\partial y}\left(k(x, y; u(x, y))\frac{\partial u}{\partial y}(x, y)\right). \quad (46)$$

Actually, this is a special case of the operator of formula (33): The coefficients a_0, a_1, a_2 here take the forms

$$a_1(x, y; \xi_0, \xi_1, \xi_2) = k(x, y; \xi_0)\,\xi_1\,,$$

$$a_2(x, y; \xi_0, \xi_1, \xi_2) = k(x, y; \xi_0)\,\xi_2\,,$$

$$a_0(x, y; \xi_0, \xi_1, \xi_2) = 0\,, \quad (47)$$

where $k = k(x, y; \xi_0)$ is a given function defined for $(x, y) \in \Omega$ and $\xi_0 \in \mathbb{R}$. Assume that the function f is such that the coefficients a_i belong to $\mathbf{CAR}(p)$ and thus satisfy the growth conditions (34).

To look for the weak solution of the boundary value problem (A, V, Q) then means to look for a function $u \in W^{1,p}(\Omega)$ such that

$$u - \varphi \in V$$

and

$$\int_\Omega k(x, y; u(x, y))\left[\frac{\partial u(x, y)}{\partial x}\frac{\partial v(x, y)}{\partial x} + \frac{\partial u(x, y)}{\partial y}\frac{\partial v(x, y)}{\partial y}\right]dx\,dy =$$

$$= <f, v>_Q + <g, v>_V \quad (48)$$

holds for all $v \in V$.

Hitherto, we have simply repeated what has already been done in the preceding paragraphs. For the sake of simplicity, we again treat the Dirichlet problem, i.e., assume that $V = W_0^{1,p}(\Omega)$ and that the functional $\mathbf{f}$ is given by the formula (37); the boundary value problem (A, V, Q) then corresponds to the problem

$$\begin{cases} Au = f & \text{on } \Omega, \\ u = \varphi & \text{on } \partial\Omega. \end{cases} \quad (49)$$

Assume that the domain Ω is divided by a curve Γ into two parts Ω_1 and Ω_2 (see the figure in Paragraph 4.3) and that both Ω_1 as well as Ω_2 belong to the class $\mathscr{C}^{0,1}$. Assume further that the definition of the function k is different on Ω_1 and Ω_2:

$$k(x, y; \xi_0) = \begin{cases} k_1(x, y; \xi_0) & \text{for} \quad (x, y) \in \Omega_1, \\ k_2(x, y; \xi_0) & \text{for} \quad (x, y) \in \Omega_2. \end{cases}$$

If both the functions k_1 and k_2 are such that the coefficients a_i in (47) satisfy the growth conditions (34), then there are no problems at all with the formulation of the weak solution of the boundary value problem (A, V, Q). We do have trouble, however, with the interpretation of the problem. As is already familiar from Paragraph 4.3, two separate problems are actually formulated in this special case instead of the boundary value problem (49), namely the problem

$$A_1 u_1 = f_1 \quad \text{on} \quad \Omega_1,$$

$$u_1 = \varphi \quad \text{on} \quad \partial\Omega_1 - \Gamma, \tag{50}$$

and the problem

$$A_2 u_2 = f_2 \quad \text{on} \quad \Omega_2,$$

$$u_2 = \varphi \quad \text{on} \quad \partial\Omega_2 - \Gamma, \tag{51}$$

where A_i are operators defined on Ω_i by the formula

$$(A_i u_i)(x, y) = -\frac{\partial}{\partial x}\left(k_i(x, y; u_i(x, y))\frac{\partial u_i(x, y)}{\partial x}\right) - \frac{\partial}{\partial y}\left(k_i(x, y; u_i(x, y))\frac{\partial u_i(x, y)}{\partial y}\right)$$

and f_i is the restriction $f|_{\Omega_i}$ $(i = 1, 2)$. Problems (50) and (51) have then to be completed by the transmission conditions

$$u_1|_\Gamma = u_2|_\Gamma,$$

$$k_1(x, y; u_1(x, y))\frac{\partial u_1}{\partial \nu}\bigg|_\Gamma = k_2(x, y; u_2(x, y))\frac{\partial u_2}{\partial \nu}\bigg|_\Gamma \tag{52}$$

[see formulas (4.12)].

We will show that all these conditions are already included in the concept of the weak solution of the boundary value problem (A, V, Q), i.e., that relation (48) together with the condition $u - \varphi \in W_0^{1,p}(\Omega)$ contain the problems (50), (51) as well as the transmission conditions (52), naturally, in so far as the solution u is sufficiently smooth.

Let then $u \in W^{1,p}(\Omega)$ be the weak solution of the boundary value problem (A, V, Q), i.e., suppose that relation (48) is valid for all $v \in V$ and let $u - \varphi \in W_0^{1,p}(\Omega)$. We denote by u_i the restriction of the function u to Ω_i; we have $u_i \in W^{1,p}(\Omega_i)$ and relation (48) could be written as

$$\int_{\Omega_1} k_1(u_1) \left[\frac{\partial u_1}{\partial x} \frac{\partial v}{\partial x} + \frac{\partial u_1}{\partial y} \frac{\partial v}{\partial y} \right] dx\, dy + \int_{\Omega_2} k_2(u_2) \left[\frac{\partial u_2}{\partial x} \frac{\partial v}{\partial x} + \frac{\partial u_2}{\partial y} \frac{\partial v}{\partial y} \right] dx\, dy =$$

$$= \int_{\Omega_1} f_1(x, y)\, v(x, y)\, dx\, dy + \int_{\Omega_2} f_2(x, y)\, v(x, y)\, dx\, dy \qquad (53)$$

[we use the shortened notation $k_i(u_i)$ for the function $k_i(x, y; u_i(x, y))$]. Assume that $k_i \in C^1(\bar{\Omega}_i \times \mathbb{R})$, and for the solution u assume that

$$u \in C^0(\bar{\Omega}), \quad u_i \in C^2(\bar{\Omega}_i), \quad i = 1, 2 ;$$

Green's theorem then implies

$$\int_{\Omega_i} k_i(u_i) \left(\frac{\partial u_i}{\partial x} \frac{\partial v}{\partial x} + \frac{\partial u_i}{\partial y} \frac{\partial v}{\partial y} \right) dx\, dy =$$

$$= \int_{\partial\Omega_i} k_i(u_i) \frac{\partial u_i}{\partial v_i} v\, dS - \int_{\Omega_i} \left[\frac{\partial}{\partial x} \left(k_i(u_i) \frac{\partial u_i}{\partial x} \right) + \frac{\partial}{\partial y} \left(k_i(u_i) \frac{\partial u_i}{\partial y} \right) \right] v\, dx\, dy , \quad (54)$$

where v_i is the outward normal to Ω_i. Relation (53) can then be written by means of formula (54) as

$$\int_{\Omega_1} (A_1 u_1 - f_1)\, v\, dx\, dy + \int_{\Omega_2} (A_2 u_2 - f_2)\, v\, dx\, dy +$$

$$+ \int_{\partial\Omega_1} k_1(u_1) \frac{\partial u_1}{\partial v_1} v\, dS + \int_{\partial\Omega_2} k_2(u_2) \frac{\partial u_2}{\partial v_2} v\, dS = 0 . \qquad (55)$$

This relation holds for every function $v \in W_0^{1,p}(\Omega)$; in particular, if $v(x) = 0$ for $x \in \bar{\Omega}_2$, then the line integrals as well as the integral over Ω_2 vanish in (55) and we obtain the relation

$$\int_{\Omega_1} (A_1 u_1 - f_1)\, v\, dx\, dy = 0 ,$$

valid for every $v \in W_0^{1,p}(\Omega_1)$. Hence, the relation

$$A_1 u_1 = f_1 \quad \text{on} \quad \Omega_1 \qquad (56)$$

follows.

If we choose v in (55) so that $v(x) = 0$ for $x \in \bar{\Omega}_1$, then the line integrals as well as the integral over Ω_1 vanish in (55), so that we obtain for every $v \in W_0^{1,p}(\Omega_2)$ the relation

$$\int_{\Omega_2} (A_2 u_2 - f_2)\, v \, dx \, dy = 0 \,,$$

which implies that

$$A_2 u_2 = f_2 \quad \text{on} \quad \Omega_2 \,. \tag{57}$$

This shows that the restriction of the weak solution u satisfies the equations in problems (50) and (51). Since $u - \varphi \in W_0^{1,p}(\Omega)$, we have $u = u_1 = \varphi$ on $\partial\Omega \cap \partial\Omega_1$ and $u = u_2 = \varphi$ on $\partial\Omega \cap \partial\Omega_2$, so that we also obtain the boundary conditions in (50) and (51).

It then remains to show that the transmission conditions are also satisfied: with respect to (56) and (57), relation (55) includes line integrals only; what is more, integration over $\partial\Omega_i$ can be divided into integration over Γ and integration over $\partial\Omega_i - \Gamma = \partial\Omega_i \cap \partial\Omega$. The integral over this second part is equal to zero, however, since $v \in W_0^{1,p}(\Omega)$ by assumption and thus $v = 0$ on $\partial\Omega_i \cap \partial\Omega$. Finally, relation (55) then has the form

$$\int_\Gamma \left[k_1(u_1) \frac{\partial u_1}{\partial v_1} + k_2(u_2) \frac{\partial u_2}{\partial v_2} \right] v \, dS = 0 \,.$$

However, the function v is arbitrary [from $V = W_0^{1,p}(\Omega)$]; hence the expression in the brackets inside the integral must vanish. Since the vectors v_1 and v_2 are oriented in opposite directions, we finally obtain the relation

$$k_1(u_1) \frac{\partial u_1}{\partial v} - k_2(u_2) \frac{\partial u_2}{\partial v} = 0 \quad \text{on} \quad \Gamma \quad (v = v_2 = -v_1) \,,$$

which is the second of the conditions (55). The first of these conditions follows from the fact that $u_1 = u|_{\Omega_1}$, $u_2 = u|_{\Omega_2}$ and $u \in C^0(\bar{\Omega})$. Thus, we have proved that the weak solution of the boundary value problem with "discontinuous" coefficients already possesses those properties which are required of the solution of the transmission problem.

We have limited ourselves to the case of the Dirichlet problem here, i.e., we chose $V = W_0^{1,p}(\Omega)$. The reader can easily discover that the same result can be obtained for other (admissible) choices of the space V as well. From the steps of the proof, it is also seen that it was not necessary to assume that the function k depends on ξ_0 alone; we could have equally assumed that

$$k = k(x, y; \xi_0, \xi_1, \xi_2) \,.$$

The simpler function was chosen merely to simplify the discussion.

SECTION 16. VARIOUS GENERALIZATIONS

16.1. The case $p = 1$. When defining the formal differential operator A in Paragraph 14.1 and the concept of the weak solution of the boundary value problem (A, V, Q) in Paragraph 15.7, we assumed that the coefficients a_α satisfy the condition

$$a_\alpha \in \textbf{CAR}(p) \quad \text{with} \quad p > 1 .$$

Consequently, the initial space for finding the weak solution was the space

$$W^{k,p}(\Omega) \quad \text{with} \quad p > 1 .$$

Examining Theorem 13.14 we see, however, that $p \geq 1$ was assumed there. It is thus also possible to introduce, without difficulty, the formal differential operator with coefficients

$$a_\alpha \in \textbf{CAR}(1) .$$

Theorem 14.2 will hold for $p = 1$ as well, and since the concept of the weak solution of a boundary value problem is based precisely on the assertion of this theorem it is possible to "reformulate" the contents of Paragraph 15.7 for $p = 1$ so that the Sobolev space

$$W^{k,1}(\Omega)$$

will then be the initial space. We recommend the reader to work through the discussion for $p = 1$ as an exercise. It must be remembered that at all points at which we used the number q, defined as $p/(p - 1)$, it is necessary to set $q = \infty$ in the case $p = 1$.

The fact that we have concentrated on the case $p > 1$ might then appear to be an end in itself. However, this is not the case: The reasons will be discussed in Paragraph 16.3 and, mainly, in Section 27. For the moment, we just give an example.

16.2. Minimal surface equation. From Paragraph 2.2 (iii), we are familiar with the problem of finding a function $u = u(x)$ defined on $\bar{\Omega} \subset \mathbb{R}^N$ which satisfies the differential equation

$$- \sum_{i=1}^N \frac{\partial}{\partial x_i} \left[(1 + |\text{grad } u|^2)^{-1/2} \frac{\partial u}{\partial x_i} \right] = 0 \quad \text{on} \quad \Omega \tag{1}$$

with the boundary condition

$$u = \varphi \quad \text{on} \quad \partial\Omega . \tag{2}$$

[The function $u = u(x)$ describes the shape of a "soap bubble" which stretches over the domain Ω and is clamped at the edge of the domain, i.e., over $\partial\Omega$, in a manner described by the function φ.]

As a matter of fact, this is the Dirichlet problem for equation (1), and the operator determined by the left-hand side of this equation is an operator of the type (15.33) with coefficients a_i determined by

$$a_0(x; \xi_0, \xi_1, ..., \xi_N) = 0,$$

$$a_i(x; \xi_0, \xi_1, ..., \xi_N) = \frac{\xi_i}{\sqrt{(1 + \xi_1^2 + ... + \xi_N^2)}}, \quad i = 1, ..., N. \tag{3}$$

It suffices to check that the coefficients a_i satisfy the growth conditions

$$|a_i(x; \xi_0, \xi_1, ..., \xi_N)| \leq g_i(x) + c_i \sum_{j=0}^{N} |\xi_j|^{p-1} \tag{4}$$

for $x \in \Omega$ and $(\xi_0, \xi_1, ..., \xi_N) \in \mathbb{R}^{N+1}$, with $g_i \in L_q(\Omega)$ and with a non-negative constant c_i, and it is possible to introduce the concept of the weak solution of the boundary value problem (1), (2).

In Example 12.14 (iii), it was shown, however, that $a_i \in \mathbf{CAR}(p)$ for arbitrary $p \geq 1$. In particular, it is then possible to choose $p = 1$ and the concept of the weak solution of the Dirichlet problem (1), (2) in the space $W^{1,1}(\Omega)$ can therefore be introduced:

Let A be the formal differential operator determined by the left-hand side of equation (1) and let φ be a function from $W^{1,1}(\Omega)$. We say that the function

$$u \in W^{1,1}(\Omega)$$

is the weak solution of the Dirichlet problem for the operator A if

(i) $u - \varphi \in W_0^{1,1}(\Omega)$,

(ii) for every $v \in W_0^{1,1}(\Omega)$ we have

$$\sum_{i=1}^{N} \int_{\Omega} (1 + |\mathrm{grad}\, u|^2)^{-1/2} \frac{\partial u}{\partial x_i} \frac{\partial v}{\partial x_i} \, dx = 0. \tag{5}$$

[This formulation corresponds to the homogeneous equation (1). Were we to consider the equation $Au = f$ on Ω, we would still have to assume that a functional $f \in (W_0^{1,1}(\Omega))^*$ is given and the expression $<f, v>_\Omega$ would appear on the right-hand side of identity (5) instead of zero.]

16.3. Remark. However, the coefficients a_i of (3) satisfy the growth conditions (4) with arbitrary parameter $p \geq 1$. It is thus possible to use

$$W^{1,p}(\Omega) \quad \text{with} \quad p > 1$$

equally well, and we can formulate the Dirichlet problem for the minimal surface equation (in the weak form) in different ways: Either by means of the space $W^{1,1}(\Omega)$

(as in Paragraph 16.2), or by means of the space $W^{1,p}(\Omega)$ with $p > 1$ (as in Paragraph 15.2). Which of these formulations should we choose?

It was already mentioned in Paragraph 14.5 (iii) that priority will be given to the formulation for the least possible p, i.e., in this case for $p = 1$. The subsequent chapters will make clear the reason for this approach. Hitherto, only the question of the formulation of a boundary value problem (in terms of weak solutions) has been treated; indeed, we did not treat the question of the existence of the weak solution at all. The conditions for the existence of a solution to be encountered in the sequel will show that the space $W^{1,p}(\Omega)$ with $p > 1$ is not suitable for the case of the minimal surface equation. It is therefore appropriate to work with the space $W^{1,1}(\Omega)$. It should be noted at once that the spaces $W^{k,1}(\Omega)$ have some unfavourable properties as compared with the spaces $W^{k,p}(\Omega)$ with $p > 1$, and that a number of problems arise for boundary value problems which call for the use of the spaces $W^{k,1}(\Omega)$ (see Chapter IV, Paragraphs 25.8 and 27.2). Thus, it was not an arbitrary choice that the boundary value problem was formulated originally for those growth conditions which led to the spaces $W^{k,p}(\Omega)$ with $p > 1$: Indeed, the difficulties hinted at above do not arise for these latter spaces (as will eventually be seen in the chapters that follow).

16.4. Generalization of the growth conditions. When defining the weak solution of a boundary value problem for a formal differential operator A of order $2k$, it was assumed that the coefficients a_α of this operator belong to the class $\mathbf{CAR}(p)$ with $p > 1$. This means, among other things, that they satisfy the growth conditions

$$\left|a_\alpha(x; \xi)\right| \leqq g_\alpha(x) + c_\alpha \sum_{|\beta| \leqq k} \left|\xi_\beta\right|^{p-1}, \tag{6}$$

where $g_\alpha \in L_q(\Omega)$ with $q = p/(p-1)$ and $c_\alpha \geqq 0$ (see Paragraphs 12.2 and 12.13). The parameter p then determines the space

$$W^{k,p}(\Omega)$$

in which we look for the weak solution.

When deriving conditions (6), in Paragraph 12.12, we started from Theorem 12.10. However, this theorem was not fully exploited: In the estimate (6), the same powers $p - 1$ appear for all the variables ξ_β while Theorem 12.10 admits different powers for different variables ξ_β. In the sequel, we will show, therefore, that the concept of the weak solution of a boundary value problem can be introduced even if the growth conditions are generalized in the above sense. We shall see that the growth conditions [i.e., the exponents in the modified estimate of type (6)] will be of prime importance for those variables ξ_β for which $|\beta| = k$, i.e., for those variables for which we substitute derivatives of the highest (k-th) order in the function $a_\alpha(x; \delta_k u(x))$.

For this, we first have to investigate some additional properties of Sobolev spaces.

16.5. Imbedding theorems. The Sobolev space $W^{1,p}(\Omega)$ was defined as the set of those functions $u \in L_p(\Omega)$ whose generalized derivatives $\partial u/\partial x_i$ also belong to $L_p(\Omega)$. Naturally, it might be expected that from the properties of the derivative $\partial u/\partial x_i$ it will be possible to derive further and better properties of the function u in addition to the fact that u belongs to $L_p(\Omega)$. In the end, this is confirmed by Example 13.4: It was shown there that for $N = 1$ and $\Omega = (a, b)$ the function $u \in W^{1,p}(a, b)$ [whose only assumed property is that it belongs to $L_p(a, b)$] is even absolutely continuous on $[a, b]$. Thus, we have

$$W^{1,p}(a, b) \subset C^0([a, b]),$$

or, in other words, the Sobolev space $W^{1,p}(a, b)$ is imbedded into the space $C^0([a, b])$.

Theorems which describe such "better" properties of functions from Sobolev spaces are therefore called imbedding theorems. We now present a summary of such results.

16.6. Theorem. *Let $\Omega \in \mathscr{C}^{0,1}$ be a domain in $\mathbb{R}^N$, k a positive integer, $p \geq 1$.*

(i) *If $kp < N$, then*

$$W^{k,p}(\Omega) \subset\subset L_q(\Omega) \text{ †} \tag{7}$$

holds for arbitrary q such that

$$1 \leq q \leq \frac{Np}{N - kp}. \tag{8}$$

(ii) *If $kp = N$, then we have*

$$W^{k,p}(\Omega) \subset\subset L_r(\Omega), \tag{9}$$

where r is an arbitrary number lying in the interval $[1, \infty)$.

(iii) *If $kp > N$, then we have*

$$W^{k,p}(\Omega) \subset\subset C^0(\overline{\Omega}). \text{ ††} \tag{10}$$

16.7. Remarks about the proof of Theorem 16.6. (i) Detailed proofs of all the assertions of Theorem 16.6 can be found, e.g., in [54], [68]. By way of illustration, we indicate below the idea of the proof for one special case. It should be remem-

---

† For the notation, see footnote on p. 78.

†† Relation (10) has to be understood as follows: If $u \in W^{k,p}(\Omega)$, where $kp > N$, then a function $v \in C^0(\overline{\Omega})$ exists such that $u(x) = v(x)$ for almost all $x \in \Omega$ (and the function v is then equal to u in the sense of the identity introduced in Paragraph 12.7) and we have

$$\|v\|_{C^0(\overline{\Omega})} \leq c\|u\|_{k,p}$$

where the constant $c > 0$ is independent of u and v.

bered, however, that two facts are to be proved: On the one hand the inclusion [e.g., of the type

$$W^{k,p}(\Omega) \subset L_q(\Omega)$$

for assertion 16.6 (i)], and on the other hand the estimate [e.g., of the type

$$\|u\|_q \leq c\|u\|_{k,p}$$

with a constant $c > 0$ independent of $u \in W^{k,p}(\Omega)$]. It is precisely this estimate which is the important thing!!

(ii) Consider the case $N = 1$, $\Omega = (a, b)$, and $k = 1$. Then $kp = p \geq 1$, so that cases (ii) and (iii) of Theorem 16.6 occur. However, we already know that

$$W^{1,p}(a, b) \subset C^0([a, b]),$$

and it thus remains to establish an estimate of the type

$$\|u\|_{C^0([a,b])} \leq c\|u\|_{1,p}. \tag{11}$$

For arbitrary $x, y \in [a, b]$, we have

$$u(x) = u(y) + \int_y^x u'(t)\,dt$$

(the function u is absolutely continuous — see Paragraph 13.4), and thus

$$|u(x)| \leq |u(y)| + \left|\int_y^x |u'(t)|\,dt\right| \leq |u(y)| + \int_a^b |u'(t)|\,dt \leq$$

$$\leq |u(y)| + (b - a)^{1-1/p}\left(\int_a^b |u'(t)|^p\,dt\right)^{1/p}$$

(in the last inequality, the Hölder inequality was applied in the case when $p > 1$ to the pair of functions u', 1). Integration of the last inequality with respect to y from a to b yields

$$(b - a)\,|u(x)| \leq \int_a^b |u(y)|\,dy + (b - a)^{2-1/p}\|u'\|_p \leq$$

$$\leq (b - a)^{1-1/p}\|u\|_p + (b - a)^{2-1/p}\|u'\|_p$$

(the Hölder inequality was again applied in the case when $p > 1$, this time to the pair of functions u, 1). Hence, we obtain the estimate

$$|u(x)| \leq c(\|u\|_p + \|u'\|_p) = c\|u\|_{1,p}$$

with the constant $c = \max\left[(b - a)^{-1/p}, (b - a)^{1-1/p}\right]$, and since x is arbitrary (in the interval $[a, b]$) and the function u is (even absolutely) continuous, we have

$$\|u\|_{C^0([a,b])} = \max_{x \in [a,b]} |u(x)| \leq c \|u\|_{1,p}$$

for every function $u \in W^{1,p}(a, b)$. This concludes the proof of assertion (iii) of Theorem 16.6 for the case when $p > 1$ (and for $k = N = 1$). For the case when $p = 1$ we have even proved something more than 16.6 (ii).

(iii) We give some examples which should bring Theorem 16.6 home to the reader.

16.8. Examples. (i) Put $N = 1$, $p > 1$. Then $kp > 1$ for every $k \in \mathbb{N}$, and thus, by Theorem 16.6 (i), we have

$$W^{k,p}(a, b) \subset\subset C^0([a, b])$$

[in fact, this has already been proved in part (ii) of Remark 16.7].

(ii) Let $N \geq 2$, $k = 1$, $p = 2$. Then $kp = 2 \leq N$, and by Theorem 16.6 (i) and (ii) we have

$$W^{1,2}(\Omega) \subset\subset L_q(\Omega),$$

where

$$q \geq 1 \quad \text{and is otherwise arbitrary if} \quad N = 2,$$

$$q \leq \frac{2N}{N - 2} \qquad\qquad \text{if} \quad N \geq 3.$$

(iii) Let $p > N$. Then

$$W^{1,p}(\Omega) \subset\subset C^0(\bar{\Omega}).$$

(iv) Let $u \in W^{k,p}(\Omega)$. This means that

$$\text{for} \quad |\beta| = k \quad \text{we have} \quad D^\beta u \in L_p(\Omega).$$

For $|\beta| = k - 1$ we have $D^\beta u \in W^{1,p}(\Omega)$ and, therefore, the following assertion is valid according to Theorem 16.6 (i): If $N > p$, then

$$\text{for} \quad |\beta| = k - 1 \quad \text{we have} \quad D^\beta u \in L_q(\Omega), \quad \text{where} \quad q = \frac{Np}{N - p}.$$

For $|\beta| = k - 2$ we have $D^\beta u \in W^{2,p}(\Omega)$ and, therefore, the following assertion is valid according to Theorem 16.6 (i): If $N > 2p$, then

$$\text{for} \quad |\beta| = k - 2 \quad \text{we have} \quad D^\beta u \in L_q(\Omega), \quad \text{where} \quad q = \frac{Np}{N - 2p}.$$

We could continue in this way and we would find out that for $|\beta| = k - j$ ($j = 0$, 1, ..., k) we have $D^\beta u \in W^{j,p}(\Omega)$ and that the following assertion then holds good:

For $|\beta| = k - j$ we have $D^\beta u \in L_q(\Omega)$, where $q = Np/(N - jp)$, as long as $N > jp$, of course, or, in other words, $N - (k - |\beta|)\, p > 0$, or again,

$$|\beta| > k - \frac{N}{p}.$$

Only assertion (i) of Theorem 16.6 has hitherto been exploited. If use is made of the remaining two assertions of this Theorem, the following lemma is obtained.

16.9. Lemma. *Let $u \in W^{k,p}(\Omega)$ and let Ω be a domain in $\mathbb{R}^N$, $\Omega \in \mathscr{C}^{0,1}$. Furthermore, let β be a multi-index, $|\beta| \leq k$. Then we have:*

(i) *If $|\beta| > k - N/p$, then*

$$D^\beta u \in L_{q(\beta)}(\Omega), \quad \text{where} \quad q(\beta) = \frac{Np}{N - (k - |\beta|)\, r}.$$

(ii) *If $|\beta| = k - N/p$, then*

$$D^\beta u \in L_{q(\beta)}(\Omega), \quad \text{where} \quad q(\beta) \geq 1 \quad \text{is arbitrary}.$$

(iii) *If $|\beta| < k - N/p$, then*

$$D^\beta u \in C^0(\overline{\Omega}).$$

(iv) *There exists a constant $c > 0$ such that for all $u \in W^{k,p}(\Omega)$ the relation*

$$\|D^\beta u\|_X \leq c\|u\|_{k,p}$$

holds, where $X = L_{q(\beta)}(\Omega)$ in cases (i) *and* (ii) *and $X = C^0(\overline{\Omega})$ in case* (iii).

16.10. Lemma 16.9 specifies how "good" the individual (generalized) derivatives of the function $u \in W^{k,p}(\Omega)$ are. By means of this lemma, it is possible to generalize Theorem 13.14 to some extent, or, more precisely, to state its assertion under somewhat weaker assumptions.

16.11. Theorem. *Let $h = h(x, \xi)$ be a function defined for $x \in \Omega$ and $\xi \in \mathbb{R}^\varkappa$, and let $h \in$ CAR. Let k be a positive integer, $p \geq 1$, $r \geq 1$, and let a non-negative continuous function $c = c(t)$, defined for $t \geq 0$, and a function $g \in L_r(\Omega)$ exist such that for all $\xi \in \mathbb{R}^\varkappa$ and for almost all $x \in \Omega$ we have*

$$|h(x; \xi)| \leq c\Big(\sum_{|\beta| < k - N/p} |\xi_\beta| \Big) \Big[g(x) + \sum_{k - N/p \leq |\beta| \leq k} |\xi_\beta|^{q(\beta)/r} \Big], \tag{14}$$

where

$$q(\beta) = \frac{Np}{N - (k - |\beta|)\, p} \quad \text{for} \quad |\beta| > k - \frac{N}{p},$$

$$q(\beta) \geq 1 \quad \text{arbitrary} \quad \text{for} \quad |\beta| = k - \frac{N}{p}. \tag{15}$$

Then we have

$$h(x; \delta_k u(x)) \in L_r(\Omega) \tag{16}$$

for every $u \in W^{k,p}(\Omega)$ and the Němyckiǐ operator $\mathscr{H}$ determined by the function h is a continuous operator from the space $W^{k,p}(\Omega)$ into $L_r(\Omega)$.

16.12. Remarks concerning Theorem 16.11. (i) If $k - N/p \leq 0$, that is if $kp \leq N$, then no multi-index β exists such that $|\beta| < k - N/p$. In this case, we modify the estimate (14): We assume that inequality (14) is satisfied with the constant $c > 0$ instead of the function $c(t)$. The assertion of the theorem is valid for this case as well.

(ii) As far as the proof of Theorem 16.11 is concerned, it would be possible to repeat what has already been said in Remark 12.11. What is easy to prove is assertion (16):

We raise inequality (14) to the r-th power and use the relation

$$(a + b)^r \leq 2^{r-1}(a^r + b^r);$$

we then obtain the inequality

$$|h(x; \xi)|^r \leq \left|c\left(\sum_{|\beta| < k - N/p} |\xi_\beta|\right)\right|^r c_1\left[|g(x)|^r + \sum_{k - N/p \leq |\beta| \leq k} |\xi_\beta|^{q(\beta)}\right]$$

or, in other words [if we substitute $D^\beta u(x)$ for ξ_β], the inequality

$$|h(x; \delta_k u(x))|^r \leq c_1 \left|c\left(\sum_{|\beta| < k - N/p} |D^\beta u(x)|\right)\right|^r \left\{|g(x)|^r + \sum_{k - N/p \leq |\beta| \leq k} |D^\beta u(x)|^{q(\beta)}\right\}.$$

According to part (iii) of Lemma 16.9, the derivatives $D^\beta u(x)$ included in the argument of the function c are continuous on $\bar{\Omega}$. Since the function c is also continuous and domain Ω is bounded, there is a constant $c_2 > 0$ such that

$$c\left(\sum_{|\beta| < k - N/p} |D^\beta u(x)|\right) \leq c_2 \quad \text{for all} \quad x \in \bar{\Omega}.$$

Consequently, we have

$$|h(x; \delta_k u(x))|^r \leq c_1 c_2 \left\{|g(x)|^r + \sum_{k - N/p \leq |\beta| \leq k} |D^\beta u(x)|^{q(\beta)}\right\}$$

and integration of this inequality over Ω yields

$$\int_\Omega |h(x; \delta_k u(x))|^r \, dx \leq c_1 c_2 \left\{\int_\Omega |g(x)|^r \, dx + \sum_{k - N/p \leq |\beta| \leq k} \int_\Omega |D^\beta u|^{q(\beta)} \, dx\right\}.$$

However, the right-hand side of this inequality is finite since $g \in L_r(\Omega)$ (by assumption) and $D^\beta u \in L_{q(\beta)}(\Omega)$ [by Lemma 16.9 (i), (ii)]; relation (16) is thus proved.

(iii) For the moment, denote by λ the number of multi-indexes of length less than $k - N/p$, and let η be the vector $\{|\xi_\beta|, |\beta| < k - N/p\}$. It is possible to replace the expression

$$c\Big(\sum_{|\beta| < k - N/p} |\xi_\beta|\Big)$$

on the right-hand side of condition (14) by the expression

$$c^*(\eta),$$

where c^* is a continuous function of λ variables, and condition (14) by the condition

$$|h(x; \xi)| \leq c^*(\eta) \Big[g(x) + \sum_{k - N/p \leq |\beta| \leq k} |\xi_\beta|^{q(\beta)/r}\Big], \tag{14*}$$

thus in particular by the condition

$$|h(x; \xi)| \leq \Big[\sum_{|\beta| < k - N/p} c_\beta(|\xi_\beta|)\Big] \Big[g(x) + \sum_{k - N/p \leq |\beta| \leq k} |\xi_\beta|^{q(\beta)/r}\Big], \tag{14**}$$

where $c_\beta = c_\beta(t)$ are continuous functions of the variable $t \geq 0$.

To be able to prove that condition (14*) already implies condition (14), it suffices to define the function $G(t)$ for $t \geq 0$ by

$$G(t) = \max_{|\xi_\beta| \leq t} c^*(\eta).$$

Since the function G is obviously continuous and non-decreasing, we have

$$c^*(\eta) \leq G\Big(\max_{|\beta| < k - N/p} |\xi_\beta|\Big) \leq G\Big(\sum_{|\beta| < k - N/p} |\xi_\beta|\Big)$$

and we obtain condition (14) with the function $c(t) = G(t)$.

16.13. The significance of Theorem 16.11 lies in the fact that it enables us to estimate (by means of the Hölder inequality) the integral

$$\int_\Omega h(x; \delta_k u(x)) \, w(x) \, dx,$$

which is finite if the function h satisfies the conditions of the theorem and the function w belongs to $L_s(\Omega)$, where $s = r/(r - 1)$ (if $r > 1$) or $s = \infty$ (if $r = 1$).

We will wish to exploit this fact for the estimation of integrals of the form

$$\int_\Omega a_\alpha(x; \delta_k u(x)) \, D^\alpha v(x) \, dx ; \quad u, v \in W^{k,p}(\Omega), \quad |\alpha| \leq k. \tag{17}$$

Hitherto, we have started from the fact that $D^\alpha v \in L_p(\Omega)$ for $v \in W^{k,p}(\Omega)$ and that it thus suffices for the function a_α to satisfy inequality (14) with the value $r = p/(p - 1)$ (for the sake of simplicity, we assume that $p > 1$; the reader can easily deal with the case $p = 1$ himself).

However, the imbedding theorems are now familiar and we know, therefore, that the function $D^\alpha v$ belongs not only to $L_p(\Omega)$ but that it even belongs to the "more agreeable" space $L_{q(\alpha)}(\Omega)$ (if $|\alpha| \geq k - N/p$) or $C^0(\bar{\Omega})$ (if $|\alpha| < k - N/p$). Hence, we may choose the number r in the estimate (14) — applied to the function a_α instead of the function h, of course — as follows:

$$r = \frac{q(\alpha)}{q(\alpha) - 1}, \quad \text{if } |\alpha| \geq k - \frac{N}{p}; \quad r = 1, \quad \text{if } |\alpha| < k - \frac{N}{p}.$$

[In the second case, the function $D^\alpha v$ is continuous, by Lemma 16.9 (iii) in fact, and so it is bounded on $\bar{\Omega}$. For the integral (17) to be finite, it is therefore sufficient that $a_\alpha(x; \delta_k u(x)) \in L_1(\Omega).$]

Consequently, it is possible to establish the following generalization of Theorem 14.2:

16.14. Theorem. *Let A be the formal differential operator of order $2k$ given by the formula*

$$(Au)(x) = \sum_{|\alpha| \leq k} (-1)^{|\alpha|} D^\alpha a_\alpha(x; \delta_k u(x)),$$

*and let the functions $a_\alpha \in$ **CAR** satisfy the following growth conditions for almost all $x \in \Omega$ and for $\xi \in \mathbb{R}^\times$:*

$$\left| a_\alpha(x; \xi) \right| \leq c_\alpha \Big(\sum_{|\beta| < k - N/p} |\xi_\beta| \Big) \big[g_\alpha(x) + \sum_{k - N/p \leq |\beta| \leq k} |\xi_\beta|^{r(\alpha,\beta)} \big], \tag{18}$$

where $p > 1$ and

(a) $c_\alpha = c_\alpha(t)$ *is a non-negative continuous function of the variable $t \geq 0$,*

$$c_\alpha = \text{const.} \quad \text{for} \quad k - \frac{N}{p} \leq 0;$$

(b) $g_\alpha \in L_s(\Omega)$, *where*

$$s = \begin{cases} \dfrac{q(\alpha)}{q(\alpha) - 1} & \text{for } |\alpha| \geq k - \dfrac{N}{p}, \\[2ex] 1 & \text{for } |\alpha| < k - \dfrac{N}{p}; \end{cases}$$

(c)
$$r(\alpha, \beta) = \begin{cases} \dfrac{[q(\alpha) - 1]\, q(\beta)}{q(\alpha)} & \text{for } |\alpha| \geq k - \dfrac{N}{p}, \\[2ex] q(\beta) & \text{for } |\alpha| < k - \dfrac{N}{p}; \end{cases}$$

(d)
$$q(\gamma) = \frac{Np}{N - (k - |\gamma|)\, p} \quad for \quad |\gamma| > k - \frac{N}{p},$$

$$q(\gamma) \geq 1 \quad arbitrary \qquad for \quad |\gamma| = k - \frac{N}{p}. \tag{19}$$

The formal differential operator A then determines the continuous operator $\mathbb{A}$, defined on the space $W^{k,p}(\Omega)$ with values in the dual space $(W^{k,p}(\Omega))^*$, given by the formula

$$<\mathbb{A}u, v> = \sum_{|\alpha| \leq k} \int_{\Omega} a_\alpha(x;\, \delta_k\, u(x))\, D^\alpha v(x)\, dx$$

for all $u, v \in W^{k,p}(\Omega)$.

16.15. Remarks. (i) If the function $a_\alpha \in$ **CAR** satisfies the growth conditions (18), we denote this by the symbol

$$a_\alpha \in \mathbf{CAR}^*(p).$$

Naturally, the growth conditions (18) can be modified in the sense of Remark 16.12 (iii).

(ii) Comparison of Theorems 14.2 and 16.14 reveals that the same result is obtained if the growth conditions (12.12) are replaced by conditions (18), i.e., if the coefficients $a_\alpha \in$ **CAR**(p) are replaced by coefficients from the class **CAR**$^*(p)$. Moreover, since the definition of the weak solution of a boundary value problem (A, V, Q) in Paragraph 15.7 was based upon the assumption $a_\alpha \in$ **CAR**(p), we see immediately that everything stated there remains valid for the new growth conditions as well.

(iii) Conditions (18) together with the "explanatory" relations (19) are not altogether clear. Therefore, in the following paragraph we shall elucidate — using several examples — the difference between conditions (18) and (12.12). At this stage, we mention one important fact: Both the growth conditions, conditions (12.12) as well as conditions (18), are "tailored" to the application of the space $W^{k,p}(\Omega)$. In the former conditions, the parameter p appeared in the form of the exponent $p - 1$ with all the variables ξ_β, while in the latter conditions it appears in this form only for those variables ξ_β with $|\beta| = k$ and, moreover, only in those functions a_α where $|\alpha| = k$, too. Indeed, if $|\gamma| = k$, then $q(\gamma) = p$, and thus

$$r(\alpha, \beta) = p - 1 \quad for \quad |\alpha| = |\beta| = k.$$

If $|\alpha| < k$ or $|\beta| < k$, then $r(\alpha, \beta) > p - 1$ and more rapid growth is thus allowed than for the conditions of the first type.

This means then that for the determination of the space $W^{k,p}(\Omega)$, in which we look for the weak solution, the growth of the coefficients a_α, with $|\alpha| = k$, with respect to the variables ξ_β with $|\beta| = k$ is decisive. [Of course, neither the growth with respect to the remaining variables nor the growth of the coefficients a_α, with $|\alpha| < k$, is arbitrary; it again depends on the parameter p, as also is shown by formulas (19), in fact.]

16.16. Examples. (i) For an ordinary second-order differential equation [i.e., for the case when $N = 1$, $k = 1$, $\Omega = (0, 1)$, see Paragraph 15.12], the growth conditions (12.12) are

$$|a_i(x; \xi_0, \xi_1)| \leq g_i(x) + c_i(|\xi_0|^{p-1} + |\xi_1|^{p-1}), \quad i = 0, 1, \tag{20}$$

where $g_i \in L_q(0, 1)$, $q = p/(p - 1)$, and the c_i are non-negative constants. The new growth conditions (18) have the form

$$|a_1(x; \xi_0, \xi_1)| \leq c_1(|\xi_0|)\,[g_1(x) + |\xi_1|^{p-1}],$$
$$|a_0(x; \xi_0, \xi_1)| \leq c_0(|\xi_0|)\,[g_0(x) + |\xi_1|^{p}], \tag{21}$$

where c_1, c_0 are non-negative continuous functions, $g_1 \in L_q(0, 1)$ with $q = p/(p - 1)$, and $g_0 \in L_1(0, 1)$.

Assume, for the moment, that an ordinary second-order differential equation is given for the coefficients a_0 and a_1 for which the conditions (21) with constant functions c_1, c_0, g_1, and g_0, hold. Then

$$a_1 \in \mathbf{CAR}(p), \quad a_0 \in \mathbf{CAR}(p + 1),$$

and, by Lemma 12.15, both a_0 and a_1 thus belong to the class $\mathbf{CAR}(p + 1)$. If we did not know that conditions (21) make it possible to work with the space $W^{1,p}(0, 1)$, we would conclude that it is necessary to use the space

$$W^{k,p+1}(0, 1).$$

[The application of the "better" space $W^{1,p+1}(0, 1)$ would not be of any more use here: In subsequent chapters, it will be seen that from the point-of-view of solvability the correct choice of the space is essential.]

For instance, should the growth conditions (20) be employed, the concept of the weak solution could not be introduced at all for the formal differential operator

$$Au = -u'' + e^u$$

since its coefficient a_0 increases exponentially:

$$a_0(x; \xi_0, \xi_1) = e^{\xi_0}.$$

Nevertheless, conditions (21) are satisfied: It suffices to choose $p = 2$ since $a_1(x; \xi_0, \xi_1) = \xi_1$, $c_1(|\xi_0|) \equiv 1$, $g_0(x) = g_1(x) \equiv 1$, and $c_0(t) = e^t$. It is therefore possible to define the concept of the weak solution which we will look for in the space

$$W^{1,2}(0, 1) .$$

(ii) For an ordinary differential equation of the fourth order [i.e., for the case when $N = 1$, $k = 2$, $\Omega = (0, 1)$], the growth conditions (12.12) are

$$\left| a_i(x; \xi_0, \xi_1, \xi_2) \right| \leq g_i(x) + c_i \big[|\xi_0|^{p-1} + |\xi_1|^{p-1} + |\xi_2|^{p-1} \big] , \quad i = 0, 1, 2 ,$$

where $g_1 \in L_q(0, 1)$, $q = p/(p - 1)$, and the c_i are non-negative constants. However, due to Theorem 16.14, everything that was said in Paragraph 15.14 can be applied just as well to the equations whose coefficients satisfy the conditions

$$\left| a_2(x; \xi_0, \xi_1, \xi_2) \right| \leq c_2(|\xi_0| + |\xi_1|) \big[g_2(x) + |\xi_2|^{p-1} \big] ,$$

$$\left| a_i(x; \xi_0, \xi_1, \xi_2) \right| \leq c_i(|\xi_0| + |\xi_1|) \big[g_i(x) + |\xi_2|^p \big] , \quad i = 0, 1 , \tag{22}$$

where c_0, c_1, c_2 are continuous functions, $g_2 \in L_q(0, 1)$ with $q = p/(p - 1)$, and $g_0, g_1 \in L_1(0, 1)$.

In concrete terms, it is possible, e.g., in the space $W^{2,2}(0, 1)$, to formulate the problem of the weak solution for the equation

$$\frac{d^4 u}{dx^4} + g\left(\left| \frac{du}{dx} \right|, |u| \right) = f \quad \text{on} \quad (0, 1)$$

with an arbitrary continuous function $g = g(s, t)$.

(iii) Consider a partial differential equation of the second order (i.e., the case when $N > 1$, $k = 1$ — see Paragraph 15.16). Then it is possible, instead of the "usual" growth conditions

$$\left| a_i(x; \xi_0, \xi_1, ..., \xi_N) \right| \leq g_i(x) + c_i \sum_{j=0}^{N} |\xi_j|^{p-1} , \quad i = 0, 1, ..., N$$

[see (15.34)], to consider the following new growth conditions:

(a) For the case when $p \leq N$:

$$\left| a_i(x; \xi_0, \xi_1, ..., \xi_N) \right| \leq c_i \big[g_i(x) + |\xi_0|^\sigma + \sum_{j=1}^{N} |\xi_j|^{p-1} \big] , \quad i = 1, ..., N ,$$

$$\left| a_0(x; \xi_0, \xi_1, ..., \xi_N) \right| \leq c_0 \big[g_0(x) + |\xi_0|^\tau + \sum_{j=1}^{N} |\xi_j|^\varrho \big] , \tag{23}$$

where $c_0, c_1, ..., c_N$ are non-negative constants, $g_i \in L_q(\Omega)$ with $q = p/(p - 1)$ for $i = 1, ..., N$, $g_0 \in L_s(\Omega)$ with $s = Np/(Np - N + p)$ when $p < N$ and arbitrary

$s > 1$ when $p = N$,

$$\sigma = \begin{cases} N(p-1)/(N-p) & \text{for } p < N , \\ s(p-1)/p & \text{for } p = N \quad (\text{arbitrary } s > 1) ; \end{cases}$$

$$\tau = \begin{cases} (Np-N+p)/(N-p) & \text{for } p < N , \\ s - 1 & \text{for } p = N \quad (\text{arbitrary } s > 1) ; \end{cases}$$

$$\varrho = \begin{cases} p-1+p/N & \text{for } p < N \\ p(s-1)/s & \text{for } p = N \quad (\text{arbitrary } s > 1) . \end{cases} \quad (24)$$

(b) For the case when $p > N$:

$$\left| a_i(x; \xi_0, \xi_1, ..., \xi_N) \right| \leq c_i(|\xi_0|) \left[g_i(x) + \sum_{j=1}^{N} |\xi_j|^{p-1} \right], \quad i = 1, 2, ..., N ,$$

$$\left| a_0(x; \xi_0, \xi_1, ..., \xi_N) \right| \leq c_0(|\xi_0|) \left[g_0(x) + \sum_{j=1}^{N} |\xi_j|^{p} \right], \quad (25)$$

where $c_0, c_1, ..., c_N$ are non-negative continuous functions, $g_i \in L_q(\Omega)$ with $q = p/(p-1)$ for $i = 1, ..., N$, $g_0 \in L_1(\Omega)$.

(iv) As an illustration of the above general case, consider the particular formal differential operator

$$Au = -\Delta u + |u|^s u ,$$

where s is a positive parameter. This corresponds to the coefficients

$$a_i(x; \xi_0, \xi_1, ..., \xi_N) = \xi_i , \quad i = 1, ..., N ,$$
$$a_0(x; \xi_0, \xi_1, ..., \xi_N) = |\xi_0|^s \xi_0$$

[see also Example 15.16 (I)].

The form of the coefficients a_i $(i = 1, ..., N)$ indicates that it is possible to choose $p = 2$ and thus to work with the space

$$W^{1,2}(\Omega) .$$

Indeed, we have

$$\left| a_i(x; \xi_0, \xi_1, ..., \xi_N) \right| = |\xi_i| = |\xi_i|^{2-1} \leq \sum_{j=1}^{N} |\xi_j|^{2-1} ,$$

which corresponds to condition (23) [with $c_i = 1$, $g_i(x) \equiv 0$] as well as to condition (25) [with $c_i(t) \equiv 1$, $g_i(x) \equiv 0$]. We are now interested in the question of for which values of the parameter s it is possible to formulate (in the weak sense) the boundary value problem for the operator A using the space $W^{1,2}(\Omega)$. To this end, we have to investigate conditions (23) and (25) for the coefficient a_0.

Since $p = 2$ and $N \geq 2$, the case $p > N$ cannot arise, i.e., conditions (25) need not be considered. From conditions (23), the exponent τ in the second condition is of importance to us. For our particular coefficient a_0, it is sufficient that $\tau \geq s + 1$; from conditions (24) it then follows that

$$s \geq 0 \quad \text{and is otherwise arbitrary} \quad \text{for} \quad N = 2 ,$$

$$s \leq \frac{2N - N + 2}{N - 2} - 1 = \frac{4}{N - 2} \quad \text{for} \quad N > 2 .$$

It is thus possible to formulate in the weak sense the boundary value problem for the operator A in the space $W^{1,2}(\Omega)$ if we have arbitrary $s \geq 0$ in the case when $N = 2$, and if $s \leq 4/(N - 2)$ when $N > 2$. Comparing this result with the result of Example 15.16 (I, II) we see that when applying the growth conditions (12.12) it would be possible to use the space $W^{1,2}(\Omega)$ only if $s = 0$.

(v) The general case from part (iii) will again be illustrated on the example of the formal differential operator

$$Au = - \sum_{i=1}^{N} \frac{\partial}{\partial x_i} \left(\left| \frac{\partial u}{\partial x_i} \right|^{p-2} \frac{\partial u}{\partial x_i} \right) + h(u) ,$$

where $p > 1$ and $h = h(t)$ is a continuous function of the real variable t [Example (iv) is obtained by choosing $p = 2$ and $h(t) = |t|^s . t$]. The coefficients corresponding to the operator A are

$$a_i(x; \xi_0, \xi_1, \ldots, \xi_N) = |\xi_i|^{p-2} \xi_i , \quad i = 1, \ldots, N ,$$

$$a_0(x; \xi_0, \xi_1, \ldots, \xi_N) = h(\xi_0) .$$

Since

$$\left| a_i(x; \xi_0, \xi_1, \ldots, \xi_N) \right| = |\xi_i|^{p-1} \leq \sum_{j=1}^{N} |\xi_j|^{p-1} \quad \text{for} \quad i = 1, \ldots, N ,$$

we see that it will again be appropriate to work with the space

$$W^{1,p}(\Omega) .$$

We examine what properties the function h must have to ensure that we are actually able to work with this space. Conditions (25) imply that in the case when $p > N$ it is not necessary to impose any further restrictions on the function h: The second of these conditions will obviously be satisfied if we choose $c_0(|t|) = |h(t)| + |h(-t)|$ and $g_0(x) \equiv 1$. In the case when $p \leq N$, the function h has also to satisfy the growth condition

$$|h(t)| \leq c|t|^\tau + d ,$$

where c and d are positive constants and τ is determined in (24).

In particular, this means that for the operator

$$-\sum_{i=1}^{N} \frac{\partial}{\partial x_i}\left(\left|\frac{\partial u}{\partial x_i}\right|^{p-2}\frac{\partial u}{\partial x_i}\right) + e^u$$

it is possible to formulate the problem of the weak solution [in $W^{1,p}(\Omega)$] only if the number p which determines the growth of the derivatives is larger than the dimension of the domain Ω, since for $p \leq N$ the condition

$$|e^t| \leq c|t|^\tau + d \quad \text{for all} \quad t \geq 0$$

is not satisfied for any non-negative numbers τ, c, d. In particular, it is thus impossible to formulate the concept of the weak solution for the formal differential equation

$$-\Delta u + e^u = f \quad \text{on} \quad \Omega$$

encountered in Paragraph 4.2; indeed, we have $p = 2$ here, and for $N \geq 2$ we then always have $p \leq N$. [Compare this result with the entirely different situation in Example (i)!]

16.17. Anisotropic spaces. The growth conditions (12.12) assumed the same growth (of the type t^{p-1}) for all the derivatives; the new growth conditions (18) anticipated different rates of growth dependent on the order of the derivative $D^\beta u$ and on the index of the coefficient a_α (i.e., growth of the type $t^{r(\alpha,\beta)}$). Of course, it was important there that derivatives of the same order always displayed the same growth in functions a_α with the same value of $|\alpha|$.

Theorem 12.10, upon which all our estimates were based, however admits different growth of the function $h(x; \xi)$ for each of the variables ξ_β (i.e., growth of the type $t^{p(\beta)}$). It turns out that it is possible to describe growths of this type, in which growth with respect to the derivative $D^\beta u$ depends on the multi-index β and not only on its length $|\beta|$ (i.e., it depends not only on the order of the derivative but also on the variables with respect to which the derivative is taken), and to introduce the concept of the weak solution for the corresponding differential operators. Such "generalized growth" assumes, naturally, the application of certain modified Sobolev spaces — the co-called anisotropic spaces.

We will not go too far into the details here and merely present a simple example by way of illustration.

16.18. Example. Let Ω be a plane domain (i.e., $N = 2$), and consider the formal differential operator of the second order

$$-\frac{\partial}{\partial x}\left(\left|\frac{\partial u}{\partial x}\right|^{p-2}\frac{\partial u}{\partial x}\right) - \frac{\partial}{\partial y}\left(\left|\frac{\partial u}{\partial y}\right|^{q-2}\frac{\partial u}{\partial y}\right) = f \quad \text{on} \quad \Omega \quad (p > 1, q > 1). \tag{26}$$

This is a special case of the equation of Paragraph 15.16; the corresponding coefficients are

$$a_0(x, y; \xi_0, \xi_1, \xi_2) = 0 \,,$$

$$a_1(x, y; \xi_0, \xi_1, \xi_2) = |\xi_1|^{p-2} \xi_1 \,,$$

$$a_2(x, y; \xi_0, \xi_1, \xi_2) = |\xi_2|^{q-2} \xi_2 \,. \tag{27}$$

If $p = q$, it is possible to define the weak solution of the boundary value problem for equation (26); we look for this solution as an element of the space

$$W^{1,p}(\Omega) \,.$$

If $p \neq q$, it is again possible to define the weak solution of the boundary value problem for equation (26); however, this time we have to work with the space

$$W^{1,r}(\Omega) \,, \quad \text{where} \quad r = \max(p, q) :$$

For the coefficients (27) we have, indeed,

$$a_1 \in \mathbf{CAR}(p) \,, \quad a_2 \in \mathbf{CAR}(q) \,,$$

and, thus, by Lemma 12.15,

$$a_i \in \mathbf{CAR}(r) \quad \text{holds for} \quad i = 0, 1, 2 \,.$$

However, this choice of the space $W^{1,r}(\Omega)$ leads to something of a loss in detail; it is more desirable to work with a space which reflects more accurately the special character of equation (26). The so-called *anisotropic Sobolev space* is just that space; it is denoted by

$$W^{1;p,q}(\Omega)$$

and defined as the set of all those $u \in L_p(\Omega) \cap L_q(\Omega)$ whose generalized derivatives of the first order satisfy

$$\frac{\partial u}{\partial x} \in L_p(\Omega) \,, \quad \frac{\partial u}{\partial y} \in L_q(\Omega) \,.$$

Assume, e.g. (without loss of generality), that $1 < p < q$ and define the norm on $W^{1;p,q}(\Omega)$ by the formula

$$\|u\|_{1;p,q} = \|u\|_q + \left\|\frac{\partial u}{\partial x}\right\|_p + \left\|\frac{\partial u}{\partial y}\right\|_q \tag{28}$$

[clearly, we then have

$$W^{1;p,q}(\Omega) \subsetneqq W^{1,p}(\Omega)] \,.$$

Define, furthermore, the space

$$W_0^{1;p,q}(\Omega)$$

to be the closure of the set $C_0^\infty(\Omega)$ in the norm (28).

It can be easily shown now that the expression

$$a(u, v) = \int_\Omega \left|\frac{\partial u}{\partial x}\right|^{p-2} \frac{\partial u}{\partial x} \frac{\partial v}{\partial x} \, dx \, dy + \int_\Omega \left|\frac{\partial u}{\partial y}\right|^{q-2} \frac{\partial u}{\partial y} \frac{\partial v}{\partial y} \, dx \, dy$$

represents, for fixed $u \in W^{1;p,q}(\Omega)$, the value of the functional $\mathbb{A}u \in (W^{1;p,q}(\Omega))^*$ at the point $v \in W^{1;p,q}(\Omega)$:

$$a(u, v) = \, <\mathbb{A}u, v> .$$

It is then again possible to define the weak solution of the boundary value problem for equation (26) in a manner entirely analogous to that used in Paragraph 15.7: Assume that we are given a space V such that

$$W_0^{1;p,q}(\Omega) \subset V \subset W^{1;p,q}(\Omega),$$

a space Q such that $V \subsetneq Q$ and $C_0^\infty(\Omega)$ is a dense set in Q, a function $\varphi \in W^{1;p,q}(\Omega)$, a functional $\mathbf{f} \in Q^*$, and a functional $\mathbf{g} \in V^*$ such that $<\mathbf{g}, v>_V = 0$ for $v \in W_0^{1;p,q}(\Omega)$.

We say that the function $u \in W^{1;p,q}(\Omega)$ is the weak solution of the boundary value problem (A, V, Q) [where A is the formal differential operator from (26)] if

(i) $u - \varphi \in V$,
(ii) for all $v \in V$, we have

$$<\mathbb{A}u, v> \, = \, <\mathbf{f}, v>_Q + \, <\mathbf{g}, v>_V .$$

Just as in Paragraph 15.16, it can be shown that the choice $V = W_0^{1;p,q}(\Omega)$ corresponds to the Dirichlet problem for equation (26), i.e., to equation (26) with the boundary condition

$$u = \varphi \quad \text{on} \quad \partial\Omega,$$

while the choice $V = W^{1;p,q}(\Omega)$ corresponds to the Neumann problem, i.e., to equation (26) with the boundary condition

$$\left|\frac{\partial u}{\partial x}\right|^{p-2} \frac{\partial u}{\partial x} v_x + \left|\frac{\partial u}{\partial y}\right|^{q-2} \frac{\partial u}{\partial y} v_y = g \quad \text{on} \quad \partial\Omega$$

(v_x, v_y are components of the unit vector of the outward normal v to $\partial\Omega$).

In terms of anisotropic spaces it is also possible to formulate problems in several variables and of higher orders. However, we shall not do this here. The fact that problems formulated in this way are also solvable will be discussed in Paragraph 32.3.

The interested reader will find references concerning the theory of anisotropic spaces, e.g., in the book [54].

16.19. Rapidly increasing coefficients. Consider, first, the ordinary differential equation

$$-u'' + e^u = f \quad \text{on} \quad (0, 1). \tag{29}$$

In Paragraph 16.16 (i) it was shown that in this case it is possible to define the weak solution of the boundary value problem for equation (29); we look for the weak solution u in the space $W^{1,2}(0, 1)$.

On the other hand, for the partial differential equation

$$-\Delta u + e^u = f \quad \text{on} \quad \Omega \subset \mathbb{R}^N, \quad N > 1, \tag{30}$$

which is a multi-dimensional analogue of equation (29), our theory does not enable us to define the weak solution $u \in W^{1,2}(\Omega)$ [see Example 16.16 (v)]†).

In spite of this, equations of the type of (30) appear quite often in the literature and describe practical problems (see Paragraph 4.2); it would thus be useful to be able to introduce the concept of the weak solution for such equations as well.

In the case of equations of the forms (29) and (30), the corresponding coefficients a_α exhibit polynomial growth, at least with respect to the first derivative [this is the growth corresponding to the choice of the space $W^{1,2}(\Omega)$, i.e. $a_\alpha \in \textbf{CAR}(2)$ for $|\alpha| = 1$]. However, in an equation having the form

$$-\left(e^{(u')^2}\right)' + e^u = f \quad \text{on} \quad (0, 1) \tag{31}$$

or

$$-\sum_{i=1}^{N} \frac{\partial}{\partial x_i} \left[u^2 \exp\left(\frac{\partial u}{\partial x_i}\right)^2 \right] = f \quad \text{on} \quad \Omega \tag{32}$$

polynomial growth is already out of the question because to equation (31) correspond the coefficients

$$a_1(x; \xi_0, \xi_1) = \exp \xi_1^2, \quad a_0(x; \xi_0, \xi_1) = \exp \xi_0,$$

while the equation (32) correspond the coefficients

$$a_i(x; \xi_0, \xi_1, ..., \xi_N) = \xi_0^2 \exp \xi_1^2 \quad (i = 1, 2, ..., N),$$
$$a_0(x; \xi_0, \xi_1, ..., \xi_N) = 0.$$

Thus, the coefficients cannot be estimated here by powers of the variables $\xi_0, \xi_1,$ or

---

†) We should add, however, that recently a number of papers have appeared in which it is shown that under certain assumptions it is possible to solve the Dirichlet problem for an equation of the type of (30) in Sobolev spaces — see, e.g., [18].,

of the variables $\xi_0, \xi_1, ..., \xi_N$, respectively; the coefficients belong neither to the class **CAR**(p) nor to the class **CAR**$^*(p)$ for any $p > 1$ [see Example 12.14 (ii)].

Nevertheless, it is sometimes possible to introduce the concept of the weak solution for such equations as well; however, the Sobolev spaces are no longer adequate and we have to introduce new spaces.

16.20. Orlicz spaces. Let $g = g(t)$ be a function defined for $t \geq 0$, continuous, increasing, and such that $g(0) = 0$ and $\lim\limits_{t \to \infty} g(t) = \infty$, and let $h = h(t)$ be the function inverse to g. For $s \geq 0$, define a pair of functions G, H by the formulas

$$G(s) = \int_0^s g(t)\, dt , \quad H(s) = \int_0^s h(t)\, dt .$$

Functions G and H of this type are called *Young functions*; we describe the pair G, H as mutually *complementary Young functions*.†)

Let Ω be a bounded domain in $\mathbb{R}^N$, G a Young function. Denote by the symbol

$$L_G(\Omega)$$

the set of all measurable functions $u = u(x)$ defined almost everywhere on Ω and such that at least one number $k > 0$ exists for which

$$\int_\Omega G(k|u(x)|)\, dx < \infty . \tag{33}$$

Furthermore, denote by the symbol

$$E_G(\Omega)$$

the set of all functions $u \in L_G(\Omega)$ for which the integral (33) is finite for all $k > 0$.

Clearly,

$$E_G(\Omega) \subset L_G(\Omega)$$

while the two sets only coincide for a very narrow class of Young functions G.

On the sets $L_G(\Omega)$ and $E_G(\Omega)$, it is possible to introduce a norm by means of the formula

$$\|u\|_G = \inf \left\{ k > 0 : \int_\Omega G\left(\frac{1}{k}|u(x)|\right) dx < 1 \right\} . \tag{34}$$

The following assertions are true:

(i) *The space $E_G(\Omega)$ with the norm $\|\cdot\|_G$ is a separable Banach space.*

(ii) *The space $L_G(\Omega)$ with the norm $\|\cdot\|_G$ is a Banach space which is separable if and only if $L_G(\Omega) = E_G(\Omega)$.*

---

† The requirements imposed on the functions G, H can be weakened substantially; see, e.g., [54].

The spaces $L_G(\Omega)$ and $E_G(\Omega)$ are called *Orlicz spaces*. If we choose $G(t) = t^p$, $p > 1$, we obtain the space $L_p(\Omega)$ from Paragraph 12.7. The function complementary to this function G is $H(t) = t^q$, where $q = p/(p-1)$. The pair of spaces $L_G(\Omega)$ and $L_H(\Omega)$ then assumes the role of the spaces $L_p(\Omega)$ and $L_q(\Omega)$ whose parameters are connected by the relation

$$\frac{1}{p} + \frac{1}{q} = 1 \,.$$

An analogue of the Hölder inequality (12.5) holds for the Orlicz spaces: *If G, H are complementary Young functions, then for $u \in L_G(\Omega)$ and $v \in L_H(\Omega)$ we have*

$$\int_\Omega |u(x)\,v(x)|\,\mathrm{d}x \le 2\|u\|_G\,\|v\|_H \,. \tag{35}$$

Thus, Orlicz spaces are a generalization of the spaces $L_p(\Omega)$. In general, they obviously have less agreeable properties, to some extent, than the spaces $L_p(\Omega)$ and are more difficult to handle. [This can also be seen from the fact that for Orlicz spaces we consider the pair $L_G(\Omega)$ and $E_G(\Omega)$; if we choose $G(t) = t^p$, $p > 1$, then $L_G(\Omega) = E_G(\Omega) = L_p(\Omega)$, i.e., we only have to deal with a single space.]

Theorem 12.10 can be generalized for Orlicz spaces:

16.21. The Němyckiĭ operator in Orlicz spaces. *Let $h = h(x, \xi)$ be a function defined for $x \in \Omega$ and $\xi \in \mathbb{R}^m$, $h \in$* **CAR***, and let complementary Young functions G, H, a function $g \in L_H(\Omega)$, and positive constants c, d exist such that for almost all $x \in \Omega$ and for all $\xi \in \mathbb{R}^m$ we have*

$$\left| h(x; \xi_1, \ldots, \xi_m) \right| \le g(x) + c \sum_{k=1}^m H^{-1}\!\left(G(d|\xi_k|) \right), \tag{36}$$

where H^{-1} is the inverse function to the Young function H. Then the function

$$h\big(x; u_1(x), \ldots, u_m(x)\big)$$

belongs to $L_H(\Omega)$ for any arbitrary m-tuple of functions $u_i \in E_G(\Omega)$ $(i = 1, \ldots, m)$.

This means that the Němyckiĭ operator $\mathscr{H}$ determined by the function h maps the Cartesian product

$$E_G(\Omega) \times E_G(\Omega) \times \ldots \times E_G(\Omega)$$

into $L_H(\Omega)$.

The proof can be found, e.g., in the book [53]. There it is also proved that the Němyckiĭ operator is continuous in a certain sense.

16.22. The Sobolev-Orlicz space and differential operators. (i) Let G be a Young function, Ω a domain in $\mathbb{R}^N$, $\Omega \in \mathscr{C}^{0,1}$, k a positive integer. By the symbols

$$W^k L_G(\Omega) \quad \text{and} \quad W^k E_G(\Omega)$$

we denote, respectively, the sets of all those functions $u \in L_G(\Omega)$, or $u \in E_G(\Omega)$, whose generalized derivatives $D^\beta u$ up to and including order k (i.e., for $|\beta| \leq k$) also belong to $L_G(\Omega)$, or to $E_G(\Omega)$.†) On the spaces $W^k L_G(\Omega)$ and $W^k E_G(\Omega)$, the norm is defined by the formula

$$\|u\|_{k,G} = \sum_{|\beta| \leq k} \|D^\beta u\|_G . \tag{37}$$

These spaces will be called the *Sobolev-Orlicz spaces*. They are again Banach spaces.

Furthermore, it is again possible to introduce the space

$$W_0^k E_G(\Omega)$$

as the closure of the set $C_0^\infty(\Omega)$ in the norm (37).

(ii) Let the formal differential operator A

$$(Au)(x) = \sum_{|\alpha| \leq k} (-1)^{|\alpha|} D^\alpha a_\alpha(x; \delta_k u(x)) \tag{38}$$

now be given and assume that the coefficients a_α belong to the class **CAR**. Let us further assume that complementary Young functions G, H, functions $g_\alpha \in L_H(\Omega)$, and positive constants c_α and d_α ($|\alpha| \leq k$) exist such that we have

$$|a_\alpha(x; \xi)| \leq g_\alpha(x) + c_\alpha \sum_{|\beta| \leq k} H^{-1}(G(d_\alpha|\xi_\beta|)) \tag{39}$$

for all $x \in \Omega$ and $\xi \in \mathbb{R}^\varkappa$.

If we now apply the results of Paragraph 16.21 [where as the function $h(x; \xi)$ we choose the functions $a_\alpha(x; \xi)$ and put $m = \varkappa$], we obtain

$$a_\alpha(x; \delta_k u(x)) \in L_H(\Omega) \quad \text{if} \quad u \in W^k E_G(\Omega) .$$

By inequality (35), the integral

$$\int_\Omega a_\alpha(x; \delta_k u(x)) D^\alpha v(x) \, dx$$

is then finite if $u \in W^k E_G(\Omega)$ and $D^\alpha v \in L_G(F)$, or, in other words, the expression

$$a(u, v) = \sum_{|\alpha| \leq k} \int_\Omega a_\alpha(x; \delta_k u(x)) D^\alpha v(x) \, dx$$

is finite for $u \in W^k E_G(\Omega)$ and $v \in W^k L_G(\Omega)$.

---

†) It is possible to introduce the generalized derivatives of a function w from an Orlicz space in the same way as was done for the functions from $L_p(\Omega)$ in Paragraph 13.2: The generalized derivative $D^\beta w$ is the function w_β for which relation (13.4) holds for all $v \in C_0^\infty(\Omega)$.

Thus, the same result has been reached as in Paragraph 12.12, the only difference being the replacement of the growth conditions (12.12) by the growth conditions (39). These latter conditions generalize the former — if we put $G(t) = t^p$, $p > 1$, we actually obtain conditions (12.12). Just as in Paragraph 12.13, we could possibly introduce the notation

$$a_\alpha \in \mathbf{CAR}(G)$$

to indicate the fact that $a_\alpha \in \mathbf{CAR}$ and that (39) holds.

It is now clear that, by analogy with Definition 15.7, we could introduce the concept of the weak solution of the boundary value problem (A, V, Q), where A is the formal differential operator from (38) with the coefficients $a_\alpha \in \mathbf{CAR}(G)$, and that the weak solution u should be an element of the space

$$W^k E_G(\Omega) \,.$$

The precise formulation is not presented here since it would still be necessary to introduce a number of new concepts. By way of illustration, we examine one concrete case.

16.23. The Dirichlet problem. Consider the formal differential operator of order $2k$ in the form

$$(Au)(x) = \sum_{|\alpha| \le k} (-1)^{|\alpha|} \, D^\alpha(g(|D^\alpha u(x)|) \, \mathrm{sgn}\, D^\alpha u(x)) \,, \tag{40}$$

where $g = g(t)$ is a continuous increasing function defined for $t \ge 0$ and such that $g(0) = 0$ and $\lim_{t \to \infty} g(t) = \infty$. It is an operator of the type (38) with the coefficients

$$a(x; \xi) = g(|\xi_\alpha|) \, \mathrm{sgn}\, \xi_\alpha \,, \quad |\alpha| \le k \,.$$

If we choose the complementary Young functions G, H by putting

$$G(t) = \int_0^t g(s) \, ds \,, \quad H(t) = \int_0^t g^{-1}(s) \, ds \,, \tag{41}$$

the growth conditions (39) will be satisfied since

$$g(t) \le 2H^{-1}(G(2t)) \quad \text{for} \quad t \ge 0 \,,$$

i.e., (39) is valid with $g_\alpha(x) \equiv 0$ and $c_\alpha = d_\alpha = 2$.

If φ is now a given function from $W^k E_G(\Omega)$, where the function G is given by formula (41), and if f is a given function from $E_H(\Omega)$, we call the function $u \in W^k E_G(\Omega)$ the weak solution of the Dirichlet problem for the equation

$$\sum_{|\alpha| \le k} (-1)^{|\alpha|} \, D^\alpha(g(|D^\alpha u(x)|) \, \mathrm{sgn}\, D^\alpha u(x)) = f(x) \quad \text{on} \quad \Omega$$

if

(i) $u - \varphi \in W_0^k E_G(\Omega)$,

(ii) for all $v \in W_0^k E_G(\Omega)$, we have

$$\sum_{|\alpha| \leq k} \int_\Omega g(|D^\alpha u(x)|) \, D^\alpha v(x) \, dx = \int_\Omega f(x) \, v(x) \, dx \,.$$

16.24. Remarks. (i) We were led to the application of Orlicz spaces by the examples of Paragraph 16.19, i.e., by the equations whose coefficients grow very rapidly (e.g., exponentially). However, Orlicz spaces are also suitable for the solution of equations whose coefficients grow very slowly (e.g., logarithmically). For slowly growing coefficients we know, as a rule, how to formulate the problem of the weak solution of a boundary value problem by means of appropriate Sobolev spaces, but these spaces are usually not suitable from the point-of-view of the solvability of the thus formulated problem. [The situation is much the same as when applying the Sobolev spaces $W^{1,p}(\Omega)$ to the minimum surface equation — see Paragraph 16.3.]

Besides, from Paragraphs 16.20 to 16.23 we see that in the theory as well as in the applications of Orlicz spaces we always work with a pair of complementary functions G, H, although only the function G appears explicitly in the formulation of the Dirichlet problem in Paragraph 16.23. If one of the functions of this pair grows rapidly, then the other one grows very slowly and at least one of them then belongs to the class which interests us.

(ii) Imbedding theorems also hold for Sobolev-Orlicz spaces. Using them, conditions (39) might be weakened, just as in Paragraphs 16.4 to 16.6 for the case of polynomial growths (12.12). We are not going to formulate the analogue of the growth conditions (18) here; interested readers are referred to the literature ([16], [40]).

(iii) Anisotropic Sobolev-Orlicz spaces could be introduced as well, just as in Paragraphs 16.17 and 16.18. Consider, e.g., the formal differential operator A of order $2k$ which has the form

$$(Au)(x) = \sum_{|\alpha| \leq k} (-1)^{|\alpha|} D^\alpha(g_\alpha(|D^\alpha u(x)|) \, \mathrm{sgn} \, D^\alpha u(x)) \,, \tag{42}$$

where $g_\alpha = g_\alpha(t)$, $|\alpha| \leq k$, are distinct functions of the same type as the function g appearing in the operator (40). The above operator is of the type (38) with coefficients

$$a_\alpha(x; \xi) = g_\alpha(|\xi_\alpha|) \, \mathrm{sgn} \, \xi_\alpha \,, \quad |\alpha| \leq k \,.$$

If we define an α-tuple of Young functions G_α by the formula

$$G_\alpha(t) = \int_0^t g_\alpha(s) \, dx \,, \quad |\alpha| \leq k \,,$$

then for the formulation of the weak solution of the boundary value problem for the operator A in (42) the anisotropic space

$$W^k E_{\vec{G}}(\Omega), \quad \vec{G} = \{G_\alpha\}_{|\alpha| \leq k},$$

is suitable; it is defined as the set of all functions $u = u(x)$ whose generalized derivatives $D^\alpha u$ satisfy the relation

$$D^\alpha u \in E_{G_\alpha}(\Omega), \quad |\alpha| \leq k.$$

The norm in the space $W^k E_{\vec{G}}(\Omega)$ can be defined by

$$\|u\|_{k,\vec{G}} = \sum_{|\alpha| \leq k} \|D^\alpha u\|_{G_\alpha}.$$

16.25. Systems of differential equations. In Section 3, a number of boundary value problems for systems of differential equations were formulated. For such problems, it is also possible to introduce the concept of the weak solution; the difference as compared with the case of a single equation lies in the fact that we look not for a single function u but for a vector function

$$u = (u_1, \ldots, u_m),$$

if we are dealing with a system of m equations for m unknown functions,[†] whose components lie in suitable Sobolev spaces:

$$u_i \in W^{k_i, p_i}(\Omega), \quad i = 1, \ldots, m. \tag{43}$$

The numbers k_i are given by the orders of the individual differential equations in the system while the numbers $p_i > 1$ are determined by the growth conditions which the coefficients of the equations must satisfy.

In general, such a system can be written in the form

$$\sum_{|\alpha| \leq k_i} (-1)^{|\alpha|} D^\alpha a_{i\alpha}(x; \delta_{k_1} u_1(x), \ldots, \delta_{k_m} u_m(x)) = f_i(x) \quad \text{on } \Omega, \quad i = 1, \ldots, m, \tag{44}$$

where $k_1, \ldots, k_m$ are positive integers. The coefficients $a_{i\alpha} = a_{i\alpha}(x; \xi^{(1)}, \ldots, \xi^{(m)})$ are functions defined for $x \in \Omega \subset \mathbb{R}^N$ and for $\xi^{(j)} \in \mathbb{R}^{\varkappa_j}$ $[j = 1, \ldots, m; \varkappa_j = \varkappa(k_j, N)]$ which satisfy the growth conditions

$$\left| a_{i\alpha}(x; \xi^{(1)}, \ldots, \xi^{(m)}) \right| \leq g_{i\alpha}(x) + c_{i\alpha} \Big[\sum_{|\beta| \leq k_1} \big| \xi_\beta^{(1)} \big|^{p_1 - 1} + \ldots + \sum_{|\beta| \leq k_m} \big| \xi_\beta^{(m)} \big|^{p_m - 1} \Big],$$

where $p_i > 1$, $g_{i\alpha} \in L_{q_i}(\Omega)$ with $q_i = p_i/(p_i - 1)$, and $c_{i\alpha}$ are non-negative constants.

---

†) Note that the number of equations need not always correspond to the number of unknown functions.

Thus, e.g., by the weak solution of the Dirichlet problem for the system (44) we understand the vector function $u = (u_1, \ldots, u_m)$ for the components u_i of which (43) holds and which is such that

(i) $u_i - \varphi_i \in W_0^{k_i, p_i}(\Omega)$, $i = 1, \ldots, m$,

(ii) for all $v_i \in W_0^{k_i, p_i}(\Omega)$ $(i = 1, \ldots, m)$, we have

$$\int_\Omega \sum_{i=1}^m \left[\sum_{|\alpha| \le k_i} a_{i\alpha}(x; \delta_{k_1} u_1(x), \ldots, \delta_{k_m} u_m(x)) \, D^\alpha v_i(x) \right] dx = \sum_{i=1}^m \int_\Omega f_i(x) \, v_i(x) \, dx \, ,$$

where φ_i are given functions from $W^{k_i, p_i}(\Omega)$ and f_i are given functions from $L_{q_i}(\Omega)$.

The boundary value problem formulated in this way corresponds to system (44) with the boundary conditions

$$u_i = \varphi_i \, , \quad \frac{\partial u_i}{\partial v} = \frac{\partial \varphi_i}{\partial v} \, , \quad \ldots, \quad \frac{\partial^{k_i - 1} u_i}{\partial v^{k_i - 1}} = \frac{\partial^{k_i - 1} \varphi_i}{\partial v^{k_i - 1}} \quad \text{on} \quad \partial\Omega \, , \quad i = 1, \ldots, m \, .$$

The reader will certainly agree that the concept of the weak solution of a system of equations is not exactly the simplest of concepts (and we have only discussed the Dirichlet problem here). Of course, the analogy with equations (i.e., with "systems" of m equations for $m = 1$) is clear; the difficulties are mainly of a formal character.

For this reason, we shall not discuss this concept in detail in what follows but instead present several examples by way of illustration.

16.26. The von Karmán equations. In Paragraph 3.2, we noted the following system of two equations of the fourth order in a plane domain

$$\left. \begin{aligned} \Delta^2 u - [u, v] &= f \\ \Delta^2 v + [u, u] &= 0 \end{aligned} \right\} \quad \text{on} \quad \Omega \tag{45}$$

(for the notation see Paragraph 3.2).

(i) We study the system (45) with the boundary conditions

$$u = 0 \, , \quad \frac{\partial u}{\partial v} = 0 \, , \quad v = 0 \, , \quad \frac{\partial v}{\partial v} = 0 \quad \text{on} \quad \partial\Omega \tag{46}$$

[i.e., this is the Dirichlet problem for the system (45) which corresponds to a clamped plate].

From the form of equations (45) it is at once clear that it is appropriate to work with the space

$$V = \{(u, v); \ u \in W_0^{2,2}(\Omega), \ v \in W_0^{2,2}(\Omega)\} \, .$$

By the weak solution of the boundary value problem (45), (46) [with the function

$f \in L_2(\Omega)]$ we understand the pair $(u, v) \in V$ such that for all pairs $(\mathscr{U}, \mathscr{V}) \in V$ we have

$$\int_\Omega (\Delta u \, \Delta \mathscr{U} - [u, v] \, \mathscr{U} + \Delta v \, \Delta \mathscr{V} + [u, u] \, \mathscr{V}) \, dx \, dy = \int_\Omega f(x, y) \, \mathscr{U}(x, y) \, dx \, dy.$$

This identity is obtained if we assume that the functions $u, v, \mathscr{U}, \mathscr{V}$ are sufficiently smooth, then multiply the first equation in (45) by the function $\mathscr{U}$, the second equation by the function $\mathscr{V}$, integrate both equations over Ω, add them and modify using Green's Theorem 13.12, exploiting the fact that both (u, v) and $(\mathscr{U}, \mathscr{V})$ belong to V.

The obligatory first condition from the definition of the weak solution, which should be of the form $(u - \varphi, v - \psi) \in V$, dissappears since the boundary conditions (46) are homogeneous and it is thus possible to choose $\varphi = \psi = 0$.

(ii) Consider system (45) with the boundary conditions

$$u = 0, \quad Mu = 0, \quad v = 0, \quad \frac{\partial v}{\partial v} = 0 \quad \text{on} \quad \partial\Omega, \tag{47}$$

where $Mu = \sigma \, \Delta u + (1 - \sigma) \, \partial^2 u / \partial v^2$, $0 \leqq \sigma < 1$ (this boundary value problem corresponds to a simply supported plate).

Here, we will work with the space

$$V = \{(u, v); \; u \in W^{2,2}(\Omega) \cap W_0^{1,2}(\Omega), \; v \in W_0^{2,2}(\Omega)\}$$

[i.e., $u \in W^{2,2}(\Omega)$, $u = 0$ on $\partial\Omega$ in the sense of traces].

By the weak solution of the boundary value problem (45), (47) we understand the pair $(u, v) \in V$ such that for all pairs $(\mathscr{U}, \mathscr{V}) \in V$ we have

$$\int_\Omega \left\{ \frac{\partial^2 u}{\partial x^2} \left(\frac{\partial^2 \mathscr{U}}{\partial x^2} + \sigma \frac{\partial^2 \mathscr{U}}{\partial y^2} \right) + 2(1 - \sigma) \frac{\partial^2 u}{\partial x \, \partial y} \frac{\partial^2 \mathscr{U}}{\partial x \, \partial y} + \frac{\partial^2 u}{\partial y^2} \left(\frac{\partial^2 \mathscr{U}}{\partial y^2} + \sigma \frac{\partial^2 \mathscr{U}}{\partial x^2} \right) + \right.$$

$$+ \frac{\partial^2 v}{\partial x^2} \left(\frac{\partial^2 \mathscr{V}}{\partial x^2} + \sigma \frac{\partial^2 \mathscr{V}}{\partial y^2} \right) + 2(1 - \sigma) \frac{\partial^2 v}{\partial x \, \partial y} \frac{\partial^2 \mathscr{V}}{\partial x \, \partial y} + \frac{\partial^2 v}{\partial y^2} \left(\frac{\partial^2 \mathscr{V}}{\partial y^2} + \sigma \frac{\partial^2 \mathscr{V}}{\partial x^2} \right) -$$

$$\left. - [u, v] \, \mathscr{U} + [u, u] \, \mathscr{V} \right\} dx \, dy = \int_\Omega f(x, y) \, \mathscr{U}(x, y) \, dx \, dy \tag{48}$$

[this identity is obtained by the same procedure as in case (i)].

(iii) Consider system (45) with the boundary conditions

$$. \quad Mu = 0, \quad Nu = 0, \quad v = 0, \quad \frac{\partial v}{\partial v} = 0 \quad \text{on} \quad \partial\Omega, \tag{49}$$

where Nu is given by formula (1.11). (This boundary value problem corresponds to a plate with free edge.)

The weak solution of the boundary value problem (45), (49) is again defined by the identity (48), this time for pairs (u, v), $(\mathscr{U}, \mathscr{V})$ from the space

$$V = \{(u, v); \; u \in W^{2,2}(\Omega), \; v \in W_0^{2,2}(\Omega)\} \, ,$$

thus also emphasizing the fact that the boundary conditions for the function v are stable while the boundary conditions for the function u are unstable.

16.27. Remark. The three boundary value problems presented above for the concrete system of two equations (45) were, perhaps, a somewhat inadequate illustration, but the scope of the book does not permit more on this. However, the analogy with boundary value problems for single equations is hopefully clear from the preceding paragraph.

In the examples of Paragraph 16.26, the space V was defined by stating the conditions for the functions u and v separately. However, when formulating the weak solution of a boundary value problem for a system of equations, we encounter problems in which the space V is also given by conditions which link the individual components of the vector function. Thus, e.g., for the system of two equations of the fourth order (for two unknown functions u, v) a condition of the type

$$(au + bv)\big|_{\partial\Omega} = 0 \tag{50}$$

could also appear (as well as further boundary conditions); see Paragraph 3.5 (ii). The space V would then be given by the requirements $u \in W^{2,2}(\Omega)$, $v \in W^{2,2}(\Omega)$, and by condition (50) (and by other conditions expressing further boundary conditions).

In the next paragraph, we will discuss an example which will be less typical; in this example, a condition will be included in the definition of the space V linking the individual components of the vector function. However, as opposed to condition (50), it will be a condition on Ω and not on $\partial\Omega$.

16.28. The Navier-Stokes equations. In Paragraph 3.3, the system (3.4) with boundary conditions (3.5) was given; there, we looked for an N-tuple of functions $u_1, \ldots, u_N$. Now, we present the weak formulation of this boundary value problem: We define the space V as follows: The vector function $v = (v_1, \ldots, v_N)$ belongs to V if

$$\begin{cases} v_i \in W_0^{1,2}(\Omega) \quad \text{for} \quad i = 1, \ldots, N \, , \\[2mm] \operatorname{div} v = \dfrac{\partial v_1}{\partial x_1} + \ldots + \dfrac{\partial v_N}{\partial x_N} = 0 \quad \text{on} \quad \Omega \end{cases}$$

$[V$ is clearly a subspace of the Cartesian product $[W_0^{1,2}(\Omega)]^N$; we define a norm on V by the formula

$$\|u\|_V = \left(\sum_{i=1}^{N} \sum_{j=1}^{N} \int_{\Omega} \left| \frac{\partial u_i(x)}{\partial x_j} \right|^2 dx \right)^{1/2} .$$

Let $\mathbf{f}$ be a functional from V^*. We say that the vector function $u \in V$ is the weak solution of the boundary value problem (3.4), (3.5) if for all $v \in V$ the relation

$$\sum_{i=1}^{N} \sum_{j=1}^{N} \int_{\Omega} \left[\nu \frac{\partial u_i(x)}{\partial x_j} \frac{\partial v_i(x)}{\partial x_j} + u_j(x) \frac{\partial u_i(x)}{\partial x_j} v_i(x) \right] dx = <\mathbf{f}, v> \tag{51}$$

is valid.

16.29. Remarks on Paragraph 16.28. The system of Navier-Stokes equations is not exactly typical of what was said in Paragraph 16.25, in view of the fact that the last equation of system (3.4), namely the equation

$$\operatorname{div} u = 0 \quad \text{on} \quad \Omega,$$

was included in the definition of the space V which usually represents the boundary conditions.

Furthermore, we assumed that the weak solution u belongs to V although we should have assumed that $u \in [W^{1,2}(\Omega)]^N$. However, this is natural; the boundary conditions (3.5) are homogeneous which means that it is possible to choose $\varphi = 0$ and the obligatory first condition in the definition of the weak solution, namely the condition

$$u - \varphi \in V,$$

becomes simply $u \in V$. [A similar situation was previously encountered in Example 16.26 (i).]

Finally, the function p completely disappeared from the formulation of the weak solution. This is, however, a consequence of the "judicious" choice of the space V: Indeed, it is possible to obtain identity (51) (in the case of sufficiently smooth functions) by the multiplication of the i-th equation in the system (3.4) by the function v_i, the summation of all the equations thus obtained, and the application of Green's Theorem 13.12. Among other things, we also obtain the expression

$$- \sum_{i=1}^{N} \int_{\Omega} \frac{\partial p(x)}{\partial x_i} v_i(x)\, dx \tag{52}$$

which is, moreover, by Theorem 13.12, equal to

$$\sum_{i=1}^{N} \int_{\Omega} p(x) \frac{\partial v_i(x)}{\partial x_i}\, dx - \sum_{i=1}^{N} \int_{\partial \Omega} p(x)\, v_i(x)\, v_i(x)\, dS = \int_{\Omega} p(x)\, \operatorname{div} v(x)\, dx \,;$$

now $v_i \in W_0^{1,2}(\Omega)$ and, therefore, the integral over $\partial \Omega$ vanishes. But, since $v \in V$, we have $\operatorname{div} v = 0$ and the integral over Ω on the right-hand side vanishes as well, and so the entire expression (52) in which the function p appears vanishes.

SECTION 17. REGULARITY OF THE WEAK SOLUTION

17.1. In this chapter, we have introduced the concept of the weak solution of a boundary value problem for the formal differential operator A of order $2k$ given by the formula

$$(Au)(x) = \sum_{|\alpha| \leq k} (-1)^{|\alpha|} D^{\alpha} a_{\alpha}(x; \delta_k u(x)) ;$$

in fact, the weak solution was a certain function

$$u \in W^{k,p}(\Omega) .$$

The concept of the weak solution was confronted all the time with the concept of the classical solution discussed in Chapter II. The classical solution was a certain function

$$u \in C^{2k}(\overline{\Omega}) ;$$

we could speak of the classical solution only under rather strong assumptions on the data of the boundary value problem, i.e., on the coefficients $a_{\alpha} = a_{\alpha}(x; \xi)$, the right-hand side $f = f(x)$, the domain Ω and its boundary $\partial\Omega$, etc.

Roughly speaking, we have shown the following:

(i) If the classical solution of a boundary value problem exists, then it is the weak solution as well.

(ii) If the weak solution $u \in W^{k,p}(\Omega)$ of a boundary value problem exists, where the data of the problem are such that the concept of the classical solution is meaningful, and if this weak solution belongs to the space $C^{2k}(\overline{\Omega})$, then it is the classical solution as well.

Assertions of the type (ii) were proved in the text; Theorem 14.7 was devoted to this question for the case of the solution of a differential equation (without boundary conditions); for the case of a boundary value problem see, e.g., Paragraphs 15.5 or 15.13.

In assertion (ii), let us now attempt to dispense with the condition that the weak solution u belongs to $C^{2k}(\overline{\Omega})$, i.e., assume only that

1) the data of the boundary value problem make it possible to introduce the concept of the classical solution;

2) the weak solution $u \in W^{k,p}(\Omega)$ of the boundary value problem exists.

We wish to know whether this weak solution is already so smooth that it is in fact the classical solution, i.e., we wish to know whether the smoothness of the data of a boundary value problem automatically implies a certain smoothness of the weak solution.

In the paragraphs which follow, we shall show that the weak solution of the Dirichlet problem for an ordinary second-order differential equation is actually the classical solution under certain conditions. This will in fact be an instance of the so-called regularity theorems.

17.2. The formulation of the problem. Let $N = 1$, $\Omega = (0, 1)$, and consider the formal differential operator of the second order

$$(Au)(x) = -\frac{d}{dx} a_1(x; u(x), u'(x)) + a_0(x; u(x), u'(x)) \tag{1}$$

with the coefficients

$$a_0, a_1 \in \mathbf{CAR^*}(p), \quad p > 1$$

[see Paragraph 16.15 (i)]. Let $\varphi(x) = c_0 + (c_1 - c_0) x$, $f \in C^0([0, 1])$, and let

$$u \in W_0^{1,p}(0, 1)$$

be the weak solution of the Dirichlet problem for the operator A, i.e., let

$$u - \varphi \in W_0^{1,p}(0, 1) \tag{2}$$

and let, for all $v \in W_0^{1,p}(0, 1)$,

$$\int_0^1 a_1(x; u(x), u'(x)) v'(x)\, dx + \int_0^1 a_0(x; u(x), u'(x)) v(x)\, dx = \int_0^1 f(x) v(x)\, dx. \tag{3}$$

We already know that this problem corresponds, in the classical formulation, to the Dirichlet problem

$$(Au)(x) = f(x) \quad \text{for} \quad x \in (0, 1), \tag{4}$$

$$u(0) = c_0, \quad u(1) = c_1. \tag{5}$$

Our aim is to prove that under certain additional conditions involving the coefficients a_0, a_1, the weak solution belongs to $C^2([0, 1])$ and solves the boundary value problem (4), (5). For the sake of simplicity, it will be assumed that $p = 2$; we recommend the reader to think out what modifications are necessary if we wish to prove the assertion on the regularity of the weak solution for general $p > 1$.

17.3. Some computations. Let, then, the formal differential operator A of (1) be given, and assume that

$$a_0, a_1 \in \mathbf{CAR^*}(2);$$

this means that

$$a_1(x; u(x), u'(x)) \in L_2(0, 1), \quad a_0(x; u(x), u'(x)) \in L_1(0, 1) \tag{6}$$

for every function $u \in W^{1,2}(0, 1)$. In what follows, let $u \in W^{1,2}(0, 1)$ be the weak solution of the Dirichlet problem for the operator A, so that (2) holds (with $p = 2$) and relation (3) is satisfied for every function $v \in W_0^{1,2}(0, 1)$.

If $w \in L_1(0, 1)$, then

$$w(x) = \frac{d}{dx} \int_0^x w(t) \, dt$$

for almost all $x \in (0, 1)$, and by the theorem on integration by parts we have, for every function $v \in W_0^{1,2}(0, 1)$,

$$\int_0^1 w(x) \, v(x) \, dx = - \int_0^1 \left[\int_0^x w(t) \, dt \right] v'(x) \, dx .$$

As the function w choose the function $a_0(x; u(x), u'(x)) - f(x)$; the function w belongs to $L_1(0, 1)$ by (6) and by the continuity of the function f on $[0, 1]$. Then

$$\int_0^1 [a_0(x; u(x), u'(x)) - f(x)] \, v(x) \, dx =$$

$$= - \int_0^1 \left\{ \int_0^x [a_0(t; u(t), u'(t)) - f(t)] \, dt \right\} v'(x) \, dx$$

and relation (3) can be written as

$$\int_0^1 \left\{ a_1(x; u(x), u'(x)) - \int_0^x [a_0(t; u(t), u'(t)) - f(t)] \, dt \right\} v'(x) \, dx = 0 \qquad (7)$$

for every $v \in W_0^{1,2}(0, 1)$.

Now define $M(x)$ by the formula

$$M(x) = a_1(x; u(x), u'(x)) - \int_0^x [a_0(t; u(t), u'(t)) - f(t)] \, dt .$$

This function belongs to $L_2(0, 1)$ since (6) holds and the integral is a continuous function of the upper bound. Relation (7) can now be written as

$$\int_0^1 M(x) \, v'(x) \, dx = 0 \quad \text{for every} \quad v \in W_0^{1,2}(0, 1) . \qquad (8)$$

Now, choose the function v as follows:

$$v(x) = \int_0^x [M(t) - c] \, dt , \quad \text{where} \quad c = \int_0^1 M(x) \, dx .$$

The function v is absolutely continuous in $[0, 1]$ and has the derivative $v'(x)$ equal to $M(x) - c$ almost everywhere in $(0, 1)$, and so $v' \in L_2(0, 1)$. Furthermore, we have $v(0) = v(1) = 0$, and thus $v \in W_0^{1,2}(0, 1)$. If relation (8) is now applied to this function v, we obtain

$$\int_0^1 M(x) \, [M(x) - c] \, dx = 0 .$$

Hence, it follows that

$$\int_0^1 [M(x) - c]^2 \, dx = \int_0^1 M(x) [M(x) - c] \, dx - c \int_0^1 [M(x) - c] \, dx = 0$$

and $M(x) = c$ thus holds for almost all $x \in [0, 1]$. In view of how the function M was defined, we see that for almost all $x \in [0, 1]$

$$a_1(x; u(x), u'(x)) = \int_0^x [a_0(t; u(t), u'(t)) - f(t)] \, dt + c \,. \tag{9}$$

This implies that the function $w(x) = a_1(x; u(x), u'(x))$ is even absolutely continuous on $[0, 1]$ since it is an indefinite Lebesgue integral.

17.4. Lemma. *Let $u \in W^{1,2}(0, 1)$ be the weak solution of the Dirichlet problem for the operator A from* (1) *with the coefficients a_0, $a_1 \in$ CAR*(2). Let $a_1 \in C^0([0, 1] \times \mathbb{R}^2)$ and let a constant $c^* > 0$ exist such that for all $x \in [0, 1]$ and for all $t_0, t, s \in \mathbb{R}$ we have*

$$[a_1(x; t_0, t) - a_1(x; t_0, s)] (t - s) \geq c^*(t - s)^2 \, \dagger) \,. \tag{10}$$

Then the weak solution u belongs to $C^1([0, 1])$.

Proof: For $x \in [0, 1]$ and $z \in \mathbb{R}$, put

$$F(x, z) = a_1(x; u(x), z) - \int_0^x [a_0(x; u(t), u'(t)) - f(t)] \, dt - c \,, \tag{11}$$

where c is the constant from (9). The function F is continuous on $[0, 1] \times \mathbb{R}$ and by condition (10) we have, for $x \in [0, 1]$ and $z_1, z_2 \in \mathbb{R}$,

$$[F(x, z_1) - F(x, z_2)] (z_1 - z_2) \geq c^*(z_1 - z_2)^2 \,. \tag{12}$$

Hence it follows, for fixed $x \in [0, 1]$, that the function $f_x(z) = F(x, z)$ is an increasing function of the variable $z \in \mathbb{R}$; it follows further from this that the function f_x takes positive as well as negative values; hence, for every $x \in [0, 1]$, there exists one and only one $z(x) \in \mathbb{R}$ such that

$$F(x, z(x)) = 0 \,. \tag{13}$$

Consequently, a function $z = z(x)$ exists which is defined for $x \in [0, 1]$ and is such that (13) holds for $x \in [0, 1]$. Moreover, (12) implies that the function $z(x)$ is continuous on $[0, 1]$: Indeed, if $\{x_n\}_{n=1}^\infty$ is a sequence of points in $[0, 1]$ such that

---

$\dagger$) In subsequent chapters, we will see that condition (10) is one of the conditions which **guarantee** the existence of the weak solution $u \in W^{1,2}(0, 1)$.

$x_n \to x_0$, then $F(x_n, z(x_n)) = 0$ and from (12) one obtains

$$\left| F(x_n, z(x_n)) - F(x_0, 0) \right| \geqq c^* \left| z(x_n) \right|$$

which implies that the sequence $\{z(x_n)\}_{n=1}^{\infty}$ is bounded. It is then possible to select a convergent subsequence $\{z(x_{n_k})\}_{k=1}^{\infty}$: $z(x_{n_k}) \to z_0$ and, since $F(x_n, z(x_n)) = 0$, we also have $F(x_0, z_0) = 0$ or, in other words, $z_0 = z(x_0)$. We have thus shown that $z(x_{n_k}) \to z(x_0)$ and, arguing by contradiction, we can show that $z(x_n) \to z(x_0)$ or, in other words, that the function z is continuous.

However, relation (9) asserts that

$$F(x, u'(x)) = 0 \quad \text{for almost all} \quad x \in [0, 1] ;$$

comparing this with relation (13) we see that

$$z(x) = u'(x) \quad \text{for almost all} \quad x \in [0, 1] .$$

For arbitrary $x \in [0, 1]$, we then have

$$u(x) = u(0) + \int_0^x u'(t) \, dt = u(0) + \int_0^x z(t) \, dt ;$$

however, this implies that $u'(x) = z(x)$ everywhere in $[0, 1]$ and since z was a continuous function we have

$$u' \in C^0([0, 1]) \quad \text{or, in other words,} \quad u \in C^1([0, 1]) .$$

This concludes the proof of the lemma and it is now possible to state the main assertion of this section.

17.5. Theorem. *Let $u \in W^{1,2}(0, 1)$ be the weak solution of the Dirichlet problem for the operator A of (1) with the right-hand side $f \in C^0([0, 1])$, with the function $\varphi(x) = c_0 + (c_1 - c_0) x$ and with the coefficients*

$$a_0 \in C^0([0, 1] \times \mathbb{R}^2) \cap \textbf{CAR}*(2) ; \quad a_1 \in C^1([0, 1] \times \mathbb{R}^2) \cap \textbf{CAR}*(2) ;$$

let a_1 satisfy condition (10). Then the function u is the classical solution of the Dirichlet problem, i.e., it belongs to $C^2([0, 1])$, satisfies equation (4) and the boundary conditions (5).

Proof: Under the assumptions of the theorem, the function $F(x, z)$ from (11) has continuous partial derivatives of the first order on $[0, 1] \times \mathbb{R}^2$. According to the classical theorem on implicit functions this means, however, that the function $z = z(x)$ which is the solution of (13) has a continuous derivative $z'(x)$. Since, moreover, $z(x) = u'(x)$ by the proof of Lemma 17.4. we obtain

$$u'' \in C^0([0, 1]) \quad \text{or} \quad u \in C^2([0, 1]) .$$

Equality (9) can now be differentiated with respect to x; this yields the relation

$$\frac{d}{dx} a_1(x; u(x), u'(x)) = a_0(x; u(x), u'(x)) - f(x)$$

which means that the function u satisfies equation (4) on $(0, 1)$. Since $u - \varphi \in W_0^{1,2}(0, 1)$ by assumption, we have

$$u(0) = \varphi(0) = c_0, \quad u(1) = \varphi(1) = c_1,$$

so that u satisfies the boundary conditions (5) as well. The proof of the theorem is thus accomplished.

17.6. The regularity of the weak solution of a boundary value problem in an ordinary differential equation was established fairly easily in the preceding paragraphs. However, it was in an entirely atypical situation. One could say that the regularity of the weak solution of a boundary value problem in partial differential equations is a rather "hard nut to crack" and it is a problem which has troubled mathematicians for quite a long time. As far back as the year 1900, David Hilbert formulated a problem of this type in his famous lecture given at the International Mathematical Congress held in Paris; it was the nineteenth of his celebrated twenty-three problems. In the past decade, Czechoslovak mathematics has contributed to the problem's (partial) solution, mainly through the results of J. Nečas.

In general, it is true to say that the answer to the question of whether the smoothness of the data of a boundary value problem implies the smoothness of the weak solution is negative. This conclusion follows from counterexamples originally constructed by the Italian mathematicians De Giorgi (see [15]), M. Miranda and E. Giusti (see [39]), from which we see that even an equation with very smooth coefficients can have a solution which is even singular — e.g., a solution of the type $u(x) = |x|^\lambda$ with $\lambda < 0$ on the domain $\Omega = \{x \in \mathbb{R}^N, |x| < 1\}$. By way of illustration, we at least present one (counter-) example here (see [39]).

17.7. Example. From Paragraph 6.5, we are familiar with the concept of the Euler equation of a functional; it was there an equation of the second order. The concept can be extended in such a manner that we arrive at equations of higher orders. If, e.g., a functional is given of the form

$$I(v) = \int_\Omega F(x; \delta_2 v(x)) \, dx, \qquad (14)$$

where $\Omega \in \mathbb{R}^N$ and $F(x; \xi)$ is a given function of $N + \varkappa(N, 2) = N + \frac{1}{2}(N + 1) \cdot (N + 2)$ variables (i.e., $x \in \Omega, \xi \in \mathbb{R}^{\varkappa(N,2)}$), and if the derivatives

$$\frac{\partial F}{\partial \xi_\alpha} \quad \text{for} \quad |\alpha| \leqq 2$$

exist, then the equation of the form

$$\sum_{|\alpha| \le 2} (-1)^{|\alpha|} \, D^\alpha a_\alpha(x; \delta_2 \, u(x)) = 0 \quad \text{on} \quad \Omega \tag{15}$$

is called the *Euler equation of the functional I*, where

$$a_\alpha(x; \xi) = \frac{\partial F}{\partial \xi_\alpha}(x; \xi), \quad |\alpha| \le 2, \quad \xi \in \mathbb{R}^{\varkappa(N,2)}. \tag{16}$$

Now choose the function $F(x; \xi)$ in such a way that

$$F(x; \delta_2 \, v(x)) = \sum_{i,j=1}^{N} \left(\frac{\partial^2 v}{\partial x_i \, \partial x_j}\right)^2 + \left[\sum_{i,j=1}^{N} \left(\delta_{ij} + \frac{4}{N-2} \frac{\frac{\partial v}{\partial x_i} \frac{\partial v}{\partial x_j}}{(1 + |\text{grad } v|^2)}\right) \frac{\partial^2 v}{\partial x_i \, \partial x_j}\right]^2,$$

where δ_{ij} is the Kronecker symbol, i.e., $\delta_{ij} = 0$ for $i \ne j$, $\delta_{ii} = 1$. It can be shown that if we choose

$$N \ge 3, \quad \Omega = \{x \in \mathbb{R}^N, \ |x| < 1\},$$

then the function

$$u(x) = |x| = (x_1^2 + x_2^2 + \ldots + x_N^2)^{1/2}$$

is the *weak* solution of the Dirichlet problem for equation (15), the coefficients a_α of which belong to **CAR***(2) and are very smooth. The reader can easily check that

$$u \in W^{2,2}(\Omega);$$

it is obvious, however, that the function u cannot be the *classical* solution of the Dirichlet problem for equation (15) (with the boundary condition

$$u = 1 \quad \text{on} \quad \partial\Omega)$$

since we even have

$$u \notin C^1(\bar{\Omega})$$

thanks to the behaviour of the function u in the neighbourhood of the point $x = 0$. [For the classical solution, we even require $u \in C^4(\bar{\Omega})$.]

17.8. The example just given does not imply, naturally, that the answer to the question concerning the smoothness of the weak solution could not be positive in some special cases (indeed, this is also confirmed by Theorem 17.5).

Therefore, let us first formulate more clearly what we actually understand by the problem of the regularity of the weak solution (for the sake of simplicity, very strong assumptions will be imposed on the data of the boundary value problem).

Let $\Omega \subset \mathbb{R}^N$, $\Omega \in \mathscr{C}^\infty$ †), $f \in C^0(\bar{\Omega})$, $a_\alpha \in C^{k+1}(\bar{\Omega} \times \mathbb{R}^\varkappa) \cap \textbf{CAR}(p)$, $|\alpha| \le k$, and let the function

$$u \in W^{k,p}(\Omega)$$

be the weak solution of the Dirichlet problem

$$\sum_{|\alpha| \le k} (-1)^{|\alpha|} D^\alpha a_\alpha(x; \delta_k u(x)) = f(x) \quad \text{on} \quad \Omega,$$

$$u = 0 \quad \text{on} \quad \partial\Omega. \tag{17}$$

Is it then the case that

$$u \in C^{k,\mu}(\bar{\Omega}) \tag{18}$$

holds††).

The solution of the regularity problem depends on the parameters N, p and k. Thus, Example 17.7 shows that the answer to question (18) is negative if

$$N \ge 3, \quad p = 2, \quad k = 2.$$

Under some additional conditions [see the assertion in Paragraph 17.9 (ii) below], it can be shown that the answer to question (18) is positive; this is so, e.g., in the cases presented in the following table:

N	k	p	Author (authors)
2	1	2	C. B. Morrey (1937) [65]
≥ 2	1	2	De Giorgi (1957) [14]
≥ 2	1	≥ 1	O. A. Ladyzhenskaja - N. N. Uralceva (1959) [55], C. B. Morrey (1960) [66]
2	≥ 1	2	J. Nečas (1966) [67]
2	≥ 1	≥ 1	J. Nečas (1969) [69]

Observe that for the case of systems of differential equations of order $2k$ on plane domains $(N = 2)$ the positive answer was obtained by J. Stará (see [88]).

17.9. Remarks. (i) The problem of the regularity of the weak solution was formulated as a question as to whether or not the weak solution u belongs to $C^{k,\mu}(\bar{\Omega})$. Naturally, not even a positive answer to this question guarantees, at this stage,

---

†) By the symbol $\mathscr{C}^\infty$ we denote the set of those domains from the class $\mathscr{C}^{0,1}$ for which the functions $a = a(y_1, \ldots, y_{N-1})$, which locally describe the boundary $\partial\Omega$, even belong to the set $C^\infty(\Delta)$ (see Paragraph 9.2).

††) The function $u \in C^0(\bar{\Omega})$ belongs to $C^{0,\mu}(\bar{\Omega})$ with $0 < \mu \le 1$ if a constant $c > 0$ exists such that

$$|u(x) - u(y)| \le c|x - y|^\mu \quad \text{for all} \quad x, y \in \bar{\Omega}.$$

By the symbol $C^{k,\mu}(\bar{\Omega})$ we denote the set of all functions $u \in C^k(\bar{\Omega})$ whose k-th derivatives $D^\alpha u$ $(|\alpha| = k)$ belong to $C^{0,\mu}(\bar{\Omega})$.

that a regular weak solution should be the classical solution, i.e., that it should belong to $C^{2k}(\overline{\Omega})$. However, for the sake of completeness, let us add that from the fact that the weak solution u belongs to $C^{k,\mu}(\overline{\Omega})$ it is already possible to derive (under the assumptions given in the formulation of the regularity problem) that this weak solution does indeed have continuous derivatives of order $2k$ (see the book [66]).

(ii) As far as the regularity of the weak solutions of *linear* equations is concerned, the reader may learn more from the book [68]; as far as *nonlinear* equations are concerned we refer to the book [86]. By way of illustration, we present one of the assertions on regularity which is to be found in the latter book:

It can be shown that *the weak solution of problem* (17) *(for the case of a plane domain* $\Omega \in \mathscr{C}^\infty$ *where* $N = 2$*) lies in the space* $C^{k,\mu}(\overline{\Omega})$ *with a suitable parameter* $\mu \in (0,1)$ *provided that the right-hand side f belongs to* $C^2(\overline{\Omega})$*, the coefficients* a_α *lie in* **CAR**(p)*, are twice continuously differentiable on* $\overline{\Omega} \times \mathbb{R}^\varkappa$ *and also satisfy the following conditions: Constants* $c_1 > 0$, $c_2 > 0$ *exist such that for all* $x \in \Omega$, $\xi \in \mathbb{R}^\varkappa$, *and* $\eta \in \mathbb{R}^\varkappa$, *the inequalities*

$$\sum_{|\alpha|=|\beta|=k} \frac{\partial a_\alpha(x,\xi)}{\partial \xi_\beta} \eta_\alpha \eta_\beta \geq c_1(1 + |\xi|)^{p-2}|\eta|^2, \; \dagger)$$

$$\sum_{i,j=1}^{2} \sum_{|\alpha|,|\beta|,|\gamma|\leq k} \left\{ \left| \frac{\partial^2 a_\alpha(x;\xi)}{\partial \xi_\beta \, \partial \xi_\gamma} \right| (1 + |\xi|)^2 + \right.$$

$$\left. + \left| \frac{\partial^2 a_\alpha(x;\xi)}{\partial \xi_\beta \, \partial x_i} \right| (1 + |\xi|) + \left| \frac{\partial^2 a_\alpha(x;\xi)}{\partial x_i \, \partial x_j} \right| \right\} \leq c_2 (1 + |\xi|)^{p-1}$$

are satisfied.

$\dagger$) In Chapter IV, we will see that this inequality is one of the conditions which guarantee the existence of the weak solution of problem (17).

CHAPTER IV

THE VARIATIONAL METHOD

SECTION 18. FIRST DERIVATIVE OF A FUNCTIONAL

18.1. Introductory notes. In the preceding paragraphs, we introduced the concept of the weak solution of a boundary value problem, presented a number of examples, and attempted to clarify the relation between the classical and the weak solutions. The problem of the existence of the classical solution was mentioned only very briefly (the classical solution was obtained by the linearization method — see Paragraph 10.7). In the present chapter, the question of whether the weak solution of a boundary value problem exists will be treated.

The method which will be described below is very natural and it can be motivated simply by the example of the equation

$$h(x) = 0, \tag{1}$$

where $h(x)$ is a continuous real function on $\mathbb{R}$. The solution of this equation can be reduced to the problem of finding the local extremum (e.g., the minimum) of the function H which is a primitive of h, i.e., for which

$$H'(x) = h(x)$$

is valid for every $x \in \mathbb{R}$. Indeed, if a point $x_0 \in R$ exists at which the function $H(x)$ assumes its local minimum, then the derivative $H'(x)$ necessarily vanishes by familiar theorems of classical analysis and x_0 is thus the solution of equation (1).

This is just the idea which we will wish to exploit to ensure the existence of the solution of the operator equation

$$\mathbb{A}u = \mathbf{f}, \tag{2}$$

where $\mathbb{A}$ is an operator defined on the Banach space X with values in the dual space X^* and $\mathbf{f}$ is a functional from X^*. In particular, we shall be interested in the case when $\mathbb{A}$ is an operator defined by means of the formal differential operator A (see Paragraphs 14.1, 14.2) and $X = V$ (see the definition of the weak solution of a boundary value problem in Paragraph 15.7). The expression

$$\mathbb{A}u - \mathbf{f}$$

will take on the role of the function h from equation (1); however, when constructing the "primitive" H the following problem is immediately encountered: What really is the "derivative" in this case?

Equation (2) is solved in the space X [if, e.g., we have the Dirichlet problem, then $X = W_0^{k,p}(\Omega)$]. Therefore, we first develop a theory of differentiation for functionals†) defined on normed linear spaces. The problem is then that of associating, with the operator $\mathbb{A}$, a functional F defined on X in such a way that its "derivative" (which will be introduced later on) is just the expression $\mathbb{A}u - \mathbf{f}$. We will try to prove that the functional F has a minimum on the space X. If the analogue of the corresponding theorem from calculus is still valid (i.e., if it holds that the derivative of the functional F vanishes at the point of the minimum), this will also serve as the proof of the existence of the weak solution of the boundary value problem for the formal differential equation $Au = \mathbf{f}$.

18.2. A historical-terminological remark. Considerations of the above type were performed (although without the appropriate mathematical justification, of course) as far back as the 18th century, especially in physics. Instead of "derivative" the term used was "variation" (which concept is sometimes used to this day). This is the reason why the method discussed in this chapter is called *variational*. The precise mathematical apparatus based on the concept of the derivative of a functional was only developed by the French mathematician R. Gâteaux in the early years of this century.

We present two important examples of functionals.

18.3. Example. Let $\Omega \subset \mathbb{R}^N$ be a bounded domain, and let the function $h(x; \xi)$ be defined for (almost) all $x \in \Omega$ and all $\xi \in \mathbb{R}$. Let $p \geq 1$, and let $h \in \mathbf{CAR}$ (see Definition 12.2). Let us assume that there exists a function $g \in L_1(\Omega)$ and a number $c \geq 0$ such that for almost all $x \in \Omega$ and for all $\xi \in \mathbb{R}$

$$|h(x; \xi)| \leq g(x) + c|\xi|^p \quad \text{††}).$$

Then

$$\Phi(u) = \int_\Omega h(x; u(x)) \, dx \tag{3}$$

---

†) Let X be a normed linear space and let F be a mapping defined on a nonempty subset M of the space X with values in $\mathbb{R}$. Such a mapping is called a *functional*. Examples of functionals are real-valued functions (where $X = \mathbb{R}$ or $X = \mathbb{R}^N$) and continuous linear functionals — see part (i). footnote †) on p. 95.

††) Observe that if, in addition, $g \in L_{(p+1)/p}(\Omega)$ holds, then we have $h \in \mathbf{CAR}(p+1)$ (see Paragraph 12.13).

is a functional defined on the space $L_p(\Omega)$. The results obtained in Paragraph 12.10 imply immediately that the functional Φ defined by formula (3) is continuous on the space $L_p(\Omega)$ since the Němyckiĭ operator

$$(\mathscr{H}u)(x) = h(x; u(x))$$

is a continuous mapping from the space $L_p(\Omega)$ into the space $L_1(\Omega)$ under the conditions given above and since the mapping

$$T(z) = \int_\Omega z(t)\, dt$$

is a continuous linear functional on the space $L_1(\Omega)$ (the functional Φ is the composition of two continuous operators and is thus continuous).

18.4. Example. Let $\Omega \subset \mathbb{R}^N$, $\Omega \in \mathscr{C}^{0,1}$, $k \in \mathbb{N}$, $p > 1$, $\varphi \in W^{k,p}(\Omega)$. Let the symbols V, Q, $\mathbf{g} \in V^*$, $\mathbf{f} \in Q^*$ have the same meaning as in the definition of the weak solution of a boundary value problem — see Paragraph 15.7. Let the function $b(x; \xi)$ be defined for almost all $x \in \Omega$ and all $\xi \in \mathbb{R}^\varkappa$. Assume that $b \in \mathbf{CAR}^*(p + 1)$ [in particular, $b \in \mathbf{CAR}(p + 1)$ may then hold].†)

Then

$$F(u) = \int_\Omega b(x; \delta_k u(x) + \delta_k \varphi(x))\, dx - <\mathbf{f}, u>_Q - <\mathbf{g}, u>_V \tag{4}$$

is a functional on the space V. ††)

In the case when $b \in \mathbf{CAR}(p + 1)$, the above assertion follows from Theorem 12.10 in a manner analogous to Example 18.3; in the case when $b \in \mathbf{CAR}^*(p + 1)$, the assertion of the imbedding theorem (see Paragraph 16.6) must also be used.

18.5. Definition. Let $F(u)$ be a functional defined on an open non-empty subset M of the linear normed space X. Let $u \in M$. For arbitrary $v \in X$,

$$f_v(t) = F(u + tv)$$

is then a real function of the real variable t defined on the open interval $(-\varepsilon, \varepsilon)$, provided $\varepsilon > 0$ is a sufficiently small number.

Assume that the function $f_v(t)$ has a derivative at the point 0, i.e., that the finite limit

$$f_v'(0) = \lim_{t \to 0} \frac{f_v(t) - f_v(0)}{t} = \lim_{t \to 0} \frac{F(u + tv) - F(u)}{t} \tag{5}$$

---

†) For the definition of the class $\mathbf{CAR}^*(p + 1)$, see Paragraph 16.15 (i); for the definition of the class $\mathbf{CAR}(p + 1)$, see Paragraph 12.13.

††) Recall that V is a closed subspace of the space $W^{k,p}(\Omega)$; V is thus a Banach space with the norm $\|u\|_{k,p}$.

exists. Put

$$dF(u; v) = f_v'(0).$$

The number $dF(u, v)$ is then called the *derivative of the functional F at the point $u \in M$ in the direction $v \in X$*.

We say, further, that the functional F has a *differential at the point $u \in M$* if $dF(u, v)$ exists for any element $v \in X$. By the differential of the functional F at the point $u \in M$ we understand the functional $dF(u)$ defined on the space X by the relation

$$dF(u)(v) = dF(u; v), \quad v \in X.$$

18.6. We now investigate under what conditions on the function $b(x; \xi)$ the functional F defined in Example 18.4 by relation (4) has a differential. Let $u \in V$ and $v \in V$. By Definition 18.5, the question then is whether or not the derivative of the function

$$f_v(t) = F(u + tv)$$

at the point $t = 0$ exists. To start with, we proceed entirely formally:

$$\frac{d}{dt} F(u + tv)\Big|_{t=0} = \frac{d}{dt}\left[\int_\Omega b(x; \delta_k u(x) + \delta_k \varphi(x) + t\delta_k v(x))\, dx\right]\Bigg|_{t=0} -$$

$$- \frac{d}{dt}\left(<\mathbf{f}, u + tv>_Q + <\mathbf{g}, u + tv>_V\right)\Big|_{t=0} =$$

$$= \int_\Omega \frac{\partial}{\partial t} b(x; \delta_k u(x) + \delta_k \varphi(x) + t\delta_k v(x))\big|_{t=0}\, dx - <\mathbf{f}, v>_Q - <\mathbf{g}, v>_V =$$

$$= \int_\Omega \sum_{|\alpha| \leq k} \frac{\partial b}{\partial \xi_\alpha}(x; \delta_k u(x) + \delta_k \varphi(x))\, D^\alpha v(x)\, dx - <\mathbf{f}, v>_Q - <\mathbf{g}, v>_V. \quad (6)$$

Clearly, we will then have to assume that the partial derivatives

$$\frac{\partial b(x; \xi)}{\partial \xi_\alpha}$$

exist for an arbitrary multi-index $\alpha = (\alpha_1, \ldots, \alpha_N)$, $|\alpha| \leq k$, for almost all $x \in \Omega$ and for all $\xi \in \mathbb{R}^\varkappa$. This justifies the last equality in (6). It thus remains to consider the validity of the relation

$$\frac{d}{dt}\left[\int_\Omega b(x; \delta_k u(x) + \delta_k \varphi(x) + t\delta_k v(x))\, dx\right]\Bigg|_{t=0} =$$

$$= \int_\Omega \frac{\partial}{\partial t} b(x; \delta_k u(x) + \delta_k \varphi(x) + t\delta_k v(x))\big|_{t=0}\, dx.$$

We are dealing with reversing the order of the operations of differentiation and integration. This interchange is possible if we assume, e.g., that

$$\frac{\partial b}{\partial \xi_\alpha} \in \mathbf{CAR}^*(p)$$

for every multi-index α, $|\alpha| \le k$ [see the considerations of Paragraph 16.13; namely, we have $u, v \in V \subset W^{k,p}(\Omega)$]. In fact, this almost proves the following theorem.

18.7. Theorem. *Let* $\Omega \subset \mathbb{R}^N$, $\Omega \in \mathscr{C}^{0,1}$. *Let the function* $b(x; \xi)$ *be defined for almost all* $x \in \Omega$ *and all* $\xi \in \mathbb{R}^\varkappa$, *and let it be such that the partial derivatives*

$$\frac{\partial b(x; \xi)}{\partial \xi_\alpha}$$

exist for almost all $x \in \Omega$, *all* $\xi \in \mathbb{R}^\varkappa$, *and all multi-indexes* α, $|\alpha| \le k$. *Assume that*

$$p > 1, \tag{7}$$

$$b \in \mathbf{CAR}^*(p+1), \quad \frac{\partial b}{\partial \xi_\alpha} \in \mathbf{CAR}^*(p) \tag{8}$$

(again for every multi-index α, $|\alpha| \le k$*).*

Then the functional F defined by formula (4) *has the derivative* $\mathrm{d}F(u, v)$ *at every point* $u \in V$ *in an arbitrary direction* $v \in V$, *and we have*

$$\mathrm{d}F(u; v) = \sum_{|\alpha| \le k} \int_\Omega \frac{\partial b}{\partial \xi_\alpha} (x; \delta_k u(x) + \delta_k \varphi(x)) \, D^\alpha v(x) \, \mathrm{d}x - \langle \mathbf{f}, v \rangle_Q - \langle \mathbf{g}, v \rangle_V. \tag{9}$$

Moreover, the differential $\mathrm{d}F(u)$ *is a continuous linear functional on V for arbitrary* $u \in V$, *i.e.,* $\mathrm{d}F(u) \in V^*$.

Proof. It merely remains to prove the part concerning the properties of the differential $\mathrm{d}F(u)$. First of all, it is immediately seen that the mapping $\mathrm{d}F(u)$ is linear. To establish its continuity it suffices to check that

$$\sup_{\|v\|_{k,p}=1} |\mathrm{d}F(u)(v)| < \infty \ \dagger). \tag{10}$$

For the sake of simplicity, let us assume that

$$\frac{\partial b}{\partial \xi_\alpha} \in \mathbf{CAR}(p).$$

Hence and from Paragraph 12.12 [particularly from inequality (12.13), where the function a_α is replaced by the function $\partial b / \partial \xi_\alpha$], it follows that a constant $c_\alpha \ge 0$

---

†) See the footnote on p. 95.

exists such that for all $u, v \in W^{k,p}(\Omega)$,

$$\int_\Omega \left| \frac{\partial b}{\partial \xi_\alpha} (x; \delta_k u(x) + \delta_k \varphi(x)) D^\alpha v(x) \right| dx \leq c_\alpha \left(1 + \sum_{|\gamma| \leq k} \left\| D^\gamma u + D^\gamma \varphi \right\|_p^{p-1} \right) \left\| D^\alpha v \right\|_p \leq$$

$$\leq c_\alpha \left(1 + \sum_{|\gamma| \leq k} \left\| D^\gamma u + D^\gamma \varphi \right\|_p^{p-1} \right) \left\| v \right\|_{k,p} ,$$

Therefore, there is a constant $c > 0$ such that for all $u, v \in V$

$$\left| dF(u)(v) \right| \leq \sum_{|\alpha| \leq k} \int_\Omega \left| \frac{\partial b}{\partial \xi_\alpha} (x; \delta_k u(x) + \delta_k \varphi(x)) \right| \left| D^\alpha v(x) \right| dx +$$

$$+ \left\| \mathbf{f} \right\|_{Q*} \left\| v \right\|_{k,p} + \left\| \mathbf{g} \right\|_{V*} \left\| v \right\|_{k,p} \leq c \left\{ 1 + \sum_{|\gamma| \leq k} \left\| D^\gamma u + D^\gamma \varphi \right\|_p^{p-1} \right\} \left\| v \right\|_{k,p} .$$

The last inequalities now establish relation (10).

For the case when

$$\frac{\partial b}{\partial \xi_\alpha} \in \mathbf{CAR}^*(p)$$

the reader may verify relation (10) as an exercise making use of the considerations given in Paragraph 16.12 (ii).

18.8. Remarks on Definition 18.5. (i) If the derivative $dF(u; v)$ exists and if $\tau \neq 0$, it is immediately seen from (5) that the derivative $dF(u; \tau v)$ then exists and that

$$dF(u; \tau v) = \tau \, dF(u; v) .$$

Thus, the differential $dF(u)$ is homogeneous. However, it need not be linear and continuous (it is possible to construct simple examples even for the case $X = \mathbb{R}^2$). But if the mapping

$$dF(u)(v) = dF(u; v)$$

is continuous and linear on X (this was the case, e.g., in Theorem 18.7), then the functional $dF(u)$ is called the *derivative of the functional F at the point u* and instead of the symbol $dF(u)$ the notation $F'(u)$ is used in line with classical notation, i.e.,

$$\langle F'(u), v \rangle = dF(u; v) .$$

(ii) The functional F investigated in Theorem 18.7 has a derivative $F'(u)$ at any arbitrary point $u \in V$.

SECTION 19. POTENTIALS OF BOUNDARY VALUE PROBLEMS

19.1. Let $p > 1$ and let

$$a_\alpha \in \mathbf{CAR}^*(p)$$

($|\alpha| \leq k$). Let V, Q, $\mathbf{f}$, $\mathbf{g}$, φ have the same meaning as in the definition of the weak solution of the boundary value problem (A, V, Q) for the formal differential operator

$$(Au)(x) = \sum_{|\alpha| \leq k} (-1)^{|\alpha|} D^\alpha a_\alpha(x; \delta_k u(x))$$

(see Paragraph 15.7). Recall that the function $\hat{u} \in W^{k,p}(\Omega)$ is called a weak solution of the boundary value problem (A, V, Q) if

(a) $u = \hat{u} - \varphi \in V$;
(b) for all $v \in V$, the identity

$$(<\mathbb{A}\hat{u}, v> =) \sum_{|\alpha| \leq k} \int_\Omega a_\alpha(x; \delta_k \hat{u}(x)) D^\alpha v(x) \, dx = <\mathbf{f}, v>_Q + <\mathbf{g}, v>_V \quad (1)$$

is satisfied.

We now modify this definition to some extent: The *weak solution of the boundary value problem* (A, V, Q) is a function $u \in V$ such that for all $v \in V$

$$\sum_{|\alpha| \leq k} \int_\Omega a_\alpha(x; \delta_k u(x) + \delta_k \varphi(x)) D^\alpha v(x) \, dx - <\mathbf{f}, v>_Q - <\mathbf{g}, v>_V = 0. \quad (2)$$

Identity (1) is thus replaced by identity (2), and instead of the function $\hat{u} \in W^{k,p}(\Omega)$ we deal with the function $u = \hat{u} - \varphi \in V$; condition (a) thus disappears. This "displacement" of the function $\hat{u}$ by the boundary condition φ is desirable mainly because we shall deal in the sequel only with the space V.†)

Now, let F be the functional defined on the space V by the formula

$$F(u) = \int_\Omega b(x; \delta_k u(x) + \delta_k \varphi(x)) \, dx - <\mathbf{f}, u>_Q - <\mathbf{g}, u>_V \quad (3)$$

(for more details see Paragraph 18.4) and compare the formula for its derivative

$$dF(u; v) = \sum_{|\alpha| \leq k} \int_\Omega \frac{\partial}{\partial \xi_\alpha} b(x; \delta_k u(x) + \delta_k \varphi(x)) D^\alpha v(x) \, dx - <\mathbf{f}, v>_Q - <\mathbf{g}, v>_V \quad (4)$$

(for more details see Paragraph 18.7) with the left-hand side of (2). If the function $b(x; \xi)$ is then chosen so that

$$\frac{\partial b(x; \xi)}{\partial \xi_\alpha} = a_\alpha(x; \xi) \quad (5)$$

---

†) The reader will certainly have realized that the weak solution of the boundary value problem (A, V, Q) (in the sense of Definition 15.7) is not the function $u \in V$ but the function $u = \hat{u} + \varphi$; the difference is purely formal.

be true, relation

$$dF(u; v) = <\mathbb{A}(u + \varphi), v> - <\mathbf{f}, v>_Q - <\mathbf{g}, v>_V \tag{6}$$

holds for all $u, v \in V$.

The problem is then the following: We know the coefficients $a_\alpha(x; \xi)$ of the formal differential operator A and our problem is to find the function $b(x; \xi)$ (i.e., the functional F) so that (5) holds. In fact, this is the problem mentioned in Paragraph 18.1, and we will solve it now.

19.2. Lemma. *Let $a_\alpha(x; \xi)$ ($|\alpha| \leq k$) be functions defined for almost all $x \in \Omega$ and all $\xi \in \mathbb{R}^\varkappa$. Let*

$$a_\alpha \in \mathbf{CAR}^*(p), \quad p > 1,$$

and let us assume that for almost all $x \in \Omega$, all multi-indexes β, $|\beta| \leq k$, and all $\xi \in \mathbb{R}^\varkappa$, the partial derivatives

$$\frac{\partial a_\alpha(x; \xi)}{\partial \xi_\beta} = a_{\alpha\beta}(x; \xi)$$

exist and

$$a_{\alpha\beta}(x; \xi) = a_{\beta\alpha}(x; \xi) \tag{7}$$

holds. Let

$$\xi_\alpha a_{\alpha\beta}(x; \xi) \in \mathbf{CAR}^*(p) . \; \dagger) \tag{8}$$

Define the function b by

$$b(x; \xi) = \int_0^1 \left[\sum_{|\alpha| \leq k} \xi_\alpha a_\alpha(x; t\xi) \right] dt . \tag{9}$$

Then

(a) $b \in \mathbf{CAR}^*(p + 1)$;

(b) *for an arbitrary multi-index β, $|\beta| \leq k$, for almost all $x \in \Omega$, and for all $\xi \in \mathbb{R}^\varkappa$, we have*

$$\frac{\partial b(x; \xi)}{\partial \xi_\beta} = a_\beta(x; \xi) .$$

The proof follows from the theorems on the integration of functions depending on parameters. The assertion $b \in \mathbf{CAR}$ is obtained, e.g., from the theorem on the continuous dependence of the integral on a parameter.

---

†) It is possible to replace this condition by the condition

$$a_{\alpha\beta} \in C^0(\bar{\Omega} \times \mathbb{R}^\varkappa) .$$

We prove assertion (b). The theorem on the derivative of an integral with respect to the parameters implies

$$\frac{\partial b(x;\xi)}{\partial \xi_\beta} = \int_0^1 a_\beta(x; t\xi) \, dt + \int_0^1 t \sum_{|\alpha| \le k} \xi_\alpha a_{\alpha\beta}(x; t\xi) \, dt =$$

$$= \int_0^1 a_\beta(x; t\xi) \, dt + \int_0^1 t \frac{d}{dt} (a_\beta(x; t\xi)) \, dt =$$

$$= \int_0^1 a_\beta(x; t\xi) \, dt + a_\beta(x; \xi) - \int_0^1 a_\beta(x; t\xi) \, dt = a_\beta(x; \xi) . \tag{10}$$

Lemma 19.2, Paragraph 19.1, and Theorem 18.7 immediately yield the main result of this paragraph.

19.3. Theorem. *Let the formal differential operator*

$$(Au)(x) = \sum_{|\alpha| \le k} (-1)^{|\alpha|} D^\alpha a_\alpha(x; \delta_k u(x))$$

be given, the coefficients of which satisfy the conditions of **Lemma 19.2.** *Let* $\varphi \in W^{k,p}(\Omega)$, V, Q, **f**, **g** *all have the same meaning as in the definition of the weak solution of the boundary value problem* (A, V, Q) — *see Paragraph 15.7. Let* $\mathbb{A}$ *be an operator defined on the space* $W^{k,p}(\Omega)$ *with values in the dual space* $(W^{k,p}(\Omega))^*$ *which is assigned to the formal differential operator* A *by means of the formula*

$$<\mathbb{A}u, v> = \sum_{|\alpha| \le k} \int_\Omega a_\alpha(x; \delta_k u(x)) \, D^\alpha v(x) \, dx$$

for every $u, v \in W^{k,p}(\Omega)$ — *see Paragraph 16.14.*

We now construct the function $b(x; \xi)$ *according to formula* (9), *i.e., put*

$$b(x; \xi) = \int_0^1 \Big[\sum_{|\alpha| \le k} \xi_\alpha \, a_\alpha(x; t\xi) \Big] \, dt \tag{9}$$

and use formula (3) *to define the functional* F *on the space* V, *i.e.,*

$$F(u) = \int_\Omega b(x; \delta_k u(x) + \delta_k \varphi(x)) \, dx - <f, u>_Q - <g, u>_V . \tag{3}$$

For all $u, v \in V$, *we then have*

$$<F'(u), v> = dF(u; v) = <\mathbb{A}(u + \varphi), v> - <f, v>_Q - <g, v>_V . \tag{11}$$

19.4. Remarks. (i) The functional F defined in Theorem 19.3 is called the *potential of the boundary value problem* (A, V, Q). In general: An operator T which maps the Banach space X into the dual space X^* is called a *potential operator* if there exists a functional F on the space X such that

$$F'(u) = T(u) \tag{12}$$

for every $u \in X$ [i.e., $<F'(u), v> = <T(u), v>$ for all $u, v \in X$]. In a similar manner, it is possible to define potential operators on an open subset M of the Banach space X. The functional F with property (12) is called the *potential of the operator* T. (The terminology derives from physical considerations.)

(ii) The condition of the existence of the derivatives $\partial a_\alpha / \partial \xi_\beta$ and their symmetry (7) [which were applied in the computation presented in (10)] are "drawbacks" of the variational method when $\xi \in \mathbb{R}^\varkappa$ with $\varkappa > 1$; we shall try to remove these conditions in Chapter V.

If we assume, however, that the derivatives of the functions $a_\alpha(x; \xi)$ exist, i.e., that $b(x; \xi)$ has partial derivatives of the second order with respect to the variables ξ_β, $|\beta| \leq k$, then condition (7) means that

$$\frac{\partial^2 b(x; \xi)}{\partial \xi_\alpha \, \partial \xi_\beta} = \frac{\partial^2 b(x; \xi)}{\partial \xi_\beta \, \partial \xi_\alpha}$$

(i.e., the interchangeability of derivatives of the second order is assumed). Moreover, the majority of "reasonable" functions possess this property.

19.5. Examples. (i) Let $N = 1$, $\Omega = (0, 1)$, and let g be a continuous function on $\mathbb{R}$ with the primitive G. Define the formal differential operator A by

$$(Au)(x) = -u''(x) + g(u(x)).$$

Then the potential of the operator $\mathbb{A}$ determined by the formal differential operator A is the functional F defined on the space $W^{1,2}(0, 1)$ by the formula

$$F(u) = \frac{1}{2} \int_0^1 [u'(x)]^2 \, dx + \int_0^1 G(u(x)) \, dx, \quad u \in W^{1,2}(0, 1).$$

Certainly, we have

$$\lim_{t \to 0} \frac{F(u + tv) - F(u)}{t} = \frac{1}{2} \int_0^1 \left[\lim_{t \to 0} \frac{[u'(x) + t \, v'(x)]^2 - [u'(x)]^2}{t} \right] dx +$$

$$+ \int_0^1 \left[\lim_{t \to 0} \frac{G(u(x) + t \, v(x)) - G(u(x))}{t} \right] dx = \int_0^1 u'(x) \, v'(x) \, dx + \int_0^1 g(u(x)) \, v(x) \, dx$$

for all $u, v \in W^{1,2}(0, 1)$.

Unlike Theorem 19.3, it is in this case not necessary to assume the existence of the derivatives of the coefficients a_α, i.e., the existence of the derivative g'. The reason for this is that the function $g = g(\xi)$ is a function of one real variable [see Remark 19.4 (ii)].

(ii) Let $N > 1$. Let g be a continuous function. Let τ be an arbitrary positive number for $N = 2$, and put

$$\tau = \frac{N + 2}{N - 2} \quad \text{for} \quad N > 2.$$

We assume that constants $c > 0$, $d > 0$ exist such that

$$|g(\xi)| \leq c + d|\xi|^{\tau}$$

for all $\xi \in \mathbb{R}$ [see Paragraph 16.16 (iii)].

Then the functional

$$F(u) = \frac{1}{2} \sum_{i=1}^{N} \int_{\Omega} \left(\frac{\partial u(x)}{\partial x_i} \right)^2 dx + \int_{\Omega} G(u(x)) \, dx \,,$$

where G is again a primitive of the function g, is the potential of the operator $\mathbb{A}$ which is determined by the formal differential operator

$$(Au)(x) = -\Delta u(x) + g(u(x)) \,.$$

(iii) Let $p > 1$. The functional

$$F(u) = \frac{1}{p} \sum_{i=1}^{N} \int_{\Omega} \left| \frac{\partial u(x)}{\partial x_i} \right|^p dx \,, \quad u \in W^{1,p}(\Omega) \,,$$

is the potential of the operator $\mathbb{A}$ which is determined by the formal differential operator

$$Au = -\sum_{i=1}^{N} \frac{\partial}{\partial x_i} \left(\left| \frac{\partial u}{\partial x_i} \right|^{p-2} \frac{\partial u}{\partial x_i} \right) \,.$$

(iv) The examples given above served to check whether the functional F is the potential of the operator $\mathbb{A}$. For the formal differential operators A of Examples (i) to (iii), one can now formulate the boundary value problem (A, V, Q) and by means of these examples determine the potentials of the given boundary value problem (A, V, Q).

SECTION 20. THE EULER NECESSARY CONDITION

20.1. Recall Theorem 19.3. Let $u_0 \in V$. Relation (19.11) implies that u_0 satisfies identity (19.2) [i.e., that $u_0 + \varphi$ is a weak solution of the boundary value problem (A, V, Q) — see Paragraph 19.1] if and only if

$$F'(u_0) \quad \text{is the zero element of the space} \quad V^* \,,$$

i.e., if

$$dF(u_0; v) = 0 \quad \text{for every} \quad v \in V.$$

It is well known that a real differentiable function has a vanishing derivative, e.g., at the points at which it attains its local extrema. We shall prove that such an assertion holds for functionals as well.

20.2. Definition. Let X be a normed linear space and let F be a functional defined on X. We say that the functional F has a *local minimum* (*maximum*) at the point $u_0 \in X$ if there is a neighbourhood $U = \{u \in X; \|u - u_0\|_X < r\}$ of the point u_0 $(r > 0)$ such that for arbitrary $u \in U - \{u_0\}$ we have

$$F(u) \geq F(u_0) \quad [F(u) \leq F(u_0)].$$

If these inequalities are strict, we speak of a *strict local minimum* (*maximum*). If the functional F has a local minimum or a local maximum at the point u_0, we say that it has a *local extremum* at the point u_0.

The fundamental assertion concerning local extrema is the theorem which now follows, the so-called Euler necessary condition for local extrema.

20.3. Theorem. *Let the functional F, defined on the linear normed space X, have a local extremum at the point $u_0 \in X$. If $dF(u_0; v)$ exists for some $v \in X$, then*

$$dF(u_0; v) = 0.$$

Proof. For $f_v(t) = F(u_0 + tv)$, we have

$$f_v'(0) = dF(u_0; v).$$

If $f_v'(0) \neq 0$, then the function $f_v(t)$ does not have a local extremum at the point 0, and so the functional F cannot have a local extremum at the point u_0.

20.4. Consider the real function $F(x) = x^3$. Although this function has a vanishing derivative at the point 0, it does not have a local extremum there. Theorem 20.3 cannot therefore have a converse. However, as this theorem shows, the investigation of the set of points at which the derivative is zero is very important. Let us therefore make the following terminological observation: The point $u_0 \in X$ is called a *critical point of the functional F* defined on X if $dF(u_0, v)$ exists for arbitrary $v \in X$ and

$$dF_0(u; v) = 0$$

holds.

Under the condition of the existence of the differential of the functional F on the entire space X, the assertion of Theorem 20.3 can also be stated as follows:

Every local extremum point of the functional F is also a critical point.

Summarizing the results of Section 19, and using Theorem 20.3, we immediately obtain the following important assertion which indicates the connection between the weak solution of a boundary value problem and the minimum of a potential:

20.5. Theorem. *Let all the assumptions of* Theorem 19.3 *be satisfied, and let the functional F defined by relation* (19.3) *have a local minimum on the space V at the point $u_0 \in V$. Then the function $u_0 \in V$ satisfies identity* (19.2), *i.e., the function $u_0 + \varphi$ is a weak solution of the boundary value problem* (A, V, Q).

20.6. In the present investigation, we were led to look for the connections between the weak solution of a boundary value problem and the minimum of a functional by analogy with certain results from the theory of functions of one real variable. A rather different analogue arising from the search for the solution of a linear operator equation is presented below: We shall state the so-called theorem on the minimum of a quadratic functional (this theorem and its consequences for the solution of the Dirichlet problem for linear differential equations are discussed at length in [80], especiálly in Chap. 9, pp. 114 and further). This theorem can take, e.g., the following form:

20.7. Theorem. *Let H be a Hilbert space with the inner product $<u, v>$ †), $f \in H$. Let T be a linear mapping from H into H satisfying the following conditions:*

$$<Tu, v> = <u, Tv> \text{ for every two elements } u, v \in H,$$
$$<Tu, u> \geq 0 \text{ for every } u \in H,$$
$$<Tu, u> = 0 \Rightarrow u = \Theta. \text{ ††)}$$

---

†) Let H be a real linear space. To an arbitrary pair $u, v \in H$, let a real number $<u, v>$ be assigned so that the following conditions hold:

1. For every $u \in H$, we have $<u, v> \geq 0$ with $<u, u> = 0$ if and only if $u = \Theta$.
2. For all elements $u, v, w \in H$, we have $<u + v, w> = <u, w> + <v, w>$.
3. For all elements $u, v \in H$, we have $<u, v> = <v, u>$.
4. For $u, v \in H$ and $\lambda \in \mathbb{R}$, we have $<\lambda u, v> = \lambda<u, v>$.

The number $<u, v>$ is called the *inner product* (of the elements u and v). It can easily be verified that $\|u\|_H = <u, u>^{1/2}$ is a norm on H. If H with the norm defined in this way is a complete (i.e., a Banach) space, then H is called a *Hilbert space*.

At first sight, it would appear that we have introduced an inconsistency in using the notation $<u, v>$: This is the symbol reserved for the value of the functional $u \in H^*$ at the point $v \in H$. According to the Riesz Theorem — see, e.g., [51] — the value of a continuous linear functional f on H at the point v is precisely the inner product of a certain element u_f and the element v, i.e., $<f, v> = <u_f, v>$ for all $v \in H$. For this reason, the use of the symbol $<u, v>$ for the inner product is logical.

††) Such a mapping T is called *positive and symmetric*.

Let the equation Tu = f have a solution $u_0 \in H$, i.e., let

$$Tu_0 = f.$$

Then the so-called quadratic functional

$$F(u) = \tfrac{1}{2} <Tu, u> - <f, u> \tag{1}$$

assumes its minimal value in H precisely at the point u_0, i.e., for all $u \in H$ we have $F(u) \geq F(u_0)$ with the equality $F(u) = F(u_0)$ being true only for $u = u_0$.

Conversely, let the functional F assume its minimal value at the point u_0 among all the elements $u \in H$. Then u_0 is the solution of the equation $Tu = f$.

20.8. In the preceding theorem, what is the relation between the functional F [see (1)] and the operator T? Let us compute the derivative of the functional F:

$$dF(u; v) = \tfrac{1}{2} \lim_{t \to 0} \frac{<T(u + tv), u + tv> - <Tu, u>}{t} -$$

$$- \lim_{t \to 0} \frac{<f, u + tv> - <f, u>}{t} = <Tu - f, v>,$$

i.e., $F'(u) = Tu - f$. Thus, F is the potential of the operator $Tu - f$.

Hence, and from Theorem 20.3, the second part of the assertion in Theorem 20.7 follows immediately: *If the functional F assumes its minimum on H at the point u_0, which is clearly a local extremum, then $F'(u_0) = 0$, i.e., $Tu_0 = f$.*

We will return to the first part of Theorem 20.7 again in Paragraph 23.9.

SECTION 21. SECOND DERIVATIVE OF A FUNCTIONAL

21.1. In the investigation of local extrema of a real function $f(x)$, the properties of the second derivative $f''(x)$ play a not insignificant role. In fact, the following is true: *Let $f'(x_0) = 0$, and let $f''(x_0) > 0$. Then the function $f(x)$ has a local minimum at the point x_0.* Also, almost conversely, we have: *Let $f(x)$ have a local minimum at x_0, and let $f''(x_0)$ exist. Then $f''(x_0) \geq 0$.* (Obviously, analogous assertions are true for local maxima.)

We thus try to derive similar assertions for a functional $F(u)$ defined on a normed linear space X. We know already (see Paragraph 18.5) what we mean by the first (directional) derivative. It is therefore reasonable to define the "second derivative" as the "first derivative of the first derivative".

21.2. Definition. Let X be a normed linear space and M a non-empty open subset of X. Let $F(u)$ be a functional defined on M, and let $u_0 \in M$, $v_1 \in X$, $v_2 \in X$. Assume that $dF(u; v_1)$ (i.e., the derivative in the direction v_1) exists for all $u \in M$. If the (finite) limit

$$\lim_{t \to 0} \frac{dF(u_0 + tv_2; v_1) - dF(u_0; v_1)}{t}$$

exists, we denote its value by $d^2F(u_0; v_1, v_2)$ and call it the *second derivative of the functional $F(u)$ at the point $u_0 \in M$* [*in the direction (v_1, v_2)*].

21.3. Example. Before going any further, we attempt the computation of the second derivative for the functional $F(u)$ of Example 18.4. By Theorem 18.7,

$$dF(u; v_1) = \sum_{|\alpha| \leqq k} \int_\Omega \frac{\partial b}{\partial \xi_\alpha} (x; \delta_k u(x) + \delta_k \varphi(x)) D^\alpha v_1(x) \, dx - \langle \mathbf{f}, v_1 \rangle_\mathcal{Q} - \langle \mathbf{g}, v_1 \rangle_V$$

holds for all $u, v_1 \in V$. When computing the second derivative, we proceed purely formally to begin with, just as in Paragraph 18.6:

$$d^2F(u_0; v_1, v_2) = \frac{d}{dt} [dF(u_0 + tv_2; v_1)]\big|_{t=0} =$$

$$= \frac{d}{dt} \left[\sum_{|\alpha| \leqq k} \int_\Omega \frac{\partial b}{\partial \xi_\alpha} (x; \delta_k u_0(x) + t\delta_k v_2(x) + \delta_k \varphi(x)) D^\alpha v_1(x) \, dx - \right.$$

$$\left. - \langle \mathbf{f}, v_1 \rangle_\mathcal{Q} - \langle \mathbf{g}, v_1 \rangle_V \right]\Bigg|_{t=0} =$$

$$= \sum_{\substack{|\alpha| \leqq k \\ |\beta| \leqq k}} \int_\Omega \frac{\partial^2 b}{\partial \xi_\alpha \partial \xi_\beta} (x; \delta_k u_0(x) + \delta_k \varphi(x)) D^\alpha v_1(x) D^\beta v_2(x) \, dx . \qquad (1)$$

We then require, for $\varphi \in W^{k,p}(\Omega)$ and for $u_0, v_1, v_2 \in V \subset W^{k,p}(\Omega)$, that the function

$$\frac{\partial^2 b}{\partial \xi_\alpha \partial \xi_\beta} (x; \delta_k u_0(x) + \delta_k \varphi(x)) D^\alpha v_1(x) D^\beta v_2(x)$$

have a finite Lebesgue integral over the set Ω. Since the functions $D^\gamma v_1(x)$, $D^\gamma v_2(x)$, $|\gamma| = k$, are — in general — only elements of the space $L_p(\Omega)$, it is necessary that the function

$$\left| \frac{\partial^2 b}{\partial \xi_\alpha \partial \xi_\beta} (x; \delta_k u_0(x) + \delta_k \varphi(x)) \right|^{p-2}$$

have a finite Lebesgue integral. For this reason, we limit ourselves to the case $p \geqq 2$. Furthermore, in the light of our experience with the computation of the first derivative, we will not need to dwell on what it is necessary to assume concerning the function $b(x; \xi)$ or on the way in which all the equalities in the formal computation (1) are justified by means of the theorem on the derivative of an integral with respect to a parameter. We thus immediately state the corresponding theorem:

21.4. Theorem. *Let* $p \geq 2$, $\Omega \subset \mathbb{R}^N$, $\Omega \in \mathscr{C}^{0,1}$. *Let the function* $b(x; \xi)$ *be defined for almost all* $x \in \Omega$ *and all* $\xi \in \mathbb{R}^\varkappa$, *and let it be such that the partial derivatives*

$$\frac{\partial b(x; \xi)}{\partial \xi_\alpha}, \quad \frac{\partial^2 b(x; \xi)}{\partial \xi_\alpha \, \partial \xi_\beta}$$

exist for almost all $x \in \mathbb{R}^N$, *all* $\xi \in \mathbb{R}^\varkappa$, *and all multi-indexes* α, β, $|\alpha| \leq k$, $|\beta| \leq k$. *Assume that*

$$b \in \mathbf{CAR}^*(p+1), \quad \frac{\partial b}{\partial \xi_\alpha} \in \mathbf{CAR}^*(p), \quad \frac{\partial^2 b}{\partial \xi_\alpha \, \partial \xi_\beta} \in \mathbf{CAR}^*(p-1) \; \dagger) \tag{2}$$

(again for all multi-indexes α, β, $|\alpha| \leq k$, $|\beta| \leq k$).

Then the functional F *defined by the formula*

$$F(u) = \int_\Omega b(x; \delta_k \, u(x) + \delta_k \, \varphi(x)) \, dx - \, <\mathbf{f}, u>_Q - \, <\mathbf{g}, u>_V \tag{3}$$

$\bigl[$*see* $(18.4)\bigr]$ *has a second derivative*

$$d^2 F(u; v_1, v_2) = \sum_{\substack{|\alpha| \leq k \\ |\beta| \leq k}} \int_\Omega \frac{\partial^2 b}{\partial \xi_\alpha \, \partial \xi_\beta} (x; \delta_k \, u(x) + \delta_k \, \varphi(x)) \, D^\alpha v_1(x) \, D^\beta v_2(x) \, dx \tag{4}$$

at every point $u \in V$.

SECTION 22. LAGRANGE CONDITIONS

The theorems which were mentioned at the beginning of the preceding section (see Paragraph 21.1) will now be formulated and proved.

22.1. Theorem. *Let* X *be a normed linear space,* $M \subset X$ *an open non-empty subset. Let* $F(u)$ *be a functional defined on the set* M *which has its local minimum at the point* $u_0 \in M$. *Assume that* $d^2 F(u_0; v, v)$ *exists for every* $v \in X$.
Then

$$d^2 F(u_0; v, v) \geq 0 .$$

---

†) These conditions are easy to remember: With every differentiation we "differentiate" the polynomial growth as well, i.e., the exponent is decreased by one. It should be noted, however, that conditions (2) concern in the first place the growth of the function b and its derivatives with respect to the variable ξ; namely, if $\partial^2 b / \partial \xi_\alpha \, \partial \xi_\beta \in \mathbf{CAR}(p-1)$ should be assumed we would have to require, furthermore, that the function $g_{\alpha\beta}(x)$ [which corresponds to the function $g_\alpha(x)$ in (12.12)] belong to $L_s(\Omega)$ with $s = p/(p-2)$.

Proof. Choose $v \in X$ arbitrary but fixed. Then the real function

$$f_v(t) = F(u_0 + tv)$$

is defined on a certain open interval $(-\varepsilon, \varepsilon)$ and has its local minimum at the point $t = 0$. Clearly,

$$f_v'(0) = dF(u_0; v) \quad \text{and} \quad f_v''(0) = d^2F(u_0; v, v).$$

According to the classical theorems mentioned in Paragraph 21.1, we have $f_v''(0) \geq 0$ which proves the required assertion.

The assertion of Theorem 22.1 can be modified in a certain way if some additional conditions are satisfied:

22.2. Theorem. *Let X be a normed linear space, $M \subset X$ an open non-empty subset. Let $F(u)$ be a functional defined on the set M such that the point $u_0 \in M$ is one of its critical points $[$i.e., $dF(u_0; v) = 0$ for every $v \in X]$. Assume, further, that a neighbourhood $\mathcal{U}$ of the point u_0 exists such that for arbitrary $u \in \mathcal{U}$ and $v \in X$ the second derivative $d^2F(u; v, v)$ exists and has the following properties:*

(a) *there exists $\lambda > 0$ such that*

$$d^2F(u_0; v, v) \geq \lambda \|v\|_X^2$$

for every $v \in X$;

(b) *the second derivative $d^2F(u; v, v)$ is continuous at the point u_0 in the following sense: For every $\varepsilon > 0$ there exists $\delta > 0$ such that*

$$|d^2F(u_0 + \tau v; v, v) - d^2F(u_0; v, v)| < \varepsilon \|v\|_X^2$$

for all $v \in X$ such that $\|v\|_X < \delta$ and for all $\tau \in [0, 1]$.

Then the functional $F(u)$ has a strict local minimum at the point u_0.

Proof. Put $f_v(t) = F(u_0 + tv)$. If the norm $\|v\|_X$ is sufficiently small, then

$$F(u_0 + v) - F(u_0) = f_v(1) - f_v(0) = \int_0^1 f_v'(t)\, dt = \int_0^1 dF(u_0 + tv; v)\, dt =$$

$$= \int_0^1 [dF(u_0 + tv; v) - dF(u_0; v)]\, dt = \int_0^1 \int_0^t d^2F(u_0 + \tau v; v, v)\, d\tau\, dt =$$

$$= \tfrac{1}{2}d^2F(u_0; v, v) + \int_0^1 \int_0^t [d^2F(u_0 + \tau v; v, v) - d^2F(u_0; v, v)]\, d\tau\, dt \geq$$

$$\geq \tfrac{1}{2}(\lambda - \varepsilon) \|v\|_X^2 > 0$$

(provided $\varepsilon > 0$ is sufficiently small), which proves the assertion of the theorem.

22.3. Example. Let $p \geq 2$, and let the function $b(x; \xi)$ satisfy all the conditions given in Theorem 21.4. Let the functional $F(u)$ defined by relation (21.3) have a local minimum at the point $u_0 \in V$. By Theorem 22.1 and 21.4, we then have

$$d^2 F(u_0; v, v) = \sum_{\substack{|\alpha| \leq k \\ |\beta| \leq k}} \int_\Omega \frac{\partial^2 b}{\partial \xi_\alpha \partial \xi_\beta} (x; \delta_k u_0(x) + \delta_k \varphi(x)) D^\alpha v(x) D^\beta v(x) \, dx \geq 0$$

for every $v \in V$.

22.4. Example. Let $p = 2$. Let a constant $\lambda > 0$ exist such that for all $\xi, \zeta \in \mathbb{R}^\varkappa$ and almost all $x \in \Omega$

$$\sum_{\substack{|\alpha| \leq k \\ |\beta| \leq k}} \frac{\partial^2 b(x; \xi)}{\partial \xi_\alpha \partial \xi_\beta} \zeta_\alpha \zeta_\beta \geq \lambda |\zeta|^2 \tag{1}$$

holds. Then assumption (a) of Theorem 22.2 is obviously satisfied for the functional F of (21.3).†)

Furthermore, let us find out whether assumption (b) of Theorem 22.2 is satisfied in our special case $(p = 2)$. Obviously,

$$\left| d^2 F(u_0 + \tau v; v, v) - d^2 F(u_0; v, v) \right| =$$

$$= \left| \sum_{\substack{|\alpha| \leq k \\ |\beta| \leq k}} \int_\Omega \left[\frac{\partial^2 b}{\partial \xi_\alpha \partial \xi_\beta} (x; \delta_k u_0(x) + \tau \delta_k v(x) + \delta_k \varphi(x)) - \right. \right.$$

$$\left. \left. - \frac{\partial^2 b}{\partial \xi_\alpha \partial \xi_\beta} (x; \delta_k u_0(x) + \delta_k \varphi(x)) \right] D^\alpha v(x) D^\beta v(x) \, dx \right| \leq$$

$$\leq \|v\|_{k,2}^2 \sum_{\substack{|\alpha| \leq k \\ |\beta| \leq k}} \left\| \frac{\partial^2 b}{\partial \xi_\alpha \partial \xi_\beta} (x; \delta_k u_0(x) + \tau \delta_k v(x) + \delta_k \varphi(x)) - \right.$$

$$\left. - \frac{\partial^2 b}{\partial \xi_\alpha \partial \xi_\beta} (x; \delta_k u_0(x) + \delta_k \varphi(x)) \right\|_\infty .$$

It then suffices to prove that the norm

$$\left\| \frac{\partial^2 b}{\partial \xi_\alpha \partial \xi_\beta} (x; \delta_k u_0(x) + \tau \delta_k v(x) + \delta_k \varphi(x)) - \frac{\partial^2 b}{\partial \xi_\alpha \partial \xi_\beta} (x; \delta_k u_0(x) + \delta_k \varphi(x)) \right\|_\infty$$

is small for all $\tau \in [0, 1]$ as long as $v \in V$ has a sufficiently small norm $\|v\|_{k,2}$. However, this is a direct consequence of the continuity of the Němyckiĭ operator $\mathcal{H}$ determined by the function $\partial^2 b / \partial \xi_\alpha \partial \xi_\beta$; if the conditions of Theorem 21.4 are satisfied, we have, namely, $\partial^2 b / \partial \xi_\alpha \partial \xi_\beta \in \mathbf{CAR}^*(1)$ and the operator $\mathcal{H}$ is thus a continuous mapping from V into the space $L_\infty(\Omega)$ — see Theorem 13.14.

---

†) We recommend the reader to carry out the computations for different examples to verify conditions (1). E.g., put $N = 1$, $k = 1$, and $b(x; \xi_0, \xi_1) = \xi_1^2 + \xi_0^2 + e^{\xi_0}$.

SECTION 23. CONVEX FUNCTIONALS

23.1. In Theorem 22.1 and 22.2, the inequality $d^2F(u; v, v) \geq 0$ appeared. We now examine the meaning of this condition. Those who know that the non-negativity of the second derivative of a real function $f(x)$ means that $f(x)$ is a convex function will surely suspect an analogue of this classical fact. Such is indeed the case.

23.2. Definition. (i) A *subset M* of a normed linear space X is called *convex* if $tu + (1 - t) v \in M$ for arbitrary $u, v \in M$ and $t \in [0, 1]$. (In other words: If the set M contains two points, then it also contains the whole straight line segment connecting those points.)

(ii) A *functional $F(u)$* defined on a convex subset M of a normed linear space X is called *convex* if

$$F(tu + (1 - t) v) \leq t F(u) + (1 - t) F(v)$$

for arbitrary elements $u, v \in M$ and for all $t \in [0, 1]$.

23.3. Theorem. *Let F be a functional defined on a convex open set $M \subset X$. Assume that for every $u \in M$ and for all $v \in X$*

$$d^2F(u; v, v) \geq 0 \tag{1}$$

holds.
Then F is a convex functional.

The proof is based on a three-fold application of the very well-known (so-called Lagrange) mean value theorem which says the following: *Let f be a continuous real function on the interval $[a, b]$ which has a derivative in the open interval (a, b). Then there exists a $\vartheta \in (0, 1)$ such that*

$$f(b) - f(a) = f'(a + \vartheta(b - a)) (b - a).$$

Let $t \in [0, 1]$, $u, v \in M$. According to the above-mentioned Lagrange Theorem, numbers $\vartheta, \zeta, v \in (0, 1)$ then exist such that

$$
\begin{aligned}
t\, F(u) &+ (1 - t)\, F(v) - F(tu + (1 - t) v) = \\
&= t[F(u) - F(u + (1 - t)(v - u))] + (1 - t)[F(v) - F(v + t(u - v))] = \\
&= -t\, dF(u + v(1 - t)(v - u); (1 - t)(v - u)) - \\
&\quad - (1 - t)\, dF(v + \vartheta t(u - v); t(u - v)) = \\
&= (1 - t)\, t(1 - \vartheta t + v - vt)\, d^2F(\zeta(v + \vartheta t(u - v)) + \\
&\quad + (1 - \zeta)(u + v(1 - t)(v - u)); u - v, u - v) \geq 0 .
\end{aligned}
\tag{2}
$$

23.4. Remarks. (i) From the computation in (2), there also follows a certain "conversion" of the assertion given in Theorem 23.3: *Let F be a convex functional defined on an open convex subset $M \subset X$. Let $d^2 F(u; v, v)$ exist for arbitrary $u \in M$ and $v \in X$. Then* (1) *is true.*

(ii) Analysis of the computation in (2) also shows that the validity of the inequality

$$dF(u; u - v) - dF(v; u - v) \geq 0 \tag{3}$$

for every $u, v \in M$ is a further sufficient condition for the convexity of the functional F.†)

Condition (3) will be applied in cases when it is not possible to speak of $d^2 F(u; v, v)$ at all, e.g. if we are dealing with a functional $F(u)$ defined by relation (21.3), where $1 < p < 2$. Condition (3) will also be encountered in Section 26 and in Chapter V.

23.5. Example. (i) Let $p \geq 2$, and let the function $b(x; \xi)$ satisfy the conditions of Theorem 21.4. If for all $\xi, \eta \in \mathbb{R}^\varkappa$ and almost all $x \in \Omega$ we have

$$\sum_{\substack{|\alpha| \leq k \\ |\beta| \leq k}} \frac{\partial^2 b(x; \xi)}{\partial \xi_\alpha \, \partial \xi_\beta} \eta_\alpha \eta_\beta \geq 0 \,, \tag{4}$$

then the functional

$$F(u) = \int_\Omega b(x; \delta_k \, u(x) + \delta_k \, \varphi(x)) \, dx \; - \; <\mathbf{f}, u>_Q - \; <\mathbf{g}, u>_V \tag{5}$$

is convex on the space V. (The assertion follows immediately from Theorem 23.3 and Theorem 21.4.)

(ii) Let $p > 1$, and let the function $b(x; \xi)$ satisfy the conditions of Theorem 18.7. If for all $\xi, \zeta \in \mathbb{R}^\varkappa$ and almost all $x \in \Omega$ we have

$$\sum_{|\alpha| \leq k} \left(\frac{\partial b(x; \xi)}{\partial \xi_\alpha} - \frac{\partial b(x; \zeta)}{\partial \xi_\alpha} \right) (\xi_\alpha - \zeta_\alpha) \geq 0 \,, \tag{6}$$

then the functional given by relation (5) is convex on the space V. [The assertion follows immediately from Theorem 18.7 and Remark 23.4 (ii).]

(iii) Condition (6) is more general than condition (4) even in the case when $p \geq 2$: The Lagrange Theorem (see the proof of Theorem 23.3) immediately implies that if (4) is valid, then (6) is valid as well.

By Theorem 20.3, every local extremum point is a critical point. For convex functionals the converse is also true as is shown by the following theorem.

---

†) It should be noted that we are dealing with a generalization of the following classical assertion: *If the derivative f' is nondecreasing, then the function f is convex.*

23.6. Theorem. *Let F be a convex functional on an open convex subset M of the normed linear space X. Let $u_0 \in M$ be a critical point of the functional F.*
Then F attains its minimum on the set M at the point u_0.

Proof. For the sake of simplicity, assume that $\Theta \in M$, $u_0 = \Theta$, and $F(\Theta) = 0$; then

$$dF(\Theta; v) = 0$$

for every $v \in X$. Let F not have its minimum at the point Θ. There exists, therefore, a point $z \in M$ such that

$$F(z) = m < 0.$$

Then

$$F(tz + (1 - t)\Theta) \leq t F(z) + (1 - t) F(\Theta) = tm$$

and

$$\frac{F(tz) - F(\Theta)}{t} \leq m$$

for every $t \in (0, 1)$. Hence, it follows that

$$dF(\Theta; z) \leq m < 0,$$

which is a contradiction.

It is easily seen that the additional assumptions $\Theta \in M$, $u_0 = \Theta$, $F(\Theta) = 0$ do not incur any loss of generality.

23.7. Example. Let the conditions of Example 23.5 be satisfied [either alternative (i) or alternative (ii)]. Denote

$$a_\alpha(x; \xi) = \frac{\partial b(x; \xi)}{\partial \xi_\alpha},$$

and let

$$(Au)(x) = \sum_{|\alpha| \leq k} (-1)^{|\alpha|} D^\alpha a_\alpha(x; \delta_k u(x))$$

be a formal differential operator of order $2k$. Then the boundary value problem (A, V, Q) has the weak solution $u_0 + \varphi \in W^{k,p}(\Omega)$ (see Paragraph 19.1) if and only if $u_0 \in V$ is the minimum of the functional F defined on the space V by the formula

$$F(u) = \int_\Omega b(x; \delta_k u(x) + \delta_k \varphi(x)) \, dx - \langle f, u \rangle_Q - \langle g, u \rangle_V, \tag{5}$$

where

$$b(x; \xi) = \int_0^1 \left[\sum_{|\alpha| \leq k} \xi_\alpha a_\alpha(x; t\xi) \right] dt.$$

In other words: The boundary value problem (A, V, Q) has at least one weak solution if and only if the potential of this problem attains at least one minimum on the space V.

23.8. Remarks. (i) A convex functional might attain its minimal value at several points (one can quite easily construct an example of a convex real function having this property). However, in any case, if a convex functional attains its minimum at the point $u_1 \in M$ and simultaneously at the point $u_2 \in M$, then it attains its minimum along the entire segment joining the points u_1, u_2; in particular, it is constant along this entire segment and has a vanishing derivative there (as long as this derivative exists). For instance, it might happen that the potential of a boundary value problem has several critical points and the boundary value problem thus has several weak solutions. However, we frequently wish to know whether the solution of the equation is determined uniquely. This leads to a more restrictive concept of "convex functional".

We say that a *functional* F defined on a convex set M of a normed linear space X is *strictly convex* if for any two points $u, v \in M$, $u \neq v$, and every $t \in (0, 1)$, we have

$$F(tu + (1 - t)v) < t F(u) + (1 - t) F(v).$$

A strictly convex functional cannot be constant along any segment lying in M. Thus, a strictly convex functional may have at most one critical point and at most one point at which it assumes its minimum.

(ii) It can easily be verified that if a functional F has a second derivative $d^2F(u; v, v)$ on an open convex set M, then F is strictly convex if and only if for an arbitrary $v \in X$, $v \neq \Theta$, and every $u \in M$ we have

$$d^2F(u; v, v) > 0.$$

(The proof of this assertion is along exactly the same lines as the proof of Theorem 23.3.)

(iii) We return to Example 23.5 (i). If a strict inequality holds in (4) for $\zeta \neq 0$, then the functional F is even strictly convex on the space V. Under this additional condition, the boundary value problem (A, V, Q) investigated in Example 23.7 has at most one weak solution.

We leave the formulation of the same assertions for case (ii) from Example 23.5 to the reader. [It suffices to assume that strict inequality holds in relation (6) for $\xi \neq \eta$.]

23.9. Back to the proof of Theorem 20.7. We have now developed so many theoretical tools and proved such a large number of general assertions that it is indeed possible to prove very easily the first part of the assertion of the theorem on the minimum of a quadratic functional (see Theorem 20.7); the proof differs from the one found in the book [80], p. 115.

Since the operator appearing in Theorem 20.7 is positive, the functional F defined in (20.1) is strictly convex [see Paragraph 23.8 (ii)]. By Theorem 23.6, every solution of the equation $Tu = f$ (i.e., every critical point of the functional F) is a point at which F assumes its minimum on H. Finally, by 23.8 (i), there exists at most one point at which the functional has its minimum.

SECTION 24. WEAK CONVERGENCE AND WEAK COMPACTNESS

24.1. The relation between the weak solution of a boundary value problem and the minimum of the potential of this problem was clarified in a rather satisfactory manner in the preceding sections. However, the question still remains unanswered: Under what conditions does the potential of a boundary value problem attain its minimum? It would seem that the following very well-known theorem is applicable:

24.2. Theorem. *Let F be a continuous functional on a compact†) subset M of the normed linear space X. Then there exists $u_0 \in M$ such that*

$$F(u_0) = \min_{u \in M} F(u),$$

i.e., $F(u_0) \leqq F(u)$ for every $u \in M$.

24.3. Recall that for the above theorem to hold the condition of continuity of the functional F is unnecessarily strong. It suffices to assume that the functional F is *lower semicontinuous* on the set M, i.e., that for every $u_0 \in M$ and for any sequence $\{u_n\}_{n=1}^{\infty}$ of elements of the set M such that $u_n \to u_0$ we have

$$F(u_0) \leqq \liminf_{n \to \infty} F(u_n).$$

24.4. Theorem 24.2 is not applicable for our purposes since compact sets are "small" in spaces of infinite dimension††): They contain no inner points. In particular, we have:

---

†) A set $M \subset X$ is called *compact* if it is possible from an arbitrary sequence $\{u_n\}_{n=1}^{\infty}$ of elements of the set M to select a subsequence $\{u_{n_k}\}_{k=1}^{\infty}$ which converges to some element $u_0 \in M$, i.e.,

$$\lim_{k \to \infty} \|u_{n_k} - u_0\|_X = 0 \quad \text{or} \quad u_{n_k} \to u_0 \quad (\text{in } X).$$

††) We say that a linear space X is of *finite dimension* if there exist elements $u_1, \ldots, u_m \in X$ such that an arbitrary element $u \in X$ can be expressed in the form

$$u = \lambda_1 u_1 + \ldots + \lambda_m u_m,$$

where $\lambda_1, \ldots, \lambda_m$ are certain real numbers. If a linear space is not of finite dimension, then we say that it is a space of infinite dimension. The spaces $C^k(\overline{\Omega})$, $L_p(\Omega)$, $W_0^{k,p}(\Omega)$, $W^{k,p}(\Omega)$, V, and other spaces considered in this book are spaces of infinite dimension.

The subset

$$B(\Theta; 1) = \{u \in X; \|u\|_X \leq 1\}$$

of a normed linear space is compact if and only if the space X is of finite dimension.

For this reason, we introduce a new idea of convergence in the normed linear space X and thus new notions of compactness and of lower semicontinuity as well, which are such that the compact sets for this convergence are larger than those for the convergence induced by the norm of the space X. In doing this, we single out a class of spaces such that the set $B(\Theta; 1)$ defined above is compact for this convergence.

In the sequel, we will assume that the linear normed space X is complete, i.e., that it is a Banach space.

24.5. Definition. Let $\{u_n\}_{n=1}^{\infty}$ be a sequence of elements of the Banach space X. Let $u_0 \in X$. We say that u_0 is the *weak limit* of the sequence $\{u_n\}_{n=1}^{\infty}$ (or that $\{u_n\}_{n=1}^{\infty}$ *converges weakly to* u_0) and we write

$$u_n \rightharpoonup u_0 \,,$$

if for every continuous linear functional $f \in X^*$ we have

$$\lim_{n \to \infty} <f, u_n> = <f, u_0> \,.$$

24.6. At first sight, it is not clear whether the above definition is reasonable. For the correctness of the definition it has to be checked, among other things, that it cannot happen that a sequence has more than one limit. However, it can indeed be proved that an arbitrary sequence of elements of the Banach space X has at most one weak limit (see [51]; see also [61]).

24.7. Some properties of weak convergence.

(i) *Let $u_n \rightharpoonup u_0$, $v_n \rightharpoonup v_0$. Then $u_n + v_n \rightharpoonup u_0 + v_0$.*

(ii) *Let $\{\lambda_n\}_{n=1}^{\infty}$ be a sequence of real numbers, $\lambda_n \to \lambda_0$; let $u_n \rightharpoonup u_0$. Then*

$$\lambda_n u_n \rightharpoonup \lambda_0 u_0 \,.$$

[Both assertions are immediate consequences of the definition. Let us prove assertion (i), for instance: For an arbitrary continuous functional $f \in X^*$ we have

$$\lim_{n \to \infty} <f, u_n> = <f, u_0> \quad \text{and} \quad \lim_{n \to \infty} <f, v_n> = <f, v_0> \,.$$

Thus,

$$\lim_{n \to \infty} <f, u_n + v_n> = \lim_{n \to \infty} <f, u_n> + \lim_{n \to \infty} <f, v_n> =$$

$$= <f, u_0> + <f, v_0> = <f, u_0 + v_0> ,$$

which proves that $u_n + v_n \rightharpoonup u_0 + v_0$.]

(iii) *Let $u_n \to u_0$; then $u_n \rightharpoonup u_0$.*

[Obviously, we have $\lim_{n \to \infty} <f, u_n - u_0> = 0$ since the functional f is continuous.]

Observe immediately that the converse assertion to (iii) does not hold, at least for spaces of infinite dimension. Indeed, there exist weakly convergent sequences which are not convergent. As an example, we mention the sequence $\{\sin nx\}_{n=1}^{\infty}$ in the space $L_2(0, \pi)$ which converges weakly to the zero element of the space $L_2(0, \pi)$ but does not converge in the norm of the space $L_2(0, \pi)$ since the distance between any two distinct elements of this sequence is equal to $\sqrt{2}$. An example of a sequence with this property can be constructed in almost any arbitrary Banach space of infinite dimension. It is possible to prove, however, that in spaces of finite dimension the concepts of weak and strong convergence coincide, i.e., that the following is true: *Let X be a Banach space of finite dimension. Let $\{u_n\}_{n=1}^{\infty}$ be a sequence of elements of the space X. Then $u_n \to u_0$ if and only if $u_n \rightharpoonup u_0$.*

Assertions (i)−(iii) were simple consequences of the definition. The following assertion is not quite so trivial.

(iv) *A weakly convergent sequence is bounded. If $u_n \rightharpoonup u_0$, then*

$$\|u_0\|_X \leq \liminf_{n \to \infty} \|u_n\|_X .$$

(For the proof see [61].)

With the aid of weak convergence we now introduce the concepts of "weakly compact set" and "weakly lower semicontinuous functional".

24.8. Definition. We say that a subset M of the Banach space X is *weakly compact* if from an arbitrary sequence $\{u_n\}_{n=1}^{\infty}$ of elements of the set M it is possible to select a subsequence $\{u_{n_k}\}_{k=1}^{\infty}$ which converges weakly to an element of the set M, i.e., there exists $u_0 \in M$ such that $u_{n_k} \rightharpoonup u_0$.

24.9. Definition. Let $M \subset X$, and let F be a functional defined on the set M. We say that F is *weakly lower semicontinuous* on M if

$$F(u_0) \leq \liminf_{n \to \infty} F(u_n)$$

for any $u_0 \in M$ and for any sequence $\{u_n\}_{n=1}^{\infty}$ of elements of the set M such that $u_n \rightharpoonup u_0$.

24.10. Examples of weakly compact sets and weakly lower semicontinuous functionals will be discussed in subsequent sections. For the time being, we note only that

(i) an arbitrary continuous linear functional $f \in X^*$ is a simple example of a weakly lower semicontinuous functional on the Banach space X;

(ii) as an example of a nonlinear weakly lower semicontinuous functional on the Banach space X, we may take the norm of the space X, i.e., the functional F defined on X by

$$F(u) = \|u\|_X$$

[see assertion 24.7 (iv)].

We shall prove the existence theorem for the minimum of a functional now. The theorem will be merely auxiliary, while the explanation of its assumptions will be found in the sections which follow.

24.11. Theorem. *Let M be a non-empty weakly compact subset of the Banach space X. Let F be a weakly lower semicontinuous functional on the set M. Then*

(a) $\inf\limits_{u \in M} F(u) > -\infty$;

(b) *there exists at least one $u_0 \in M$ such that*

$$F(u_0) = \inf_{u \in M} F(u) .$$

Proof. If we prove assertion (b), then assertion (a) will be proved as well. Let $\{u_n\}_{n=1}^{\infty}$ be a sequence of elements from M such that

$$\lim_{n \to \infty} F(u_n) = \inf_{u \in M} F(u) . \tag{1}$$

[A sequence having property (1) is usually called a *minimizing sequence* — see also Section 28.] Since the set M is weakly compact, there exist a subsequence $\{u_{n_k}\}_{k=1}^{\infty}$ and an element u_0 such that $u_{n_k} \rightharpoonup u_0$. By assumption, the functional F is weakly lower semicontinuous on the set M. This and (1) together imply

$$F(u_0) \leq \liminf_{n \to \infty} F(u_{n_k}) = \lim_{n \to \infty} F(u_n) = \inf_{u \in M} F(u) . \tag{2}$$

We clearly have

$$F(u_0) \geq \inf_{u \in M} F(u) . \tag{3}$$

Inequalities (2) and (3) show that

$$F(u_0) = \inf_{u \in M} F(u) ,$$

and the proof is complete.

SECTION 25. REFLEXIVE SPACES

25.1. We now clarify the statement:

"*M is a weakly compact subset of the Banach space X*",

which was important for the assertion of Theorem 24.11.

Obviously, every compact subset of the Banach space X is weakly compact as well. However, the converse is not true: The set

$$M = \{\sin nx\}_{n=0}^{\infty}$$

is weakly compact in the space $L_2(0, \pi)$ but is not compact [see Paragraph 24.7 (iii)]. In spaces of finite dimension, the concepts of "weak compactness" and "compactness" obviously coincide.

Since *every weakly compact set is weakly closed†*), we first study weakly closed sets. To start with, consider the relation between weakly closed sets and closed sets††). Obviously, every weakly closed set is also closed, since any convergent sequence is also weakly convergent. In general, a closed set need not also be weakly closed. As an example, we again refer to the set

$$M = \{\sin nx\}_{n=1}^{\infty}$$

in the space $L_2(0, \pi)$ which is closed but not weakly closed (since the zero function which is the weak limit of the sequence $\{\sin nx\}_{n=1}^{\infty}$ is not an element of the set M). However, the following very simple sufficient condition holds:

25.2. Theorem. *Every convex closed set is also weakly closed.*

25.3. Remarks. The proof of Theorem 25.2 is based on the following intuitive (but nontrivial and deep) assertion: If K is a closed convex set of the Banach space X and $u_0 \in X$ is an element such that $u_0 \notin K$, then it is possible "to decompose the space X into two half-spaces with one containing the set K and the other containing the element u_0". More precisely, the following theorem holds:

(i) Mazur Theorem (for the proof see [51]). *Let K be a closed convex non-empty set, $u_0 \in X$, $u_0 \notin K$. Then a continuous linear functional $f \in X^*$ and real numbers $c, d, c > d$, exist such that*

$$<f, u_0> = c \quad and \quad <f, u> \leqq d$$

for any $u \in K$.

---

†) A subset M of the Banach space X is *weakly closed* if the weak limit of any weakly convergent sequence of elements of the set M is an element of the set M.

††) Recall that a subset M of the Banach space X is *closed* if the limit of any (strongly) convergent sequence of elements of the set M is an element of the set M.

("The boundary of the half-spaces" mentioned above consists of the set

$$\left\{ u \in X; \, <f, u> \, = \frac{c + d}{2} \right\}.\,)$$

(ii) Theorem 25.2 can now be proved by contradiction: Suppose that K is a closed convex non-empty set which is not weakly convergent. Then there is a sequence $\{u_n\}_{n=1}^{\infty}$ of elements of the set K with $u_n \to u_0$ and $u_0 \notin K$. Let f be a continuous linear functional whose existence is guaranteed by the Mazur Theorem. Then

$$d < c = \, <f, u_0> \, = \lim_{n \to \infty} <f, u_n> \, \leq d \, ,$$

which is the desired contradiction.

For the material of this book, the class of Banach spaces introduced below is very important.'

25.4. Definition. A Banach space X is called *reflexive* if any bounded†) and weakly closed subset of X is weakly compact.

25.5. According to Theorem 25.2, every convex bounded and closed subset of a reflexive Banach space is weakly compact. Thus, weakly compact sets of a reflexive space exist which contain inner points at which it is possible to differentiate functionals and apply the results of Sections 20, 22, as well as of Theorem 24.11.

From what was said above about weakly compact and weakly closed sets, it follows immediately that every space of finite dimension is a reflexive Banach space. However, do reflexive spaces of infinite dimension exist at all? Are Sobolev spaces (which are of importance for the development of the theory of weak solutions of boundary value problems) reflexive Banach spaces?

25.6. Before answering the principal question of the preceding paragraph, we add one further remark. The reader who came to this book already familiar with the foundations of functional analysis is perhaps surprised by the definition of reflexive Banach space presented here. Definition 25.4 is not usual: a different definition is usually found in the literature. At first sight, that definition appears to be in no way connected with our definition. The usual development encountered in textbooks of functional analysis (for the details see, e.g., [51])is the following:

(i) If X is a Banach space, then the space X^* of all continuous linear functionals defined on X with the norm introduced in the footnote on p. 95 is again Banach space.

---

†) Recall that a subset M of a Banach space X is *bounded* if a constant $K > 0$ exists such that for all $u \in M$ we have

$$\|u\|_X \leq K \, .$$

Thus, it is possible to construct the Banach space $(X^*)^*$ (written X^{**}) of all continuous linear functionals on X^*; furthermore it is also possible to construct the spaces $(X^{**})^* = X^{***}$, $(X^{***})^* = X^{****}$, etc.

(ii) We define a special mapping K (called the *canonical mapping*) of the space X into the space X^{**} as follows: For $x \in X$, $K(x) = x^{**}$ is an element of the space X^{**} (this means that x^{**} is a continuous linear functional on the space X^*) such that for all elements $x^* \in X^*$ (i.e., for all continuous linear functionals on the space X) we have

$$x^{**}(x^*) = x^*(x).$$

In the case when the range of the canonical mapping K is the entire space X^{**}, the space X is called *reflexive*. In other words, a reflexive space is a Banach space X which can be identified with its second dual X^{**} by means of the canonical mapping.

(iii) One of the most important assertions is the so-called

Eberlein-Šmuljan Theorem:

A Banach space X is reflexive if and only if any bounded and weakly closed subset of X is weakly compact.

We see now that it was just the necessary and sufficient condition of the Eberlein-Šmuljan Theorem which was chosen as the definition of a reflexive space in Paragraph 25.4, since this will be particularly useful in the sequel.

25.7. Some important assertions concerning reflexive spaces. Examples.

(i) *A closed subspace of an arbitrary reflexive space is itself a reflexive space.*

(ii) *A Cartesian product of reflexive spaces is a reflexive space.*

(iii) *Every Hilbert space* (see the footnote on p. 181) *is a reflexive space.*

(iv) *The space $L_p(\Omega)$ is a reflexive space if and only if $p > 1$.*

(v) *The spaces $C^k(\overline{\Omega})$ $(k = 0, 1, 2, \ldots)$ are not reflexive.*

(vi) *For $p > 1$, $k \in \mathbb{N}$, the Sobolev spaces $W^{k,p}(\Omega)$, $W_0^{k,p}(\Omega)$ are reflexive.*

(vii) *The spaces $W^{k,1}(\Omega)$, $W_0^{k,1}(\Omega)$ are not reflexive.*

(viii) *The space V from the definition of the weak solution of a boundary value problem* (see Paragraph 15.7) *is reflexive for $p > 1$.* [The proof follows directly from assertions (vi) and (i).]

The proofs of assertions (iv), (v), (vi), and (vii) can be found in [54].

25.8. Remark. In the next section and in Chapter V, we shall prove the existence of a solution of nonlinear operator equations in reflexive spaces; reflexivity will be essential. In applications to boundary value problems in differential equations, the assertion given in 25.7 (vi), (viii) will then be of importance.

From assertion 25.7 (vii), it is now obvious why we limited ourselves to the case $p > 1$ in the formulation of the weak solution of a boundary value problem. It is also seen what we meant in Paragraph 16.3 — when defining the weak solution of a boundary value problem for the case $p = 1$ (e.g., for minimal surfaces) — by saying that the Sobolev space $W_0^{1,1}(\Omega)$ possesses "some disagreeable properties".

SECTION 26. EXISTENCE THEOREMS

Making use of the results of the preceding section we can modify Theorem 24.11 in the following way:

26.1. Theorem. *Let M be a non-empty, convex, closed, and bounded subset of a reflexive Banach space X. Let F be a weakly lower semicontinuous functional on the set M. Then*

(a) $\displaystyle\inf_{u \in M} F(u) > -\infty$;

(b) *there exists at least one $u_0 \in M$ such that*

$$F(u_0) = \inf_{u \in M} F(u) .$$

26.2. Theorem 24.11 follows directly from Theorem 25.2 and Definition 25.4. This clarifies those conditions on the existence of the minimum of a functional which relate to the set M. It remains to explain the conditions concerning the functional F. First, a necessary and sufficient condition for the functional F to be weakly lower semicontinuous is proved.

26.3. Lemma. *Let X be a Banach space and M a weakly closed subset of X. Let F be a functional defined on the set M.*
   Then F is weakly lower semicontinuous on M if and only if the set

$$E(a) = \{u \in M;\ F(u) \leq a\}$$

is weakly closed for arbitrary $a \in \mathbb{R}$.

Proof. Let F be a weakly lower semicontinuous functional on the set M. Let $a \in \mathbb{R}$, and let $\{u_n\}_{n=1}^{\infty}$ be a sequence of elements of the set $E(a)$ such that $u_n \rightharpoonup u_0 \in M$. Then

$$F(u_0) \leq \liminf_{n \to \infty} F(u_n) \leq a$$

and thus $u_0 \in E(a)$, i.e., the set $E(a)$ is weakly closed.

On the other hand, let the set $E(a)$ be weakly closed for arbitrary $a \in \mathbb{R}$ and suppose that the functional F is not weakly lower semicontinuous on the set M. Then an element $u_0 \in M$ and a sequence $\{u_n\}_{n=1}^{\infty}$ of elements of the set M exist such that $u_n \rightharpoonup u_0$ and

$$\liminf_{n \to \infty} F(u_n) < F(u_0) .$$

Choose $a \in \mathbb{R}$ so that the inequalities

$$\liminf_{n \to \infty} F(u_n) < a < F(u_0)$$

hold. Then there exists a subsequence $\{u_{n_k}\}_{k=1}^{\infty}$ of the sequence $\{u_n\}_{n=1}^{\infty}$ such that

$$u_{n_k} \in E(a), \quad k = 1, 2, \dots .$$

Since $E(a)$ is a weakly closed set, we have $u_0 \in E(a)$. Then

$$F(u_0) \leqq a < F(u_0),$$

which is a contradiction; the functional F is thus weakly lower semicontinuous on the set M.

26.4. Compare now the conditions of Theorem 26.1 with Lemma 26.3. The set $E(a)$ is weakly closed if it is, e.g., closed and convex. When is the set $E(a)$ closed and convex for arbitrary $a \in \mathbb{R}$? If the functional F is continuous on the set M, $E(a)$ will obviously be a closed set for any $a \in \mathbb{R}$. An easy computation shows that if the functional F is convex on a convex set M, then $E(a)$ is a convex set for every $a \in \mathbb{R}$. In this way, applying Theorem 25.2. we obtain the following simple sufficient condition:

26.5. Theorem. *A continuous convex functional F on a closed convex set M is weakly lower semicontinuous on M.†)*

Combining Theorems 26.1 and 26.5 we obtain an existence theorem for the minimum of a functional with very intuitive assumptions.

26.6. Theorem. *Let M be a non-empty, convex, closed, and bounded subset of a reflexive Banach space X. Let F be a continuous and convex functional defined on the set M. Then:*

(a) $\inf\limits_{u \in M} F(u) > -\infty$;

---

†) It is not true that every continuous functional is at the same time weakly lower semicontinuous. As an example of a continuous functional which is not weakly lower semicontinuous we have, on the space $L_2(0, 1)$, the functional

$$F(u) = 1 - \int_0^1 u^2(x) \, dx .$$

(b) *there exists at least one* $u_0 \in M$ *such that*

$$F(u_0) = \inf_{u \in M} F(u) \; ;$$

(c) *if, moreover, F is a strictly convex functional on M* [see Paragraph 23.8 (i)], *then there exists presicely one* u_0 *with the property* (b).

[Assertion (c) is an immediate consequence of the considerations of Paragraph 23.8 (i).]

26.7. The condition that the set M be bounded is essential for the validity of the assertions of Theorems 26.1 and 26.6. Indeed, if, e.g., $F(u) = e^u$ and $M = X = \mathbb{R}$, then the assertion of Theorem 26.6 is not valid for this real function. The condition that the set M be bounded can thus be removed only if some additional condition concerning the functional F is imposed.

26.8. Theorem. *Let X be a reflexive Banach space, and let F be a functional defined on X such that*

$$\lim_{\|u\|_X \to \infty} F(u) = \infty \; . \tag{1}$$

Suppose that one of the following conditions is satisfied:

(I) *F is a continuous and convex functional on X;*
(II) *F is a weakly lower semicontinuous functional on X.*

Then

(a) $\inf_{u \in X} F(u) > -\infty$;

(b) *there exists at least one* $u_0 \in X$ *such that*

$$F(u_0) = \inf_{u \in X} F(u) \; ;$$

(c) *if condition* (I) *is satisfied and, moreover, if the functional F is strictly convex on X, then there exists precisely one* u_0 *with the property* (b).

Proof. Let

$$d > \inf_{u \in X} F(u) \, .$$

By condition (1) (called the *coerciveness of the functional F*) an $r > 0$ exists such that for all $u \in X$ for which $\|u\|_X \geq r$ we have $F(u) \geq d$. Put

$$M = \{u \in X; \; \|u\|_X \leq r\} \, .$$

Then

$$\inf_{u \in M} F(u) = \inf_{u \in X} F(u) \, ,$$

and thus, by Theorem 26.1 (or by Theorem 26.6), $u_0 \in M$ exists such that

$$F(u_0) = \inf_{u \in M} F(u) = \inf_{u \in X} F(u),$$

which finishes the proof.

26.9. Since our main aim is to prove theorems on the existence of the weak solution of boundary value problems in nonlinear differential equations, we shall formulate the consequences of Theorem 26.8 in terms of the solvability of operator equations. For ease of expression, we present one further definition which deals with concepts whose importance is particularly stressed by Chapter V.

26.10. Definition. The operator T which maps a Banach space X into the dual space X^* is called

(i) *bounded* if the image of every bounded subset of the space X is a bounded subset of the set X^*;

(ii) *monotone* if

$$<Tu - Tv,\ u - v> \geq 0$$

for any pair of points $u, v \in X$;

(iii) *coercive* if

$$\lim_{\|u\|_X \to \infty} \frac{<Tu,\ u>}{\|u\|_X} = \infty.$$

26.11. Theorem. *Let X be a reflexive Banach space. Let T be an operator defined on X with values in X^* which is potential, bounded, monotone, coercive.*
Then $TX = X^*$, i.e., the equation

$$Tu = f \tag{2}$$

has a solution for arbitrary $f \in X^*$.

Proof. Let $f \in X^*$, and let F_0 be the potential of the operator T. Then the operator $Tu - f$ is the derivative of the functional $F(u) = F_0(u) - <f, u>$.

We shall prove that the functional F satisfies the conditions of Theorem 26.8 (alternative II).

A. *The functional F is weakly lower semicontinuous on X* since if $u, v \in X$, then by the Lagrange mean value theorem (see the proof of Theorem 23.3) there exists $t \in [0, 1]$ such that

$$F(u) - F(v) = <T(v + t[u - v]),\ u - v>\ ;$$

thus

$$F(u) - F(v) = \,<Tv, \ u - v> + \,<T(v + t[u - v]) - Tv, \ u - v> \,=$$

$$= \,<Tv, \ u - v> + \frac{1}{t} \,<T(v + t[u - v]) - Tv, \ t(u - v)> \,\geqq$$

$$\geqq \,<Tv, \ u - v>$$

since

$$<T(v + t[u - v]) - Tv, \ t(u - v)> \,\geqq 0$$

by the monotony of the operator T. Thus,

$$F(u) - F(v) \geqq \,<Tv, \ u - v> \tag{3}$$

for all $u, v \in X$. If then $v_n \rightarrow v$, i.e., in particular, if

$$\lim_{n \to \infty} <Tv, \ v_n> \,= \,<Tv, \ v> \,,$$

then inequality (3) implies the relation

$$\liminf_{n \to \infty} F(v_n) \geqq F(v) - \,<Tv, \ v> \,+ \lim_{n \to \infty} <Tv, \ v_n> \,= F(v).$$

B. *The functional F is coercive* $\big[$i.e., it satisfies condition (1) of Theorem 26.8$\big]$: For arbitrary $u \in X$, $u \neq \Theta$,

$$F(u) = F(\Theta) + \int_0^1 <T(tu), \ tu> \frac{dt}{t} \,=$$

$$= F(\Theta) + \int_0^{\|u\|_X} \left\langle T\left(\tau \frac{u}{\|u\|_X}\right), \ \tau \frac{u}{\|u\|_X} \right\rangle \frac{d\tau}{\tau} \tag{4}$$

holds because $Tu - f$ is the derivative of the functional F. Since T is a coercive operator, there exists $\tau_0 > 0$ such that

$$\frac{1}{\tau} \left\langle T\left(\tau \frac{u}{\|u\|_X}\right), \ \tau \frac{u}{\|u\|_X} \right\rangle = \frac{1}{\left\| \dfrac{\tau u}{\|u\|_X} \right\|_X} \left\langle T\left(\tau \frac{u}{\|u\|_X}\right), \ \tau \frac{u}{\|u\|_X} \right\rangle \geqq 1$$

for arbitrary $\tau \geqq \tau_0$ and $u \in X$, $u \neq \Theta$. Furthermore,

$$\sup_{\substack{\tau \in \langle 0, \tau_0 \rangle \\ u \in X, u \neq \Theta}} \left\| T\left(\tau \frac{u}{\|u\|_X}\right) \right\|_X = m < \infty$$

(the operator T is bounded) and we thus obtain, from (4),

$$F(u) = F(\Theta) + \int_0^{\tau_0} \left\langle T\left(\tau \frac{u}{\|u\|_X}\right), \, \tau \frac{u}{\|u\|_X} \right\rangle \frac{d\tau}{\tau} +$$

$$+ \int_{\tau_0}^{\|u\|_X} \left\langle T\left(\tau \frac{u}{\|u\|_X}\right), \, \tau \frac{u}{\|u\|_X} \right\rangle \frac{d\tau}{\tau} \geq F(\Theta) - \tau_0 m + \|u\|_X - \tau_0 \, ,$$

or, in other words, $F(u) \to \infty$ as $\|u\|_X \to \infty$.

The conditions of Theorem 26.8 are thus verified; consequently, there exists $u_0 \in X$ such that

$$F(u_0) = \inf_{u \in X} F(u) \, .$$

The assertion of the theorem now follows directly from the Euler necessary condition (see Theorem 20.3).

26.12. Remark. If, moreover, the operator T is *strictly monotone*, i.e., if

$$<Tu - Tv, \, u - v> \, > 0$$

holds for all $u, v \in X$, $u \neq v$, then equation (2) has precisely one solution for arbitrary $f \in X^*$. Indeed, should two different solutions u and v of equation (2) exist for some $f \in X^*$, then $Tu = Tv = f$, i.e., $Tu - Tv = \Theta$ and

$$0 = \, <Tu - Tv, \, u - v> \, > 0 \, ,$$

which is a contradiction.

26.13. With the aid of Theorem 26.11, we shall now prove the existence of a weak solution of the boundary value problem (A, V, Q). Thus, let

$$(Au)(x) = \sum_{|\alpha| \leq k} (-1)^{|\alpha|} \, D^\alpha a_\alpha(x; \delta_k \, u(x))$$

be a formal differential operator of order $2k$; furthermore, let

$$p > 1 \, , \tag{5}$$

$$a_\alpha \in \mathbf{CAR}^*(p) \, . \tag{6}$$

Let V be a space such that

$$W_0^{k,p}(\Omega) \subset V \subset W^{k,p}(\Omega) \, ,$$

let $V \subsetneq Q$ and let $\mathbf{f} \in Q^*$, $\varphi \in W^{k,p}(\Omega)$, $\mathbf{g} \in V^*$ (for further details see Paragraph 15.7). To the formal differential operator we can assign an operator $\mathbb{A}$ which maps the space

$W^{k,p}(\Omega)$ into $\left(W^{k,p}(\Omega)\right)^*$ (see Paragraphs 14.2 and 16.14) and is such that

$$< Au, v> = \int_\Omega \sum_{|\alpha| \leq k} a_\alpha(x; \delta_k\, u(x))\, D^\alpha v(x)\, dx$$

for every $u, v \in W^{k,p}(\Omega)$.

Define the operator T on the space V as follows: For $u \in V$, let Tu be an element of the space V^* such that

$$< Tu, v> \; = \; < A(u + \varphi), v> \; - \; <f, v>_Q \; - \; <g, v>_V \qquad (7)$$

holds for all $v \in V$.

To prove that the boundary value problem (A, V, Q) has at least one weak solution it suffices to show that the equation

$$Tu = \Theta \qquad (8)$$

has at least one solution in the space V [since the set of all solutions of equation (8) is identical with the set of all weak solutions of the boundary value problem (A, V, Q)]. Thus, it suffices to ascertain when the operator T and the space V satisfy the assumptions of Theorem 26.11.

(i) **Reflexivity of the space** V: If the number p satisfies conditions (5), then the space V is reflexive by 25.7 (vii).

(ii) **Potentiality of the operator** T: The existence of the potential of the boundary value problem (A, V, Q) was investigated in Section 19. By Theorem 19.3, the operator T defined by relation (7) is potential if for all multi-indexes $\alpha, \beta, |\alpha|, |\beta| \leq k$, for almost all $x \in \Omega$, and for all $\xi \in \mathbb{R}^\varkappa$, the partial derivatives

$$\frac{\partial a_\alpha(x; \xi)}{\partial \xi_\beta} = a_{\alpha\beta}(x; \xi)$$

exist and if the condition of "symmetry"

$$a_{\alpha\beta}(x; \xi) = a_{\beta\alpha}(x; \xi) \qquad (9)$$

and the condition

$$\xi_\alpha a_{\alpha\beta}(x; \xi) \in \boldsymbol{CAR}^*(p) \qquad (10)$$

are valid.

(iii) **Boundedness of the operator** T: This fact follows from condition (6), as proved in Paragraph 12.12 [inequality (12.13)] for the case $a_\alpha \in \boldsymbol{CAR}(p)$; for the general case see Paragraphs 16.11 to 16.15.

(iv) Monotony of the operator T: It is immediately seen that if

$$\sum_{|\alpha|\leq k} \left[a_\alpha(x;\xi) - a_\alpha(x;\zeta)\right](\xi_\alpha - \zeta_\alpha) \geq 0 \tag{11}$$

holds for all $\xi, \zeta \in \mathbb{R}^\varkappa$ and for almost all $x \in \Omega$, then the operator T is monotone since

$$<Tu - Tv, u - v> = <\mathbb{A}(u + \varphi) - \mathbb{A}(v + \varphi), u - v> =$$

$$= \sum_{|\alpha|\leq k} \int_\Omega \left(a_\alpha(x; \delta_k u(x) + \delta_k \varphi(x)) - a_\alpha(x; \delta_k v(x) + \delta_k \varphi(x))\right)\left(D^\varkappa u(x) - D^\varkappa v(x)\right) dx \geq 0$$

[when deriving the last inequality we exploit condition (11)].

If, in particular, $p = 2$, then the operator T is monotone if

$$\sum_{\substack{|\alpha|\leq k \\ |\beta|\leq k}} a_{\alpha\beta}(x;\xi)\,\zeta_\alpha\zeta_\beta \geq 0 \tag{12}$$

holds for all $\xi, \zeta \in \mathbb{R}^\varkappa$ and for almost all $x \in \Omega$. [Compare conditions (11), (12) with conditions (23.4), (23.6) which ensure the convexity of the functional F defined by relation (23.5).]

(v) Coerciveness of the operator T: This is the last condition of Theorem 26.11, which we have not examined as yet. The problem in question is thus to find "reasonable" conditions on the coefficients $a_\alpha(x;\xi)$ which would ensure the validity of the relation

$$\lim_{\|u\|_{k,p}\to\infty} \frac{1}{\|u\|_{k,p}} \sum_{|\alpha|\leq k} \int_\Omega a_\alpha(x; \delta_k u(x) + \delta_k \varphi(x))\, D^\varkappa u(x)\, dx = \infty. \tag{13}$$

We shall show that relation (13) is valid if $a_\alpha \in \mathbf{CAR}\,(p)$ and if there exist constants $c_1 > 0$, $c_2 > 0$, $c_3 \geq 0$ [$c_2 \geq 0$ is sufficient in the case when $V = W_0^{k,p}(\Omega)$] such that for all $\xi \in \mathbb{R}^\varkappa$ and for almost all $x \in \Omega$

$$\sum_{|\alpha|\leq k} a_\alpha(x;\xi)\,\xi_\alpha \geq c_1 \sum_{|\alpha|=k} |\xi_\alpha|^p + c_2|\xi_{(0,\ldots,0)}|^p - c_3 \tag{14}$$

holds.†) The proof will only be given for the case $V = W_0^{k,p}(\Omega)$; the general case can be proved similarly. The norm

$$\|\|u\|\|_{k,p,0} = \left(\sum_{|\beta|=k} \|D^\beta u\|_p^p\right)^{1/p}$$

is equivalent to the norm $\|u\|_{k,p}$ on the space $W_0^{k,p}(\Omega)$ (the proof is the same as the proof given in Lemma 13.7). We can therefore substitute this new norm in condition

---

†) Note that in the case of the Neumann problem [i.e., $V = W^{1,2}(0, \pi)$] for the formal differential equation $-u'' = f$ condition (14) is satisfied with $c_2 = 0$; condition (13) is not satisfied, however. The addendum to the effect that c_2 might vanish in the case of the Dirichlet problem is thus essential. If $a_\alpha \in \mathbf{CAR^*}\,(p)$, then condition (14) need not guarantee the validity of relation (13).

(13). It is easily checked that a constant $d > 0$ exists such that

$$\frac{1}{\|\|u\|\|_{k,p,0}} \int_\Omega \sum_{|\alpha| \leq k} a_\alpha(x; \delta_k\, u(x) + \delta_k\, \varphi(x))\, D^\alpha u(x)\, dx \geq$$

$$\geq c_1 \frac{\|u + \varphi\|_{k,p,0}^p}{\|\|u\|\|_{k,p,0}} - d\, \frac{\|\varphi\|_{k,p,0} \|u + \varphi\|_{k,p,0}^{p-1}}{\|\|u\|\|_{k,p,0}} ;$$

(13) now follows easily.

Thus, we proved the following theorem on the existence of the weak solution of the boundary value problem (A, V, Q).

26.14. Theorem. *Let* $k \in \mathbb{N}$, $p > 1$, *and suppose that the coefficients* $a_\alpha(x; \xi)$ *satisfy the following conditions:*

$$a_\alpha(x; \xi) \in \mathbf{CAR}^*(p) ; \tag{6}$$

$$a_{\alpha\beta}(x; \xi) = a_{\beta\alpha}(x; \xi) ; \tag{9}$$

$$\xi_\alpha\, a_{\alpha\beta}(x; \xi) \in \mathbf{CAR}^*(p) ; \tag{10}$$

$$\sum_{|\alpha| \leq k} [a_\alpha(x; \xi) - a_\alpha(x; \zeta)]\, (\xi_\alpha - \zeta_\alpha) \geq 0 ; \tag{11}$$

$$\lim_{\|u\|_{k,p} \to \infty} \frac{1}{\|u\|_{k,p}} \sum_{|\alpha| \leq k} \int_\Omega a_\alpha(x; \delta_k\, u(x) + \delta_k\, \varphi(x))\, D^\alpha u(x)\, dx = \infty. \tag{13}$$

Then at least one weak solution of the boundary value problem (A, V, Q) *exists. If, moreover, equality holds in condition* (11) *only for* $\xi = \zeta$, *then the boundary value problem* (A, V, Q) *has precisely one weak solution.*

26.14½. Remark. The reader who is familiar with the theory of linear equations will certainly have met the concept of *elliptic* equation before. Here, this concept has only now appeared and will not appear again in the sequel. However, an analysis of conditions (11) [or, rather, (12)] and (14) would easily show that for the case of linear equations, i.e., of equations with coefficients

$$a_\alpha(x; \xi) = \sum_{|\beta| \leq k} a_{\alpha\beta}(x)\, \xi_\beta ,$$

these conditions express the so-called *ellipticity* condition:

$$\sum_{\substack{|\alpha| \leq k \\ |\beta| \leq k}} a_{\alpha\beta}(x)\, \zeta_\alpha \zeta_\beta \geq c \sum_{|\alpha| \leq k} |\zeta_\alpha|^2 , \quad c > 0 .$$

We can therefore assert that the boundary value problem investigated in Theorem 26.14 with an operator T which is monotone and coercive (see Paragraph 26.13) is actually a boundary value problem for a nonlinear elliptic equation.

26.15. Examples.

(i) Let

$$Au = -\sum_{i=1}^{N} \frac{\partial}{\partial x_i} \left(\left| \frac{\partial u}{\partial x_i} \right|^{p-2} \frac{\partial u}{\partial x_i} \right)$$

and $f \in L_q(\Omega)$. Then the Dirichlet problem for the formal differential equation

$$Au = f \quad \text{on} \quad \Omega$$

has precisely one weak solution in the space $W^{1,p}(\Omega)$ for an arbitrary boundary condition $\varphi \in W^{1,p}(\Omega)$. (Verify the conditions of Theorem 26.14!)

(ii) Let $f \in L_1(0, 1)$ and let $g \in C^1(\mathbb{R})$ be a nondecreasing function on $\mathbb{R}$. Then the formal Dirichlet problem

$$\begin{cases} -u''(x) + g(u(x)) = f(x), & x \in (0, 1), \\ u(0) = u(1) = 0 \end{cases} \tag{15}$$

satisfies all the conditions of Theorem 26.14 and thus has at least one weak solution $u_0 \in W_0^{1,2}(0, 1)$.

If, moreover, the function g is increasing, then precisely one weak solution of the formal boundary value problem (15) exists for arbitrary $f \in L_1(0, 1)$.

(iii) Define the formal differential operator A by the relation

$$(Au)(x) = -\frac{d}{dx}(a_1(x; u(x), u'(x))) + a_0(x; u(x), u'(x)).$$

Let the functions $a_1(x; \xi_0, \xi_1)$, $a_0(x; \xi_0, \xi_1)$ be continuous on $[0, 1] \times \mathbb{R}^2$, and let the following growth conditions, the conditions of potentiality, monotony and coerciveness, be satisfied, which ensure the applicability of Theorem 26.14.

Growth conditions: A constant $c_1 > 0$ and a continuous function $g(\xi_0)$ on $\mathbb{R}$ exist such that for all $x \in [0, 1]$, $\xi_0, \xi_1 \in \mathbb{R}$, we have

$$|a_1(x; \xi_0, \xi_1)| \leq c_1(g(\xi_0) + |\xi_1|), \tag{16}$$

$$|a_0(x; \xi_0, \xi_1)| \leq c_1(g(\xi_0) + |\xi_1|^2). \tag{17}$$

Potentiality conditions: For $i = 0, 1$, the partial derivatives

$$\frac{\partial a_1(x; \xi_0, \xi_1)}{\partial \xi_i} = a_{1i}(x; \xi_0, \xi_1),$$

$$\frac{\partial a_0(x; \xi_0, \xi_1)}{\partial \xi_i} = a_{0i}(x; \xi_0, \xi_1)$$

exist and

$$a_{10}(x; \xi_0, \xi_1) = a_{01}(x; \xi_0, \xi_1), \tag{18}$$

$$\xi_i \, a_{ij}(x; \xi_0, \xi_1) \in \mathbf{CAR}^*(2) \quad (i, j = 0, 1) \tag{19}$$

hold.

Monotony and coerciveness condition: Constants $c_2 > 0$, $c_3 > 0$ [it is enough just that $-c_3 < c_2$ in the case when $V = W_0^{1,2}(0, 1)$] exist so that for all $x \in [0, 1]$, $\xi_0, \zeta_0, \xi_1, \zeta_1 \in \mathbb{R}$, we have

$$(a_1(x; \xi_0, \xi_1) - a_1(x; \zeta_0, \zeta_1))(\xi_1 - \zeta_1) + (a_0(x; \xi_0, \xi_1) - a_0(x; \zeta_0, \zeta_1))(\xi_0 - \zeta_0) \geqq$$
$$\geqq c_2|\xi_1 - \zeta_1|^2 + c_3|\xi_0 - \zeta_0|^2. \tag{20}$$

If the assumptions given above are satisfied, then, by Theorem 26.14, the boundary value problem $(A, V, L_1(0, 1))$ for the formal differential equation

$$Au = f \quad \text{on} \quad (0, 1)$$

has precisely one weak solution $u_0 \in W^{1,2}(0, 1)$ for every $f \in L_1(0, 1)$.

(iv) As an exercise, the reader could work out the generalizations of Example (iii) in the following two directions:

I. It is possible to consider boundary value problems for ordinary differential equations of higher orders [and look for the solution in the spaces $W^{k,2}(0, 1)$].

II. It is possible to consider those growth conditions and potentiality, monotony and coerciveness conditions under which we look for the weak solution of a boundary value problem in an ordinary differential equation in the space $W^{k,p}(0, 1)$, $p \neq 2$ [making use of Theorem (26.14)].

26.16. Generalization of the potentiality conditions. In Paragraph 19.5, we have shown on several examples that there exist potentials of boundary value problems without as strong conditions being valid as were applied in Paragraph 26.13 (ii), in Theorem 26.14, and in Examples 26.15 (ii), (iii). (Differential operators were concerned for which the nonlinearity depended on "one variable" only.) If we apply the results from Paragraph 19.5 in Paragraph 26.13, we obtain, e.g., assertions such as the following:

(i) Let $f \in L_1(0, 1)$, and let g be a continuous nondecreasing function on $\mathbb{R}$. Then the formal Dirichlet problem (15) has at least one weak solution $u_0 \in W_0^{1,2}(0, 1)$.

If, moreover, the function g is increasing, then precisely one weak solution of the formal boundary value problem (15) exists for arbitrary $f \in L_1(0, 1)$. [Compare the conditions of this example with the conditions imposed on the function g in Example 26.15 (ii)!]

(ii) Let $g(\xi)$ be a continuous nondecreasing function on $\mathbb{R}$, $f \in L_2(\Omega)$, and suppose that $c > 0$ exists such that

$$|g(\xi)| \leq c(1 + |\xi|^\tau)$$

holds for all $\xi \in \mathbb{R}$ $(\Omega \subset \mathbb{R}^N, N > 1, \Omega \in \mathscr{C}^{0,1})$, where τ is an arbitrary positive number for $N = 2$; for $N > 2$, we have

$$\tau = \frac{N + 2}{N - 2}.$$

Then the Dirichlet problem for the formal differential equation

$$-\Delta u(x) + g(u(x)) = f(x) \quad \text{on} \quad \Omega$$

has at least one weak solution. If g is increasing, then precisely one weak solution exists.

(iii) Let the conditions of (ii) be satisfied. Then the boundary value problem $(A, V, L_2(\Omega))$, where A is the formal differential operator defined by the relation

$$(Au)(x) = -\Delta u(x) + u(x) + g(u(x)),$$

has a weak solution for every right-hand side $f \in L_2(\Omega)$.

26.17. Existence of the classical solution of a boundary value problem. First of all, note that the regularity problem of the weak solution $u_0 \in W^{k,p}(\Omega)$ of the boundary value problem (A, V, Q) was formulated in Section 17 as the question whether the function u_0 is an element of the space $C^{k,\mu}(\Omega)$. One of the reasons why we are interested in the smoothness of "only" the k-th derivatives of the solution of a differential equation of order $2k$ lies in the fact that only derivatives of order k appear in the potential

$$F(u) = \int_\Omega b(x; \delta_k u(x) + \delta_k \varphi(x)) \, dx - <\mathbf{f}, u>_Q - <\mathbf{g}, u>_V$$

of the boundary value problem (A, V, Q). Under fairly reasonable conditions (see Paragraph 23.7), the points of the minimum of the potential F and the weak solutions of the boundary value problem (A, V, Q) coincide. In the regularity problem, we then ask whether the function $u_0 \in W^{k,p}(\Omega)$ for which the functional F assumes its minimum is smooth. As observed in Paragraph 17.9 (i), the weak solution of the boundary value problem (A, V, Q) which satisfies the condition

$$u_0 \in W^{k,p}(\Omega) \cap C^{k,\mu}(\bar{\Omega}),$$

is already the classical solution.

Thus, if to the conditions of Theorem 26.14 we add further conditions which ensure the regularity of the weak solution [e.g., if $\Omega \subset \mathbb{R}^2$ and if we add the conditions mentioned in Paragraph 17.9 (ii)], we prove the existence of that weak solution $u_0 \in$ $\in W^{k,p}(\Omega)$ of the boundary value problem (A, V, Q) which is, moreover, such that $u_0 \in C^{k,\mu}(\overline{\Omega})$. Thus, it is already the classical solution. The theorems which follow concerning the existence of the classical solution of a boundary value problem in ordinary differential equations are, in particular, immediate consequences of the assertion in Example 26.15 (ii) and of Theorem 17.5.

26.18. Theorem. *Let*

$$(Au)(x) = -\frac{d}{dx}(a_1(x; u(x), u'(x))) + a_0(x; u(x), u'(x))$$

be a formal differential operator whose coefficients $a_1(x; \xi_0, \xi_1)$, $a_0(x; \xi_0, \xi_1)$ *are continuous on* $[0, 1] \times \mathbb{R}^2$. *Assume that besides*

the growth conditions: (16), (17);
the potentiality conditions: (18), (19);
the conditions of monotony and coerciveness: (20),
the regularity conditions

$$f \in C^0([0, 1]), \quad \varphi \in C^2([0, 1]), \quad a_1 \in C^1([0, 1] \times \mathbb{R}^2) \tag{21}$$

are also satisfied.

Then there exists precisely one function $u_0 \in C^2([0, 1])$ *which is the weak solution of the boundary value problem* (A, V, Q) *and which satisfies the differential equation*

$$-\frac{d}{dx}(a_1(x; u_0(x), u_0'(x))) + a_0(x; u_0(x), u_0'(x)) = f(x)$$

and the boundary conditions $u_0(0) = \varphi(0)$, $u_0(1) = \varphi(1)$.

26.19. Theorem. *Let* $f \in C^0([0, 1])$, *and let* $g(\xi)$ *be a continuous nondecreasing function on* $\mathbb{R}$. *Then the boundary value problem*

$$\begin{cases} -u''(x) + g(u(x)) = f(x), & x \in (0, 1), \\ u(0) = u(1) = 0 \end{cases} \tag{22}$$

has at least one classical solution $u_0 \in C^2([0, 1])$.

If, moreover, the function $g(\xi)$ *is increasing on* $\mathbb{R}$, *then the boundary value problem* (22) *has precisely one classical solution for arbitrary* $f \in C^0([0, 1])$.

Proof. The existence of the weak solution is proved in Example 26.16 (i); this solution is a classical solution by (the regularity) Theorem 17.5. Assume that there exist two distinct classical solutions $u_1, u_2 \in C^2([0, 1])$ of problem (22). Then

$$-[u_1(x) - u_2(x)]'' + g(u_1(x)) - g(u_2(x)) = 0 ;$$

if we multiply this equality by the function $(u_1(x) - u_2(x))$, we obtain — integrating by parts — the relation

$$0 = \int_0^1 [u_1'(x) - u_2'(x)]^2 \, dx + \int_0^1 [g(u_1(x)) - g(u_2(x))] \, [u_1(x) - u_2(x)] \, dx > 0;$$

this is a contradiction. Thus, the considered problem (22) has precisely one classical solution.

26.20. Remark concerning the proof of Theorem 26.19. We return to the proof of the uniqueness of the classical solution of boundary value problem (22). In Example 26.16 (i), it was shown that the weak solution of the Dirichlet problem is determined uniquely if the function g is increasing.

In the definition of the weak solution of the Dirichlet problem (see Paragraph 15.2), the function φ appears which characterizes the boundary conditions (see Paragraph 15.5). To be able then to define the weak solution with the boundary condition $u(0) = u(1)$, we first have to choose the function φ. In Paragraph 15.4, it was shown that it makes no difference which function is chosen from the space $W_0^{1,2}(0, 1)$ (only the traces of this function are important). However, we do not yet know what influence this arbitrariness in the choice of the function φ has on the uniqueness of the solution. In the definition of the classical solution, the function φ does not appear at all. However, since we get at the classical solution with the aid of the regularity theorem by way of the weak solution, it could happen that this will influence the uniqueness of the classical solution. Theorem 26.19 just ensures that the classical solution will be determined uniquely. More precisely:

Let $f \in C^0([0, 1])$. The function φ can be chosen, e.g., as

$$\varphi(x) = 0 \quad \text{for} \quad x \in [0, 1],$$

and we obtain precisely one weak solution u_1 which is the classical solution of problem (22). However, the function φ can be chosen in other ways as well, e.g.,

$$\varphi(x) = x(1 - x),$$

and we again obtain precisely one weak solution u_2 of problem (22), which is again the classical solution. Moreover, Theorem 26.19 says that

$$u_1(x) = u_2(x) \quad \text{for} \quad x \in [0, 1].$$

26.21. Examples. The boundary value problems

$$\begin{cases} -u''(x) + u^3(x) = f(x), & x \in (0, 1), \\ u(0) = u(1) = 0; \end{cases} \tag{23}$$

$$\begin{cases} -u''(x) + e^{u(x)} = f(x), & x \in (0, 1), \\ u(0) = u(1) = 0 ; \end{cases} \tag{24}$$

$$\begin{cases} -u''(x) + u(x) + e^{u(x)} = f(x), & x \in (0, \pi), \\ u(0) = u(\pi) = 0 ; \end{cases} \tag{25}$$

$$\begin{cases} -u''(x) + u(x) + \operatorname{arctg} u(x) = f(x), & x \in (0, \pi), \\ u(0) = u(\pi) = 0 ; \end{cases} \tag{26}$$

$$\begin{cases} -u''(x) - \mu u^+(x) + \nu u^-(x) = f(x), & x \in (0, \pi), \\ u(0) = u(\pi) = 0 , \end{cases} \tag{27}$$

where $0 \geq \mu \geq \nu$, $u^+(x) = \max\{u(x), 0\}$, $u^-(x) = \max\{-u(x), 0\}$, have precisely one classical solution $u \in C^2([0, 1])$ [or $u \in C^2([0, \pi])$] for every $f \in C^0([0, 1])$ [or $f \in C^0([0, \pi])$, respectively].

We shall encounter these problems again in the sequel. In problems (25) to (27) we solve the Dirichlet problem on the interval $[0, \pi]$. This is not only for pedagogical reasons (for the reader to appreciate that intervals other than the interval $[0, 1]$ with which we worked in the problems investigated earlier can be considered as well) but also from the formal viewpoint: In Chapter VI, it will be better to work with the interval $[0, \pi]$ than with the interval $[0, 1]$.

26.22. Remark. Some sufficient conditions for the existence of the classical solution of the boundary value problem (22) were already investigated in Paragraph 10.7. In assertion 10.7 (ii) (by means of the linearization method) as well as in Theorem 26.19 (by means of the variational method and the theorem on the regularity of the weak solution), we found out that problem (22) has at least one (or even precisely one) classical solution for every $f \in C^0([0, 1])$. The difference in the conditions imposed on the function $g(\xi)$ in the two approaches is clear from the following table:

Linearization method	Variational method
$g(\xi)$ satisfies the Lipschitz condition on $\mathbb{R}$ with a constant $c < 1$	$g(\xi)$ is a continuous and nondecreasing (increasing) function on $\mathbb{R}$

Thus, we immediately see that none of the examples (23) to (27) can be solved by the linearization method and the application of the Banach contraction principle (see Paragraph 10.6). On the other hand, however, there also exist boundary value problems which have a solution in accordance with Paragraph 10.7 but to which it is not yet possible to apply the variational method and the regularity theorem. As an example, we mention the boundary value problem

$$\begin{cases} -u''(x) + \tfrac{1}{2}\sin u(x) = f(x), & x \in (0, 1), \\ u(0) = u(1) = 0. \end{cases} \tag{28}$$

Here, the function $g(\xi) = \tfrac{1}{2}\sin\xi$ is not nondecreasing but it satisfies, on $\mathbb{R}$, the Lipschitz condition with the constant $\tfrac{1}{2}$.

The consequences investigated so far of the abstract existence theorems for problem (22) require that the function $g(\xi)$ be nondecreasing [this because the operator T should be monotone — see Paragraph 26.13 (iv)]. Now, we try to show that the condition of the monotony of the function $g(\xi)$ is unnecessarily strong.

26.23. Monotony in the principal part. (i) Let $G(\xi)$ be a primitive (function) of the function $g(\xi)$ on $\mathbb{R}$, let $f \in L_1(0, 1)$, and put

$$F(u) = \frac{1}{2}\int_0^1 [u'(x)]^2\,\mathrm{d}x + \int_0^1 G(u(x))\,\mathrm{d}x - \int_0^1 f(x)\,u(x)\,\mathrm{d}x \tag{29}$$

for $u \in W_0^{1,2}(0, 1)$. The functional defined in this way is obviously [see Example 19.5 (i)] the potential of the boundary value problem $[A, W_0^{1,2}(0, 1), L_1(0, 1)]$ where the formal differential operator A is defined by the formula

$$(Au)(x) = -u''(x) + g(u(x)). \tag{30}$$

To be able to prove the existence of the weak solution of the mentioned boundary value problem, we will want to show that the functional F is weakly lower semi-continuous on the space $W_0^{1,2}(0, 1)$. Let, then, $\{u_n\}_{n=1}^{\infty}$ be a sequence of elements of the space $W_0^{1,2}(0, 1)$ such that

$$u_n \rightharpoonup u_0 \quad \text{in} \quad W_0^{1,2}(0, 1). \tag{31}$$

We shall prove that

$$F(u_0) \le \liminf_{n \to \infty} F(u_n). \tag{32}$$

Assertion 24.7 (iv) implies that

$$\frac{1}{2}\int_0^1 [u_0'(x)]^2\,\mathrm{d}x = \tfrac{1}{2}\|u_0\|_{1,2,0}^2 \le \tfrac{1}{2}\liminf_{n \to \infty}\|u_n\|_{1,2,0}^2 = \tfrac{1}{2}\liminf_{n \to \infty}\int_0^1 [u_n'(x)]^2\,\mathrm{d}x.$$

To prove inequality (32) it then suffices to show that

$$\int_0^1 G(u_0(x))\,\mathrm{d}x = \lim_{n \to \infty}\int_0^1 G(u_n(x))\,\mathrm{d}x. \tag{33}$$

If we prove that a sequence $\{u_n\}_{n=1}^{\infty}$ which satisfies (31) converges on the interval $[0, 1]$ uniformly to u_0, i.e., $u_n \to u_0$ in the space $C^0([0, 1])$, then the theorems on the interchange of the limit and the integral sign immediately yield equality (33). In fact, we have:

(ii) *If $u_n \rightharpoonup u_0$ in the space $W^{1,2}(0, 1)$, then $u_n \to u_0$ in the space $C^0([0, 1])$ (i.e., the sequence $\{u_n\}_{n=1}^{\infty}$ converges to the element u_0 uniformly on the interval $[0,1]$).* (For the details, see Paragraph 26.24.)

Should we manage to find some conditions which guarantee that the functional F be coercive on the space $W_0^{1,2}(0, 1)$ (and for this it is sufficient — according to part B of the proof of Theorem 26.11 — that the derivative T of the functional F be a coercive operator), then it will be possible to use Theorem 26.8 and the Euler necessary condition (see Theorem 20.3) for the proof of the existence of the weak solution of the boundary value problem $(A, W_0^{1,2}(0, 1), L_1(0, 1))$.

This procedure yields directly the following theorems on the existence of the solutions of boundary value problems in ordinary differential equations.

(iii) *Let $g(\xi)$ be a continuous function on $\mathbb{R}$ such that for all $\xi \in \mathbb{R}$ we have*

$$g(\xi)\,\xi \geq 0 . \tag{34}$$

Then at least one weak solution of the Dirichlet problem

$$-u''(x) + g(u(x)) = f(x), \quad x \in (0, 1), \tag{35}$$
$$u(0) = u(1) = 0$$

exists for every $f \in L_1(0, 1)$. If, moreover, $f \in C^0([0, 1])$, then the boundary value problem (22) has at least one classical solution.

Proof. In view of what was said in part (i), it suffices to prove that the operator T, whose value at the point $u \in W_0^{1,2}(0, 1)$ is an element $Tu \in (W_0^{1,2}(0, 1))^*$ such that for all $v \in W_0^{1,2}(0, 1)$ we have

$$<Tu, v> = \int_0^1 u'(x)\,v'(x)\,dx + \int_0^1 g(u(x))\,v(x)\,dx , \tag{36}$$

is coercive. This follows immediately from the inequality

$$\frac{<Tu, u>}{\|u\|_{1,2,0}} = \|u\|_{1,2,0} + \frac{\displaystyle\int_0^1 g(u(x))\,u(x)\,dx}{\|u\|_{1,2,0}} \geq \|u\|_{1,2,0} .$$

(iv) *Let $g(\xi)$ be a continuous and bounded function on $\mathbb{R}$. Then the Dirichlet problem for the formal differential equation (35) has at least one weak solution for every $f \in L_1(0, 1)$. If, moreover, $f \in C^0([0, 1])$, then boundary value problem (22) has at least one classical solution.* [This assertion could be used for the investigation of the existence of the solution of boundary value problem (28).]

Proof. The coerciveness of the operator T defined by relation (36) follows from the fact that

$$\frac{<Tu, u>}{\|u\|_{1,2,0}} = \|u\|_{1,2,0} + \frac{\displaystyle\int_0^1 g(u(x))\,u(x)\,dx}{\|u\|_{1,2,0}} \geqq$$

$$\geqq \|u\|_{1,2,0} - \sup_{\xi \in \mathbb{R}} |g(\xi)| \frac{\|u\|_2}{\|u\|_{1,2,0}} \geqq \|u\|_{1,2,0} - \sup_{\xi \in \mathbb{R}} |g(\xi)| .$$

[In the above computation, use was made of the inequality

$$\|u\|_2 \leqq \|u\|_{1,2,0} \tag{37}$$

which is valid for every $u \in W_0^{1,2}(0, 1)$ — see the proof of Lemma 13.7.]

(v) *Let $g(\xi)$ be a continuous function on $\mathbb{R}$ with the following property: $c \in [0, 1)$ and $d \geqq 0$ exist such that for all $\xi \in \mathbb{R}$ we have*

$$|g(\xi)| \leqq c|\xi| + d . \tag{38}$$

Then the homogeneous Dirichlet problem for the formal differential equation (35) has at least one weak solution for every $f \in L_1(0, 1)$. If, moreover, $f \in C^0([0, 1])$, then boundary value problem (22) has at least one classical solution.

[Every function $g(\xi)$ which satisfies the conditions of the linearization method satisfies conditions (38) as well. Assertion (v) is thus more general than the linearization method. Assertion (v) might also be applied to boundary value problem (27) in the case when $\mu < 1$, $v < 1$. Under these conditions, the assertion is also applicable to the homogeneous Dirichlet problem

$$\begin{cases} -u''(x) - \mu\, u^+(x) + v\, u^-(x) + h(u(x)) = f(x) , & x \in (0, \pi) , \\ u(0) = u(\pi) = 0 , \end{cases}$$

where $h(\xi)$ is a continuous and bounded function on $\mathbb{R}$.]

Proof. The coerciveness of the operator T defined by relation (36) follows from the fact that

$$\frac{<Tu, u>}{\|u\|_{1,2,0}} = \|u\|_{1,2,0} + \frac{\displaystyle\int_0^1 g(u(x))\,u(x)\,dx}{\|u\|_{1,2,0}} \geqq \|u\|_{1,2,0} - \frac{\displaystyle\int_0^1 |g(u(x))|\,|u(x)|\,dx}{\|u\|_{1,2,0}} \geqq$$

$$\geqq \|u\|_{1,2,0} - c\frac{\|u\|_2^2}{\|u\|_{1,2,0}} - d\frac{\|u\|_2}{\|u\|_{1,2,0}} \geqq (1 - c)\,\|u\|_{1,2,0} - d ,$$

where relation (37) was again applied in the last inequality.

(vi) The preceding assertions generalize the result presented in Theorem 26.19 as well as the result of Paragraph 10.17 (ii). The operator T was not monotone; indeed, the following condition was not satisfied [see condition (11)]: For all $\xi_1, \zeta_1, \xi_0, \zeta_0 \in \mathbb{R}$, we have

$$(\xi_1 - \zeta_1)^2 + (g(\xi_0) - g(\zeta_0))(\xi_0 - \zeta_0) \geqq 0.$$

However, it satisfies a certain weaker condition which is called monotony in the principal part. To be more precise: The formal differential operator

$$(Au)(x) = \sum_{|\alpha| \leqq k} (-1)^{|\alpha|}\, a_\alpha(x;\, \delta_{k-1}\, u(x),\, \hat{\delta}_k\, u(x)), \quad x \in \Omega,$$

is said to be *monotone in the principal part* if for all $\zeta \in \mathbb{R}^{\varkappa(N, k-1)}$, $\xi, \hat{\xi} \in \mathbb{R}^m$, where $m = \varkappa(N, k) - \varkappa(N, k-1)$ (for the notation, see Paragraph 7.2), and for almost all $x \in \Omega$ we have

$$\sum_{|\alpha|=k} (a_\alpha(x;\, \zeta,\, \xi) - a_\alpha(x;\, \zeta,\, \hat{\xi}))(\xi_\alpha - \hat{\xi}_\alpha) \geqq 0. \tag{39}$$

In assertions (i)–(v), the formal differential operator

$$(Au)(x) = -u''(x) + g(u(x))$$

is monotone in the principal part since condition (39) is of the form

$$(\xi_1 - \hat{\xi}_1)^2 \geqq 0.$$

The results given in (iii)–(v) could also be generalized to boundary value problems in ordinary and partial differential equations of higher orders. We leave the detailed analysis by the variational method to the reader as an exercise; in Chapter V, we return to these considerations and analyse — using the so-called topological method — the case of partial differential equations as well. If, however, the reader wishes to apply the variational method to partial differential operators which are monotone only in their principal part, then he will need an assertion similar to implication (ii) for the Sobolev spaces $W^{k,p}(\Omega)$. Since such assertions are going to be used, we discuss them in the following paragraph.

26.24. Compact imbedding theorem. Previously (e.g., in the footnote on p. 78), we introduced the symbol for the imbedding

$$X \subsetneqq Y$$

for Banach spaces X, Y such that $X \subset Y$ and the identity mapping is a continuous operator from the space X to the space Y (i.e., a constant $c > 0$ exists such that for all $u \in X$ we have

$$\|u\|_Y \leqq c\|u\|_X).$$

(i) We say that the Banach space X is *compactly imbedded* into the space Y if

(a) $X \subset Y$;

(b) any sequence $\{u_n\}_{n=1}^{\infty}$ of elements of the Banach space X which converges *weakly* in the space X to $u_0 \in X$ (i.e., $u_n \rightharpoonup u_0$ in X) converges *strongly* in the space Y to u_0 (i.e., $u_n \to u_0$ in Y).

The fact that the space X is compactly imbedded into the space Y is denoted by the symbol

$$X \subset\subset Y.$$

(ii) It is easily checked that if the space X is compactly imbedded into the space Y (i.e., $X \subset\subset Y$), then the space X is continuously imbedded into Y (i.e., $X \subset Y$).

Furthermore, it is possible to prove easily that if X is a reflexive Banach space and Y an arbitrary Banach space, then the relation $X \subset\subset Y$ is equivalent to the following pair of conditions:

(a) $X \subset Y$;

(b′) an arbitrary *bounded* subset of the space X is contained in a *compact* subset of the space Y. (This is the origin of the term "compact imbedding".)

(iii) The assertion presented in Paragraph 26.23 (ii) can then be written simply as

$$W^{1,2}(0, 1) \subset\subset C^0([0, 1]).$$

In general, we can formulate the following so-called compact imbedding theorem for Sobolev spaces:

(iv) Let $\Omega \subset \mathbb{R}^N$, $\Omega \in \mathscr{C}^{0,1}$. Let $p > 1$, $k \in \mathbb{N}$. Then the following is true:

I. $$W^{k,p}(\Omega) \subset\subset L_r(\Omega)$$

if

$$N > 1, \quad kp < N, \quad and \quad \frac{1}{r} > \frac{1}{p} - \frac{k}{N};$$

II. $$W^{k,p}(\Omega) \subset\subset L_r(\Omega)$$

if

$$N > 1, \quad kp = N, \quad and \quad r > 1 \quad is \ arbitrary;$$

III. $$W^{k,p}(\Omega) \subset\subset C^0(\bar{\Omega})$$

if

$$N \geqq 1, \quad kp > N.$$

The proof of this assertion can be found, e.g., in [54] and in [68].

218

(v) *For* $\Omega \in \mathscr{C}^{0,1}$ *and* $k \geq 2$,

$$W^{k,p}(\Omega) \subsetneqq\subsetneqq W^{k-1,p}(\Omega)$$

also holds.

Using this assertion together with the results given in (iv), the reader may find — as an exercise — the relations that must exist between the parameters k, p, l, r, N for the imbeddings

$$W^{k,p}(\Omega) \subsetneqq\subsetneqq W^{l,r}(\Omega),$$
$$W^{k,p}(\Omega) \subsetneqq\subsetneqq C^{l}(\bar{\Omega})$$

to hold.

For example, we have

$$W^{k,p}(0,1) \subsetneqq\subsetneqq C^{k-1}([0,1]).$$

SECTION 27. MINIMAL SURFACES

27.1. In Section 26, the theorem on the existence of the minimum of a functional was used to prove theorems which under certain conditions ensure the existence of a weak solution of a boundary value problem in a nonlinear differential equation. The existence of the minimum of a functional was thus merely an auxiliary tool and in Chapter V we shall actually see that other methods also exist by means of which it is possible to prove that a boundary value problem has a weak solution.

However, a considerable number of physical and geometrical problems are not formulated in the "language of differential equations" but directly as problems of finding the minimum of a certain functional. For instance, the minimal surface problem is a classical problem of the calculus of variations of this type. In this section, we discuss this problem briefly.

Let the domain Ω be a bounded subset of the space $\mathbb{R}^N$, and let the function φ be defined on $\partial\Omega$. Put

$$\mathscr{F}(\xi) = (1 + |\xi|^2)^{1/2} \quad \text{for} \quad \xi \in \mathbb{R}^N \tag{1}$$

and define the functional F by the formula

$$F(u) = \int_\Omega \mathscr{F}(\text{grad } u(x)) \, dx. \tag{2}$$

The problem is to find a function u_0 defined on $\bar{\Omega}$ for which the functional F attains its minimal value among a certain class of functions u such that

$$u|_{\partial\Omega} = \varphi. \tag{3}$$

For $N = 2$ and $u \in C^1(\bar{\Omega})$, $F(u)$ stands for the area of the surface of the graph of the function u. We are thus looking for that surface which has the least area among a certain class of surfaces which satisfy the given boundary condition (3) on $\partial\Omega$. For this reason, the problem is called the *minimal surface problem* and the functional $F(u)$ the *functional of the surface.*

The interested reader who would like to devote more time to this problem is referred to [37] (where the proofs of the assertions given below are carried out), and in particular to the monograph by J. C. C. Nitsche [75], where examples of various minimal surfaces are given, among other things.

27.2. In what kind of space should one look for the solution? (i) First, we consider whether or not it is possible to apply to the solution of the minimal surface problem the results derived in the foregoing sections (in particular, in Sections 18 through 25).

The function $\mathcal{F}(\xi)$ given by relation (1) is continuous on $\mathbb{R}^N$ and even has continuous partial derivatives of all orders. Furthermore, for all $\xi \in \mathbb{R}^N$, we have

$$|\mathcal{F}(\xi)| \leq 1 + |\xi| \tag{4}$$

and (as can be easily derived) for every $p \geq 1$ and for every $\xi \in \mathbb{R}^N$ we also have

$$|\mathcal{F}(\xi)| \leq 2 + |\xi|^p. \tag{5}$$

Thus, the growth conditions are satisfied and the functional of the surface is defined on every space $W^{1,p}(\Omega)$, $p > 1$ (this is a special case of the functionals which were investigated in Example 18.4), and also on the space $W^{1,1}(\Omega)$ (see Section 16).

Since the function $\mathcal{F}(\xi)$ is convex on the space $\mathbb{R}^N$ (because — as the reader may easily verify — we have

$$\sum_{i,j=1}^N \frac{\partial^2 \mathcal{F}(\xi)}{\partial \xi_i \, \partial \xi_j} \zeta_i \zeta_j \geq 0$$

for all ξ, $\zeta \in \mathbb{R}^N$), the functional F is also convex on the space $W^{1,p}(\Omega)$, $p > 1$, as well as on the space $W^{1,1}(\Omega)$.

For it to be possible to apply Theorem 26.8, it is necessary that $p > 1$ [i.e., that the space $W^{1,p}(\Omega)$ be reflexive]. A further important condition in Theorem 26.8 is that the functional F_0 defined by the relation

$$F_0(v) = F(v + \varphi) = \int_\Omega [1 + |\text{grad } v(x) + \text{grad } \varphi(x)|^2]^{1/2} \, dx$$

[we assume that the function φ is extended from $\partial\Omega$ to $\bar\Omega$ so that it is an element of the space $W^{1,p}(\Omega)$] be coercive on the space $W_0^{1,p}(\Omega)$. First of all, it can esily be shown that for every $v \in W_0^{1,p}(\Omega)$ $(p \geq 1)$ we have

$$F_0(v) \leq \text{meas } \Omega + \|v\|_{1,1,0} + \|\varphi\|_{1,1}.$$

If we choose $p > 1$, the above inequality implies that the functional F_0 is not coercive: Indeed, it is possible to construct a sequence $\{u_n\}_{n=1}^\infty$ of elements of the space $W_0^{1,p}(\Omega)$

such that

$$\lim_{n \to \infty} \|u_n\|_{1,p,0} = \infty$$

while

$$\sup_{n \in \mathbb{N}} \|u_n\|_{1,1,0} = c < \infty,$$

so that

$$F_0(u_n) \leqq \text{meas } \Omega + c + \|\varphi\|_{1,1}.$$

If we choose $p = 1$, the functional F_0 is coercive on $W_0^{1,1}(\Omega)$ since the inequality

$$F_0(v) \geqq \|v\|_{1,1,0} - \|\varphi\|_{1,1}$$

implies that

$$\lim_{\|v\|_{1,1,0} \to \infty} F_0(v) = +\infty.$$

However, *the space* $W_0^{1,1}(\Omega)$ *is not reflexive* [see Paragraph 25.7 (vii)].

From the above, we see the type of difficulties which arise when solving the minimal surface problem. The methods of Sections 18 through 25 are not suitable. Therefore, we have to proceed in a slightly different manner: We will look directly for the minimum of the functional of the surface in the largest of the Sobolev spaces under consideration, i.e., in the space $W^{1,1}(\Omega)$. Evidently, equality (3) will be understood in the sense of the traces (see Paragraphs 13.8 through 13.10).

(ii) **Definition.** We say that the function $u_0 \in W^{1,1}(\Omega)$ is a *weak solution of the minimal surface problem* if the functional F [see (2)] attains its minimal value on the set

$$\{u \in W^{1,1}(\Omega); \ u = \varphi \text{ on } \partial\Omega \text{ in the sence of traces}\}$$

precisely for the function u_0.

Just as in Example 18.4 and by applying the results given in (i), it is possible to prove the following:

(iii) **Lemma.** *The functional of a surface is continuous and convex on the space* $W^{1,1}(\Omega)$.

27.3. The classical solution. (i) Let $\varphi \in C(\partial\Omega)$. We say that the function

$$u_0 \in C^2(\Omega) \cap C^0(\bar{\Omega})$$

is the *classical solution of the minimal surface problem*, if it satisfies the differential equation

$$\sum_{i=1}^{N} \frac{\partial}{\partial x_i} \left(\frac{\dfrac{\partial u(x)}{\partial x_i}}{(1 + |\text{grad } u(x)|^2)^{1/2}} \right) = 0 \quad \text{on} \quad \Omega \tag{6}$$

and the condition

$$u = \varphi \quad \text{on} \quad \partial\Omega$$

(see Paragraphs 4.4 and 6.6).

(ii) **Remark.** Equation (6) is called the *Euler equation of the functional of a sur-face*. It has the following meaning: If the functional F attains its minimum on the set

$$\{v \in C^2(\bar{\Omega}); \; v|_{\partial\Omega} = \varphi\},$$

at the point u_0, then functional

$$F_0(v) = F(v + u_0) \tag{7}$$

attains its minimum on the Banach space

$$X = \{v \in C^2(\bar{\Omega}); \; v|_{\partial\Omega} = 0\}$$

[with the norm of the space $C^2(\bar{\Omega})$] at the point Θ. We easily establish that the func-tional F_0 has a derivative in any direction $v \in X$, that

$$0 = dF_0(\Theta; v) = \int_\Omega \sum_{i=1}^N \frac{\dfrac{\partial u_0(x)}{\partial x_i} \dfrac{\partial v(x)}{\partial x_i}}{(1 + |\operatorname{grad} u_0(x)|^2)^{1/2}} \, dx$$

holds (see Theorem 20.3), and that by Green's theorem (see Paragraph 11.1) we have

$$\int_\Omega v(x) \left[\sum_{i=1}^N \frac{\partial}{\partial x_i} \left(\frac{\dfrac{\partial u_0(x)}{\partial x_i}}{(1 + |\operatorname{grad} u_0(x)|^2)^{1/2}} \right) \right] dx = 0.$$

This last equality is valid not only for all $v \in X$ but also for arbitrary $v \in C(\bar{\Omega})$; if we put

$$v(x) = \sum_{i=1}^N \frac{\partial}{\partial x_i} \left(\frac{\dfrac{\partial u_0(x)}{\partial x_i}}{(1 + |\operatorname{grad} u_0(x)|^2)^{1/2}} \right),$$

we obtain

$$\int_\Omega \left[\sum_{i=1}^N \frac{\partial}{\partial x_i} \left(\frac{\dfrac{\partial u_0(x)}{\partial x_i}}{(1 + |\operatorname{grad} u_0(x)|^2)^{1/2}} \right) \right]^2 dx = 0,$$

implying that the function u_0 satisfies the differential equation (6) on the set Ω.

Conversely, the following also holds: If the function $u_0 \in C^2(\overline{\Omega})$ satisfies equation (6) on the set Ω, then Θ is the critical point of the functional F_0. Since the functional F_0 is convex on the space X, Θ is the point at which the functional F_0 attains its minimum on the space X (see Theorem 23.6).

27.4. The relation between the classical and the weak solutions of the minimal surface problem. (i) Let $u_0 \in C^2(\Omega) \cap C^0(\overline{\Omega})$ be the classical solution of the minimal surface problem. Even though the set $C^2(\Omega) \cap C^0(\overline{\Omega})$ is not a subset of the space $W^{1,1}(\Omega)$ it is possible to prove that

$$u_0 \in W^{1,1}(\Omega)$$

(for the proof, see [37]).

(ii) *Every weak solution $u_0 \in W^{1,1}(\Omega)$ of the minimal surface problem for which $u_0 \in C^2(\Omega) \cap C^0(\overline{\Omega})$ is the classical solution as well.*

Proof. We proceed in a manner entirely analogous to that of Paragraph 27.3 (ii). If the function $u_0 \in W^{1,1}(\Omega)$ is the weak solution of the minimal surface problem, then the functional F_0 defined on $W_0^{1,1}(\Omega)$ by relation (7) attains its minimum at Θ; by Theorem 20.3, we then have

$$0 = dF_0(\Theta; v) = \int_\Omega \sum_{i=1}^{N} \frac{\dfrac{\partial u_0(x)}{\partial x_i} \dfrac{\partial v(x)}{\partial x_i}}{(1 + |\text{grad } u_0(x)|^2)^{1/2}} \, dx \, .$$

The proof is concluded along the same lines as in Paragraph 27.3 (ii), under the assumption that

$$u_0 \in C^2(\Omega) \cap C^0(\overline{\Omega}) \, .$$

27.5. In Paragraph 17.6, we mentioned the nineteenth Hilbert problem. As the twentieth problem, David Hilbert framed the question whether all "regular functionals on a certain class of functions with reasonable boundary conditions" attain their minima. He was convinced that it should be possible to accomplish the proof of the existence of the minimizing element at the possible expense of having to propose some generalizations (e.g., of the concept of the derivative, etc.). This hypothesis turned out to be false, to some extent: the functional of a surface, which is "regular" in the Hilbert sense, serves as a counterexample.

Simple examples showing that the minimal surface problem has no solution on a nonconvex domain are based on the Bernstein method (of 1912).

27.6. The nonexistence of the solution of a problem. (i) *Let $R_1 > R_0 > 0, 0 < \psi_0 < \psi_1 < 2\pi$, and put*

$$\Omega = \{(x, y) \in \mathbb{R}^2; \ x = \varrho \cos \psi, \ y = \varrho \sin \psi, \ R_0 < \varrho < R_1, \psi_0 < \psi < \psi_1\} \, .$$

Put

$$K(R_0) = \{(x, y) \in \mathbb{R}^2; \ x = R_0 \cos \psi, \ y = R_0 \sin \psi, \ \psi \in (\psi_0, \psi_1)\}$$

and choose the function φ so that

$$\varphi(x, y) = - R_0 \arccos \frac{(x^2 + y^2)^{1/2}}{R_0}, \quad (x, y) \in \partial\Omega - K(R_0),$$

and

$$\max_{(x,y) \in K(R_0)} \varphi(x, y) > 0.$$

*Then the minimal surface problem for the domain Ω and for the boundary con-
dition φ does not possess a classical solution.*

(ii) A more general assertion can be proved (see [20]): For every plane domain Ω which is not convex, it is possible to construct a continuous boundary condition φ such that the corresponding minimal surface problem does not possess a classical solution.

(iii) It can be proved that for the domain Ω and the boundary condition φ from (i) not even the weak solution of the minimal surface problem exists.

In concluding this section, we also present one positive result concerning the solution of the minimal surface problem. In view of the preceding paragraph, it will come as no surprise that the set Ω is convex. However, we also assume a specific form for the boundary condition φ.

27.7. The bounded slope condition. Let $\Omega \subset \mathbb{R}^N$, let $K \geq 0$, and let function φ be defined on $\partial\Omega$. We say that φ satisfies the *bounded slope condition* with the constant K if, for every $z \in \partial\Omega$, there exist two functions

$$\Pi_z^+(x_1, \ldots, x_N) = a_1^+ x_1 + \ldots + a_N^+ x_N + d^+,$$
$$\Pi_z^-(x_1, \ldots, x_N) = a_1^- x_1 + \ldots + a_N^- x_N + d^-$$

$(a_i^+, a_i^-, d^+, d^- \in \mathbb{R})$ such that

(a) $\Pi_z^+(z) = \varphi(z) = \Pi_z^-(z)$;

(b) $\sup\limits_{z \in \partial\Omega} |\text{grad } \Pi_z^+(x)| \leq K$,

$\sup\limits_{z \in \partial\Omega} |\text{grad } \Pi_z^-(x)| \leq K$;

(c) $\Pi_z^-(x) \leq \varphi(x) \leq \Pi_z^+(x)$ for all $x \in \partial\Omega$.

27.8. Remarks. (i) It is easy to prove that every function which satisfies the bounded slope condition with the constant K also satisfies the Lipschitz condition with the same constant K on $\partial\Omega$.

(ii) It is not true, in general, that a function φ which satisfies the Lipschitz condition on the boundary $\partial\Omega$ of a convex set Ω satisfies the bounded slope condition as well. Functions of this type are studied in great detail in [41], [42] where it is also proved that the bounded slope condition describes a certain "smoothness" of the function φ. Along the boundaries of "nice" convex sets (e.g., circles, spheres) the function φ satisfies the bounded slope condition "if and only if it is the restriction to $\partial\Omega$ of some function which has, on Ω, first derivatives which satisfy the Lipschitz condition on Ω". (The assertion in the quotation marks is not quite accurate; a precise formulation would require the introduction of several new concepts. For more details, see [41].)

(iii) It is possible to prove that if the function φ is not a restriction (to $\partial\Omega$) of some linear function and if it satisfies the bounded slope condition with some constant K, then the set Ω is convex.

The promised positive result concerning the existence of the solution of the minimal surface problem is included in the following theorem which was proved by G. Stampacchia and P. Hartman in [43].

27.9. Theorem. *Let $\Omega \subset \mathbb{R}^N$ be a convex domain, $\Omega \in \mathscr{C}^{0,1}$. Let the function φ be defined on $\partial\Omega$, and let it satisfy the bounded slope condition there with a constant $K \geq 0$.*
Then there exists precisely one $u_0 \in W^{1,1}(\Omega)$ such that

$$F(u_0) = \inf_{u \in M} F(u),$$

where F is the functional of the surface and

$$M = \{u \in W^{1,1}(\Omega);\ u = \varphi \text{ on } \partial\Omega \text{ in the sense of traces}\}.$$

Moreover,

(a) *the function u_0 satisfies the Lipschitz condition on $\overline{\Omega}$ with the constant K;*

(b) *the function u_0 is not only the weak solution of the minimal surface problem but also its classical solution and even*

$$u_0 \in C^{\infty}(\Omega).$$

27.10. Remarks. (i) The assertion of Theorem 27.9 holds not only for the functional of a surface but also for all functionals of the type

$$\int_{\Omega} \mathscr{F}(\operatorname{grad} u(x))\, \mathrm{d}x,$$

where $\mathscr{F} \in C^{\infty}(\mathbb{R}^N)$ is a strictly convex function with the following property:

Positive constants c_1, c_2, c_3 exist such that

$$c_1|\xi| - c_2 \leqq \mathscr{F}(\xi) \leqq c_3(1 + |\xi|)$$

holds for arbitrary $\xi \in \mathbb{R}^N$.

(ii) In the paper $[49]$, *ultraweak* solutions of the minimal surface problem are defined and it is proved that for a large class of sets (even domains which are not convex are included) and for all boundary conditions from the space $L_1(\partial\Omega)$ ultraweak solutions of the minimal surface problem exist. (Spaces in which we look for ultraweak solutions are constructed in $[87]$.)

SECTION 28. EXCURSION ON NUMERICAL METHODS

28.1. Let X be a Banach space and F a functional defined on X. By a variational problem we understand, in this section, the problem of finding an element $u_0 \in X$ such that

$$F(u_0) = \inf_{u \in X} F(u) . \tag{$\mathscr{P}_0$}$$

The element u_0 is called the *solution of the variational problem* $(\mathscr{P}_0)$. In Section 26, we got to appreciate the significance of the problem $(\mathscr{P}_0)$ for the solvability of boundary value problems and we formulated several important assertions (see Paragraph 26.8) concerning the question of when problem $(\mathscr{P}_0)$ has at least one or precisely one solution. We now discuss the numerical solution of problem $(\mathscr{P}_0)$. Within the scope of this book, it is not possible to discuss in detail all the numerical methods for the solution of problem $(\mathscr{P}_0)$; this section is to be understood therefore as an excursion on variational numerical methods. The reader may find a detailed analysis and further numerical methods in the literature which is recommended in the course of the exposition.

We shall discuss one of the most frequently used methods — the *Ritz method*, which yields directly an algorithm that can be realized on computers. Its principal idea is simple: Instead of looking for the minimum of the functional F on the entire space X, we look for its minimum on suitable subspaces of the space X in which we know how to solve the variational problem. We now formulate this idea precisely:

To every $n \in \mathbb{N}$, let a closed subspace X_n of the space X be assigned. The problem of finding an element $u_n \in X_n$ so that

$$F(u_n) = \inf_{u \in X_n} F(u_n) , \tag{$\mathscr{P}_n$}$$

holds is called the *Ritz approximation of problem* $(\mathscr{P}_0)$ and the element $u_n \in X_n$ is called the solution of problem $(\mathscr{P}_n)$.

From both the practical and theoretical points-of-view, the basic problems immediately present themselves:

(a) the problem of the existence and uniqueness of the solution of the problem $(\mathscr{P}_n)$,
(b) the relation between the solutions of the problems $(\mathscr{P}_0)$ and $(\mathscr{P}_n)$.

Problem (a) has already been solved in Theorem 26.8: If X is a reflexive Banach space, then its closed subspace X_n is a reflexive Banach space as well [see Paragraph 25.7 (i)] and Theorem 26.8 (alternative I) immediately yields the following assertion:

28.2. Theorem. *Let X be a reflexive Banach space, and let the functional F defined on the space X satisfy the following conditions:*

(a) *F is continuous and strictly convex on X;*
(b) *F is coercive on X, i.e.,*

$$\lim_{\|u\|_X \to \infty} F(u) = +\infty .$$

Then each of the problems $(\mathscr{P}_0)$ and $(\mathscr{P}_n)$ has precisely one solution u_0 and u_n, respectively.

28.3. We now treat problem (b) of Paragraph 28.1. We investigate under what conditions is

$$\lim_{n \to \infty} \|u_0 - u_n\|_X = 0 \tag{1}$$

true. If (1) is valid, then we say that the Ritz method converges for problem $(\mathscr{P}_0)$ and the system of subspaces X_n and that the solutions u_n of problems $(\mathscr{P}_n)$ approximate the solution of problem $(\mathscr{P}_0)$ in the sense of the norm of the space X. We introduce yet another concept:

28.4. Definition. We say that the elements $v_n \in X_n$, $n \in \mathbb{N}$, constitute a *minimizing sequence* for the functional F if

$$\lim_{n \to \infty} F(v_n) = \inf_{u \in X} F(u) \; \dagger) . \tag{2}$$

28.5. Theorem. *Let the assumptions of Theorem 28.2 be satisfied. Moreover, suppose that for every $v \in X$ there exist elements $v_n \in X_n$, $n \in \mathbb{N}$, such that*

$$\lim_{n \to \infty} \|v - v_n\|_X = 0 . \tag{3}$$

Then the elements $u_n \in X_n$, $n \in \mathbb{N}$ [satisfying $(\mathscr{P}_n)$], whose existence is ensured by Theorem 28.2, constitute a minimizing sequence for the functional F.

Proof. For the solution u_0 of the problem $(\mathscr{P}_0)$ there exist, by condition (3), elements $v_n \in X_n$ such that

$$\lim_{n \to \infty} \|u_0 - v_n\|_X = 0 .$$

---

†) Compare with the definition of a minimizing sequence given on p. 194.

Since the functional F is continuous on the space X, we have

$$\lim_{n \to \infty} F(v_n) = F(u_0) . \tag{4}$$

Furthermore, the inequalities

$$F(u_0) \leq F(u_n) \leq F(v_n) \tag{5}$$

are satisfied since

$$F(u_0) = \inf_{u \in X} F(u) \leq F(u_n) = \inf_{v \in X_n} F(v) \leq F(v_n) .$$

Passing to the limit as $n \to \infty$ in the inequalities (5), and applying relation (4), we immediately obtain the assertion of the theorem.

28.6. Remark. Condition (3) of Theorem 28.5 makes sense intuitively and defines the relation between the spaces X and X_n. The fact that an arbitrary element $v \in X$ can be approximated to any degree of accuracy by an element $v_n \in X_n$ means that the subspaces X_n almost completely "exhaust" the space X. To be precise: The union

$$\bigcup_{n=1}^{\infty} X_n$$

constitutes a dense subset of the space X.

We now state and prove an important assertion on the convergence of the Ritz method for the problem $(\mathscr{P}_0)$.

28.7. Theorem. *Let X be a Hilbert space, and let F be a continuous functional on the space X which has a second derivative $d^2 F(u; v, v)$ in every direction $(v, v) \in$ $\in X \times X$. Assume, further, that a constant $c > 0$ exists such that for all $u, v \in X$ we have*

$$d^2 F(u; v, v) \geq c\|v\|_X^2 . \tag{6}$$

Let the subspaces X_n of the space X satisfy condition (3) of Theorem 28.5. Then:

(a) *there exists precisely one solution $u_0 \in X$ of problem $(\mathscr{P}_0)$;*
(b) *for every $n \in \mathbb{N}$, there exists precisely one solution $u_n \in X_n$ of problem $(\mathscr{P}_n)$;*
(c) *the Ritz method converges for problem $(\mathscr{P}_0)$, i.e.,*

$$\lim_{n \to \infty} \|u_0 - u_n\|_X = 0 . \tag{1}$$

[For the sake of simplicity, we assume in the theorem that X is a Hilbert space — see the footnote on p. 181. The reason for this lies mainly in the fact that condition (6) is used which is only typical of Hilbert spaces. We will not deal with its generalization and thus with the generalization of Theorem 28.7 to the case of Banach spaces†).]

---

†) Note, however, that these generalizations are carried out in the literature quoted below.

Proof. If we remember that a Hilbert space is a reflexive Banach space [see Paragraph 27.7 (ii)] and that condition (6) ensures that the functional F is strictly convex and coercive on the space X [computations analogous to the computations in (26.3) and (26.4) are involved], then we see immediately that assertions (a) and (b) are included in Theorem 28.2. It remains to prove assertion (c).

Let a fixed non-negative integer n be chosen, and define a real function f on $\mathbb{R}$ by the rule

$$f(t) = F(u_0 + t(u_n - u_0)).$$

From the Taylor formula it follows that

$$f(1) = f(0) + f'(0) + \tfrac{1}{2}f''(\vartheta),$$

where $0 < \vartheta < 1$, i.e.,

$$F(u_n) = F(u_0) + dF(u_0; u_n - u_0) +$$
$$+ \tfrac{1}{2}d^2F(u_0 + \vartheta(u_n - u_0); u_n - u_0, u_n - u_0). \tag{7}$$

Since the functional F has its minimum at the point $u_0 \in X$, we have

$$dF(u_0; u_n - u_0) = 0$$

by Theorem 20.3. From this and from condition (6), relation (7) yields the inequality

$$F(u_n) \geqq F(u_0) + \frac{c}{2}\|u_n - u_0\|_X^2 \tag{8}$$

which holds for arbitrary $n \in \mathbb{N}$. However, by Theorem 28.5, the elements u_n, $n \in \mathbb{N}$, constitute a minimizing sequence for the functional F, i.e.,

$$\lim_{n \to \infty} F(u_n) = \inf_{u \in X} F(u) = F(u_0).$$

Thus, passing to the limit as $n \to \infty$ in inequality (8), one obtains the desired assertion.

28.8. The solution of problem $(\mathscr{P}_n)$. The most frequent and most important case arises in practice when the spaces X_n are of finite dimension $N(n)$ †). In this case then, elements $e_1^n, \ldots, e_{N(n)}^n$ from X_n exist such that an arbitrary element $v \in X_n$ can be uniquely written in the form

$$v = c_1 e_1^n + \ldots + c_{N(n)} e_{N(n)}^n,$$

---

†) Recall that the space X is a space of finite dimension k if there exist elements $e_1, \ldots, e_k$ such that an arbitrary element $u \in X$ can be written uniquely in the form

$$u = c_1 e_1 + \ldots + c_k e_k,$$

where $c_1, \ldots, c_k$ are real numbers. For more details, see [51]. (Cf. the footnote on p. 191.)

where

$$c = (c_1, \ldots, c_{N(n)}) \in \mathbb{R}^{N(n)}.$$

Now define a real function $\mathscr{F}_n$ on the space $\mathbb{R}^{N(n)}$ by the rule

$$\mathscr{F}_n(c_1, \ldots, c_{N(n)}) = F\left(\sum_{i=1}^{N(n)} c_i e_i^n\right).$$

To find the solution u_n of problem $(\mathscr{P}_n)$ then means finding the element

$$c^n = (c_1^n, \ldots, c_{N(n)}^n) \in \mathbb{R}^{N(n)}$$

such that

$$\mathscr{F}_n(c^n) = \inf_{c \in \mathbb{R}^{N(n)}} \mathscr{F}_n(c). \qquad (\mathscr{P}_n^*)$$

If we succeed in finding a solution $c^n \in \mathbb{R}^{N(n)}$ of problem $(\mathscr{P}_n^*)$, then the element

$$u_n = c_1^n e_1^n + \ldots + c_{N(n)}^n e_{N(n)}^n$$

will be a solution of problem $(\mathscr{P}_n)$.

If the assumptions of Theorem 28.7 are satisfied, then the function $\mathscr{F}_n$ is strictly convex on the space $\mathbb{R}^{N(n)}$, and thus, by Theorem 23.6 and Theorem 20.3, the vector

$$c^n = (c_1^n, \ldots, c_{N(n)}^n) \in \mathbb{R}^{N(n)}$$

is the solution of problem $(\mathscr{P}_n^*)$ if and only if all the partial derivatives of the first order of the function $\mathscr{F}_n$ vanish at c^n. Thus, the problem of finding the solution of problem $(\mathscr{P}_n^*)$ is equivalent to the problem of finding the solution of the system

$$\frac{\partial \mathscr{F}_n(c_1, \ldots, c_{N(n)})}{\partial c_1} = 0,$$

$$\frac{\partial \mathscr{F}_n(c_1, \ldots, c_{N(n)})}{\partial c_2} = 0,$$

$$\cdots\cdots\cdots\cdots\cdots \qquad (\mathscr{S})$$

$$\frac{\partial \mathscr{F}_n(c_1, \ldots, c_{N(n)})}{\partial c_{N(n)}} = 0.$$

The system $(\mathscr{S})$ is a system of $N(n)$ algebraic (generally nonlinear) equations. [Note that if, moreover, the functional F is quadratic (see Paragraphs 20.6 and 20.7), then the system $(\mathscr{S})$ is a system of linear algebraic equations.]

28.9. The Ritz method. From the practical point-of-view, it is important that the system $(\mathscr{S})$ be as simple as possible. The form of the system $(\mathscr{S})$ depends on the actual choice of the subspaces X_n. A suitable choice of these subspaces will be demonstrated on examples. However, we first carry out one simplification. We say that the sequence $\{e_i\}_{i=1}^{\infty}$ of elements of a Hilbert space X constitutes a basis of this space if

(a) for every $n \in \mathbb{N}$, the set $e_1, \ldots, e_n$ is linearly independent†);
(b) for every $u \in X$ and every $\varepsilon > 0$ a non-negative integer n and real numbers $c_1, \ldots, c_n$ exist such that

$$\|u - (c_1 e_1 + \ldots + c_n e_n)\|_X < \varepsilon \, .$$

Let then $\{e_i\}_{i=1}^{\infty}$ be a basis of the Hilbert space X, and define, for every $n \in \mathbb{N}$, the subspace X_n as the set of all the elements $u \in X$ which are of the form

$$u = c_1 e_1 + \ldots + c_n e_n$$

(where $c_1, \ldots, c_n$ are real numbers). We easily check that the subspaces X_n, $n \in \mathbb{N}$, satisfy condition (3) of Theorem 28.5 and that

$$X_m \subset X_n$$

holds for $n > m$.

28.10. Example. Let

$$X = W_0^{1,2}(0, 1) \, \dagger\dagger) \, .$$

Let $f \in L_1(0, 1)$; for $u \in W_0^{1,2}(0, 1)$, put

$$F(u) = \frac{1}{2} \int_0^1 |u'(x)|^2 \, dx + \frac{1}{4} \int_0^1 u^4(x) \, dx - \int_0^1 f(x) \, u(x) \, dx \, . \tag{9}$$

From the results given in Paragraphs 19.4 and 19.5, it follows that the functional F is the potential of the Dirichlet problem

$$\begin{cases} -u''(x) + u^3(x) = f(x) \, , & x \in (0, 1) \\ u(0) = u(1) = 0 \, . \end{cases} \tag{10}$$

---

†) We say that the elements $e_1, \ldots, e_n \in X$ constitute a linearly independent set if for any real numbers $c_1, \ldots, c_n$ such that

$$c_1 e_1 + \ldots + c_n e_n = 0$$

it must hold that

$$c_1 = c_2 = \ldots = c_n = 0 \, .$$

††) Recall that the space $W_0^{1,2}(0, 1)$ is a Hilbert space with the inner product

$$\langle u, v \rangle_{1,2,0} = \int_0^1 u'(x) \, v'(x) \, dx \, , \quad u, v \in W_0^{1,2}(0, 1)$$

and with the norm

$$\|u\|_{1,2,0} = \left(\int_0^1 |u'(x)|^2 \, dx \right)^{1/2} \, , \quad u \in W_0^{1,2}(0, 1) \, .$$

As shown in Paragraph 21.4, the functional F defined by relation (9) possesses both first and second derivatives on the space $W_0^{1,2}(0, 1)$ and for all $u, v \in W_0^{1,2}(0, 1)$ we have

$$dF(u; v) = \int_0^1 u'(x) v'(x) \, dx + \int_0^1 u^3(x) v(x) \, dx - \int_0^1 f(x) v(x) \, dx \, ,$$

$$d^2F(u; v, v) = \int_0^1 |v'(x)|^2 \, dx + 3 \int_0^1 u^2(x) v^2(x) \, dx \, .$$

It is then immediately seen that the functional F satisfies all the assumptions of Theorem 28.7.

The sequence of functions e_i, $i = 1, 2, \ldots$, which are defined by the rule

$$e_i(x) = x^i(1 - x) \, ,$$

constitutes a basis of the space $W_0^{1,2}(0, 1)$ (see [64]). Thus, if we construct the subspaces X_n with the aid of these functions and according to the method described in Paragraph 28.9, condition (3) of Theorem 28.5 will be satisfied. If we rewrite the system $(\mathscr{S})$ for this concrete case, we obtain the following system of nonlinear equations ($c_1, \ldots, c_n$ are unknown numbers):

$$\sum_{k=1}^n c_k \int_0^1 [x^k(1 - x)]' \, [x^j(1 - x)]' \, dx + \int_0^1 \Big[\sum_{k=1}^n c_k x^k(1 - x) \Big]^3 x^j(1 - x) \, dx =$$

$$= \int_0^1 f(x) x^j(1 - x) \, dx \, , \quad j = 1, \ldots, n \, . \tag{11}$$

In each of the equations of system (11), all the unknowns $c_1, \ldots, c_n$ appear; this is rather unpleasant from the computational point of view. (We recommend the reader to write out system (11) for the cases $n = 3, 4, 5$.)

The question then arises whether it is possible to choose the spaces X_n so that each of the equations of the system $(\mathscr{S})$ depend on only a "small number" of unknowns. We will show that this is possible.

Let n be a non-negative integer, and put $x_i = 1/n$ for $i = 0, 1, \ldots, n$ and $I_j = [x_j, x_{j+1}]$ for $j = 0, 1, \ldots, n - 1$. Furthermore, define the spaces X_n as follows:

X_n is the set of functions u continuous on the interval $[0, 1]$ which are linear on every interval $[x_i, x_{i+1}]$ and for which

$$u(0) = u(1) = 0 \, ;$$

the dimension of the space X_n is

$$N(n) = n - 1 \, .$$

Let $e_i \in X_n$, $i = 1, ..., n - 1$, be functions such that

$$e_i(x_j) = \begin{cases} 1 & \text{for} \quad i = j, \\ 0 & \text{for} \quad i \neq j, \end{cases}$$

$j = 0, ..., n$. It is easily established that the set $\{e_i\}_{i=1}^{n-1}$ constitutes a basis of the space X_n and that for all $v \in X_n$ we have

$$v(x) = \sum_{j=1}^{n-1} v(x_j) e_j(x), \quad x \in [0, 1].$$

The system $(\mathscr{S})$ constructed for this basis will now itself be a system for the unknown values $u_n(x_j)$ of the solution of problem $(\mathscr{P}_n)$. It is also crucial that the function $e_i(x)$ vanishes outside the interval $I_{i-1} \cup I_i = [(i-1)/n, (i+1)/n]$. We then have

$$e_i(x) e_j(x) = e_i'(x) e_j'(x) = 0$$

for $i, j = 1, ..., n - 1$, $|i - j| > 1$ at every point x of the interval $[0, 1]$ (with the obvious exception, for derivatives, of the points $x_1, ..., x_{n-1}$ which constitute a set of measure zero). Therefore, in each of the equations

$$\sum_{i=1}^{n-1} c_i \int_0^1 e_i'(x) e_j'(x) \, dx + \int_0^1 [\sum_{i=1}^{n-1} c_i \, e_i(x)]^3 \, e_j(x) \, dx = \int_0^1 f(x) e_j(x) \, dx \qquad (12)$$

$(j = 1, ..., n - 1)$ of system $(\mathscr{S})$ only the unknowns c_{j-1}, c_{j+1} appear apart from c_j. Furthermore, we put

$$c_0 = c_n = 0.$$

By computation, we find that equation (12) has the form

$$-nc_j + 2nc_{j+1} + \frac{1}{20n} c_{j-1}^3 + \frac{2}{5n} c_j^3 + \frac{1}{20n} c_{j+1}^3 + \frac{3}{20n} c_{j-1} c_j^2 +$$

$$+ \frac{1}{10n} c_{j-1}^2 c_j + \frac{1}{10n} c_j c_{j+1}^2 + \frac{3}{20n} c_j^2 c_{j+1} = \alpha_j,$$

where

$$\alpha_j = \int_0^1 f(x) e_j(x) \, dx$$

for $j = 1, ..., n - 1$.

If we compute the solution

$$c_1^n, ..., c_{n-1}^n$$

from these equations, and if we put

$$u_n(x) = c_1^n \, e_1(x) + ... + c_{n-1}^n \, e_{n-1}(x), \quad x \in [0, 1],$$

we obtain the solution of problem $(\mathscr{P}_n)$ (see Paragraph 28.8). We now clearly wish to know whether

$$\lim_{n \to \infty} \|u_n - u_0\|_{1,2,0} = 0 .$$

For this, it suffices to show, by Theorem 28.7, that the spaces X_n satisfy condition (3) of Theorem 28.5. First of all, we note the following inequality:

Let $\psi \in C^2([a, b])$ and let

$$\omega(x) = \frac{\psi(b) - \psi(a)}{b - a} (x - a) + \psi(a) .$$

Then

$$\max_{x \in \langle a,b \rangle} |\psi'(x) - \omega'(x)| \leq (b - a) \max_{x \in \langle a,b \rangle} |\psi''(x)| . \tag{13}$$

(This inequality follows immediately from the Lagrange mean value theorem — see p. 187.)

We shall now prove that the spaces X_n satisfy condition (3). Let $v \in W_0^{1,2}(0, 1)$ and $\varepsilon > 0$. We shall show that there exist $n \in \mathbb{N}$ and $v_n \in X_n$ such that

$$\|v - v_n\|_{1,2,0} < \varepsilon . \tag{14}$$

Since the set $C_0^\infty(0, 1)$ is dense in the space $W_0^{1,2}(0, 1)$ (see Paragraph 13.5), there exists a function $w \in C_0^\infty(0, 1)$ such that

$$\|v - w\|_{1,2,0} < \varepsilon/2 . \tag{15}$$

Let $n \in \mathbb{N}$ be arbitrary, and construct a function $v_n \in X_n$ such that

$$v_n(x_i) = w(x_i)$$

for all $i = 0, \ldots, n$. Then we have

$$\|w - v_n\|_{1,2,0}^2 = \sum_{i=0}^{n-1} \int_{x_i}^{x_{i+1}} |w'(x) - v_n'(x)|^2 \, dx \leq$$

$$\leq \sum_{i=0}^{n-1} \frac{1}{n^2} \max_{x \in \langle 0,1 \rangle} |w''(x)|^2 (x_{i+1} - x_i) = \frac{1}{n^2} \max_{x \in \langle 0,1 \rangle} |w''(x)|^2$$

(to estimate the integral we made use of inequality (13) for $a = x_i$, $b = x_{i+1}$, $\omega = v_n$, $\psi = w$). From this, it now follows that for sufficiently large $n \in \mathbb{N}$ we have

$$\|w - v_n\|_{1,2,0} < \varepsilon/2 .$$

This inequality together with (15) proves the desired assertion.

28.11. Remarks on Example 28.10. (i) System (12) was fairly agreeable. It was by no means essential there that the dividing points of the interval $[0, 1]$ were chosen at equal distances apart, i.e., that an equidistant division of the interval $[0, 1]$ was selected.

(ii) The spaces X_n were the simplest which could have been chosen for the given example. It is also possible to choose spaces of functions which are polynomials of higher degree on every interval I_i. E.g., one can choose

$$X_n = \{v \in C^1([0, 1]); \; v(0) = v(1) = 0, \; v|_{I_i} \text{ is a polynomial}$$

$$\text{of the third degree for all } i = 0, ..., n - 1\} .$$

A basis of this space whose dimension is $2n$ consists of the functions

$$e_1, ..., e_{n-1}, \quad \psi_0, ..., \psi_n$$

such that

$$e_i(x_j) = \begin{cases} 1 & \text{for} \quad i = j \\ 0 & \text{for} \quad i \neq j \end{cases}, \quad e_i'(x_j) = 0, \quad i = 1, ..., n - 1, \; j = 0, ..., n ;$$

$$\psi_i(x_j) = 0, \quad \psi_i'(x_j) = \begin{cases} 1 & \text{for} \quad i = j \\ 0 & \text{for} \quad i \neq j \end{cases}, \quad i, j = 0, ..., n .$$

Every function $v \in X_n$ can be written in the form

$$v(x) = \sum_{j=1}^{n-1} v(x_j) \, e_j(x) + \sum_{j=0}^{n} v'(x_j) \, \psi_j(x), \quad x \in [0, 1] .$$

We recommend the reader to apply the spaces X_n described above to the example investigated in Paragraph 28.10.

(iii) In practice, the question of how rapidly the solutions u_n of the problems $(\mathscr{P}_n)$ converge to the solution u_0 of problem $(\mathscr{P}_0)$ is very important. This question is closely related to the regularity of the solution of equations. If, e.g., $f \in C^0([0, 1])$, then $u_0 \in C^2([0, 1])$ (see Theorem 17.5) and using this it can be proved that a constant $c > 0$ exists such that for all $n \in \mathbb{N}$ we have

$$\|u_0 - u_n\|_{1,2,0} \leq c/n .$$

If, e.g., $u_0 \in C^4([0, 1])$, then we even have

$$\|u_0 - u_n\|_{1,2,0} \leq c/n^3 .$$

28.12. The finite element method. Hitherto, we have been interested in the construction of spaces X_n for the case when X was the space $W_0^{1,2}(0, 1)$. We could proceed similarly even in the case when $X = W^{k,2}(\Omega)$, $\Omega \subset \mathbb{R}^N$, $\Omega \in \mathscr{C}^{0,1}$. We divide the set Ω into a finite number of open subsets Ω_i, $i = 1, \ldots, N(n)$, such that their diameter

$$\text{diam } \Omega_i = \sup_{x, y \in \Omega_i} |x - y|$$

is less than $1/n$ and such that

$$\bar{\Omega} = \bigcup_{i=1}^{n} \bar{\Omega}_i, \quad \Omega_i \cap \Omega_j = \emptyset \quad \text{for} \quad i \neq j.$$

Each of the sets $\bar{\Omega}_i$ is called a *finite element*. The space X_n will consist of functions whose restrictions to Ω_i are smooth functions, for instance polynomials in N variables, and satisfy certain conditions on the "interface of the sets Ω_i and Ω_j" $(i \neq j)$. For greater intuitive appeal, we treat the case of a plane domain Ω, and let Ω be a polygon with the boundary $\partial\Omega$. For every $n \in \mathbb{N}$, we perform a triangulation $\mathscr{T}_n$ of the set $\bar{\Omega}$, i.e., we put

$$\bar{\Omega} = \bigcup_{i=1}^{N(n)} \bar{K}_i,$$

where the K_i are open triangles such that

$$\text{diam } K_i \leq 1/n$$

for every $K_i \in \mathscr{T}_n$ [i.e., for $i = 1, \ldots, N(n)$]. Moreover, assume that precisely one of the following situations arises for the mutual position of the triangles K_i, $K_j \in \mathscr{T}_n$ $(i \neq j)$:

    (a) the closures of two distinct triangles have no common point;
    (b) the closures of two distinct triangles have only one vertex in common;
    (c) the closures of two distinct triangles have an entire side in common.

Denote by $\vartheta(n)$ the minimal internal angle found in the triangles of the triangulation $\mathscr{T}_n$. In the sequel, we shall assume that the system of triangulations $\{\mathscr{T}_n; n \in \mathbb{N}\}$ satisfies the following condition: A constant $\gamma > 0$ exists such that for all $n \in \mathbb{N}$ we have

$$\vartheta(n) \geq \gamma. \tag{16}$$

The spaces X_n will be sets of functions whose restrictions to K_i are polynomials of the k-th order. Below, we give examples of spaces X_n for the cases $k = 1$ and $k = 3$. We show with the aid of which parameters (values of functions and of derivatives at given points) can such functions be constructed on the individual triangles $K_i \in \mathscr{T}_n$. The continuity of the function $v \in X_n$ is ensured on the set $\bar{\Omega}$ by choosing the values of the parameters (used for the construction of the function) to be equal at the common vertices. The reader will find the details in [9] and [94].

28.13. Example $(k = 1)$. Let K be an open triangle with vertices Q_1, Q_2, Q_3. Let $P_1(K)$ be the set of all polynomials of the first degree defined on K, i.e., $p \in P_1(K)$

if

$$p(x, y) = \alpha_0 + \alpha_1 x + \alpha_2 y, \quad (x, y) \in \overline{K}.$$

It is easily shown that the function $p(x, y) \in P_1(K)$ is uniquely determined by its values at the vertices Q_1, Q_2, Q_3. The values $p(Q_1), p(Q_2), p(Q_3)$ serve as parameters by means of which the function $p(x, y)$ is constructed.

That function $p \in P_1(K)$ for which

$$p(Q_i) = v(Q_i), \quad i = 1, 2, 3,$$

is called the *Lagrange interpolation of the function* $v \in C^0(\overline{K})$. The function $p(x, y)$ constructed in this way is denoted by $\Pi_K v$. Clearly, Π_K is a linear mapping from the space $C^0(\overline{K})$ into $P_1(K)$ and

$$\|v - \Pi_K v\|_{W^{1,2}(K)} \leq c\, h_K \|v\|_{W^{2,2}(K)} \tag{17}$$

holds for arbitrary functions $v \in W^{2,2}(K)$ ($h_K = \text{diam } K$ and $c > 0$ is a constant independent of v and h_K). Define the spaces X_n as follows:

$$X_n = \{v \in C^0(\overline{\Omega}); \ v|_{\overline{K}_i} \in P_1(K_i) \ \text{ for all } \ K_i \in \mathcal{T}_n\}. \tag{18}$$

Obviously,

$$X_n \subset W^{1,2}(\Omega).$$

Let $v \in W^{2,2}(\Omega)$. Construct the function $v_n \in X_n$ in the following way:

$$v_n|_{\overline{K}_i} = \Pi_{K_i} v.$$

Applying inequality (17), we then obtain

$$\|v - v_n\|_{W^{1,2}(\Omega)} \leq \frac{c}{n} \|v\|_{W^{2,2}(\Omega)}.$$

Thus, the function v_n is arbitrarily close to the function v provided n is a sufficiently large non-negative integer. Hence, making use of the fact that the set $W^{2,2}(\Omega)$ is dense in the space $W^{1,2}(\Omega)$, it follows that the spaces X_n, $n \in \mathbb{N}$, satisfy condition (3).

We can construct the basis functions just as in Example 28.10. If $\{Q_i\}_{i=1}^{M(n)}$ are all the vertices of all the triangles of the triangulation $\mathcal{T}_n$, we construct the functions

$$e_j \in X_n, \quad j = 1, \ldots, M(n),$$

so that

$$e_i(Q_j) = \begin{cases} 1 & \text{for } i = j, \\ 0 & \text{for } i \neq j. \end{cases}$$

28.14. Example $(k = 3)$. Let K be an open triangle with vertices Q_1, Q_2, Q_3 and with center of gravity Q_0. Let $P_3(K)$ be the set of polynomials of the third degree defined on $\overline{K}$, i.e., $p \in P_3(K)$ if

$$p(x, y) = \alpha_0 + \alpha_1 x + \alpha_2 x^2 + \alpha_3 x^3 + \alpha_4 xy + \alpha_5 xy^2 + \alpha_6 x^2 y + \alpha_7 y +$$
$$+ \alpha_8 y^2 + \alpha_9 y^3 , \quad (x, y) \in \overline{K} .$$

The function $p(x, y) \in P_3(K)$ is uniquely determined by the values at the vertices and at the center of gravity and by the values of the first partial derivatives at the vertices of the triangle K. The function $\Pi_K v \in P_3(K)$ for which

$$\Pi_K v(Q_i) = v(Q_i) , \quad i = 0, 1, 2, 3 ;$$

$$\frac{\partial \Pi_K v(Q_i)}{\partial x} = \frac{\partial v(Q_i)}{\partial x} ,$$

$$\frac{\partial \Pi_K v(Q_i)}{\partial y} = \frac{\partial v(Q_i)}{\partial y} , \quad i = 1, 2, 3 ,$$

is called the *Hermite interpolation of the function* $v \in C^1(\overline{K})$. Just as in the preceding example, the relation

$$\|v - \Pi_K v\|_{W^{3,2}(K)} \leqq c \, h_K \|v\|_{W^{4,2}(K)}$$

holds for every function $v \in W^{4,2}(K)$. If we put

$$X_n = \{v \in C^1(\overline{\Omega}); \ v|_{K_i} \in P_3(K_i) \text{ for every triangle } K_i \in \mathcal{T}_n\} ,$$

then

$$X_n \subset W^{1,2}(\Omega)$$

and the spaces X_n, $n \in \mathbb{N}$, again satisfy condition (3) since the set $W^{4,2}(\Omega)$ is dense in the space $W^{1,2}(\Omega)$.

28.15. Remark. For the sake of simplicity, we have assumed that X is a Hilbert space. The case when X is a Banach space together with further generalizations and a more detailed exposition can be found in [10].

28.16. Remark on the solution of system $(\mathscr{S})$. Hitherto, we have not been concerned with the question which is fundamental from the practical point-of-view: How to solve system $(\mathscr{S})$ numerically? These problems are discussed at length, e.g., in the books [8] and [76] where the reader will find a variety of methods applicable to the numerical solution of problem $(\mathscr{P}_n)$ and system $(\mathscr{S})$.

By way of illustration, we present a method which belongs among the so-called *minimization methods* and which is described in detail in [83]. Choose, arbitrarily, the vector

$$c^0 = (c_1^0, ..., c_{N(n)}^0) \in \mathbb{R}^{N(n)} .$$

We present the algorithm for the construction of the sequence $\{c^n\}_{n=1}^{\infty}$ which converges to the solution of system $(\mathcal{S})$. If we know the vector

$$c^m = \left(c_1^m, \ldots, c_{N(n)}^m\right) \in \mathbb{R}^{N(n)},$$

we calculate the components of the vector

$$c^{m+1} = \left(c_1^{m+1}, \ldots, c_{N(n)}^{m+1}\right)$$

as follows: Let the function

$$\mathscr{F}_n\left(c_1^{m+1}, \ldots, c_{i-1}^{m+1}, \xi, c_{i+1}^m, \ldots, c_{N(n)}^m\right)$$

of the variable ξ on $\mathbb{R}$ take its minimum at the point $\tilde{c}_i^{m+1}$. Put, then,

$$c_1^{m+1} = c_i^m + \omega\left(\tilde{c}_i^{m+1} - c_i^m\right),$$

where $0 < \omega \leq 2$.

Here ω is the so-called relaxation parameter. If we choose $\omega = 1$ and if F is a quadratic functional, we obtain the so-called Gauss-Seidel iterative method (see, e.g., [91]).

28.17. One more numerical method. In the foregoing paragraphs, we reduced the "infinite dimensional" nonlinear problem $(\mathscr{P}_0)$ to a "finite dimensional" problem $(\mathscr{P}_n)$ which was again nonlinear. However, it is also possible to proceed otherwise:

The functional F, which is not quadratic in general, is approximated at a chosen fixed point u_1 by some quadratic functional F_1 and instead of the problem $(\mathscr{P}_0)$ we look for the minimum of the "near" quadratic functional F_1. Much is known about the minimum of quadratic functionals and the answer to this question is available in the literature, for instance in [80]. Assume that u_2 is the point at which the functional F_1 attains its minimum. At this point, replace the functional F by the "near" quadratic functional F_2 and find the point u_3 at which the functional F_2 attains its minimum. We proceed inductively in this manner and construct a sequence of points u_n, $n = 1, 2, \ldots$, at which certain "near" quadratic functionals F_n, $n = 1, 2, \ldots$, attain their minima. Our aim here is to formulate conditions for the functional F and to define the "nearness" of the quadratic functionals F_n to F in such a way that the sequence $\{u_n\}_{n=1}^{\infty}$ converges to the solution of problem $(\mathscr{P}_0)$.

One of these methods is the so-called Katchanov method, the convergence of which was proved in [37] and in the paper [31]. In [31], the method is applied to the solution of a problem from the theory of plastic deformations. The generalization of this method to the so-called Katchanov-Galerkin method is presented in [30] (at every stage we look for the minimum of a "near" quadratic functional on a subspace of finite dimension). In [48], numerical calculations carried out on an ODRA computer for the solution of a magnetic field problem are described (see Paragraph 2.2).

CHAPTER V

THE TOPOLOGICAL METHOD

SECTION 29. EXISTENCE THEOREMS

29.1. As mentioned in Chapter IV [Paragraph 19.4(ii)], we shall now try to eliminate the obstacle which appears when applying the variational method to boundary value problems in partial differential equations. This obstacle consists of the so-called *potentiality conditions*, i.e., the assumption that the coefficients a_α of the formal differential operator

$$(Au)(x) = \sum_{|\alpha| \leq k} (-1)^{|\alpha|} D^\alpha a_\alpha(x; \delta_k u(x)), \quad x \in \Omega,$$

are differentiable and that they satisfy the requirement of symmetry:

$$\frac{\partial a_\alpha}{\partial \xi_\beta} = \frac{\partial a_\beta}{\partial \xi_\alpha}.$$

We shall establish the same assertion as in Theorem 26.11 but without the condition that the operator T is potential. At the same time, we shall analyse operators which are only monotone in the principal part in more depth [as promised in Paragraph 26.23 (vi)]. Thanks to these considerations, the existence of the weak solution will be proved under weaker conditions than obtained in the preceding chapter. The abstract method of the solution of operator equations which will be explained below is usually called the *topological method* since it is based on the properties of a certain topological invariant (the so-called degree of a mapping) — see Section 30. (The present section will be useful to the reader who wishes to understand the principal ideas upon which the whole theory is based. The reader who is interested merely in the existence theorems and not in how they are proved need not read Section 30.)

We shall not deal with numerical methods for non-potential equations; interested readers are referred to the literature quoted in Section 28, namely to the paper [10].

We first present an example of a boundary value problem.

29.2. Example. Let $f \in L_1(0, 1)$, and let us investigate the Dirichlet problem

$$\begin{cases} u^{(IV)} + \dfrac{1}{\pi} \operatorname{arctg} u' = f & \text{on } (0, 1), \\ u(0) = u(1) = u'(0) = u'(1) = 0. \end{cases} \tag{1}$$

On the space $W_0^{2,2}(0, 1)$, we define an operator T with values in the space $(W_0^{2,2}(0, 1))^*$ such that for all $u, v \in W_0^{2,2}(0, 1)$ we have

$$<Tu, v> = \int_0^1 u''(x) v''(x) \, dx + \frac{1}{\pi} \int_0^1 \text{arctg } u'(x) v(x) \, dx - \int_0^1 f(x) v(x) \, dx \, .$$

Then the function $u_0 \in W_0^{2,2}(0, 1)$ is the weak solution of problem (1) if and only if

$$Tu_0 = \Theta \, .$$

The operator T is bounded, coercive and monotone in the principal part [see Paragraph 26.23 (vi)]. (These properties could quite easily be verified as an exercise.) However, the operator T is not potential since

$$a_0(x; \xi_0, \xi_1, \xi_2) = \frac{1}{\pi} \text{arctg } \xi_1 \, ,$$

$$a_1(x; \xi_0, \xi_1, \xi_2) = 0 \, ,$$

$$a_2(x; \xi_0, \xi_1, \xi_2) = \xi_2$$

and

$$\frac{\partial a_1}{\partial \xi_0} = 0 \, , \quad \frac{\partial a_0}{\partial \xi_1} \neq 0 \, .$$

It is therefore not possible to apply the method described in Paragraph 26.23 to boundary value problem (1). The existence of the weak solution of boundary value problem (1) will, however, be a consequence of Theorem 29.5 presented below.

We now state a very simple theorem on the existence of the solution of operator equations which embraces non-potential operators as well.

29.3. Theorem. *Let H be a Hilbert space with the inner product $<u, v>$, and let T be an operator defined on H with values in H and satisfying the following conditions: there exist numbers $m > 0$, $M > 0$, $M > m$ such that*

$$\|Tu - Tv\|_H \leq M \|u - v\|_H \tag{2}$$

(i.e., the operator T satisfies on H the Lipschitz condition with the constant M) and

$$<Tu - Tv, u - v> \geq m \|u - v\|_H^2 \, \dagger) \tag{3}$$

hold for all $u, v \in H$.

---

† In Paragraph 26.10, we defined what we meant by the statement that an operator T which maps a Banach space X into the dual space X^* is monotone. In the case of a Hilbert space H, this then means that it is possible to introduce the concept of monotony for the mapping $T: H \to H^*$. In the footnote on p. 181, we concluded, however, that by means of the so-called Riesz theorem on the representation of a continuous linear functional on H the space H^* can be identified with the space H and it is possible to write the inner product instead of the value of the functional at a point. This identification $H = H^*$ will be used henceforth because it leads to simplified expressions.

Note, nevertheless, that an operator $T: H \to H$ which satisfies condition (3) is usually called strongly monotone.

Then the equation

$$Tu = f \qquad (4)$$

has precisely one solution for every $f \in H$ and it is possible to construct this solution by the method of successive approximations.

Proof. Let $f \in H$, and let $\varepsilon > 0$. Define the operator A_ε by the relation

$$A_\varepsilon u = u - \varepsilon(Tu - f).$$

For arbitrary $u, v \in H$, we then have

$$\|A_\varepsilon u - A_\varepsilon v\|_H^2 = \|u - v\|_H^2 - 2\varepsilon < Tu - Tv, u - v> + \varepsilon^2 \|Tu - Tv\|_H^2 \leqq$$
$$\leqq (1 - 2\varepsilon m + \varepsilon^2 M^2) \|u - v\|_H^2.$$

Thus, if we choose $\varepsilon > 0$ so that

$$\varepsilon < \frac{2m}{M^2},$$

and if we put

$$k = (1 - 2\varepsilon m + \varepsilon^2 M^2)^{1/2},$$

then the operator A_ε is a contractive mapping [see Paragraph 10.6 (i)] with a constant $k < 1$. From this it follows that by the Banach contraction principle [see Paragraph 10.6 (i) again] there exists precisely one $u \in H$ (which is the limit of the sequence of successive approximations) such that

$$A_\varepsilon u = u,$$

i.e., such that

$$u - \varepsilon(Tu - f) = u,$$

and thus

$$Tu = f.$$

29.4. Remark. In the preceding theorem, it was essential that the operator T was defined on a Hilbert space. For the application of the theorem to the Dirichlet problem

$$\begin{cases} -\dfrac{d}{dx} a_1(x; u(x), u'(x)) + a_0(x; u(x), u'(x)) = f(x), & x \in (0, 1), \\ u(0) = u(1) = 0 \end{cases}$$

this means that for the coefficients $a_0(x; \xi_0, \xi_1)$, $a_1(x; \xi_0, \xi_1)$ we have

$$a_1, a_0 \in \mathbf{CAR^*}(2).$$

As an exercise, it is possible to verify that the operator T so defined that for all $u, v \in W_0^{1,2}(0, 1)$ we have

$$<Tu, v>_{1,2} = \int_0^1 a_1(x; u(x), u'(x)) \, v'(x) \, dx + \int_0^1 a_0(x; u(x), u'(x)) \, v(x) \, dx \, \dagger)$$

satisfies condition (2) if there exists a constant $M > 0$ such that for all $x \in [0, 1]$ and all $\xi_0, \zeta_0, \xi_1, \zeta_1 \in \mathbb{R}$

$$\left| a_i(x; \xi_0, \xi_1) - a_i(x; \zeta_0, \zeta_1) \right| \leq M(\left| \xi_0 - \zeta_0 \right| + \left| \xi_1 - \zeta_1 \right|), \quad i = 0, 1 \, ,$$

holds. [The conditions of monotony and coerciveness — i.e., the fulfilment of condition (3) — were discussed, e.g., in Paragraph 26.15 (iii).]

[Theorem 29.3 can also be applied to obtain the existence of the weak solution of boundary value problems of higher orders. Thus, for instance, the boundary value problem

$$u^{(\mathrm{IV})} + u' = f \quad \text{on} \quad (0, 1) \, ,$$
$$u(0) = u(1) = u'(0) = u'(1) = 0$$

has, by Theorem 29.3, precisely one weak solution $u \in W_0^{2,2}(0, 1)$ for every $f \in$ $\in L_1(0, 1)$. (It is not possible to apply the variational method to this boundary value problem since — just as for boundary value problem (1) — the condition of "symmetry" of the derivatives of the coefficients is not satisfied. Verify this!)]

The conditions on the coefficients of the formal differential operator are thus rather limiting. This is due to the fact that the Banach contraction principle was applied. This is, no doubt, a very useful theorem (the solution can be found by the method of successive approximations), but it is not the most suitable tool for the problems investigated here.

The following two theorems will provide the basic means of obtaining an assertion on the existence of the weak solution of a boundary value problem in this section. The first of these theorems (Theorem 29.5) is usually associated with the name of the American mathematician F. E. Browder, the second is named after the French mathematicians J. Leray and J.-L. Lions. (In this section, we discuss applications of these theorems to boundary value problems while the method of their proof is relegated to the next section.)

29.5. Browder theorem. *Let X be a reflexive Banach space. Let T be an operator defined on X with values in X^*, and let the following conditions be satisfied$\dagger\dagger$):*

$\dagger$) It must be remembered here that we make use of the convention adopted in the footnote on p. 240. Hence, we write, e.g., $<Tu, v>_{1,2}$ [i.e., the inner product in the space $W^{1,2}(0, 1)$] instead of $<Tu, v>$, i.e., instead of the value of the functional Tu at the point v.

$\dagger\dagger$) For the terminology, see also Paragraph 26.10.

(a) *T is a bounded operator, i.e., the image of any bounded subset of the space X is a bounded subset of the space X*;*

(b) *the operator T is demicontinuous, i.e., for arbitrary $u_0 \in X$ and any sequence $\{u_n\}_{u=1}^{\infty}$ of elements of the space X such that*

$$u_n \to u_0 \quad in \quad X$$

we have

$$Tu_n \to Tu_0 \quad in \quad X^* ;$$

(c) *the operator T is coercive, i.e.,*

$$\lim_{\|u\|_X \to \infty} \frac{<Tu, u>}{\|u\|_X} = \infty ; \tag{5}$$

(d) *the operator T is monotone on the space X, i.e., for all $u, v \in X$ we have*

$$<Tu - Tv, u - v> \geq 0 . \tag{6}$$

Then the equation

$$Tu = f \tag{7}$$

has at least one solution $u \in X$ for every $f \in X^*$. If, moreover, inequality (6) is strict for all $u, v \in X$, $u \neq v$, then equation (7) has precisely one solution $u \in X$ for every $f \in X^*$.

29.6. Leray-Lions theorem. *Let X be a reflexive Banach space. Let T be an operator defined on X with values in X*, and let the following conditions be satisfied:*

(a) *the operator T is bounded;*

(b) *the operator T is demicontinuous;*

(c) *the operator T is coercive.*

Let a bounded mapping Φ exist from the space $X \times X$ into the space X* such that

(d) *$\Phi(u, u) = Tu$ for every $u \in X$;*

(e) *for all $u, w, h \in X$ and any sequence $\{t_n\}_{n=1}^{\infty}$ of real numbers such that*

$$t_n \to 0 ,$$

we have

$$\Phi(u + t_n h, w) \to \Phi(u, w) ;$$

(f) *for all $u, w \in X$, we have*

$$<\Phi(u, u) - \Phi(w, u), u - w> \geq 0$$

(the so-called *condition of monotony in the principal part*);

(g) *if* $u_n \rightharpoonup u$ *and*

$$\lim_{n \to \infty} \; <\Phi(u_n, u_n) - \Phi(u, u_n), u_n - u> \; = 0 \,,$$

then we have

$$\Phi(w, u_n) \rightharpoonup \Phi(w, u)$$

for arbitrary $w \in X$;

(h) *if* $w \in X$, $u_n \rightharpoonup u$, $\Phi(w, u_n) \rightharpoonup z$, *then*

$$\lim_{n \to \infty} \; <\Phi(w, u_n), u_n> \; = \; <z, u> \,.$$

Then the equation

$$Tu = f \tag{7}$$

has at least one solution $u \in X$ *for every* $f \in X^*$.

The conditions of Theorem 29.5 are relatively simple. They generalize in a natural manner the conditions of Theorem 26.11. However, conditions (d)–(h) of Theorem 29.6 are somewhat unintuitive at first sight. We hope that the meaning of all the conditions will be clear after the application of the two theorems to boundary value problems in differential equations.

29.7. Application of Theorem 29.5 to boundary value problems. First, let us compare the conditions of Theorems 26.11 and 29.5: We see immediately that the condition of potentiality of the operator T in Theorem 26.11 is replaced in Theorem 29.5 by condition (b), i.e., by a condition of some kind of continuity of the operator T. Therefore, the application of Theorem 29.5 to a boundary value problem will be similar to that in Paragraph 26.13 where Theorem 26.11 was applied.

Thus, let

$$(Au)(x) = \sum_{|\alpha| \leq k} (-1)^{|\alpha|} D^\alpha a_\alpha(x; \delta_k u(x))$$

be a formal differential operator of order $2k$, and let $p > 1$. Let V be a space such that

$$W_0^{k,p}(\Omega) \subset V \subset W^{k,p}(\Omega) \,,$$

let $V \subsetneq Q$, and let $\mathbf{f} \in Q^*$, $\varphi \in W^{k,p}(\Omega)$, $\mathbf{g} \in V^*$ (for more details see Paragraph 15.7).

Define the operator T on the space V as follows: For $u \in V$, let Tu be an element of the dual space V^* such that

$$<Tu, v> \; = \sum_{|\alpha| \leq k} \int_\Omega a_\alpha(x; \delta_k u(x) + \delta_k \varphi(x)) D^\alpha v(x) \, dx - <\mathbf{f}, v>_Q - <\mathbf{g}, v>_V \tag{8}$$

holds for all $v \in V$.

Remember that for the operator T on the space V to be definable it is necessary that the coefficients $a_\alpha(x; \xi)$ of the formal differential operator A satisfy the growth conditions

$$a_\alpha \in \textbf{CAR}^*(p) \tag{9}$$

(see Paragraphs 14.2 and 16.15).

If (9) is satisfied, then the operator T is automatically bounded [for the proof, see Paragraph 26.13 (iii)]. This also immediately implies that condition (b) of Theorem 29.5 is satisfied: If $u_n \to u_0$ in the space V, then

$$a_\alpha(x; \delta_k\, u_n(x) + \delta_k\, \varphi(x)) \to a_\alpha(x; \delta_k\, u_0(x) + \delta_k\, \varphi(x))$$

in the space $L_{r(\alpha)}(\Omega)$ (see Theorem 16.11). Thus, for arbitrary $v \in V$ and for arbitrary α, $|\alpha| \leq k$, we have

$$\lim_{n \to \infty} \int_\Omega a_\alpha(x; \delta_k\, u_n(x) + \delta_k\, \varphi(x))\, D^\alpha v(x)\, dx =$$

$$= \int_\Omega a_\alpha(x; \delta_k\, u_0(x) + \delta_k\, \varphi(x))\, D^\alpha v(x)\, dx ,$$

and thus, for arbitrary $v \in V$, we have

$$\lim_{n \to \infty} <Tu_n, v> = <Tu_0, v> .$$

However, this last relation shows that

$$Tu_n \to Tu_0 \quad \text{in the space} \quad V^* .$$

That conditions (c) and (d) are satisfied is guaranteed (just as in Paragraph 26.13) by the conditions of monotony and coerciveness (26.11) and (26.13), i.e., for the coefficients $a_\alpha(x; \xi)$ we assume: For all $\xi, \zeta \in \mathbb{R}^\times$ and for almost all $x \in \Omega$ we have

$$\sum_{|\alpha| \leq k} (a_\alpha(x; \xi) - a_\alpha(x; \zeta))\,(\xi_\alpha - \zeta_\alpha) \geq 0 ; \tag{10}$$

the relation

$$\lim_{\|u\|_{k,p} \to \infty} \frac{1}{\|u\|_{k,p}} \sum_{|\alpha| \leq k} \int_\Omega a_\alpha\, (x;\, \delta_k u(x) + \delta_k \varphi(x))\, D^\alpha u(x)\, dx = \infty \tag{11}$$

holds [let us remark that the validity of condition (26.14) is sufficient for (11) to hold if $a_\alpha \in \textbf{CAR}(p)$].

This verifies the conditions of Theorem 29.5 and we thus obtain the following theorem on the existence of a weak solution of the boundary value problem (A, V, Q). (After reading Theorem 29.8, compare its conditions with the conditions of Theorem 26.14 and appreciate the significance of the topological method!)

29.8. Theorem. *Let $k \in \mathbb{N}$, $p > 1$, and assume that the coefficients $a_\alpha(x; \xi)$ satisfy the following conditions:*

$$a_\alpha \in \mathbf{CAR}^*(p) ; \tag{9}$$

$$\sum_{|\alpha| \leq k} (a_\alpha(x; \xi) - a_\alpha(x; \zeta)) (\xi_\alpha - \zeta_\alpha) \geq 0 ; \tag{10}$$

$$\lim_{\|u\|_{k,p} \to \infty} \frac{1}{\|u\|_{k,p}} \sum_{|\alpha| \leq k} \int_\Omega a_\alpha(x; \delta_k u(x) + \delta_k \varphi(x)) D^\alpha u(x)\, dx = \infty . \tag{11}$$

Then at least one weak solution of the boundary value problem (A, V, Q) exists. If, moreover, equality holds in condition (10) for $\xi = \zeta$ only, then the boundary value problem (A, V, Q) has precisely one weak solution.

29.9. Remark. As a useful exercise, one could go through the examples given in Paragraphs 26.15 and 26.16 again, applying Theorem 29.5 to them instead of the variational method.

29.10. Application of Theorem 29.6 to boundary value problems. Let the symbols p, V, $\mathbf{f}$, Q, φ, A, $\mathbf{g}$, T have the same meaning as in Paragraph 29.7. Since the assumptions (a)–(c) are the same in Theorems 29.5 and 29.6, it follows from Paragraph 29.7 that they are satisfied if (9) and (11) hold.

We now analyze assumptions (d)–(h) of Theorem 29.6. In the first place, it is necessary to define an operator Φ on the space $V \times V$ which takes values in the space V^*. The operator T is defined on V by relation (8), i.e., for all $u, v \in V$

$$<Tu, v> = \int_\Omega \sum_{|\alpha| \leq k} a_\alpha(x; \delta_k u(x) + \delta_k \varphi(x)) D^\alpha v(x)\, dx - <\mathbf{f}, v>_Q - <\mathbf{g}, v>_V . \tag{8}$$

Now define the operator Φ on the space $V \times V$ as follows: For $u, v \in V$, let $\Phi(u, w)$ be an element of the space V^* such that for all $v \in V$ we have

$$<\Phi(u, w), v> =$$

$$= \int_\Omega \sum_{|\alpha| = k} a_\alpha(x; \delta_{k-1} w(x) + \delta_{k-1} \varphi(x), \hat{\delta}_k u(x) + \hat{\delta}_k \varphi(x)) D^\alpha v(x)\, dx +$$

$$+ \int_\Omega \sum_{|\alpha| \leq k-1} a_\alpha(x; \delta_k w(x) + \delta_k \varphi(x)) D^\alpha v(x)\, dx - <\mathbf{f}, v>_Q - <\mathbf{g}, v>_V \tag{12}$$

(recall that $\hat{\delta}_k w = \{D^\gamma w; |\gamma| = k\}$ — see Paragraph 7.2). Comparing relations (8) and (12), we immediately see that assumption (d) of Theorem 29.6 is valid, i.e., that

$$\Phi(u, u) = Tu$$

for every $u \in V$. In a manner analogous to that in which condition (b) of Theorem 29.5 was verified in Paragraph 29.7, it is possible to verify that condition (e) of Theorem 29.6 is satisfied as well. If the coefficients $a_\alpha(x; \xi)$ satisfy the condition of monotony in the principal part [see Paragraph 26.23 (vi)], i.e., if

$$\sum_{|\alpha| \leq k} (a_\alpha(x; \zeta, \xi) - a_\alpha(x; \zeta, \hat{\xi}))(\xi_\alpha - \hat{\xi}_\alpha) \geq 0 \tag{13}$$

holds for all $\zeta \in \mathbb{R}^{\varkappa(N, k-1)}$, $\xi, \hat{\xi} \in \mathbb{R}^m$, where $m = \varkappa(N, k) - \varkappa(N, k-1)$ (for the notation, see Paragraph 7.2), and for almost all $x \in \Omega$, we immediately see that condition (f) of Theorem 29.6 is satisfied [put

$$\zeta = \delta_{k-1} u(x) + \delta_{k-1} \varphi(x),$$
$$\xi = \hat{\delta}_k u(x) \quad + \hat{\delta}_k \varphi(x),$$
$$\hat{\xi} = \hat{\delta}_k w(x) \quad + \hat{\delta}_k \varphi(x)$$

in (13) and integrate the resulting inequality over the set Ω]. If conditions (9), (11) and (13) are satisfied, then conditions (g) and (h) of Theorem 29.6 are satisfied as well (for the proof see, e.g., [70]). Observe that to verify condition (g) some rather involved theorems from the theory of the Lebesgue integral are needed; in the verification of condition (h), theorems on the compact imbedding of Sobolev spaces (see Paragraph 26.24) play an essential role. We thus obtain the assertion which follows.

29.11. Theorem. *Let $\Omega \subset \mathbb{R}^N$, $\Omega \in \mathscr{C}^{0,1}$. Let $k \in \mathbb{N}$, $p > 1$, and assume that the coefficients $a_\alpha(x; \xi)$ satisfy the following conditions:*

$$a_\alpha \in \mathbf{CAR}^*(p) ; \tag{9}$$

$$\lim_{\|u\|_{k,p} \to \infty} \frac{1}{\|u\|_{k,p}} \sum_{|\alpha| \leq k} \int_\Omega a_\alpha(x; \delta_k u(x) + \delta_k \varphi(x)) \, D^\alpha u(x) \, dx \; = \; \infty ; \tag{11}$$

$$\sum_{|\alpha| = k} (a_\alpha(x; \zeta, \xi) - a_\alpha(x; \zeta, \hat{\xi}))(\xi_\alpha - \hat{\xi}_\alpha) \geq 0 . \tag{13}$$

Then there exists at least one weak solution of the boundary value problem (A, V, Q) †).

29.12. Remarks. (i) Of the Theorems 26.14, 29.8, and 29.11 on the existence of the weak solution of the boundary value problem (A, V, Q), Theorem 29.11 is the most general and Theorem 26.14 the least general.

(ii) As a very useful exercise, it is again possible to analyze the assertions of Paragraph 26.23, but now from the point-of-view of the application of Theorem 29.11. [Most probably, the remark of Paragraph 26.23 (vi) as well as the concept of the differential operator which is monotone in the principal part are already clearer by now.]

---

†) Observe that in the case of equations with operators which are monotone only in the principal part it is not possible, in general, to say anything regarding the uniqueness of the solution.

(iii) If we add, to the conditions of Theorems 29.8 and 29.11, further conditions which ensure the regularity of the weak solution (see Section 17), it is possible to generalize, e.g., Theorems 26.18 and 26.19 on the existence of the classical solution of a boundary value problem.

SECTION 30. THE BROUWER AND THE LERAY-SCHAUDER DEGREE OF A MAPPING

The following assertion, which will also be important for Chapter VI, is basical for the proof of Theorems 29.5 and 29.6 (as will be seen in Paragraph 30.16).

30.1. Theorem. *Let* $r > 0$. *Denote by*

$$B(r) = \{x \in \mathbb{R}^N; |x| < r\}$$

the sphere in the space $\mathbb{R}^N$, *denote its boundary by* $\partial B(r)$:

$$\partial B(r) = \{x \in \mathbb{R}^N; |x| = r\} .$$

Let F be a continuous mapping defined on $\overline{B(r)}$ *with values in* $\mathbb{R}^N$ *such that*

$$F(x) \neq 0 \quad \text{for every} \quad x \in \partial B(r) .$$

Then an integer

$$d[F(x); B(r), 0]$$

[*called the Brouwer degree of the mapping F with respect to the sphere* $B(r)$ *and the point* 0 — *or just the degree of the mapping F*, for short] *exists such that:*

(a) $d[x; B(r), 0] = 1$;

(b) *if*

$$d[F(x); B(r), 0] \neq 0 ,$$

then an $x_0 \in B(r)$ *exists such that*

$$F(x_0) = 0 .$$

(c) **(Invariance with respect to homotopy.)** *Let* $h(x, t)$ *be a continuous mapping of the set* $\overline{B(r)} \times [0, 1]$ *into* $\mathbb{R}^N$ *such that for all* $t \in [0, 1]$ *and for all* $x \in \partial B(r)$ *we have* $h(x, t) \neq 0$. *Then*

$$d[h(x, 0); B(r), 0] = d[h(x, 1); B(r), 0] \,\dagger) .$$

---

†) Two continuous mappings F_0 and F_1 on the set $\overline{B(r)}$ are said to be *homotopic* if a continuous mapping $h(x, t)$ exists on $\overline{B(r)} \times [0, 1]$ such that for all $x \in \overline{B(r)}$

$$h(x, 0) = F_0(x) , \quad h(x, 1) = F_1(x)$$

and for all $x \in \partial B(r)$ and all $t \in [0, 1]$

$$h(x, t) \neq 0 .$$

A mapping $h(x, t)$ with the properties given above is called a *homotopy* of the mappings F_0 and F_1.

(d) *If, moreover, the mapping F is odd [i.e , if*

$$F(x) = -F(-x)$$

for all $x \in \overline{B(r)}$] then

$$d[F(x); B(r), 0]$$

is an odd (and thus non-zero) number.

30.2. Remark on the significance and application of the degree of a mapping.
Consider Theorem 30.1. This is a theorem which ensures the existence of the solution
of the equation $F(x) = 0$ but does not furnish any formula for the calculation of the
degree $d[F(x); B(r), 0]$. The significance of the degree of a mapping is clear when one
examines property (b):

Let a mapping F on the space $\mathbb{R}^N$ be given. Our task is to find out whether the
equation

$$F(x) = 0 \tag{1}$$

has a solution. If equation (1) has a solution on the boundary $\partial B(r)$ of the sphere
$B(r)$, then no further investigation is necessary. If $F(x) \neq 0$ for all $x \in \partial B(r)$ (which
is the other alternative), then Theorem 30.1 indicates the possibility of further progress. Namely, if we succeed in discovering that the mapping F is of non-zero degree
with respect to the sphere $B(r)$ and the point 0, then it follows from property (b)
of the degree of the mapping that the considered equation (1) has at least one solution
in the set $B(r)$. The significance of the Brouwer degree of a mapping lies in this fact.

But how is it possible to discover that the degree of an actual mapping F is non-
zero? First of all, we know — see property (d) of Theorem 30.1 — that every odd
mapping is of non-zero degree [in particular, this is true for the identical mapping —
see property (a)]. Moreover, if the mapping F is not odd, property (c) suggests
a further possibility: We can try to establish a "homotopic connection" of our mapping F with some odd mapping (see the footnote on p. 248).

The procedure indicated here will be carried out several times in what follows (see
the proofs of Theorems 30.4 – 30.6).

30.3. On the construction of the degree of a mapping. Theorem 30.1 is one of the
important assertions of algebraic topology. There are several methods for the construction of the degree of a mapping

$$d[F(x); B(r), 0]$$

with the properties given in Theorem 30.1. The construction could also be made
with the aid of the tools of mathematical analysis, i.e., by means of calculus. The
detailed proof will not be presented here (the reader is referred, e.g., to [36] or
[52]). We present only the basic ideas of the construction of the Brouwer degree of
a mapping.

Step I of the construction of the Brouwer degree:

Assume that

(α) the mapping

$$F(x) = (F_1(x), \ldots, F_N(x))$$

is continuous on $\overline{B(r)}$, $F(x) \neq 0$ for all $x \in \partial B(r)$;

(β) all the partial derivatives

$$\frac{\partial F_i(x)}{\partial x_j}$$

($i, j = 1, \ldots, N$) are continuous on $B(r)$;

(γ) the equation

$$F(x) = 0$$

[i.e., the system of equations $F_i(x) = 0$, $i = 1, \ldots, N$] has only a finite number of solutions $\xi^{(1)}, \ldots, \xi^{(m)}$ in the set $B(r)$ and the Jacobian $J_F(x)$, i.e., the determinant of the matrix

$$\left(\frac{\partial F_i(x)}{\partial x_j} \right)_{i,j=1,\ldots,N},$$

is non-zero at each of the points $\xi^{(1)}, \ldots, \xi^{(m)}$. In this case, put

$$d[F(x); B(r), 0] = \sum_{i=1}^{m} \frac{J_F(\xi^{(i)})}{|J_F(\xi^{(i)})|}.$$

Step II: *The removal of condition* (γ).

Let the mapping $F(x)$ satisfy conditions (α), (β). It is necessary to construct a sequence of mappings $\{F_n(x)\}_{n=1}^{\infty}$ defined on $\overline{B(r)}$ such that

(i) $F_n(x)$ satisfy conditions (α), (β), (γ) for every $n \in \mathbb{N}$;

(ii) $\lim\limits_{n \to \infty} \max\limits_{x \in \overline{B(r)}} |F_n(x) - F(x)| = 0$.

[The existence of a sequence $\{F_n(x)\}_{n=1}^{\infty}$ with the properties (i), (ii) is implied by the so-called Sard theorem, see, e.g., [36], p. 13.]

By step I, the degree

$$d[F_n(x); B(r), 0]$$

is defined for every mapping F_n; it can be shown that a limit

$$\lim_{n \to \infty} d[F_n(x); B(r), 0]$$

exists and that the value of this limit is the same for all sequences $\{F_n(x)\}_{n=1}^{\infty}$ with properties (i), (ii). Therefore, we may put

$$d[F(x); B(r), 0] = \lim_{n\to\infty} d[F_n(x); B(r), 0].$$

Step III: *The removal of condition* (β).

Let the mapping $F(x)$ satisfy condition (α). According to the so-called Weierstrass theorem on the uniform approximation of a continuous function by means of polynomials it is possible to construct a sequence of mappings F_n, $n \in \mathbb{N}$, such that

(a) F_n satisfies conditions (α), (β) for every $n \in \mathbb{N}$;

(b) $\lim_{n\to\infty} \max_{x\in\overline{B(r)}} |F_n(x) - F(x)| = 0$.

By step II, the degree

$$d[F_n(x); B(r), 0]$$

is defined for every mapping F_n, and it can be shown that a finite limit

$$\lim_{n\to\infty} d[F_n(x); B(r), 0]$$

exists and that the value of this limit is the same for all sequences $\{F_n(x)\}_{n=1}^{\infty}$ with the properties (a), (b). Therefore, we may define

$$d[F(x); B(r), 0] = \lim_{n\to\infty} d[F_n(x); B(r), 0].$$

The number

$$d[F(x); B(r), 0]$$

defined in this way is an integer (we twice passed to limits of sequences of integers), and it can be shown that it actually possesses all the properties mentioned in Theorem 30.1.

The construction indicated above shows that the computation of the degree of a concrete mapping is almost impossible! Now, properties (c) and (d) from Theorem 30.1 come into their own. Their application (indicated in Remark 30.2) will be illustrated in the theorems which immediately follow.

30.4. Brouwer fixed point theorem. *Let F be a continuous mapping on $\overline{B(r)}$ which maps the sphere $\overline{B(r)}$ into $\overline{B(r)}$, i.e.,*

$$F(\overline{B(r)}) \subset \overline{B(r)}.$$

Then there exists an $x_0 \in \overline{B(r)}$ such that

$$F(x_0) = x_0$$

(i.e., x_0 is a fixed point of the mapping F — see Paragraph 10.6).

Proof. In the case when there exists an $x_0 \in \partial B(r)$ such that $F(x_0) = x_0$, there is nothing more to be proved.

Suppose, therefore, that

$$x - F(x) \neq 0$$

for every $x \in \partial B(r)$. In this case, the degree

$$d[x - F(x); B(r), 0]$$

is defined. Put

$$h(x, t) = x - t\, F(x)$$

for $x \in \overline{B(r)}$ and $t \in [0, 1]$. Clearly, $h(x, t)$ is a continuous mapping on $\overline{B(r)} \times [0, 1]$. Assume that $\tilde{x} \in \partial B(r)$ and $\tilde{t} \in [0, 1]$ exist such that

$$\tilde{x} - \tilde{t}\, F(\tilde{x}) = 0 \,.$$

Then

$$0 = \left| \tilde{x} - \tilde{t}\, F(\tilde{x}) \right| \geqq \left| \tilde{x} \right| - \tilde{t} \left| F(\tilde{x}) \right| \geqq (1 - \tilde{t})\, r \geqq 0$$

since $\left| F(\tilde{x}) \right| \leqq r$ and $\left| \tilde{x} \right| = r$. Thus, $\tilde{t} = 1$. This, however, contradicts the assumption that $x - F(x) \neq 0$ on $\partial B(r)$. Thus,

$$h(x, t) \neq 0$$

for all $x \in \partial B(r)$ and for all $t \in [0, 1]$. Properties (a) and (b) of Theorem 30.1 yield immediately that

$$1 = d[x; B(r), 0] = d[x - F(x); B(r), 0] \,.$$

Property (b) of Theorem 30.1 can therefore be applied: It follows from this that $x_0 \in B(r)$ exists such that

$$F(x_0) = x_0 \,,$$

and the proof is finished.

30.5. Theorem. *Let F be a continuous mapping on $\overline{B(r)}$ with values in $\mathbb{R}^N$ such that for all $x \in \partial B(r)$ we have*

$$<F(x), x> \leqq 0 \;\dagger)$$

[or, rather, that for all $x \in \partial B(r)$ we have

$$<F(x), x> \geqq 0] \,.$$

Then there exists at least one $x_0 \in \overline{B(r)}$ such that

$$F(x_0) = x_0 \,.$$

---

†) The symbol $<x, y>$ denotes the inner product on the space $\mathbb{R}^N$, i.e., for $x = (x_1, \ldots, x_N)$, $y = (y_1, \ldots, y_N)$ we have

$$<x, y> = x_1 y_1 + \ldots + x_N y_N \,.$$

The proof is entirely analogous to the proof of the Brouwer Theorem 30.4. As a direct consequence, we have the following theorem:

30.6. Theorem. *Let F be a continuous mapping on $\overline{B(r)}$ with values in $\mathbb{R}^N$ and such that for all $x \in \partial B(r)$ we have*

$$<F(x), x> \leq <x, x>$$

[or, rather, that for all $x \in \partial B(r)$ we have

$$<F(x), x> \geq <x, x>].$$

Then there exists at least one $x_0 \in \overline{B(r)}$ such that

$$F(x_0) = 0.$$

30.7. Some generalizations. (i) Since any two normed linear spaces of the same finite dimension are isomorphic, it is possible to replace the space $\mathbb{R}^N$ in Theorems 30.1 and 30.4 by an arbitrary Banach space of finite dimension; in Theorems 30.5 and 30.6 we can then replace the space $\mathbb{R}^N$ by an arbitrary Hilbert space of finite dimension.

(ii) In the Brouwer Theorem 30.4, it is possible to replace the sphere $\overline{B(r)}$ by a closed, bounded, non-empty convex subset of a Banach space of finite dimension.

The space X^* dual to the Banach space X of finite dimension has the same dimension as X [the spaces X and X^* are then isomorphic — see (i) above], thus it is possible to generalize Theorem 30.6. This generalization will be very useful for the proof of Theorems 29.5 and 29.6.

30.8. Theorem. *Let F be a continuous mapping defined on the Banach space X of finite dimension with values in X^*. Assume that there exists a real function $c(r)$, defined on the interval $(0, \infty)$, such that*

$$\lim_{r \to \infty} c(r) = \infty$$

and such that

$$<F(u), u> \geq c(\|u\|_X) \|u\|_X$$

holds for all $u \in X$.

Then $F(X) = X^*$, i.e., the equation

$$F(u) = f$$

has at least one solution in the space X for arbitrary $f \in X^*$.

Proof: Let $f \in X^*$. In the case when $X = X^* = \mathbb{R}^N$ and when $<u, v>$ is the inner product in $\mathbb{R}^N$, there exists $r > 0$ such that the operator $T: \mathbb{R}^N \to \mathbb{R}^N$ defined by the relation

$$Tu = F(u) - f$$

satisfies all the conditions of Theorem 30.6. Thus, the equation $Tu = 0$ — i.e., $F(u) = $ $= f$ — has at least one solution. In the general case, the assertions of Paragraph 30.7 (i), (ii) must be employed.

30.9. Theorem 30.8 turns out to be sufficient for the proof of Theorem 29.5 and Theorem 29.6. However, we think that its application to these proofs will be clearer if the considerations hitherto undertaken in the current section are generalized still further to a certain extent. The generalization is not essential at this point, but will be very useful in the next chapter.

Consider the question of whether, by chance, the assertion of the Brouwer Theorem 30.4, together with Remark 30.7 (i), holds without the condition that the Banach space X be of finite dimension. As it stands, this is not true! A considerable number of counter-examples not presented here show this — the reader may consult, e.g. [36]. However, a generalization of the suggested type is possible for quite a large and useful class of operators which "behave" in a "finite-dimensional way".

30.10. Definition. Let E be a subset of a Banach space X. An operator T defined on E with values in X is called *completely continuous* on E if

(a) T is a continuous operator on E;

(b) for any bounded set $M \subset E$, $\overline{T(M)}$ is a compact set in the space X.

Fixed points of completely continuous operators are dealt with in the following theorem.

30.11. Schauder Theorem. *Let K be a closed non-empty convex bounded subset of a Banach space X. Let T be a completely continuous operator defined on K such that*

$$T(K) \subset K .$$

Then there exists at least one $u_0 \in K$ such that

$$Tu_0 = u_0 .$$

Proof. Recall that if the set $\overline{M} \subset X$ is compact, then, for every $\varepsilon > 0$, points $v_1, \ldots, v_\varrho \in M$ exist such that for any $u \in M$ we have

$$\min_{i=1,\ldots,\varrho} \|u - v_i\|_X < \varepsilon .$$

The set $\{v_1, \ldots, v_\varrho\}$ is called an *ε-net of the set M* (see, e.g., [51]).

Let $\bar{M}$ be compact in X, and let $\{v_1, \ldots, v_\varrho\}$ be an ε-net of the set M. For $u \in M$, put

$$F_\varepsilon u = \frac{\sum\limits_{i=1}^{\varrho} m_i(u)\, v_i}{\sum\limits_{i=1}^{\varrho} m_i(u)}, \tag{2}$$

where

$$m_i(u) = \begin{cases} \varepsilon - \|u - v_i\|_X & \text{if } \|u - v_i\|_X \le \varepsilon, \\ 0 & \text{if } \|u - v_i\|_X > \varepsilon. \end{cases}$$

Further, put $M = T(K)$. Then

$$\|Tu - F_\varepsilon Tu\|_X = \frac{\left\|\sum\limits_{i=1}^{\varrho} m_i(Tu)\, Tu - \sum\limits_{i=1}^{\varrho} m_i(Tu)\, v_i\right\|_X}{\sum\limits_{i=1}^{\varrho} m_i(Tu)} \le \frac{\sum\limits_{i=1}^{\varrho} m_i(Tu)\, \|Tu - v_i\|_X}{\sum\limits_{i=1}^{\varrho} m_i(Tu)} < \varepsilon,$$

i.e., for arbitrary $\varepsilon > 0$ and for every $u \in K$ we have

$$\|Tu - F_\varepsilon Tu\|_X < \varepsilon. \tag{3}$$

For $n \in \mathbb{N}$, let X_n stand for the linear hull†) of a $1/n$-net of the set $T(K)$ and of at least one element of the set K. The linear space X_n is a Banach space of finite dimension (the same norm being used in X_n as in X of course). Put

$$K_n = K \cap X_n, \quad T_n(u) = F_{1/n} Tu \quad \text{for} \quad u \in K_n.$$

The set K_n is obviously closed (in X_n), convex, bounded, and non-empty; the operator T_n is continuous on K_n and

$$T_n(K_n) \subset K_n$$

holds by (2) since the set K_n is convex. Thus, by the Brouwer Theorem 30.4 and by Remark 30.7 (i), there exists an element $u_n \in K_n \subset K$ for every $n \in \mathbb{N}$ such that

$$T_n u_n = u_n.$$

Moreover, relation (3) implies

$$\|Tu_n - u_n\|_X = \|Tu_n - T_n u_n\|_X < \frac{1}{n},$$

---

†) By the linear hull of the set of points $u_1, \ldots, u_m$ we understand the set of all points of the form

$$\lambda_1 u_1 + \ldots + \lambda_m u_m,$$

where $\lambda_1, \ldots, \lambda_m$ are arbitrary real numbers.

and thus

$$\lim_{n \to \infty} \| Tu_n - u_n \|_X = 0 . \tag{4}$$

Since $Tu_n \in \overline{T(K)}$ and $\overline{T(K)}$ is a compact set, a subsequence $\{u_{n_k}\}_{k=1}^{\infty}$ and a point $u_0 \in \overline{T(K)}$ exist (see the footnote on p. 191) such that

$$Tu_{n_k} \to u_0 \quad \text{in} \quad X . \tag{5}$$

Since

$$\| u_{n_k} - u_0 \|_X \leq \| u_{n_k} - Tu_{n_k} \|_X + \| Tu_{n_k} - u_0 \|_X ,$$

relations (4) and (5) also imply that

$$u_{n_k} \to u_0 \quad \text{in} \quad X .$$

Since the operator T is continuous, we have

$$Tu_{n_k} \to Tu_0 \quad \text{in} \quad X . \tag{6}$$

Relations (5) and (6) show that

$$Tu_0 = u_0 ,$$

which proves the theorem.

30.12. Remark. The reader who read through Section 28 of this book will certainly have spotted an analogy with the Ritz method (i.e., a "finite-dimensional" approximation of the considered problem) in the proof of the Schauder Theorem on the fixed point of a completely continuous operator. This type of proof of the existence of the solution of a nonlinear operator equation will be encountered again in Paragraph 30.16.

30.13. The linearization method revisited. (i) In Paragraph 10.7, we looked for the classical solution of the boundary value problem

$$\begin{cases} -u''(x) + g(u(x)) = f(x) & \text{for} \quad x \in (0, 1), \\ u(0) = u(1) = 0 \end{cases} \tag{7}$$

by the linearization method, applying the Banach contraction principle. We now repeat the considerations carried out in Paragraph 10.7; to prove that the operator B defined by relation (10.15) has a fixed point in the space $C^0([0, 1])$ we now use the Schauder Theorem 30.11 instead of the Banach contraction principle. Let g be a continuous real function. The Arzèla criterion of compactness in the space $C^0([0, 1])$ (see, e.g., [51]) immediately yields that the operator B is completely continuous on the space $C^0([0, 1])$. It thus suffices to find $r > 0$ such that

$$B(K) \subset K , \tag{8}$$

where
$$K = \{u \in C^0(\langle 0, 1\rangle); \|u\|_{C^0} \leqq r\} .$$

We immediately see that inclusion (8) will be satisfied, e.g., if for the function
$$\psi(\varrho) = \max_{(t,\xi)\in[0,1]\times[-\varrho,\varrho]} |f(t) - g(\xi)|$$
there exists an $r > 0$ such that
$$\psi(r) \leqq r .$$

Hence, the Schauder Theorem 30.11 together with the theoretical considerations concerning the linearization method which were given in Paragraph 10.7 imply the assertion which follows.

(ii) Let $f \in C^0([0, 1])$, and let g be a continuous function on $\mathbb{R}$. Assume that there exists an $r > 0$ such that
$$\max_{(t,\xi)\in[0,1]\times[-r,r]} |f(t) - g(\xi)| \leqq r . \tag{9}$$

Then the boundary value problem (7) has at least one classical solution.

The existence of the classical solution of boundary value problem (7) has already been proved in Paragraph 26.23 (v), but the proof there was by the variational method and under the assumption that positive constants $c, d, c < 1$, exist such that for all $\xi \in \mathbb{R}$
$$|g(\xi)| \leqq c|\xi| + d \tag{10}$$
holds. Since condition (9) in assertion (ii) follows from condition (10) as the reader easily sees, we have actually proved assertion 26.23 (v) by a different method.

(iii) The linearization method, together with the Schauder fixed point theorem, is (unlike the application of the Banach contraction principle) a powerful tool in the theory of partial differential equations as well. For more on this topic, see, e.g., [55].

By the same method as was used in the proof of the Schauder Theorem, it is also possible to generalize the concept of the Brouwer degree of a mapping.

30.14. Theorem. *Let X be a Banach space, $r > 0$, and*
$$B(r) = \{u \in X; \|u\|_X < r\} .$$

Let F be a completely continuous operator defined on $\overline{B(r)}$ with values in X and such that
$$Fu \neq u$$
for every $u \in \partial B(r)$. Then an integer
$$d[u - Fu; B(r), \Theta]$$

exists [called *the Leray-Schauder degree of the mapping* $u - Fu$ *with respect to the sphere* $B(r)$ *and the point* Θ, or simply *the degree of the mapping* $u - Fu$, *for short*] *such that*

(a) $d[u; B(r), \Theta] = 1$.

(b) *If*

$$d[u - Fu; B(r), \Theta] \neq 0,$$

then there exists $u_0 \in B(r)$ *such that*

$$Fu_0 = u_0.$$

(c) *If* G *is a completely continuous mapping on* $\overline{B(r)}$, *again with values in* X, *and if*

$$u - Fu - tGu \neq \Theta$$

holds for every $u \in \partial B(r)$ *and for every* $t \in [0, 1]$, *then*

$$d[u - Fu; B(r), \Theta] = d[u - Gu - Fu; B(r), \Theta].$$

(d) *If, moreover, the operator* F *is odd* [*i.e., if* $F(u) = -F(-u)$ *for all* $u \in \overline{B(r)}$], *then the degree*

$$d[u - Fu; B(r), \Theta]$$

is an odd (*and thus non-zero*) *number.*

30.15. Remarks. (i) If $X = \mathbb{R}^N$, then the Brouwer and the Leray-Schauder degrees of a mapping are identical.

(ii) The manner of application of the Leray-Schauder degree of a mapping is the same as the manner of application of the Brouwer degree (see Remark 30.2). The Leray-Schauder degree will be used in Chapter VI.

30.16. In concluding this section, we discuss the proofs of Theorems 29.5 and 29.6. We indicate the principal ideas of the proof of Theorem 29.5. The proof of Theorem 29.6 is similar; however, it is technically more demanding and the reader can find it, e.g., in [57].

Thus, let T be an operator defined on a reflexive Banach space X with values in X^* such that

(a) *T is bounded*;

(b) *T is demicontinuous*;

(c) *T is coercive*;

(d) *T is monotone.*

Stage I. We wish to prove that if $f \in X^*$ is chosen arbitrary but fixed, then the equation

$$Tu = f \tag{11}$$

has at least one solution. The operator

$$T_f u = Tu - f$$

again satisfies all the conditions of Theorem 29.5. Thus, we can work with the operator T_f instead of the operator T; in what follows, we again write T instead of T_f. Therefore, it suffices to show that if conditions (a) through (d) are satisfied, then the equation

$$Tu = \Theta \tag{12}$$

has at least one solution.

Stage II. We construct an "approximation of the infinite-dimensional equation (12) by an equation in a space of finite dimension". More precisely: Let Λ be the family of all subspaces of finite dimension in the space X. If $F \in \Lambda$, define the operator j_F for $u \in F$ by the relation

$$j_F u = u .$$

Obviously, the operator j_F has values in the space X and is linear and continuous on F.

If M, N are two Banach spaces and S is a continuous linear operator defined on M with values in N, then there exists precisely one continuous linear operator S^* defined on N^* with values in M^* such that

$$<v, Su>_N = <S^*v, u>_M$$

for all $u \in M$ and $v \in N^*$ (the expression on the left-hand side stands for the value of the continuous linear functional $v \in N^*$ at the point $Su \in N$; the expression on the right-hand side represents the value of the functional $S^*v \in M^*$ at the point $u \in M$). The existence and the basic properties of the operator S^* (which is called the *adjoint operator* to S) are proved, e.g., in [51].

Let us then construct the operator j_F^* adjoint to the operator j_F. The operator j_F^* is continuous and linear on X^* with values in F^*. For $u \in F$, put

$$T_F u = j_F^*(Tu) .$$

This defines a mapping T_F of the space F into the space F^*.

Stage III. It is easy to show [making use of condition (b) and of the fact that a continuous linear operator maps a weakly convergent sequence onto a weakly convergent sequence] that the operator T_F is continuous on a Banach space F of finite dimension (in which strong and weak convergence coincide — see Paragraph 24.7) and that it maps the space F into the dual space F^*. Furthermore, we shall show that the equation

$$T_F u = \Theta \tag{13}$$

has at least one solution in the space F. For this, it suffices — by Theorem 30.8 — to find a real function $c(r)$ defined for $r \geq 0$ and such that

$$\lim_{r \to \infty} c(r) = \infty$$

and

$$<T_F u, u> \geq c(\|u\|_X) \|u\|_X .$$

holds for all $u \in F$.

Stage IV. The construction of the function $c(r)$ with the properties mentioned above is accomplished as follows: Put

$$c(r) = \inf_{\substack{u \in X \\ \|u\|_X = r}} \frac{<Tu, u>}{\|u\|_X} .$$

By condition (c) (the coerciveness of operator T), we have

$$\lim_{r \to \infty} c(r) = \infty .$$

Furthermore,

$$<T_F u, u> = <Tu, j_F u> = <Tu, u> \geq c(\|u\|_X) \|u\|_X \tag{14}$$

is valid for arbitrary $u \in F$, since $j_F u = u$ for $u \in F$.

Thus, Theorem 30.8 ensures that for an arbitrary $F \in \Lambda$ there exists at least one $u_F \in F$ which satisfies equation (13), i.e.,

$$T_F(u_F) = \Theta .$$

Stage V (a priori estimate). There exists an $r_0 > 0$ such that

$$\|u_F\|_X \leq r_0 \tag{15}$$

holds for arbitrary $F \in \Lambda$ and for every solution $u_F \in F$ of equation (13). Indeed, should such an r_0 not exist, there would be a sequence $\{u_n\}_{n=1}^{\infty}$ of solutions of equation (13) with $F = F_n$ $(n = 1, 2, \ldots)$ such that

$$\lim_{n \to \infty} \|u_n\|_X = \infty .$$

Thus,

$$\lim_{n \to \infty} c(\|u_n\|_X) = \infty$$

by assumption. This leads to a contradiction in view of inequality (14):

$$c(\|u_n\|_X) \|u_n\|_X \leq 0 = <T_{F_n} u_n, u_n > .$$

Stage VI. Let $F_0 \in \Lambda$ and

$$\Lambda_{F_0} = \{F \in \Lambda; F_0 \subset F\} .$$

We denote by $\mathcal{U}_{F_0}$ the set of all elements $u \in X$ which are solutions of equation (13) for some $F \in \Lambda_{F_0}$. Furthermore, let $\overline{\mathcal{U}}_{F_0}^w$ be the weak closure of the set $\mathcal{U}_{F_0}$ (i.e., the least weakly closed set which contains $\mathcal{U}_{F_0}$ — see footnote on p. 195). One of the important properties of reflexive Banach spaces is the so-called *finite intersection property* (see, e.g., [51]). This immediately implies that an element $u_0 \in X$ exists such that

$$u_0 \in \bigcap_{F_0 \in \Lambda} \overline{\mathcal{U}}_{F_0}^w . \tag{16}$$

We shall show that u_0 is the solution of equation (12).

Stage VII. Let $v \in X$. Choose $F_0 \in \Lambda$ so that $v \in F_0$, and let $F \in \Lambda_{F_0}$. If u_F is a solution of equation (13), then condition (d) implies that

$$0 \leqq \; <Tv - Tu_F, v - u_F> \; = \; <Tv, v - u_F> \; - \; <Tu_F, v - u_F> \; =$$

$$= \; <Tv, v - u_F> \; - \; <Tu_F, j_F(v - u_F)> \; =$$

$$= \; <T, v - u_F> \; - \; <T_F u_F, v - u_F> \; = \; <Tv, v - u_F> .$$

Thus,

$$0 \leqq \; <Tv, v - u> \tag{17}$$

holds for arbitrary $u \in \mathcal{U}_{F_0}$. Passing to the limit, this shows that inequality (17) is valid even for arbitrary $u \in \overline{\mathcal{U}}_{F_0}^w$. In particular, we then have

$$0 \leqq \; <Tv, v - u_0> . \tag{18}$$

The point $v \in X$ was chosen arbitrarily at the beginning of this stage so that inequality (18) is valid for any $v \in X$.

Stage VIII (the so-called **Minty trick**). If we put $v = u_0 + tw$ in inequality (18) for arbitrary $w \in X$ and $t > 0$, we obtain

$$0 \leqq \; <T(u_0 + tw), tw> \; = \; t<T(u_0 + tw), w> ,$$

i.e.,

$$0 \leqq \; <T(u_0 + tw), w> .$$

By passing to the limit as $t \to 0+$, we obtain — applying condition (b) — the inequality

$$0 \leqq \; <Tu_0, w> , \tag{19}$$

which is valid for all $w \in X$. Thus, it is possible to replace the element w in (19) by the element $-w$, i.e.,

$$0 \leqq \; <Tu_0, -w> \; = \; - <Tu_0, w> \, . \tag{20}$$

(19) and (20) imply that for every $w \in X$ we have

$$<Tu_0, w> \; = 0 \, ,$$

i.e.,

$$Tu_0 = \Theta \, ,$$

and the proof is accomplished.

SECTION 31. GENERAL BOUNDARY CONDITIONS FOR SECOND ORDER ORDINARY DIFFERENTIAL EQUATIONS

31.1. Formulation of the problem. In Paragraph 15.12, the various choices of the spaces V such that

$$W_0^{1,2}(0, 1) \subset V \subset W^{1,2}(0, 1)$$

represented different types of boundary conditions in the formulation of the weak solution of the boundary value problem (A, V, Q). The formal differential operator A was there given by the formula

$$(Au)(x) = -\frac{d}{dx} [a_1(x; u(x), u'(x))] + a_0(x; u(x), u'(x)) \, .$$

As observed in Paragraph 15.12 (IV), it is not possible, in general, to characterize in the weak formulation of the boundary value problem the formal differential equation

$$Au = f \quad \text{on} \quad (0, 1)$$

with the boundary conditions

$$\alpha \, u(0) + \beta \, u'(0) = a \, ,$$
$$\gamma \, u(1) + \delta \, u'(1) = b \, .$$

In this section, we investigate the existence of the classical solutions of such boundary value problems by applying the weak solution (for a certain Neumann problem) and the regularity theorem.

Let $f \in C^0([0, 1])$, and let $a, b, \alpha, \beta, \gamma, \delta \in \mathbb{R}$. For the sake of simplicity, assume that the coefficients $a_1(x; \xi_0, \xi_1)$, $a_0(x; \xi_0, \xi_1)$ satisfy similar conditions as in Theorem 26.18 (with the exception of the conditions of potentiality which — as we know from Section 29 — can be removed applying the topological method, i.e., the Browder Theorem 29.5.) Thus, we assume that

$$a_1 \in C^1([0, 1] \times \mathbb{R}^2) \, , \quad a_0 \in C^0([0, 1] \times \mathbb{R}^2)$$

holds and, further, that $a_i \in CAR^*(2)$, i.e., that there exist a continuous function g on $\mathbb{R}$ and a constant $c_1 > 0$ so that

$$|a_1(x; \xi_0, \xi_1)| \leq c_1(g(\xi_0) + |\xi_1|), \tag{1}$$

$$|a_0(x; \xi_0, \xi_1)| \leq c_1(g(\xi_0) + |\xi_1|^2) \tag{2}$$

hold for all $x \in [0, 1]$ and for all $\xi_0, \xi_1 \in \mathbb{R}$.

We are looking for a function $u \in C^2([0, 1])$ which satisfies the equation

$$-\frac{d}{dx}[a_1(x; u(x), u'(x))] + a_0(x; u(x), u'(x)) = f(x) \tag{3}$$

on the interval $(0, 1)$ and also satisfies the boundary conditions

$$\begin{cases} \alpha\, u(0) + \beta\, u'(0) = a, \\ \gamma\, u(1) + \delta\, u'(1) = b. \end{cases} \tag{4}$$

Under some additional conditions, the existence of the (classical) solution of the boundary value problem (4), (5) is proved in Theorem 26.18 for the case when $\beta = \delta = 0$, $\alpha \neq 0$, $\gamma \neq 0$ [see also Remarks 29.9 and 29.12 (iii)]. The remaining alternatives for the choice of the constants α, β, γ, δ will now be discussed.

31.2. We begin by investigating the following problem which is at first sight in no way connected with boundary value problem (3), (4)†):

Let h_1, h_0 be two continuous functionals on the space $W^{1,2}(0, 1)$ such that for all functions $u_1, u_2 \in W^{1,2}(0, 1)$ we have

$$(h_1(u_1) - h_1(u_2))(u_1(1) - u_2(1)) - (h_0(u_1) - h_0(u_2))(u_1(0) - u_2(0)) \geq 0. \tag{5}$$

Define an operator T on the space $W^{1,2}(0, 1)$ with values in $W^{1,2}(0, 1)$†† in such a way that for all $u, v \in W^{1,2}(0, 1)$ we have

$$<Tu, v>_{1,2} = \int_0^1 a_1(x; u(x), u'(x))\, v'(x)\, dx +$$

$$+ \int_0^1 a_0(x; u(x), u'(x))\, v(x)\, dx + h_1(u)\, v(1) - h_0(u)\, v(0).$$

The operator T is continuous on the space $W^{1,2}(0, 1)$. Assume, further, that there exist constants $c_2 > 0$, $c_3 > 0$ such that for all $x \in [0, 1]$ and $\xi_0, \xi_1, \zeta_0, \zeta_1 \in \mathbb{R}$ we have

$$[a_1(x; \xi_0, \xi_1) - a_1(x; \zeta_0, \zeta_1)](\xi_1 - \zeta_1) +$$

$$+ [a_0(x; \xi_0, \xi_1) - a_0(x; \zeta_0, \zeta_1)](\xi_0 - \zeta_0) \geq c_2|\xi_1 - \zeta_1|^2 + c_3|\xi_0 - \zeta_0|^2. \tag{6}$$

---

†) In fact, we shall carry out in detail the work mentioned in Paragraph 15.16 (pp. 123 and 124).

††) Since we deal with the Hilbert space $H = W^{1,2}(0, 1)$, we identify H and H^* — see the footnote on p. 240.

If condition (6) holds, then the operator T is strongly monotone on the space $W^{1,2}(0, 1)$ (see Paragraph 29.3), in particular, it is purely monotone and coercive. The Browder Theorem 29.5 then immediately implies the following:

31.3. Lemma. *If the conditions* (1), (2), (5), *and* (6) *mentioned above are satisfied, then there exists exactly one function* $u_0 \in W^{1,2}(0, 1)$ *such that*

$$< Tu_0, v >_{1,2} = \int_0^1 f(x)\, v(x)\, dx \tag{7}$$

holds for all $v \in W^{1,2}(0, 1)$.

Just as in Theorem 17.5, we also obtain the assertion on the regularity of the solution u_0:

31.4. Lemma. *The solution* u_0 *of problem* (7), *the existence of which is ensured by Lemma 31.3, is an element of the space* $C^2([0, 1])$.

31.5. Since $u_0 \in C^2([0, 1])$, integration by parts yields, from relation (7) and from the definition of the operator T, the relation

$$\int_0^1 \left\{ - \frac{d}{dx} \left[a_1(x; u_0(x), u_0'(x)) \right] + a_0(x; u_0(x), u_0'(x)) - f(x) \right\} v(x)\, dx +$$

$$+ \left[h_1(u_0) + a_1(1; u_0(1), u_0'(1)) \right] v(1) - \left[h_0(u_0) + a_1(0; u_0(0), u_0'(0)) \right] v(0) = 0. \tag{8}$$

Thus,

$$\int_0^1 \left\{ - \frac{d}{dx} \left[a_1(x; u_0(x), u_0'(x)) \right] + a_0(x; u_0(x), u_0'(x)) - f(x) \right\} v(x)\, dx = 0 \tag{9}$$

holds for every function $v \in C_0^\infty(0, 1)$, i.e.,

$$- \frac{d}{dx} \left[a_1(x; u_0(x), u_0'(x)) \right] + a_0(x; u_0(x), u_0'(x)) = f(x) \tag{10}$$

for every $x \in [0, 1]$. The solution of problem (7) is then the solution of equation (3). Substitution of (10) into (8) yields

$$\left[h_1(u_0) + a_1(1; u_0(1), u_0'(1)) \right] v(1) - \left[h_0(u_0) + a_1(0; u_0(0), u_0'(0)) \right] v(0) = 0$$

for every $v \in W^{1,2}(0, 1)$; thus,

$$h_1(u_0) = -a_1(1; u_0(1), u_0'(1)), \tag{11}$$

$$h_0(u_0) = -a_1(0; u_0(0), u_0'(0)). \tag{12}$$

From equations (11), (12), we see how to choose the functionals $h_1(u)$, $h_0(u)$ so that the function $u_0(x)$ which is the solution of problem (7) may satisfy the boundary conditions (4). Let $\beta\delta \neq 0$. We put

$$h_1(u) = -a_1\left(1; u(1), \frac{b - \gamma\, u(1)}{\delta}\right), \tag{13}$$

$$h_0(u) = -a_1\left(0; u(0), \frac{a - \alpha\, u(0)}{\beta}\right) \tag{14}$$

for $u \in W^{1,2}(0, 1)$. [Obviously, $h_0(u)$, $h_1(u)$ are continuous functionals on the space $W^{1,2}(0, 1)$.] Then we have

$$a_1\left(1; u_0(1), \frac{b - \gamma\, u_0(1)}{\delta}\right) = a_1(1; u_0(1), u_0'(1)),$$

$$a_1\left(0, u_0(0), \frac{a - \alpha\, u_0(0)}{\beta}\right) = a_0(0; u_0(0), u_0'(0)).$$

In condition (6), put $\xi_0 = \zeta_0 = u_1(1)$, $\xi_1 = [b - \gamma\, u_0(1)]/\delta$, $\zeta_1 = u_0'(1)$, $x = 1$. This immediately yields

$$\frac{b - \gamma\, u_0(1)}{\delta} = u_0'(1). \tag{15}$$

Similarly, we obtain

$$\frac{a - \alpha\, u_0(0)}{\beta} = u_0'(0). \tag{16}$$

Equations (15) and (16) show that the function u_0 satisfies condition (4) and is the solution of equation (3) (as shown above).

It will not have escaped the attentive reader that condition (5) has not yet been verified. For it to hold, we assume, further, that

$$(a_1(x; \xi_0, \xi_1) - a_1(x; \zeta_0, \zeta_1))\,(\xi_1 - \zeta_1) \geqq 0 \tag{17}$$

for all $\xi_0, \xi_1, \zeta_0, \zeta_1 \in \mathbb{R}$, $x \in [0, 1]$. [For instance, if the function a_1 is independent of the variable ξ_0, then (17) is a consequence of condition (6).] From this, we obtain

$$-\frac{\gamma}{\delta}\left[a_1\left(1; u_1(1), \frac{b - \gamma\, u_1(1)}{\delta}\right) - \right.$$

$$\left. - a_1\left(1; u_2(1), \frac{b - \gamma\, u_2(1)}{\delta}\right)\right](u_1(1) - u_2(1)) \geqq 0, \tag{18}$$

$$- \frac{\alpha}{\beta} \left[a_1 \left(0; u_1(0), \frac{a - \alpha u_1(0)}{\beta} \right) - \right.$$

$$\left. - a_1 \left(0; u_2(0), \frac{a - \alpha u_2(0)}{\beta} \right) \right] (u_1(0) - u_2(0)) \geqq 0 \qquad (19)$$

for arbitrary $u_1, u_2 \in W^{1,2}(0, 1)$.

Thus, if the conditions

$$\beta \delta \neq 0, \quad \frac{\gamma}{\delta} \geqq 0, \quad \frac{\alpha}{\beta} \leqq 0 \qquad (20)$$

are satisfied, then condition (5) is satisfied as well. In the same way, it is possible to establish that condition (5) is also satisfied if either

$$\alpha \neq 0, \quad \beta = 0, \quad \delta \neq 0, \quad \frac{\gamma}{\delta} \geqq 0 \qquad (21)$$

or

$$\beta \neq 0, \quad \gamma \neq 0, \quad \delta = 0, \quad \frac{\alpha}{\beta} \leqq 0 \qquad (22)$$

is valid. The next theorem now follows.

31.6. Theorem. *Let* $f \in C^0([0, 1])$, $a_1 \in C^1([0, 1] \times \mathbb{R}^2)$, $a_0 \in C^0([0, 1] \times \mathbb{R}^2)$. *Let* $a, b, \alpha, \beta, \gamma, \delta \in \mathbb{R}$. *Assume, further, that*

$$\beta \delta \neq 0, \quad \frac{\gamma}{\delta} \geqq 0, \quad \frac{\alpha}{\beta} \leqq 0 \qquad (20)$$

or

$$\alpha \neq 0, \quad \beta = 0, \quad \delta \neq 0, \quad \frac{\gamma}{\delta} \geqq 0 \qquad (21)$$

or

$$\beta \neq 0, \quad \gamma \neq 0, \quad \delta = 0, \quad \frac{\alpha}{\beta} \leqq 0; \qquad (22)$$

$$|a_1(x; \xi_0, \xi_1)| \leqq c_1(g(\xi_0) + |\xi_1|^2); \qquad (1)$$

$$|a_0(x; \xi_0, \xi_1)| \leqq c_1(g(\xi_0) + |\xi_1|^2); \qquad (2)$$

(i.e., $a_i \in$ **CAR***(2), $i = 0, 1$);

$$[a_1(x; \xi_0, \xi_1) - a_1(x; \zeta_0, \zeta_1)] (\xi_1 - \zeta_1) +$$
$$+ [a_0(x; \xi_0, \xi_1) - a_0(x; \zeta_0, \zeta_1)] (\xi_0 - \zeta_0) \geqq c_2 |\xi_1 - \zeta_1|^2 + c_3 |\xi_0 - \zeta_0|^2 \qquad (6)$$

(where c_1, c_2, c_3 *are positive constants);*

$$[a_1(x; \xi_0, \xi_1) - a_1(x; \zeta_0, \zeta_1)] (\xi_1 - \zeta_1) \geqq 0. \qquad (17)$$

Then there exists precisely one function $u_0 \in C^2([0, 1])$ which satisfies the differential equation

$$-\frac{d}{dx}[a_1(x; u(x), u'(x))] + a_0(x; u(x), u'(x)) = f(x) \quad for \quad x \in (0, 1) \qquad (3)$$

and also the boundary conditions

$$\begin{cases} \alpha \, u(0) + \beta \, u'(0) = a, \\ \gamma \, u(1) + \delta \, u'(1) = b. \end{cases} \qquad (4)$$

31.7. Remarks. (i) Let $\alpha \geq 0$, $\gamma \geq 0$, $\alpha^2 + \beta^2 > 0$, $\gamma^2 + \delta^2 > 0$. In those cases which are not included in the assumptions (20) to (22) of Theorem 31.6, we can easily construct examples (e.g., on the basis of the differential equation $-u'' + u = = 0$) proving that the assertion of the above theorem need not hold in general.

(ii) Existence of a classical solution of the boundary value problem (3), (4) can be investigated in a similar way even in the case

$$a_1, a_0 \in \mathbf{CAR}^*(p), \quad p \neq 2.$$

(iii) The method used is typical for ordinary differential equations of the second order. Nevertheless, it can be transferred (with certain technical difficulties) also to equations of $2k$-th order of the form

$$\sum_{i=0}^{k}(-1)^i \frac{d^i}{dx^i} \, a_i(x; u(x), u'(x), \ldots, u^{(k)}(x)) = f(x) \quad for \quad x \in (0, 1)$$

with the corresponding boundary value conditions [among other conditions of the type

$$\alpha_0 \, u(0) + \alpha_1 \, u'(0) + \ldots + \alpha_k \, u^{(k)}(0) = a,$$

$$\beta_0 \, u(1) + \beta_1 \, u(1) + \ldots + \beta_k \, u^{(k)}(1) = b].$$

SECTION 32. SUMMARY OF CHAPTERS IV AND V. SOME ADDITIONAL REMARKS

32.0. Summary. In Chapters IV and V, several theorems were presented which guarantee the existence and, eventually, also the uniqueness of the weak solution of the boundary value problem (A, V, Q), i.e., the existence of a function $u_0 \in V$ satisfying relation (15.8). To prove these theorems either the variational method (see Chapter IV) or the topological method (see Chapter V) was used. From the survey which follows below, it is clear which of the conditions imposed on the coefficients a_α of the formal differential operator A is essential for which method.

(a) **Growth conditions** [see (15.4)]. These conditions serve to make the definition of the concept of the weak solution possible at all (see Sections 12 – 15). They must therefore be satisfied for the application of either method.

(b) **Reflexivity of the space** V (see Section 25). This again is a requirement which is necessary for the application of the variational method (see Theorem 26.11) as well as for the application of the topological method (see Theorems 29.5 and 29.6).

The condition of reflexivity can no doubt be avoided at the price of certain modifications — see Section 27; however, it was just in that section that we saw, when investigating the existence of the solution of the minimal surface problem, the difficulties associated with problems which have to be solved in non-reflexive spaces.

(c) **Coerciveness conditions** [see (26.14)]. These are further conditions which are exploited in the variational method as well as in the topological method. Boundary value problems in some nonlinear differential equations whose coefficients do not satisfy the coerciveness conditions will be treated briefly in Chapter VI.

(d) **Monotony conditions** [see (26.11)]. Both methods require these conditions. However, as shown in Paragraph 26.23 and in Theorem 29.6, the monotony conditions can be weakened in both approaches to the so-called conditions of monotony in the principal part.

(e) **Potentiality conditions** [see Paragraph 26.13 (ii)]. This is an assumption which is essential for the application of the variational method; the topological method does not need these conditions. Note further that in the case of "simple nonlinearities" (see, e.g., Paragraph 26.16) the potentiality conditions are satisfied automatically.

The existence of the weak solution for the boundary value problem (A, V, Q) is proved by the variational method in Paragraphs 26.13 and 26.14, and by the topological method in Paragraphs 29.7 through 29.11. The uniqueness of the weak solution is proved in Paragraphs 26.14 and 29.8.

32.1. Further application of calculus. In Definition 18.5, we introduced one of the ways defining the derivative of a functional on a general normed linear space. This was the so-called Gâteaux derivative. The definition corresponds to the concept of the partial derivative for functions in N real variables (as we saw in Chapter IV). However, this is not the only way of defining the derivative of functionals: We could also exploit similarities with the theory of real functions in N real variables and generalize the definition of total differential. This generalization will be extended even to operators.

(i) **Definition.** Let X, Y be Banach spaces. Let the operator T be defined on X with values in Y. Let $u_0 \in X$. We say that the operator T has a *Fréchet* (or total) *differential* at the point u_0 if there exists a continuous linear operator from the space X into the space Y — we shall denote it by $T'(u_0)$ — such that

$$\lim_{u \to u_0} \frac{\|Tu - Tu_0 - T'(u_0)(u - u_0)\|_Y}{\|u - u_0\|_X} = 0 .$$

The operator $T'(u_0)$ is called the *Fréchet derivative of the mapping T at the point u_0.*

The basic properties of the Fréchet differential will not be given in the book (the reader who is interested in differential calculus in general normed spaces is referred to the books [89], [90], where he will find adequate material on this topic). Nevertheless, we want to demonstrate one frequently used method for establishing the existence of the solution of boundary value problems in nonlinear differential equations. We first introduce one more concept, however.

(ii) **Definition of the partial differential.** Let X_1, X_2, Y be Banach spaces, and let T be an operator defined on the Cartesian product $X_1 \times X_2$ with values in Y. Let $(a_1, a_2) \in X_1 \times X_2$, and define

$$T_{a_2}(u_1) = T(u_1, a_2), \quad u_1 \in X_1 ,$$

$$T_{a_1}(u_2) = T(a_1, u_2), \quad u_2 \in X_2 .$$

The operator T_{a_2} maps the space X_1 into the space Y; the operator T_{a_1} maps the space X_2 into the space Y. If the operator T_{a_2} has a total differential at the point $a_1 \in X_1$, we will denote it by $T_1'(a_1, a_2)$ and call it the *partial total differential of the operator T at the point* (a_1, a_2) with respect to the first variable. Similarly, we define the partial total differential $T_2'(a_1, a_2)$ of the operator T at the point (a_1, a_2) with respect to the second variable.

The following assertion is a very important theorem known as the **Hildebrandt-Graves Theorem on implicit functions.**

(iii) **Theorem.** *Let X_1, X_2, Y be Banach spaces, and let the operator T defined on $X_1 \times X_2$ with values in Y satisfy the following conditions:*

(a) *T is continuous at the point $(u_0, v_0) \in X_1 \times X_2$;*

(b) *$T(u_0, v_0) = \Theta$;*

(c) *the partial total differential $T_2'(u_0, v_0)$ exists and is a continuous linear mapping of the space X_2 onto the space Y;*

(d) *T_2' is a continuous mapping at the point (u_0, v_0) in the following sense:*

For all sequences of elements $u_n \in X_1$, $v_n \in X_2$ such that

$$u_n \to u_0 \quad in \quad X_1 ,$$

$$v_n \to v_0 \quad in \quad X_2$$

we have

$$\lim_{n \to \infty} \sup_{\substack{h \in X_2 \\ \|h\|_{X_2} \leq 1}} \left\| T_2'(u_n, v_n) h - T_2'(u_0, v_0) h \right\|_Y = 0 .$$

Then there exist positive numbers ε, δ such that for every $u \in X_1$,

$$\|u - u_0\|_{X_1} < \delta ,$$

precisely one $v(u) \in X_2$ exists,

$$\|v(u) - v_0\|_{X_2} < \varepsilon ,$$

which satisfies the equation

$$T(u, v(u)) = \Theta .$$

(For the proof see, e.g., [89].)

(iv) Example. To illustrate the application of the implicit function theorem we make use of the following boundary value problem. Let $f \in C^0([0, 1])$ and consider the Dirichlet problem

$$\begin{cases} -u'' - u^3 = f & \text{on} \quad (0, 1) , \\ \quad u(0) = u(1) = 0 . \end{cases} \tag{1}$$

The theory outlined in Chapters IV and V cannot be applied to this example, since the problem is not coercive [cf. Example 26.21 — the boundary value problem (26.23), see also Section 37]. Put

$$X_1 = C^0([0, 1]) ,$$
$$X_2 = \{u \in C^2([0, 1]); u(0) = u(1) = 0\} ,$$

and

$$T(f, u) = -u'' - u^3 - f .$$

The operator T maps the Cartesian product $X_1 \times X_2$ into the space $Y = X_1$. Clearly, $T(\Theta, \Theta) = \Theta$, and

$$T_2'(\Theta, \Theta) h = -h'' , \quad h \in X_2 .$$

It is easily checked that all the conditions of the implicit function theorem are satisfied. For a function $f \in C^0([0, 1])$ of sufficiently small norm [in the space $C^0([0, 1])$], there therefore exists at least one (or even precisely one) solution which lies "near" the null function.

In Chapter VI, we will prove that problem (1) has an infinite number of solutions for any arbitrary right-hand side $f \in C^0([0, 1])$ — see Theorem 37.2. (However, by the above, for a "small" right-hand side f, there exists precisely one "small" solution.)

As an appropriate exercise, it is possible to apply the implicit function theorem to the determination of the nontrivial conditions imposed on the function $a(x; \xi_0, \xi_1)$

so that it may be possible to prove, just as above, that the boundary value problem

$$\begin{cases} -u''(x) - a(x; u(x), u'(x)) = f(x), & x \in (0, 1), \\ u(0) = u(1) = 0 \end{cases}$$

has at least one classical solution for a sufficiently "small" right-hand side $f \in C^0([0, 1])$.

(v) By means of this method, it is also possible to prove the existence of the solution in the case of noncoercive nonlinear partial differential equations. The implicit function theorem is thoroughly exploited for these equations in the book [92]. However, its drawback lies in the fact that the existence of the solution is obtained for "sufficiently small" right-hand sides only.

32.2. Some generalizations of monotone operators. The topological method is more general than the variational method. However, the variational method is simpler and has considerable importance in numerical methods. A complete list of publications dealing with the variational and the topological methods, either from the theoretical or the applicational points-of-view, would be inordinately long for inclusion in this book. In a considerable number of papers the concept of the monotone operator has been generalized. We have already met with the generalization to "operators monotone in the principal part" (see the Leray-Lions Theorem 29.6). We now present one more generalization.

(i) **Definition.** Let T be an operator defined on the Banach space X with values in the dual space X^*. We say that T is *a pseudo-monotone operator* if the following conditions are satisfied:

(a) The operator T is bounded [see Definition 26.10 (i)].

(b) If

$$u_n \to u \quad \text{in} \quad X$$

and

$$\limsup_{n \to \infty} <Tu_n, u_n - u> \leq 0,$$

then

$$\liminf_{n \to \infty} <Tu_n, u_n - v> \geq <Tu, u - v>$$

holds for any $v \in X$.

(ii) It can be proved that every demicontinuous (see Paragraph 29.5) monotone operator A is pseudo-monotone. On the other hand, the operator $C = A + B$, where A is a demicontinuous monotone operator and B is completely continuous, is pseudo-monotone but is not monotone in general. Every operator which satisfies the conditions of the Leray-Lions Theorem 29.6 is pseudo-monotone. In spaces of finite dimension, every continuous operator is pseudo-monotone.

The following assertion generalizes Theorem 29.6:

(iii) *Let X be a reflexive Banach space and T a pseudo-monotone coercive operator defined on X and with values in X*. Then*

$$T(X) = X^* ,$$

i.e., the equation Tu = f has at least one solution for every right-hand side $f \in X^*$.

The proofs of the assertions given here can be found, e.g., in $[59]$.

32.3. Anisotropic problems. In Example 16.18, the concept of the weak solution of boundary value problems of the type

$$-\frac{\partial}{\partial x}\left(\left|\frac{\partial u}{\partial x}\right|^{p-2}\frac{\partial u}{\partial x}\right) - \frac{\partial}{\partial y}\left(\left|\frac{\partial u}{\partial y}\right|^{q-2}\frac{\partial u}{\partial y}\right) = f \quad \text{on} \quad \Omega ,$$

$$u|_{\partial\Omega} = 0 , \tag{2}$$

was formulated with the aid of so-called anisotropic Sobolev spaces (see Paragraph 16.17); here Ω was a plane domain, $1 < p < q$, and $f \in L_{q^*}(\Omega)$ with

$$\frac{1}{q^*} + \frac{1}{q} = 1 .$$

We define the operator T on the space $W_0^{1;p,q}(\Omega)$ so that for all $u, v \in W_0^{1;p,q}(\Omega)$ we have

$$< Tu, v> = \int_\Omega \left|\frac{\partial u(x, y)}{\partial x}\right|^{p-2} \frac{\partial u(x, y)}{\partial x}\frac{\partial v(x, y)}{\partial x}\, dx\, dy +$$

$$+ \int_\Omega \left|\frac{\partial u(x, y)}{\partial y}\right|^{q-2} \frac{\partial u(x, y)}{\partial y}\frac{\partial v(x, y)}{\partial y}\, dx\, dy .$$

It is easy to verify that the space $W_0^{1;p,q}(\Omega)$ is reflexive and that the operator T satisfies, on the space $W_0^{1;p,q}(\Omega)$, all the conditions of the Browder Theorem 29.5 (in particular, it is purely monotone and coercive). Then:

(i) The boundary value problem (2) has precisely one weak solution for arbitrary $f \in L_{q^*}(\Omega)$.

(ii) As a very useful exercise, it is possible to prove the existence of the weak solution of boundary value problem (2) by the variational method. The investigation of problems more general than the Dirichlet problem (2) is again entirely analogous to the procedure of Sections 26 and 29.

For more details on problems of this type, see $[59]$.

32.4. Equations in Sobolev-Orlicz spaces. By means of the topological method, it is possible to prove the existence of the solution for boundary value problems with coefficients with strong (or weak) growth — see Paragraph 16.19. On carrying out certain modifications, it is also possible to use the variational method. However, for such problems both methods call for the explanation of some deeper properties of the Sobolev-Orlicz spaces, in particular, some properties of their dual spaces. These problems lie outside the scope of our book and we shall not treat them here. We direct the reader's attention to selected papers in journals:

(a) The application of the topological method: [16], [40].
(b) The application of the variational method: [46], [47].

To illustrate the approach, we formulate one example to which it is possible to apply the topological method discussed in this chapter (see [40]). As far as the notation is concerned, see Paragraphs 16.22 and 16.23.

(i) Example. Let $\Omega \in \mathbb{R}^N$, $\Omega \in \mathscr{C}^{0,1}$, and let g be a continuous, increasing and odd function defined on $\mathbb{R}$ such that

$$\lim_{\xi \to \infty} g(\xi) = \infty .$$

Put

$$G(t) = \int_0^t g(s)\, \mathrm{d}s ,$$

and let the formal differential operator A be defined by the formula

$$Au = \sum_{|\alpha| \leq k} (-1)^{|\alpha|}\, D^\alpha(g(D^\alpha u)) .$$

Then, for every $\mathbf{f} \in (W_0^k\, E_G(\Omega))^*$, there exists at least one $u \in W_0^k\, E_G(\Omega)$ which satisfies, in the weak sense, the Dirichlet problem for the formal differential equation

$$Au = \mathbf{f} \quad \text{on} \quad \Omega$$

with a homogeneous boundary condition, i.e., for which

$$\sum_{|\alpha| \leq k} \int_\Omega g(D^\alpha u(x))\, D^\alpha v(x)\, \mathrm{d}x = <\mathbf{f}, v>$$

holds for every $v \in W_0^k\, E_G(\Omega)$.

(ii) Remark. The boundary value condition of the above example (see also Paragraph 16.23 with $\varphi = 0$) has a solution, in particular, for arbitrary $f \in E_H(\Omega)$, where G and H are complementary Young functions.

CHAPTER VI

NONCOERCIVE PROBLEMS

SECTION 33. VANISHING NONLINEARITIES. REGULAR CASE

33.1. Classification of nonlinearities. In previous chapters, the solution of a boundary value problem for a nonlinear differential equation was transformed into the solution of an abstract operator equation in an appropriate Banach space $V \subset \subset W^{k,p}(\Omega)$; for the existence of the solution, it was always essential here that the given operator be *coercive* (see Theorems 26.11, 29.5, 29.6). In practice, however, problems also occur for which coerciveness is disturbed. In this chapter, we show that it is sometimes possible to prove the existence of the solution for such problems as well. We shall investigate the existence of the solution of the Dirichlet problem

$$-u''(x) - g(u(x)) = f(x), \quad x \in (0, \pi), \tag{1}$$

$$u(0) = u(\pi) = 0. \tag{2}$$

The fact that ordinary differential equations on the interval $(0, \pi)$ are considered in this chapter is, of course, in no way essential; simpler notation is the principal reason for restricting attention to them here. For the same reason, the function $g(u(x))$ appears with a minus sign [the function $g(\xi)$ will be called the *nonlinearity of the boundary value problem* (1), (2)] in contradistinction to Section 26 where equation (1) was considered with a plus sign. The methods of proof will just be illustrated on the very simple problem (1), (2). Eventual possible generalizations to more complicated problems or to boundary value problems in partial differential equations will either be mentioned without proof or references to the literature will be given.

The nonlinearity g will always be a *continuous function on* $\mathbb{R}$.

On the Sobolev space $W_0^{1,2}(0, \pi)$, we work with the inner product

$$<u, v>_{1,2,0} = \int_0^\pi u'(x)\, v'(x)\, dx, \quad u, v \in W_0^{1,2}(0, \pi),$$

and the norm

$$\|u\|_{1,2,0} = \left(\int_0^\pi |u'(x)|^2\, dx \right)^{1/2}, \quad u \in W_0^{1,2}(0, \pi)$$

(see Paragraph 13.7).

In the case of problem (1), (2), the requirement of coerciveness means that the condition

$$\lim_{\|u\|_{1,2,0} \to \infty} \left\{ \|u\|_{1,2,0} - \frac{1}{\|u\|_{1,2,0}} \int_0^\pi g(u(x))\, u(x)\, dx \right\} = \infty \tag{3}$$

is satisfied.

It has already been shown that the boundary value problem (1), (2) satisfies condition (3) [and the boundary value problem (1), (2) has, therefore, a weak solution for every right-hand side $f \in L_1(0, \pi)$] if one of the following conditions is satisfied:

(a) $g(\xi)\, \xi \leq 0$ for every $\xi \in \mathbb{R}$ [see Paragraph 26.23 (iii)]†);

(b) there exist constants $c_1 \geq 0$, $c_2 \geq 0$, $\sigma \geq 0$, $\sigma < 1$, such that

$$|g(\xi)| \leq c_1 + c_2 |\xi|^\sigma$$

for all $\xi \in \mathbb{R}$ [this is a direct consequence of the assertion in Paragraph 26.23 (v)];

(c) $g(\xi) = \lambda \xi + \tilde{g}(\xi)$, where $\lambda < 1$ and the function $\tilde{g}(\xi)$ satisfies condition (b)††).

We assume now that the limits

$$\mu = \lim_{\xi \to \infty} \frac{g(\xi)}{\xi}, \quad \nu = \lim_{\xi \to -\infty} \frac{g(\xi)}{\xi} \tag{4}$$

exist, and we consider the following types of nonlinearities:

I. Vanishing nonlinearity: $\mu = \nu \in \mathbb{R}$.

[E.g., the differential equation

$$-u'' - u + \operatorname{arctg} u = f\,;$$

cf. Example (26.26). In this case, $g(\xi) = \xi - \operatorname{arctg} \xi$.]

II. Jumping nonlinearity: $\mu \neq \nu$.

[E.g., the differential equation (26.27), i.e.,

$$-u'' - \mu u^+ + \nu u^- = f$$

---

†) It is even possible to work with the following condition: There exists a number A such that $g(\xi)\, \xi \leq A$ holds for all $\xi \in \mathbb{R}$.

††) This condition has not been considered elsewhere. The fact that it also implies the coerciveness of the operators considered follows from the following assertion: *For $\lambda < 1$, there exists a constant $c_\lambda > 0$ such that*

$$\int_0^\pi |u'(x)|^2\, dx - \lambda \int_0^\pi u^2(x)\, dx \geq c_\lambda \int_0^\pi |u'(x)|^2\, dx$$

holds for all $u \in W_0^{1,2}(0, \pi)$.

for general parameters $\mu, \nu \in \mathbb{R}$, or the equation

$$-u'' - u + e^u = f\,,$$

cf. Example (26.25). In the first case, we have

$$g(\xi) = \begin{cases} \mu\xi & \text{for} \quad \xi \geq 0\,, \\ \nu\xi & \text{for} \quad \xi < 0\,; \end{cases}$$

in the second case, $g(\xi) = \xi - e^\xi$.]

III. Rapid nonlinearity: $\mu = \nu = \infty$.

[E.g., the differential equation

$$-u'' - u^3 = f\,,$$

cf. Example (26.23). In this case, $g(\xi) = \xi^3$.]

33.2. Vanishing nonlinearity. Assume that the two limits in relation (4) are finite and equal. Denote their common value by λ:

$$\lambda = \mu = \nu\,.$$

The function g will be written in the form

$$g(\xi) = \lambda\xi - \psi(\xi)\,.$$

Now, define the operators L_λ and S on the space $W_0^{1,2}(0,\pi)$ with values in $W_0^{1,2}(0,\pi)$ †) by means of the following integral identities:

$$<L_\lambda u, v>_{1,2,0} = \int_0^\pi u'(x)\, v'(x)\, \mathrm{d}x - \lambda \int_0^\pi u(x)\, v(x)\, \mathrm{d}x\,,$$

$$<Su, v>_{1,2,0} = \int_0^\pi \psi(u(x))\, v(x)\, \mathrm{d}x\,, \quad u, v \in W_0^{1,2}(0,\pi)\,.$$

To show that there exists at least one weak solution of the problem (1), (2) for an arbitrary right-hand side $f \in L_1(0,\pi)$ means finding at least one solution of the operator equation

$$L_\lambda u + Su = z \tag{5}$$

for arbitrary $z \in W_0^{1,2}(0,\pi)$, since the relation

$$<\mathbb{A}u, v> = <f, v>$$

---

†) Throughout this chapter, the identification $H = H^*$ is made for Hilbert spaces H (see the footnote on p. 240).

by which the weak solution was defined has the form

$$<L_\lambda u + Su, v>_{1,2,0} = \int_0^\pi f(x)\, v(x)\, dx$$

(see Paragraph 15.4) and the relation between $z \in W_0^{1,2}(0, \pi)$ and $f \in L_1(0, \pi)$ is given by the integral identity

$$<z, v>_{1,2,0} = \int_0^\pi f(x)\, v(x)\, dx\,, \quad v \in W_0^{1,2}(0, \pi)\,.$$

The following assertion is the principal result of this section:

33.3. Theorem. *Let there exist constants $c_1 \geqq 0$, $c_2 \geqq 0$, and σ, $0 \leqq \sigma < 1$, such that*

$$|\psi(\xi)| \leqq c_1 + c_2 |\xi|^\sigma \tag{6}$$

holds for all $\xi \in \mathbb{R}$. Let $\lambda \in \mathbb{R}$ be such that

$$\lambda \neq n^2 \quad \text{for every} \quad n \in \mathbb{N}\,. \tag{7}$$

Then the boundary value problem (1), (2) *[with the function $g(\xi) = \lambda\xi - \psi(\xi)$] has at least one weak solution for arbitrary $f \in L_1(0, \pi)$. If, moreover, $f \in C^0([0, \pi])$, then the boundary value problem* (1), (2) *has at least one classical solution.*

33.4. On the proof of Theorem 33.3. (i) First of all, note that the final assertion of Theorem 33.3 is a direct consequence of the existence of the weak solution and of the regularity theorem (see Paragraph 17.5).

We prove below that the operator equation (5) has at least one solution in the space $W_0^{1,2}(0, \pi)$ for arbitrary right-hand sides $z \in W_0^{1,2}(0, \pi)$. For this, we investigate the properties of the operators L_λ and S which were defined in Paragraph 33.2.

(ii) Properties of the operator L_λ. The operator L_λ can be written in the form

$$L_\lambda u = u - \lambda Bu\,,$$

where the operator B which maps the space $W_0^{1,2}(0, \pi)$ into the space $W_0^{1,2}(0, \pi)$ is defined by the integral identity

$$<Bu, v>_{1,2,0} = \int_0^\pi u(x)\, v(x)\, dx\,, \quad u, v \in W_0^{1,2}(0, \pi)\,.$$

The operator B is plainly linear; it is also completely continuous [this is implied by the compact imbedding $W_0^{1,2}(0, \pi) \subset\subset C^0([0, \pi])$ — see Paragraph 26.24 (iii)]. We see, further, that the equation

$$L_\lambda u = \Theta$$

has a non-zero solution in the space $W_0^{1,2}(0, \pi)$ if and only if $\lambda = n^2$, where $n \in \mathbb{N}$:

Indeed, an arbitrary weak solution of the boundary value problem

$$-u'' - \lambda u = 0 \quad \text{on} \quad (0, \pi), \tag{8}$$

$$u(0) = u(\pi) = 0 \tag{9}$$

is a classical solution as well (according to the regularity theorem — see Paragraph 17.5). The solution of equation (8) has the following form:

$$\begin{cases} u(x) = \alpha \sin \lambda^{1/2}x + \beta \cos \lambda^{1/2}x & \text{for} \quad \lambda > 0, \\ u(x) = \alpha x + \beta & \text{for} \quad \lambda = 0, \\ u(x) = \alpha\, e^{(-\lambda)^{1/2}x} + e^{-(-\lambda)^{1/2}x} & \text{for} \quad \lambda < 0. \end{cases} \tag{10}$$

Hence, it can now be seen — following a trivial computation — that a non-zero function of the form (10) which satisfies the boundary conditions (9) must have the form

$$u(x) = \alpha \sin \lambda^{1/2}x, \quad \lambda = n^2, \quad n \in \mathbb{N}, \quad \alpha \neq 0.$$

However, since we assume that $\lambda \neq n^2$ for every $n \in \mathbb{N}$, the equation $L_\lambda u = \Theta$ is only satisfied for $u = \Theta$. Thus, the so-called Fredholm Theorems (see, e.g., [51]) imply that the operator L_λ maps the space $W_0^{1,2}(0, \pi)$ onto the entire space $W_0^{1,2}(0, \pi)$; moreover, the inverse mapping L_λ^{-1} exists and is continuous on the space $W_0^{1,2}(0, \pi)$.

(iii) **Properties of the operator** S. It can be proved — in a way entirely analogous to that applied in (ii) to ascertain that B is a completely continuous operator — that the nonlinear operator S is completely continuous. Condition (6) immediately implies that

$$\|Su\|_{1,2,0} \leqq \tilde{c}_1 + \tilde{c}_2\|u\|_{1,2,0}^\sigma \tag{11}$$

for all $u \in W_0^{1,2}(0, \pi)$.

(iv) It suffices to show that the operator $u + L_\lambda^{-1}Su$ maps the space $W_0^{1,2}(0, \pi)$ onto the entire space $W_0^{1,2}(0, \pi)$ †). Thus, let w be an arbitrary but fixed function from $W_0^{1,2}(0, \pi)$, and let us investigate whether the solution of equation

$$u = w - L_\lambda^{-1}Su \tag{12}$$

exists. Put

$$Fu = w - L_\lambda^{-1}Su.$$

The function $u \in W_0^{1,2}(0, \pi)$ is a solution of equation (12) if and only if it is a fixed point of the operator F. The existence of a fixed point of the operator F is proved by means of the Schauder Theorem 30.11.

---

†) In fact, the operator $L_\lambda + S$ maps the space $W_0^{1,2}(0, \pi)$ onto the entire space $W_0^{1,2}(0, \pi)$ if and only if the operator $I + L_\lambda^{-1}S$ possesses the same property, I being the identity mapping.

(v) *The operator F is completely continuous* because the operator L_λ^{-1} is continuous and the operator S is completely continuous. To verify all the conditions of the Schauder Theorem 30.11 it suffices to find $r_0 > 0$ such that

$$F(K) \subset K,$$

where

$$K = \{u \in W_0^{1,2}(0, \pi); \|u\|_{1,2,0} \leq r_0\}. \tag{13}$$

Now let $r > 0$ and $u \in W_0^{1,2}(0, \pi)$, $\|u\|_{1,2,0} \leq r$. Inequality (11) then yields

$$\|Fu\|_{1,2,0} \leq \|w\|_{1,2,0} + \|L_\lambda^{-1}\| \, \|Su\|_{1,2,0} \leq \alpha + \beta\|u\|_{1,2,0} \leq \alpha + \beta r^\sigma \; \dagger).$$

Since $\sigma \in [0, 1)$, there exists $r_0 > 0$ such that

$$\alpha + \beta r_0^\sigma \leq r_0.$$

The set K from (13) thus satisfies the condition $F(K) \subset K$, and by the Schauder Theorem on fixed points of a completely continuous operator the operator F has a fixed point in the set K. In view of what was said in (iv), this finishes the proof of the entire theorem.

The procedure given above can be generalized to boundary value problems in nonlinear partial differential equations as well, and in just the same way as in Paragraph 33.3 it is possible to prove the next assertion:

33.5. Theorem. *Define the formal differential operator $\mathscr{L}$ by the formula*

$$\mathscr{L}u = -\sum_{i,j=1}^{N} \frac{\partial}{\partial x_i}\left(a_{ij}(x)\frac{\partial u}{\partial x_j}\right).$$

Let $a_{ij}(x) = a_{ji}(x) \in L_\infty(\Omega)$ for $i, j = 1, 2, \ldots, N$, and assume that there exists $m > 0$ such that

$$\sum_{i,j=1}^{N} a_{ij}(x)\,\xi_i\xi_j \geq m\sum_{j=1}^{N}\xi_j^2$$

holds for all $\xi_i \in \mathbb{R}$ and almost all $x \in \Omega$. Let the continuous real function ψ satisfy the following condition: There exists $\sigma, 0 \leq \sigma < 1$, such that

$$|\psi(\xi)| \leq c_1 + c_2|\xi|^\sigma, \quad \xi \in \mathbb{R}. \tag{6}$$

Let $\lambda \in \mathbb{R}$.

$\dagger)$

$$\|L_\lambda^{-1}\| = \sup_{\|u\|_{1,2,0}=1} \|L_\lambda^{-1}u\|_{1,2,0}$$

is the norm of the continuous linear operator L_λ^{-1} (see, e.g., [51]).

If the formal linear Dirichlet problem

$$\begin{cases} \mathscr{L}u - \lambda u = 0 & on \quad \Omega \\ \quad u|_{\partial\Omega} = 0 \end{cases} \tag{14}$$

has only the trivial (i.e., the null) weak solution, then the nonlinear boundary value problem

$$\begin{cases} (\mathscr{L}u)(x) - \lambda\, u(x) + \psi(u(x)) = f(x) & on \quad \Omega, \\ \qquad\qquad\qquad\qquad u|_{\partial\Omega} = 0 \end{cases} \tag{15}$$

has at least one weak solution for arbitrary $f \in L_2(\Omega)$.

33.6. Remarks. (i) A more detailed analysis of part (v) in Paragraph 33.4 reveals that it is even possible to put $\sigma = 1$ in condition (6). In this case, it is necessary, however, to assume that the constant $c_2 > 0$ is "sufficiently small". The reader might compute, as an exercise, how large the constant c_2 can be (for $\sigma = 1$) so that the method described in Paragraph 33.4 be applicable to this case as well.

(ii) Theorem 33.5 can be generalized to general boundary value problems in nonlinear partial differential equations of order $2k$. The procedure is analogous to the procedure of Paragraph 33.4. For more details see, e.g., [36].

(iii) In Theorem 33.5, it was assumed that problem (14) possesses only the trivial weak solution. The verification of this assumption is substantially more difficult in the case of partial differential equations than in the case of ordinary differential equations; of course, for certain special types of domains and operators this verification is possible. For instance, if $N = 2$, $\Omega = (0, \pi) \times (0, \pi)$, then the equation

$$-\Delta\, u(x, y) - \lambda\, u(x, y) = 0 \quad \text{on} \quad \Omega$$

with the boundary condition

$$u|_{\partial\Omega} = 0$$

has a nontrivial weak solution if and only if λ is a positive integer of the form

$$\lambda = m^2 + n^2, \quad m, n \in \mathbb{N}.$$

In this case, the weak (and — as can be seen at once — even the classical) solutions of this problem are the functions of the form

$$u(x, y) = \sum_{\substack{j^2 + k^2 = \lambda \\ j, k \in \mathbb{N}}} \alpha_{j,k} \sin jx \sin ky, \quad \alpha_{j,k} \in \mathbb{R}.$$

33.7. A final remark. During the years 1967 and 1968, there appeared initial attempts to remove the condition of coerciveness with which we became acquainted in detail in Chapters IV and V, and the so-called "Fredholm alternative for nonlinear operators" was formulated. Generalizations to nonlinear operators of results of linear functional analysis (see, e.g., [36]), known since the early years of this century, were in question. The problems investigated throughout the present section are typical examples of problems covered by this abstract theory. The Fredholm alternative for nonlinear operators was probably first formulated independently by S. I. Pokhozhaev [77] and J. Nečas [71] as follows:

"*If the equation $Tu = \Theta$ has only the trivial solution, then the equation $Tu + + Su = f$ has at least one solution for arbitrary right-hand side f.*"

(Of course, the operators T and S have to satisfy a number of conditions.)

The problem was further modified and adapted in a number of papers. The reader will find references to the literature and more details concerning the entire range of such problems in [36]. There, the applications of the abstract theory to the solvability of boundary value problems in nonlinear partial differential equations of the type

$$-\sum_{i=1}^{N} \frac{\partial}{\partial x_i}\left(\left|\frac{\partial u(x)}{\partial x_i}\right|^{p-2}\frac{\partial u(x)}{\partial x_i}\right) - \lambda|u(x)|^q\, u(x) + \psi(u(x)) = f(x)$$

are also given and investigated in detail.

SECTION 34. VANISHING NONLINEARITIES. SINGULAR CASE

34.1. Preliminary considerations. Notation. We return to the Dirichlet problem

$$\begin{cases} -u''(x) - \lambda\, u(x) + \psi(u(x)) = f(x)\,, & x \in (0, \pi)\,, \\ u(0) = u(\pi) = 0 \end{cases} \tag{1}$$

investigated in Theorem 33.3. Let $n \in \mathbb{N}$ be chosen fixed, and let $\lambda = n^2$ [i.e., condition (33.7) is not satisfied]. In this case, the operator equation

$$L_\lambda u = \Theta$$

with the operator L_λ defined in Paragraph 33.2 possesses a non-trivial solution: All its solutions are of the form

$$u(x) = \alpha \sin nx\,, \quad \alpha \in \mathbb{R}\,.$$

The inverse operator L_λ^{-1} does not exist and it is thus not possible to apply the method described in Paragraph 33.4.

(i) We summarize some properties of the operator L_λ in this singular case. *Put*

$$X = \{v \in W_0^{1,2}(0, \pi); \ <v(x), \sin nx>_{1,2,0} = 0\} ,$$

$$Y = \{\alpha \sin nx; \ \alpha \in \mathbb{R}\} .$$

Then the equation

$$L_\lambda u = z \tag{2}$$

has a solution for $z \in W_0^{1,2}(0, \pi)$ *if and only if* $z \in X$. *If* $z \in X$, *then precisely one* $u \in X$ *exists which is the solution of equation* (2). By the symbol K_λ, we denote the operator which assigns the solution $u \in X$ of equation (2) to the element $z \in X$. The operator K_λ (usually called the *right inverse of the operator* L_λ) is a continuous linear mapping from the space X into the space X.

(ii) Let P be an operator defined on the space $W_0^{1,2}(0, \pi)$ by the formula

$$(Pu)(x) = \frac{2}{\pi n} \left(\int_0^\pi u'(\tau) \cos n\tau \, d\tau \right) \sin nx .$$

Clearly, P is a continuous linear mapping from the space $W_0^{1,2}(0, \pi)$ onto the space Y such that $Pu = u$ for every $u \in Y$. $[P$ is the so-called *projection* of the space $W_0^{1,2}(0, \pi)$ onto the space $Y.]$ We put, further,

$$P^c u = u - Pu .$$

The operator P^c is the projection of the space $W_0^{1,2}(0, \pi)$ onto the space X.

(iii) Let S be the operator defined in Paragraph 33.2, and let us investigate for which $z \in W_0^{1,2}(0, \pi)$ the operator equation

$$L_\lambda u + Su = z \tag{3}$$

has a solution. Equation (3) can be written in the form of the system

$$PL_\lambda u + PSu = Pz , \tag{4_1}$$

$$P^c L_\lambda u + P^c Su = P^c z . \tag{4_2}$$

If we write $u = Pu + P^c u$ and if we put $v = Pu$, $w = P^c u$, then system (4) reduces to the system

$$PL_\lambda v + PL_\lambda w + PS(v + w) = Pz , \tag{5_1}$$

$$P^c L_\lambda v + P^c L_\lambda w + P^c S(v + w) = P^c z . \tag{5_2}$$

Noting that $L_\lambda v = \Theta$ for every $v \in Y$ and that $L_\lambda w \in X$ for every $w \in X$, and therefore that $PL_\lambda w = \Theta$ and $P^c L_\lambda w = L_\lambda w$, we may write

$$PS(v + w) = Pz , \tag{6_1}$$

$$L_\lambda w + P^c S(v + w) = P^c z . \tag{6_2}$$

instead of (5). From the properties of the right inverse K_λ, it can be shown that equation (6_2) is equivalent to the equation

$$w + K_\lambda P^c S(v + w) = K_\lambda P^c z \,.$$

Thus, equation (3) has the solution $u_0 \in W_0^{1,2}(0, \pi)$ if and only if the system

$$PS(v + w) = Pz \,, \tag{7_1}$$

$$w = -K_\lambda P^c S(v + w) + K_\lambda P^c z \ \dagger) \tag{7_2}$$

has the solution $(v_0, w_0) \in Y \times X$, in which case, $u_0 = v_0 + w_0$.

We therefore investigate for which $z \in W_0^{1,2}(0, \pi)$ system (7) has a solution. [By the above, we will thus identify those $z \in W_0^{1,2}(0, \pi)$ for which equation (3) has a solution.] For this investigation, we utilize the Schauder fixed-point Theorem 30.11. To this end, we first rewrite system (7) in a more suitable form. It is easily checked that system (7) has a solution if and only if the system

$$v - \varepsilon PS(v - K_\lambda P^c S(v + w) + K_\lambda P^c z) + \varepsilon Pz = v \,, \tag{8_1}$$

$$w = -K_\lambda P^c S(v + w) + K_\lambda P^c z \tag{8_2}$$

has a solution for some $\varepsilon > 0$. This last system is now in the correct form for the application of the fixed point theorem. For $\varepsilon > 0$, we define an operator V_ε on the space $Y \times X$ by the formula

$$V_\varepsilon(v, w) = (\tilde{v}, \tilde{w}) \,, \tag{9}$$

where

$$\tilde{v} = v - \varepsilon PS(v - K_\lambda P^c S(v + w) + K_\lambda P^c z) + \varepsilon Pz \,,$$
$$\tilde{w} = -K_\lambda P^c S(v + w) + K_\lambda P^c z \,.$$

For arbitrary $\varepsilon > 0$, the operator V_ε clearly maps the space $Y \times X$ into the space $Y \times X$. System (8) has the solution (v_0, w_0) if and only if (v_0, w_0) is a fixed point of the operator V_ε (for some $\varepsilon > 0$). The aim of this section is, therefore, to find sufficient conditions under which the operator V_{ε_0} has a fixed point for some $\varepsilon_0 > 0$.

34.2. Theorem. *Let ψ be a continuous and bounded function on $\mathbb{R}$ such that*

$$\lim_{\xi \to \infty} \psi(\xi) = \psi(\infty) \in \mathbb{R} \,, \tag{10}$$

$$\lim_{\xi \to -\infty} \psi(\xi) = \psi(-\infty) \in \mathbb{R} \,. \tag{11}$$

$\dagger)$ The system of equations (7) is frequently called the bifurcation system for equation (3).

Let $n \in \mathbb{N}$. Assume that

$$\psi(-\infty) < \psi(\xi) < \psi(\infty) \tag{12}$$

holds for all $\xi \in \mathbb{R}$.

Then the boundary value problem

$$\begin{cases} -u''(x) - n^2 u(x) + \psi(u(x)) = f(x), & x \in (0, \pi), \\ u(0) = u(\pi) = 0 \end{cases} \tag{13}$$

has at least one weak solution for $f \in L_1(0, \pi)$ if and only if the inequalities

$$\psi(-\infty) \int_0^\pi (\sin nx)^+ \, dx - \psi(\infty) \int_0^\pi (\sin nx)^- \, dx < \int_0^\pi f(x) \sin nx \, dx <$$

$$< \psi(\infty) \int_0^\pi (\sin nx)^+ \, dx - \psi(-\infty) \int_0^\pi (\sin nx)^- \, dx \; \dagger) \tag{14}$$

are satisfied.

Proof. Let $f \in L_1(0, \pi)$, and denote by z an element of the space $W_0^{1,2}(0, \pi)$ such that for all $v \in W_0^{1,2}(0, \pi)$ we have

$$<z, v>_{1,2,0} = \int_0^\pi f(x) \, v(x) \, dx \, . \tag{15}$$

(i) We show, first of all, that inequalities (14) are necessary for the existence of the weak solution. If the function $u_0 \in W_0^{1,2}(0, \pi)$ is a weak solution of problem (13), then it is also the solution of the operator equation (3), i.e.,

$$L_\lambda u_0 = z - S u_0 \, .$$

This means, however, that $z - S u_0 \in X$ [see Paragraph 34.1 (i)], i.e., that

$$<z - S u_0, \sin nx>_{1,2,0} = 0 \, ;$$

this can be written as

$$\int_0^\pi f(x) \sin nx \, dx = \int_0^\pi \psi(u_0(x)) \sin nx \, dx \, .$$

At the same time, we have

$$\int_0^\pi \psi(u_0(x)) \sin nx \, dx < \psi(\infty) \int_0^\pi (\sin nx)^+ \, dx - \psi(-\infty) \int_0^\pi (\sin nx)^- \, dx$$

$\dagger)$ Recall that for the function $u(x)$ we put $u^+(x) = \max(u(x), 0)$ and $u^-(x) = \max(-u(x), 0)$.

and

$$\int_0^\pi \psi(u_0(x)) \sin nx \, dx > \psi(-\infty) \int_0^\pi (\sin nx)^+ \, dx - \psi(\infty) \int_0^\pi (\sin nx)^- \, dx \,,$$

which together imply inequalities (14).

(ii) Now, we shall show that the inequalities (14) are also sufficient conditions for the existence of the solution of boundary value problem (13). Thus, let the function $f \in L_1(0, \pi)$ satisfy inequalities (14), and let $z \in W_0^{1,2}(0, \pi)$ be the function defined by relation (15). By what was said in Paragraph 34.1 (iii), it suffices to show that there exists an $\varepsilon_0 > 0$ such that the operator V_{ε_0} [see (9)] has a fixed point in the space $Y \times X$.

First of all, it is clear that, for any $\varepsilon > 0$, V_ε is a completely continuous operator from the space $Y \times X$ into $Y \times X$. To satisfy the conditions of the Schauder Theorem 30.11, it suffices to show that a non-empty convex set $\mathcal{K} \subset Y \times X$ and a number $\varepsilon_0 > 0$ exist such that

$$V_{\varepsilon_0}(\mathcal{K}) \subset \mathcal{K} \,.$$

Condition (12) implies that

$$\sup_{\substack{v \in Y \\ w \in X}} \| -S(v + w) + z \|_{1,2,0} = \gamma < \infty \,,$$

$$\sup_{\substack{v \in Y \\ w \in X}} \| -K_\lambda P^c S(v + w) + K_\lambda P^c z \|_{1,2,0} = \gamma_1 < \infty \,,$$

$$\sup_{\substack{v \in Y \\ w \in X}} \| PS(v + w) - Pz \|_{1,2,0} = \gamma_2 < \infty \,.$$

Because the relations

$$\lim_{t \to \infty} \, <S(t \sin n\tau + w(\tau)) - z, \, \sin n\tau>_{1,2,0} =$$

$$= \psi(\infty) \int_0^\pi (\sin n\tau)^+ \, d\tau - \psi(-\infty) \int_0^\pi (\sin n\tau)^- \, d\tau - \int_0^\pi f(\tau) \sin n\tau \, d\tau > 0 \,,$$

$$\lim_{t \to -\infty} \, <S(t \sin n\tau + w(\tau)) - z, \, \sin n\tau>_{1,2,0} =$$

$$= \psi(-\infty) \int_0^\pi (\sin n\tau)^+ \, d\tau - \psi(\infty) \int_0^\pi (\sin n\tau)^- \, d\tau - \int_0^\pi f(\tau) \sin n\tau \, d\tau < 0$$

hold for all $w \in X$, $\|w\|_{1,2,0} \leq \gamma_1$, a number $\delta > 0$ exists and it is possible to find $t_0 > 0$ such that

$$<S(v + w) - z, v>_{1,2,0} \geq \delta t_0/2$$

holds for all $v \in Y$, $\|v\|_{1,2,0} \geq t_0/2$, and for all $w \in X$, $\|w\|_{1,2,0} \leq \gamma_1$. Hence, it follows that for every $w \in X$, for arbitrary $v \in Y$ such that

$$t_0/2 \leq \|v\|_{1,2,0} \leq t_0 \,,$$

and for $\varepsilon > 0$ such that

$$\varepsilon \leq \delta t_0/\gamma_1^2 \,,$$

we have

$$\|v - \varepsilon PS(v - K_\lambda P^c S(v + w) + K_\lambda P^c z) + \varepsilon Pz\|_{1,2,0}^2 =$$

$$= \|v\|_{1,2,0}^2 - 2\varepsilon <S(v - K_\lambda P^c S(v + w) + K_\lambda P^c z) - z, v>_{1,2,0} +$$

$$+ \varepsilon^2 \|PS(v - K_\lambda P^c S(v + w) + K_\lambda P^c z) - Pz\|_{1,2,0}^2 \leq$$

$$\leq t_0^2 - \varepsilon \delta t_0 + \varepsilon^2 \gamma_1^2 \leq t_0^2 \,.$$

For $w \in X$, $v \in Y$, such that

$$\|v\|_{1,2,0} \leq t_0/2$$

and $\varepsilon > 0$ such that

$$\varepsilon \leq t_0/2\gamma_2 \,,$$

we have

$$\|v - \varepsilon PS(v - K_\lambda P^c S(v + w) + K_\lambda P^c z) + \varepsilon Pz\|_{1,2,0} \leq$$

$$\leq \|v\|_{1,2,0} + \varepsilon \|PS(v - K_\lambda P^c S(v + w) + K_\lambda P^c z) - Pz\|_{1,2,0} \leq$$

$$\leq t_0/2 + \varepsilon \gamma_2 \leq t_0 \,.$$

Thus, if

$$\varepsilon_0 = \min \{\delta t_0/\gamma_1^2, \, t_0/2\gamma_2\}$$

and

$$\mathscr{K} = \{(v, w) \in Y \times X; \, \|v\|_{1,2,0} \leq t_0, \, \|w\|_{1,2,0} \leq \gamma_1\} \,,$$

then the above computations imply

$$V_{\varepsilon_0}(\mathscr{K}) \subset \mathscr{K} \,.$$

($\mathscr{K}$ is clearly a non-empty closed convex and bounded subset of the space $Y \times X$.)
This concludes the proof.

34.3. Remarks. (i) Recall inequalities (14). As mentioned in Paragraph 34.1 (i), the boundary value problem

$$\begin{cases} -u'' - n^2 u = f & \text{on} \ (0, \pi) \,, \\ u(0) = u(\pi) = 0 \end{cases}$$

has a weak solution if and only if the right-hand side $f \in L_1(0, \pi)$ satisfies the condition

$$\int_0^\pi f(x) \sin nx \, dx = 0$$

[i.e., $<z, \sin nx>_{1,2,0} = 0$, where $z \in W_0^{1,2}(0, \pi)$ is defined by relation (15)]. Denote the set of all such functions $f \in L_1(0, \pi)$ by the symbol M. By Theorem 34.2, the nonlinear boundary value problem (13) has a solution if and only if $f \in L_1(0, \pi)$ is an element of a certain "band" $\mathcal{B}$ surrounding the set M ["the dimensions of this band" are given by the nonlinearity ψ: The smaller the absolute values of the limits $\psi(\infty)$, $\psi(-\infty)$, the more the band $\mathcal{B}$ tends to the set M]. In any case, the set $\mathcal{B}$ is an open subset of the space $L_1(0, \pi)$.

(ii) Condition (12) can be generalized in the following sense: *The assertion of Theorem 34.2 remains true if*

$$\psi(-\infty) \leqq \psi(\xi) \leqq \psi(\infty)$$

for every $\xi \in \mathbb{R}$ and

$$\psi(-\infty) < \psi(0) < \psi(\infty).$$

By the same method [i.e., by the application of the Schauder Theorem 30.11 to obtain the existence of the solution of the bifurcation system (7)], it is possible to prove the existence of the weak solution of boundary value problems in nonlinear partial differential equations of order $2k$. We limit ourselves to the formulation of the principal result; the proof is given in [33].

34.4. Theorem. *Let $\Omega \subset \mathbb{R}^N$, $\Omega \in \mathscr{C}^{0,1}$. Let V be a closed subspace of the space $W^{k,2}(\Omega)$ such that*

$$W_0^{k,2}(\Omega) \subset V \subset W^{k,2}(\Omega).$$

Let

$$a_{\alpha\beta}(x) \in L_\infty(\Omega), \quad a_{\alpha\beta}(x) = a_{\beta\alpha}(x) \tag{16}$$

$(|\alpha|, |\beta| \leq k)$. *Assume that there exists $c > 0$ such that*

$$\sum_{|\alpha|=|\beta|=k} a_{\alpha\beta}(x)\, \xi_\alpha \xi_\beta \geq c \sum_{|\alpha|=k} |\xi_\alpha|^2 \tag{17}$$

for all $\xi_\alpha \in \mathbb{R}$ $(|\alpha| = k)$ and for almost all $x \in \Omega$. Let

$$b_{\alpha\beta} \in L_\infty(\partial\Omega), \quad b_{\alpha\beta} = b_{\beta\alpha} \quad (|\alpha|, |\beta| < k). \tag{18}$$

Denote by $\mathscr{N}$ the set of all $w \in V$ such that for all $v \in V$

$$\sum_{|\alpha|,|\beta| \leq k} \int_\Omega a_{\alpha\beta}(x)\, D^\alpha w(x)\, D^\beta v(x)\, dx + \sum_{|\alpha|,|\beta| < k} \int_{\partial\Omega} b_{\alpha\beta}(x)\, D^\alpha w(x)\, D^\beta v(x)\, dS = 0$$

is true and assume that

$$\mathscr{N} \neq \{\Theta\}. \tag{19}$$

Let M be a non-empty set of multi-indexes of length at most $k - 1$. For $\alpha \in M$, let ψ_α be a continuous function on $\mathbb{R}$; put

$$\lim_{\xi \to \infty} \psi_\alpha(\xi) = \psi_\alpha(\infty),$$

$$\lim_{\xi \to -\infty} \psi_\alpha(\xi) = \psi_\alpha(-\infty)$$

and assume, moreover, that

$$-\infty < \psi_\alpha(-\infty) \leq \psi_\alpha(\xi) \leq \psi_\alpha(\infty) < \infty \tag{20}$$

for all $\xi \in \mathbb{R}$.

For $w \in \mathcal{N}$, let

$$\mathcal{L}(w) = \sum_{\alpha \in M} \left(\psi_\alpha(\infty) \int_\Omega [D^\alpha w(x)]^+ \, dx - \psi_\alpha(-\infty) \int_\Omega [D^\alpha w(x)]^- \, dx \right).$$

Then the following is true:

(a) If $f \in L_2(\Omega)$ is such that

$$\int_\Omega f(x)\, w(x)\, dx < \mathcal{L}(w) \tag{21}$$

holds for all $w \in \mathcal{N}$, $w \neq \Theta$, then the boundary value problem

$$\sum_{|\alpha|,|\beta| \leq k} \int_\Omega a_{\alpha\beta}(x)\, D^\alpha u(x)\, D^\beta v(x)\, dx + \sum_{|\alpha|,|\beta| < k} \int_{\partial\Omega} b_{\alpha\beta}(x)\, D^\alpha u(x)\, D^\beta v(x)\, dS +$$

$$+ \sum_{\alpha \in M} \int_\Omega \psi_\alpha(D^\alpha u(x))\, D^\alpha v(x)\, dx = \int_\Omega f(x)\, v(x)\, dx \tag{22}$$

$(v \in V)$ has at least one solution $u \in V$.

(b) If problem (22) has a solution for $f \in L_2(\Omega)$, then

$$\int_\Omega f(x)\, w(x)\, dx \leq \mathcal{L}(w)$$

for every $w \in \mathcal{N}$.

(c) If the relation $\leq$ is replaced in (20) by the strict inequality $<$ for at least one $\alpha \in M$, then (21) is the necessary and sufficient condition for the existence of the weak solution of the boundary value problem (22) with the right-hand side $f \in L_2(\Omega)$.

When investigating the existence of the solution of boundary value problem (13), it is also possible to consider unbounded nonlinearities ψ where

$$\psi(\infty) = \infty, \quad \psi(-\infty) = -\infty$$

holds for the limits (10) and (11). In view of what was said in Remark 34.3 (i), one can think of the "band" $\mathscr{B}$ "inflating" so that it fills up the entire space. The boundary value problem (13) could then have a weak solution for every right-hand side $f \in$ $\in L_1(0, \pi)$. In fact, such an assertion is true under certain conditions:

34.5. Theorem. *Let* ψ *be a continuous monotone odd function on* $\mathbb{R}$. *Let constants* $c_1 > 0$, $c_2 > 0$,

$$c_2 < \tfrac{3}{4}\pi^{1/2}\big[2^{1/2}\big(\pi^{1/2} + 8\big)\big]^{-1}, \tag{23}$$

exist such that

$$|\psi(\xi)| \leqq c_1 + c_2|\xi| \tag{24}$$

holds for all $\xi \in \mathbb{R}$, *and let*

$$\lim_{\xi \to \infty} \psi(\xi) = \infty. \tag{25}$$

Then the boundary value problem (13) *has at least one weak solution for arbitrary* $f \in L_1(0, \pi)$.

34.6. Remarks. (i) If condition (24) is replaced by the growth condition

$$|\psi(\xi)| \leqq c_1 + c_2|\xi|^\sigma, \quad 0 < \sigma < 1,$$

then restriction (23) concerning the magnitude of the constant c_2 can be ignored.

(ii) The proof of Theorem 34.5 is given in [22]. There, the boundary value problem (22) with unbounded nonlinearities ψ_α is also examined.

(iii) Observe, further, that if, e.g.,

$$\psi(\infty) = \psi(-\infty) = 0,$$

then the important inequalities (14) in Theorem 34.2 have no meaning. But even in this case, it is possible to proceed in the same way as in Paragraph 34.1 and in the proof of Theorem 34.2 (see [24], [28]):

34.7. Theorem. *Let* ψ *be a continuous bounded and odd function on* $\mathbb{R}$. *Assume that there exists* $\zeta > 0$ *so that*

$$\lim_{\xi \to \infty} \xi^2 \min_{\tau \in [\zeta, \xi]} \psi(\tau) = \infty.$$

Then at least one weak solution of the boundary value problem (13) *exists for every* $f \in L_1(0, \pi)$ *such that*

$$\int_0^\pi f(x) \sin nx \, dx = 0.$$

34.8. Remarks. (i) The function

$$\psi(\xi) = \frac{\xi}{1 + \xi^2}, \quad \xi \in \mathbb{R},$$

is a typical example of a function which satisfies the conditions of Theorem 34.7 and does not satisfy the conditions of Theorem 34.2 (we choose $\zeta = 1$ in this case).

(ii) Results analogous to Theorem 34.7 also hold for boundary value problems in nonlinear partial differential equations of the second order (see [12], [32], [50]).

34.9. A final remark. The problems investigated in this section were first examined by E. M. Landesman and A. C. Lazer [56]. In their work, Theorem 34.4 is proved for the case of $k = 1$, homogeneous Dirichlet conditions, and the dimension of the space $\mathcal{N}$ equal to one. The last condition was removed by S. A. Williams [93], while a different proof appeared in [45]. J. Nečas [73] proved an abstract theorem which is applicable to general boundary value problems in nonlinear partial differential equations of arbitrary order. These problems are systematically studied in [23], where further references related to these problems are also to be found (e.g., the works of the Belgian mathematician J. Mawhin which will be mentioned again in Section 38). At present, there is quite a number of (as yet unpublished) papers along these lines and intensive research in the field continues. We are thus dealing with problems which are quite up-to-date.

SECTION 35. JUMPING NONLINEARITIES WITH FINITE JUMPS

35.1. The nonlinearity $g(\xi)$ from equation (33.1) will now be considered in the form

$$g(\xi) = \mu \xi^+ - \nu \xi^- - \psi(\xi),$$

where $\mu, \nu \in \mathbb{R}$ and ψ is a continuous bounded function on $\mathbb{R}$. Recall that

$$\xi^+ = \max\{\xi, 0\}, \quad \xi^- = \max\{-\xi, 0\}.$$

It is obvious that

$$\mu = \lim_{\xi \to \infty} \frac{g(\xi)}{\xi}, \quad \nu = \lim_{\xi \to -\infty} \frac{g(\xi)}{\xi}.$$

We investigate the existence of the solution of the Dirichlet problem

$$\begin{cases} -u''(x) - \mu u^+(x) + \nu u^-(x) + \psi(u(x)) = f(x), & x \in (0, \pi), \\ u(0) = u(\pi) = 0. \end{cases} \tag{1}$$

Thus, let $f \in L_1(0, \pi)$. We look for $u \in W_0^{1,2}(0, \pi)$ such that the integral identity

$$\int_0^\pi u'(x) \, v'(x) \, dx - \mu \int_0^\pi u^+(x) \, v(x) \, dx + v \int_0^\pi u^-(x) \, v(x) \, dx +$$

$$+ \int_0^\pi \psi(u(x)) \, v(x) \, dx = \int_0^\pi f(x) \, v(x) \, dx \tag{2}$$

be satisfied for arbitrary $v \in W_0^{1,2}(0, \pi)$. On the space $W_0^{1,2}(0, \pi)$, we define the operators S and $T_{\mu,v}$ with values in $W_0^{1,2}(0, \pi)$ so that

$$<T_{\mu,v}(u), v>_{1,2,0} = \mu \int_0^\pi u^+(x) \, v(x) \, dx - v \int_0^\pi u^-(x) \, v(x) \, dx , \tag{3}$$

$$<Su, v>_{1,2,0} = \int_0^\pi \psi(u(x)) \, v(x) \, dx \tag{4}$$

holds for all $v \in W_0^{1,2}(0, \pi)$.

35.2. Properties of the operators S and $T_{\mu,v}$.

(i) *The operator $T_{\mu,v}$ is completely continuous on $W_0^{1,2}(0, \pi)$.*

(ii) *The operator S is completely continuous on $W_0^{1,2}(0, \pi)$.*

(iii) $\displaystyle\sup_{u \in W_0^{1,2}(0,\pi)} \|Su\|_{1,2,0} = \gamma < \infty .$

(iv) *For every $t \geq 0$ and $u \in W_0^{1,2}(0, \pi)$, we have*

$$T_{\mu,v}(tu) = t T_{\mu,v}(u) .$$

[Assertions (i), (ii) can be proved in the same way as in Paragraph 33.4, assertions (iii), (iv) are obvious.]

35.3. Let $z \in W_0^{1,2}(0, \pi)$ be a function such that

$$<z, v>_{1,2,0} = \int_0^\pi f(x) \, v(x) \, dx \tag{5}$$

holds for all $v \in W_0^{1,2}(0, \pi)$. To investigate the existence of the weak solution of problem (1) means to investigate the existence of the solution of the operator equation

$$u - T_{\mu,v}(u) + Su = z \tag{6}$$

in the space $W_0^{1,2}(0, \pi)$. To this end, we use the Leray-Schauder degree of a mapping (see Paragraph 30.14).

However, we first determine the set A_{-1} of all parameters $(\mu, v) \in \mathbb{R}^2$ such that the equation

$$u - T_{\mu,v}(u) = \Theta \tag{7}$$

has a non-trivial solution in the space $W_0^{1,2}(0, \pi)$. We exclude this set since the Leray-Schauder degree

$$d\big[u - T_{\mu,v}(u); B(1), \Theta\big] \tag{8}$$

of the operator $u - T_{\mu,v}(u)$, with respect to the unit sphere $B(1)$ in the space $W_0^{1,2}(0, \pi)$ which has its center at the origin and with respect to the point Θ (see Paragraph 30.14), is not defined for the parameters $(\mu, v) \in A_{-1}$.

We now determine the set A_{-1}.

35.4. Lemma. *Let $\mu, v \in \mathbb{R}$. Then the Dirichlet problem*

$$\begin{cases} -u'' - \mu u^+ + v u^- = 0 & \text{on } (0, \pi), \\ u(0) = u(\pi) = 0 \ \dagger) \end{cases} \tag{9}$$

has a non-zero weak solution if and only if one of the following conditions is satisfied:

(a) $\mu = 1$, v *arbitrary*;

(b) μ *arbitrary*, $v = 1$;

(c) $\mu > 1$, $v > 1$, $\dfrac{\mu^{1/2} v^{1/2}}{\mu^{1/2} + v^{1/2}} \in \mathbb{N}$;

(d) $\mu > 1$, $v > 1$, $\dfrac{v^{1/2}(\mu^{1/2} - 1)}{\mu^{1/2} + v^{1/2}} \in \mathbb{N}$;

(e) $\mu > 1$, $v > 1$, $\dfrac{\mu^{1/2}(v^{1/2} - 1)}{\mu^{1/2} + v^{1/2}} \in \mathbb{N}$.

Proof. First of all, observe that by the regularity Theorem 17.5 every weak solution $u_0 \in W_0^{1,2}(0, \pi)$ of problem (9) is a classical solution, i.e.,

$$u_0 \in C^2(0, \pi) \cap W_0^{1,2}(0, \pi).$$

The remaining part of the proof consists essentially of calculation. If u_0 is a non-zero classical solution of the boundary value problem (9), then — in view of the uniqueness theorem for solutions of the initial value problem in ordinary differential equations — the function $u_0(x)$ has only a finite number of zeros in the interval $[0, \pi]$: In fact,

---

†) I.e., equation (7).

if $u_0(x_0) = 0$, then $u_0'(x_0) \neq 0$ (by the theorem mentioned above) and there exists therefore a neighbourhood of the point x_0 which contains no other zero of the function u_0.

If the function u_0 has no zero in the interval $(0, \pi)$, then either (a) or (b) is true since u_0 is the solution of the equation

$$-u'' - \lambda u = 0,$$

where either $\lambda = \mu$ [if $u_0(x) > 0$ everywhere in $(0, \pi)$] or $\lambda = v$ [if $u_0(x) < 0$ everywhere in $(0, \pi)$]. If the function u_0 has at least one zero in the interval $(0, \pi)$, then $\mu > 0$, $v > 0$, and u_0 is a periodic function with the period

$$\pi \left(\frac{1}{\mu^{1/2}} + \frac{1}{v^{1/2}} \right).$$

This result can easily be verified as follows: On every interval in which $u_0(x) > 0$, we have

$$u_0(x) = \alpha \sin \mu^{1/2}(x - \zeta), \quad \alpha > 0, \quad \zeta \in \mathbb{R};$$

similarly,

$$u_0(x) = \beta \sin v^{1/2}(x - \omega), \quad \beta > 0, \quad \omega \in \mathbb{R},$$

on the intervals in which $u_0(x) < 0$. Hence, it follows that at least one of the equations

$$\ell \left(\frac{1}{\mu^{1/2}} + \frac{1}{v^{1/2}} \right) = 1,$$

$$\ell \left(\frac{1}{\mu^{1/2}} + \frac{1}{v^{1/2}} \right) + \frac{1}{\mu^{1/2}} = 1, \tag{*}$$

$$\ell \left(\frac{1}{\mu^{1/2}} + \frac{1}{v^{1/2}} \right) + \frac{1}{v^{1/2}} = 1$$

is satisfied by the positive integer ℓ. This means, however, that at least one of the conditions (a)−(e) is satisfied.

Conversely, if one of the conditions (a)−(e) is satisfied, then we "glue" together a non-zero classical (and thus also weak) solution of the boundary value problem (9) using the functions

$$\alpha \sin \mu^{1/2}(x - \zeta), \quad \alpha > 0, \quad \zeta \in \mathbb{R},$$

and

$$\beta \sin v^{1/2}(x - \omega), \quad \beta < 0, \quad \omega \in \mathbb{R}.$$

35.5. The set A_{-1} is represented by bold lines in Fig. 35.5 [they are the graphs of the straight lines $\mu = 1$, $v = 1$ and of the hyperbolas described by relations (*) in Paragraph 35.4 for $m = 1$]. The degree (8) can be defined for parameters (μ, v)

from the set $A_0 = \mathbb{R}^2 - A_{-1}$. As we shall see below, parameters $(\mu, \nu) \in A_0$ such that the degree (8) is non-zero are the best to work with. The set of all such parameters (μ, ν) is denoted by A_1 [it is the hatched part of Fig. 35.5; for more details see 35.11 (ii)]. The properties of the sets A_0, A_1 are discussed in the following lemmas.

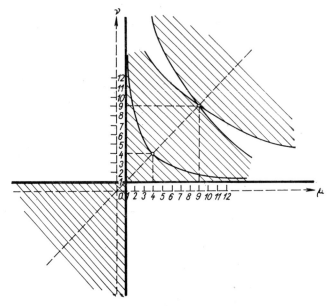

Fig. 35.5

35.6. Lemma. *For every* $(\mu, \nu) \in A_0$, *there exists a constant* $c_1(\mu, \nu) > 0$ *such that*

$$\| u - T_{\mu,\nu}(u) \|_{1,2,0} \geq c_1(\mu, \nu) \| u \|_{1,2,0}$$

holds for all $u \in W_0^{1,2}(0, \pi)$.

Proof. Let $(\mu, \nu) \in A_0$ and assume that for this pair of parameters the assertion of the lemma does not hold. In that case, there exists a sequence $\{u_n\}_{n=1}^{\infty}$ of elements of the space $W_0^{1,2}(0, \pi)$ such that

$$\| u_n \|_{1,2,0} = 1$$

and

$$\lim_{n \to \infty} \| u_n - T_{\mu,\nu}(u_n) \|_{1,2,0} = 0. \tag{10}$$

Since the operator $T_{\mu,\nu}$ is completely continuous [see Paragraph 35.2 (i)], a subsequence $\{u_{n_k}\}_{k=1}^{\infty}$ and a function $w_0 \in W_0^{1,2}(0, \pi)$ exist such that

$$T_{\mu,\nu}(u_{n_k}) \to w_0 \quad \text{in} \quad W_0^{1,2}(0, \pi).$$

Hence, and from (10), one obtains

$$u_{n_k} \to w_0 \quad \text{in} \quad W_0^{1,2}(0, \pi) .$$

The continuity of the operator $T_{\mu,\nu}$ implies that

$$w_0 - T_{\mu,\nu}(w_0) = \Theta .$$

Furthermore, $\|w_0\|_{1,2,0} = 1$. The function w_0 is thus a nontrivial weak solution of the Dirichlet problem (9). But this is in contradiction with the fact that $(\mu, \nu) \in A_0$ since the null function is the only weak solution of problem (9) for parameters $(\mu, \nu) \in A_0$.

35.7. Lemma. *If $(\mu, \nu) \in A_1$, then the operator equation (6) has a solution in the space $W_0^{1,2}(0, \pi)$ for arbitrary right-hand sides $z \in W_0^{1,2}(0, \pi)$ [i.e., the boundary value problem (1) has at least one solution for every $f \in L_1(0, \pi)$].*

Proof. Let $z \in W_0^{1,2}(0, \pi)$ be an arbitrary but fixed chosen function. Lemma 35.6 and Paragraph 35.2 (iii) imply that

$$\|u - T_{\mu,\nu}(u) + t(Su - z)\|_{1,2,0} \geqq \|u - T_{\mu,\nu}(u)\|_{1,2,0} - \|Su\|_{1,2,0} - \|z\|_{1,2,0} \geqq$$

$$\geqq c_1(\mu, \nu) \|u\|_{1,2,0} - \gamma - \|z\|_{1,2,0} \tag{11}$$

for every $t \in [0, 1]$ and $u \in W_0^{1,2}(0, \pi)$. Thus, there exists $r > 0$ such that

$$u - T_{\mu,\nu}(u) + t(Su - z) \neq \Theta$$

for every $u \in W_0^{1,2}(0, \pi)$, $\|u\|_{1,2,0} = r$, and for every $t \in [0, 1]$. Since the operator $T_{\mu,\nu}$ satisfies the assertion given in Paragraph 35.2 (iv), we have

$$d[u - T_{\mu,\nu}(u); B(r), \Theta] = d[u - T_{\mu,\nu}(u); B(1), \Theta] \neq 0 .$$

The inequalities (11) imply that it is possible to make use of the invariance of the Leray-Schauder degree of a mapping with respect to homotopy (see Paragraph 30.14), thus

$$d[u - T_{\mu,\nu}(u) + Su - z; B(r), \Theta] = d[u - T_{\mu,\nu}(u); B(r), \Theta] \neq 0 .$$

According to assertion 30.14, this completes the proof of the lemma.

35.8. Remark. In the preceding lemma, a very important result was presented but the condition $(\mu, \nu) \in A_1$ remains rather obscure. Now, recall Remarks 30.2 and 30.15 where we said that the computation of the degree is not possible from the definition. In the case under examination we are able, however, to describe the set A_1 precisely. First of all, we note the following:

35.9. Lemma. *On every connected part of the set A_0, the function*

$$r(\mu, v) = d[u - T_{\mu,v}(u); B(1), \Theta]$$

is constant.

(This lemma is a consequence of assertion 30.14 concerning the homotopic invariance of the Leray-Schauder degree of a mapping.)

35.10. Lemma. *Let the connected part B of the set A_0 contain a point of the straight line $\mu = v$, i.e., let $\lambda \in \mathbb{R}$ exist such that $(\lambda, \lambda) \in B$. Then $B \subset A_1$.*

Proof. The operator $u - T_{\lambda,\lambda}(u)$ is odd; by Theorem 30.14, the degree $d[u - T_{\lambda,\lambda}(u); B(1), \Theta]$ is thus an odd (i.e., non-zero) number. Hence, it follows that $(\lambda, \lambda) \in A_1$, and thus — by Lemma 35.9 — the entire set B is contained in the set A_1.

35.11. Remarks. (i) It is even possible to show that the degree (8) is either $+1$ or -1 for points of the set A_1.

(ii) Compare the results hitherto obtained with Fig. 35.5. By Lemma 35.10, the hatched parts of the figure are the sets of those parameters (μ, v) where the degree (8) is non-zero. Thus, by Lemma 35.7, for parameters (μ, v) belonging to the hatched part, the boundary value problem (1) has at least one weak solution for arbitrary right-hand sides $f \in L_1(0, \pi)$. However, there still remain "blank regions" in the figure, i.e., those connected parts of the set A_0 where it is indeed possible to define the degree (8) but we do not know yet whether it is zero or non-zero. We now turn our attention to just these sets of parameters.

35.12. Lemma. *Let $(\mu, v) \in A_0$ be a pair such that for some $\tilde{z} \in W_0^{1,2}(0, \pi)$ the equation*

$$u - T_{\mu,v}(u) = \tilde{z}_n \tag{12}$$

does not have a solution in the space $W_0^{1,2}(0, \pi)$. Then there exists $z \in W_0^{1,2}(0, \pi)$ such that equation (6) also has no solution in the space $W_0^{1,2}(0, \pi)$.

Proof. Let $(\mu, v) \in A_0$. First, we show that the range $\mathscr{R}$ of the operator $u - T_{\mu,v}(u)$ is a closed subset of the space $W_0^{1,2}(0, \pi)$. Let

$$u_n - T_{\mu,v}(u_n) = z_n$$

and assume that

$$z_n \to z_0 \quad \text{in} \quad W_0^{1,2}(0, \pi).$$

Lemma 35.6 implies that

$$\sup_{n \in \mathbb{N}} \|u_n\|_{1,2,0} < \infty$$

and thus (the operator $T_{\mu,\nu}$ is completely continuous) a subsequence $\{u_{n_k}\}_{k=1}^{\infty}$ and a function $w \in W_0^{1,2}(0, \pi)$ exist such that

$$T_{\mu,\nu}(u_{n_k}) \to w .$$

Then $u_{n_k} \to z_0 + w = u_0$, and, therefore, $T_{\mu,\nu}(u_{n_k}) \to T_{\mu,\nu}(u_0)$. Hence, it now follows easily that

$$u_0 - T_{\mu,\nu}(u_0) = z_0 ,$$

i.e., $z_0 \in \mathscr{R}$.

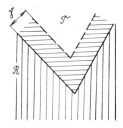

Fig. 35.12

Moreover, the set $\mathscr{R}$ is positive homogeneous, i.e., if $z \in \mathscr{R}$, then the entire half line tz for $t \geq 0$ is a part of $\mathscr{R}$. Let then $\mathscr{R}$ not be the entire space $W_0^{1,2}(0, \pi)$. The idea behind the proof of the fact that not even the range of the operator $u - T_{\mu,\nu}(u) + Su$ fills up the entire space $W_0^{1,2}(0, \pi)$ is most clear from Fig. 35.12. Since $\mathscr{R} \neq W_0^{1,2}(0, \pi)$, there exists an open "funnel" $\mathscr{T}$ such that equation (12) has no solution for $\tilde{z} \in \mathscr{T}$. But what can the nonlinear operator S "do" with the set $\mathscr{R}$? The operator S satisfies assertion 35.2 (iii) so that the range of the operator $u - T_{\mu,\nu}(u) + Su$ can "inflate", as compared with the set $\mathscr{R}$, maximally to the distance γ from $\mathscr{R}$. However, this enlargement of the set $\mathscr{R}$ cannot fill up the entire "funnel" $\mathscr{T}$. (A detailed proof in which the triangle inequality is the most powerful tool is left to the reader.)

The significance of Lemma 35.12 is clear from the assertions which follow.

35.13. Remarks. (i) Let (μ, ν) lie in the "blank regions" of Fig. 35.5. Then there exists $f \in L_1(0, \pi)$ so that the boundary value problem

$$\begin{cases} -u'' - \mu u^+ + \nu u^- = f & \text{on } (0, \pi), \\ u(0) = u(\pi) = 0 \end{cases} \tag{13}$$

has no weak solution.

[The proof is accomplished by constructing the function $f(x)$ by means of the so-called comparison theorems for ordinary second-order differential equations. See [12].]

(ii) Assertion (i) and Lemma 35.12 then imply that there exists $f \in L_1(0, \pi)$ for (μ, v) from the "blank regions" of Fig. 35.5 so that the boundary value problem (1) has no weak solution [in this case, the degree (8) is null].

(iii) E. N. Dancer [13] showed that, even for parameters $(\mu, v) \in A_{-1}$, there exists $f \in L_1(0, \pi)$ so that the boundary value problem (13) has no weak solution.

The results of this section can now be assembled in the following theorem.

35.14. Theorem. *The boundary value problem* (1) *has at least one weak solution for an arbitrary right-hand side* $f \in L_1(0, \pi)$ *if and only if the pair of parameters* (μ, v) *lies in the hatched parts of* Fig. 35.5.

To the family of problems investigated in this section, there also belongs the following assertion which says, essentially, how many solutions exist.

35.15. Theorem. *Let the function* $g \in C^2(\mathbb{R})$ *satisfy the following conditions:*

(a) $g(0) = 0$;

(b) $g''(\xi) > 0$ *for every* $\xi \in \mathbb{R}$;

(c) $0 < \lim\limits_{\xi \to -\infty} \dfrac{g(\xi)}{\xi} < 1$;

(d) $1 < \lim\limits_{\xi \to \infty} \dfrac{g(\xi)}{\xi} < 4$.

Then there exists a closed set $M \neq \emptyset$ *in the space* $C^0([0, 1])$ *such that*

$$C^0([0, 1]) - M = B_1 \cup B_2$$

$(B_1 \neq \emptyset \neq B_2)$ *and the following holds:*

(I) *If* $f \in B_1$, *then the boundary value problem*

$$\begin{cases} -u''(x) - g(u(x)) = f(x), & x \in (0, \pi), \\ u(0) = u(\pi) = 0 \end{cases} \tag{14}$$

has no (*classical*) *solution;*

(II) *if* $f \in B_2$, *then problem* (14) *has exactly two solutions;*

(III) *if* $f \in M$, *then problem* (14) *has exactly one solution.*

35.16. Remark. Theorem 35.15 which was proved in [2] for the case of boundary value problems in partial differential equations was a rather surprising result at the time since it was the first attempt to investigate nonlinear equations in which the corresponding operator had Leray-Schauder degree zero. In Theorem 35.15, the result is of only theoretical significance and does not enable us to obtain a description of those right-hand sides $f \in C^0([0, 1])$ for which problem (14) possesses a solution. A method by which it is possible to obtain sufficient conditions on $f \in L_1(0, \pi)$ for the boundary value problem to have a weak solution is presented in [25].

The results of A. Ambrosetti and G. Prodi from [2] have been generalized in various directions, e.g., in [7], [25], [62], [78]. In all these works, however, cases are investigated where the interval with endpoints μ, ν contains the number 1. More general cases of the choice of the parameters μ, ν for the boundary value problem (1) are studied in [27] where it is shown that assumptions (c), (d) are essential for the validity of the assertion of Theorem 35.15. A generalization of the results from [27] and an almost complete characterization of the pairs of parameters μ, $\nu \in \mathbb{R}$ for which the boundary value problem (1) has a solution for an arbitrary right-hand side is included in [12]. There, some results are also given on boundary value problems in partial differential equations; these results are completed in certain directions in [26]. For instance, it is possible to give sufficient (but not necessary) conditions on the parameters μ, $\nu \in \mathbb{R}$ for the corresponding boundary value problem to have a solution for arbitrary right-hand sides. Generally speaking, it can be said, however, that in the investigation of boundary value problems of the type

$$\begin{cases} -\Delta u - \mu u^+ + \nu u^- = f & \text{on} \quad \Omega, \\ u|_{\partial\Omega} = 0 \end{cases}$$

satisfactory results have not yet been obtained, indeed, not even in the case of $N = 2$ and $\Omega = (0, \pi) \times (0, \pi)$ is the form of the set A_{-1} known: We cannot describe the set of all pairs $(\mu, \nu) \in \mathbb{R}^2$ for which the Dirichlet problem

$$\begin{cases} -\Delta u - \mu u^+ + \nu u^- = 0 & \text{on} \quad \Omega, \\ u|_{\partial\Omega} = 0 \end{cases}$$

has a nontrivial solution.

SECTION 36. JUMPING NONLINEARITIES WITH INFINITE JUMPS

36.1. A typical example of the boundary value problems investigated in this section is the Dirichlet problem

$$\begin{cases} -u'' - u + e^u = f & \text{on} \quad (0, \pi), \\ u(0) = u(\pi) = 0. \end{cases} \tag{1}$$

In this case, we thus have (see Paragraph 33.1)

$$g(\xi) = \xi - e^\xi$$

and

$$\mu = \lim_{\xi \to \infty} \frac{g(\xi)}{\xi} = -\infty, \quad \nu = \lim_{\xi \to -\infty} \frac{g(\xi)}{\xi} = 1.$$

For simplicity's sake, only classical solutions will be considered. The following assertions embody the principal results.

36.2. Theorem. *Let ψ be a continuous nondecreasing function on $\mathbb{R}$. Let $f \in C^0([0, \pi])$. Then the solution of the Dirichlet problem*

$$\begin{cases} -u''(x) - u(x) + \psi(u(x)) = f(x), & x \in (0, \pi), \\ u(0) = u(\pi) = 0 \end{cases} \tag{2}$$

exists if and only if there exists $w_0 \in C^2([0, \pi])$, $w_0(0) = w_0(\pi) = 0$ so that

$$\int_0^\pi f(x) \sin x \, dx = \int_0^\pi \psi(w_0(x)) \sin x \, dx \tag{3}$$

holds.

36.3. Theorem. *Let ψ be a continuous nondecreasing function on $\mathbb{R}$, and let*

$$\psi(-\infty) < \psi(\xi) < \psi(\infty) \tag{4}$$

for all $\xi \in \mathbb{R}$. Then the boundary value problem (2) *has at least one classical solution if and only if*

$$2\psi(\infty) > \int_0^\pi f(x) \sin x \, dx > 2\psi(-\infty) \ \dagger) \tag{5}$$

holds.

36.4. Remark. Theorem 36.3 immediately implies that the boundary value problem (1) has a solution if and only if

$$\int_0^\pi f(x) \sin x \, dx > 0.$$

36.5. On the proof of Theorem 36.3. First of all, we show that the assertion of Theorem 36.3 follows from Theorem 36.2.

(i) Let the Dirichlet problem (2) have the solution $u_0 \in C^2([0, \pi])$, $u_0(0) = u_0(\pi) = 0$. By the assertion in Paragraph 34.1 (i), we then have

$$\int_0^\pi f(x) \sin x \, dx = \int_0^\pi \psi(u_0(x)) \sin x \, dx ,$$

and the validity of relation (5) is immediately seen from inequalities (4).

(ii) Let inequalities (5) be valid. By Theorem 36.2, it suffices to find $w_0 \in C^2([0, \pi])$, $w_0(0) = w_0(\pi) = 0$, so that (3) be valid. By inequalities (5) it is possible to find a constant $c \in \mathbb{R}$ so that $2\,\psi(c)$ is "approximately" equal to the number

$$a = \int_0^\pi f(x) \sin x \, dx .$$

---

†) If, moreover, the function ψ is bounded, then Theorem 36.3 is a special case of Theorem 34.2.

Using the constant function c, we construct the function $w_0 \in C^2([0, \pi])$, $w_0(0) = $
$= w_0(\pi) = 0$, in the manner indicated in Fig. 36.5 and so that we also have

$$a = \int_0^\pi \psi(w_0(x)) \sin x \, dx .$$

(The fact that the construction of a function w_0 with the properties mentioned above
is possible follows from the properties of the Lebesgue integral.) It is thus shown —
on the basis of Theorem 36.2 (as yet unproved) — that problem (2) has at least one
classical solution.

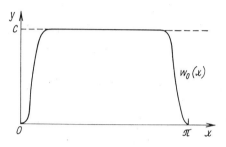

Fig. 36.5

36.6. On the proof of Theorem 36.2. (i) If the boundary value problem (2) has
a solution $w_0 \in C^2([0, \pi])$, $w_0(0) = w_0(\pi) = 0$, then the function w_0 satisfies condition (3) [this was already proved in Paragraph 36.5 (i)].

(ii) Let $w_0 \in C^2([0, \pi])$, $w_0(0) = 0 = w_0(\pi) = 0$, exist such that condition (3)
holds. Put

$$P(x) = f(x) - \psi(w_0(x)), \quad x \in [0, \pi] .$$

Then

$$f(x) - \psi(u(x)) \leq P(x), \quad x \in [0, \pi] , \qquad (6)$$

is true for an arbitrary function $u \in C^2([0, \pi])$ with $u(0) = u(\pi) = 0$ such that

$$w_0(x) \leq u(x) \quad \text{for every} \quad x \in [0, \pi] .$$

Similarly:

$$P(x) \leq f(x) - \psi(u(x)), \quad x \in [0, \pi] , \qquad (7)$$

is true for every function $u \in C^2([0, \pi])$ with $u(0) = u(\pi) = 0$ such that

$$u(x) \leq w_0(x) \quad \text{for every} \quad x \in [0, \pi] .$$

(iii) The boundary value problem

$$\begin{cases} -v'' - v = P & \text{on} \ (0, \pi), \\ \quad v(0) = v(\pi) = 0 \end{cases} \qquad (8)$$

has at least one solution $v_0 \in C^2([0, \pi])$ since

$$\int_0^\pi P(x) \sin x \, dx = 0$$

[this result follows from the considerations of Paragraph 34.1 (i)]. Choose $\gamma \in \mathbb{R}$ so that

$$\gamma \sin x + v_0(x) \geq w_0(x) \tag{9}$$

for every $x \in [0, \pi]$. The existence of such a γ clearly follows easily from the properties of the function $\sin x$ on the interval $[0, \pi]$. Now, put

$$u_+(x) = \gamma \sin x + v_0(x), \quad x \in [0, \pi].$$

Then, obviously,

$$u_+(0) = u_+(\pi) = 0, \tag{10}$$

and, moreover, by (8), (9), and (6), we have

$$-u''_+(x) - u_+(x) = -v''_0(x) - v_0(x) = P(x) \geq f(x) - \psi(u_+(x)),$$

i.e.,

$$-u''_+(x) - u_+(x) + \psi(u_+(x)) \geq f(x). \tag{11}$$

A function $u_+ \in C^2([0, \pi])$ which satisfies relations (10), (11) is usually called the *upper solution of the Dirichlet problem* (2).

Similarly, we choose $\delta \in \mathbb{R}$ so that

$$u_-(x) = \delta \sin x + v_0(x) \leq w_0(x), \quad x \in [0, \pi].$$

This function $u_- \in C^2([0, \pi])$ satisfies the boundary conditions

$$u_-(0) = u_-(\pi) = 0 \tag{12}$$

and the inequalities

$$-u''_-(x) - u_-(x) + \psi(u_-(x)) \leq f(x), \quad x \in (0, \pi) \tag{13}$$

[a function u_- with the properties (12), (13) is called the *lower solution of the Dirichlet problem* (2)]. Plainly

$$u_-(x) \leq u_+(x), \quad x \in [0, \pi]. \tag{14}$$

(iv) We have succeeded in finding, in a very simple way, the lower solution u_- and the upper solution u_+ of problem (2) so that inequality (14) holds. Many theorems exist which confirm the existence of the solution in such cases. One such assertion is the theorem below which also yields the final part of the proof of Theorem 36.2. (We will not return to the proof of Theorem 36.2 again since everything will be clear from what follows.)

36.7. Theorem. *Let* $\Phi(x; \xi)$ *be a continuous function on* $[0, \pi] \times \mathbb{R}$, *and assume that there exist functions*

$$u_+ \in C^2([0, \pi]), \quad u_+(0) = u_+(\pi) = 0,$$
$$u_- \in C^2([0, \pi]), \quad u_-(0) = u_-(\pi) = 0,$$

such that for all $x \in [0, \pi]$

$$u_-(x) \leq u_+(x), \tag{15}$$
$$-u_-''(x) \leq \Phi(x; u_-(x)), \quad x \in (0, \pi) \tag{16}$$

(the function u_- *is the so-called lower solution),*

$$-u_+''(x) \geq \Phi(x; u_+(x)), \quad x \in (0, \pi) \tag{17}$$

(the function u_+ *is the so-called upper solution).*

Then a function

$$u_0 \in C^2([0, \pi]), \quad u_0(0) = u_0(\pi) = 0,$$

exists such that

$$u_-(x) \leq u_0(x) \leq u_+(x), \quad x \in [0, \pi], \tag{18}$$
$$-u_0''(x) = \Phi(x; u_0(x)), \quad x \in (0, \pi), \tag{19}$$

hold.

36.8. On the proof of Theorem 36.7. Just as in Paragraph 10.7, we construct the Green's function

$$K(t, s) = \begin{cases} -\dfrac{1}{\pi} t(\pi - s), & 0 \leq s \leq t, \\[2mm] -\dfrac{1}{\pi}(\pi - t) s, & t \leq s \leq \pi. \end{cases}$$

It can be shown that the homogeneous Dirichlet problem for equation (19) has a solution if and only if the integral equation

$$u(x) = -\int_0^\pi K(x, s)\, \Phi(s; u(s))\, ds \tag{20}$$

has a solution (see Paragraph 10.7). We investigate whether at least one solution of the integral equation (20) exists.

(i) First of all, assume, further, that the function $\Phi(x; \xi)$ is bounded on the set $[0, \pi] \times \mathbb{R}$, i.e., that there exists $M > 0$ such that

$$|\Phi(x; \xi)| \leq M$$

for all $x \in [0, \pi]$ and for all $\xi \in \mathbb{R}$. We put $X = C^0([0, \pi])$ †) and define the operator T from the space X into X by the formula

$$(Tu)(x) = -\int_0^\pi K(x, s) \, \Phi(s; u(s)) \, ds .$$

Since

$$\sup_{(t,s) \in [0,\pi] \times [0,\pi]} |K(t, s)| = \pi ,$$

we have

$$|(Tu)(x)| \leq \pi^2 M$$

for every $x \in [0, \pi]$ and $u \in X$. Thus, the operator T maps the closed bounded nonempty and convex set

$$\mathcal{K} = \{u \in X; |u(x)| \leq \pi^2 M\}$$

into $\mathcal{K}$. Moreover, T is completely continuous on $\mathcal{K}$ (the considerations are similar to those of Paragraph 30.13). The Schauder Theorem 30.11 then implies that the operator T has at least one fixed point u_0 in $\mathcal{K}$, i.e., the integral equation (20) has a solution $u_0 \in \mathcal{K}$. Just as in Paragraph 10.7, we show that this solution satisfies equation (19) and that

$$u_0(0) = u_0(\pi) = 0 .$$

(ii) We show that even without the additional condition of the boundedness of the function $\Phi(x; \xi)$ there exists a solution $u_0 \in C^2([0, \pi])$, $u_0(\pi) = 0$, of equation (19) which, moreover, satisfies the inequalities (18). Define a function $F(x; \xi)$ on the set $[0, \pi] \times \mathbb{R}$ by the formula

$$F(x; \xi) = \begin{cases} \Phi(x; u_+(x)) - \dfrac{\xi - u_+(x)}{1 + \xi^2} & \text{if } \xi > u_+(x), \\[2mm] \Phi(x; \xi) & \text{if } u_-(x) \leq \xi \leq u_+(x), \\[2mm] \Phi(x; u_-(x)) - \dfrac{\xi - u_-(x)}{1 + \xi^2} & \text{if } \xi < u_-(x). \end{cases}$$

Since the function $\Phi(x; \xi)$ is continuous, the function $F(x; \xi)$ is continuous and bounded on the set $[0, \pi] \times \mathbb{R}$. Thus, according to (i), there exists a function $u_0 \in \in C^2([0, \pi])$, $u_0(0) = u_0(\pi) = 0$, such that

$$-u_0''(x) = F(x; u_0(x)) , \quad x \in (0, \pi) .$$

---

†) In the space X, we use the norm

$$\|u\|_X = \max_{x \in [0, \pi]} |u(x)|$$

(see Paragraph 10.4).

We show that the function u_0 satisfies equation (19) and the inequalities (18). From the definition of the function $F(x; \xi)$ it follows that for this it is enough to prove the inequalities (18). Assume, therefore, that these inequalities do not hold. Then, e.g., $x_0 \in (0, \pi)$ exists such that

$$u_0(x_0) > u_+(x_0) \, .$$

There thus exist two points $x_1, x_2 \in [0, \pi]$ such that

$$0 \leq x_1 < x_0 < x_2 \leq \pi \quad \text{and} \quad u_0(x_i) = u_+(x_i) \quad (i = 1, 2)$$

and, moreover,

$$u_0(x) > u_+(x)$$

for every $x \in (x_1, x_2)$. The difference

$$u_0(x) - u_+(x)$$

attains its positive maximum on the interval $[x_1, x_2]$ at the point $\bar{x} \in (x_1, x_2)$. Thus,

$$u_0'(\bar{x}) = u_+'(\bar{x}) \quad \text{and} \quad u_0''(\bar{x}) - u_+''(\bar{x}) \leq 0 \, .$$

Furthermore,

$$0 \geq u_0''(\bar{x}) - u_+''(\bar{x}) = -\Phi(\bar{x}; u_+(\bar{x})) + \frac{u_0(\bar{x}) - u_+(\bar{x})}{1 + u_0^2(\bar{x})} - u_+''(\bar{x}) \geq$$

$$\geq -\Phi(\bar{x}; u_+(\bar{x})) + \frac{u_0(\bar{x}) - u_+(\bar{x})}{1 + u_0^2(\bar{x})} + \Phi(\bar{x}; u_+(\bar{x})) = \frac{u_0(\bar{x}) - u_+(\bar{x})}{1 + u_0^2(\bar{x})} > 0 \, ,$$

which is a contradiction. Consequently, $u_0(x) \leq u_+(x)$ for all $x \in [0, \pi]$. Arguing along similar lines, it is possible to prove that

$$u_-(x) \leq u_0(x)$$

for every $x \in [0, \pi]$. This finishes the proof of Theorem 36.7.

36.9. Remark. The literature dealing with assertions analogous to Theorem 36.7 is very extensive. We note only that an essentially more general version of Theorem 36.7 is included in [84]. Under the assumption of the existence of the upper and lower solutions of boundary value problems in nonlinear partial differential equations of the second order, the existence of the solution can also be proved (see, e.g., [1], [82]).

It follows from the above remarks that the method of the foregoing paragraphs can be applied equally to more general problems. It is even possible to use it in the proof of the existence of a solution of a general boundary value problem in nonlinear differential equations of the second order such that the "linearized problem" with zero right-hand side only has solutions which do not change sign. These problems are studied very intensively in the paper [50] where the proof of the following assertions is also given.

36.10. Theorem. *Let $f(x; \xi)$ be a continuous function on $[0, \pi] \times \mathbb{R}$. Assume the following:*

I. *A number $s_+ \in \mathbb{R}$ and a continuous bounded function $g_+(x; \xi)$ on $[0, \pi] \times \mathbb{R}$ exist so that for every function $u \in C^2([0, \pi])$, $u(0) = u(\pi) = 0$, such that*

$$u(x) > s_+ \sin x \quad for \quad x \in (0, \pi),$$

we have

$$f(x; u(x)) \leq g_+(x; u(x))$$

and

$$\int_0^\pi g_+(x; u(x)) \sin x \, dx \leq 0.$$

II. *A number $s_- \in \mathbb{R}$ and a continuous bounded function $g_-(x; \xi)$ on $[0, \pi] \times \mathbb{R}$ exist such that if $u \in C^2([0, \pi])$, $u(0) = u(\pi) = 0$, and*

$$u(x) < s_- \sin x \quad for \ all \quad x \in (0, \pi),$$

then

$$f(x; u(x)) \geq g_-(x; u(x))$$

and

$$\int_0^\pi g_-(x; u(x)) \sin x \, dx \geq 0 \ \dagger).$$

Then there exists at least one classical solution of the problem

$$\begin{cases} -u''(x) - u(x) = f(x; u(x)), & x \in (0, \pi), \\ u(0) = u(\pi) = 0. \end{cases} \tag{21}$$

36.11. Example. For boundary value problems in partial differential equations we can prove, e.g., the following assertion: *Let $N = 2$, $\Omega = (0, \pi) \times (0, \pi)$, and $f \in C^0(\bar{\Omega})$. Then the Dirichlet problem*

$$\begin{cases} -\Delta u(x, y) - 2u(x, y) + e^{u(x,y)} = f(x, y) & on \quad \Omega, \\ u|_{\partial\Omega} = 0 \end{cases} \tag{22}$$

has a solution if and only if

$$\int_\Omega f(x, y) \sin x \sin y \, dx \, dy > 0. \tag{23}$$

---

†) Assumption I ensures the existence of the upper solution, while assumption II ensures the existence of the lower solution.

In particular, this means then that for

$$f(x, y) = \alpha \sin x \sin y$$

the problem (22) has a solution if $\alpha > 0$. If $\alpha \leq 0$, then the Dirichlet problem (22) has no solution for such a right-hand side.

36.12. A further remark. In Theorems 36.2, 36.3, 36.10 (or, rather, in Example 36.11) it was essential that the considered boundary value problem in the equation

$$-u'' - u = 0 \quad \text{on} \quad (0, \pi)$$

(or, rather, in the equation $-\Delta u - 2u = 0$ on Ω) only have nontrivial solutions which do not change sign in the interval $(0, \pi)$ (or, rather, on the set Ω)†). In Paragraph 36.6, this fact was exploited several times, e.g., to derive inequality (9). Note that in the case when $n \in \mathbb{N}$, $n \neq 1$, nothing is known about the existence of the solution of boundary value problems of the type

$$\begin{cases} -u'' - n^2 u + e^u = f \quad \text{on} \quad (0, \pi), \\ u(0) = u(\pi) = 0 . \end{cases}$$

SECTION 37. RAPID NONLINEARITIES

37.1. In concluding the analysis of the solvability of boundary value problems of the type

$$\begin{cases} -u''(x) - g(u(x)) = f(x), \quad x \in (0, \pi), \\ u(0) = u(\pi) = 0 , \end{cases} \tag{1}$$

we examine the case when g is continuous on $\mathbb{R}$ and

$$\lim_{\xi \to \pm\infty} \frac{g(\xi)}{\xi} = \infty . \tag{2}$$

The basic result is the following assertion:

37.2. Theorem. *If condition (2) is satisfied, then the Dirichlet problem (1) has an infinite number of classical solutions for every right-hand side $f \in C^0([0, \pi])$.*

37.3. The idea of the proof of Theorem 37.2. We are not going to prove Theorem 37.2 since the method of its proof differs radically from the methods analyzed in this book. We confine ourselves merely to explaining the principal ideas, since the technical processing of the details is somewhat lenghty (the proof is given, e.g., in [19], [34]).

---

†) In [29], such problems are investigated by other methods. Even there, it is essential that the nontrivial solution of the linear part of the differential operator does not change sign in Ω.

(i) Over and above the conditions of Theorem 37.2, we assume, moreover, that the function g satisfies on $\mathbb{R}$ the *local Lipschitz condition*, i.e., if we choose an interval $[a, b] \subset \mathbb{R}$, then a constant $K = K(a, b) > 0$ exists such that

$$|g(\xi_1) - g(\xi_2)| \leq K|\xi_1 - \xi_2| \tag{3}$$

is true for all $\xi_1, \xi_2 \in [a, b]$.

Let $f \in C^0([0, \pi])$, and let us investigate the existence of the solution of the system of ordinary differential equations

$$\begin{cases} u'(x) = v(x), \\ v'(x) = -f(x) - g(u(x)) \end{cases} \tag{4}$$

with the initial condition

$$u(0) = 0, \quad v(0) = t, \tag{5}$$

where $t \in \mathbb{R}$. The additional condition (3) ensures (due to the generally familiar existence and uniqueness theorems for the solution of an initial value problem in systems of ordinary differential equations of the first order — see, e.g., [11]) that there exists precisely one solution

$$W(x, t) = (u_t(x), v_t(x))$$

of the initial value problem (4), (5) for arbitrary $t \in \mathbb{R}$, and this solution is defined on the maximal interval $J_t \subset [0, \pi]$, $0 \in J_t$.

(ii) Condition (2) ensures that $J_t = [0, \pi]$ for arbitrary $t \in \mathbb{R}$. The same condition implies

$$\lim_{t \to \pm\infty} \left(\inf_{x \in [0, \pi]} |W(x, t)| \right) = \infty, \tag{6}$$

where

$$|W(x, t)| = (u_t^2(x) + v_t^2(x))^{1/2}.$$

(iii) If t is then sufficiently large in absolute values, it follows from (6) that $W(x, t) \neq 0$ for every $x \in [0, \pi]$. For sufficiently large t, the function $W(x, t)$ can be expressed in the form

$$W(x, t) = |W(x, t)| (\cos r_t(x), -\sin r_t(x)) \tag{7}$$

and the real function

$$R(t) = r_t(\pi) - r_t(0)$$

is continuous on the set of all t of sufficiently large absolute value.

(iv) From (7), we see immediately that the boundary value problem (1) has a solution if and only if the equation

$$r_t(\pi) = (2n + 1)\frac{\pi}{2}$$

has a solution for some integer n and sufficiently large t. Since $r_t(0)$ is an odd multiple of the number $\pi/2$ [because $u_t(0) = 0$], it suffices to establish the number of solutions of the equation

$$R(t) = k\pi \quad (k \text{ integer, } t \text{ sufficiently large}).\tag{8}$$

Since $R(t)$ is continuous for t sufficiently large, equation (8) will have solutions for an infinite number of integers k if

$$\lim_{t \to \pm\infty} R(t) = \infty \ ;\tag{9}$$

the boundary value problem (1) will then also have an infinite number of solutions. Using somewhat delicate estimates together with comparison theorems for ordinary differential equations, it is possible to derive relation (9) and to show that condition (3) is superfluous.

37.4. Remarks. Applying the method indicated in Paragraph 37.3, the assertion of Theorem 37.2 can be generalized to boundary conditions of the form

$$\alpha\, u(0) + \beta\, u'(0) = 0\,,$$
$$\gamma\, u(\pi) + \delta\, u'(\pi) = 0$$

($\alpha, \beta, \gamma, \delta$ are given real numbers). Also, it is not necessary to consider classical solutions; without altering the method, it can be shown that there exists an infinite number of solutions in the Carathéodory sense (see [11]) for an arbitrary right-hand side $f \in L_1(0, \pi)$.

According to a personal communication, analogous problems in nonlinear partial differential equations have recently been investigated by S. I. Pokhozhaev who proved the same assertion as in Theorem 37.2 for the Dirichlet problem

$$-\Delta u(x) + g(u(x)) = f(x)\,, \quad x \in \Omega\,,$$
$$u\big|_{\partial\Omega} = 0\,.$$

SECTION 38. PERIODIC PROBLEMS

38.1. Let $T \in \mathbb{R}$. A real function $u(x)$ defined on $\mathbb{R}$ is called a *T-periodic function* if

$$u(x + T) = u(x)$$

for every $x \in \mathbb{R}$.

In practice (particularly in electrical engineering), T-periodic solutions of ordinary differential equations and T-periodic solutions of systems of ordinary differential equations are of considerable importance. It can be said without exaggeration that results known for boundary value problems can be carried over to periodic problems. Also, conversely: What is not yet solved for boundary value problems is also not known in the case of periodic problems. Thus, e.g., the results of Sections 33 – 37 can be carried over, by means of the same methods (but using spaces of T-periodic functions and other modifications), to the existence of T-periodic solutions of the differential equation

$$u''(x) = f(x; u(x), u'(x)) .$$

These problems were studied very intensively by the Belgian mathematician Jean Mawhin who developed the theory of the so-called *coincidence degree of a mapping*. This method is similar to that used to prove the existence of the solution in Section 34. J. Mawhin and several other mathematicians applied the theory of the degree of a mapping and fixed point theorems to the proof of the existence of T-periodic solutions of nonlinear ordinary differential equations of the second order, for the T-periodic solvability of systems of nonlinear differential equations of higher orders, and for related problems. J. Mawhin reports on these results very clearly and in detail in his text [63] where we also find a bibliographical and historical review. Below, we present without proof existence theorems for T-periodic solutions of nonlinaer differential equations. In the quoted literature, it is then possible to find not only the proofs but also eventual generalizations and further references to papers which discuss these problems.

38.2. Theorem. *Let* $a_1, ..., a_{2k-1}$ *be real numbers such that*

$$(-1)^j a_{2k-2j} \leqq 0 \quad (j = 1, ..., k-1) \ \dagger) .$$

Let h *and* g *be continuous functions on* $\mathbb{R}$. *Assume that the finite limits*

$$g(-\infty) = \lim_{\xi \to -\infty} g(\xi), \quad g(\infty) = \lim_{\xi \to \infty} g(\xi)$$

exist and that

$$g(-\infty) < g(\xi) < g(\infty)$$

holds for all $\xi \in \mathbb{R}$. *Let* f *be a continuous* T-*periodic function on* $\mathbb{R}$.
   Then the so-called Liénard equation

$$-(-1)^k u^{(2k)}(x) + a_{2k-1} u^{(2k-1)}(x) + ... + a_1 u'(x) + h(u(x)) u'(x) +$$
$$+ g(u(x)) = f(x)$$

---

†) No further conditions are imposed on the coefficients with odd subscripts.

has at least one T-periodic solution if and only if

$$g(-\infty) < \frac{1}{T} \int_0^T f(x)\,dx < g(\infty).$$

(For the proof, see [35].)

38.3. Remark. As far as the *T*-periodic solvability of ordinary differential equations with jumping nonlinearities is concerned, i.e., of equations of the type

$$-u''(x) - \mu\,u^+(x) + v\,u^-(x) + \psi(u(x)) = f(x)$$

(with a periodic and continuous right-hand side *f*), the same is known as in the case of the boundary value problem in Section 35 (see [12], [13]). The application of a procedure analogous to the method of Section 35 is again in question.

38.4. Theorem. *Let g be a continuous function on* $\mathbb{R}$ *such that*

$$\lim_{\xi \to \pm\infty} \frac{g(\xi)}{\xi} = \infty.$$

Let f be a continuous T-periodic function on $\mathbb{R}$*. Then at least one T-periodic solution of the equation*

$$-u''(x) - g(u(x)) = f(x), \quad x \in \mathbb{R}$$

exists.

(For the proof, see [34]; we note that the idea of the proof is the same as in Paragraph 37.3 — it exploits, moreover, the properties of the Brouwer degree of a mapping.)

CHAPTER VII

VARIATIONAL INEQUALITIES

SECTION 39. FORMULATION OF THE PROBLEM

39.1. Introduction. Let A be a formal differential operator of order $2k$,

$$(Au)(x) = \sum_{|\alpha| \leq k} (-1)^{|\alpha|} D^\alpha a_\alpha(x; \delta_k u(x)), \quad x \in \Omega, \tag{1}$$

with the coefficients

$$a_\alpha \in \mathbf{CAR}^*(p), \quad p > 1,$$

and let $\mathbb{A}$ be an operator from $W^{k,p}(\Omega)$ into the dual space $(W^{k,p}(\Omega))^*$ assigned to the (differential) operator A and given by the formula

$$<\mathbb{A}u, v> = \int_\Omega \Big[\sum_{|\alpha| \leq k} a_\alpha(x; \delta_k u(x)) D^\alpha v(x) \Big] dx, \quad u, v \in W^{k,p}(\Omega). \tag{2}$$

We recall the boundary value problem (A, V, Q) which was introduced in Paragraph 15.7; for simplicity's sake, we assume that the function φ which appears among the data of this problem vanishes. Then the function

$$u \in W^{k,p}(\Omega)$$

is the weak solution of this boundary value problem if

$$u \in V$$

(in fact, we have $\varphi = \Theta$) and if the relation

$$<\mathbb{A}u, v> = <\mathbf{f}, v>_Q + <\mathbf{g}, v>_V \tag{3}$$

is valid for all $v \in V$ (for the details and the notation see Paragraph 15.7).

In Section 19, we showed that to find the weak solution of the boundary value problem (A, V, Q) means to find a point at which the functional

$$F(w) = \int_0^1 <\mathbb{A}(tw), w> dt - <\mathbf{f}, w>_Q - <\mathbf{g}, w>_V \tag{4}$$

attains its minimum on the space $V \subset W^{k,p}(\Omega)$: If $u_0 \in V$ is a function such that

$$F(u_0) = \inf_{w \in V} F(w) \,,$$

then the function u_0 (under certain additional conditions) is a weak solution of problem (A, V, Q) as well (see Theorems 19.3 and 20.5).

For simplicity's sake we assumed that $\varphi = \Theta$. We now introduce one more simplification: Assume that the operator A from (1) is linear, i.e., that the coefficients $a_\alpha(x; \xi)$ are of the form

$$a_\alpha(x; \xi) = \sum_{|\beta| \leq k} a_{\alpha\beta}(x) \, \xi_\beta \,,$$

where $a_{\alpha\beta} \in L_\infty(\Omega)$ are given functions and where, moreover,

$$a_{\alpha\beta}(x) = a_{\beta\alpha}(x) \tag{5}$$

holds for $|\alpha|, |\beta| \leq k$. In this case, we choose $p = 2$ and work with the space V:

$$W_0^{k,2}(\Omega) \subseteq V \subseteq W^{k,2}(\Omega) \,;$$

the operator $\mathbb{A}$ is then also linear and, moreover, by (5), we have

$$<\mathbb{A}u, v> \ = \ <\mathbb{A}v, u> \tag{6}$$

for all pairs $u, v \in W^{k,2}(\Omega)$. The functional F from (4) is then simplified further: In fact, for $t \in \mathbb{R}$, we have

$$<\mathbb{A}(tw), w> \ = \ t<\mathbb{A}w, w>$$

and, consequently,

$$F(w) = \tfrac{1}{2}<\mathbb{A}w, w> \ - \ <\mathbf{f}, w>_Q \ - \ <\mathbf{g}, w>_V \,. \tag{7}$$

To find the weak solution of the boundary value problem for a linear operator A then means to find the point at which the so-called quadratic functional F of (7) attains its minimum — see also Theorem 20.7.

39.2. The extremum of a function with respect to a set. In motivating the variational method discussed in Chapter IV, we were governed by the very simple analogy with the theory of functions of one real variable: To find the solutions of the equation

$$h(t) = 0 \,,$$

where h is a (continuous) function defined on $\mathbb{R}$, means to find the local extrema of a function H which is primitive to h, i.e., for which

$$H'(t) = h(t) \,, \quad t \in \mathbb{R} \,.$$

When investigating the extrema of real functions, we do not always seek the minimum of the function H on the entire space $\mathbb{R}$, but — e.g. — the minimum of the function H on some subset M of the space $\mathbb{R}$ which is specified in advance. We then speak of the *minimum of the function H with respect to the set M* (or of an extreme or a minimum *subject to a constraint*: the constraint is precisely the condition $t \in M$).

We therefore examine whether it is also possible to exploit the analogy with the extremum of a function with respect to a set when looking for the minimum of a functional:

When applying the variational method, we looked, in Chapter IV, for a point $u_0 \in V$ for which

$$F(u_0) = \inf_{w \in V} F(w) .$$

Now, let K be a subset of the space V, and let us look for an element $u_0 \in K$ such that

$$F(u_0) = \inf_{w \in K} F(w) . \tag{8}$$

When

$$K = V$$

we exploited the fact — when investigating problem (8) — that the element u_0 satisfied the relation

$$<\mathbb{A}u_0, v> = <\mathbf{f}, v>_Q + <\mathbf{g}, v>_V$$

for every $v \in V$, i.e., that the function u_0 was a weak solution of the boundary value problem (A, V, Q). Now, we assume that

$$K \subsetneqq V$$

and that K is a closed convex set (see Paragraph 23.2). If $u_0 \in K$ is an element for which (8) is valid and if v is an arbitrary (but fixed) element from K, we also have

$$w = u_0 + t(v - u_0) = (1 - t) u_0 + tv \in K$$

for $t \in [0, 1]$. Consider the function

$$f_v(t) = F(u_0 + t(v - u_0)) , \tag{9}$$

defined for $t \in [0, 1]$. It is easily established that, by our conditions, the function $f_v(t)$ has a derivative $f_v'(t)$ at each point of the interval $[0, 1]$ [at the endpoints 0 and 1 the symbols $f_v'(0)$ and $f_v'(1)$ stand for right-hand and left-hand derivatives, respectively]. Since (8) holds, the function f_v attains its minimum on the interval $[0, 1]$ at the point $t = 0$. We therefore have

$$f_v'(0) \geqq 0 . \tag{10}$$

Note that equality does not generally hold in inequality (10): In fact, we seek the minimum of the function $f_v(t)$ on the interval $[0, 1]$ only, i.e., the minimum with respect to the set $M = [0, 1]$ is being considered. For instance, the function $h(t) = t$ attains its minimum with respect to the interval $[0, 1]$ at the point $t = 0$ while $h'(0) = = 1 > 0$. The inequality sign in (10) is thus material.

What, however, is the significance of relation (10)? Consider the functional F of (7). Then

$$f_v(t) = \tfrac{1}{2} <\mathbb{A}(u_0 + t(v - u_0)), u_0 + t(v - u_0) > - $$
$$- <\mathbf{f}, u_0 + t(v - u_0)>_Q - <\mathbf{g}, u_0 + t(v - u_0)>_V,$$

and since the operator $\mathbb{A}$ is linear and $\mathbb{A}w$, $\mathbf{f}$, and $\mathbf{g}$ are linear functionals we have

$$f_v(t) = \tfrac{1}{2} <\mathbb{A}u_0, u_0> + \tfrac{1}{2}t <\mathbb{A}u_0, v - u_0> +$$
$$+ \tfrac{1}{2}t <\mathbb{A}(v - u_0), u_0> + \tfrac{1}{2}t^2 <\mathbb{A}(v - u_0), v - u_0> -$$
$$- <\mathbf{f}, u_0>_Q - t <\mathbf{f}, v - u_0>_Q - <\mathbf{g}, u_0>_V -$$
$$- t <\mathbf{g}, v - u_0>_V =$$
$$= F(u_0) + t\{\tfrac{1}{2} <\mathbb{A}u_0, v - u_0> + \tfrac{1}{2} <\mathbb{A}(v - u_0), u_0> -$$
$$- <\mathbf{f}, v - u_0>_Q - <\mathbf{g}, v - u_0>_V\} + \tfrac{1}{2}t^2 <\mathbb{A}(v - u_0), v - u_0>.$$

Since, by (6),

$$<\mathbb{A}(v - u_0), u_0> = <\mathbb{A}u_0, v - u_0>,$$

we finally obtain

$$f_v'(0) = <\mathbb{A}u_0, v - u_0> - <\mathbf{f}, v - u_0>_Q - <\mathbf{g}, v - u_0>_V$$

and condition (10) which characterizes the elements $u_0 \in K$ for which (8) is true takes the form:

$$<\mathbb{A}u_0, v - u_0> \geqq <\mathbf{f}, v - u_0>_Q + <\mathbf{g}, v - u_0>_V \qquad (11)$$

for every $v \in K$.

39.3. Remark. Relation (11) is called a *variational inequality*; the element $u_0 \in K$ is its solution. We have arrived at this inequality under rather special conditions $(\varphi = \Theta, \mathbb{A}$ is a linear operator); it is possible to remove these conditions, but the condition that the function $f_v(t)$ from (9) has a derivative (i.e., that the functional F is the potential of the operator $\mathbb{A}$) is very important.

Naturally, relation (11) can be formally written without this last condition, just as we managed without the condition of potentiality in Chapter V. But inequality (11) cannot then be derived by means of the variational problem, i. e., an extremal problem with the so-called constraint condition $u_0 \in K$, nor is the term variational inequality the most apt. Nevertheless, the term will be used in the sequel since it is already common in the literature.

We give below quite general formulation of the problem of "solving a variational inequality".

39.4. The solution of the variational inequality. Let V be a Banach space, K a closed convex subset of the space V, and T an operator (generally nonlinear) which maps K into the dual space V^*.

To solve the variational inequality then means: *To find $u \in K$ so that*

$$< Tu, v - u > \geqq 0 \tag{12}$$

is true for all $v \in K$.

39.5. Example. Let $k \in \mathbb{N}$, $p > 1$, and choose the space V so that

$$W_0^{k,p}(\Omega) \subsetneqq V \subsetneqq W^{k,p}(\Omega).$$

Let K be a closed convex subset of the space V, $\mathbb{A}$ the operator given by formula (2), and $\mathbf{f}$ a functional from V^*. If we choose the operator T in the following manner:

$$Tw = \mathbb{A}w - \mathbf{f}, \quad w \in V,$$

then inequality (12) assumes the form

$$< \mathbb{A}u - \mathbf{f}, v - u > \geqq 0$$

or, in other words,

$$< \mathbb{A}u, v - u > \geqq < \mathbf{f}, v - u > . \tag{13}$$

In more detail: The function $u \in K$ is the solution of the variational inequality (13) if

$$\sum_{|\alpha| \leqq k} \int_\Omega a_\alpha(x; \delta_k u(x)) \, D^\alpha(v(x) - u(x)) \, dx \geqq < \mathbf{f}, v - u > \tag{14}$$

holds for all $v \in K$.

If, e.g., the operator $\mathbb{A}$ is determined by the formal Laplace operator

$$-\Delta w = - \sum_{i=1}^N \frac{\partial^2 w}{\partial x_i^2}$$

and if

$$< \mathbf{f}, v > = \int_\Omega f(x) \, v(x) \, dx ,$$

we put $k = 1$, $p = 2$, and relation (14) takes the form

$$\sum_{i=1}^{N} \int_{\Omega} \frac{\partial u(x)}{\partial x_i} \frac{\partial (v(x) - u(x))}{\partial x_i} \, dx \geqq \int_{\Omega} f(x) \, (v(x) - u(x)) \, dx \, .$$

39.6. Remark. Inequality (13), or rather (14), differs to some extent from relation (11): The term with the functional $\mathbf{g} \in V^*$ is missing and the functional $\mathbf{f}$ is now regarded not as an element of Q^* but as an element of V^*. The two relations will be the same, however, if the following (simplifying) assumption is made:

Assume that the space Q which appears in the definition of the weak solution of the boundary value problem (A, V, Q) is the same as the space V:

$$Q = V \, ,$$

and add together the two functionals $\mathbf{f}$ and $\mathbf{g}$, defined on V now, to get a single functional which is again denoted by $\mathbf{f}$.

Making this assumption and comparing the variational inequality (13), e.g., with relation (15.8) from the definition of the weak solution of the boundary value problem (A, V, Q), a certain (even close) relationship is evident. In what follows, it will be seen that the concept of "the solution of variational inequality (14)" generalizes the concept of "the weak solution of boundary value problem (A, V, Q)", and that the two concepts coincide if we choose $K = V$ (and $Q = V$) (see also Paragraph 40.3). The relationship between the two concepts is also borne out by the following assertion:

(i) *Let u_0 be the solution of the variational inequality (13), i.e., let*

$$<\mathbb{A} u_0, v - u_0> \geqq <\mathbf{f}, v - u_0> \tag{15}$$

hold for all $v \in K$. If the element u_0 lies inside the set K, then

$$<\mathbb{A} u_0, w> \, = \, <\mathbf{f}, w> \tag{16}$$

holds for all $w \in V$. †)

Since relation (16) is in fact a representation of the equation

$$\mathbb{A} u = \mathbf{f} \, ,$$

this means that inequality (15) is related, first of all, to the possible existence of a solution on the boundary of the set K. This is in line with the manner in which we reached the variational inequality in Paragraph 39.2.

---

†) By saying that the element u_0 lies inside K we mean that for any given element $w \in V$ a number $\varepsilon > 0$ exists such that $u_0 + tw \in K$ for $t \in (-\varepsilon, \varepsilon)$. Hence, the reader may easily derive equation (16) himself — it suffices to choose $v = u_0 + tw$ in (15).

In Section 41, we shall show that the "concrete" variational inequality $[(13)$ or $(14)]$ can be re-interpreted as a certain boundary value problem. However, we first examine certain general properties of the abstract variational inequality (12).

SECTION 40. MORE ON THE DEFINITION OF THE SOLUTION OF A VARIATIONAL INEQUALITY

40.1. The case $K = V$. Let $u \in K$ be a solution of the variational inequality (39.12), i.e., let

$$<Tu, v - u> \geqq 0 \tag{1}$$

hold for every $v \in K$, and let $K = V$ (V is obviously a convex set). Let $w \in V$ be arbitrary; then

$$w + u \in K \quad \text{and also} \quad -w + u \in K,$$

since $K = V$ is a linear space. Putting $v = w + u$ in (1), we obtain the inequality

$$<Tu, w> \geqq 0; \tag{2}$$

putting $v = -w + u$ in (1), we obtain the inequality

$$<Tu, -w> \geqq 0,$$

or, in other words (Tu is a linear functional),

$$<Tu, w> \leqq 0. \tag{3}$$

Inequalities (2) and (3) imply the equality

$$<Tu, w> = 0; \tag{4}$$

since $w \in V$ was arbitrary, we obtain the relation

$$Tu = \Theta.$$

If thus u is the solution of variational inequality (1) and $K = V$, then Tu is the zero element of the space V^*. The converse implication can easily be proved as well; the following assertion thus holds:

40.2. Lemma. *If $K = V$, then the variational inequality*

$$<Tu, v - u> \geqq 0, \quad v \in V, \tag{1}$$

is equivalent to the identity

$$<Tu, v> = 0, \quad v \in V. \tag{5}$$

40.3. Remark. If we choose V and T as in Paragraph 39.5, then the variational inequality

$$<\mathbb{A}u, v - u> \geqq <\mathbf{f}, v - u>, \quad v \in V,$$

is equivalent, for $K = V$, to the identity

$$<\mathbb{A}u, v> = <\mathbf{f}, v>, \quad v \in V.$$

In this case, Lemma 40.2 then says that the weak solution of the boundary value problem is the same, for $K = V$, as the solution of the variational inequality [the boundary value problem (A, V, V) is in question here — see Paragraph 39.6].

40.4. The cone. Let V be a Banach space. We say that the closed set $K \subset V$ is a *cone* with vertex at the point Θ if

$$v + w \in K, \quad tv \in K$$

holds for every pair of elements $v, w \in K$ and for every $t \geqq 0$.

Clearly, every cone is a convex set.

40.5. Theorem. *Let K be a cone with vertex at the point Θ. Then the element $u \in K$ is the solution of the variational inequality*

$$<Tu, v - u> \geqq 0, \quad v \in K, \tag{1}$$

if and only if the following two relations are satisfied:

$$<Tu, v> \geqq 0 \quad \text{for every} \quad v \in K \tag{6}$$

and

$$<Tu, u> = 0. \tag{7}$$

Proof. (a) Let (6) and (7) hold. Subtracting equality (7) from inequality (6), we obtain

$$<Tu, v> - <Tu, u> \geqq 0,$$

or, in other words (Tu is a linear functional),

$$<Tu, v - u> \geqq 0 \quad \text{for every} \quad v \in K,$$

i.e., (1) holds.

(b) Let (1) hold for every $v \in K$. Choosing, in particular,

$$v = 2u$$

(this is possible since $u \in K$ and K is a cone) we have $v - u = u$, and thus

$$<Tu, u> \geqq 0. \tag{8}$$

Choosing $v = \Theta$ in (1) we have

$$< Tu, -u > \geqq 0 ,$$

or, in other words,

$$< Tu, u > \leqq 0 . \tag{9}$$

Inequalities (8) and (9) imply equality (7).

The addition of inequality (1) to equality (7) now yields (6).

40.6. Remarks. (i) If we again choose V and T as in Paragraph 39.5, Theorem 40.5 says that if K is a cone with vertex at the point Θ, then the variational inequality

$$< \mathbb{A}u, v - u > \geqq <\mathbf{f}, v - u> , \quad v \in K , \tag{10}$$

is equivalent to the pair of relations

$$< \mathbb{A}u, v > \geqq <\mathbf{f}, v> \quad \text{for every} \quad v \in K \tag{11}$$

and

$$< \mathbb{A}u, u > = <\mathbf{f}, u> . \tag{12}$$

(ii) In the sequel, we will not work with the "abstract" variational inequality (1) but with the variational inequality in the "concrete" form (10). Formally, this situation differs to some extent from the situation in Chapters IV, V, and VI, where we dealt with a general operator T. The reader will certainly realize, however, that the special form of the operator $\mathbb{A}$ — see formula (39.2) — as well as of the space V plays no essential role, and (if he wishes) he could substitute the expression

$$Tu$$

for the expression

$$\mathbb{A}u - \mathbf{f}$$

everywhere in the sequel and deal with a general Banach space V.

40.7. "Nonlinearity" of the variational inequality. We have arrived at variational inequality (10) in a rather natural manner in the case of the operator $\mathbb{A}$ being linear. It should be stressed, however, that the problem of solving the variational inequality (10) is generally a nonlinear problem; this is true even if the operator is linear: In fact, if u_1 is the solution of the variational inequality with the "right-hand side" $\mathbf{f}_1 \in V^*$, i.e., if

$$< \mathbb{A}u_1, v - u_1 > \geqq <\mathbf{f}_1, v - u_1> \quad \text{for every} \quad v \in K ,$$

and if u_2 is the solution of the variational inequality with the "right-hand side" $\mathbf{f}_2 \in V^*$, i.e., if

$$< \mathbb{A}u_2, v - u_2 > \geqq <\mathbf{f}_2, v - u_2> \quad \text{for every} \quad v \in K ,$$

it cannot be said that the variational inequality with the "right-hand side"

$$\mathbf{f} = c_1\mathbf{f}_1 + c_2\mathbf{f}_2 \in V^*$$

$(c_1, c_2 \in \mathbb{R})$ necessarily has the solution

$$u = c_1 u_1 + c_2 u_2 .$$

Indeed, the set K need not be a linear space in general; it is then possible that

$$u \notin K .$$

For variational inequalities, the difference between the linear and nonlinear character is weakened. However, it is possible to "linearize" a nonlinear problem in a certain sense: The solution $u \in K$ of the variational inequality (10) appears in both terms of the expression

$$<\mathbb{A}u, v - u> ;$$

here, the expression

$$<\mathbb{A}u, w>$$

is linear in the second term (i.e.,

$$<\mathbb{A}u, c_1 w_1 + c_2 w_2> = c_1 <\mathbb{A}u, w_1> + c_2 <\mathbb{A}u, w_2>$$

holds for $w_1, w_2 \in K$, $c_1, c_2 \in \mathbb{R}$) while this is not generally true with respect to the first term in so much as the operator $\mathbb{A}$ may not be linear. However, under certain assumptions it is possible to "transfer" the solution from the left ("nonlinear") term of the expression $<\mathbb{A}u, w>$ to the right ("linear") term; this follows from the assertion below.

40.8. Theorem. *Let K be a closed convex subset of a Banach space V, $\mathbb{A}$ an operator from K to V^*, $\mathbf{f} \in V^*$. Let the operator $\mathbb{A}$ be continuous and monotone (i.e.,*

$$<\mathbb{A}v - \mathbb{A}w, v - w> \geqq 0 \tag{13}$$

holds for all pairs $v, w \in K$). Then the element $u \in K$ is the solution of the variational inequality

$$<\mathbb{A}u, v - u> \geqq <\mathbf{f}, v - u>, \quad v \in K, \tag{10}$$

if and only if

$$<\mathbb{A}v, v - u> \geqq <\mathbf{f}, v - u> \tag{14}$$

holds for every $v \in K$.

Proof: Let (10) hold for every $v \in K$. Since

$$\mathbb{A}v = \mathbb{A}u + \mathbb{A}v - \mathbb{A}u ,$$

we have

$$<Av, v - u> = <Au, v - u> + <Av - Au, v - u> .$$

The second term on the right-hand side is non-negative by (13), and thus

$$<Av, v - u> \geq <Au, v - u> .$$

Inequality (14) now follows immediately from (10).

(b) Let (14) hold for every $v \in K$. In particular, choose here

$$v = (1 - t) u + tw ,$$

where $w \in K$ is arbitrary and $t \in [0, 1]$. Then

$$v - u = t(w - u) \quad \text{and} \quad v = u + t(w - u)$$

and (14) implies

$$<Av, v - u> = <A(u + t(w - u)), t(w - u)> =$$
$$= t <A(u + t(w - u)), w - u> \geq$$
$$\geq <f, v - u> = <f, t(w - u)> = t <f, w - u> .$$

For $t > 0$, we then have

$$<A(u + t(w - u)), w - u> \geq <f, w - u> . \tag{15}$$

Now, let $t \to 0+$; since the operator A is continuous, we have

$$\lim_{t \to 0+} <A(u + t(w - u)), w - u> = <Au, w - u> .$$

Hence, and from relation (15), it follows that

$$<Au, w - u> \geq <f, w - u> .$$

Since $w \in K$ was arbitrary, we obtain the variational inequality (10).

40.9. Remarks. (i) From the proof of the foregoing theorem, one immediately sees that the condition of continuity of the operator A is unnecessarily strong: It would suffice to assume that the function

$$h(t) = <A(u + tv), w>$$

is a continuous function of the variable t at the point $t = 0$ for every triple $u, v, w \in K$. In particular, it would then suffice to assume that the operator A is demicontinuous (see Paragraph 29.5).

(ii) Hitherto, nothing has been said on the existence of the solution of the variational inequality. We leave this problem until Section 43; we observe, however, the condition of the monotony of the operator $\mathbb{A}$ which induces some sort of relationship with the existence theorems of Chapters IV and V. Under the assumption of Theorem 40.8, it is now possible to characterize the set of all the solutions of the variational inequality (10):

40.10. Theorem. *Let the conditions of* Theorem 40.8 *be satisfied. Then the set of all the solutions of the variational inequality* (10) *is convex and closed.*

Proof: Let $u_1, u_2 \in K$ be two solutions of the variational inequality (10), i.e., for every $v \in K$ let

$$<\mathbb{A}u_i, v - u_i> \geqq <f, v - u_i>, \quad i = 1, 2.$$

By Theorem 40.8,

$$<\mathbb{A}v, v - u_i> \geqq <f, v - u_i>, \quad i = 1, 2, \tag{16}$$

then holds for every $v \in K$. Now, put

$$u = tu_1 + (1 - t)u_2, \quad t \in [0, 1].$$

Then

$$<\mathbb{A}v, v - u> = <\mathbb{A}v, tv - tu_1 + (1 - t)v - (1 - t)u_2> =$$
$$= <\mathbb{A}v, t(v - u_1)> + <\mathbb{A}v, (1 - t)(v - u_2)> =$$
$$= t<\mathbb{A}v, v - u_1> + (1 - t)<\mathbb{A}v, v - u_2> \geqq$$
$$\geqq t<f, v - u_1> + (1 - t)<f, v - u_2> =$$
$$= <f, t(v - u_1) + (1 - t)(v - u_2)> = <f, v - u>$$

[making use of relations (16) and of the fact that $f \in V^*$ and $\mathbb{A}v \in V^*$]. By Theorem 40.8, this means, however, that the element u is also a solution of the variational inequality (10) and the set of all solutions is thus convex.

Now, let $\{u_n\}_{n=1}^{\infty}$ be a sequence of solutions of the variational inequality (10). Thus,

$$<\mathbb{A}u_n, v - u_n> \geqq <f, v - u_n>,$$

and, by Theorem 40.8,

$$<\mathbb{A}v, v - u_n> \geqq <f, v - u_n> \tag{17}$$

also holds for every $v \in K$ and for every $n \in \mathbb{N}$. If $u_n \to u$ as $n \to \infty$, then $u \in K$ because K is a closed set and $u_n \in K$. Passing to the limit, inequalities (17) yield

$$<\mathbb{A}v, v - u> \geqq <f, v - u>, \quad v \in K$$

($\mathbb{A}v$ and f are continuous functionals). By Theorem 40.8, this means, however, that u also satisfies the variational inequality (10) — the set of all the solutions is thus closed.

SECTION 41. EXAMPLES

41.1. Ordinary differential operator of the second order. Choose $\Omega = (0, 1)$, $k = 1$, $p = 2$, $V \subset W^{1,2}(0, 1)$,

$$<f, v> = \int_0^1 f(x) \, v(x) \, dx \,, \quad f \in L_1(0, 1) \,, \quad \dagger)$$

$$<Av, w> = \int_0^1 v'(x) \, w'(x) \, dx \,.$$

To solve the variational inequality then means to find an element $u \in K$, for a given closed convex set $K \subset V$, so that

$$\int_0^1 u'(x) \, [v'(x) - u'(x)] \, dx \geq \int_0^1 f(x) \, [v(x) - u(x)] \, dx \tag{1}$$

holds for all $v \in K$.

(i) Choose

$$K = V = W_0^{1,2}(0, 1) \,. \tag{2}$$

Variational inequality (1) is then equivalent, by Lemma 40.2, to the identity

$$\int_0^1 u'(x) \, v'(x) \, dx = \int_0^1 f(x) \, v(x) \, dx$$

which is to hold for every $v \in W_0^{1,2}(0, 1)$.

As is familiar from Paragraph 15.4, this identity corresponds to the Dirichlet problem

$$\begin{cases} -u'' = f \quad \text{on} \quad (0, 1) \,, \\ \quad u(0) = u(1) = 0 \,. \end{cases} \tag{3}$$

To solve variational inequality (1) then means, in the case of (2), to find the (weak) solution of the boundary value problem (3).

(ii) Choose

$$V = W^{1,2}(0, 1)$$

and

$$K = \{v \in W^{1,2}(0, 1); \, v(0) \geq 0, \, v(1) \geq 0\} \,. \tag{4}$$

With this choice of the set K, the variational inequality (1) then corresponds to the following "boundary value problem":

$$\begin{cases} -u'' = f \quad \text{on} \quad (0, 1) \,, \\ \quad u(0) \geq 0 \,, \quad u(1) \geq 0 \,, \quad u'(0) \leq 0 \,, \quad u'(1) \geq 0 \,, \\ \quad u(t) \, u'(t) = 0 \quad \text{for} \quad t = 0, 1 \,. \end{cases} \tag{5}$$

$\dagger$) Indeed, this formula defines a continuous linear functional f since the function $v \in V^*$ belongs to the Sobolev space $W^{1,2}(0, 1)$ and is thus even continuous on $[0, 1]$ — see Paragraph 13.4.

We show that this is true: First of all, it is easy to show that the set K from (4) is not only convex but that it is even a cone (see Paragraph 40.4). By Theorem 40.5, or — rather — by Remark 40.6 (i), relation (1) is then equivalent to the pair of relations

$$\int_0^1 u'(x) \, v'(x) \, dx \geqq \int_0^1 f(x) \, v(x) \, dx, \tag{6}$$

$$\int_0^1 [u'(x)]^2 \, dx = \int_0^1 f(x) \, u(x) \, dx, \tag{7}$$

where $u \in K$ is the solution and $v \in K$ is arbitrary.

Assume now that the solution u of the variational inequality (1) exists and that it is sufficiently smooth, e.g., that

$$u \in C^2([0, 1]).$$

Relation (6) holds for every $v \in K$; in particular, it thus holds for every $v \in C_0^\infty(0, 1)$ since we then have $v(0) = v(1) = 0$, and thus $v(0) \geqq 0$ as well as $v(1) \geqq 0$. Furthermore, (6) holds for the function $-v$ as well, since $-v(0) = -v(1) = 0 \geqq 0$. For this second choice, we obtain from (6) the inequality

$$\int_0^1 u'(x) \, v'(x) \, dx \leqq \int_0^1 f(x) \, v(x) \, dx.$$

This, together with (6), implies that the identity

$$\int_0^1 u'(x) \, v'(x) \, dx = \int_0^1 f(x) \, v(x) \, dx$$

is valid for every $v \in C_0^\infty(0, 1)$. Rewriting the left-hand side according to Green's formula (i.e., by integration by parts) we obtain the relation

$$\int_0^1 [-u''(x)] \, v(x) \, dx = \int_0^1 f(x) \, v(x) \, dx$$

or, in other words, the relation

$$\int_0^1 [-u''(x) - f(x)] \, v(x) \, dx = 0.$$

Since $v \in C_0^\infty(0, 1)$ was arbitrary, the function u satisfies the equation

$$-u'' = f \quad \text{on} \quad (0, 1). \tag{8}$$

The first line of (5) is thus derived.

We now return again to inequality (6) choosing, however, $v \in K$ arbitrarily [thus: $v(0) \geqq 0$, $v(1) \geqq 0$]. Rewriting the left-hand side of (6) using Green's formula again, we obtain the inequality

$$\int_0^1 \left[-u''(x)\right] v(x)\,dx + \left[u'(1)\,v(1) - u'(0)\,v(0)\right] \geqq \int_0^1 f(x)\,v(x)\,dx\,.$$

Relation (8) implies that the two integrals are equal, and we thus have

$$u'(1)\,v(1) - u'(0)\,v(0) \geqq 0 \quad \text{for every} \quad v \in K\,. \tag{9}$$

Choosing, in particular, v so that $v(1) = 1$ and $v(0) = 0$ [or $v(1) = 0$ and $v(0) = 1$], relation (9) yields the condition

$$u'(1) \geqq 0 \quad [\text{or} -u'(0) \geqq 0, \text{ respectively}]\,. \tag{10}$$

This, together with the condition $u \in K$, gives the second line of (5).

Relation (9) was derived from inequality (6). In exactly the same way, the relation

$$u'(1)\,u(1) - u'(0)\,u(0) = 0$$

is derived from equality (7). However, since $u \in K$ [i.e., $u(0) \geqq 0, u(1) \geqq 0$] and since (10) holds, we have

$$0 \leqq u'(1)\,u(1) = u'(0)\,u(0) \leqq 0\,.$$

But this is possible if and only if

$$u'(1)\,u(1) = u'(0)\,u(0) = 0\,,$$

which is the third line of (5).

(iii) Choose

$$V = W_0^{1,2}(0, 1)$$

and

$$K = \{v \in W_0^{1,2}(0, 1);\ |v'(x)| \leqq 1 \text{ almost everywhere in } (0, 1)\}\,. \tag{11}$$

For this choice of the set K (which is not a cone this time), variational inequality (1) corresponds to the following "boundary value problem":

$$\begin{cases} -u'' = f \quad \text{on} \quad \Omega_1\,, \\ |u'| = 1 \quad \text{on} \quad (0, 1) - \Omega_1\,, \\ u(0) = u(1) = 0\,, \end{cases} \tag{12}$$

where $\Omega_1 = \{x \in (0, 1);\ |u'(x)| < 1\}$ is a set determined by the solution $u \in K$. (See also Example 42.6.)

41.2. Remark. We shall again return to the elucidation of the meaning of "boundary value problems" (5) and (12) when investigating the analogous problem for the case of partial differential equations — see Paragraph 41.4.

41.3. Ordinary differential operator of the fourth order. Again choose $\Omega = (0, 1)$, $p = 2$, but $k = 2$ and $V = W^{2,2}(0, 1) \cap W_0^{1,2}(0, 1)$. Furthermore, choose $\mathbf{f} = \Theta$ and

$$<Av, w> = \int_0^1 [\lambda u''(x) v''(x) - u'(x) v'(x)] \, dx$$

$(\lambda \in \mathbb{R})$. Finally, choose

$$K = \{v \in V; v(x_1) \geq 0, v(x_2) \geq 0\} ,$$

where $0 < x_1 < x_2 < 1$.

To solve the variational inequality means to find $u \in K$ so that

$$\int_0^1 \{\lambda u''(x) [v''(x) - u''(x)] - u'(x) [v'(x) - u'(x)]\} \, dx \geq 0 \qquad (13)$$

holds for all $v \in K$.

Note that here the problem is not only to find the solution $u \in K$ but to find out, first of all, whether there is a value $\lambda \in \mathbb{R}$ such that a nontrivial solution u exists [we immediately see, indeed, that the function $u(x) \equiv 0$ always satisfies the variational inequality (13)].

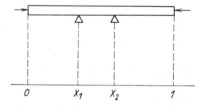

Fig. 41.3

The variational inequality (13) describes a simply supported beam of length 1 which is supported, moreover, also at the points $x = x_1$ and $x = x_2$ so that it cannot deflect downwards under the action of the deforming force. The deforming force and the material properties of the beam are represented by the constant λ; thus we are dealing with the "boundary value problem"

$$\begin{cases} \lambda u^{(IV)} - u = 0 \quad \text{on} \quad (0, x_1) \cup (x_1, x_2) \cup (x_2, 1) ; \\ u(0) = u''(0) = u(1) = u''(1) = 0 , \\ u(x_i) \geq 0, \ u'''(x_i +) - u'''(x_i -) \leq 0 , \\ [u'''(x_i +) - u'''(x_i -)] \, u(x_i) = 0 , i = 1, 2 \end{cases}$$

(see also Fig. 41.3).

41.4. Partial differential operator of the second order. Choose $\Omega \subset \mathbb{R}^N$, $N > 1$, $k = 1$, $p = 2$, $V \subset W^{1,2}(\Omega)$,

$$<f, v> = \int_\Omega f(x)\, v(x)\, dx \quad \text{with} \quad f \in L_2(\Omega),\qquad (14)$$

$$<\mathbb{A}v, w> = \int_\Omega \left[\sum_{i=1}^N \frac{\partial v(x)}{\partial x_i} \frac{\partial w(x)}{\partial x_i} + v(x)\, w(x)\right] dx \qquad (15)$$

[this corresponds to the formal differential operator of the second order with the coefficients

$$a_i(x; \xi_0, \xi_1, \ldots, \xi_N) = \xi_i, \quad i = 0, 1, \ldots, N,$$

i.e., to the operator $-\Delta u + u$]. To solve the variational inequality then means to find $u \in K$ so that

$$\int_\Omega \left[\sum_{i=1}^N \frac{\partial u(x)}{\partial x_i} \frac{\partial [v(x) - u(x)]}{\partial x_i} + u(x)\, [v(x) - u(x)]\right] dx \geq$$

$$\geq \int_\Omega f(x)\, [v(x) - u(x)]\, dx \qquad (16)$$

holds for all $v \in K$.

(i) Choose

$$K = V = W_0^{1,2}(\Omega). \qquad (17)$$

By Lemma 40.2, the variational inequality (16) is then equivalent to the identity

$$\int_\Omega \left[\sum_{i=1}^N \frac{\partial u(x)}{\partial x_i} \frac{\partial v(x)}{\partial x_i} + u(x)\, v(x)\right] dx = \int_\Omega f(x)\, v(x)\, dx$$

which should hold for all functions $v \in W_0^{1,2}(\Omega)$.

As we already know from Paragraph 15.16, this identity corresponds to the boundary value problem

$$\begin{cases} -\Delta u + u = f & \text{on } \Omega, \\ u|_{\partial\Omega} = 0. \end{cases} \qquad (18)$$

To solve the variational inequality (16) in the case of (17) then means to find the weak solution of the Dirichlet problem (18).

(ii) Choose

$$V = W^{1,2}(\Omega)$$

and

$$K = \{v \in W^{1,2}(\Omega);\ v|_{\partial\Omega} \geq 0 \text{ in the sense of traces}\}. \qquad (19)$$

For this choice, the variational inequality (16) corresponds to the following "boundary value problem":

$$\begin{cases} -\Delta u + u = f \quad \text{on} \quad \Omega, \\[2mm] u \geq 0 \quad \text{on} \quad \partial\Omega, \quad \dfrac{\partial u}{\partial v} \geq 0 \quad \text{on} \quad \partial\Omega, \\[2mm] u\,\dfrac{\partial u}{\partial v} = 0 \quad \text{on} \quad \partial\Omega. \end{cases} \tag{20}$$

We prove the above statement†): First of all, it can be shown easily that the set K from (19) is not only convex but that it is even a cone (see Paragraph 40.4). By Theorem 40.5 [or, rather, by Remark 40.6 (i)], relation (16) is then equivalent to the pair of relations

$$\int_\Omega \left[\sum_{i=1}^N \frac{\partial u(x)}{\partial x_i} \frac{\partial v(x)}{\partial x_i} + u(x)\,v(x) \right] dx \geq \int_\Omega f(x)\,v(x)\,dx, \tag{21}$$

$$\int_\Omega \left[\sum_{i=1}^N \left(\frac{\partial u(x)}{\partial x_i} \right)^2 + u^2(x) \right] dx = \int_\Omega f(x)\,u(x)\,dx, \tag{22}$$

where $u \in K$ is the solution and $v \in K$ is arbitrary.

Assume now that the solution u of variational inequality (16) exists and that it is sufficiently smooth, e.g., that

$$u \in C^2(\bar\Omega).$$

Relation (21) holds for every $v \in K$; in particular, it holds for every $v \in C_0^\infty(\Omega)$ since we then have $v|_{\partial\Omega} = 0$, and thus $v|_{\partial\Omega} \geq 0$. Furthermore, (21) holds for the function $-v$ as well since we also have $(-v)|_{\partial\Omega} = 0 \geq 0$; thus, $-v \in K$. For this choice, relation (21) reduces to the inequality

$$\int_\Omega \left[\sum_{i=1}^N \frac{\partial u(x)}{\partial x_i} \frac{\partial v(x)}{\partial x_i} + u(x)\,v(x) \right] dx \leq \int_\Omega f(x)\,v(x)\,dx,$$

which together with (21) says that the identity

$$\int_\Omega \left[\sum_{i=1}^N \frac{\partial u(x)}{\partial x_i} \frac{\partial v(x)}{\partial x_i} + u(x)\,v(x) \right] dx = \int_\Omega f(x)\,v(x)\,dx$$

holds for every $v \in C_0^\infty(\Omega)$. Rewriting this identity using Green's formula (11.1), we arrive at the relation

$$\int_\Omega [-\Delta u(x) + u(x) - f(x)]\,v(x)\,dx = 0.$$

---

†) Compare the formulation, the boundary value problem, and also what follows with Example 41.1 (ii).

Since the function $v \in C_0^\infty(\Omega)$ was arbitrary, the function u satisfies the equation

$$-\Delta u + u - f = 0 \quad \text{on} \quad \Omega ; \tag{23}$$

the first line of (20) is thus derived.

We now return to inequality (21) once more, but choose $v \in K$ arbitrarily (thus, $v|_{\partial\Omega} \geq 0$). Rewriting the left-hand side using Green's formula again, we obtain the inequality

$$\int_\Omega [-\Delta u(x) + u(x)] v(x) \, dx + \int_{\partial\Omega} \frac{\partial u(x)}{\partial v} v(x) \, dS \geq \int_\Omega f(x) v(x) \, dx .$$

From relation (23), it immediately follows, however, that the two integrals over Ω are equal. Thus,

$$\int_{\partial\Omega} \frac{\partial u(x)}{\partial v} v(x) \, dS \geq 0 \quad \text{for all} \quad v \in K . \tag{24}$$

But $v|_{\partial\Omega} \geq 0$ by assumption; therefore, we have also $\partial u/\partial v \geq 0$ on $\partial\Omega$: In fact, if $\partial u(x_0)/\partial v < 0$ for some $x_0 \in \partial\Omega$, we could easily construct a function $v \in K$ for which (24) is not valid [e.g., we could choose $v(x) > 0$ for x in a neighbourhood of the point x_0, $v(x) = 0$ for every other $x \in \partial\Omega$]. Thus,

$$u \geq 0 \quad \text{on} \quad \partial\Omega$$

(since $u \in K$) and

$$\frac{\partial u}{\partial v} \geq 0 \quad \text{on} \quad \partial\Omega ,$$

which is the second line of (20).

Relation (24) was derived from relation (21). In the same way, we prove that equality (22) implies the equality

$$\int_{\partial\Omega} \frac{\partial u(x)}{\partial v} u(x) \, dS = 0$$

for the solution $u \in K$. Since both factors are non-negative functions, we have

$$u \frac{\partial u}{\partial v} = 0 \quad \text{on} \quad \partial\Omega . \tag{25}$$

This shows that (20) is valid.

41.5. Remarks. (i) Let us discuss further boundary condition (25): It says that either $u(x) = 0$ or $\partial u(x)/\partial v = 0$ at every point $x \in \partial\Omega$. In other words: The solution $u \in K$ splits the boundary $\partial\Omega$ into two parts — the part Γ on which $u|_\Gamma = 0$, and the part $\partial\Omega - \Gamma$ on which $u > 0$ and thus $\partial u/\partial v = 0$. Problem (20) is then some sort of "mixed problem" of the kind encountered, e.g., in Paragraph 15.16 (I-3): We have

$$u = 0 \quad \text{on} \quad \Gamma, \quad \frac{\partial u}{\partial v} = 0 \quad \text{on} \quad \partial\Omega - \Gamma.$$

The difference, as compared with Paragraph 15.16 (besides the further conditions $u \geq 0$ and $\partial u/\partial v \geq 0$ on $\partial\Omega$) obviously lies in the fact that the partition of the boundary $\partial\Omega$ into two parts is not given beforehand but is determined by the solution u.

We shall return to this question again in Paragraphs 42.2 and 42.3.

(ii) The variational inequality of Example 41.4 (ii) has its origin in mechanics. The boundary conditions of problem (20) can even be non-homogeneous: In the formulation of the problem — see the beginning of Paragraph 41.4 — we change only the functional $\mathbf{f} \in V^*$: Instead of (14), we put

$$<\mathbf{f}, v> = \int_\Omega f(x) \, v(x) \, dx + \int_{\partial\Omega} g(x) \, v(x) \, dS,$$

where $f \in L_2(\Omega)$ and $g \in L_2(\partial\Omega)$ (it can be shown that then $\mathbf{f} \in V^*$, in fact), and leave all the other data unchanged. The corresponding variational inequality then corresponds to a "boundary value problem" which only differs from (20) in the final conditions: They will be of the form

$$u \geq 0 \quad \text{on} \quad \partial\Omega, \quad \frac{\partial u}{\partial v} \geq g \quad \text{on} \quad \partial\Omega,$$

$$u \left(\frac{\partial u}{\partial v} - g \right) = 0 \quad \text{on} \quad \partial\Omega,$$

so that we have a "mixed problem" again, with the boundary conditions

$$u = 0 \quad \text{on} \quad \Gamma, \quad \frac{\partial u}{\partial v} = g \quad \text{on} \quad \partial\Omega - \Gamma.$$

Here, Γ is again a certain unknown subset of the boundary $\partial\Omega$ which depends on the solution u.

41.6. Operators of the second order revisited. Consider once more variational inequality (16) from Example 41.4 with

$$V = W^{1,2}(\Omega);$$

however, this time we choose

$$K = \{v \in W^{1,2}(\Omega); \ v \geq 0 \quad \text{almost everywhere on} \quad \Omega\}. \tag{26}$$

Assume that the solution of variational inequality (16) exists and that it is sufficiently smooth, e.g., that

$$u \in C^2(\bar{\Omega}),$$

and put

$$\Omega_0 = \{x \in \Omega;\ u(x) = 0\},$$
$$\Omega_1 = \{x \in \Omega;\ u(x) > 0\},$$
$$M = \partial\Omega_1 \cap \partial\Omega_0,\quad \Gamma_1 = \partial\Omega \cap \partial\Omega_1$$

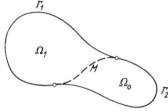

Fig. 41.6

(see Fig. 41.6)†). Inequality (16) then corresponds to the following "boundary value problem":

$$\begin{cases} -\Delta u + u = f \quad \text{on} \quad \Omega_1,\\[4pt] \qquad u = 0 \quad \text{on} \quad \Omega_0,\\[4pt] u = 0 \quad \text{on} \quad M,\quad \dfrac{\partial u}{\partial v} = 0 \quad \text{on} \quad M,\quad \dfrac{\partial u}{\partial v} \geq 0 \quad \text{on} \quad \Gamma_1,\\[8pt] u\dfrac{\partial u}{\partial v} = 0 \quad \text{on} \quad \Gamma_1. \end{cases} \tag{27}$$

We indicate the proof of our assertion here: Let then $u \in K$ be the solution of variational inequality (16) with K determined by (26); choose $\varphi \in C_0^\infty(\Omega_1)$ and write $\mathfrak{M} = \operatorname{supp} \varphi$. Since $\mathfrak{M}$ is a compact set, $\mathfrak{M} \subsetneqq \Omega_1$, and u is positive on Ω_1, a number $\eta > 0$ exists such that

$$u(x) \geq \eta > 0 \quad \text{for} \quad x \in \mathfrak{M}.$$

If we now choose the function v as

$$v = u \pm \varepsilon\varphi, \tag{28}$$

we will certainly have, for sufficiently small $\varepsilon > 0$,

$$v(x) \geq 0 \quad \text{for} \quad x \in \Omega,\quad \text{i.e.,}\quad v \in K.\ \dagger\dagger)$$

---

†) We note that Fig. 41.6 serves as no more than a guide since we know nothing about the structure of the sets Ω_0 and Ω_1.

††) It suffices to choose
$$\varepsilon < \eta\big[\max_{x \in \mathfrak{M}} |\varphi(x)|\big]^{-1}.$$

Relation (16) holds for every $v \in K$; substituting v from (28), we obtain $v - u = $ $= \pm \varepsilon \varphi$ and (16) reduces to

$$\pm \varepsilon \int_{\Omega_1} \left[\sum_{i=1}^{N} \frac{\partial u(x)}{\partial x_i} \frac{\partial \varphi(x)}{\partial x_i} + u(x)\, \varphi(x) \right] dx \geqq \pm \varepsilon \int_{\Omega_1} f(x)\, \varphi(x)\, dx$$

(it suffices to integrate over Ω_1 because $\varphi(x) = 0$ for $x \in \Omega_0$). By means of Green's formula we obtain the relation

$$\pm \varepsilon \int_{\Omega_1} \left[-\Delta u(x) + u(x) - f(x) \right] \varphi(x)\, dx \geqq 0$$

or, in other words $-$ since $\varepsilon > 0$ $-$

$$\int_{\Omega_1} \left[-\Delta u(x) + u(x) - f(x) \right] \varphi(x)\, dx = 0 \quad \text{for every} \quad \varphi \in C_0^\infty(\Omega_1).$$

This means that the function u satisfies the equation

$$-\Delta u + u = f \quad \text{on} \quad \Omega_1. \tag{29}$$

Since the set K from (26) is obviously a cone again, it is possible to use the two relations (21) and (22) instead of inequality (16). Here, it suffices to integrate over Ω_1 in (22) and on the left-hand side of (21) because $u(x) = 0$ for $x \in \Omega_0$. If we now rewrite the left-hand side of (21) using Green's formula, and if we use relation (29), we obtain $-$ just as in Paragraph 41.4 (ii) $-$ the inequality

$$\int_{\partial \Omega_1} \frac{\partial u(x)}{\partial v} v(x)\, dS \geqq \int_{\Omega_0} f(x)\, v(x)\, dS \tag{30}$$

which holds for every $v \in K$. Hence, we derive the "boundary conditions" of (27):

(a) Choose $v \in K$ so that $v(x) = 0$ for $x \in \Omega_0$. Then $v|_M = 0$ holds as well and (30) yields

$$0 \leqq \int_{\partial \Omega_1} \frac{\partial u(x)}{\partial v} v(x)\, dS = \int_{\Gamma_1} \frac{\partial u(x)}{\partial v} v(x)\, dS + \int_M \frac{\partial u(x)}{\partial v} v(x)\, dS = \int_{\Gamma_1} \frac{\partial u(x)}{\partial v} v(x)\, dS,$$

and thus

$$\frac{\partial u}{\partial v} \geqq 0 \quad \text{on} \quad \Gamma_1$$

because $v \geqq 0$ on Γ_1.

(b) The condition $u = 0$ on M is satisfied automatically because $u(x) = 0$ for $x \in \Omega_0$ and $M \subset \partial \Omega_0$.

(c) (22) implies that equality holds in (30) if we choose $v = u$. Thus,

$$\int_{\partial\Omega_1} \frac{\partial u(x)}{\partial v} u(x) \, dS = \int_{\Omega_0} f(x) \, u(x) \, dS = 0$$

since $u = 0$ on Ω_0. Furthermore,

$$\int_{\partial\Omega_1} \frac{\partial u(x)}{\partial v} u(x) \, dS = \int_{\Gamma_1} \frac{\partial u(x)}{\partial v} u(x) \, dS + \int_M \frac{\partial u(x)}{\partial v} u(x) \, dS = \int_{\Gamma_1} \frac{\partial u(x)}{\partial v} u(x) \, dS$$

since $u = 0$ on M. Thus,

$$\int_{\Gamma_1} \frac{\partial u(x)}{\partial v} u(x) \, dS = 0$$

and since we have $\partial u/\partial v \geq 0$ as well as $u \geq 0$ on Γ_1, the relation

$$\frac{\partial u}{\partial v} u = 0 \quad \text{must hold on} \quad \Gamma_1 .$$

(d) Since $u(x) = 0$ on Ω_0 and $u(x) > 0$ on Ω_1, $\partial u/\partial v \leq 0$ necessarily holds on M (under certain conditions concerning the smoothness of the curve M). At the same time, it can be proved — just as in (a) — that $\partial u/\partial v \geq 0$ on M. From these two inequalities, the last of the "boundary conditions" in (27) follows:

$$\frac{\partial u}{\partial v} = 0 \quad \text{on} \quad M .$$

41.7. Operators of the second order revisited for the third time. Choose $k = 1$, $p = 2$, $V = W_0^{1,2}(\Omega)$, **f** by (14), and put

$$<\mathbb{A}v, w> = \int_\Omega \left[\sum_{i=1}^N \frac{\partial v(x)}{\partial x_i} \frac{\partial w(x)}{\partial x_i} \right] dx .$$

To solve the variational inequality then means to find $u \in K$ such that

$$\int_\Omega \left[\sum_{i=1}^N \frac{\partial u(x)}{\partial x_i} \frac{\partial (v(x) - u(x))}{\partial x_i} \right] dx \geq \int_\Omega f(x) \, (v(x) - u(x)) \, dx \tag{31}$$

holds for all $v \in K$.

(i) Let Φ be a given function defined on $\bar\Omega$ and let $\Phi|_{\partial\Omega} \leq 0$. Choose

$$K = \{v \in W_0^{1,2}(\Omega) ; \quad v \geq \Phi \quad \text{almost everywhere on} \quad \Omega\} .$$

The variational inequality (31) then corresponds to the following "boundary value problem":

$$\begin{cases} -\Delta u - f \geqq 0 \quad \text{on} \quad \Omega, \quad u \geqq \Phi \quad \text{on} \quad \Omega, \\ (-\Delta u - f)(u - \Phi) = 0 \quad \text{on} \quad \Omega, \\ u = 0 \quad \text{on} \quad \partial\Omega. \end{cases}$$

In other words: If we put

$$\Omega_0 = \{x \in \Omega; u(x) = \Phi(x)\},$$
$$\Omega_1 = \{x \in \Omega; u(x) > \Phi(x)\},$$

then u satisfies the equation

$$-\Delta u = f \quad \text{on} \quad \Omega_1$$

with the "boundary conditions"

$$u = 0 \quad \text{on} \quad \partial\Omega \cap \partial\Omega_1, \quad u = \Phi \quad \text{on} \quad \partial\Omega_1 \cap \partial\Omega_0.$$

The sets Ω_0 and Ω_1 are again not given beforehand, of course, but are determined by the solution u.

(ii) Choose

$$K = \{v \in W_0^{1,2}(\Omega); \ |\text{grad } v| \leq 1 \quad \text{almost everywhere on} \quad \Omega\}.$$

If we put

$$\Omega_0 = \{x \in \Omega; |\text{grad } u(x)| = 1\},$$
$$\Omega_1 = \{x \in \Omega; |\text{grad } u(x)| < 1\},$$

with $u \in K$ being the solution of variational inequality (31), then this inequality corresponds to the following "boundary value problem": The function u satisfies the equation

$$-\Delta u = f \quad \text{on} \quad \Omega_1$$

with the boundary condition $u|_{\partial\Omega} = 0$ and with certain transmission conditions on $M = \partial\Omega_0 \cap \partial\Omega_1$.

41.8. Remarks. (i) The last example describes the situation which occurs in the theory of so-called *elasto-plastic deformations*: The set Ω_0 is the so-called domain of plasticity while Ω_1 is the so-called domain of elasticity.

(ii) The examples of Paragraphs 41.6 and 41.7 had the common property that they led to the solution of a boundary value problem in a differential equation on a certain new domain $\Omega_1 \subset \Omega$ which is not known beforehand and which is determined by the solution $u \in K$. In fact, we have here a certain similarity with the free boundary problem discussed in Section 5: The domain Ω is indeed known, but the "curve" M dividing the sets Ω_1 and Ω_0 is not known†).

(iii) In all the examples above, a linear operator $\mathbb{A}$ was considered. The reader will certainly be able to construct additional examples with nonlinear operators $\mathbb{A}$ easily himself. Difficulties which will arise will not have their origin in the essence of the matter, but will be of a technical nature since the difference between a linear and nonlinear problem is suppressed for variational inequalities, as already mentioned in Remark 40.7.

41.9. Free boundary problem. In Paragraph 5.2, a problem treating seepage of water through a dam was formulated. Below, we retain the notation introduced in that paragraph; let Q be the rectangle $ABCD$, $V = W^{1,2}(Q)$, and

$$K = \{v \in W^{1,2}(Q); \ v \geq 0 \text{ almost everywhere in } Q,$$
$$v = g \text{ on } \partial Q \text{ in the sense of traces}\},$$

where the function g is defined on ∂Q as follows:

$$g(x, y) = \begin{cases} \frac{1}{2}(y_1 - y)^2 & \text{on} \quad AE, \\ \frac{1}{2}(y_2 - y)^2 & \text{on} \quad BF, \\ \frac{1}{2}y^2 + \frac{1}{2}(y_2 - y_1)^2 \, x/a & \text{on} \quad AB, \\ 0 & \text{on} \quad ED \cup DC \cup CF \end{cases}$$

(see Fig. 5.2).

Let $w \in K$ be the solution of the variational inequality

$$\int_Q \left[\frac{\partial w}{\partial x} \frac{\partial(v - w)}{\partial x} + \frac{\partial w}{\partial y} \frac{\partial(v - w)}{\partial y} \right] dx \, dy \geq - \int_Q (v - w) \, dx \, dy, \quad v \in K, \text{ ††)} \quad (32)$$

and put

$$\Omega = \{(x, y) \in Q; \ w(x, y) > 0\} \tag{33}$$

(on the basis of the foregoing examples, the reader will easily deduce that the solu-

---

†) Our considerations were to a certain extent inaccurate: Namely, we know nothing about the character of the sets Ω_0 and Ω_1, it is not even clear whether the set $M = \partial\Omega_0 \cap \partial\Omega_1$ is a curve, etc. To be sure, we assumed — when applying Green's formula, for instance — that $\Omega_1 \in \mathscr{C}^{0,1}$; this was based partly on wishful thinking, but also partly on physical considerations. Let us add that the problem of a more detailed characterization of the sets Ω_1 and Ω_0 is currently being studied — see, e.g., [21].

††) For simplicity's sake, we omit the arguments x, y from the functions v and w.

tion w — as long as it is sufficiently smooth — satisfies the equation

$$-\Delta w = -1 \quad \text{on} \quad \Omega\,).$$

As shown recently in [3], the solution w of the variational inequality (32) already determines the solution u of the free boundary problem: The domain Ω from (33) is described precisely by means of the desired function φ which characterizes the free boundary:

$$\Omega = \{(x, y) \in \mathbb{R}^2;\ x \in (0, a),\ y \in (0, \varphi(x))\}\,,$$

and the solution u is given as follows:

$$u(x, y) = y - \frac{\partial w(x, y)}{\partial y}\,.$$

41.10. Partial differential operator of the fourth order. Choose $\Omega \subset \mathbb{R}^2$, $k = 2$, $p = 2$, $V = W^{2,2}(\Omega)$, $\mathbf{f}$ as in (14), and

$$<\mathbb{A}v, w> = \int_\Omega \left[\frac{\partial^2 v}{\partial x^2} \frac{\partial^2 w}{\partial x^2} + 2(1 - \sigma) \frac{\partial^2 v}{\partial x\, \partial y} \frac{\partial^2 w}{\partial x\, \partial y} + \frac{\partial^2 v}{\partial y^2} \frac{\partial^2 w}{\partial y^2} + \right.$$
$$\left. + \sigma \left(\frac{\partial^2 v}{\partial x^2} \frac{\partial^2 w}{\partial y^2} + \frac{\partial^2 v}{\partial y^2} \frac{\partial^2 w}{\partial x^2}\right)\right] dx\, dy\,.$$

Furthermore, choose

$$K = \{v \in W^{2,2}(\Omega);\ v \geqq 0 \text{ on } \partial\Omega \text{ in the sense of traces}\}\,,$$

If $u \in K$ is the solution of the variational inequality

$$<\mathbb{A}u, v - u> \geqq <\mathbf{f}, v - u>\,, \quad v \in K\,,$$

and if, e.g., $u \in C^4(\bar{\Omega})$, then u solves the following problem from the theory of elasticity (the so-called Signorini problem — see Paragraph 5.3):

$$\begin{cases} \Delta^2 u = f \quad \text{on} \quad \Omega\,, \\ Mu = 0 \quad \text{on} \quad \partial\Omega\,, \\ u \geqq 0 \quad \text{and} \quad Nu \geqq 0 \quad \text{on} \quad \partial\Omega\,, \\ u\, Nu = 0 \quad \text{on} \quad \partial\Omega\,. \end{cases}$$

The last condition says that $Nu(x) = 0$ for $u(x) \neq 0$; a sort of "mixed problem" is again present here just as in Example 41.4 (ii) (for the meaning of the symbols M and N, see Paragraph 5.3).

Further examples can be found in the book [59]; see also [17].

SECTION 42. SOME SPECIAL RESULTS

42.1. Theorem. *Let V be a Hilbert space, A a continuous linear operator from V to V* which is coercive, i.e.,*

$$\lim_{\|v\|_V \to \infty} \frac{<Av, v>}{\|v\|_V} = \infty .$$

Let K, $\tilde{K}$ be two convex subsets of the space V, $f \in V^*$, and let u, $\tilde{u}$ be the solutions of the variational inequalities with respect to K, $\tilde{K}$, i.e., $u \in K$,

$$<Au, v - u> \geqq <f, v - u> \quad \text{for all} \quad v \in K , \tag{1}$$

and $\tilde{u} \in \tilde{K}$

$$<A\tilde{u}, v - \tilde{u}> \geqq <f, v - \tilde{u}> \quad \text{for all} \quad v \in \tilde{K} . \tag{2}$$

Assume that elements $w \in K$ and $\tilde{w} \in \tilde{K}$ exist such that

$$\begin{cases} w + \tilde{w} = u + \tilde{u} , \\ <A(w - \tilde{u}), w - u> = 0 . \end{cases} \tag{3}$$

Then

$$w = u \quad (\text{and thus } \tilde{w} = \tilde{u}) .$$

Proof: Choose $v = w$ in (1), choose $v = \tilde{w}$ in (2); then

$$<Au, w - u> \geqq <f, w - u> ,$$
$$<A\tilde{u}, \tilde{w} - \tilde{u}> \geqq <f, \tilde{w} - \tilde{u}> .$$

Since $w - u = -(\tilde{w} - \tilde{u})$ by (3), addition of the above two inequalities yields a zero on the right-hand side, and thus

$$<Au - A\tilde{u}, w - u> \geqq 0 .$$

But the operator A is linear; therefore

$$Au - A\tilde{u} = A(u - \tilde{u}) = A(u - w + w - \tilde{u}) = A(u - w) + A(w - \tilde{u}) ,$$

so that we obtain the relation

$$<A(u - w), w - u> + <A(w - \tilde{u}), w - u> \geqq 0 .$$

By (3), the second term on the left-hand side vanishes; thus, we have

$$<A(u - w), w - u> \geqq 0 ,$$

or, in other words,

$$<A(u - w), u - w> \leqq 0 . \tag{4}$$

The assertion of the theorem is now proved by contradiction: Assume that $u \neq w$, i.e., that $\|u - w\|_V > 0$, and put

$$v_n = n(u - w), \quad n \in \mathbb{N}.$$

Inequality (4) implies that

$$\frac{<\mathbb{A}v_n, v_n>}{\|v_n\|_V} = \frac{n^2 <\mathbb{A}(u - w), u - w>}{n\|u - w\|_V} \leq 0;$$

at the same time, however, the coerciveness of the operator $\mathbb{A}$ implies that

$$\frac{<\mathbb{A}v_n, v_n>}{\|v_n\|_V} \to \infty \quad \text{for} \quad n \to \infty,$$

because $\|v_n\|_V = n\|u - w\|_V$.

This is a contradiction; therefore, $u = w$.

42.2. Aplication of Theorem 42.1. The foregoing theorem is somewhat artificial. However, it serves to prove an interesting assertion.

Therefore, let us recall the variational inequality

$$\int_\Omega \left[\sum_{i=1}^N \frac{\partial u(x)}{\partial x_i} \frac{\partial (v(x) - u(x))}{\partial x_i} + u(x)\,(v(x) - u(x)) \right] dx \geq$$

$$\geq \int_\Omega f(x)\,(v(x) - u(x))\,dx, \quad v \in K, \tag{5}$$

with the solution $u \in K$, where

$$K = \{v \in W^{1,2}(\Omega);\ v \geq 0 \quad \text{on} \quad \partial\Omega \quad \text{in the sense of traces}\}. \tag{6}$$

This inequality was encountered in Paragraph 41.4 (ii) and it was shown that its solution $u \in K$ is at the same time (if it is sufficiently smooth) the solution of the boundary value problem

$$\begin{cases} -\Delta u + u = f & \text{on} \quad \Omega, \\ u = 0 & \text{on} \quad \Gamma, \\ \dfrac{\partial u}{\partial v} = 0 & \text{on} \quad \partial\Omega - \Gamma, \end{cases} \tag{7}$$

where the set $\Gamma \subset \partial\Omega$ is not known beforehand and is determined by the solution u.

Now, let S be an arbitrary but fixed (and "reasonable") subset of the boundary $\partial\Omega$, and denote by u_S the weak solution of the mixed boundary value problem

$$\begin{cases} -\Delta u_S + u_S = f & \text{on } \Omega, \\ u_S = 0 & \text{on } S, \\ \dfrac{\partial u_S}{\partial v} = 0 & \text{on } \partial\Omega - S, \end{cases} \tag{8}$$

i.e., let

(i) $u_S \in W_S$, where

$$W_S = \{v \in W^{1,2}(\Omega), \ v|_S = 0 \text{ in the sense of traces}\} ; \tag{9}$$

(ii) for all $v \in W_S$,

$$\int_\Omega \left[\sum_{i=1}^N \frac{\partial u_S(x)}{\partial x_i} \frac{\partial v(x)}{\partial x_i} + u_S(x) \, v(x) \right] dx = \int_\Omega f(x) \, v(x) \, dx . \tag{10}$$

We now have the following theorem:

42.3. Theorem. *Let $u \in K$ be the solution of variational inequality* (5) *with the set K given by formula* (6). *Then*

$$u(x) = \sup_{S \subset \partial\Omega} u_S(x), \quad x \in \Omega . \ \dagger)$$

Proof: Let $u \in K$ be the solution of inequality (5), and let

$$\Gamma = \{x \in \partial\Omega; \ u(x) = 0\} .$$

Then

$$u = u_\Gamma ,$$

where the solution of inequality (5) appears on the left-hand side while the solution of the mixed problem (8) for $S = \Gamma$ appears on the right-hand side. Thus, it suffices to prove that for any other $S \subset \partial\Omega$

$$u_S \leq u \quad \text{holds almost everywhere on } \Omega . \tag{11}$$

Let then the set $S \subset \partial\Omega$ be arbitrary (but "reasonable"). Using the notation of (41.14) and (41.15), relation (10) can be written as follows:

$$\langle \mathbb{A}u_S, v \rangle = \langle \mathbf{f}, v \rangle . \tag{12}$$

Put, further,

$$W_S = \tilde{K} .$$

---

†) The supremum is taken over all "reasonable" subsets $S \subset \partial\Omega$.

Since $\tilde{K}$ is a linear space, identity (12) is equivalent to the inequality

$$<\mathbb{A}u_S, v - u_S> \geq <\mathbf{f}, v - u_S>,$$

valid for every $v \in \tilde{K}$.

Theorem 42.1 can now be applied; we choose $\tilde{K} = W_S$, $\tilde{u} = u_S$, K is given by formula (6), and inequality (5) has the form

$$<\mathbb{A}u, v - u> \geq <\mathbf{f}, v - u> \quad \text{for every} \quad v \in K.$$

The assumptions of Theorem 42.1 are satisfied because the space V is the Hilbert space $W^{1,2}(\Omega)$, the operator $\mathbb{A}$ is linear and also coercive since

$$<\mathbb{A}v, v> = \|v\|_{1,2}^2,$$

or — in other words —

$$\frac{<\mathbb{A}v, v>}{\|v\|_{1,2}} = \|v\|_{1,2} \to \infty \quad \text{for} \quad \|v\|_{1,2} \to \infty.$$

Choose then

$$w = \max\{u, \tilde{u}\}, \quad \tilde{w} = \min\{u, \tilde{u}\}.$$

First of all, we have $w \in K$ because $u \in K$, so that $u \geq 0$ on $\partial\Omega$, and $w \geq u$ by definition. Furthermore, we have $\tilde{w} \in \tilde{K}$, and also

$$w + \tilde{w} = u + \tilde{u}.$$

Thus, it remains to prove that

$$<\mathbb{A}(w - \tilde{u}), w - u> = 0.$$

Put

$$g = u - \tilde{u}.$$

Then

$$g^+ = \max\{g, 0\} = \max\{u - \tilde{u}, 0\} = w - \tilde{u},$$
$$g^- = -\min\{g, 0\} = -\min\{u - \tilde{u}, 0\} = \max\{\tilde{u} - u, 0\} = w - u,$$

and thus

$$<\mathbb{A}(w - \tilde{u}), w - u> = <\mathbb{A}g^+, g^->.$$

However, we have

$$<\mathbb{A}g^+, g^-> = \sum_{i=1}^{N} \int_{\Omega} \frac{\partial g^+(x)}{\partial x_i} \frac{\partial g^-(x)}{\partial x_i} \, dx + \int_{\Omega} g^+(x) g^-(x) \, dx = 0$$

since at least one factor in each of the integrals vanishes.

By Theorem 42.1, we thus have

$$u = w = \max\{u, u_S\},$$

and this is nothing but relation (11).

42.4. Remark. In fact, Theorem 42.3 also gives certain "instructions" about how to find (approximately) the solution $u \in K$ of variational inequality (5): It suffices to solve a sufficiently large number of mixed problems (8) and to consider the supremum of all their solutions.

However, these instructions can be difficult to carry out if $\Omega \subset \mathbb{R}^N$ with $N > 1$; it is simpler if $N = 1$ since there are only four possibilities for the choice of the set $S \subset \partial\Omega$: If $\Omega = (0, 1)$, then the boundary $\partial\Omega$ consists of the points 0 and 1 and we can construct the solution of the equation

$$-u'' + u = f \quad \text{on} \quad (0, 1) \tag{13}$$

with the following boundary conditions:

(i) $$u(0) = u(1) = 0$$

(denote this solution by u_1; it corresponds to the choice $S = \{0, 1\}$, i.e., $S = \partial\Omega$);

(ii) $$u'(0) = u'(1) = 0$$

(denote this solution by u_2; it corresponds to the choice $S = \emptyset$);

(iii) $$u'(0) = u(1) = 0$$

(denote this solution by u_3; it corresponds to the choice $S = \{1\}$);

(iv) $$u(0) = u'(1) = 0$$

(denote this solution by u_4; it corresponds to the choice $S = \{0\}$).

The variational inequality which corresponds to equation (13) is now satisfied, following Theorem 42.3, by the function

$$u(x) = \max\{u_1(x), u_2(x), u_3(x), u_4(x)\}.$$

42.5. Regularity of the solution of the variational inequality. When interpreting, in Section 41, the solution $u \in K$ of the variational inequality as the solution of a certain boundary value problem it was assumed that u is a sufficiently smooth function.

In Section 17, the regularity of the weak solutions of boundary value problems was discussed and it was shown that at least in the case of ordinary differential equations the weak solution is already the classical solution if also the data of the boundary value problem are smooth (see Theorem 17.5). The situation is entirely different for variational inequalities as is shown by the following example.

42.6. Example. Consider variational inequality (41.1) with the function $f(x) = 4$ for $x \in (0, 1)$; the set K is chosen as in (41.11). The reader can easily check that this inequality is satisfied by the function $u \in K$ defined as follows:

$$u(x) = \begin{cases} x & \text{for } x \in \left[0, \frac{1}{4}\right], \\ -2x^2 + 2x - \frac{1}{8} . & \text{for } x \in \left(\frac{1}{4}, \frac{3}{4}\right), \\ 1 - x & \text{for } x \in \left[\frac{3}{4}, 1\right]. \end{cases}$$

(Draw a figure!) Obviously, $u \in K$; here we have

$$\Omega_1 = \{x \in (0, 1); \ |u'(x)| < 1\} = \left(\frac{1}{4}, \frac{3}{4}\right).$$

However, the function u does not belong to $C^2([0, 1])$ because its second derivative u'' is discontinuous at the points $x = \frac{1}{4}$ and $x = \frac{3}{4}$.

Consequently, the solution of the variational inequality (41.1) is not regular although its data are smooth: $f \in C^\infty([0, 1])$, and the coefficients $a_i = a_i(x; \xi_0, \xi_1)$ of the formal differential operator A which determines the operator $\mathbb{A}$ are also smooth since

$$a_1(x; \xi_0, \xi_1) = \xi_1, \quad a_0(x; \xi_0, \xi_1) = 0.$$

42.7. Remark. For the solutions of variational inequalities we thus cannot expect the regularity that we have for the weak solutions of boundary value problems (with smooth data). For variational inequalities one additional element joins the data of the problem: the convex set K. For the sake of completeness, we add that the "non-regularity" of the solution u in Example 42.6 is not due to the nature of the set K employed [there, the condition $u \in K$ meant that $|u'(x)| \leq 1$ almost everywhere in $(0, 1)$]: in fact, there also exist examples of "irregular" solutions of variational inequalities with other types of sets K, see [60].

SECTION 43. EXISTENCE THEOREMS

43.1. Hitherto, it has been assumed throughout that the variational inequality has a solution and only in Example 42.6 was this solution actually presented. We now present a result which gives conditions under which a solution actually exists. The reader will again spot the close connection with Chapters IV and V since he encountered conditions for the existence of a solution (albeit, in a somewhat modified form) in the existence theorems for the weak solution of a boundary value problem.

43.2. Theorem. *Let V be a reflexive Banach space, K a convex set in V and $\mathbb{A}$ an operator from K into V^* with the following properties:*

(a) $\mathbb{A}$ *is continuous;*

(b) $\mathbb{A}$ *is bounded (i.e., it maps bounded sets from K onto bounded sets in V^*);*

(c) $\mathbb{A}$ *is monotone (i.e., we have*

$$<\mathbb{A}v - \mathbb{A}w, \, v - w> \geqq 0 \tag{1}$$

for all pairs of elements $v, w \in K$);

(d) $\mathbb{A}$ *is coercive on K (i.e., there exists an element $v_0 \in K$ such that*

$$\lim_{\substack{\|v\|_V \to \infty \\ v \in K}} \frac{<\mathbb{A}v, \, v - v_0>}{\|v\|_V} = \infty). \tag{2}$$

Then for every $\mathbf{f} \in V^*$, an element $u \in K$ exists, such that for all $v \in K$ we have

$$<\mathbb{A}u, \, v - u> \geqq <\mathbf{f}, v - u> . \tag{3}$$

[In other words: *The variational inequality* (3) *has a solution for every $\mathbf{f} \in V^*$.*]

43.3. Remarks on Theorem 43.2. (i) The resemblance of Theorem 43.2 to the Browder Theorem 29.5 and its application to the proof of the existence of the weak solution of a boundary value problem (see Paragraph 29.7) is obvious.

The only new concept here is the concept of *coerciveness with respect to the set K* which appears in condition (d): Hitherto, we have dealt with "ordinary" coerciveness under which the zero element Θ is chosen for the element v_0.

(ii) Obviously, condition (d) is essential, only if the convex set K is unbounded. We recommend the reader to check that all the operators $\mathbb{A}$ which correspond to the examples investigated in Section 41 satisfy condition (d), namely with the element $v_0 = \Theta$.

(iii) Just as in the case of existence theorems for the weak solution of a boundary value problem (see Sections 29 and 32), the conditions can be weakened further; we refer to the literature ([59], [60]).

(iv) The proof of Theorem 43.2 will be indicated later (see Paragraphs 43.5 to 43.11); different types of proofs of the existence of a solution will then be presented, namely those which are in a certain sense constructive, i.e., which actually give a method for the construction of the solution u. However, we can prove the uniqueness theorem for the solution at once.

43.4. Theorem. *Let the operator $\mathbb{A}$ be strictly monotone (i.e., let*

$$<\mathbb{A}v - \mathbb{A}w, \, v - w> \, > 0$$

for $v, w \in K$, $v \neq w$). Then variational inequality (3) *has at most one solution.*

Proof: Assume that inequality (3) possesses two solutions $u_1, u_2 \in K$, i.e., let

$$<\mathbb{A}u_1, v - u_1> \geqq <\mathbf{f}, v - u_1> ,$$

$$<\mathbb{A}u_2, v - u_2> \geqq <\mathbf{f}, v - u_2>$$

hold for all $v \in K$. In the first inequality, choose $v = u_2$, in the second $v = u_1$, and add the resulting inequalities. We then get

$$<\mathbb{A}u_1 - \mathbb{A}u_2, u_2 - u_1> \geqq 0 ,$$

and, consequently,

$$<\mathbb{A}u_1 - \mathbb{A}u_2, u_1 - u_2> \leqq 0 .$$

Since the operator $\mathbb{A}$ is strictly monotone, $u_1 = u_2$ must hold and the theorem is proved.

43.5. Method of successive approximations. We shall assume that V is a Hilbert space and we therefore write H instead of V. In this case, $H^* = H$ (see the footnote on p. 240), and the operator $\mathbb{A}$ will thus be regarded as a mapping from H into H.

We show that under certain conditions concerning the operator $\mathbb{A}$ (stronger than the conditions of Theorem 43.2) the problem of finding the solution of variational inequality (3) is equivalent to the problem of solving a certain operator equation with an operator B which is contractive. The Banach contraction principle (see Paragraph 10.6) can then be applied. (The same idea is applied here as in Theorem 29.3; there and in Paragraph 10.6 the advantages and drawbacks of the contraction principle are discussed.)

We introduce the concept of projection: Let K be a closed convex set in the Hilbert space H. Then precisely one element $P_K w \in K$ exists, for every $w \in H$, such that

$$\left\| w - P_K w \right\|_H = \inf_{v \in K} \left\| w - v \right\|_H . \tag{4}$$

The element $P_K w$ thus realizes the minimum of the functional

$$F(v) = \left\| w - v \right\|_H$$

on K; its existence is ensured, e.g., by Theorem 26.1 or by Theorem 26.8 because a Hilbert space is a reflexive Banach space and the functional F is lower semicontinuous as well as (in the case of an unbounded set K) coercive [i.e., it satisfies relation (26.1) — see Theorem 26.8].

The element $P_K w$, which is called the *projection of the element $w \in H$ onto the set K,* is characterized by the fact that

$$<w - P_K w, v - P_K w> \leqq 0 \quad \text{holds for every} \quad v \in K . \tag{5}$$

This assertion can easily be proved; it is also evident, however, from Fig. 43.5: The left-hand side of (5) is just the cosine of the angle α between the lines connecting the point $P_K w$ with the point w and with the (arbitrary) point $v \in K$, respectively, and we have $\cos \alpha \leq 0$ since $\alpha \geq 90°$ necessarily holds. Conversely, for every other point $\tilde{w} \in K$, $w \neq P_K w$, there clearly exists a point $\tilde{v} \in K$ so that the angle between the lines connecting the point $\tilde{w}$ with the points w and $\tilde{v}$ is less than $90°$.

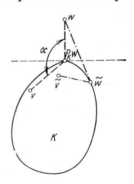

Fig. 43.5

43.6. Theorem. *Let H be a Hilbert space, K a closed convex set in H, $\mathbb{A}$ an operator from K into H, $\mathbf{f} \in H$, $\gamma > 0$. The element $u \in K$ is the solution of variational inequality* (3) *if and only if*

$$u = P_K(u - \gamma(\mathbb{A}u - \mathbf{f})), \tag{6}$$

i.e., if u is the fixed point of the operator B given by the formula

$$Bu = P_K(u - \gamma(\mathbb{A}u - \mathbf{f})). \tag{7}$$

Proof: Put $w = u - \gamma(\mathbb{A}u - \mathbf{f})$. In view of (5), relation (6) is equivalent to the fact that $u \in K$ and

$$<(u - \gamma(\mathbb{A}u - \mathbf{f})) - u, \ v - u> \ \leq 0 \quad \text{for all} \quad v \in K.$$

However, this last inequality is nothing but inequality (3) since it can be written as

$$-\gamma <\mathbb{A}u - \mathbf{f}, \ v - u> \ \leq 0,$$

where $-\gamma < 0$.

We are now ready to prove an analogue of Theorem 29.3:

43.7. Theorem. *Let the conditions of Theorem 43.6 be satisfied, and let the operator $\mathbb{A}$ have the following properties: Constants $M > 0$ and $m > 0$ exist such that*

$$\|\mathbb{A}v - \mathbb{A}w\|_H \leq M\|v - w\|_H \tag{8}$$

and

$$<\mathbb{A}v - \mathbb{A}w, \ v - w> \ \geq m\|v - w\|_H^2 \tag{9}$$

hold for all $v, w \in K$. Then there exists exactly one solution $u \in K$ of variational inequality (3) for every $\mathbf{f} \in H$.

If γ is chosen so that $0 < \gamma < 2m/M^2$ and if u_0 is an arbitrary element from K, then

$$u = \lim_{n \to \infty} u_n,$$

where

$$u_{n+1} = P_K(u_n - \gamma(\mathbb{A}u_n - \mathbf{f})), \quad n = 0, 1, \dots.$$

Proof: In view of Theorem 43.6, it suffices to verify that the operator B defined by formula (7) is a contractive operator. Since $\|P_K v - P_K w\|_H \leq \|v - w\|_H$ holds for every two elements $v, w \in H$, we obtain — by means of (8) and (9) —

$$\|Bv - Bw\|_H^2 \leq \|v - \gamma(\mathbb{A}v - \mathbf{f}) - w + \gamma(\mathbb{A}w - \mathbf{f})\|_H^2 =$$
$$= \|v - w - \gamma(\mathbb{A}v - \mathbb{A}w)\|_H^2 =$$
$$= \|v - w\|_H^2 - 2\gamma <v - w, \mathbb{A}v - \mathbb{A}w> + \gamma^2\|\mathbb{A}v - \mathbb{A}w\|_H^2 \leq$$
$$\leq \|v - w\|_H^2 - 2\gamma m\|v - w\|_H^2 + \gamma^2 M^2\|v - w\|_H^2 =$$
$$= (1 - 2\gamma m + \gamma^2 M^2) \|v - w\|_M^2 .$$

If $0 < \gamma < 2m/M^2$, the operator B is a contractive operator with the constant

$$\sqrt{(1 - 2\gamma m + \gamma^2 M^2)} < 1$$

and the assertion of the theorem follows from the Banach contraction principle.

43.8. The Ritz (Galerkin) method. When seeking the element $u \in X$ which realizes the minimum of the functional F on the Banach space X, the procedure in Section 28 was to transform our "infinite-dimensional" problem into a problem in spaces of finite dimension: We found a sequence of spaces $X_n \subset X$ whose dimensions were finite, and solved the problem of finding an element $u_n \in X_n$ so that

$$F(u_n) = \inf_{v \in X_n} F(v)$$

holds. The proof of the Browder Theorem 29.5 is also based on a similar idea. Also, since Theorem 43.2 closely resembles Theorem 29.5, it is possible to use the procedure indicated in Paragraph 30.16 for its proof as well. We shall not go into the details of the method here; in principle, it consists of constructing a suitable sequence $\{V_n\}_{n=1}^{\infty}$ of n-dimensional Banach spaces of the *separable* space V and solving a "finite dimensional" variational inequality instead of variational inequality (3), i.e., we look for $u_n \in K_n$ so that

$$<\mathbb{A}u_n, v - u_n> \geq <\mathbf{f}, v - u_n>$$

holds for all $v \in K_n$, where $K_n = K \cap V_n$. The solution u of variational inequality (3) is then obtained as the (weak) limit of the sequence $\{u_n\}_{n=1}^{\infty}$.

43.10. The penalty method. Under certain conditions, the problem of finding a solution of the variational inequality is equivalent to the problem of finding a point at which the functional F attains its minimum with respect to a certain set K; the condition $u \in K$ is sometimes called a *constraint condition* (or simply a *constraint*). Sometimes, we can do without this constraint condition: Instead of looking for a solution $u \in K$ such that

$$F(u) = \inf_{v \in K} F(v) ,$$

where $K \subset V$, we look for the point $u_\varepsilon \in V$ which realizes the minimum of a certain new functional F_ε on the whole space V, i.e., we look for the point $u_\varepsilon \in V$ for which

$$F_\varepsilon(u_\varepsilon) = \inf_{v \in V} F_\varepsilon(v) ;$$

here, we put

$$F_\varepsilon(v) = F(v) + \frac{1}{\varepsilon} \varphi(v) , \quad \varepsilon > 0 ,$$

where φ is a functional on V for which

$$\varphi(v) = 0 \quad \text{for} \quad v \in K , \quad \varphi(v) > 0 \quad \text{for} \quad v \notin K .$$

Under certain assumptions, it can be shown that the element $u \in K$ is the (weak) limit of the system of functions u_ε as $\varepsilon \to 0+$.

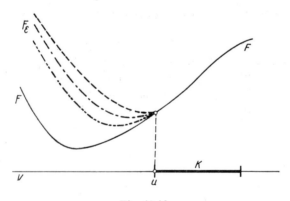

Fig. 43.10

The functional φ is the so-called *penalty functional*; with its aid, the variational problem with a constraint can be replaced by a variational problem without a constraint. The situation is illustrated, simplified, in Fig. 43.10: The straight line in the lower part of the figure represents the space V, its boldly drawn part the set K. The functional F which attains its minimum with respect to the set K at the point $u \in K$ is replaced by a new functional $F_\varepsilon = F + (1/\varepsilon) \varphi$ to the left of the point u (three possibilities are shown in the figure which correspond to three distinct choices of the parameter ε). It is clear that, for a suitable choice of this parameter, the point $u \in K$ is indeed the minimum of the new functional F_ε *with respect to the whole space V.*

The idea which is sketched above originated in the equivalence of the variational inequality with the variational problem. A similar procedure will also be used now for the general problem of finding the solution of the variational inequality:

Let the conditions of Theorem 43.2 be satisfied; assume, moreover, that the operator $\mathbb{A}$ maps V into V^* (i.e., that it is defined on the whole space V), and that a continuous bounded monotone operator β exists which again maps V into V^* and is such that

$$\beta v = \Theta \quad \text{if and only if} \quad v \in K ; \tag{10}$$

the operator β is called the *penalty operator* (corresponding to the set $K \subset V$).

Let $\varepsilon > 0$ be arbitrary, and let us look for the point $u_\varepsilon \in V$ so that

$$<\mathbb{A} u_\varepsilon + \frac{1}{\varepsilon} \beta u_\varepsilon, v> \ = \ <\mathbf{f}, v> \tag{11}$$

holds for all $v \in V$ (i.e., so that the equation

$$\mathbb{A} u_\varepsilon + \frac{1}{\varepsilon} \beta u_\varepsilon = \mathbf{f}$$

is satisfied in V). Thus, inequality (3) is replaced on K by the equation (identity) (11) on V.

Under our assumptions, the solutions u_ε of problem (11) exist and converge to the solution u of variational inequality (3). We prove this assertion under the restriction that the set K contains the zero element Θ and that it is possible to choose $v_0 = \Theta$ in condition (d) of Theorem 43.2; this restriction leads to no essential loss of generality but simplifies the working.

43.11. Theorem. *Let the conditions of* Theorem 43.2 *be satisfied; let the operator* $\mathbb{A}$ *be defined on V, let β be the penalty operator corresponding to the set K, let $\Theta \in K$, and let $v_0 = \Theta$ in condition 43.2* (d).

Then there exists a solution u_ε of problem (11) *for every $\varepsilon > 0$ and a sequence $\{\varepsilon_n\}_{n=1}^\infty$ such that $\varepsilon_n \to 0+$ and u_{ε_n} converges weakly to the solution u of variational inequality* (3).

Proof: The operator $B_\varepsilon = \mathbb{A} + (1/\varepsilon) \beta$ is continuous and monotone for given $\varepsilon > 0$ because the operators $\mathbb{A}$ and β are continuous and monotone. The operator B_ε is also coercive because (10) implies that $\beta \Theta = \Theta$ (in fact, $\Theta \in K$), and, furthermore, we have

$$<B_\varepsilon v, v> \ = \ <\mathbb{A} v, v> + \frac{1}{\varepsilon} <\beta v, v> \ =$$

$$= \ <\mathbb{A} v, v> + \frac{1}{\varepsilon} <\beta v - \beta \Theta, v - \Theta> \ \geq \ <\mathbb{A} v, v>$$

(the operator β is monotone) so that

$$\frac{<B_\varepsilon v, v>}{\|v\|_V} \geqq \frac{<\mathbb{A}v, v>}{\|v\|_V} \to \infty$$

for $\|v\|_V \to \infty$ (note that $v_0 = \Theta$).

Thus, the operator B_ε satisfies the conditions of the Browder Theorem 29.5 according to which an element $u_\varepsilon \in V$ exists for $\mathbf{f} \in V^*$ so that

$$B_\varepsilon u_\varepsilon = \mathbf{f},$$

i.e., that (11) is valid for every $v \in V$.

For every $\varepsilon > 0$, we then have

$$<\mathbb{A}u_\varepsilon, u_\varepsilon> \leqq <B_\varepsilon u_\varepsilon, u_\varepsilon> = <\mathbf{f}, u_\varepsilon> \leqq \|\mathbf{f}\|_{V^*} \|u_\varepsilon\|_V,$$

or, in other words,

$$\frac{<\mathbb{A}u_\varepsilon, u_\varepsilon>}{\|u_\varepsilon\|_V} \leqq \|\mathbf{f}\|_{V^*}.$$

But this means that the set of elements u_ε ($\varepsilon > 0$) is bounded since the converse would lead to a contradiction with the coerciveness of the operator $\mathbb{A}$. Since the space V is reflexive, the set $\{u_\varepsilon; \varepsilon > 0\}$ is contained in a weakly compact set of the space V, i.e., there exists a sequence $\{\varepsilon_n\}_{n=1}^\infty$, $\varepsilon_n > 0$, $\varepsilon_n \to 0$, such that the sequence of elements u_{ε_n}, $n \in \mathbb{N}$, converges weakly to some element $u_0 \in V$.

We now examine the properties of the element u_0. First of all, we have

$$<\beta v - \beta u_{\varepsilon_n}, v - u_{\varepsilon_n}> \geqq 0 \tag{12}$$

for every $v \in V$ because the operator β is monotone. (11) implies that

$$\beta u_{\varepsilon_n} = \varepsilon_n(\mathbf{f} - \mathbb{A}u_{\varepsilon_n}),$$

and — since the operator $\mathbb{A}$ is bounded — the sequence $\{\mathbb{A}u_{\varepsilon_n}\}_{n=1}^\infty$ is bounded and thus

$$\beta u_{\varepsilon_n} \to \Theta \quad \text{for} \quad n \to \infty.$$

Passing to the limit, (12) yields:

$$<\beta v, v - u_0> \geqq 0 \quad \text{for every} \quad v \in V.$$

Choose $v = u_0 + tw$, where $t > 0$ and $w \in V$; then $v - u_0 = tw$ and

$$<\beta(u_0 + tw), w> \geqq 0.$$

By the continuity of the operator β, it follows from this, letting $t \to 0+$, that

$$<\beta u_0, w> \geqq 0 \quad \text{for every} \quad w \in V.$$

This inequality then holds for the element $-w$ as well so that we obtain

$$<\beta u_0, w> \;\leqq 0 \quad \text{for every} \quad w \in V;$$

thus, we have $<\beta u_0, w> \;= 0$, or, in other words, $\beta u_0 = \Theta$. According to (10), this means that

$$u_0 \in K.$$

We show further, that the element u_0 is the solution of variational inequality (3). (10), (11) and the monotony of the operators $\mathbb{A}$ and β imply:

$$<\mathbb{A}v - \mathbf{f}, v - u_{\varepsilon_n}> \;=\; <\mathbb{A}v - \mathbb{A}u_{\varepsilon_n}, v - u_{\varepsilon_n}> + <\mathbb{A}u_{\varepsilon_n} - \mathbf{f}, v - u_{\varepsilon_n}> \;=$$

$$=\; <\mathbb{A}v - \mathbb{A}u_{\varepsilon_n}, v - u_{\varepsilon_n}> + \frac{1}{\varepsilon_n} <\beta v - \beta u_{\varepsilon_n}, v - u_{\varepsilon_n}> \;\geqq 0$$

for every $v \in K$, and, letting $n \to \infty$, we thus have

$$<\mathbb{A}v - \mathbf{f}, v - u_0> \;\geqq 0 \quad \text{for every} \quad v \in K.$$

But by Theorem 40.8, this is equivalent to inequality (3), and the theorem is thus proved.

43.12. Remark. If, moreover (in addition to the conditions of Theorem 43.12), the operator $\mathbb{A}$ is strictly monotone, the elements $u_\varepsilon \in V$ are uniquely determined and

$$u_\varepsilon \to u_0 \quad \text{for} \quad \varepsilon \to 0+$$

[i.e., $\lim_{\varepsilon \to 0+} \mathbf{g}(u_\varepsilon) = \mathbf{g}(u_0)$ for every $\mathbf{g} \in V^*$]; it is thus not necessary to look for the particular sequence $\{\varepsilon_n\}_{n=1}^{\infty}$ in this case.

43.13. Examples. (i) Consider variational inequality (41.16) and choose

$$K = \{v \in W_0^{1,2}(\Omega); \; v \geqq 0 \text{ almost everywhere on } \Omega\}.$$

It is then possible to choose the operator β as follows:

$$<\beta v, w> \;=\; -\int_\Omega v^-(x)\, w(x)\, dx,$$

where $v^-(x) = -\min(v(x), 0)$. Here, $V = W_0^{1,2}(\Omega)$ and relation (11) means that

$$\sum_{i=1}^{N} \int_\Omega \frac{\partial u_\varepsilon(x)}{\partial x_i} \frac{\partial v(x)}{\partial x_i}\, dx + \int_\Omega u_\varepsilon(x)\, v(x)\, dx - \frac{1}{\varepsilon} \int_\Omega u_\varepsilon^-(x)\, v(x)\, dx = \int_\Omega f(x)\, v(x)\, dx$$

holds for every $v \in W_0^{1,2}(\Omega)$. As we know from Paragraph 15.16, this means that u_ε is the weak solution of the Dirichlet problem

$$
\begin{cases}
-\Delta u_\varepsilon + u_\varepsilon - \dfrac{1}{\varepsilon} u_\varepsilon^- = f \quad \text{on} \quad \Omega, \\[2mm]
u_\varepsilon\big|_{\partial\Omega} = 0 .
\end{cases}
$$

(ii) Consider again variational inequality (41.16) from Example 41.4 (ii), again with the set K given by (41.19). Then it is possible to choose the penalty operator β as follows:

$$
<\beta v, w> \; = \; -\int_{\partial\Omega} v^-(x)\, w(x)\, \mathrm{d}S .
$$

Here, $V = W^{1,2}(\Omega)$, and relation (11) means that for every $v \in W^{1,2}(\Omega)$ we have

$$
\sum_{i=1}^{N} \int_\Omega \frac{\partial u_\varepsilon(x)}{\partial x_i} \frac{\partial v(x)}{\partial x_i}\, \mathrm{d}x + \int_\Omega u_\varepsilon(x)\, v(x)\, \mathrm{d}x - \frac{1}{\varepsilon}\int_{\partial\Omega} u_\varepsilon^-(x)\, v(x)\, \mathrm{d}S = \int_\Omega f(x)\, v(x)\, \mathrm{d}x .
$$

As we know from Paragraph 15.16, this means that u_ε is the weak solution of the "Newton problem"

$$
-\Delta u_\varepsilon + u_\varepsilon = f \qquad \text{on} \quad \Omega,
$$

$$
\frac{\partial u}{\partial v} - \frac{1}{\varepsilon} u_\varepsilon^- = 0 \quad \text{on} \quad \partial\Omega .
$$

43.14. Remarks. (i) If V is a Hilbert space, the penalty operator β can be constructed by means of the projection defined in Paragraph 43.5:

$$
\beta v = v - P_K v, \quad v \in V .
$$

Then the penalty functional φ is given by the formula

$$
\varphi(v) = \tfrac{1}{2}\|v - P_K v\|^2 .
$$

(ii) Both the examples of Paragraph 43.13 confirm what was previously said in Paragraph 40.7: Namely, that the problem of solving the variational inequality is a nonlinear problem even for the linear formal differential operator A. In Example 43.13 (i), the nonlinear term u^- appears in the equation; in Example 43.13 (ii), it appears in the boundary condition.

The reader will certainly easily construct additional examples for himself: See also the book [59] by J.-L. Lions where one can not only find a number of additional examples but also become more thoroughly acquainted, and in greater detail, with the whole range of problems associated with variational inequalities. In fact, the present chapter was conceived as no more than introduction to this important field, and the authors hope that — just like the previous chapters — it fulfilled its purpose.

REFERENCES

[1] H. Amann: On the existence of positive solutions for non-linear elliptic boundary value problems. Indiana Univ. Math. Journal 21, 1971, 125—146.

[2] A. Ambrosetti - G. Prodi: On the inversion of some differentiable mappings with singularities between Banach spaces. Annali Mat. Pura Appl. 93, 1973, 231—247.

[3] C. Baiocchi - V. Comincioli - E. Magenes - G. A. Pozzi: Free boundary problems in the theory of fluid flow through porous media: Existence and uniqueness theorems. Annali Mat. Pura Appl. 97, 1973, 1—82.

[4] V. Barbu: Nonlinear Semigroups and Differential Equations in Banach Spaces. Editura Academiei, Noordhoff Internat. Publ., 1976.

[5] F. E. Browder: Existence and uniqueness theorems for solutions of nonlinear boundary value problems. Proc. Amer. Math. Soc., Symp. in Appl. Math. 17, 1965, 24—29.

[6] F. E. Browder: Existence theory for boundary value problems for quasi-linear elliptic systems with strongly non-linear lower order terms. Proc. Amer. Math. Soc., Symp. Partial Differential Equations 23, 1973, 269—286.

[7] M. S. Berger - E. Podolak: On the solutions of a nonlinear Dirichlet problem. Indiana Univ. Math. Journal 24, 1975, 837—846.

[8] J. Céa: Optimization: Théorie et Algorithmes. Dunod, Paris, 1971.

[9] P. Ciarlett - P. A. Raviart: General Lagrange and Hermite interpolations in R^n with applications to finite element methods. Arch. Rat. Mech. Anal. 46, 1972, 217—249.

[10] P. G. Ciarlett - A. Schultz - R. S. Varga: Numerical methods of higher order accuracy for nonlinear boundary value problems. In: Monotone operators theory. Numer. Math. 13, 1969, 51—77.

[11] E. A. Coddington - N. Levinson: Theory of Ordinary Differential Equations. McGraw-Hill, New York—Toronto—London, 1955.

[12] E. N. Dancer: On the Dirichlet problem for weakly nonlinear elliptic partial differential equations. Proc. Royal Soc. Edinburgh, 76A, 1977, 283—300.

[13] E. N. Dancer: Boundary-value problems for weakly nonlinear ordinary differential equations (in preparation).

[14] E. De Giorgi: Sulla differenziabilità e l'analiticttà delle estremali degli integrali multipli regolari. Mem. Accad. Sci. Torino 3, 1957, 25—43.

[15] E. De Giorgi: Un esempio di estremali discontinue per un problema variazionale di tipo ellittico. Boll. Unione Mat. Ital. (4), 1, 1968, 135—137.

[16] T. Donaldson: Nonlinear elliptic boundary value problems in Orlicz-Sobolev spaces. Journal Differential Equations 10, 1971, 507—528.

[17] G. Duvaut - J. - L. Lions: Inequalities in Mechanics and Physics. Springer Verlag, Berlin—Heidelberg—New York, 1976.

[18] D. E. Edmunds - V. B. Moscatelli - J. R. L. Webb: Strongly nonlinear elliptic operators in unbounded domains. Publ. Math. Univ. Bordeaux, Année 1973—1974, Fasc. 4, 5—32.

[19] H. Ehrmann: Über die Existenz der Lösungen von Randwertaufgaben bei gewöhnlichen nichtlinearen Differentialgleichungen zweiter Ordnung. Math. Ann. 134, 1957, 167—194.

[20] R. Finn: Remarks relevant to minimal surfaces and to surfaces of prescribed mean curvature. Journ. d'anal. mat. 14, 1965, 139—160.

[21] A. Friedman: The shape and smoothness of the free boundary for some elliptic variational inequalities. Indiana Univ. Math. Journal 25, 1976, 103—118.

[22] S. Fučík: Surjectivity of operators involving linear non-invertible part and compact perturbation. Funkc. Ekvacioj 17, 1974, 73—83.

[23] S. Fučík: Nonlinear equations with non-invertible linear part. Czechoslovak Math. Journal 24, 1974, 467—495.

[24] S. Fučík: Further remark on a theorem by E. M. Landesman and A. C. Lazer. Comment. Math. Univ. Carolinae 15, 1974, 259—272.

[25] S. Fučík: Remarks on a result by A. Ambrosetti and G. Prodi. Boll. Unione Mat. Ital. 11. 1975, 259—267.

[26] S. Fučík: Solvability and nonsolvability of weakly non-linear equations. Proceedings of the Summer School "Theory of Nonlinear Operators. Constructive Aspects" held in September 1975 at Berlin. Abhandlungen der Akademie der Wissenschaften der DDR, Berlin, 1977, 1, 57—68.

[27] S. Fučík: Boundary value problems with jumping nonlinearities. Čas. pěst. mat. 101, 1976, 69—87.

[28] S. Fučík: Remarks on some nonlinear boundary value problems. Comment. Math. Univ. Carolinae 17, 1976, 721—730.

[29] S. Fučík: Remarks on superlinear boundary value problems. Bull. Austral. Math. Soc. 16, 1977, 181—188.

[30] S. Fučík - A. Kratochvíl - J. Nečas: Kačanov-Galerkin method. Comment. Math. Univ. Carolinae 14, 1973, 651—659.

[31] S. Fučík - A. Kratochvíl - J. Nečas: Kačanov's method and its application. Rev. Roum. Math. Pures et Appl. 20, 1975, 907—916.

[32] S. Fučík - M. Krbec: Boundary value problems with bounded nonlinearity and general nullspace of the linear part. Math. Z. 155, 1977, 129—138.

[33] S. Fučík - M. Kučera - J. Nečas: Ranges of nonlinear asymptotically linear operators. Journal Differential Equations 17, 1975, 375—394.

[34] S. Fučík - V. Lovicar: Periodic solutions of the equation $x''(t) + g(x(t)) = p(t)$. Čas. pěst. mat. 100, 1975, 160—175.

[35] S. Fučík - J. Mawhin: Periodic solutions of some nonlinear differential equations of higher order. Čas. pěst. mat. 100, 1975, 276—283.

[36] S. Fučík - J. Nečas - J. Souček - V. Souček: Spectral Analysis of Nonlinear Operators. Springer Verlag, Berlin—Heidelberg—New York; JČSMF, Praha, 1973.

[37] S. Fučík - J. Nečas - V. Souček: Einführung in die Variationsrechnung. Teubner, Leipzig, 1977.

[38] H. Gajewski - K. Gröger - K. Zacharias: Nichtlineare Operatorgleichungen und Operator-differentialgleichungen. Akademie-Verlag, Berlin 1974.

[39] E. Giusti - M. Miranda: Un esempio di soluzioni discontinue per un problema di minimo relativo ad un integrale regolare del calcolo delle variazioni. Boll. Unione Mat. Ital. (4), 1, 1968, 219—226.

[40] J. P. Gossez: Nonlinear elliptic boundary value problems for equations with rapidly or slowly increasing coefficients. Trans. Amer. Math. Soc. 190, 1974, 163—205.

[41] P. Hartman: On the bounded slope condition. Pac. J. Math. 18, 1966, 495—511.

[42] P. Hartman: Convex sets and the bounded slope condition. Pac. J. Math. 25, 1968, 511—522.

[43] P. Hartman - G. Stampacchia: On some nonlinear elliptic differential functional equations. Acta Math. 115, 1966, 271—310.

[44] P. Hess: On nonlinear mappings of monotone type with respect to two Banach spaces. J. Math. Pures et appl. 52, 1973, 285—298.

[45] P. Hess: On a theorem by Landesman and Lazer. Indiana Univ. Math. Journal 23, 1974, 827—829.

[46] J. Kačur: On the existence of the weak solution for nonlinear differential equations of elliptic type. Comment. Math. Univ. Carolinae 11, 1970, 137—181.

[47] J. Kačur: On boundedness of the weak solution for some class of quasilinear partial differential equations. Čas. pěst. mat. 98, 1973, 43—55.

[48] J. Kačur - J. Nečas - J. Polák - J. Souček: Convergence of a method for solving the magnetostatic field in nonlinear media. Apl. mat. 13, 1968, 456—465.

[49] J. Kačur - J. Nečas - J. Souček: The ultraweak solutions of variational problems over spaces W_1^K. (Unpublished text.)

[50] J. L. Kazdan - F. W. Warner: Remarks on some quasilinear elliptic equations. Comm. Pure Appl. Math. 28, 1975, 567—597.

[51] A. N. Kolmogorov - S. V. Fomin: Introductory Real Analysis. (Revised edition.) Prentice-Hall, Englewood Cliffs, 1970.

[52] M. A. Krasnosel'skiĭ: Topological Methods in the Theory of Nonlinear Integral Equations. Macmillan, New York, 1964.

[53] M. A. Krasnosel'skiĭ - Ya. B. Rutickiĭ: Convex Functions and Orlicz Spaces. Noordhoff, Groningen, 1961.

[54] A. Kufner - O. John - S. Fučík: Function Spaces. Academia, Praha; Noordhoff, Groningen; 1977.

[55] O. A. Ladyzhenskaja - N. N. Uralceva: Linear and Quasilinear Equations of Elliptic Type. Academic Press, New York, 1968.

[56] E. M. Landesman - A. C. Lazer: Nonlinear perturbations of linear elliptic boundary value problems at resonance. Journal Math. Mech. 19, 1970, 609—623.

[57] J. Leray - J.-L. Lions: Quelques résultats de Višik sur les problémes elliptiques nonlinéaires par les méthodes de Minty-Browder. Bull. Soc. Math. France 93, 1965, 97—107.

[58] J.-L. Lions: Contrôle Optimal de Systèmes Gouvernés par des Équations aux Dérivées Partielles. Dunod, Paris, 1968.

[59] J.-L. Lions: Quelques Méthodes de Résolution des Problémes aux Limites Non Linéaires. Dunod, Paris, 1969.

[60] J.-L. Lions: On inequalities in partial derivatives. (In Russian.) Uspekhi Mat. Nauk 2 (158), 1971, 205—263.

[61] L. A. Ljusternik - V. I. Sobolev: Elements of Functional Analysis. (In Russian.) Nauka, Moscow, 1975.

[62] A. Manes - A. Micheletti: Un'estensione della teoria variazionale classica degli autovalori per operatori ellittici del secondo ordine. Boll. Unione Mat. Ital. 7, 1973, 285—301.

[63] J. Mawhin: Nonlinear perturbations of Fredholm mappings in normed spaces and applications to differential equations. Trabalho de Matematica No 61, Universidad de Brasilia, 1974.

[64] S. G. Michlin: Variationsmethoden in der Mathematischen Physik. Deutscher Verlag der Wissenschaften, Berlin, 1960.

[65] C. B. Morrey: Existence and differentiability theorems for the solutions of variational problems for multiple integrals. Bull. Amer. Math. Soc. 46, 1940, 439—458.

[66] C. B. Morrey: Multiple Integrals in the Calculus of Variations. Springer Verlag, Berlin—Heidelberg—New York, 1966.

[67] J. Nečas: On the existence and regularity of solutions of nonlinear elliptic equations. Proceedings of Equadiff II., Slov. ped. nakl., Bratislava, 1967, 101—119.

356

[68] J. Nečas: Les Méthodes Directes en Théorie des Équations Elliptiques. Academia, Praha 1967.

[69] J. Nečas: Sur la régularité des solutions variationnelles des équations elliptiques non-linéaires d'ordre $2k$ en deux dimensions. Ann. Scuola Norm. Sup. Pisa 21, 1967, 427—457.

[70] J. Nečas: Les équations elliptiques non linéaires. Czechoslovak Math. Journal 19, 1969, 252—274.

[71] J. Nečas: Sur l'alternative de Fredholm pour les opérateurs non-linéaires avec applications aux problèmes aux limites. Ann. Scuola Norm. Sup. Pisa 23, 1969, 331—345.

[72] J. Nečas: Fredholm alternative for nonlinear operators and application to partial differential equations. Čas. pěst. mat. 97, 1972, 65—71.

[73] J. Nečas: On the ranges of nonlinear operators with linear asymptotes which are not invertible. Comment. Math. Univ. Carolinae 14, 1973, 63—72.

[74] J. Nečas - I. Hlaváček: Introduction to the Mathematical Theory of Elastic and Elastico-Plastic Bodies. Elsevier, Amsterdam (in preparation).

[75] J. C. C. Nitsche: Vorlesungen über Minimalflächen. Springer Verlag, Berlin—Heidelberg—New York, 1975.

[76] J. M. Ortega - W. C. Rheinboldt: Iterative Solutions of Nonlinear Equations in Several Variables. Academic Press, New York, 1970.

[77] S. I. Pokhozhaev: On the solvability of nonlinear equations with odd operators. (In Russian.) Funkcionalnyj analiz i prilož. 1, 1967, 66—73.

[78] E. Podolak: On the range of operator equations with an asymptotically linear term. Indiana Univ. Math. Journal 25, 1976, 1127—1137.

[79] K. Rektorys: Survey of Applicable Mathematics. Iliffe, London, 1969.

[80] K. Rektorys: Variational Methods in Mathematics, Science and Engineering. Reidel, Dordrecht, 1977.

[81] S. Saks: Theory of the Integral. Warszawa—Lwów, 1937.

[82] D. H. Sattinger: Topics in stability and bifurcation theory. Lecture Notes in Mathematics No. 309, Springer Verlag, Berlin—Heidelberg—New York, 1973.

[83] S. Schechter: Relaxation methods for convex problems. SIAM Journal Numer. Anal. 5, 19, 601—612.

[84] K. Schmitt: A nonlinear boundary value problem. Journal Differential Equations 7, 1970, 527—537.

[85] L. Schwartz: Mathematics for the Physical Sciences. Addison-Wesley, Reading, 1966.

[86] I. V. Skrypnik: Nonlinear Elliptic Equations of Higher Order. (In Russian.) Naukova dumka, Kiev, 1973.

[87] J. Souček: Spaces of functions on domain Ω whose k-th derivatives are measures defined on $\overline{\Omega}$. Čas. pěst. mat. 97, 1972, 10—46.

[88] J. Stará: Regularity results for nonlinear elliptic systems in two dimensions. Ann. Scuola Norm. Sup. Pisa 25, 1971, 163—190.

[89] M. M. Vajnberg: Variational Methods for the Study of Nonlinear Operators. Holden-Day, San Francisco, 1964.

[90] M. M. Vajnberg: The Variational Method and the Method of Monotone Operators in the Theory of Nonlinear Equations. (In Russian.) Nauka, Moscow, 1972.

[91] R. Varga: Matrix Iterative Analysis. Prentice Hall, New York, 1962.

[92] O. Vejvoda et al.: Partial Differential Equations. Time Periodic Solutions. Sijthoff & Noordhoff, Alphen (in preparation).

[93] S. A. Williams: A sharp sufficient condition for solution of a nonlinear boundary value problem. Journal Differential Equations 8, 1970, 580—586.

[94] M. Zlámal: On the finite element method. Numer. Math. 12, 1968, 394—409.

INDEX

adjoint operator, 259
adjoint space, 95
Airy function, 25
anisotropic problems, 272
anisotropic spaces, 146

Banach contraction principle, 64
Banach space, 62
bifurcation system, 283
biharmonic operator, 16, 24
boundary conditions, 46, 50, 51
boundary condition of s-th order, 51
boundary value problem, 51
bounded operator, 201
bounded set, 196
bounded slope condition, 223
Brouwer degree of a mapping, 248
Brouwer fixed point theorem, 251
Browder theorem, 242

canonical mapping, 197
Carathéodory property, 74
Cartesian product of spaces, 79
classical solution of a boundary value
    problem, 65
classical solution of a differential equation, 45
classical solution of the minimal surface
    problem, 220
closed set, 195
coefficient of equation, 33, 40
coercive operator, 201
coerciveness of a functional, 200
coerciveness with respect to a set, 344
compact imbedding, 216
compact set, 191
complementary Young functions, 150
complete normed linear space, 62
completely continuous operator, 254
cone, 319
continuous linear functional, 95
continuous operator, 79
convex functional, 187
convex subset, 187

critical point of a functional, 180
creep, 24

deflection of a membrane, 17
degree of a mapping, 248, 258
demicontinuous operator, 243
dense subset, 77
derivative in the direction of the outward
    normal, 15
derivative in the direction of the tangent, 15
derivative of a functional, 172
derivative of a functional, second, 183
differential equation of order $2k$ in divergent
    form, 40
differential equation of second order in di-
    vergent form, 33
differential of a functional, 172
differential operator, 62, 94
Dirichlet problem, 52, 122, 153
distribution of temperature, 17
divergence of a vector, 34
domain with a Lipschitz boundary, 47
dual space, 95

Eberlein-Šmuljan theorem, 197
elasto-plastic deformation, 20, 24, 73
equation of a bar, 16
equation of a plate, 17
equation of gas flow, 21
equation of minimal surface, 30, 37, 131
equations in Sobolev-Orlicz spaces, 273
equivalence of norms, 88
equivalent norms, 88
Euler equations, 37
Euler necessary condition for local extrema,
    180

finite dimension, 191
finite element, 235
finite element method, 234
fixed point of an operator, 64
fixed point principle, 64

formal differential operator, 94
formal differential operator of order $2k$, 203
formal differential operator of order $2k$
  (example on the minimum), 189
Fréchet derivative, 269
Fréchet differential (of an operator), 268
Fredholm alternative, 281
free boundary problem, 30
function with polynomial growth, 82
functional, 95, 182, 187, 190, 191, 193
fundamental sequence, 63

Galerkin method, 347
Gauss-Seidel method, iterative, 238
generalized derivative, 85
gradient of a function, 19
Green's formula, 69
Green's function of a boundary value
  problem, 66
Green's theorem, 93

Hermite interpolation of a function, 237
Hilbert space, 181
Hildebrandt-Graves theorem on the implicit
  function, 269
Hölder inequality, 77
homotopic mapping, 248
homotopy of a mapping, 248

imbedding theorems, 134
implicit function theorem, 269
inner product, 181
interpolation of a function, 236, 237
invariance with respect to homotopy, 248

jumping nonlinearity, 275
jumping nonlinearity with finite jumps, 290
jumping nonlinearity with infinite jumps, 299

Katchanov method, 238

Lagrange conditions, 184
Lagrange interpolation of a function, 236
Laplace operator, 16
Lebesgue integrable function, 74
length of a multi-index, 38
Leray-Lions theorem, 243
Leray-Schauder degree of a mapping, 258
linear hull, 255

linearization method, 256
Lipschitz condition, 44
local extremum, 180
local maximum of a functional, 180
local minimum of a functional, 180
lower semicontinuous functional, 191

mapping, 181, 197, 248
maximum of a functional, 180
Mazur theorem, 195
method of successive approximations, 345
minimal surface, 218
minimal surface problem, 21, 219
minimizing sequence, 226
minimum of a functional, 180
minimum of a quadratic functional, 181
Minty trick, 261
mixed problem, 123
Monge-Ampère equation, 23, 36
monotone operator, 201
monotony in the principal part, 213, 247
multi-index, 38

Navier-Stokes equations, 25
Němyckiĭ operator, 75, 151
Neumann problem, 54, 123
Newton problem, 55, 123
nonlinear biharmonic operator, 24
nonlinear Laplace operator, 16
nonlinearity, 275, 276, 290, 299, 307
norm of an element, 62
normed linear space, 62

operator, 62
operator, adjoint, 259
operator, biharmonic, 16
operator, biharmonic, nonlinear, 24
operator, bounded, 201
operator, coercive, 201
operator, completely continuous, 254
operator, continuous, 79
operator, demicontinuous, 243
operator, differential, 62, 94
operator, formal differential, 94
operator, Laplace, 16
operator, monotone, 201
operator, Němyckiĭ, 151
operator, nonlinear Laplace, 22

operator, penalty, 349
operator, potential of, 178
operator, pseudo-monotone, 271
operator, strictly monotone, 203, 216
operator, strongly monotone, 240
operator equation, 62
Orlicz spaces, 150

partial differential of an operator, 269
penalty functional, 348
penalty method, 348
penalty operator, 349
periodic problems, 309
Plateau problem, 21
Poisson equation, 17, 34
positive homogeneous set, 297
positive mapping, 181
potential flow of gases, 22
potential of a boundary value problem, 177
potential of an operator, 178
potential operator, 177
problem of the Signorini type, 32
problem with oblique derivative, 55
pseudo-monotone operator, 271

quadratic functional, 182

rapid nonlinearity, 276, 307
reflexive space, 196
regularity of the solution of a variational
    inequality, 342
regularity of the weak solution, 160
Ritz method, 347

Schauder fixed point theorem, 254
seepage, 30
separable space, 77
Sobolev-Orlicz space, 151
Sobolev space, 88
Sobolev space, anisotropic, 272

solution of a variational inequality, 316
space, 62, 77, 88, 95, 146, 150, 181, 191, 196,
    272
space of finite dimension, 191
space of infinite dimension, 191
stable boundary conditions, 51
stationary magnetic field, 21
strict local maximum of a functional, 180
strict local minimum of a functional, 180
strictly convex functional, 190
strictly monotone operator, 203
successive approximations, 345
support of a function, 44
symmetric mapping, 181

T-periodic function, 309
theorem on the minimum of a quadratic
    functional, 181
total differential, 268
trace of a function, 92
transmission conditions, 29
transmission problem, 28, 127

ultraweak solution, 225
unstable boundary conditions, 51

vanishing nonlinearity, 275
variation of a functional, 170
variational inequality, 315
von Kármán equations, 25, 156

weak convergence, 192
weak limit of a sequence, 192
weak solution of a boundary value problem,
    105
weak solution of the Dirichlet problem, 101
weakly closed set, 195
weakly compact set, 193
weakly lower semicontinuous functional, 139

Young functions, 150